Great Stories of
Mystery
and
Suspense

Great Stories of
Mystery
and
Suspense

Selected and condensed by the editors of
The Reader's Digest

The Reader's Digest Association
Pleasantville, New York
Montreal, Sydney, Cape Town, Hong Kong

CONTENTS

A Kiss
Before Dying

A CONDENSATION OF
THE BOOK BY

Ira
Levin

ILLUSTRATED BY JIM SHARPE

Dorothy . . . Ellen . . . Marion . . . the three daughters of Leo Kingship, copper magnate. Three pretty, intelligent young women with lots of money, and more to come when the old man is gone. Three natural targets for a cold-blooded fortune hunter.

But Dorothy spoils everything by getting pregnant, and she must go. Ellen comes too close to the truth about her sister's "suicide," so she too must die. Now it's Marion's turn . . . but the whole thing is preposterous. There's nothing amiss with Marion's fiancé, nothing that Kingship can quite put his finger on anyway. . . .

A shattering, spellbinding first novel from the author who went on to write *Rosemary's Baby* and *The Boys from Brazil*.

One: Dorothy

HIS plans had been running so beautifully, so damned beautifully, and now *she* was going to smash them all. Hate erupted and flooded through him, gripping his face with jaw-aching pressure. That was all right, though; the lights were out.

She kept on sobbing weakly in the dark, her cheek pressed against his bare chest, her tears and her breath burning hot. He wanted to push her away.

Finally his face relaxed. His legs were quivering the way they always did when things took a crazy turn and caught him unprepared. He lay still for a moment, waiting for the trembling to subside, then he put his arm around her and stroked her back. With his free hand he drew the blanket up around her shoulders. "Crying isn't going to do any good," he told her gently.

Obediently, she tried to stop, rubbing her eyes with the worn binding of the blanket and catching her breath in long choking gasps. "It's just . . . the holding it in for so long. I've known for weeks. I didn't want to say anything until I was sure."

His hand on her back was warm. "No mistake possible?"

"No."

"How far?"

"Two months almost." She lifted her cheek from his chest. "What are we going to do?" she asked.

"You didn't give the doctor your right name, did you?"

"No. He knew I was lying though. It was awful."

"If your father ever finds out . . ."

She lowered her head again and repeated the question. "What are we going to do?"

"Listen, Dorrie," he said. "I know you want me to say we'll get married right away—tomorrow. And I want to marry you. More than anything else in the world." He paused, planning his words with care. "But if we marry this way, me not even meeting your father first, and then a baby comes seven months later . . . You know what he'd do."

"He couldn't *do* anything," she protested. "I'm over eighteen. Eighteen's all you have to be out here. What could he do?"

"I'm not talking about an annulment or anything like that."

"Then what? What do you mean?" she appealed.

"The money," he said. "Dorrie, what about him—him and his holy morals? Your mother makes a single slip; he finds out about it eight years later and divorces her, not caring about you and your sisters, not caring about her bad health. Well, what do you think he would do to you? He'd forget you ever existed. You wouldn't see a penny."

"I don't *care*," she said earnestly. "Do you think I care?"

"But I do, Dorrie." His hand began moving gently on her back again. "Not for me, but for you. What will happen to us? We'll both have to quit school; you for the baby, me to work. And what will I be? A clerk? Or an oiler in some textile mill or something? Living in a furnished room with paper drapes?"

"It doesn't matter."

"It does! You're only nineteen and you've had money all your life. You don't know what it means not to have it. I do. We'd be at each other's throats in a year."

She began sobbing again.

He closed his eyes and spoke dreamily. "I had it planned so beautifully. I would have come to New York this summer. I could have gotten him to like me. You would have told me what he's interested in, what he likes—" He stopped short, then continued. "And after graduation we would have been married. Or even this summer. We could have come back here in September for our last two years. A little apartment of our own, right near the campus . . ."

She lifted her head from his chest. "Why are you saying these things?" she begged.

"I want you to see how wonderful it could have been."

"Do you think I don't see?" The sobs twisted her voice. "But I'm pregnant. I'm two months pregnant. We *have* to get married now. We don't have any choice."

"We *do* have a choice, Dorrie," he said. /

He felt her body stiffen against his. She began shaking her head violently from side to side.

"Listen, Dorrie!" he pleaded. "No operation. Nothing like that." He caught her jaw in one hand, holding her head rigid. "There's a guy on campus, Hermy Godsen. He works in his uncle's drugstore. He could get some pills."

"Pills . . ." She shook her head. "Oh, God, I don't know."

He put his arms around her. "Baby, I *love* you. I wouldn't let you take anything that might hurt you."

She collapsed against him. "I don't know. . . . I don't know."

He said, "It would be so wonderful"—his hand caressing—"a little apartment of our own. Don't you see, baby? We've got to try!" He had discovered that when he called her baby and held her in his arms he could get her to do practically anything.

Finally she said, "What if the pills don't work?"

He took a deep breath. "If they don't work"—he kissed the corner of her mouth—"if they don't work we'll get married right away and to hell with your father and Kingship Copper Incorporated. I swear we will, baby."

HE WAS born in Menasset, on the outskirts of Fall River, Massachusetts; the only child of a father who was an oiler in a textile mill and a mother who sometimes had to take in sewing when the money ran low. At an early age he became conscious of his good looks—the blondness of his hair, the clear blue of his eyes. His parents argued a great deal, usually over the time and money his mother devoted to dressing him.

His mother had never encouraged him to play with the children of the neighborhood, and his first few days at school were agony. The boys made fun of his perfect clothes and the obvious care he took to avoid the puddles in the schoolyard. One day, when he could bear it no longer, he went up to the ringleader and spat on his shoes. The ensuing fight was brief but wild. At the end of it he had the ringleader flat on his back and was kneeling on his chest, banging his head against the ground. A teacher came running and broke up the fight. After that, everything was all right.

His marks were good, which made his mother glow and even won reluctant praise from his father. His marks became still better when he started sitting next to a brilliant girl who neglected to cover her paper during examinations.

His school days were the happiest of his life; the girls liked him for his looks and his charm; the teachers liked him because he was polite and attentive; to the boys he showed just enough dislike of both girls and teachers to make them like him too. At home, he was a god.

When he started dating, it was with girls from the better part of town. His mother began to talk about his marrying a rich man's daughter. She only said it jokingly, of course, but she said it more than once.

He was president of his senior class in high school and was graduated with honors in mathematics and science. In the school yearbook he was named the best dancer, the most popular, and the most likely to succeed. His parents gave a party for him, which was attended by many young people from the better part of town.

Two weeks later he was drafted.

For the first few days of basic training he cursed the blind system which had dropped him into the infantry, where he was surrounded by coarse, comic-book-reading idiots. After a while he read comic books too, and made a few friends, buying them beers in the PX.

When he was shipped out of San Francisco, he vomited all the way across the Pacific, and he knew it was only partly from the lift and drop of the ship. He was sure he was going to be killed.

On an island still partially occupied by the Japanese, he became separated from his company and stood terrified in the midst of a silent jungle, desperately shifting this way and that, not knowing in which direction safety lay. A rifle slapped, sending a bullet keening past his ear. Jagged bird screams split the air. He rolled under a bush, sick with the certainty that this was the moment of his death.

He saw a gleam in a tree up ahead, and knew that that was where the sniper waited. He found himself inching forward under the bushes, dragging his rifle with one hand. His legs were trembling so badly that he was sure the sniper would hear the leaves rustling under them.

Finally, when he was only twenty feet from the tree, he could discern the figure crouched in it. He lifted his rifle; he aimed, and fired. A rifle dropped from the tree, and he saw the sniper slide down a vine and drop to the ground with his hands high in the air—a little man grotesquely festooned with leaves and branches, his lips emitting a terrified singsong chatter.

Keeping the rifle trained on the Japanese soldier, he stood up. The man was as scared as he was; his face twitched wildly and his knees shivered. More scared, in fact, for the front of his pants was dark with a spreading stain.

He watched the wretched figure with contempt. His own legs steadied. The rifle was weightless, like an extension of his arms. Quite slowly, he squeezed the trigger, watching attentively as a red hole blossomed and swelled in the chest of the enemy soldier. The little man slid to the jungle floor.

After looking at the slain enemy for a minute or so, he turned and walked away, his step as easy and certain as when he had crossed the stage of the high school auditorium to accept his diploma.

15

IN JANUARY OF 1947 he left the army with the Bronze Star and a Purple Heart for a shell fragment which had traced a thin scar over his ribs. Returning home, he found that his father had been killed two weeks before in an automobile accident.

He was offered several jobs in Menasset, but rejected them as being of too little promise. His father's insurance money was sufficient to support his mother, and she was taking in sewing again besides, so after two months of drawing admiration from the townspeople and twenty dollars a week from the federal government, he decided to go to New York. Some of the neighbors expressed surprise that he did not intend to go to college, especially when the government would pay for it. He felt, however, that college would only be an unnecessary stopover on the road to certain success.

His first job in New York was in a publishing house, where the personnel manager assured him there was a fine future for the right man. Two weeks, however, was all he could take of the shipping room.

His next job was with a department store, where he was a salesclerk in the menswear department. The only reason he remained there an entire month was that he was able to buy his clothes at a twenty percent discount.

By the end of August, when he had been in New York five months and had had six jobs, he was still alone; unadmired and with no tangible sign of success.

In September he enrolled in a drama school under the GI bill. The instructors expressed great hopes for him at first; he was handsome, intelligent, and had a fine speaking voice. He had great hopes too, at first. Then he discovered how much work and study were involved in becoming an actor. The exercises the instructors gave—"Look at this photograph and act out the emotions it brings to mind"—struck him as ridiculous.

In December, on his twenty-second birthday, he met an attractive widow. She was in her forties and she had a good deal of money. In the weeks that followed, he weaned himself away from the drama school and devoted his afternoons to squiring her on shopping tours, some of which were for him. Unfortunately, he learned from the elevator operator in her apartment house that he was only one of a series of young men, each of whom had been replaced with regularity at the end of six months. At the end of five months, when she began to exhibit less curiosity about how he spent his time when he was not with her, he anticipated her move and told her that he had to return home because his mother was deathly ill.

He did return home, and spent the early part of June lounging around the house, making a new plan. He decided to go to college after all. He took a summer job in a local dry goods store because, while the GI bill would cover his tuition, his living expenses would be high; he was going to attend a good school.

He finally chose Stoddard University in Blue River, Iowa, which was supposed to be something of a country club for the children of the midwestern wealthy. There was no difficulty in his gaining admission. He had such a fine high school record.

In his first year he met a lovely girl, a senior, the daughter of the vice-president of an internationally organized farm equipment concern. They took walks together, cut classes together, and slept together. In May she told him that she was engaged to a boy back home and she hoped he hadn't taken it too seriously.

In his sophomore year he met Dorothy Kingship.

HE GOT the pills, two grayish-white capsules, from Hermy Godsen. They cost him five dollars.

At eight o'clock he met Dorothy at their regular meeting place, a tree-shrouded bench between the Fine Arts and Pharmacy buildings. He sat down beside her and kissed her cheek. After a moment he said, "I got them."

He took the envelope from his pocket and put it into Dorothy's hand. "You're to take both of them together," he said. "You're liable to get a little fever, and you'll probably feel nauseous."

She put the envelope in her coat pocket. "What's in them?" she asked.

"Quinine, some other things. I'm not sure." He paused. "They can't hurt you."

He saw that she was staring off at something beyond the Fine Arts Building. He turned and followed her gaze to a winking red light miles away. It marked the local radio station's transmitting tower, which stood atop Blue River's tallest structure, the Municipal Building—where the Marriage License Bureau was. He touched her hands and found them cold. "Don't worry, Dorrie. Everything will be all right."

He walked her back across the campus. Opposite the low modern shape of the girls' dormitory, they kissed good-night. "See you in class tomorrow," he said. She nodded, and kissed him again. She was trembling. "Look, baby, there's nothing to worry about. If they don't work, we get married." She was waiting for him to say more. "And I love you very much," he said.

He returned to his room and sat with his elbows planted on the bridge table, his head in his hands. Oh, God, the pills must work! They *will* work!

He got up and went to the bureau and opened the bottom drawer. From under the neatly folded pajamas he took two pamphlets whose supple covers gleamed with a copper finish.

On first meeting Dorothy and discovering that she was a daughter of the president of Kingship Copper Incorporated, he had written a businesslike letter to the organization's New York office. In it he represented himself as contemplating an investment in Kingship Copper (which was not entirely untrue) and requested descriptive brochures of its holdings.

When the pamphlets arrived, he opened their envelope with ceremonial care. They proved wonderful, crammed with photographs: mines and furnaces, concentrators and converters, reversing mills, rolling mills, rod mills and tube mills. He read them a hundred times and knew every caption by heart. He returned to them at odd moments, like a woman with her love letters.

Tonight they were no good. "Open-cut mine in Landers, Michigan. From this single mine, a yearly output . . ."

What angered him most was that the responsibility for the entire situation rested with Dorothy. He had wanted to take her to his room only once—a down payment guaranteeing the fulfillment of a contract. It was Dorothy, with her passive, orphan hunger, who had wished for further visits. It really was her fault! Damn her!

If the pills didn't work . . . Leave school? Ditch her? It would be futile. Even if she should be reluctant to seek him out, her father would hasten to do so. Of course there could be no legal action (or could there?), but Kingship could still cause him plenty of trouble. "Watch out for this young man. He's no good. I feel it my duty as a parent to warn you . . ." And what would be left for him then?

The pills had to work. That was all there was to it.

THE book of matches was white, with *Dorothy Kingship* stamped on it in copper leaf. Every Christmas Kingship Copper gave personalized matches to its executives, customers and friends. It took Dorothy four strokes to light the match, and when she held it to her cigarette the flame trembled as though in a breeze. She sat back, trying to relax, but she couldn't tear her eyes from the open bathroom door, the white envelope waiting on the edge of the sink, the glass of water.

She closed her eyes. If only she could speak to Ellen about it. A letter had come that morning: "The weather has been beautiful . . . president of the refreshment committee for the Junior Prom"—another of the meaningless mechanical notes that had been drifting between them since Christmas and the argument. If only she could get Ellen's advice, talk to her the way they used to talk. . . .

Dorothy had been five and Ellen six when Leo Kingship divorced his wife. A third sister, Marion, was ten. When the three girls lost their mother, first through the divorce and then through her death a year later, Marion felt the loss most deeply of all. As the years passed she grew solitary and withdrawn.

Dorothy and Ellen, however, turned to each other for the affection which they received neither from their father nor from the series of governesses to whom he transferred the custody the courts had granted him. The two sisters went to the same schools and camps, joined the same clubs, and attended the same dances. Where Ellen led, Dorothy followed.

But when Ellen entered Caldwell College, in Caldwell, Wisconsin, and Dorothy made plans to follow her there the next year, Ellen said no; Dorothy should grow up and become self-reliant. Their father agreed, self-reliance being a trait he valued. Dorothy was sent to Stoddard, slightly more than a hundred miles from Caldwell.

A few visits were made, the length of time between them increasing progressively, until Dorothy announced that her first year of college had made her completely self-reliant. Finally, this past Christmas, there had been an argument. It had started over nothing—"If you wanted to borrow my blouse, you might at least have asked me!"—and had swollen because Dorothy had been in a depressed mood all during her vacation. When the girls returned to school, the letters between them faded to brief, infrequent notes.

There was still the telephone. Dorothy found herself staring at it. She could get Ellen on the line in an instant. . . . But no; why should she be the one to give in first and chance a rebuff? Besides, now that she had calmed down, what was there to hesitate about? She would take the pills; if they worked, all well and good. If not, marriage.

She went to the hall door and locked it, feeling a slight thrill in the unaccustomed and somewhat melodramatic act. In the bathroom, she took the envelope from the edge of the sink and tilted the capsules into her palm. She lifted the glass, clapped the pills into her mouth, and drained the water in a single draft.

HE SAT in the back of the classroom, in the second seat from the window. It was the first class of the morning, a daily social science lecture, and their only class together this semester. Today of all days she could have made an effort to be on time. Didn't she know he'd be frozen in an agony of suspense?

The door at the side of the room opened quietly. His head jerked around.

She looked awful. Her face was pasty white and there were gray arcs under her eyes. With a barely perceptible motion she shook her head.

Oh, God! He heard her coming around behind him, slipping into the seat on his left. He heard the scratching of a pen on paper, and finally the sound of a page being torn from a pad.

He turned. Her hand was extended toward him, holding a folded piece of blue-lined paper. She was watching him, her wide eyes anxious.

He took the paper, opened it in his lap, and read, "I had a terrible fever and I threw up. But nothing happened."

After a few minutes he was able to turn to Dorothy, give her a reassuring smile, and form the words "Don't worry" with silent lips.

When the bell sounded, they left the room with the other students and stood outside in the shadow of the building.

The color was beginning to return to Dorothy's cheeks. She spoke quickly. "It'll be all right. I know it will. You won't have to quit school. You'll get more money from the government, won't you? With a wife?"

"A hundred and five a month." He couldn't keep the sourness out of his voice.

"Others get along on it . . . the ones in the trailer camp."

He put his books down on the grass. The important thing was to get time, time to think. He was afraid his knees were going to start shaking. He took her by the shoulders, smiling. "You just don't worry about anything." He took a breath. "Friday afternoon we'll go down to the Municipal—"

"Friday?"

"Baby, it's Tuesday. Three days won't make any difference now." He fingered the collar of her coat. "Be practical. There are so many things to be taken care of. If we get married Friday, we can have the weekend for a honeymoon. I'm going to get us a reservation at the New Washington House."

She touched his hand. "I . . . I know it isn't the way we wanted it, but . . . you're happy, aren't you?"

"Well, what do you think?" He looked at his watch. "You have a ten o'clock, don't you?"

"*Solamente el Español.* I can cut it."

"Don't. We'll have better reasons to cut our morning classes." She squeezed his hand. Reluctantly, she turned to go.

"Oh, Dorrie . . ."

"Yes?"

"You haven't said anything to your sister, have you?"

"Ellen? No."

"Well, you better not. Not until after we're married."

"I thought I'd tell her before. We've been so close. I'd hate to do it without letting her know."

"She's liable to tell your father. He might try to stop us."

"All right. Whatever you say."

"Afterward you can call her up. We'll tell everybody."

A final smile, and then she was walking to the sun-bright path, her hair glinting gold. He picked up his books and walked away in the opposite direction. A braking car screeched somewhere, making him start. It sounded like a bird in a jungle.

LEANING on the rail of the Morton Street Bridge, he looked down at the river and smoked a cigarette. The dilemma had finally caught up with him and engulfed him like the filthy water that pounded the abutments of the bridge. Marry her or leave her. A wife and a child and no money, or be hounded and blackballed by her father. Then what? There would be no place to go to but home.

He thought of his mother. Years of complacent pride, and then she sees him clerking in a dry goods store. Or even some lousy mill! He'd seen what love she'd had for his father burn itself into bitterness and contempt. Was that in store for him too? Oh, God! Why hadn't the damned pills killed the girl?

If only he could get her to undergo an operation. But no, even if he pleaded and argued, she'd still want to consult Ellen before taking such a drastic measure. And suppose something happened, suppose she died. Her death wouldn't do him a bit of good.

Not if she died that way.

After a while he picked up his books and went into a dingy riverside restaurant. He sat at a little corner table and ordered a ham sandwich and coffee. The first thing that had entered his mind was the Colt .45 he had taken on leaving the army. But assuming he wanted to do it, a gun would be no good. It would have to look like an accident, or suicide. If it looked like anything else, he would be the first one the police would suspect.

He thought of poison. But where would he get it? Hermy Godsen? No. Maybe the Pharmacy Building. The supply room there shouldn't be too hard to get into. He would have to do some research at the library, to see which poison . . .

There were so many details—assuming he wanted to do it. Today was Tuesday; the marriage could be postponed no later than Friday or she might get worried and call Ellen. It would require a great deal of careful planning. He took out his memorandum book and fountain pen and began writing:

1. Gun (n.g.)
2. Poison
   a. Selection
   b. Obtaining
   c. Administering
   d. Appearance of (1) accident
      or (2) suicide

Assuming, of course, that he wanted to do it. At present it was all purely speculative. A mental exercise.

But his stride, when he left the restaurant and headed back through town, was relaxed and sure and steady.

He reached the campus at three o'clock and went directly to the library. In the card catalogue he found listed six books likely to contain the information he wanted. Rather than have a librarian get them for him, he registered at the desk and went into the stacks himself.

At the end of an hour he had a list of five toxic chemicals likely to be found in the Pharmacy Building supply room, any one of which would be suitable for the rudimentary plan he had formulated.

He left the library and went to the University Bookstore, where he asked the clerk for a copy of *Pharmaceutical Techniques*, the laboratory manual used by the advanced pharmacy students. "Pretty late in the semester," the clerk commented, returning from the rear of the store with the green-covered manual in his hand. "Lose yours?"

"No. It was stolen."

"Oh. Anything else?"

"Yes. I'd like some envelopes, please. For letters."

The clerk put a pack of white envelopes on the book. "That's a dollar fifty and twenty-five. Plus tax—a dollar seventy-nine."

The College of Pharmacy was housed in one of Stoddard's old buildings, three stories of ivy-masked brick. Although he had never taken classes there, he had been through its basement many times as a shortcut to the Fine Arts Building. At either side of the building were steps leading down to a long corridor which cut straight through the basement, where the supply room was located. Keys to the supply-room door were in the possession of the faculty of the College of Pharmacy and advanced students who had received permission to work without supervision.

He came in at the main entrance and crossed the hall to the lounge, going directly to the coatrack in the corner. Removing his corduroy jacket, he hung it on one of the hooks, then put his books on the shelf above. Tucking the manual under his arm, he went downstairs to the basement corridor.

On the wall a few feet beyond the supply room was a bulletin board. He walked over to it and stood looking at the notices tacked there. His back was turned slightly toward the end of the corridor, so that from the corner of his eye he could see the central stairwell. He held the manual under his left arm. At his side, his key chain dangled from his right hand.

Presently a girl appeared, coming toward him. There was a

lab manual in her hand. She had lanky brown hair and horn-rimmed glasses. She was taking a brass key from the pocket of her smock. He moved to the supply-room door, not looking at the approaching girl. His attention was on his keys, shuffling through them, apparently looking for a certain one. It seemed as though he didn't become conscious of the girl's presence until she had inserted her key in the lock and pushed the door partially open, smiling up at him. "Oh . . . thanks," he said, tucking the keys back in his pocket. He followed the girl in and closed the door behind them.

It was a small room with counters and shelves filled with labeled bottles and boxes and odd-looking apparatuses. The girl touched a wall switch, making fluorescent tubes wink to life. She went to the side of the room and opened her manual on a counter there. "Are you in Aberson's class?" she asked.

He went to the opposite side. He stood with his back to the girl, facing a wall of bottles. "Yes," he said.

Faint clinkings of glass and metal sounded in the room. "How's his arm?"

"About the same, I guess," he said. He touched the bottles, pushing them against each other, so that the girl's curiosity should not be aroused.

Each bottle had a white label with black lettering. A few bore an additional label that glared POISON in red. Among these he found the one he wanted. WHITE ARSENIC—As_4O_6—POISON.

He turned slowly until he could see the girl from the corner of his eye. She was pouring some yellow powder from the tray of a balance into a glass cup. He turned back to the wall and opened his manual on the counter. He appeared to study the meaningless pages of diagrams and instructions.

At last the girl's movements took on sounds of finality; the balance being put away, a drawer closing. He leaned more closely over the manual, following the lines of print with a careful finger. Her footsteps moved to the door. "So long," she said.

"So long."

The door opened and closed. He looked around. He was alone.

He took his handkerchief and three of the envelopes from his pocket. With the handkerchief draped over his right hand, he lifted the arsenic bottle from the shelf, put it on the counter, and removed the stopper. He poured about a tablespoonful of the flourlike powder into an envelope; it fell in whispering puffs. He folded the envelope into a tight pack, folded that into a second envelope, and pocketed it.

After he had stoppered and replaced the bottle, he moved slowly around the room, reading the labels on drawers and boxes. He found what he wanted within several minutes: a box filled with empty gelatin capsules, glittering like oval bubbles. He took six of them, to be on the safe side, put them into the third envelope, and slipped it gently into his pocket. Then, when everything appeared as he had found it, he took the manual from the counter, turned out the lights, and left the room.

After retrieving his books and jacket, he left the campus. He felt secure; he had devised a course of action and had executed its initial steps with speed and precision. Of course it was still only a tentative plan and he was in no way committed to carry it through. He would see how the next steps worked out.

He met Dorothy at eight o'clock. They went to the Uptown, where a Joan Fontaine picture was playing. He was not especially fond of movies, and he disliked pictures that were founded on exaggerated emotions. Tonight, however, he surrendered all his attention to the picture, as though answers to eternal mysteries were hidden in the windings of its plot. He enjoyed it immensely.

Afterward he went home and made up two capsules. One of the books he had read that afternoon had listed the lethal dose of arsenic as varying from one tenth to one half of a gram. By rough computation, he estimated that the two capsules contained a total of five grams. The police would never believe that Dorrie had taken a lethal dose of arsenic by accident. It would have to look like suicide. There would have to be a note or something equally convincing. Because if they ever started an investigation, the girl who had let him into the supply room would always be able to identify him.

HE FOLLOWED HIS regular routine on Wednesday, attending all his classes, but he was no more a part of the life and activity that surrounded him than a diver in his diving bell. He had unconsciously dropped the pretense of being undecided as to whether or not he would actually go through with his plans. There remained only the problem of the note, and he was determined to solve it.

A Spanish class was his last of the day, and the latter half of it was devoted to a short unannounced examination. Because it was his poorest subject, he forced himself to concentrate on translating a page of a florid Spanish novel. But in the midst of his writing the idea came to him. It rose up fully formed, a perfect plan, unlikely to fail and unlikely to arouse Dorothy's suspicion. By ten o'clock the following morning Dorothy would have written her suicide note.

That evening, his landlady having gone to an Eastern Star meeting, he brought Dorothy back to his room. During the two hours they spent there, he was as warm and tender as she had ever wished him to be. Afterward they went to a small restaurant near the campus. Seated in one of the blue-painted wall booths, they had cheeseburgers and chocolate malteds, while Dorothy chattered on about her visions of a warm and happy life in the trailer camp. He waited for a pause in the monologue.

"Oh, by the way," he said, "do you still have that picture I gave you? The one of me?"

"Of course I do."

"Well, let me have it back for a couple of days. I want to have a copy made to send to my mother."

She took out a green wallet from the pocket of her coat. "Have you told your mother about us?"

"No, I haven't."

"Why not?"

He thought for a moment. "Well, as long as you can't tell your family until after, I thought I wouldn't tell my mother. Keep it our secret." He smiled. "You haven't told anyone, have you?"

"No," she said. She was holding a few snapshots she had taken from the wallet. He looked at the top one from across the table. It was of Dorothy and two other girls—her sisters, he supposed. Seeing his glance, she passed the picture to him. "The middle one is Ellen, and Marion's on the end."

The three girls were standing in front of a car, a Cadillac, he noticed. The sun was behind them, their faces shadowed, but he could still discern a resemblance among them. All had the same wide eyes and prominent cheekbones. "Who's the prettiest?" he asked. "After you, I mean."

"Ellen," Dorothy said. "And before me. Marion could be very pretty too, only she wears her hair like this." She pulled her hair back severely and frowned. "She's the intellectual. Remember?"

"Oh. The Proust fiend."

She handed him the next snapshot, which was of her father. "Grrrrr," he growled, and they both laughed. Then she said, "And this is my fiancé," and passed him his own picture.

He looked at it speculatively. "I don't know," he drawled. "Looks kind of dissolute to me."

"But so handsome," she said. "So very handsome." He smiled and pocketed the picture with a satisfied air.

Back in his room, he held the photograph over an ashtray and touched a lighted match to its lowest corner. It was a good picture of him; he hated to burn it, but he had written "To Dorrie, with all my love" across the bottom of it.

As USUAL, she was late for their nine o'clock social science class. Her seat on his left was still empty when the lecturer mounted the platform and began talking about the city manager form of government.

He had everything in readiness. His pen was poised over the notebook opened before him and the Spanish novel *La Casa de las Flores Negras* was balanced on his knee. A sudden heart-stopping thought hit him; what if she picked today to cut? Tomorrow was the deadline. This was the only chance he would have to get the suicide note, and he had to have it by tonight.

At ten past nine, though, she appeared; out of breath, her

books under her arm, a smile for him lighting her face the moment she eased through the door. Tiptoeing across the room, she was still smiling as she sorted her books, keeping a notebook and a small assignment pad before her.

When she saw the book that he held open on his knee, her eyebrows lifted questioningly. He closed the book, keeping his fingers between the pages, and tilted it toward her so that she could see the Spanish title. Then he opened it again and indicated the two exposed pages and his notebook, meaning that that was how much translation he had to do. He pointed to the lecturer and to her notebook—she should take notes and he would copy them later. She nodded.

After he had worked for a quarter of an hour, he tore a piece of paper about two inches square from a notebook page. With a finger stabbing a passage of the novel, he began shaking his head and tapping his foot in impatient perplexity.

Dorothy turned to him inquiringly. He lifted his finger in a gesture that asked her to wait a moment. He began to write, squeezing words onto the small piece of paper, words that he was apparently copying from the novel. When he was through, he passed the paper to her.

"Traducción, por favor," he had headed it. Translation, please. *"Querido, Espero que me perdonares por la infelicidad que causaré. No hay ninguna otra cosa que puedo hacer."*

She gave him a mildly puzzled glance, because the sentences were quite simple, but she tore a page from her assignment pad and wrote: "Darling, I hope you will forgive me for the unhappiness that I will cause. There is nothing else that I can do."

She handed him the translation. He read it and nodded. *"Muchas gracias,"* he whispered.

He tucked the paper carefully into the pocket on the inner cover of the notebook and closed it. Dorothy crumpled the paper on which he had written the Spanish and dropped it to the floor. From the corner of his eye he saw it land. There was another bit of paper near it, and some cigarette butts. At the end of the day they would all be swept together and burned.

THEY WERE NOT TO see each other that evening. Dorothy wanted to wash her hair and pack a small valise for their weekend honeymoon at the New Washington House. But at eight thirty he called her.

"Listen, Dorrie. Something's come up. I've got to see you right away."

"But I can't come out. I just washed my hair. Can't you come to the lounge downstairs?"

"No. Listen, you know that place where we had the cheeseburgers last night? Gideon's? Well, meet me there. At nine. I'll explain everything."

He opened the bottom drawer of his bureau and took two envelopes from under the pajamas. One envelope was stamped, sealed and addressed:

> Miss Ellen Kingship
> North Dormitory
> Caldwell College
> Caldwell, Wisconsin

He had typed the address that afternoon in the Student Union lounge, on one of the typewriters available for general student use. In the envelope was the translated note that Dorothy had written in class that morning. The other envelope contained the two capsules filled with arsenic.

He put one envelope in each of the inner pockets of his jacket, and with a final glance in the mirror, he left to meet Dorothy.

Gideon's was practically empty when he arrived. Across the room, Dorothy sat with her hands clasped around a cup of coffee, gazing down at it as though it were a crystal ball. She had a white kerchief tied about her head. The hair that showed in front was a series of flattened damp rings, each transfixed by a bobby pin. She had no makeup on. Her pallor and the closeness of her hair made her seem younger.

"What is it?" she asked anxiously, as he eased into the seat opposite her.

He kept his voice low, matter-of-fact. "When I got back to my place this afternoon, there was a message from Hermy Godsen."

Her hands squeezed tighter around the coffee cup. "Hermy Godsen . . ."

"He made a mistake with those pills the other day. His uncle switched things around in the drugstore or something. Those pills weren't what they were supposed to be."

"What were they?" She sounded frightened.

"Some kind of emetic. You said you threw up."

She breathed relief. "Well that's all *over* with. They didn't hurt me."

"That's not the point, baby. I saw Hermy just before I called you. He gave me the right pills, the ones we should have had last time."

Her face sagged. "No."

"Well, there's nothing tragic. We're right where we were Monday, that's all. It's a second chance. If they work, everything's rosy. If not, we can still get married tomorrow." He stirred his coffee slowly, watching it swirl. "I've got them with me. You can take them tonight."

"But I don't *want* a second chance. I don't *want* any more *pills*."

"Baby, baby," he soothed, "do we have to go through it all again? It's you I'm thinking of. You, not me."

"No." She stared at him. "If you were thinking of me, you'd want what I want."

"What *do* you want, baby? To starve? This is no movie; this is real."

"We *wouldn't* starve. You'd get a good job even if you didn't finish school. You're smart, you're—"

"Look at you, Dorrie—a pair of shoes to match every outfit, a handbag to match every pair of shoes. You can't—"

"Do you think that matters? Do you think I care?" Her hands flew to her face. "I believe, I truly believe, that if two people really love each other, then nothing else matters very much."

He drew a handkerchief from his breast pocket and touched it to her hand. She took it and held it against her eyes. "Baby, I believe that too. You know I do," he said gently. She patted her eyes with the handkerchief. "I'll get a night job. We'll manage to get along, and we'll be happy. But let's be just a little realistic, Dorrie. We'll be even happier if we can get married this summer with your father's approval. And all you have to do for us to have a chance at that extra happiness is just take these pills." He reached into an inner pocket and brought out the envelope, pressing it to make sure it was the right one.

She folded the handkerchief, turned it in her hands, and gave it back to him. "Since Tuesday morning I've been dreaming about tomorrow. It changed everything . . . the whole world."

"I know you're disappointed, Dorrie. But you've got to think of the future." He extended the envelope to her. She made no move to accept it. He put it on the table between them.

He spoke with cool authority as she stared at the envelope. "If you refuse to take them, Dorothy, you're being stubborn, unrealistic and unfair. Unfair more to yourself than to me."

Her eyes lifted to meet his.

"Please, baby . . ."

She took the envelope and pushed it into the handbag on the bench beside her. He reached across the table and caressed the back of her hand.

Afterward they walked to her dormitory in silence, divorced by the privacy of their thoughts.

He kissed her good-night and went to a nearby bar, where he drank two glasses of beer and tore a paper napkin into a delicate filigreed square. When half an hour had passed, he stepped into the telephone booth and called Dorothy.

She answered after two rings. "Hello?"

"Hello, Dorrie?" Silence at her end. "Dorrie, did you do it?"

A pause. "Yes."

"When?"

"A few minutes ago."

He drew a deep breath. "Whatever happens, don't get frightened. It'll just mean that the pills are working. Don't call anyone."

He paused, waiting for her to say something. "You're not angry with me, are you, Dorrie?"

"No."

"You'll see, it'll all be for the best."

"I know. I'm sorry I was stubborn."

"That's all right, baby. Don't apologize."

There was a silence for a moment and then she said, "Well, good night."

"Good-by, Dorothy," he said.

He paid for his beers and walked back to her dorm. In the corner mailbox he posted the suicide note to Ellen Kingship.

STRIDING into the classroom Friday morning, he felt weightless and tall and wonderful. It was a beautiful day; sunlight poured into the room and bounced off the metal chairs to spangle the walls and ceiling. Taking his seat in the back of the room, he stretched his legs all the way out, watching the other students crowd in.

Three girls stood off to the side and whispered excitedly. He wondered if they could possibly be talking about Dorothy. It was unlikely that she would be found before one o'clock or so. If his luck *really* held, she would not be discovered until a frantic phone call from Ellen led to the discovery. Then everything would be neat and in its proper order.

There would be an autopsy, of course. It would reveal the presence of a great deal of arsenic and a two-month pregnancy—the way and the why of her suicide. That and the note would more than satisfy the police. Oh, they would make a perfunctory check of the local drugstores, but it would net them only a fat zero. Would they look for the man in the case, the lover?

He would certainly be dragged into that, but Dorothy hadn't told anyone they were going steady, so other men would be involved too. There was the redheaded one she'd been chatting with the day he first saw her and learned that she was Dorothy Kingship of Kingship Copper, and the one she'd started knitting argyle socks for, and every man she'd dated once or twice—they would *all* be brought into it. There would be suspicion directed at every one of them, proof against none.

The door opened, creating a draft that lifted the pages of his notebook. He turned to see who it was. It was Dorothy.

Shock burst over him, hot as a wave of lava. He half rose, blood pushing to his face. Sweat dotted his body and crawled like a million insects. He knew distress was written on his face in swollen eyes and burning cheeks, written for her to see, but he couldn't stop it. She was looking at him wonderingly.

What happened? Oh, God! She didn't take the pills! She couldn't have! She lied! The bitch! The lying bitch! The note on its way to Ellen . . . Oh, my God!

He heard her sliding into her seat. Her frightened whisper— "What's wrong? What's the matter?" He tried to speak. *"What is it?"* Students were turning to look.

Finally he scraped out, "Nothing. I'm all right." He touched the side where she knew he had the army scar. "It gives me a twinge once in a while."

"I thought you were having a heart attack," she whispered.

"No. I'm all right." He kept looking at her, his hands clutching his knees in rigid restraint. Oh, God, what could he do? The bitch! She had planned also, planned to get married!

He saw the anxiety for him melt from her face. She ripped a page from her assignment pad, scribbled on it, and passed it to him. "The pills didn't work."

The liar! The damned liar! He crumpled the paper and squeezed it in his hand, fingernails biting into his palm.

His danger was so enormous he couldn't grasp it all at once. Ellen would receive the note—when? This afternoon? And call Dorothy—"What does this mean? Why did you write this?" "Write what?" Then Ellen would read the note over the phone and Dorothy would recognize it.

What explanation could he invent? Or would she see the truth—blurt out the whole story to Ellen—call her father. If she hadn't thrown the pills away, there would be proof! Attempted murder.

There was no figuring her now. She was an unknown quantity. He'd thought he could predict every little twitch of her brain, and now . . .

He could feel her looking at him, waiting for some kind of reaction to the words she'd written. He tore paper from his notebook and pulled open his pen. He had to make it sound natural. "Okay. We tried, that's all. Now we get married as per schedule."

He handed it to her. She read it and turned to him, and her face was warm and radiant as the sunlight. He pressed a smile back at her, praying she wouldn't notice the stiffness of it.

It still wasn't too late. He looked at his watch; nine twenty. The earliest Ellen could get the note would be . . . three o'clock. Five hours and forty minutes. In five hours and forty minutes she must be dead.

At ten o'clock they left the building arm in arm, going out into the crystalline air that rang with the shouts of between-class students.

"Does your side still hurt you?" Dorothy asked.

"A little," he said.

"Do you get those twinges often?"

"No. Don't worry." He looked at his watch. "You're not marrying an invalid."

They stepped off the path onto the lawn. "When will we go?" She pressed his hand.

"This afternoon. Around four."

She was hugging her arms and smiling. "I *can't* go to my classes! I'm cutting."

"Good. I am too. Stay with me."

"What do you mean?"

"Until we go down to the Municipal Building. We'll spend the day together."

"I can't, darling. Not the whole day. I have to get back to the dorm, finish packing."

He smiled. "You can give me *some* of your time, anyway. Until lunch." Suddenly he stopped walking.

"What is it?"

"Dorrie, why should we wait until four o'clock? Let's go now!"

"Get married *now?*"

"Well, after you pack and dress and everything. Look, you go back to the dorm and get ready. What do you say?"

"Oh, yes! Yes!"

"I'll call you up in a little while and tell you when I'll pick you up."

"Yes. Yes." She stretched up and kissed his cheek excitedly. "I love you so much," she whispered. She hurried away, flashing a smile back over her shoulder.

He watched her go. Then he turned and looked beyond the Fine Arts Building toward the Blue River Municipal Building; the tallest building in the city; fourteen stories above the hard concrete sidewalk.

He checked to make sure Dorothy was out of sight, then went to a telephone booth in the Fine Arts Building. He dialed the number of the Marriage License Bureau. "Hello. I'm calling to find out what hours the bureau is open today."

"Till noon and from one to five thirty."

"Closed between twelve and one?"

"That's right."

"Thank you." He hung up, dropped another coin into the phone, and dialed Dorothy's dorm. When they buzzed her room, there was no answer. He replaced the receiver, wondering what could have detained her.

On his way home he stopped in at a luncheonette and called Dorothy again. This time she answered.

"Hi. What took you so long? I called a couple of minutes ago."

"I stopped on the way. I had to buy a pair of gloves." She sounded breathless and happy.

"Oh. Listen, it's twenty-five after ten now. Can you be ready at twelve?"

"Well, I don't know. I want to take a shower. . . ."

"Twelve fifteen?"

"Okay."

"That's the girl. I'll be waiting for you outside the dorm at a quarter after twelve. On University Avenue. Use the side door, bring your valise, and don't sign out."

"Gee, we're practically eloping." She laughed warmly. "A quarter after twelve then."

"Right. We'll be downtown by twelve thirty."

"Good-by, groom."

"So long, bride."

HE DRESSED meticulously in his navy-blue suit, with black shoes and socks, a white shirt, and a simple pearl-gray tie. Viewing himself in the mirror, he wished he could exchange his face, temporarily, for one less distinctive. There were times, he realized, when being so handsome was a definite handicap.

At five minutes past twelve he was on University Avenue, across the street from the dorm. At twelve fifteen the dormitory door opened and Dorothy appeared. For once in her life she was punctual.

She was beautiful. Her suit was dark green, with a bow of white silk sparkling at the throat. Her shoes and purse were brown alligator, and there was a froth of dark green veil floating in her feathery golden hair. When she reached him, he grinned and took the valise from her hand. "All brides are beautiful," he said, "but you especially."

"*Gracias, señor.*" She looked as though she wanted to kiss him.

The lower eight floors of the Blue River Municipal Building were given over to city and county offices. The remaining six floors were rented to lawyers, doctors and dentists. Viewed from above, the building was a hollow square, an air shaft plunging down through the core of it. From the side, setbacks at the eighth and twelfth stories gave it the appearance of three blocks of decreasing size piled one atop the other.

It was twelve thirty when they mounted the steps and pushed through the central revolving door. He dropped a pace behind Dorothy, letting her lead the way to the directory board at the side of the crowded lobby. "There it is," she said triumphantly. "Marriage License Bureau—six oh four."

As they approached the elevators, he stepped back a bit, allowing Dorothy to enter first. He was the first to leave the car at the sixth floor, followed by two men with briefcases who walked briskly to the right. "Hey, wait for me!" Dorothy protested as the elevator door clanged shut behind her. She had been the last to leave the car. He had turned to the left and walked some fifteen feet, for all the world as though he were alone. He turned, appearing flustered, as she caught up with him and gaily took his arm. Over her head he watched the men with the briefcases disappear as they turned at the end of the corridor.

"Where were you running?" Dorothy teased.

"Sorry," he smiled. "Nervous bridegroom." They walked along arm in arm, Dorothy reciting the numbers on the doors as they passed. "Six twenty, six eighteen, six sixteen . . ." When they reached 604, he tried the door. It was locked. They read the hours listed on the frosted glass panel and Dorothy moaned dejectedly.

"Damn," he said. "I should have called to make sure." He put down the valise and looked at his watch. "Twenty-five to one."

"Twenty-five minutes," Dorothy said. "I guess we might as well go downstairs."

"Those crowds . . ." he muttered, then paused. "Hey, I've got an idea."

"What?"

"The roof. Let's go up on the roof. It's such a beautiful day, I bet we'll be able to see for miles!"

"Are we allowed?"

"If nobody stops us, we're allowed." He picked up the valise. "Come on, get your last look at the world as an unmarried woman."

She smiled and they began walking, retracing their path back to the bank of elevators where, in a few moments, there glowed above one of the doors a white arrow pointing upward.

When they left the car at the fourteenth floor, they were again separated by the other alighting passengers. In the corridor, they waited until these had hurried around the turns or into offices, and then Dorothy said, "Let's go," in a conspiratorial whisper.

They had to make a half circuit of the building until they found a door marked STAIRWAY. It opened onto a landing with black metal stairs leading up and down. Dim light sifted through a dirt-fogged skylight. They walked up. A heavy metal door confronted them. He tried the knob.

"Is it locked?"

"I don't think so."

He put his shoulder to the door and pushed. It gave, groaning open. A slice of electric-blue sky hit their eyes, blinding after the obscurity of the stairway. There was the quick flutter of pigeons' wings.

He picked up the valise, stepped over a ledge, and put the valise down on the other side. Then he extended a hand to Dorothy. Gesturing toward the expanse of roof, he gave her a mock bow and his best smile. "Enter, mam'selle," he said.

Taking his hand, she stepped gracefully over the ledge and onto the black tar of the roof.

HE WASN'T nervous at all. Everything was going to be perfect. No mistakes. He just *knew* it. He hadn't felt so good since—God, since high school!

"Come look at this," Dorothy said. She was standing a few feet away, her back toward him, the alligator purse tucked under one arm. Her hands rested on the waist-high parapet that edged the roof. He came up behind her. "Isn't it something?" she said. The city sprawled before them, clear and sharp in the brilliant sunlight. "Look"—Dorothy pointed to a green spot far away—"I think that's the campus." He put his hands on her shoulders. A white-gloved hand reached up to touch his. He looked down at the top of her head, the dark green veiling buoyant in the yellow hair. She tilted her head back and smiled up at him.

When her eyes returned to the panorama, he moved to her side and, putting an arm about her shoulders, he leaned over the parapet. Two stories below, the red-tiled floor of the twelfth-story setback extended like a shelf across the width of the building and around its other three sides. That was bad; a two-story drop wasn't what he wanted. He turned and surveyed the roof.

It was perhaps a hundred and fifty feet square, dotted with chimneys and ventilator pipes and edged by the brick parapet with its flat white stone coping a foot wide. On the right, the KBRI tower reared up like a small Eiffel Tower. In the center of the roof, another brick parapet rimmed the air shaft, a square some thirty feet across.

Leaving Dorothy, he walked across to the air shaft. He leaned over the parapet. Four walls funneled down to a tiny areaway fourteen stories below, its corners banked with trash cans and wooden crates. Three sides of the shaft were striped with windows. The fourth, which evidently backed on the elevator shafts, was blank, windowless. This was the spot. The south side of the air shaft. He slapped the top of the parapet, his lips pursed thoughtfully.

Dorothy came up behind him and took his arm. "It's so quiet," she said.

They began walking slowly. When they reached the northern rim of the roof they were able to see the river, and with the sky reflected in it, it was really blue, as blue as the rivers painted on maps. "Do you have a cigarette?" she asked.

He reached into his pocket and touched a pack of Chesterfields. Then his hand came out empty. "No, I don't. Do you have any?"

"They're buried in here someplace." She dug into her purse, pushing aside a gold compact and a turquoise handkerchief, and finally produced a crushed pack of Tareytons. They each took one. He lit them and she returned the pack to her purse.

"Dorrie, there's something I want to tell you." She was blowing a stream of smoke against the sky, hardly listening. "It's about the pills."

Her face jerked around, going white. "What?"

"I'm glad they didn't work," he said, smiling. "I really am."

She looked at him uncomprehendingly. "You're glad?"

"Yes. When I called you last night, I was going to tell you not to take them, but you already had." Come on, he thought. Get it off your chest, Dorrie. It must be killing you.

Her voice was shaky. "Why? You were so . . . What made you change your mind?"

"I don't know. I thought it over. I suppose I'm as anxious to get married as you are." He examined his cigarette. When he looked up again, her cheeks were flushed and her eyes glistened. "What's the matter, Dorrie?"

"Please . . . don't be angry. I—I didn't take them." The words poured from her lips. "You said you were going to get a night job and I knew we could manage, everything would work out, and I was counting on it so much, *so* much." She paused. "You aren't angry, are you?" she beseeched. "You understand?"

"Sure, baby. I told you I was glad they didn't work."

He took the neatly folded handkerchief from his breast pocket and touched it to her eyes. "Dorrie, what did you do with the pills?"

"Threw them away." She smiled shamefacedly.

"Where?" he asked casually, replacing the handkerchief.

"Flushed them down the john."

That was what he wanted to hear. There would be no questions about why she had taken such a messy way out when she had already gone to the trouble of obtaining poison. He dropped his cigarette and stepped on it. Dorothy, taking a final puff, did the same with hers.

He looked down at the two butts, hers edged with lipstick, his clean. He picked his up. Splitting it down the middle with his thumbnail, he let the tobacco blow away and rolled the paper into a tiny ball. He flicked it out over the parapet. "That's the way we used to do it in the army," he said.

He took her arm. They turned and walked leisurely away from the edge of the roof. When they reached the south side of the air shaft, he stood with his back against the parapet, braced his hands on the top of it, and hitched himself up.

"Don't sit there," Dorothy said apprehensively.

"Why not?" he asked, glancing at the white stone coping. "You sit on a bench this wide and you don't fall off." He patted the stone on his left. "Come on."

"No," she said, touching her skirt. "My suit . . ."

He took out his handkerchief, whipped it open, and spread it on the stone beside him. "Sir Walter Raleigh," he said.

She hesitated a moment, then gave him her purse. Turning her back to the parapet, she gripped the top on either side of the handkerchief and lifted herself up. "There," he said, putting his arm around her waist. She turned her head slowly, peeking over her shoulder. "Don't look down," he warned. "You'll get dizzy."

He put the purse on the stone to his right and they sat in silence for a moment, watching two pigeons as they came out from behind the staircase shed. After a minute he took his arm from her waist and put his hand over hers as it gripped the front of the stone between them. He braced his other hand on the coping and eased himself down from the parapet. Before she could do likewise he swung around and faced her, his waist against her knees, his hands covering both of hers. He smiled at her and she smiled back.

His hands moved to her knees, cupped them, his fingertips caressing under the hem of her skirt.

"We'd better be going, hadn't we, darling?" she said.

"In a minute, baby. We still have time."

His eyes caught hers, held them, as his hands descended and moved behind to rest on the slope of her calves. Her white-gloved hands still clasped the front of the coping firmly.

"That's a beautiful blouse," he said, looking at the fluffy silk bow at her throat. "Is it new?"

"New? It's as old as the hills."

His gaze became critical. "The bow is a little off-center."

One hand left the stone and rose to finger the bow. "No," he said, "now you've got it worse." Her other hand detached itself from the top of the parapet.

His hands moved down over her silken calves, as low as he could reach without bending. His right foot dropped back, poised on the toe in readiness. He held his breath.

She adjusted the bow with both hands. "Is that any bett—"

With cobra speed he ducked—hands streaking down to catch

her heels—stepped back and straightened up, lifting her legs high. For one frozen instant as his hands shifted, their eyes met, stupefied terror bursting in hers, a cry rising in her throat. With all his strength he pushed against her legs.

Her shriek of petrified anguish trailed down into the shaft like a burning wire. He closed his eyes. The scream died. Silence, then an awful deafening crash. Wincing, he remembered the cans and crates piled far below.

He opened his eyes to see his handkerchief billowing as the breeze pulled it free from the stone's rough surface. He snatched it up. Wheeling, he raced to the stairway door, grabbed the valise with one hand, and pulled the door open, wiping the knob with the handkerchief as he did so.

He clattered down flight after flight of black metal steps, the valise banging against his legs, his right hand burning over the banisters. His heart galloped and the image of whirling walls dizzied him. When he finally stopped, he was on the seventh-floor landing.

He clung to the newel post, gasping. The phrase "physical release of tension" danced in his mind. That was why he had run that way—physical release of tension—not panic, not panic. Putting down the valise, he caught his breath. After a few straightening tugs at his jacket, he picked up the valise, opened the door, and stepped out into the corridor.

Every door was open. People had rushed across the hall to the offices whose windows faced the air shaft. Walking toward the elevators at a moderate pace, he glanced in at each office and saw the backs of people crammed around the windows, their voices a murmur of excitement and tense speculation.

Shortly after he reached the bank of elevators, a down car came. He squeezed in and faced the front. Behind him the other passengers avidly exchanged fragments of information, the customary elevator coldness shattered by the violence at their backs.

The easy bustle of normality filled the lobby. Most of the people there were unaware of any disturbance. Swinging the valise lightly, he made his way across the marbled expanse and out

into the bright afternoon. As he jogged down the steps that fronted the building, two policemen passed him, going up. At the foot of the steps he turned and watched the blue uniforms vanish into a revolving door. He wondered how dangerous it would be for him to go back, mingle with the crowd, see her. . . . He decided against it.

A university bus came by and stopped for a red light. Swinging himself on, he paid his fare and walked to the rear. He stood looking out the window. When the bus had gone about four blocks, a white ambulance clanged by, the pitch of its bell dropping as it passed.

THE Stoddard baseball pep rally began at nine that night in an empty lot next to the stadium, but the news of a student's suicide put a damper on the entire affair. In the orange glow of the bonfire, the students spread their blankets and sat huddled in conversation. The manager of the baseball team and the members of the cheerleading squad tried vainly to make the rally what it should be. They spurred the boys to the gathering of more and more fuel, throwing on crates and cartons until the flaming pillar was so high it threatened to topple, but it was to no avail. Cheers wavered and died before half the school's name was spelled out.

He had not attended many rallies before, but he attended this one. He walked the dark streets from his rooming house at a leisurely pace, bearing a carton in his arms.

In the afternoon he had emptied Dorothy's valise. Then, although it was a warm day, he had donned his trench coat, and after filling its pockets with bottles and small containers of cosmetics, he left the house with the valise, stripped of the tags bearing Dorothy's name and address. He had gone downtown and checked the valise in a locker at the bus terminal. From there he had walked to the Morton Street Bridge, where he dropped the locker key and then the cosmetics bottles, one by one, into the umber water, opening them first so that trapped air would not keep them afloat. On his way home from the bridge he stopped at a grocery store, where he secured a corrugated paper carton. Into the carton he packed the pharmacy lab manual, the Kingship Copper pamphlets, the tags from the valise, and the few articles of clothing that Dorothy had packed for their brief honeymoon: a cocktail dress of gray taffeta, a pair of black suede pumps, stockings, a half-slip, bra and panties, two handkerchiefs, a pair of pink satin mules, a pink negligee and a nightgown—silk and lace, delicate, scented. . . .

He carried the carton to the rally and picked his way through the reclining figures in the darkness. Stepping gingerly between blue-jeaned legs, he advanced to the flaming center of the field.

The heat and the glare were intense in the clearing that surrounded the roaring twelve-foot fire. He stood for a moment, staring at the flames. Suddenly a cheerleader came dashing around from the other side of the clearing. "That's the boy," he cried, and seized the carton from his hands. He swung the carton toward the flames. "All the way to the top!" he shouted.

He stood watching as the carton turned black, sheets of flame sliding up its sides and ripping through its top.

FROM the Blue River *Clarion-Ledger;* Friday, April 28, 1950:

STODDARD COED DIES IN PLUNGE
MUNICIPAL BUILDING TRAGEDY FATAL TO DAUGHTER OF COPPER MAGNATE

Dorothy Kingship, 19-year-old Stoddard University sophomore, was killed today when she fell or jumped from the roof of the 14-story Blue River Municipal Building. The attractive blond girl, whose home was in New York City, was a daughter of copper magnate Leo Kingship, president of Kingship Copper Inc.

At 12:58 p.m. workers in the building were startled by a loud scream and a crashing sound from the wide air shaft which runs through the structure. Rushing to their windows, they saw the contorted figure of a young woman. Dr. Harvey C. Hess, of 57 Woodbridge Circle, who was in the lobby at the time, reached the scene seconds later to pronounce the girl dead.

The police, arriving shortly thereafter, found a purse resting on the 3½-foot wall that encircles the air shaft on the roof of the building. In the purse were a birth certificate and a university registration card which served to identify the girl. Police also found a fresh cigarette butt on the roof, stained with lipstick of the shade Miss Kingship wore, leading them to conclude that she had been on the roof for several minutes prior to the plunge which ended her life.

Rex Cargill, an elevator operator, told police that he believes he took Miss Kingship to the 6th or 7th floor half an hour before the tragedy, but because of the lunch-hour crowds none of the operators could recall what passengers they took to the 14th floor. The roof can be reached by the fire staircase as well.

According to Stoddard's Dean of Students, Clark D. Welch, Miss Kingship was doing satisfactory work in all her studies. Shocked residents of the dormitory where she lived could offer no reason why she might have taken her own life. They described her as quiet and withdrawn. "Nobody knew her well," said one girl.

From the Blue River *Clarion-Ledger;* Saturday, April 29, 1950:

COED'S DEATH WAS SUICIDE
SISTER RECEIVES NOTE IN MAIL

Dorothy Kingship, the Stoddard coed who plunged from the roof of the Municipal Building yesterday afternoon, was a suicide, Chief of Police Eldon Chesser told reporters last night. An unsigned note in a handwriting definitely established to be that of the dead girl was received through the mail late yesterday afternoon by her sister, Ellen Kingship, a student in Caldwell, Wisconsin. Although the exact wording of the note has not been made public, Chief Chesser characterized it as "a clear expression of suicidal intent."

On receiving the note, Ellen Kingship attempted to reach her sister by telephone. The call was transferred to Stoddard's Dean of Students, Clark D. Welch, who informed Miss Kingship of the 19-year-old girl's death. Miss Kingship left immediately for Blue River, arriving here yesterday evening. Her father, Leo Kingship, is expected to arrive some time today.

Also from the *Clarion-Ledger;* Saturday, April 29, 1950:

LAST PERSON TO SPEAK TO SUICIDE DESCRIBES HER AS TENSE, NERVOUS

by LaVerne Breen

"She laughed a lot and was smiling the whole time she was in my room. I thought at the time that she was very happy about something, but now I realize that those were all symptoms of some terrible strain." Thus Annabelle Koch, Stoddard sophomore, describes the behavior of Dorothy Kingship two hours before the latter's suicide.

"Dorothy knocked on the door around a quarter past eleven," says Miss Koch. "She came in and I was a little surprised, because we hardly knew each other. She asked if I would loan her the belt to my green suit. I should mention that we both have the same green suit. I got mine in Boston and she got hers in New York, but they're exactly the same. Anyway, she asked if I would loan her my belt because the buckle of hers was broken. I hesitated at first, because it's my new spring suit, but she seemed to want it so badly that I finally gave it to her. She thanked me and left.

"Now here's the strange part," Miss Koch continued. "Later, when the police came and searched her room for a note, *they found my belt on her desk!* I recognized it by the way the gold finish was rubbed off the buckle. The police kept the belt.

"I was very puzzled by Dorothy's actions. She had pretended to want my belt, but she hadn't used it at all. She was wearing her green suit when . . . when it happened. The police checked and her belt buckle wasn't the least bit broken. It all seemed very mysterious.

"She must have been desperate for someone to talk with. If only I'd recognized the signs at the time. I can't help feeling that if I had gotten her to talk out her troubles, maybe all this wouldn't have happened."

HE FOUND the last six weeks of the school year disappointingly flat. He had expected the excitement created by Dorothy's death to linger in the air like the glow of a rocket; instead, it had faded almost immediately. As for the newspapers, a short paragraph announcing Leo Kingship's arrival in Blue River marked the last time the Kingship name appeared in the *Clarion-Ledger*. There was no word of an autopsy nor of Dorothy's pregnancy. Keeping it out of the papers must have cost Kingship plenty.

He told himself he should be rejoicing. If there had been any kind of inquiry, he certainly would have been sought for questioning. But there had been no questions, no suspicion. Everything had fallen into place perfectly. Except that business of the belt. That puzzled him. Why on earth had Dorothy taken another girl's belt when she hadn't wanted to wear it? Maybe she really did want to talk to someone—about the wedding—and then had thought better of it. But Annabelle Koch's interpretation of it only strengthened the picture of a suicide. He should be walking on air, smiling at strangers. Instead, there was this dull, leaden, let-down feeling.

His depression became worse when he returned to Menasset early in June. Here he was again, right where he'd been last summer and the summer before. Dorothy's death and all his planning hadn't advanced him in the slightest.

He became impatient with his mother's badgering. Did he have pictures of the girls he'd gone out with at school?—expecting them to be the most beautiful, the most sought after. Did he belong to this club, to that club?—expecting him to be the president of each. What was his standing in philosophy, in English, in Spanish?—expecting him to be the leader in all. One day he lost his temper. "It's about time you realized I'm not the king of the world!" he shouted, storming from the room.

He took a job in a haberdashery shop for the summer. Though it didn't take his mind off things, he began to slough off his dejection. He still had the newspaper clippings about Dorothy's death, locked in a small gray strongbox he kept in his bedroom closet. He took them out once in a while, smiling at the officious certainty of the police and the half-baked theorizing of Annabelle Koch. Once he whispered it aloud: "I got away with murder!"

So what if he wasn't rich yet! Hell, he was only twenty-four.

Two: Ellen

LETTER from Annabelle Koch to Leo Kingship:

March 5, 1951

Dear Mr. Kingship,

I suppose you are wondering who I am, unless you remember my name from the Blue River newspapers. I am the student at Stoddard who loaned a belt to your daughter Dorothy last April just before her death. I was the last person to speak to her. I would not bring up this subject as I am sure it must be very painful to you, except that I have a good reason.

As you may recall from the newspaper account, Dorothy and I had the same green suit. She came to my room and asked to borrow my belt. I loaned it to her and later the police found it (or what I thought was it) in her room. By the time they got around to returning it to me it was quite late in the season, so I did not wear the green suit again last year.

Now spring is approaching and last night I tried on my green suit again and it fitted perfectly. But when I put on the belt I found to my surprise that it was Dorothy's belt all along. You see, the notch that is marked from the buckle is two notches too big for my waist. Dorothy was quite slender but I am even more so. When the police first showed it to me I thought it was mine because the gold finish on the buckle was rubbed off. I should have realized that since both suits were made by the same manufacturer the finish would have come off of *both* buckles. So now it seems that Dorothy could not wear her own belt for some reason and was wearing mine instead when she died. I cannot understand it. At the time I thought she only pretended to need my belt because she wanted to speak to me.

Now that I know the belt is Dorothy's I would feel funny wearing it. I thought of throwing it away but I would feel funny doing that also, so I am sending it to you in a separate package and you can keep it or dispose of it as you see fit.

Yours truly,
Annabelle Koch

51

Letter from Leo Kingship to Ellen Kingship:

March 8, 1951

My dear Ellen,

Yesterday being Wednesday, Marion came here to dinner. I showed her a letter which I received yesterday and she suggested that I send it on to you. You will find it enclosed. Read it now, and then continue with my letter.

Now that you have read Miss Koch's letter, I will explain why I forwarded it. I well remember your attitude last April, when you refused to believe that Dorothy's death had been a suicide. You felt that if Dorothy had committed suicide you were in some way responsible, and so it was several weeks before you were able to accept her death for what it was.

This letter from Miss Koch makes it clear that Dorothy went to the girl because, for some peculiar reason of her own, she did want her belt; she was *not* in desperate need of someone to whom she could talk. She had made up her mind to do what she was going to do, and there is absolutely no reason for you to believe that she would have come to you first if you two had not had that argument the previous Christmas. You are not responsible; no one is but Dorothy herself.

The knowledge that Miss Koch's original interpretation of Dorothy's behavior was erroneous will, I hope, rid you of any feelings of self-recrimination that may remain.

Your loving
Father

Letter from Ellen Kingship to Bud Corliss:

March 12, 1951

Dear Bud,

Here I sit in the club car, trying to keep my writing hand steady against the motion of the train and trying to give an explanation of why I am making this trip to Blue River.

First of all, this trip is not impulsive! I thought about it all last night. Second of all, I will not be missing work, because you are going to take complete notes in each class. Now I'll fill in a little background.

You already know that Dorothy originally wanted to come to Caldwell and that I opposed it for her own good, or so I convinced myself at the time. Since her death I've wondered whether it wasn't pure selfishness on my part. My life at home had been restrained, both by my father's strictness and Dorothy's dependence on me. So when I got to Caldwell I really let go. During my first three years I was the rah-rah girl; beer parties, hanging around with the Big Wheels, etc. You wouldn't have recognized me. So, as I say, I'm not sure whether I prevented Dorothy from coming in order to encourage her independence or to avoid losing mine, Caldwell being the small everybody-knows-what-everybody-else-is-doing type place that it is.

From the letter I received from my father Saturday morning, you know of his analysis of my reaction to Dorothy's death. He is absolutely right. I didn't want to admit it was suicide because that meant that I was partly responsible. But I also had other reasons for doubting it was suicide. The note she sent me, for instance. It was her handwriting but it didn't sound like her. It was kind of stilted, and she addressed me as "Darling," when before it had always been "Dear Ellen" or "Dearest Ellen." The fact that she carried her birth certificate with her also bothered me, but the police explained that a suicide will often take pains to make sure he is immediately identified. She had other identification in her wallet, but that didn't make any impression on them. And when I told them that she just wasn't the suicidal type, they didn't even bother to answer me.

When the autopsy revealed that Dorothy was pregnant I finally had to accept the fact that she committed suicide—and that I was to blame, but only partly. Dorothy's pregnancy meant that another person had deserted her too—the man. If I knew anything about Dorothy it was that she did not treat sex lightly. The fact that she was pregnant meant that there was a man whom she had loved and had intended to marry.

Now early in the December before her death, Dorothy had written me about a man she had met in her English class. She had been going out with him for quite some time, and this was the Real Thing. She said she would give me all the details over Christmas vacation. But we had an argument then, and when we returned to school our letters were almost like business letters. So

I never even learned his name. All I knew about him was that he had been in her English class in the fall term, and that he was handsome—tall, blond, and blue-eyed.

I told my father about this man, urging him to find out who he was and punish him somehow. He refused, saying that it was impossible to prove he was the one who had gotten Dorothy into trouble, and futile even if we could prove it.

That's how things stood until Saturday, when I received my father's letter with the one from Annabelle Koch enclosed. Which brings us to my big scene. Why couldn't Dorothy wear her own belt? Why had she lied about it and taken Annabelle's instead? My father was content to let it pass, saying she had "some peculiar reason of her own," but I wanted to know what that reason was, because there were three other inconsequential things which Dorothy did on the day of her death that puzzled me then and that still puzzled me. Here they are:

1. At 10:15 that morning she bought an inexpensive pair of white gloves in a shop across the street from her dormitory. (The owner reported it to the police after seeing her picture in the papers.) She was wearing them when she died, yet in the bureau in her room was a beautiful pair of handmade white gloves, perfectly spotless, that Marion had given her the previous Christmas.

2. Dorothy was a careful dresser. She was wearing her green suit when she died. With it she wore an old, inexpensive white silk blouse whose floppy bow was all wrong for the suit. Yet in her closet was a white silk blouse which had been specially made to go with the suit.

3. Dorothy was wearing dark green, with brown and white accessories. Yet the handkerchief in her purse was bright turquoise. In her room were at least a dozen handkerchiefs that would have matched her outfit perfectly.

At the time of her death I mentioned these points to the police. They dismissed them as quickly as they had dismissed the others I brought up. Their comeback was, "You can't figure a suicide."

Annabelle Koch's letter added a fourth incident which followed the pattern of the other three. Her own belt was perfectly all right, but Dorothy wore Annabelle's instead. In each case she rejected an appropriate item for one that was less appropriate. Why?

I batted that problem around in my head all day Saturday and

Saturday night, too. Suddenly, light broke. It came to me so startlingly that I shot straight up in bed. The out-of-style blouse, the gloves she'd bought that morning, Annabelle Koch's belt, the turquoise handkerchief . . . something old, something new, something borrowed, and something blue.

It might—I keep telling myself—be a coincidence. But in my heart I don't believe that.

Dorothy went to the Municipal Building because that is where you go to get married—and she carried her birth certificate with her to prove she was over eighteen. And you don't make a trip like that alone. Dorothy can only have gone with one person—the man who made her pregnant, the man she loved—the handsome blue-eyed blond of her English class. He got her up to the roof somehow. I'm almost certain that's the way it was.

The note? All it said was "I hope you will forgive me for the unhappiness I will cause. There is nothing else that I can do." Where is there mention of suicide? She was referring to the marriage! She knew Father would disapprove of a hasty step like that, but there was nothing else she could do because she was pregnant.

"Something old, something new" was enough to set me going, but it would never be enough to make the police reclassify a suicide as an unsolved murder. So I'm going to find this man and do some very cautious Sherlocking. As soon as I turn up anything that supports my suspicions, I promise to go straight to the police.

I'll wind this letter up later, when I'll be able to tell you where I'm staying and what progress, if any, I've made. I have a pretty good idea of how to begin. Wish me luck.

DEAN Welch rose as the door opened and Ellen Kingship entered. She was neat; he liked that. And quite pretty. Red-brown hair in thick bangs, brown eyes, a smile whose restraint acknowledged the unfortunate past.

"Miss Kingship," he murmured with a nod, indicating the visitor's chair. "Your father is well, I hope."

"Very well, thank you."

The dean said, "I had the pleasure of meeting him . . . last year." There was a moment of silence. "If there's anything I can do for you . . ."

She shifted in the stiff-backed chair. "We—my father and I—are trying to locate a certain man, a student here." The dean's eyebrows lifted in polite curiosity. "He lent my sister a fairly large sum of money a few weeks before her death. She wrote me about it. I happened to come across her checkbook last week and it reminded me of the incident. There's nothing in the checkbook to indicate that she ever repaid the debt, and we thought he might have felt awkward about claiming it."

The dean nodded.

"The only trouble," Ellen said, "is that I don't recall his name. But I do remember Dorothy mentioning that he was in her English class during the fall semester, and that he was blond. We thought perhaps you could help us locate him. It was a fairly large sum of money. . . ." She took a deep breath.

"I see," said the dean. "Can do," he snapped with military briskness. He jabbed one of the buttons on the interoffice speaker.

The door opened and an efficient-looking woman stepped into the room. "Miss Platt," the dean said, "get the program card of Kingship, Dorothy, fall semester, 1949. See which English section she was in and bring me the folders of all the male students who were enrolled in that section."

"Yes, sir," she said, and went out.

The dean turned back to Ellen. "Surely you haven't come to Blue River solely for this purpose?" he said.

"I'm visiting friends." She opened her handbag. "May I smoke?"

"By all means." He pushed a crystal ashtray to her side of the desk. Ellen lit her cigarette with a match from a white folder on which *Ellen Kingship* was printed in copper letters.

The dean regarded the matchbook thoughtfully. "Your conscientiousness in financial matters is admirable," he said, smiling. "If only everyone we dealt with were similarly conscientious." He examined a bronze letter opener. "We are at present beginning the construction of a new gymnasium and field house. Several people who pledged contributions have failed to live up to their words."

Ellen shook her head sympathetically.

"Perhaps your father would be interested in making a contribution," the dean speculated. "A memorial to your sister . . ."

"I'll be glad to mention it to him."

"Would you? I would appreciate that." He replaced the letter opener. "Such contributions are tax deductible," he added.

Miss Platt knocked and entered with a stack of manila folders in her arm. She set them before the dean. "English fifty-one," she said, "section six. Seventeen male students."

"Fine," said the dean. He opened the top folder and leafed through its contents until he came to an application form. There was a photograph pasted in the corner of it. "Dark hair," he said, and put the folder on his left.

When he had gone through all of them, there were two piles. "Twelve with dark hair and five with light," the dean said.

Ellen leaned forward. "Dorothy once wrote me that he was handsome."

The dean drew the pile of five folders to him and opened the first one. He lifted out the application form and turned it toward Ellen. The face was chinless. She shook her head.

The second was an emaciated young man with thick eyeglasses. The third was fifty-three and his hair was white.

The dean opened the fourth folder. "Gordon Gant," he said. "Does that sound like the name?" He turned the application form toward her.

The young man in the photograph was blond and unarguably handsome. "I think so," she said. "Yes, I think he—"

"Or could it be Dwight Powell?" the dean asked, displaying another application form.

This photograph showed a square-jawed, serious-looking young man with a cleft chin and pale eyes. Also blond and handsome.

"Which name sounds familiar?" the dean asked.

Ellen looked from one picture to the other. Two. It would slow her up a little, that's all.

She left the dean's office with her purse in one hand and a slip of paper in the other. On it were written the addresses and telephone numbers of Gordon Gant and Dwight Powell.

FROM A RESTAURANT nearby, Ellen made her first call.

"Hello?" the voice was a woman's; dry, middle-aged.

"Hello." Ellen swallowed. "Is Gordon Gant there?"

"No." Snapped out sharply.

"Who is this?"

"His landlady."

"When do you expect him back?"

"Won't be back till late tonight." The woman's voice was quick with annoyance. There was a click as she hung up.

He would be gone all day. Go there? . . . A single conversation with the landlady might establish that Gant was the one who had gone with Dorothy. Or, by elimination, it might prove that Powell was the one. Speak to the landlady . . . but under what pretext?

Why, any pretext! Provided the woman believed it, what harm could the wildest story do?

THE house where Gordon Gant lived, 1312 West Twenty-sixth, was the third one from the corner; mustard colored, with brown trim. Ellen walked up the cracked concrete path that led to the porch. There she read the nameplate on the mailbox: MRS. MINNA ARQUETTE. The doorbell was the old-fashioned kind; a fan-shaped metal tab protruded from the center of the door. Drawing a deep breath, she gave the tab a quick twist.

Presently footsteps sounded inside. The woman who came to the door was tall and lank, with frizzy gray hair clustered above a long equine face. She looked Ellen up and down. "Yes?"

"You must be Mrs. Arquette," Ellen declared.

"That's right." The woman twitched a sudden smile, displaying teeth of an unnatural perfection.

Ellen smiled back at her. "I'm Gordon's cousin. Didn't he mention that I'd be here today?"

"Why, no. He didn't say anything about a cousin. Not a word."

"That's funny. I wrote him I'd be passing through. I'm on my way to Chicago and I purposely came this way so I could stop off and see him. He must have forgotten to—"

"When did you write him?"

Ellen hesitated. "The day before yesterday. Saturday."

"Oh." The smile flashed again. "Gordon leaves the house early in the morning and the first mail don't come till ten. Your letter is probably sitting in his room this minute."

"Ohh . . ."

"He isn't here right—"

"Couldn't I come in for a few minutes, anyway?" Ellen interrupted. "I took the wrong bus from the station and I had to walk about ten blocks."

Mrs. Arquette took a step back into the house. "Of course. Come on in."

"Thank you very much." Ellen crossed the threshold, entering a dimly lit hallway.

"Miz Arquette?" a voice called from the back of the house.

"Coming!" she answered. She turned to Ellen. "You mind sitting in the kitchen?"

"Not at all," Ellen said. The Arquette teeth shone again, and Ellen followed the tall figure down the hallway.

The kitchen was painted the same mustard color as the exterior of the house. There was a white porcelain-topped table in the middle of the room, with a set of anagrams laid out on it. An elderly bald-headed man with thick eyeglasses sat at the table, pouring out the last of a bottle of Dr. Pepper. "This is Mr. Fishback from next door," said Mrs. Arquette. "We play anagrams."

"Nickel a word," added the old man.

"This is Miss . . ." Mrs. Arquette waited.

"Gant," said Ellen.

"Miss Gant, Gordon's cousin."

"How do you do," said Mr. Fishback. "Gordon's a nice boy." He raised his glasses to look at Ellen. "It's your go," he said to Mrs. Arquette. Mrs. Arquette stared at the letters on the table. "Where you on your way from?" she asked Ellen.

"California."

"I didn't know Gordon had family in the West."

"No, I was just visiting there. I'm from the East."

"Oh." Mrs. Arquette looked at Mr. Fishback.

"How is Gordon these days?" Ellen asked.

"Oh, fine," said Mrs. Arquette. "Busy as a bee, what with school and the program."

"The program?"

"You mean you don't know about Gordon's program?"

"Well, I haven't heard from him in quite a while."

"Why, he's had it for almost three months now!" Mrs. Arquette drew herself up grandly. "He plays records and talks. A disc jockey. The Discus Thrower he's called. Every night except Sunday, from eight to ten over KBRI."

"That's wonderful!" Ellen exclaimed.

"Why, he's a real celebrity," the landlady continued. "And girls he don't even know calling him up at all hours. Stoddard girls. They call up just to hear his voice over the telephone."

Ellen fingered the edge of the table. "Is Gordon still going out with that girl he wrote me about last year?" she asked.

"Which one's that?"

"A blond girl, short, pretty. Gordon mentioned her in a few of his letters last year. I thought he was really interested in her. But he stopped writing about her in April."

"Well, I'll tell you," Mrs. Arquette said, "I don't ever get to see the girls Gordon goes out with." She turned over a letter. "What was that girl's name? You tell me her name I can probably tell you if he's still going out with her, because sometimes when he's using the phone over by the stairs there, I can't help hearing part of the conversation."

The game of anagrams went on in silence for a minute. Finally Ellen said, "I think this girl's name was Dorothy."

Mrs. Arquette waved a go-ahead at Mr. Fishback. "Dorothy . . ." Her eyes narrowed. "No . . . I haven't heard him talking to any Dorothy lately."

The wooden squares clicked softly as Mrs. Arquette maneuvered them about. "I think," said Ellen, "that he must have broken up with this Dorothy in April, when he stopped writing about her. He must have been in a bad mood around the end of

April. Worried, nervous . . ." She looked at Mrs. Arquette questioningly.

"Not Gordon," she said. "He had real spring fever last year. Going around humming. I joshed him about it." Mr. Fishback fidgeted impatiently. "Oh, go ahead," Mrs. Arquette said.

Mr. Fishback pounced on the anagrams. "You missed one!" he cried. "F-A-N-E. Fane!"

"What're you talking about, fane? No such word!" Mrs. Arquette turned to Ellen. "You ever hear of a word 'fane'?"

"You should know better'n to argue with me!" Mr. Fishback shrilled. "I don't know what it means, but I know it's a word. Look it up in the dictionary!"

"That little pocket one with nothing in it? Every time I look up one of your words and it ain't there you blame it on the dictionary!"

Ellen looked at the two glaring figures. "Gordon must have a dictionary," she said. She stood up. "I'll be glad to get it if you'll tell me which room is his."

"That's right," Mrs. Arquette said decisively. "He *does* have one." She rose. "You sit down, dear. I know just where it is."

"May I come along then? I'd like to see Gordon's room. He's told me what a nice place—"

"Come on," said Mrs. Arquette, stalking out of the kitchen.

They sped up the dark wood stairs, Mrs. Arquette in the fore muttering indignantly.

The room at the head of the stairway was bright with flowered wallpaper. There were a green-covered bed, a desk, a dresser, easy chair, bookcase . . . Mrs. Arquette, having snatched a book from the top of the desk, stood by the window ruffling the pages. Ellen moved to the desk and scanned the titles of the books ranked across its top for a diary or a notebook.

"Oh, shoot," said Mrs. Arquette. She stood with her forefinger pressed to the open dictionary. " 'Fane,' " she read, " 'a temple; hence a church.' " She slammed the book shut. "Where does he get words like that?"

Ellen eased over to the dresser, where three envelopes were

fanned out. Mrs. Arquette glanced at her. "The one without a return address must be yours." She went to the door. "Coming?"

They trudged down the stairs and walked slowly into the kitchen.

Ellen took her purse and coat from the chair in which she had sat. "I guess I'll be going now," she said dispiritedly.

"Going?" Mrs. Arquette looked up, the thin eyebrows arching. "Well, for goodness' sake, aren't you going to wait for Gordon?" She looked at the clock above the refrigerator. "It's ten after two," she said. "His last class ended at two o'clock. He should be here any minute."

Ellen went cold. She couldn't speak. Finally she managed to gasp, "You . . . you told me he would be gone all day."

Mrs. Arquette looked injured. "Why, I never told you no such thing! Why on earth have you been sitting here if you're not waiting for him?"

"The telephone . . ."

The landlady's jaw dropped. "Was that you? Around one o'clock?"

Ellen nodded helplessly.

"Well, why didn't you tell me it was you? I thought it was one of those fool girls. Whenever some girl calls and won't give a name I tell them he's gone for the day. Even if he's here. He told me to. He . . ." The dull eyes, the thin-lipped mouth became grim, suspicious. "If you thought he was out for the day," she demanded slowly, "then why did you come here at all?"

"I . . . I wanted to meet you. Gordon wrote so much . . ."

"Why were you asking all those questions?" Mrs. Arquette stood up. Suddenly she was holding Ellen's arms, her long bony fingers clutching painfully.

"Let go of me. . . . Please . . ."

"Why were you snooping in his room?" Her horselike face pressed close to Ellen's, her eyes swelling with anger. "What did you want in there? You take something while my back was turned?"

Behind Ellen, Mr. Fishback's chair scraped and his voice piped frightenedly, "Why'd she want to steal anything from her own cousin?"

"Who says she's his cousin?" Mrs. Arquette snapped.

They heard the front door slam and footsteps on the stairs. "Gordon!" Mrs. Arquette shouted. "Gordon!"

The footsteps stopped. "What is it, Mrs. Arquette?" The landlady released Ellen and turned and ran down the hallway.

Ellen stood motionless, hearing the excited rasping of Mrs. Arquette's voice. "She said she was your cousin and kept asking all kinds of questions about what girls you were going out with last year, and she even tricked me into taking her to your room. She was looking at your books and letters. . . ." Mrs. Arquette's voice suddenly flooded the kitchen. "There she is!"

Ellen turned. Mrs. Arquette stood with one arm lifted, pointing in accusation. Gant was in the doorway, tall and spare in a pale blue topcoat, books in one hand. He looked at her for a moment, then his lips curved into a smile.

He stepped into the room, putting his books on the refrigerator without taking his eyes from Ellen. "Why, Cousin Hester," he marveled softly, his eyes flicking up and down in considered appraisal. "You've passed through adolescence magnificently." He ambled around the table, placed his hands on Ellen's shoulders, and kissed her fondly on the cheek.

"You mean she really *is* your cousin?" Mrs. Arquette gasped.

"Arquette, my love," said Gant, moving to Ellen's left, "ours was a communal teething ring."

Ellen eyed him crazily, her face flushed. Her gaze moved to Mrs. Arquette at the left of the table, to the hallway beyond it, to the coat and purse in her hands. She darted to the right and through the door and down the hallway. Wrenching open the heavy front door, she fled from the house.

Oh, God, everything messed up! She clenched her teeth, feeling the hot pressure of tears behind her eyes, her whole being compressed with unreasoned fury at herself.

Gant caught up with her and matched her strides with long easy legs. "You ever read the Saint stories?" he asked. "I used to. Old Simon Templar was *always* running into beautiful women with strange behavior patterns. Once one of them swam to his yacht in the middle of the night. Said she was a channel swimmer gone astray. Turned out to be an insurance investigator." He caught her arm. "Cousin Hester, I have the most insatiable curiosity—"

She pulled her arm free. They had reached an intersecting avenue and she had spotted a cruising taxi. She waved and the cab began a U-turn. "It was a joke," she said tightly. "I'm sorry. I did it on a bet."

"That's what the girl on the yacht told the Saint." His face went serious. "Fun is fun, but why all the questions about my sordid past?"

The cab pulled up. "Look here, cousin, don't be fooled by my disc jockey dialogue. I want to know what you're up to." He braced his hand against the door of the cab.

"Please," she moaned exhaustedly, tugging at the handle. The cabbie appeared at the front window, looking up at them and appraising the situation. "Hey, mister," he said. His voice was a menacing rumble.

With a sigh, Gant released the door. Ellen opened it, ducked in and slammed it closed, sinking into soft worn leather. She waited until the cab had left Gant standing at the curb before telling the driver her destination.

At the New Washington House, where she had registered before calling on the dean, Ellen seated herself at the writing table by the window of her room. She took her fountain pen and the letter to Bud from her purse and stared at the addressed but still unsealed envelope. She debated whether or not to mention the story of the Gant fiasco.

There was a knock at the door. She jumped to her feet. "Who is it?"

"Towels," a high feminine voice answered.

Ellen crossed the room and grasped the doorknob. "I'm not dressed. Could you leave them outside, please?"

"All right," the voice said.

She stood there for two minutes before she opened the door. Gant lounged with one elbow against the wall. "Hi, Cousin Hester," he said. "I believe I mentioned my insatiable curiosity."

She tried to close the door, but his foot was in the way. He smiled. "Much fun. Follow that cab!" His right hand described a zigzag course. "Shades of Warner Brothers. The driver got such a kick out of it he almost refused the tip. I told him you were running away from my bed and board."

"Get away!" she whispered fiercely. "I'll call the manager!"

"Look, Hester"—the smile dropped—"I think I could have you arrested for illegal entry or something like that, so why don't you invite me in for a small confab? If you're worried about what the bellhops will think, you can leave the door open." He pushed gently on the door, forcing Ellen to retreat a step. He strolled to the bed and sat down on the edge of it.

"What . . . what do you want?"

"An explanation."

She swung the door all the way open and remained standing in the doorway, as though it were his room and she the visitor. "It's . . . very simple. I'm from Caldwell College. I listen to your program all the time so I thought I'd try to meet you."

"And when you meet me you run away."

"Well, what would you have done? I didn't plan it *that* way. I pretended to be your cousin because I . . . I wanted to get information about you—what kind of girls you like . . ."

Rubbing his jaw doubtfully, he stood up. "How did you find out where I live?"

"From one of the girls here."

"Who?"

"Annabelle Koch. She's a friend of mine."

"Annabelle." He had recognized the name. He squinted at Ellen incredulously. "Hey, is this really on the level?"

"Yes." She looked down at her hands. "I know it was a crazy thing to do, but I like your program so much. . . ." When she looked up again he was by the window.

Suddenly he turned and stared at the hallway beyond her, his eyes baffled. When she looked, there was nothing out of the ordinary to be seen. She turned back toward Gant. He was facing the window again.

"Well, Hester," he said, "that was a flattering explanation and one I shall long remember." He glanced at the partly open bathroom door. "Do you mind if I utilize your facilities?" he asked. Before she could say anything, he had ducked into the bathroom and closed the door. The lock clicked.

Drawing a deep, steadying breath, Ellen crossed the room to the writing table, which was bare except for her purse. Bare . . . the letter to Bud! Gant had been standing near the table and he had tricked her into turning toward the hallway . . .

Frantically she hammered on the bathroom door. "Give me that letter! Give it to me!"

Several seconds passed before Gant's deep-toned voice said, "My curiosity is especially insatiable when it comes to phony cousins with flimsy stories."

He finally came out, folding the letter carefully into its envelope. He put it on the writing table and smiled somewhat uncomfortably. "As my grandmother said when the man on the phone asked for Lana Turner, 'Boy, have you got the wrong number.'"

Ellen did not move.

"Look," he said. "I didn't even know your sister. I said hello to her once or twice. I didn't even know her name until her picture was in the papers."

Ellen didn't move.

"How the hell am I supposed to convince you that I never went out with your sister?"

"You can't," Ellen said. "You might as well go."

"There were other blond guys in the class," he insisted. He snapped his fingers. "There was one she used to come in with all the time! Cary Grant chin, tall . . ."

"Dwight Powell?"

"That's right!" He stopped short. "Is he on your list?"

She hesitated a moment, and then nodded.

"He's the one!"

Ellen looked at him suspiciously.

He threw up his hands. "Okay. I give up. You'll see, it was Powell." He moved toward the door; Ellen backed into the hallway. "You couldn't use a Watson, could you?"

"I'm sorry, but . . ."

He shrugged. "Well, good luck." He turned and walked down the hallway.

Ellen went into her room and slowly closed the door.

It's 7:30 now, Bud, and I'm comfortably settled in a very nice room at the New Washington House.

I spent several hours today in the waiting room of the dean of students. When I finally got to him I told a fabulous story about an unpaid debt which Dorothy owed to a handsome blond in her fall English class. After much digging through records and examining a rogues' gallery of application photos, we came up with the man—Mr. Dwight Powell of 1520 West 35th Street, on whom the hunting season opens tomorrow morning.

How's that for an efficient start?

Love,
Ellen

Later she paused in her undressing and pushed the button marked KBRI on the bedside radio. Gant's voice swelled into the room. ". . . another session with The Discus Thrower, or as our engineer puts it, 'Puff and pant with Gordon Gant.' On to the agenda. The first disc of the evening is an oldie, and it's dedicated to Miss Hester Holmes of Caldwell, Wisconsin."

A jumpy orchestral introduction burst from the radio and faded under the singing of a sugary, little-girl voice:

> *"Button up your overcoat—*
> *When the wind is free*
> *Take good care of yourself—*
> *You belong to me!"*

"HELLO?" THE VOICE was a woman's.

"Hello," Ellen said. "Is Dwight Powell there?"

"No, he isn't."

"When do you expect him back?"

"I couldn't say for sure. He works over at Folger's between his classes and afterwards, but I don't know to what time he works. If you have a message for him, I can leave him a note."

"No, thanks. I have a class with him in a couple of hours, so I'll see him then. It wasn't anything important."

"Okay. Good-by."

"Good-by."

She picked up the telephone book, turned to the Fs, and found Folger Drugs listed at 1448 University Avenue.

It was between Twenty-eighth and Twenty-ninth streets; a squat brick structure with a long green sign stretched across its brow: FOLGER DRUGS. Drawing herself up, she pushed open the door and went in.

Dwight Powell was behind the counter of the soda fountain, wearing a snug white mess jacket, and a white cap over the waves of his fine blond hair. He was squirting whipped cream from a metal canister onto a gummy-looking sundae. There was a sullen set to his lips that made it clear he disliked his job.

Ellen walked toward the far end of the counter. As she passed Powell, she sensed him glance up. She went on to an empty section, took off her coat, and seated herself.

Powell approached along the gangway behind the counter. He put a glass of water and a paper napkin before her. His eyes were deep blue, the skin immediately below them gray-shadowed. "Yes, miss?" he said.

She looked at the pictures of sandwiches fixed to the mirrored wall. The grill was directly opposite her. "A cheeseburger," she said, looking at him. "And a cup of coffee."

"Cheeseburger and coffee," he said. He turned and opened a locker under the grill, taking out a patty of meat on a piece of waxed paper. Kicking the locker door shut, he slapped the meat onto the grill. She watched his face in the mirror. He glanced up

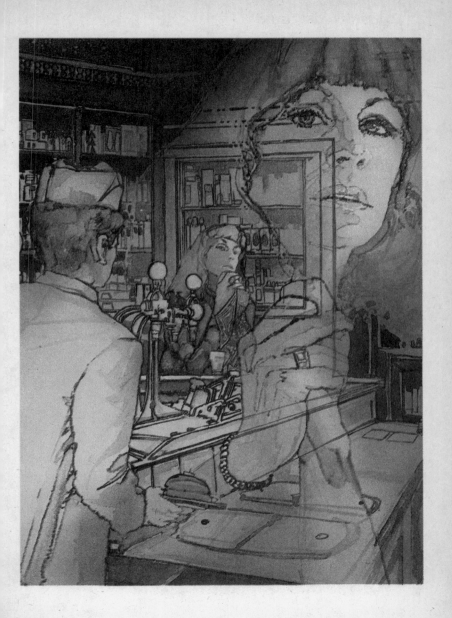

and smiled. She returned the smile faintly; I am not interested, but I am not completely *un*interested.

He put the two halves of a roll face down beside the hamburger and turned to Ellen. "Coffee now or later?"

"Now, please."

He poured the steaming liquid slowly into her cup. "You go to Stoddard?" he asked.

"No, I don't."

He rested the coffeepot on the marble and with his free hand brought a jigger of cream up from under the counter.

"You?" Ellen asked.

He nodded, picked up a spatula, and turned the hamburger. He opened the locker again and took out a slice of American cheese, which he put on top of the meat. They looked at each other in the mirror as he arranged the roll and a pickle on a plate. "You haven't been in here before, have you?" he said.

"No. I've only been in Blue River a couple of days."

"Oh. Staying or passing through?"

"Staying. If I can find a job as a secretary."

"Where you from?" he asked, setting the plate before her.

"Des Moines."

"It should be easier to find a job there than it is here."

She shook her head. "All the girls look for jobs in Des Moines."

"You have relatives here?"

She shook her head. "Don't know a soul in town. Except the woman at the employment agency."

A spoon tapped against a glass down the counter. "Damn," he muttered. "Maybe you want *my* job?" He stalked away.

In a few minutes he returned. He began scraping the top of the grill with the edge of the spatula. The grill was perfectly clean but he continued scraping it, watching Ellen in the mirror. She dabbed at her lips with the napkin. "Check, please," she said.

He turned, taking a pencil and a green pad from a clip on his belt. "Listen," he said, not looking up from his writing, "there's a very good revival at the Paramount tonight. *Lost Horizon*. You want to see it?"

"I . . ."

"You said you didn't know anybody in town."

She seemed to debate for a moment. "All right," she said finally.
He looked up and smiled. "Swell. Where can I meet you?"

"The New Washington House. In the lobby."

"Eight o'clock okay?" He tore the check from the pad. "My
name is Dwight," he said. "As in Eisenhower. Dwight Powell."
He looked at her, waiting.

"Mine is Evelyn Kittredge."

"Hi," he said, smiling. She flashed a broad smile in return.
Something flickered over Powell's face. Surprise? Memory?

"What's wrong?" Ellen asked. "Why do you look at me that
way?"

"Your smile," he said uneasily. "Exactly like a girl I used to
know. . . ."

There was a pause, then Ellen said, "Joan Bacon or Bascomb
or something. I've been in this town only two days and two people have told me I look like this Joan—"

"No," Powell said, "this girl's name was Dorothy." He folded
the check and tucked it into his pocket. "Lunch is on me."

Ellen was standing, putting on her coat. "Eight o'clock in the
New Washington lobby," Powell reiterated. "Is that where you're
staying?"

"Yes." She made herself smile again. She could see his mind
following the path. Stranger in town, staying at a hotel . . .
"Thanks for lunch."

"See you tonight, Evelyn."

"Eight o'clock," she said. She turned and walked toward the
front of the store, feeling his eyes on her back. Outside, she
found that her knees were shaking.

ELLEN was in the lobby at seven thirty, so that Powell would
not have to ask the desk clerk to ring Miss Kittredge's room. He
arrived at five of eight. He had ascertained that *Lost Horizon*
went on at 8:06, so they took a cab to the theater although it was
only five blocks away. Midway through the picture Powell put

his arm around Ellen, resting his hand on her shoulder. She kept seeing it from the corner of her eye, the hand that had caressed Dorothy's body, had pushed powerfully . . . maybe . . .

The Municipal Building was three blocks from the theater and less than two from the New Washington House. They passed it on their way back to the hotel. "Is that the tallest building in the city?" Ellen asked, looking at Powell.

"Yes," he said. His eyes were focused some twenty feet ahead on the sidewalk.

"How high is it?"

"Fourteen stories." The direction of his gaze had not altered. Ellen thought, When you ask a person the height of something that's in his presence, he instinctively turns to look at it. Unless he has some reason for not wanting to look at it.

Afterward, they sat in a booth in the hotel's cocktail lounge and drank whiskey sours. Their conversation was intermittent. The taut buoyancy with which Powell had begun the evening had faded in passing the Municipal Building, had risen again on entering the hotel, and now was waning steadily.

They spoke about jobs. Powell disliked his but was saving his money for a summer study tour of Europe. What was he studying? His major was English. What did he plan to do with it? He wasn't sure. Advertising, maybe, or get into publishing. His plans for the future seemed sketchy.

They spoke about girls. "I'm sick of these college girls," he said. "Immature. They take everything too seriously." He weighed his words carefully, twisting the stem of the third cocktail glass between long restless fingers. "You get one of them on your neck," he said, the blue eyes clouded, "and you can't get her off." He watched his hand. "Not without making a mess."

Ellen closed her eyes, her hands damp on the black tabletop.

"You can't help feeling sorry for people like that," he went on, "but you've got to think of yourself first."

"People like what?" she said, not opening her eyes.

"People who throw themselves on other people . . ." There was the slap of his hand hitting the tabletop. Ellen opened her eyes.

"Look, let's get out of here," he said.

"You mean go to another place?" Ellen asked.

"If you want to," he said unenthusiastically.

Ellen reached for the coat beside her. "If you don't mind, I'd just as soon we didn't. I was up very early this morning."

"Okay," Powell said. "I'll escort you to your door."

At the door of her room his arm went around her. His lips came toward her and she turned away, catching the kiss on her cheek. "Don't be coy," he said flatly. He caught her jaw in his hand and kissed her mouth hard.

"Let's go in . . . have a cigarette," he said.

She shook her head. "Honestly, I'm dead tired." It was a refusal, but the modest curling of her voice implied that things might be different some other night.

He drew her close, both arms around her, his chin over her shoulder as if to avoid seeing her smile.

"Do I still remind you of that girl?" she asked. And then, "I'll bet she was another girl you went out with just once."

"No," he said, "I went out with her for a long time." He pulled back. "Who says I'm going out with you just once? You doing anything tomorrow night?"

"No."

"Same time, same place?"

"If you'd like."

He kissed her cheek and held her close again. "What happened?" she asked.

"What do you mean?" His words vibrated against her temple.

"That girl. Why did you stop going with her?" She tried to make it light, casual. "Maybe I can profit by her mistakes."

"Oh." There was a pause. "It was like I said downstairs. We got too involved. Had to break it off." She heard him take a deep breath. "She was very immature," he added.

He kissed her again. She closed her eyes sickly.

Easing from his arms, she turned and put the key in the door without looking at him. "Tomorrow night at eight," he said. "Good night, Evvie."

She opened the door behind her and stepped back, forcing a smile to her lips. "Good night." She shut the door.

She was sitting motionlessly on the bed when the telephone rang five minutes later. It was Gant.

"Keeping late hours, I see."

She sighed. "Is it a relief to talk to you!"

"Well!" he said, stretching the word. "Well, well, *well!* I gather that my innocence has been conclusively established."

"Yes. Powell's the one who was going with her. And I'm right about it not being suicide. I know I am. He keeps talking about girls who throw themselves on other people and take things too seriously and things like that." The words tumbled out quickly.

"Good Lord, your efficiency astounds me. Where did you get your information?"

"From him. I picked him up in the drugstore where he works. I'm Evelyn Kittredge, unemployed secretary, of Des Moines."

There was a long silence from Gant's end of the line. "Tell all," he said finally, wearily.

She repeated as accurately as she could the remarks Powell had made in the hotel bar.

When Gant spoke again he was serious. "Listen, Ellen, this doesn't sound like anything to play around with."

"Why? As long as he thinks I'm Evelyn Kittredge—"

"How do you know he does?"

"If he suspected who I am, he wouldn't have said the things he did."

"No, I guess he wouldn't have," Gant admitted reluctantly. "What do you plan to do now?"

"I have another date with him tomorrow night. If I can get him talking about her 'suicide,' maybe he'll let drop one of those things that he couldn't know unless he was with her. If I can prove he was anywhere near her at the time, it should be enough to start the police digging."

"Will you please tell me how the hell you expect to get him to talk in such detail without making him suspicious?"

"I have to try," she argued. "What else is there to do?"

Gant thought for a moment. "Look, be careful, will you?" he said. "And if it's at all possible, call me tomorrow evening, just to let me know how things are going. My hair grays easily."

"All right."

"Good night, Ellen."

"Good night, Gordon."

ELLEN looked up and smiled across the lobby at Powell's approaching figure. "Hi," he said, dropping down beside her on the leather divan. "You certainly don't keep your dates waiting."

"Some of them I do."

He smiled. "How's the job-hunting?"

"Pretty good," she said. "I think I've got something. With a lawyer."

"Swell. You'll be staying in Blue River then, right?"

"It looks that way."

"Swell." He drew the word out caressingly. Then his eyes flicked to his wristwatch. "We'd better get on our horses. I passed the Glo-Ray Ballroom on my way over here and there was a line all the way—"

"Oh," she lamented.

"What's the matter?"

Her face was apologetic. "I've got an errand to do first. This lawyer. I have to bring him a letter. He's going to be at his office till eight thirty." She sighed. "I'm awfully sorry."

"Okay," he said cheerfully. They stood up. "Where is this lawyer?" Powell asked, helping her on with her coat.

"Not far from here," Ellen said. "The Municipal Building."

When they reached the steps that fronted the Municipal Building, Powell stopped. "I'll wait for you down here, Evvie." His jaw was rigid, the words coming out stiffly.

"I wanted you to come up with me," she said. "I thought it was kind of odd, his telling me to bring this letter in the evening. He's a greasy-looking character. You're my protection."

"Oh," Powell said.

Ellen pushed around through the revolving door, and after a

moment Powell followed her toward the only lighted elevator.

"Fourteen," Ellen said to the operator.

When the light jumped to 14, the car came to a smooth stop.

Ellen stepped out into the deserted corridor, Powell following her. "It's this way," Ellen said, moving toward the right. "Room fourteen oh five." They walked to the bend of the corridor and made a right turn. "It won't take long. I just have to give him the letter."

She went to an unlighted door on the right. Its frosted panel was inscribed FREDERIC H. CLAUSEN, ATTORNEY-AT-LAW. Powell came up behind her as she futilely tried the knob. "How do you like that?" she said bitterly. "Not even a quarter after and he said he'd be here till eight thirty." (Earlier, the secretary on the telephone had said, "The office closes at five.")

"What now?" Powell asked.

"I guess I'll bring it over in the morning," she said. "It's a shame about the dancing." Her gaze drifted to a door across the corridor, the door marked STAIRWAY. Her eyes lighted. "You know what I'd like to do?" she asked.

"What?" He smiled.

She smiled back at him. "Go up to the roof."

"What do you want to do that for?" he asked slowly.

"It's a perfect night. The view must be tre*men*dous." She crossed the corridor, pushed the door open, and looked back, waiting for him to follow.

"Evvie, I . . . Heights make me dizzy."

"You don't have to look down," she said lightly. "You don't even have to go near the edge. Oh, come on! You'd think I was asking you to go over Niagara Falls in a barrel or something!" She backed through the doorway onto the landing, holding the door, waiting for him.

He came toward her with a slow, trancelike helplessness.

They climbed the steps to a dark metal door with a warning painted on it in large white letters: ENTRANCE STRICTLY FORBIDDEN EXCEPT IN EMERGENCY. Powell read it aloud, stressing the words "strictly forbidden."

"Signs," Ellen said disdainfully. She tried the knob. "It's stuck," she said. "Give it a try."

He drew back and slammed his shoulder against the door full force. It flew open, almost dragging him with it. He stumbled across the high threshold onto the tarred deck. "Okay, Evvie," he said, holding the door wide. "Come look at your gorgeous moon."

Ellen glanced at Powell's upturned profile and involuntarily she drew away. A sick wave swept over her. It's all right, she told herself. I'm safe. I'm all right, I'm Evelyn Kittredge.

She went to the wall at the outer edge of the roof. Abrading her hands against the roughness of the coping, she gasped lungfuls of the cold night air. This roof is where he killed her. He's bound to betray himself—enough to go to the police. She looked at the panorama below, the myriad lights glittering off into the blackness. "Dwight, come look."

He walked toward the parapet but stopped short of it.

"Isn't it beautiful?" She spoke without looking back.

"Yes," he said.

He looked at the sky for a moment, while a breeze plucked softly at the tower cables, and then he turned slowly around until he was facing the air shaft. He stared at the parapet. Then he began to walk, his legs carrying him forward with relentless efficiency. Setting his hands on the cool stone of the coping, he leaned over.

Ellen felt his absence. She turned around and probed the quarter-moon obscurity. Then the tower light flashed on, its crimson glow showing him at the wall of the air shaft, and her heart jumped chokingly. She began moving toward him, her steps noiseless on the resilient tar.

He looked down. A few yellow beams from lighted windows crisscrossed the square funnel of the shaft. One light far below, at the very bottom, illuminated the small gray concrete square that was the focus of the converging walls.

"I thought heights made you dizzy."

He whirled. Ellen was beside him.

There were sweat beads on his brow. A nervous smile shot

to his lips. "They do," he said, "but I can't help looking. Self-torture . . ." The smile faded. He took a deep breath. "You ready to go now?" he asked.

"We just got here," Ellen protested lightly. She turned and walked toward the eastern rim of the roof. Powell followed reluctantly. "It's nice up here. Have you ever been here at night?" she asked.

"No," he said. "I've never been here before at all."

She turned to the outer parapet and leaned over, looking down at the shelf of the setback two stories below. "Last year," she said slowly, "I think I read about some girl falling from here."

"Yes," Powell said. His voice was dry. "A suicide. It wasn't an accident."

"Oh." Ellen kept looking at the setback. "I don't see how she could have gotten killed," she said. "It's only two stories."

He lifted a hand, the thumb pointing back over his shoulder. "Over there . . . the shaft."

"Oh, that's right." She straightened up. "I remember now. The Des Moines newspapers gave it a very big write-up. She was a Stoddard girl, wasn't she?"

"Yes," he said.

"Did you know her?"

"Why do you ask?"

"I just thought you might have known her. That's a natural thing to think, both going to Stoddard."

"Yes," he said sharply. "I knew her and she was a very nice girl. Now let's talk about something else." He squinted at his wristwatch. "Look," he said brusquely, "it's twenty-five to nine. I've had enough of this magnificent view." He turned abruptly, heading for the staircase housing.

Ellen hurried after him. "We can't go yet," she wheedled, catching his arm as he passed the air shaft.

"Why not?"

"I . . . I want a cigarette."

"Oh, for . . ." His hand jerked toward a pocket, then stopped short. "I don't have any. Come on, we'll get some downstairs."

"I have some," she said quickly. She opened her purse, smiling at Powell, saying inanely, "It'll be nice to smoke a cigarette up here." She fumbled in her purse. "Here," she offered. He snatched the cigarette grimly.

As she dug for another one, she apparently became aware of the air shaft for the first time. She turned toward it slightly. "Is this where . . . ?" She turned back to him.

His jaw tightened. "Listen, Evvie," he said, "I asked you not to talk about it. Now will you just do me that one favor? Will you, please?" He jabbed the cigarette between his lips. "Can't you understand? I *knew* the girl."

She struck a match and held it to his cigarette. The orange glow lighted his face and showed his blue eyes simmering with strain, the jaw muscles tight. . . . One more jab, one more jab. "They never did say why she did it, did they? I'll bet she was pregnant," she said.

His face flared from flame orange to raw red as the match died and the tower light flashed on. "All right!" he blazed. "All right! You know why I won't talk about it? Why I didn't even want to come into this damn building?" He flung away his cigarette. "Because the girl who committed suicide here was the girl I told you about last night! The one you smile like!"

His eyes dropped from her face to the matchbook in her left hand and she saw them dilate with shock. Then the tower light faded and she could see him only as a dim form. Suddenly his hand caught her left wrist, gripping it with paralyzing pressure. The purse slid out from under her arm and thudded to her feet. Futilely her right hand flailed at him. He was forcing her fingers open, prying the matches from her grasp.

"What are you doing?" she cried, flexing her hand, trying to recall the imprint on the object she had been holding.

Then the tower light flashed on again and she saw the matchbook resting in the palm of his hand, with the copper letters glinting sharp and clear: *Ellen Kingship.*

Fear engulfed her. She swayed sickly, her back against the hard edge of the air-shaft parapet.

"Her sister . . ." he faltered. "Her sister . . ." He stared at the matchbook with glazed incomprehension. He looked up at her. "What is this?" he asked dully. "What do you want from me?"

"Nothing . . . nothing," she said. He was standing between her and the stairway shed. If only she could circle around him . . .

He rubbed his forehead. "You . . . you pick me up . . . you ask me questions about her . . . you get me up here . . ." Now his voice was entreating. "What do you *want* from me?"

"Nothing," she repeated, warily sidestepping.

"Then why did you *do* this?" His body flexed to move forward.

"Stop!" she cried. "If anything happens to me," she said, forcing herself to speak slowly, evenly, "there's somebody else who knows all about you. He knows I'm with you tonight, so if anything happens, anything at all . . ."

"If anything . . . ?" His brow furrowed. "What are you talking about?"

"You know what I mean. If I fall . . ."

"Why should you?" He stared unbelievingly. "You think I'd . . ." One hand gestured limply toward the parapet. "Dear God," he whispered. "What are you, crazy?"

She was a good fifteen feet from him. She began edging away from the parapet. He pivoted slowly, following her cautious path.

"This person is waiting downstairs," she said. "If I'm not down in five minutes, he's calling the police."

He slapped his forehead exhaustedly. "I give up," he moaned. "You want to go downstairs? Well, go ahead!" He turned and backed to the air-shaft parapet, leaving her a clear path to the door. "Go on!"

She moved toward the door slowly, suspiciously, knowing that he could still cut her off. He didn't move.

"If I'm supposed to be arrested," he said, "I'd just like to know what for. Or is that too much to ask?"

She made no answer until she had stepped over the ledge and had the door open in her hand. Then she turned and said, "I expected you to be a convincing actor. You had to be, to make Dorothy believe you were going to marry her."

"What?" This time his surprise seemed deeper, painful. "Now listen. I never said *anything* to make her believe I was going to marry her. That was all on *her* side, all *her* idea."

"You think I'm bluffing. All right." She glared. "I'll itemize it for you. One: she was pregnant. Two: you didn't want—"

"*Pregnant?*" It hit him like a rock. He leaned forward. "Dorothy was *pregnant?* Is *that* why she killed herself?"

"She didn't kill herself!" Ellen cried. "You killed her!" She pulled the door shut, turned and ran.

She ran clatteringly down the metal steps, clutching at the banister and swinging around the turn at each landing. Before she had gone two and a half flights she heard him thundering down after her, shouting, "*Evvie! Ellen! Wait!*" She kept running with heart pounding and legs aching until at last she reached the lobby. She pushed exhaustedly out through the heavy revolving door and down more steps. She ran left toward Washington Avenue and down the small-town, night-deserted street. She could hear him shouting, "*Wait! Wait!*" She wheeled around the corner and saw the hotel down the block with its glass doors glowing. At last she reached them and a man smiling amusedly held one of them open. Finally she was in the lobby.

She was dying to drop into one of the chairs, but she went straight to a phone booth. If Gant went to the police with her—Gant, who was a local celebrity—then they'd be more inclined to listen to her, believe her, investigate. She seized the phone book and flipped to the Ks. There it was: KBRI . . . 345-1000.

As she opened her purse to hunt for coins, Powell confronted her. He was flushed and panting, his blond hair wild. He looked at her with a sick-dog, pleading expression and said softly, hurtfully, "Ellen, I loved her."

"I have a phone call to make," she said, "if you'll please get out of the way."

"I've got to talk to you," he pleaded. "Was she? Was she really pregnant?"

"You know she was."

"The papers said nothing! Nothing." Suddenly his brow furrowed and his voice dropped low, intense. "How long had she been pregnant?"

"Two months." She glared at him.

He let out a tremendous weight-dropping sigh of relief. "I was in New York! I was in New York all last spring!"

That shook her, but only for a moment. Then she said, "I suppose you could figure out a way to prove you were in Egypt, if you wanted to."

"For God's sake!" he hissed, exasperated. "Will you just let me speak to you for five minutes?" He glanced around. A man was staring at them. "People are listening," he said. "Just come into the cocktail lounge for five minutes. I couldn't do anything to you there, if that's what you're worried about."

Most of the booths in the black-walled lounge were empty. Glasses clinked and the soft piano dallied with some Gershwin themes. They took the seats they had occupied the night before. Ellen sat back stiffly and silently. Over whiskey sours, Powell began to speak, slowly and with embarrassment.

"I met Dorothy a couple of weeks after classes began last year," he said. "She was in the back of the English class, where she always sat. Going out of the room at the end of the class, I told her I'd forgotten to take down the assignment and would she give it to me. I think she knew it was just an excuse to talk, but still she responded so . . . so eagerly it surprised me. I mean, usually a pretty girl will take a thing like that lightly, give you smart answers, you know . . . But she was so . . . unsophisticated, she made me feel a little guilty.

"Well, anyway, we went out that Saturday night, and we really had a nice time. We went out again the next Saturday night and two times the week after that, until finally we were seeing each other almost every night. Once we got to know each other, she was a lot of fun. Happy. I liked her.

"In November she spent a few nights in my room." He glanced up, his eyes meeting Ellen's squarely. "You know what I mean?"

"Yes," she said coolly, impassive as a judge.

"This is a hell of a thing to tell a girl's sister."

"Go on."

"She was a *nice* girl," he said. "It was just that she was . . . love-starved." His glance fell. "She told me about things at home, about her mother—your mother—about how she'd wanted to go to school with you."

A tremor ran through her; she told herself it was only the vibration caused by someone sitting down in the booth behind her.

"Things went on that way for a while," Powell continued. "She was really in love, hanging onto my arm and smiling up at me all the time. I mentioned once I liked argyle socks; she knitted me three pairs of them." He scratched the tabletop carefully. "I loved her, too, only it wasn't the same. It was . . . sympathy love. I felt sorry for her.

"The middle of December she started to talk about marriage. She wanted me to go to New York with her. Meet the family. She kept bringing it up and finally there was a showdown.

"I told her I wasn't ready to get tied down yet, and she said if it was the future I was worrying about, her father would find a place for me. I didn't want that, though. I had ambitions.

"There was a scene. I told her it was all over. She cried and said I'd be sorry, and all the things a girl says. That's the way it ended. Couple of days later she left for New York."

Ellen said, "All during that vacation she was in such a bad mood. Sulking, picking arguments . . ."

"After vacation," Powell continued, "it was bad. We still had that class together. So I decided I'd had enough of Stoddard and applied for a transfer to NYU."

He saw the downcast expression on Ellen's face. "What's the matter?" he said. "Don't you believe me? I can prove all this. I've got a transcript from NYU."

"I believe you," Ellen said dully. "That's just the trouble."

He gave her a baffled look, and then continued. "Just before I left, toward the end of January, she was starting to go with another guy. I saw—"

"Another man?" Ellen leaned forward.

"I saw them together a couple of times. It hadn't been such a big blow to her after all, I thought. I left for New York with a nice clean conscience."

"Who was he?" Ellen asked.

"I don't know. I think he was in one of my classes. Let me finish. I read about her suicide the first of May, just a paragraph in the New York papers. I raced up to Times Square and got a *Clarion-Ledger* at that out-of-town newspaper stand.

"Can you imagine how I felt? I didn't think she had done it just on account of me, but I did think that it was a sort of a . . . general despondency. Which I was a major cause of. I felt responsible.

"My work fell off after that. I told myself it was because of the transfer to NYU and all the courses I had to make up. Anyway, I decided to come back to Stoddard in September, to get myself straightened out." He smiled wryly.

"It was a mistake. Every time I saw one of the places we used to go to, or the Municipal Building . . ." He frowned. "It got to the point where I found myself going out of my way to walk past the building, needling myself, like looking into the air shaft tonight, visualizing her. . . ."

"I know," Ellen said. "I wanted to look too. I guess it's a natural reaction."

"Well . . . that's it. Now you tell me she did it because she was pregnant . . . two months. It's a rotten thing, of course, but it makes me feel a whole lot better. I mean, there's a limit to responsibility." He drained the rest of his drink. "I don't know where you got the idea that I killed her."

"Someone did kill her," Ellen said. He looked at her wordlessly. The piano paused between selections, and in the sudden stillness she could hear faint rustlings in the booth behind her.

Leaning forward, she began telling Powell of the ambiguously worded note, of the birth certificate, of something old, something new, something borrowed and something blue.

He was silent until she had finished. Then he said, "My God . . . it *can't* be a coincidence."

"This man you saw her with," Ellen said. "You're sure you don't know who he was?"

"I think he was in one of my classes that semester, but the two times I saw them together were fairly late in January, when exams had started and there were no more classes, so I couldn't make sure. And right afterward I left for New York."

"And you don't know his name?"

"I don't know it," Powell said, "but I can find it out." He smiled. "You see, I've got his address—last year's, that is.

"One afternoon I dropped into a luncheonette across from the campus. I didn't notice them until I'd sat down at the counter, and then I didn't want to leave because Dorothy had already seen me in the mirror. I was sitting at the end of the counter, then two girls, then Dorothy and this guy.

"The minute she saw me she started talking to him and touching his arm a lot; you know, trying to show me she had someone new. Then, when they were ready to leave, she turned to him and said in a louder-than-necessary voice, 'Come on, we can drop our books at your place.' To show me how chummy they were, I figured.

"As soon as they were gone, one of the girls commented to the other about how good-looking he was. The other one agreed, and then she said something like, 'He was going with so-and-so last year. It looks as if he's only interested in the ones who have money.'

"Well, I figured that if Dorothy was a sitting duck because she was on the rebound from me, then I ought to make sure she wasn't being taken in by some gold digger. So I left the luncheonette and followed them to a house a few blocks north of the campus. I copied down the address on the cover of one of my notebooks. I thought I would call up later and find out his name. I never did it though."

"But you still have the address?" Ellen asked anxiously.

"I'm pretty sure I do. I've got all my old notebooks in a suitcase in my room. We can go over there and get it right now if you want."

She stood up. "There's still a phone call I'd like to make before we go."

"To your assistant? The one who was waiting downstairs ready to call the police if you didn't show up in five minutes?"

"That's right," she admitted, smiling. "He wasn't waiting downstairs, but there really is someone."

She went to the phone booth at the back of the dimly lit room and called KBRI.

"May I speak to Gordon Gant, please?"

"I'm sorry," the operator said, "but Mr. Gant's program is on the air now. If you call again at ten o'clock, you might be able to catch him before he leaves the building."

"Well, would you take a message for him? It's important."

The operator said that she would. Ellen told her to tell Mr. Gant that Miss Kingship said that Dwight Powell was all right but had an idea as to who wasn't, and Miss Kingship was going to Powell's home and would be there at ten o'clock, when Mr. Gant could call her. "I don't have the telephone number," she said, "but the address is on West Thirty-fifth Street. You'll be sure he gets the message?"

"Of course I will," the woman declared frostily.

Powell was feeding coins into a small silver tray held by the waiter when Ellen returned to their booth. She reached for her coat. An empty coat sleeve slapped over the top of the booth partition as her hand groped for it. "Excuse me," she said, glancing back over her shoulder. Then she saw that the next booth had been vacated. There were an empty cocktail glass and a dollar bill on the table, and a paper napkin which had been carefully torn into a delicate lacework web.

Powell helped her with the obstinate sleeve. "Ready?" he asked, putting on his own coat.

"Ready," she said.

It was nine fifty when the cab pulled up in front of Powell's house. As the cab departed, Powell unlocked the door and followed Ellen into a pleasant-looking living room full of chintz-covered maple furniture. "You'd better stay down here," Powell said, going toward a staircase. "Everything's in a mess upstairs. My landlady is in the hospital and I wasn't expecting company." He paused on the first step. "There's some instant coffee in the kitchen back there. You want to fix some?"

"All right," Ellen said, slipping out of her coat.

Powell went up the stairs and into his room. He opened the top drawer of the bureau and rummaged around until he found the paper he wanted. Pulling it free with a flourish, he went into the hall and leaned over the banister. "Ellen!" he called.

In the kitchen, Ellen adjusted the gas flame. "Coming!" she answered. She hurried into the living room. "Got it already?" she asked, going to the stairs.

Powell's head and shoulders jutted into the stairwell. "Not yet," he said. "But I thought you'd like to see this." He let go of a sheet of paper and it came fluttering down. "Just in case you have any lingering doubts."

Picking up the paper, she saw that it was a photostat of his NYU record. "If I had any lingering doubts," she said, "I wouldn't be here, would I?"

"True," Powell said, and vanished back into his room. He reached under the bed and dragged a heavy suitcase out and lifted the lid. The suitcase was filled with textbooks, a bottle of Canadian Club, golf shoes . . . The notebooks were underneath.

There were nine of them; pale green, spiral-bound notebooks. The address was penciled on the seventh one, on the back cover, rubbed and smudged, but still legible. He turned around, his mouth opening to form Ellen's name in a triumphant shout.

But the shout didn't come. The exultant expression clung to his face for a moment, like a stopped movie, and then it cracked and slid slowly away, like snow cracking and sliding from a canted roof.

The closet door was open and a man in a trench coat stood framed there.

He was tall and blond, and a gun bulked large in his gloved right hand. He was sweating. Not cold sweat, though; hot healthy sweat from standing in an airless closet in a trench coat. He also wore brown leather gloves with a fuzzy lining and elastic cuffs that held in the heat even more; his hands were sweating so much that the fuzzy linings were sodden.

Well, say something, he thought, enjoying the slow, stupid melting of Dwight Powell's face. Start talking. Start pleading. Probably can't. Probably he's all talked out after all that chatter in the cocktail lounge.

Powell stared at the gun. "You're the one . . . with Dorothy," he said.

The man with the gun stepped closer. "The notebook, *por favor*," he said, extending his left hand. "And don't try anything."

He took the notebook that Powell held out, dropped back a step, and pressed it against his side, bending it in half lengthwise, cracking the cover, never taking his eyes or the gun off Powell. "I'm awfully sorry you found this. I was hoping you wouldn't." He stuck the folded notebook into his coat pocket.

"You really killed her," Powell said.

"Let's keep the voices low." He moved the gun admonishingly. "We don't want to disturb the girl detective, do we?" It annoyed him the way Powell was standing there so blankly. "Maybe you don't realize it, but this is a real gun. It's loaded, and I'm going to kill you with it."

Powell didn't say anything. He just went on looking at the gun.

"You're such a great one for analyzing yourself—tell me, how do you feel now? I bet your knees are shaking, aren't they? Cold sweat all over you?"

Powell said, "She thought she was going there to get married."

"Forget about her! You've got yourself to worry about." Why wasn't he trembling? Didn't he have brains enough?

"Why did you kill her?" Powell's eyes finally lifted from the gun. "If you didn't want to marry her, you could have just left her. That would have been better than killing her."

"Shut up about her! What's the matter with you? You think I'm bluffing?"

Powell leaped forward.

A loud explosion roared, and lead tore into his chest.

ELLEN HAD RETURNED to the kitchen and was looking out a window when she suddenly wondered where the pleasant breeze was coming from, with the window closed.

There was a shadowed alcove in a rear corner of the room. She went to it and saw the back door, with the pane of glass nearest the knob smashed in and lying in fragments on the floor. She wondered if Dwight knew about it. You'd think he would have swept up the—

That was when she heard the shot. It smacked loudly through the house, and as the sound died the ceiling light shivered as if something upstairs had fallen. Then there was silence.

"Dwight?" Ellen called.

There was no answer.

She went into the living room and moved hesitantly to the staircase. She called the name louder. "Dwight?"

The silence held for another moment. Then a voice said, "It's all right, Ellen. Come on up."

She hurried up the stairs with her heart drumming. "In here," the voice said from the right.

The first thing she saw was Powell lying on his back in the middle of the room, limbs sprawled loosely. His jacket had fallen away from his chest. On his white shirt blood was flowing from a black core over his heart.

She steadied herself against the jamb. Then she raised her eyes to the man who stood beyond Powell, the man with the gun in his hand. He shifted the gun from the firing position to a flat appraising weight on his gloved palm. "I was in the closet," he said, looking her straight in the eye, answering the unasked questions. "He opened that suitcase and took out this gun. He was going to kill you. I jumped him. The gun went off."

"No . . . Oh, God . . ." She rubbed her forehead dizzily. "But how . . . how did you . . . ?"

He put the gun in the pocket of his coat. "I was in the cocktail lounge," he said. "Right behind you. I heard him talking you into coming up here. I left while you were in the phone booth."

"He told me he—"

89

"I heard what he told you. He was a good liar."

"But I believed him. I believed him."

"That's just your trouble," he said with an indulgent smile. "You believe everybody."

He came toward her, stepping between Powell's legs.

She said, "But I still don't understand. How were you there, in the lounge?"

"I was waiting for you in the lobby. I missed you when you left the hotel with him. Got there too late. But I waited around. What else could I do?"

He stood before her with his arms wide, like a soldier returning home. "Just be glad you gave me his address. I may have thought you were being a fool, but I wasn't going to take any chances on having you get your head blown off."

She threw herself into his arms, sobbing with relief. The leather-gloved hands patted her back comfortingly. "It's all right, Ellen," he said softly. "Everything's all right now."

She buried her cheek against his shoulder. "Oh, Bud," she sobbed, "thank God for you, Bud!"

THE telephone rang downstairs.

"Don't answer it," he said as she started to draw away.

There was a lifeless glaze to her voice. "I know who it is."

"No, don't answer it. Listen"—his hands were solid and convincing on her shoulders—"someone is sure to have heard that shot. The police will probably be here in a few minutes. Reporters too." He let that sink in. "You don't want the papers to make a big story out of this, do you? Dragging up everything about Dorothy, pictures of you . . ."

"There's no way to stop them."

"There is. I have a car downstairs. I'll take you to the hotel and then come right back. If the police haven't shown up yet, I'll call them. Then you won't be here for the reporters to jump on, and I'll refuse to talk until I'm alone with the police." He led her out into the hallway.

The telephone stopped ringing.

"I wouldn't feel right about leaving," she said as they started down the stairs.

"Why not? I'm the one who did it, not you. I'll say Powell was drunk and started a fight with me, or something like that. I'm not going to lie about your being here; I'll need you to back up my story. All I want to do is prevent the papers from having a field day with this." He turned to her as they descended into the living room. "Trust me, Ellen," he said, touching her hand.

She sighed deeply, gratefully letting tension and responsibility drop from her shoulders.

He picked up her coat and held it for her. "Where did you get a car?" she asked dully.

He gave her her purse. "I borrowed it from a friend." Turning off the lights, he opened the door to the porch. "Come on," he said, "we haven't got too much time."

He had parked the car some fifty feet down the block. He opened the door for Ellen, then went around to the other side and slipped in behind the wheel. Ellen sat silently. "You feel all right?" he asked.

"Yes," she said, her voice thin and tired. "It's just that . . . he was going to kill me." She sighed. "At least I was right about Dorothy. I *knew* she didn't commit suicide." She was silent again for a moment. "Anyway, there's a sort of silver lining to all this," she said.

"What's that?" He shifted gears and the car glided forward.

"Well, you saved my life," she said. "That should cut short whatever objections my father might have, when you meet him and we speak to him about us."

After they had been driving down Washington Avenue for a few minutes he said, "Listen, Ellen, this is going to be a lousy business. I'll be held for manslaughter."

"But you didn't mean to kill him! You were trying to get the gun away from him."

"I know, but they'll still have to hold me . . . all kinds of red tape." He stole a quick glance at the downcast figure beside him. "Ellen, when we get to the hotel, you could just pick up your things and check out. We could be back in Caldwell in a couple of hours."

"Bud!" Her voice was sharp with surprised reproach. "We couldn't do a thing like that!"

"Why not? Powell killed your sister, didn't he? He got what was coming to him. Why should we have to get mixed up—"

"We can't do it," she protested. "Aside from its being such a— a *wrong* thing to do, suppose they found out anyway that you . . . killed him. They'd never believe the truth, not if you ran away."

"I don't see how they could find out it was me," he said. "I'm wearing gloves, so there can't be any fingerprints. And nobody saw me there, except you and him."

"But suppose they *did* find out! Or suppose they blamed someone else for it! How would you feel then?" He was silent. "As soon as I get to the hotel, I'll call my father. Once he's heard the story, I know he'll take care of lawyers and everything. I guess it *will* be a terrible business. But to run away . . ."

"It was a foolish suggestion," he said. "I only tried it as a last resort." Suddenly he swung the car in a wide left turn from brightly lighted Washington Avenue to the darkness of a northbound road.

"Shouldn't you stay on Washington?" Ellen said.

"Quicker this way. Avoid traffic."

"WHAT I can't understand," she said, tapping her cigarette on the edge of the dashboard tray, "is why he didn't do anything to me on the roof." She was settled comfortably, turned toward Bud with her left leg drawn up under her, the cigarette suffusing her with sedative warmth.

"You must have been pretty conspicuous, going there at night," he said. "He was probably afraid that an elevator man or someone would remember his face."

"But wouldn't it have been less risky than taking me back to his house and . . . doing it there?"

"Maybe he was going to force you into a car and drive you out into the country someplace."

"He didn't have a car."

"He could have stolen one. It's not such a hard thing to steal a car."

"The lies he told me! 'I was in New York. I felt responsible.' " She mashed the cigarette into the ashtray, shaking her head bitterly. "Oh, my God!" she gasped.

He flicked a glance at her. "What is it?"

Her voice was sick. "He showed me his transcript . . . from NYU. He *was* in New York."

"That was probably a fake. You can fake something like that."

"But suppose it wasn't. Suppose he was telling the truth!"

"He was coming after you with a gun. Isn't that proof enough he was lying?"

"Are you sure, Bud? Are you sure he didn't—maybe take the gun out to get at something else? The notebook he mentioned? Oh, God, if he really didn't kill Dorothy . . ." She was silent for a moment. Then she said positively, "The police will investigate. They'll prove he killed Dorothy!"

Shifting uncomfortably, she drew her folded leg out from under her. She squinted at her watch in the dashboard's glow. "It's twenty-five after ten. Shouldn't we be there already?"

He didn't answer her.

She looked out the window. There were no more streetlights, no more buildings. There was only the pitch-blackness of empty fields under the starry sky. "Bud, this isn't the way into town."

He didn't answer her.

"Bud, you're going the wrong way!"

"WHAT do you want from *me?*" Chief of Police Eldon Chesser asked blandly. He lay supine, his long legs supported beneath the ankles by an arm of the chintz-covered sofa.

"Get after the car. That's what I want," Gordon Gant said, glaring at him from the middle of the living room.

"Ha," said Chesser. "Ha ha. A dark car is all the man next door knows. After he called about the shot, he saw a man and a woman leave the house and get into a dark car. You know how many dark cars there are driving around town with a man and a woman in them?"

Gant paced malevolently. "So what are we supposed to do?"

"Wait, is all. I notified the highway boys, didn't I? Why don't you sit down?"

"Sure, sit down," Gant snapped. "She's liable to be murdered! Last year her sister—now her."

"Here we go again," Chesser said. His brown eyes closed in weariness. "There *was* no murder last year," he said flatly.

Gant resumed his pacing.

"You might as well sit down," Chesser said. "There ain't a damn thing we can do but wait."

Gant sat down in a chair across the room.

"What is she? Your girl friend?" Chesser asked.

"No," Gant said. He remembered the letter he had read in Ellen's room. "No, there's some guy in Wisconsin."

BEHIND the racing island of the headlights' reach, the car arrowed along the highway. Ellen was huddled against the door, her body knotted tight. He drove with his left hand. On the seat between them, snakelike, lay his gloved right hand with the gun in it, the muzzle riveted against her hip.

He had told her everything, in a bitter voice, glancing frequently at her face in the darkness. He told her about the pills and the note and the roof and why it had been necessary to kill Dorothy, and why it had then been the most logical course to transfer to Caldwell and go after *her*, Ellen, knowing how to make himself the man she was waiting for—not only the most logical course but also the most satisfying, the most compensatory for past bad luck.

He told her these things with irritation and contempt; this girl with her hands over her mouth in horror had had everything given her on a silver platter; she didn't know what it was to live on a swaying catwalk over the chasm of failure, stealing perilously inch by inch toward the solid ground of success so many miles away.

She listened to him as though part of her were already dead. She listened, and then she cried, because she was so sickened and beaten and shocked that there was nothing else she could do to express it all. Her cries were long throat-dragging animal moans; more sound and shaking than actual tears.

"I *told* you not to come," he said querulously. "I *begged* you to stay in Caldwell, didn't I?" He glanced at her as though expecting an affirmation. "But *no*. You had to be the girl detective! Well, this is what happens to girl detectives." His eyes returned to the highway. "If you only *knew* what I've gone through since Monday," he said through clenched teeth, remembering how the world had dropped out from under him Monday morning when Ellen had phoned—"Dorothy didn't commit suicide! I'm leaving for Blue River!" It made him sick just thinking about it.

Ellen said faintly, "They'll catch you."

After a moment's silence he said, "You know how many don't get caught? More than fifty percent, that's how many." After another moment he said, "How are they going to catch me? Fingerprints? None. Witnesses? None. Motive? None that they know about. They won't even think of me." He glanced at her to see her reaction; none was visible.

His gaze returned to the road and his face clouded again. "That letter of yours—how I sweated till it came! When I first started to read it I thought I was safe; you were looking for someone she'd met in her English class in the fall, I didn't meet her till January, and it was in philosophy. But then I realized who that guy you were looking for actually was—Old Argyle Socks, my predecessor. We'd had math together, and he'd seen me with Dorrie. I thought he might know my name. I knew that if he ever convinced you he didn't have anything to do with Dorrie's murder . . . if he ever mentioned my name to you . . ."

"Please," she said. "Please . . ."

Suddenly he slowed the car to a halt, then swung around in a wide curve, almost going off the edge of the asphalt into the dirt of a field that swept off to meet the blackness of the sky. He set the emergency brake and left the motor running.

"Please . . ." she said.

He opened the door on his left. "You had to be smart." He stepped out onto the asphalt, keeping the gun aimed at her huddled figure. "Come here," he said. "Come out on this side."

"Please . . ."

The gun made an irritated gesture. "Come out."

She pulled herself across the seat, clutching her purse. She stepped out onto the asphalt.

The gun directed her in a semicircular path until she stood with the field at her back, the gun between her and the car.

"Please," she said, holding up the purse in a futile shielding gesture, "please . . ."

From the *Clarion-Ledger*; Thursday, March 15, 1951:

DOUBLE SLAYING HERE
Police Seek Mystery Gunman

Within a period of two hours last night, an unknown gunman committed two brutal murders. His victims were Ellen Kingship, 21, of New York City, and Dwight Powell, 23, of Chicago, a junior at Stoddard University.

Powell's slaying occurred at 10:00 p.m., in the home of Miss Elizabeth Honig, 1520 West 35th St., where Powell was a roomer. As police reconstruct the events, Powell, entering the house at 9:50 in the company of Miss Kingship, went to his second-floor room, where he encountered an armed burglar who had earlier broken into the house through the back door.

The medical examiner established the time of Miss Kingship's death as somewhere near midnight. Her body was discovered at 7:20 this morning by Willard Herne, 11, of nearby Randalia, as he was crossing a field. Police learned from Gordon Gant, KBRI announcer and a friend of Miss Kingship's, that she was the sister of Dorothy Kingship, who last April committed suicide by jumping from the roof of the Blue River Municipal Building.

Leo Kingship, president of Kingship Copper Inc. and father of the slain girl, is expected to arrive in Blue River this afternoon, accompanied by his daughter, Marion Kingship.

AT THE END OF THE school year Bud returned to Menasset and sat around the house in somber depression. His mother tried to combat his sullenness and then began to reflect it. They argued, like hot coals boosting each other into flame. To get out of himself, he reclaimed his old job at the haberdashery shop, standing behind a glass display counter from nine to five thirty.

One day in July he took a small gray strongbox from his closet. He unlocked it on his desk and took out the newspaper clippings about Dorothy's death. He tore them into small pieces and dropped them into the wastebasket. He did the same with the clippings on Ellen and Powell. Then he took out the Kingship Copper pamphlets; he had written away for them a second time when he started to go with Ellen. As his hands gripped them, ready to tear, he smiled ruefully. Dorothy, Ellen . . .

It was like thinking Faith, hope . . . and charity pops into the mind to fulfill the sequence.

Dorothy, Ellen . . . Marion.

Slowly he put the pamphlets down on his desk, mechanically smoothing the creases his hands had made. He pushed the strongbox to the back of the desk and sat down. He headed a sheet of paper MARION and divided it into two columns with a vertical line. He headed one column PRO, the other CON.

There were so many things to list under PRO: months of conversations with Dorothy, months of conversations with Ellen; all studded with passing references to Marion; her likes, her dislikes, her opinions, her past. He knew her like a book without even having met her; lonely, bitter, living alone. . . . A perfect setup.

He couldn't think of a thing to list under CON.

That night he tore up the sheet and began another one, of Marion Kingship's characteristics, opinions, likes and dislikes. In every spare moment he pushed his mind back to conversations with Dorothy and Ellen, dredging words, phrases and sentences up from the pool of his memory. As the list grew, his spirits swelled. Sometimes he would take the paper from the strongbox even when he had nothing to add, just to admire it—the keenness, the planning, the potency displayed. "You're crazy," he told himself aloud one day, looking at the list. "You're a crazy nut," he said affectionately.

"I'M NOT going back to school," he told his mother one day in August.

"What?" She stood small and thin in the doorway of his room, one hand frozen in midpassage over her straggly gray hair.

"I'm going to New York in a few weeks."

"You got to finish school," she said plaintively. "What is it, you got a job in New York?"

"I don't, but I'm going to get one. I've got an idea I want to work on. A . . . a project, sort of."

"Bud," she said nervously, "you're past twenty-five. You got to finish school and get yourself started someplace. You can't—"

"Look, will you just let me live my own life?"

She stared at him. "That's what your father used to give me," she said quietly, and went away.

He stood by his desk for a few moments, hearing the angry clanking of cutlery in the kitchen sink.

A few minutes later he went into the kitchen. His mother was at the sink, her back toward him. "Mom," he said pleadingly, "you know I'm as anxious as you are to see myself get someplace. I wouldn't quit school if this idea wasn't something important." He went over and sat down at the table, facing her back. "If it doesn't work, I'll finish school next year. I *promise* I will, Mom."

"What kind of idea is it?" she asked slowly. "An invention?"

"I can't tell you," he said regretfully. "It's only in the . . . the planning stage. I'm sorry."

She sighed and wiped her hands on a towel. "Can't it wait till next year? When you'd be through with school?"

"Next year might be too late, Mom."

She went around behind him and laid her hands on his shoulders. She stood there for a moment, looking down at his anxiously upturned face. "Well," she said, "I guess it must be a *good* idea."

He smiled up at her happily.

Three: Marion

WHEN Marion Kingship graduated from Barnard, her father offhandedly mentioned the fact to the head of the advertising agency which handled the Kingship Copper account, and Marion was offered a job as a copywriter. Although she wanted very much to write advertising copy, she refused the offer. Eventually she managed to find a position with a small New York agency where she was assured that she would be permitted to submit copy for some of the smaller accounts, provided that it did not interfere with her secretarial duties.

A year later, when Dorothy inevitably followed Ellen's lead and went off to football cheers and campus kisses at a midwestern Twentieth Century-Fox playground, Marion found herself alone in an eight-room apartment with her father, the two of them like charged metal pellets that pass but never touch. She decided, in spite of her father's disapproval, to find a place of her own.

She rented a two-room apartment on the top floor of a converted brownstone in the East Fifties. Because the rooms were small, she could not take all her possessions with her. Those that she did take were the fruit of a thoughtful selection. She told herself she was choosing the things she liked best, but as she hung each picture and placed each book upon the shelf, she saw it through the eyes of a visitor who would someday come to her apartment, a visitor as yet unidentified except as to his sex. Every article was an index to herself; the furniture and the lamps (modern but not modernistic), the reproduction of her favorite painting (Charles Demuth's *My Egypt*), the records (some jazz and some Stravinsky and Bartók, but mostly the melodic themes of Grieg and Brahms and Rachmaninoff), and the books—especially the books, for what better index of the personality is there? Had she been an artist she would have painted a self-portrait; instead, she decorated two rooms, charging them with objects which some visitor, someday, would recognize and understand.

There were visitors. Dorothy and Ellen came when they were

home on vacation, unconvincingly envying Marion as a woman of the world. Her father came, puffing from the three flights of stairs, looking dubiously at the small living-bedroom and smaller kitchen. A man came once; a bright young junior account executive; very nice, very intelligent. His interest in the apartment manifested itself in sidelong glances at the studio couch.

When Dorothy committed suicide, Marion returned to her father's apartment for two weeks, and when Ellen died, she stayed with him for a month. They could not get close to each other, no matter how they tried. At the end of the month he suggested with a diffidence unusual in him that she move back permanently. She couldn't; the thought of relinquishing her own apartment was unimaginable, but after that she had dinner at her father's three evenings a week.

One Saturday morning in September the telephone rang. Marion, on her knees, polishing the underside of a plate glass coffee table, rose to her feet and went to the telephone.

"Hello." It was a man's voice. "Is this Marion Kingship?"

"Yes."

"You don't know me. I was . . . a friend of Ellen's." Marion felt suddenly awkward; a friend of Ellen's; someone handsome and fast-talking—and dull underneath; someone *she* wouldn't care for, anyway. "My name," the man continued, "is Burton Corliss. Bud Corliss."

"Oh, yes. Ellen told me about you." ("I love him so much," Ellen had said during the visit that had proved to be her last, "and he loves me too.")

"I wonder if I could see you," he said. "I have something that belonged to Ellen. One of her books. She lent it to me just before . . . before she went to Blue River, and I thought you might like to have it."

Probably some popular novel, Marion thought, and then, hating herself for her smallness, said, "Yes, I'd like very much to have it."

For a moment there was a silence. Then, "I could bring it over now," he said. "I'm in the neighborhood."

"No," she said quickly. "I'm going out."

"Well, then, sometime tomorrow . . ."

"I . . . I won't be in tomorrow either." She shifted uncomfortably, ashamed that she didn't want him in her apartment. He was probably likable enough, and he'd loved Ellen and Ellen was dead, and he was going out of his way to give her Ellen's book. "We could meet someplace this afternoon," she offered.

"Fine," he said. "That would be fine."

"I'm going to be . . . around Fifth Avenue."

"Then suppose we meet, say, in front of the statue at Rockefeller Center, the one of Atlas holding up the world."

"All right."

"At three o'clock?"

"Yes. Three o'clock. Thank you very much for calling. It's very nice of you."

IN THE shadow of the towering bronze statue, he stood with his back to the pedestal, immaculate in gray flannel, a paper-wrapped package under his arm. He watched the passing crowds carefully, trying to recall the snapshot Dorothy had shown him so long ago. "Marion could be very pretty, only she wears her hair like this." He smiled, remembering Dorrie's fierce frown as she pulled her hair back primly.

He recognized her when she was still a hundred feet away. She was tall and thin and dressed much like the women around her: a brown suit, a gold scarf, a shoulder-strap handbag. Her pulled-back hair was brown. She had Dorothy's large brown eyes, but in her drawn face they were too large, and the high cheekbones that had been so beautiful in her sisters were, in Marion, too sharply defined. As she came nearer, she saw him and approached with an uncertain, questioning smile.

"Marion?"

"Yes." She offered her hand hesitantly. "How do you do," she said, directing a smile at a point somewhere below his eyes.

"Hello," he said. "I've been looking forward to meeting you."

They went to a determinedly Early American cocktail lounge

around the corner. Marion, after some indecision, ordered a daiquiri, he a martini.

"I . . . I can't stay long, I'm afraid," she said, sitting erect on the edge of her chair, her fingers stiff around the cocktail glass.

"Where are they always running, these beautiful women?" he inquired smilingly—and immediately saw that it was the wrong approach; she smiled tensely and seemed to grow more uncomfortable. After a moment he began again. "You're with an advertising agency, aren't you?"

"Camden and Galbraith," she said. "Are you still at Caldwell?"

"No."

"I thought Ellen said you were a junior."

"I was, but I had to quit school." He sipped his martini. "My father is dead. I didn't want my mother to work anymore."

"Oh, I'm sorry."

"Maybe I'll be able to finish up next year. Or I may go to night school. Where did you go to school?"

"Barnard. Are you from New York?"

"Massachusetts."

Every time he tried to steer the conversation around to her, she turned it back toward him. Or to the weather. Or to a waiter who bore a startling resemblance to Claude Rains.

Eventually she asked, "Is that the book?"

"Yes. *Dinner at Antoine's*. Ellen wanted me to read it. There are some personal notes she scribbled on the flyleaf, so I thought you might like to have it." He passed the package to her.

"Personally," he said, "I go for books that have a little more meaning."

Marion stood up. "I'll have to be leaving now," she said apologetically.

"But you haven't finished your drink yet."

"I'm sorry," she said quickly, looking down at the package in her hands. "I have an appointment. A business appointment."

He rose. "But—"

"I'm sorry." She looked at him uncomfortably.

He put money on the table.

They walked back to Fifth Avenue. At the corner she offered her hand again. "It's been very nice meeting you, Mr. Corliss," she said. "Thank you for the drink. And the book. I appreciate it. Very thoughtful." She turned and melted into the stream of people.

SUNDAY afternoon Marion went to the Museum of Modern Art. Two men were in the room that held the Lehmbruck sculptures, but they went out soon after Marion entered, leaving her alone in the cool gray cube with the two statues, the male and the female, their bodies elongated and gauntly beautiful.

"Hello." The voice was behind her, pleasantly surprised.

Bud Corliss smiled in the doorway.

"Hello," Marion said confusedly.

"It really *is* a small world," he said, coming to her. "How are you?"

"Fine, thank you." There was an uncomfortable pause. "How are you?" she added.

"Fine, thanks."

They turned to the male statue. Why did she feel so clumsy? Because he was handsome? Because he had been part of Ellen's circle—had shared football cheers and campus kisses?

"Do you come here often?" he asked.

"Yes."

"So do I."

The statue embarrassed her now, because Bud Corliss was standing beside her. She turned away and moved toward the figure of the kneeling woman. He followed. What brought him here? You'd think he'd be strolling in Central Park with some poised flawless Ellen on his arm.

After a moment he said, "I'm surprised to find you here."

"Why?"

"Well, Ellen wasn't the museum type."

"Sisters aren't exactly alike," she said.

"No, I guess not." He approached the kneeling figure.

"The Fine Arts department at Caldwell had a small museum," he said. "Mostly reproductions and copies. I dragged Ellen there once or twice. Thought I'd indoctrinate her." He shook his head. "No luck."

"She wasn't interested in art."

"No," he said. "It's funny the way we try to push our tastes on people we like."

A man and woman with two children in tow came bursting into the room.

"Let's move on," he suggested. "It's Sunday. No business appointments to run to." He smiled at her; a very nice smile, soft and reassuring. "I'm alone; you're alone." He took her elbow gently. "Come on," he said.

They went through the third floor and half of the second, and then they went down to the main floor and out through the glass doors to the garden behind the museum.

When they had looked at all the statues there, they sat on one of the benches at the back of the garden and lit cigarettes.

"You and Ellen were going steady, weren't you?"

"Not exactly. We had a great many things in common, but they were mainly surface things: having the same classes, knowing the same people . . . things having to do with Caldwell. Once we were through with college, though, I don't think we would've gotten married." He stared at his cigarette. "I was fond of Ellen. I liked her better than any girl I've ever known. I was miserable when she died. But . . . I don't know. . . . We weren't really well suited." He paused. "I hope I'm not offending you."

Marion shook her head, watching him.

"Everything was like that museum business. She wasn't interested in anything serious. It was the same thing with books or politics. She always wanted to be *doing* something."

"She'd led a restricted life at home. I guess she was making up for it."

"Yes," he said. "And then, she was four years younger than I." He put out his cigarette. "But she was the sweetest girl I've ever known."

They sat in silence for a moment. Then they began to talk again; about how many interesting things there were to do in New York, what a pleasant place the museum was, about the Matisse exhibit that was coming soon.

"Do you know who I like?" he asked.

"Who?"

"I don't know if you're familiar with his work," he said. "Charles Demuth."

Leo Kingship sat with his elbows propped on the table, his fingers interlocked around a glass of milk. "You've been seeing him frequently, haven't you?" he said, trying to sound casual.

With elaborate care, Marion placed her coffee cup in the saucer and then looked across the crystal and silver and damask at her father.

"Bud?" she said, knowing it was Bud he meant.

Kingship nodded.

"Yes," Marion said squarely, "I've been seeing him frequently." She paused. "He's calling for me tonight."

"This job of his," Kingship said, setting down the milk. "What are its prospects?"

After a cold moment Marion said, "If his executive training program works out, he should be a section manager in a few months. Why all the questions?" She smiled with her lips only.

Kingship removed his glasses. His blue eyes wrestled uncomfortably with Marion's cool stare. "You brought him here to dinner, Marion," he said. "You never brought anyone to dinner before. Doesn't that entitle me to ask a few questions?"

"He lives in a rooming house," Marion said. "When he doesn't eat with me, he eats alone. So I brought him to dinner one night."

"The nights you don't dine here, you dine with him?"

"Yes, most of them. We eat together because we enjoy each other's company," she said firmly.

"Then I do have a right to ask some questions, don't I?" Kingship pointed out quietly.

"He's someone I like. Not someone applying for a job with

Kingship Copper." She plucked a cigarette from a silver cup and lit it with a silver lighter. "You don't like him, do you?"

"I didn't say that."

"Because he's poor," she said.

There was silence for a moment.

"Oh, yes," Kingship said, "he's poor all right. He took pains to mention it exactly three times the other night. And that anecdote he dragged in, about the woman his mother did sewing for."

"What's wrong with his mother taking in sewing?"

"Nothing, Marion, nothing. It's the way he alluded to it so casually, so very casually. Do you know who he reminded me of? There's a man at the club who has a bad leg, limps a little. Every time we play golf he says, 'You boys go on ahead. Old Peg Leg'll catch up with you.' So everyone walks extra slowly and you feel like a heel if you beat him."

"I'm afraid the similarity escapes me," Marion said. She rose from the table and went toward the living room, leaving Kingship to rub a hand despairingly over the few yellow-white hairs that thinly crossed his scalp.

In the living room there was a large window that looked out over the East River. Marion stood before it, one hand on the thick cloth of the draperies. She heard her father come into the room behind her.

"Marion, believe me, I only want to see you happy." He spoke awkwardly. "I know I haven't always been so . . . concerned, but haven't I . . . done better since Dorothy and Ellen . . ."

"I know," she admitted reluctantly. She fingered the draperies. "But I'm practically twenty-six, a grown woman. You don't have to treat me as if—"

"I just don't want you rushing into anything, Marion."

"I'm not," she said softly. "Why do you dislike him?" she asked.

"I don't dislike him. He . . . I don't know, I . . ."

She turned from the window and faced Kingship at the side of the room. "You know, you really should be grateful to Bud," she said. "I'll tell you something. I didn't want him to have dinner here. But he insisted. 'He's your father,' he said. 'Think of his feelings.' You see, Bud is strong on family ties, even if I'm not. So you should be grateful to him, not antagonistic."

"All right," Kingship said. "He's probably a wonderful boy. I just want to make sure you don't make any mistakes."

Marion's eyes stung him. "I like Bud," she said slowly, her voice tight. "I like him very much. So if you do *anything*, anything at all, to make him feel unwelcome or unwanted, to make him feel that he's not good enough for me, I swear to God I'll never speak to you again as long as I live."

She turned back to the window. He looked futilely at her rigid back and then sank into a chair with a weary sigh.

A few minutes later the chimes of the front door sounded. Marion left the window and crossed the room toward the double door that led to the foyer.

"Marion." Kingship stood up. "Ask him to stay a few minutes, have a drink."

A moment passed. "All right," Marion said. At the doorway she hesitated for a second. "I'm sorry I spoke the way I did." She went out.

Kingship watched her go. Then he straightened up, put a smile on his face, turned and walked toward the doorway, extending his right hand. "Good evening, Bud," he said.

MARION's birthday fell on a Saturday early in November. After lunch with her father at a discreetly elegant restaurant off Park Avenue, Marion spent some time at a beauty salon and then returned to her apartment. Late in the afternoon the buzzer sounded. She pressed the button that released the door downstairs. A few moments later a messenger appeared at her door with a florist's box.

In it, under green waxed paper, was a white orchid. The card with it said simply "Bud." Standing before a mirror, Marion held the orchid experimentally to her hair, her waist and her shoulder.

Bud arrived promptly at six. He rang Marion's doorbell in two quick jabs and stood waiting in the stuffy hallway, removing a speck of lint from the lapel of his navy-blue coat. Soon Marion appeared, radiant, the orchid glowing white on her black coat. They clasped each other's hands. Wishing her the happiest of birthdays, he kissed her on the cheek.

They went to a steak house on Fifty-second Street. The prices on the menu seemed exorbitant to Marion, because she was seeing them through Bud's eyes. She suggested that he order for both of them. They had onion soup and sirloin steaks, preceded by champagne cocktails. "To you, Marion."

From the restaurant they took a taxi to the theater where *Saint Joan* was playing. They sat in the orchestra, sixth row center. During the intermission Marion was unusually voluble, her doelike eyes glittering brightly as she talked of Shaw and the acting and a celebrity in the row in front of them.

Afterward—because, she told herself, Bud had already spent so much money that evening—Marion suggested for the first time that they go to her apartment.

"I FEEL like a pilgrim who's finally being permitted to enter the shrine," he said.

"It's nothing fancy," Marion said as she slipped the key into the lock. "Really. They call it two rooms but it's more like one, the kitchen is so tiny."

She stepped into the apartment and reached for a wall switch beside the door. Lamps filled the room with diffused light. Bud entered, closing the door behind him. Marion turned to watch his face. His eyes were ranging over the deep gray walls, the blue and white striped draperies, the limed oak furniture. He gave an appreciative murmur.

"It's very small," Marion said.

"But nice," he said. "*Very* nice."

"Thank you." She turned away from him, unpinning the orchid from her coat, suddenly as ill at ease as when they first met. She put the corsage on a sideboard and started to remove her coat. He helped her. "Beautiful furniture," he said over her shoulder.

She hung their coats in the closet mechanically, and then turned to the mirror over the sideboard. With fumbling fingers

she pinned the orchid to the shoulder of her russet suit. Her eyes focused beyond her own reflection, on Bud's image. She watched as he crossed the room to stand before the low bookcase and look at the picture on the wall above it. "Our old friend Demuth," he said. As she turned from the mirror he glanced at her, smiling.

"I never could figure out why he called a picture of a grain elevator *My Egypt*," Bud said, looking at the picture again.

"Is that what it is? I was never sure."

"It's a beautiful picture, though."

Marion turned toward the kitchen, her face flushed with pleasure. "Would you like something to drink?" she asked. "There's nothing but wine."

"Perfect." He took a small tissue-wrapped box from his pocket. "Happy birthday, Marion."

"Oh, Bud, you shouldn't have!"

"I shouldn't have," he mimicked, "but aren't you glad I did?"

There were silver earrings in the box, simple polished triangles. "Oh, they're lovely!" Marion exclaimed, and kissed him.

She hurried to the mirror to try them on. He came up behind her, looking at her reflection. When she had fastened both earrings, he turned her around. "Lovely is right," he said.

When the kiss ended he said, "Now where's that wine we were talking about?"

Marion went to the kitchen and returned with a raffia-covered bottle of Bardolino and two glasses on a tray. Bud, his jacket off, was closing the cover of the phonograph. He crossed the room and sat beside Marion on the blue-covered studio couch. The first deep notes of the Rachmaninoff Second Piano Concerto sounded.

Leaning back against the thick bolster that ran along the wall, Bud scanned the room, now softly lighted by a single lamp. "Everything's so perfect here," he said. "Why haven't you asked me up before?"

"I don't know," she said. "I . . . I thought maybe you wouldn't like it."

"How could I not like it?" he said.

His FINGERS WORKED dexterously down the row of buttons on her suit. Her hands closed over his, restraining them.

"Bud, I've never . . . done anything before."

"I know that, darling. You don't have to tell me that."

"I've never loved anyone before."

"Neither have I. I've never loved anyone. Not until you."

"Not even Ellen?"

"Only you. I swear it."

He kissed her again.

Her hands freed his and rose to find his cheeks.

FROM *The New York Times;* Monday, December 24, 1951:

MARION J. KINGSHIP TO BE WED SATURDAY

Miss Marion Joyce Kingship, daughter of Mr. Leo Kingship of Manhattan and the late Phyllis Hatcher, will be married to Mr. Burton Corliss, son of Mrs. Joseph Corliss of Menasset, Massachusetts, and the late Mr. Corliss, on the afternoon of Saturday, December 29, in the home of her father.

Miss Kingship was graduated from the Spence School in New York and is an alumna of Barnard College. Until last week she was with the advertising agency of Camden and Galbraith.

The prospective bridegroom, who served with the Army during the Second World War and attended Caldwell College in Caldwell, Wisconsin, has recently joined the domestic sales division of Kingship Copper Inc.

Miss Richardson looked up and saw that it was the pest again. "Mr. Kingship is still at lunch," she said frigidly.

"Dear lady, he was at lunch at twelve o'clock. It is now three o'clock."

Miss Richardson looked grim. "Tomorrow is Christmas," she said. "Mr. Kingship is interrupting a four-day weekend by coming in today. He gave me strict orders not to disturb him on any account."

The blond young man sighed. Slinging his folded coat over

one shoulder, he drew a slip of paper from the rack next to Miss Richardson's telephone. "May I?" he asked. He then removed Miss Richardson's pen from its onyx holder and began to write. When he had finished, he folded the paper carefully into quarters and handed it to Miss Richardson. "Give him this," he said.

Miss Richardson glared at him. Then she calmly unfolded the paper and read it.

Uncomfortably, she looked up. "Dorothy and Ellen . . . ?" she said softly. "What's your name?"

"Just give him that, please, like the angel you are."

Miss Richardson glanced at the paper and refolded it. She moved to a heavily paneled door. "All right," she said darkly, "but you'll see. He gave me strict orders." Gingerly she tapped on the door. Opening it, she slipped in with the paper held appeasingly before her.

She reappeared a minute later with a betrayed expression on her face. "Go ahead," she said sharply, holding the door open.

At the faint sound of the door closing, Leo Kingship looked up from the slip of paper in his hand. He squinted anxiously at the young man approaching him across the paneled and carpeted room.

"Oh," he said. "You." He looked down at the slip of paper and crumpled it, his expression of anxiety turning to relief and then to annoyance. "No wonder you wouldn't give your name to Miss Richardson."

Smiling, the young man dropped into the visitor's chair.

"But I'm afraid I've forgotten it," Kingship said. "Grant?" he ventured.

"Gant. Gordon Gant."

"I'm extremely busy, Mr. Gant," Kingship said firmly, "so if this information about Dorothy and Ellen"—he held up the crumpled slip of paper—"consists of the same theories you were expounding back in Blue River, I don't want to listen. I realize your motives were of the best; you had taken a liking to Ellen. But barging into my hotel room so soon after Ellen's death . . . bringing up the past at such a moment . . ." He looked at Gant appealingly. "Do you think I wouldn't have liked to believe that Dorothy didn't take her own life?"

"She didn't."

"The note," he said wearily. "The note . . ."

"A couple of sentences that could have referred to a dozen things beside suicide. Or that she could have been tricked into writing." Gant leaned forward. "Dorothy went to the Municipal Building to get married. Ellen's theory was right; the fact that Ellen was killed proves it."

"It does no such thing," Kingship snapped. "There was no connection. You heard the police—"

"A housebreaker!" Gant said, and added flatly, "It was the same person both times."

Kingship braced his hands tiredly on the desk, looking down at the papers there. "Why do you insist on reviving all this?" he asked. "Would you please go now."

Gant made no move to rise. "I'm home on vacation," he said. "Home is White Plains. I didn't spend an hour on the train just to rehash what was already said last March."

"What, then?" Kingship looked warily at Gant.

"There was an article in this morning's *Times* . . . the society page."

"My daughter?"

Gant nodded. "What do you know about Bud Corliss?"

Kingship eyed him in silence. "Know about him?" he said slowly. "What do you mean, know about him?"

"Do you know that he and Ellen were going together?"

"Of course." Kingship straightened up. "What are you driving at?"

Gant sat silently for a moment; then he began to speak in the easy, fluid, announcer's voice. "When she left Caldwell," he said, "Ellen wrote a letter to Bud Corliss. I happened to read that letter soon after Ellen arrived in Blue River. It made quite an impression on me, since it described a murder suspect whom I resembled much too closely for comfort." He smiled. "I read the letter twice, and carefully, as you can imagine.

"On the night Ellen was killed, Police Chief Chesser asked me if Ellen was my girl friend. It was probably the only constructive thing he ever did during his entire career, because it set me thinking about my 'rival,' Bud Corliss. Partly to take my mind off Ellen, who was God-knows-where with an armed killer, and partly because I liked her and wondered what kind of a man she liked, I thought about that letter. There were several bits of information in it that I was able to fit together into an even bigger piece of information about Bud Corliss."

"Go ahead," Kingship said.

Gant leaned back comfortably. "First of all, Ellen wrote Bud that she wouldn't fall behind in her work while away from Caldwell because she would be able to get all the notes from him. Now, Ellen was a senior, and if Bud shared *all* her classes, it meant in all probability that he was a junior or a senior.

"Secondly, at one point in the letter Ellen described her behavior during her first three years at Caldwell, how she had been 'the rah-rah girl.' Then she said, 'You wouldn't have recognized me.' Which meant, as clearly as could possibly be, that Bud had not known her during those first three years.

"Thirdly, Caldwell is a very small college; everyone knows everybody else and knows what they are doing.

"So, we add one, two and three: Bud Corliss, who is at least in his third year of college, was a stranger to Ellen at the beginning of her fourth year, despite the fact that they both attended a very small school. All of which can be explained in only one way: *Bud Corliss was a transfer student, and he transferred to Caldwell in September of 1950, at the beginning of Ellen's fourth year and after Dorothy's death.*"

Kingship frowned. "I don't see what—"

"We come now to today, December 24, 1951," Gant said. "And there, on the society page of *The New York Times*, it says that Miss Marion Kingship is to wed Mr. Burton Corliss. Imagine my surprise. It looks to me, says I, as though the new member of the domestic sales division was determined not to be disqualified from the Kingship Copper sweepstakes."

"Now look here, Mr. Gant—"

"I considered," Gant went on, "how when one sister was killed he proceeded directly to the next one. Two out of three. Not a bad score. And then I thought, Three daughters out of three would have been an even better score for Mr. Burton Corliss. I wondered whether it could have been Stoddard that he transferred from—whether he might have been a student there in the spring of 1950, at the time of Dorothy's death."

Kingship stood up, staring at Gant.

"A random thought," Gant said. "Wildly improbable. But easily removed from the realm of doubt. A simple matter of consulting the Stoddard yearbook for 1950." He displayed a large blue book. "In the sophomore section," he said, "there are photographs of Dorothy Kingship and of Dwight Powell, both of whom are now dead." He opened the book to a page marked by a strip of newsprint, turned the volume around, and put it on the desk. "There was also another interesting photograph." He recited the inscription beside it from memory: "Corliss, Burton, Menasset, Mass., Liberal Arts."

Kingship sat down again. He looked at the photograph in the yearbook. Then he looked up again.

"What is this supposed to be leading up to?" he asked stolidly.

"May I ask you one question, Mr. Kingship, before I answer that? Corliss never told you he went to Stoddard, did he?"

"No. But we've never discussed things like that," he explained quickly. "He must have told Marion. Marion must know."

"I don't think she does. Marion gave them the information for that announcement in the *Times*, didn't she? The bride-to-be usually does."

"Well?"

"Well, there's no mention of Stoddard. And in the other announcements it's mentioned when someone's attended more than one school."

"Maybe she just didn't bother to tell them."

"Maybe. Or maybe she doesn't know. Maybe Ellen didn't know either."

"Which means?" Kingship challenged.

"Which means that he must have been involved with Dorothy in some way. Why else would he conceal it?" Gant looked down at the book in his lap. "There was a man who wanted Dorothy out of the way because he had gotten her pregnant. . . ."

Kingship stared at him. "Come on," he said. "That's crazy."

"All right," Gant said, "it's crazy. But if he didn't tell Marion he went to Stoddard, then in some way he must have been involved with Dorothy. And if he was involved with Dorothy, and then Ellen, and now with Marion, then he was certainly good and determined to marry one of your daughters! Any one!"

The smile left Kingship's face slowly, draining it of expression.

"That *isn't* so crazy, I take it," Gant said.

Kingship straightened up. "I will have to speak to Marion," he said. "She's at her place, packing. She's giving up her apartment, staying with me until the wedding." He put on his jacket. "He *must* have told her about Stoddard."

When they came out of the office, Miss Richardson looked up from a magazine.

"That's all for today, Miss Richardson. If you'll just clear my desk. And Merry Christmas, Miss Richardson."

They walked down a long corridor, on the walls of which were black and white photographs of mines, smelters, refineries, furnaces and rolling mills.

Waiting for the elevator Kingship said, "I'm sure he told her."

"GORDON Gant?" Marion said. "Don't I know that name?" She backed into the room, smiling.

"Blue River." Kingship's voice was wooden as when he had performed the introduction, and his eyes were not quite on Marion's. "I think I told you about him."

"Oh, yes. You knew Ellen, wasn't that it?"

"That's right," Gant said. He wished he hadn't been so damned eager when Kingship had asked him to come up; the *Times* photo of Marion had offered no hint of the I'm-getting-married radiance that glowed all over her.

She gestured at the living room despairingly. "I'm afraid there isn't even a place to sit down." She moved toward a chair on which some shoe boxes were piled.

"Don't bother," Kingship said. "We just stopped by. Only for a minute."

"You haven't forgotten tonight, have you?" Marion asked. "You can expect us at seven or so. Mrs. Corliss is arriving at five, and I guess she'll want to stop at her hotel first." She turned to Gant. "My prospective mother-in-law," she said significantly.

He smiled wanly and didn't say anything.

"To what do I owe the pleasure of this visit?" Marion inquired.

After a moment Gant said, "I knew Dorothy too. But only slightly."

"Oh," Marion said. She looked down at her hands.

"She was in one of my classes. I go to Stoddard." He paused. "I don't think Bud was ever in any of my classes, though."

She looked up. "Bud?"

"Bud Corliss. Your . . ."

She shook her head, smiling. "Bud was never at Stoddard," she corrected him.

"He was, Miss Kingship."

"No," she insisted amusedly, "he went to Caldwell."

"He went to Stoddard, *then* to Caldwell."

Marion smiled quizzically at Kingship, as though expecting him to offer some explanation for the obstinacy of the caller he had brought.

"He was at Stoddard, Marion," Kingship said heavily. "Show her the yearbook, Gant."

Gant opened the book and handed it to Marion, pointing to the picture.

"Well, for goodness' sake," she said. "I have to apologize. I never knew . . ." She glanced at the cover of the yearbook. "In 1950."

"He's in the '49 book too," Gant said. "He went to Stoddard for two years and then transferred to Caldwell."

"Isn't that funny?" she said. "Maybe he knew Dorothy." She

sounded pleased, as though this were yet another bond between her and her fiancé.

"He never mentioned it to you at all?" Gant asked.

"Why, no, he never said a . . ."

Slowly she looked up from the book, becoming aware for the first time of the strain and discomfort of the two men. "What's the matter?" she asked curiously. "Why are the two of you standing there as if . . ." There was a tightening movement in her throat. "Is this why you came up here, to tell me this?" she asked.

"We . . . we only wondered if you knew, that's all."

"Why?" she asked.

"Why should Bud conceal it?" Gant asked.

"*Conceal* it?" Marion said. "What kind of a word is that? He didn't *conceal* it; it just didn't come up."

"Why should the girl he's marrying not know he spent two years at Stoddard," Gant rephrased implacably, "unless he was involved with Dorothy?"

"*Involved*? With *Dorothy*?" Her eyes, wide with incredulity, probed into Gant's, and then swung slowly, narrowing, to Kingship. "What is this? How much are you paying him?" she asked coldly.

"He came to me of his own accord, Marion!"

Gant said, "I saw the announcement in the *Times*."

Marion glared at her father. "You think I don't know you?" she said bitterly. "He was *involved* with Dorothy—is he supposed to be the one who got her in trouble?—and he was *involved* with Ellen, and now he's *involved* with me—all for the money, all for your precious money. That's what's going on—*in your mind!*"

"You've got it wrong, Miss Kingship," Gant said. "That's what's going on in *my* mind, not your father's."

"See?" Kingship said. "He came to me of his own accord."

Marion stared at Gant. "Just who are you? What makes this your business?"

"I knew Ellen. I met her when she came to Blue River to try to find Dorothy's killer."

"So I understand," she snapped. "Do you know Bud?"

"I've never had the pleasure."

"Then will you please explain to me what you're doing here, making accusations against him behind his back! Are you jealous of Bud? Is that it? Because Ellen preferred him to you?"

"That's right," Gant said dryly. "I'm consumed with jealousy."

Kingship edged toward the door, signaling Gant with his eyes.

"Yes," Marion said, "you'd both better go."

"All right." Kingship hesitated. "You're still coming tonight, aren't you, Marion?" he asked.

Her lips clenched. She thought for a moment. "Only because I don't want to hurt Bud's mother's feelings," she said finally.

"All right, Marion," Kingship said. "All right." He followed Gant into the hall and turned to close the door.

The two men went to a drugstore on Lexington Avenue, where Gant ordered coffee and cherry pie, and Kingship a glass of milk.

"So far, so good," Gant said.

Kingship was gazing at a paper napkin he held. "What do you mean?"

"We know he didn't tell her about Stoddard. That makes it practically certain that—"

Kingship set his glass of milk down firmly. "A man is innocent until he's proved guilty."

"Then we've got to find proof, don't we?"

"You see? You're assuming he's a fortune hunter before you've started."

"I'm assuming a hell of a lot more than that," Gant said. "What are you going to do?"

Kingship was looking at the napkin again. "Nothing."

"You're going to let them get married?"

"I couldn't stop them, even if I wanted to. They're both over twenty-one."

"You could hire detectives. There are four days yet. They might find something."

"Might," Kingship said. "If there's anything to find. Or Bud might get wind of it and tell Marion."

Gant smiled. "You're afraid of her, aren't you?" he said.

Kingship sighed. "Let me tell you something," he said, not looking at Gant. "I had a wife and three daughters. Two daughters were taken from me. My wife I pushed away myself. Maybe I pushed one of the daughters too. So now I have only one daughter. I'm fifty-seven years old and I have one daughter and some men I play golf with. That's all."

After a moment Kingship turned to Gant, his face set rigidly. "What about you?" he demanded. "What *is* your real interest in this affair? Maybe you just enjoy showing people what a clever fellow you are."

"Maybe," Gant said. "Also maybe I think he killed your daughters and I've got this quixotic notion that murderers should be punished."

Kingship finished his milk. "I think you'd better just go back to Yonkers and enjoy your vacation."

"White Plains." Gant scraped together the syrupy remains of the pie with the side of his fork. "Do you have ulcers?" he asked, glancing at the empty milk glass.

Kingship nodded.

Gant leaned back on his stool and surveyed the man beside him. "And about thirty pounds overweight, I'd say. I should estimate that Bud has you figured for ten more years. Or maybe he'll get impatient in three or four years and try to hurry you on."

Kingship got off his stool. He put a dollar on the counter. "Good-by, Mr. Gant," he said, and strode away.

IN WRITING to his mother, Bud had made only vague allusions to Kingship's money. He had looked forward eagerly, therefore, to the moment when he could introduce her to Marion and her father, and to the magnificence of Kingship's duplex apartment, knowing that in light of the coming marriage she would regard such splendor as evidence not of Kingship's capabilities but of his own.

The evening, however, was a disappointment.

Not that his mother's reaction was anything less than he had anticipated; with mouth partially opened, she drew in her breath with soft sibilance, as though seeing not one but a series of miracles; the formally attired servant—a butler!—the velvety depth of the carpets, the wallpaper of textured cloth, the leather-bound books, the golden clock, the silver tray from which the butler served champagne—champagne!

No, his mother's reaction was warming and wonderful. What made the evening a disappointment was the fact that Marion and her father had apparently had an argument; Marion spoke to him only when appearances made it inescapable. And furthermore, the argument must have been about her marriage, since Kingship addressed Bud with hesitant, unfocused eyes, while Marion was determinedly, defiantly effusive, clinging to him and calling him 'dear' and 'darling.' Dinner was dismal.

The first faint worry began to irritate Bud like a pebble in his shoe.

Later, it being Christmas Eve, they went to church, and after church Bud expected to take his mother back to her hotel while Marion returned home with her father. But Marion, to his annoyance, insisted on accompanying them, so Kingship went off by himself as Bud squired the two women to the lobby of his mother's hotel. Bud kissed his mother good-night and, still holding Bud's hand, Mrs. Corliss kissed Marion on the cheek.

During the taxi ride back to her father's apartment, Marion was silent.

"What's the matter, darling?"

"Nothing," she said, smiling unconvincingly.

He had intended to leave her at the door of the apartment, but the pebble of worry was assuming the proportions of a sharp stone; he went in with her. Kingship had already retired. They went into the living room, where Bud lit cigarettes while Marion turned on the radio.

She told him that she liked his mother very much. He said he was glad, and he could tell that his mother liked her too. They began to speak of the future, and he sensed from the stiff casualness of her voice that she was working up to something. He leaned back with his eyes half closed. It couldn't be anything important! It couldn't be! He had slighted her somehow, forgotten something he had promised to do, that was all.

She worked the conversation around to children. "Two," she said. "Then one can go to Barnard and one to Caldwell."

Caldwell. Something about Caldwell. Ellen.

"Or maybe," Marion went on, "they could go to Stoddard and then transfer to Caldwell." She leaned forward, smiling, and pressed her cigarette into an ashtray.

Stoddard! And transfer to Caldwell. Transfer to Caldwell . . .

They sat side by side silently for a moment.

"That's what I did," he said. "Transferred from Stoddard to Caldwell."

"Did you?" She sounded surprised.

"Of course," he said. "I told you."

"No, you didn't. You never said—"

"I did, honey. I'm sure I told you. I went to Stoddard University and then to Caldwell."

"Why, that's where my sister Dorothy went, Stoddard! Don't tell me you *knew* her."

"No. Ellen showed me her picture, though, and I think I remember seeing her around. I'm sure I told you, that first day, in the museum."

"No, you didn't. I'm positive."

"Well, I was at Stoddard two years. And you mean to say you didn't—" Marion's lips stopped the rest of the sentence, kissing him fervidly, atoning for doubt.

THERE was still no real danger. Trouble maybe; the wedding plans might be blown up, but there was no *danger*, no police danger. Marion's questions only meant that Kingship had somehow learned he'd been at Stoddard.

But why so late? If Kingship wanted to check on him, why hadn't he done it sooner? Why today? . . . The announcement in the *Times* . . . of course! Someone had seen it, someone who'd been at Stoddard. The son of one of Kingship's friends or someone like that. "My son and your future son-in-law were at Stod-

123

dard together." So Kingship puts two and two together; Dorothy, Ellen, Marion—gold digger. He tells Marion, and that was the cause of their argument.

Still, what could Kingship do, with only suspicions? They must be only suspicions; the old man couldn't know for sure that he'd known Dorothy. Could he *make* certain? How? The kids at Stoddard, mostly seniors now, would they remember who Dorothy had gone with? They might. But it's Christmas vacation! They're scattered all over the country. And only four days to the wedding.

All he had to do was sit tight and keep his fingers crossed. Tuesday, Wednesday, Thursday, Friday . . . *Saturday*. If worst came to worst, so he was after the money; that was all Kingship could ever prove. And there's no law against going after a rich girl, is there?

And if best came to best, the wedding would go off as per schedule. Then what could Kingship do even if the kids at Stoddard did remember? Divorce? Annulment? Not if Marion couldn't be persuaded to seek one. What, then? Maybe Kingship would try to buy him off. . . .

Now *there* was a thought. How much would Kingship be willing to pay to free his daughter from the big bad gold digger? Quite a lot, probably.

But not nearly as much as Marion would have someday.

THE Corliss house in Menasset was a shabby gray box, one story, the sills of its darkened windows furred with snow. It was set back only a few yards from the sidewalk; the snow between door and sidewalk was undisturbed. Gordon Gant went around to the back. What a hell of a way to spend Christmas night, he thought. He went up on the small back porch. He tried the door; it was locked. The window next to it was locked also. He took a roll of Scotch tape from his pocket. Tearing off a ten-inch length, he pressed it across one of the window's dozen panes.

After he had crosshatched the glass with several strips, he struck the pane with his gloved fist. The broken glass sagged, held in place by the tape. Gant withdrew a section of tape and glass from the window and, reaching through, unfastened the latch and raised the lower section.

He took a pencil flashlight from his pocket and climbed through the open window, closing it after him.

The flashlight's disk of pallid light glided swiftly over a cramped and shabby kitchen. Gant moved forward, treading softly on worn linoleum. He came to the living room. There were pictures of Bud all over; Bud as a child, Bud at high school graduation, Bud in a private's uniform. He passed Mrs. Corliss' bedroom; a bottle of lotion on the dresser, an empty dress box on the bed, a wedding picture on the night table. The fourth room he came to was Bud's.

He inspected the titles of some books on a shelf; they were mainly college texts and a few classic novels. He sat behind the desk and went through the drawers one at a time. No letters, no calendars with appointments written in, no address books with names crossed out. He rose from the desk and went to the dresser. Half the drawers were empty. The others contained summer shirts and swimming trunks, a couple of pairs of argyle socks, underwear, tarnished cuff links, bow ties with broken clips. Perfunctorily he opened the closet. On the floor in the corner there was a small gray strongbox.

He took it out and put it on the desk. It was locked. He lifted and shook it. The contents shifted, sounding like packets of paper. He wrapped the box in newspaper, hoping that it didn't contain Mrs. Corliss' life's savings.

He returned to the kitchen, opened the window, and climbed out onto the back porch. He closed the window and, with the strongbox under his arm, moved quietly between the houses to the sidewalk.

Leo Kingship returned to his apartment at ten o'clock on Wednesday night, having worked late in order to compensate for some of the lost hours Christmas had entailed. "Is Marion in?" he asked the butler, giving him his coat.

"Out with Mr. Corliss. She said she'd be in early, though. There's a Mr. Dettweiler waiting in the living room."

"Dettweiler?" Kingship frowned.

"He said Miss Richardson sent him about the securities. He has a little strongbox with him."

As Kingship went into the living room, Gordon Gant rose from a comfortable chair adjacent to the fireplace. "Hello," he said pleasantly.

Kingship looked at him for a moment. His hands clenched at his sides. "Get out of here," he said. "If Marion comes in . . ."

"Exhibit A," Gant pronounced, raising a gleaming copper pamphlet in each hand, "in the case against Bud Corliss."

"I don't want to . . ." The sentence hung unfinished. Apprehensively, Kingship came forward. He took the pamphlets from Gant's hands. "Our publications . . ."

"In the possession of Bud Corliss," Gant said. "Kept in a strongbox which until last night resided in a closet in the Corliss house in Menasset, Massachusetts." He gave a light kick to the strongbox on the floor beside him. There were four oblong manila envelopes inside. "I stole it," Gant said.

"You're crazy." Kingship sat heavily on a couch that faced the fireplace. He stared at the pamphlets. "Oh, God," he said.

Gant resumed his seat next to the couch. "Observe the condition of exhibit A, if you will. Frayed around the edges, soiled by many finger marks, center pages worked loose from the staples. I would say he had had the pamphlets for quite some time. I would say he drooled over them considerably."

"That . . . that son of a bitch!" Kingship spoke the phrase distinctly, as though not accustomed to using it.

Gant prodded the strongbox with his toe. "The history of Bud Corliss, a drama in four envelopes," he said. "Envelope one: newspaper clippings of the high school hero; class president, chairman of the prom committee, most likely to succeed and so on and so forth. Envelope two: honorable discharge from the army, Bronze Star, Purple Heart. Envelope three: college days; transcripts from Stoddard and Caldwell. Envelope four: two well-read brochures describing the magnitude of Kingship Copper Incorporated, and this"—he drew a folded sheet of blue-lined yellow paper from his pocket and passed it to Kingship—"which I can't make head or tail of."

Kingship unfolded the paper. He read halfway down it. "What is it?"

"I'm asking you."

He shook his head.

"It must have some bearing on the pamphlets," Gant said. "It was in the same envelope with them."

Kingship shook his head and handed the paper back to Gant. "How am I supposed to tell Marion?" he asked. "She *loves* him." He looked at Gant dismally. Then slowly his face smoothed out. He glanced at the pamphlets and back at Gant, his eyes narrowing. "How do I know these were in the strongbox? How do I know that you didn't put them there yourself?"

Kingship got up and went to a telephone on a carved table across the room. He dialed a number.

In the silence of the room the clicks of the phone were audible. "Hello? Miss Richardson? This is Mr. Kingship. I'd like to ask a favor of you. A big favor, I'm afraid. And absolutely confidential. Would you please go down to the office—" An unintelligible twittering emanated from the phone. "I wouldn't ask you, only it's terribly important, and I—" There was more twittering. "Go to the public relations department," Kingship said. "Go through the files and see whether we've ever sent any promotional publications to . . . Bud Corliss."

"Burton Corliss," Gant said.

"Or Burton Corliss. Yes, that's right—Mr. Corliss. I'm at my home, Miss Richardson. Call me as soon as you find out. Thank you very much. I appreciate this." He hung up.

Gant shook his head wryly. "We're really grasping at straws, aren't we?"

"I have to be sure," Kingship said. "You have to be sure of your evidence in a thing like this."

"You're sure already, and you know damn well you are," Gant

said. "Mr. Kingship, I am right about this much. Will you admit
that I might be right all the way?"

"What all the way?"

"About Dorothy and Ellen." Kingship drew an irritated breath.
Gant continued quickly. "He didn't tell Marion he went to Stoddard. He *must* have been mixed up with Dorothy. He *must* be the
one who got her pregnant. He killed her, and Powell and Ellen
somehow found out it was him and he had to kill them too."

"The note . . ."

"He could have tricked her into writing it! It's been done before. There was a case in the papers just last month about a guy
who did it, and for the same reason."

Kingship shook his head. "I'd believe it of him," he said. "After
what he's done to Marion, I'd believe anything of him. But
there's a flaw in your theory, a big flaw."

"What?" Gant demanded.

"He's after the money, isn't he?"

Gant nodded.

"Well," Kingship said, "if he were the one who'd gotten Dorothy into trouble, and if she were ready to marry him, then why
would he have killed her? He would have gone ahead and married her and gotten in on the money."

Gant looked at him wordlessly.

"You were right about this," Kingship said, lifting the pamphlets, "but you're wrong about Dorothy. All wrong."

After a moment Gant rose. He turned and paced up to the
window. He looked through it dully, gnawing his lower lip.

WHEN the door chimes toned, Gant turned from the window.
Kingship was standing before the fireplace, holding the pamphlets
at his side, his face averted from Gant's watching eyes.

They heard the front door open, and then voices. ". . . come
in for a while?"

"I don't think so, Marion. We'll have to get up early tomorrow." There was a long silence. "I'll be in front of my place at
seven thirty."

"You'd better wear a dark suit. A smelter must be a filthy place." Another silence. "Good night, Bud."

"Good night."

The door closed.

Kingship wound the pamphlets into a cylinder. "Marion," he called, but it came out too low. "Marion," he called again louder.

"Coming," her voice answered cheerfully.

The two men waited, suddenly conscious of a clock's ticking.

She appeared in the wide doorway. Her cheeks were luminous from the cold outside. "Hi," she said. "We had a—"

She saw Gant. Her hands froze, dropped. Then she whirled and was gone.

Kingship hurried to the doorway and into the foyer. "Marion!" She was halfway up the curving white staircase. "Marion!" he shouted grimly, commanding.

She stopped, facing rigidly up the stairs, one hand on the banister. "Well?"

"Come down here," he said. "I have to speak to you. This is extremely important." A moment passed. "Come into the living room," he said.

"All right." She turned and descended the stairs with regal coldness. "You can speak to me. Before I go upstairs and pack and get out of here."

Kingship returned to the living room. Gant was standing uncomfortably in the middle of the room, his hand on the back of the couch. Kingship went to his side.

Marion came into the room and sat down on a chair at the end of the couch. She crossed her legs carefully, smoothing the red wool of her skirt. She looked up at them. "Well?" she said.

Kingship shifted uneasily, withering under her gaze. "Mr. Gant went to . . ." He turned to Gant helplessly.

Gant said, "Yesterday, absolutely without your father's knowledge, I went to Menasset. I broke into your fiancé's home—"

"No!"

"And I took from it a strongbox I found in the closet in his room. I brought it home and jimmied the cover."

Marion's eyes flashed. "What did you find? The plans of the atom bomb?"

Kingship walked to the end of the couch and handed her the pamphlets, awkwardly unrolling them.

"They're old," Gant said. "He's had them for some time."

Kingship said, "He hasn't been back to Menasset since you started going with him. He had them before he met you."

She smoothed the pamphlets carefully in her lap. Some of the corners were folded over. She bent them straight. "Ellen must have given them to him."

"Ellen never had any of our publications, Marion. You know that. She was as little interested as you are."

She began turning the pages of one of the pamphlets; casually, as though it were a magazine in a waiting room. "All right," she said stiffly, "maybe it *was* the money that attracted him at first." Her lips formed a strained smile. "For once in my life I'm grateful for your money." She turned a page. "What is it they say? It's as easy to fall in love with a rich girl as with a poor girl." And another page. "You really can't blame him too much, coming from such a poor family." She stood up and tossed the pamphlets on the couch. "Is there anything else you wanted?" Her hands were trembling slightly.

"Anything else?" Kingship stared. "Isn't that enough?"

"Enough?" she inquired. "Enough for me to call off the wedding? No." She shook her head. "No, it isn't enough."

"Marion, you *can't* marry him now."

"No? Come down to City Hall Saturday morning!"

"He's a no-good scheming—"

"Oh, yes! You always know just who's good and who's bad, don't you! You knew Mother was bad and you got rid of her, and you would have found out that Dorothy was bad and that's why she killed herself. Haven't you done enough with your good and bad?"

"You're *not* going to marry a man who's only after you for your money!"

"He *loves* me! Don't you understand English? I love him! I

don't care *what* brought us together! We think alike! Feel alike! We like the same books, the same plays, the same music, the same—"

"The same food?" Gant cut in. "Would you both be fond of Italian and Armenian food?" She turned to him, her mouth ajar. He was unfolding a sheet of blue-lined yellow paper. "And those books," he said, looking at the paper. "Would they include the works of Proust, Thomas Wolfe, Carson McCullers?"

Her eyes widened. "How did you . . . ? What is that?" She suddenly sat down on the couch.

"This was in the strongbox with the pamphlets," he said. "In the same envelope." He handed her the yellow paper. "I'm sorry," he said.

She looked at him confusedly, and then looked down at the paper.

Proust, T. Wolfe, C. McCullers, *Madame Bovary, Alice in Wonderland,* Eliz. B. Browning—Read!
Art (Mostly modern)—Hopley or Hopper, DeMeuth (sp?), Renoir, VanGogh. Read general books on mod. art
Jealous of E.?
Italian & Armenian food—Look up restaurants in NYC
Theater: Shaw, T. Williams—serious stuff

She read barely a quarter of the closely written page, her cheeks draining of color. Then she folded the paper with trembling care. "Well," she said, not looking up, "haven't I been the . . . trusting soul." She smiled crazily at her father as he came around the end of the couch to stand helplessly beside her. "I should have known, shouldn't I?" The blood rushed back to her cheeks, burning red. Her eyes were swimming and her fingers were suddenly mashing and twisting the paper with steel strength. "Too good to be true." She smiled, tears starting down her cheeks. Her hands released the yellow fragments and flew to her face. She began to cry.

Kingship sat beside her, his arm about her bowed shoulders.

"Marion . . . Marion . . . Be glad you didn't find out too late."

Her back was shaking under his arm. "You don't understand," she sobbed through her hands. "You can't understand. . . ."

WHEN the tears had stopped she sat numbly, her fingers knotted around the handkerchief Kingship had given her, her eyes on the pieces of yellow paper on the carpet.

"Do you want me to take you upstairs?" Kingship asked.

"No. Please . . . just . . . just let me sit here."

He rose and joined Gant, who had walked over to the window. They were silent for a while, looking at the lights beyond the river. Finally Kingship said, "I'll do *something* to him. I swear to God, I'll do *something*."

A minute passed. Gant said, "Mr. Kingship, what would you have done if Dorothy had married without first consulting you, and then had had a baby . . . too soon?"

After a moment Kingship said, "I don't know."

"He would have thrown her out," Marion said quietly. The two men turned. She was still looking at the papers on the floor.

"I don't think I would have thrown her out," Kingship protested.

"You would have," Marion said tonelessly.

"Well," Kingship said, "shouldn't a couple be expected to assume the responsibilities of marriage, as well as the . . ." He left the sentence unfinished.

Gant lit a cigarette. "There you are," he said. "That's why he killed her. She must have told him about you. He knew he wouldn't get near the money if he married her, and if he didn't marry he would get into trouble, so . . . Then he decides to have a second try, with Ellen, but she starts to investigate Dorothy's death and, through Powell, gets too close to the truth. And so he tries a third time."

"Bud?" Marion said. She spoke the name blankly, her face showing the barest flicker of surprise, as though her fiancé had been accused of having imperfect table manners.

Kingship turned to Gant, the resolution fading from his eyes.

"We're not even sure he *knew* Dorothy, let alone he was the one she was . . . seeing. We have to be *sure*."

The telephone rang.

Kingship went to the carved table and lifted the receiver. "Hello?" There was a long pause. "When?" he asked. There was another pause, then, "Thank you very much."

Gant looked at Kingship. He was standing beside the table, his pink face rigid. "Miss Richardson," he said. "Promotional literature was sent to Burton Corliss in Caldwell, Wisconsin, on October 16, 1950."

"Just when he must have started his campaign with Ellen," Gant said.

Kingship nodded. "But that was the second time," he said slowly. "Promotional literature was also sent to Burton Corliss on February 6, 1950, in Blue River, Iowa."

Gant said, "Dorothy . . ."

Marion moaned.

GANT remained after Marion had gone upstairs. "We're still in the same boat Ellen was in," he said. "The police have Dorothy's suicide note and all we have are suspicions and a flock of circumstantial evidence."

Kingship held one of the pamphlets. "I'll get him somehow," he said. "I'll make sure, and I'll get him."

Gant said, "We've either got to find out how he got Dorothy to write that suicide note, or else find the gun he used on Powell and Ellen. And before Saturday."

Kingship looked at the photograph on the pamphlet's cover. "The smelter . . ." Sorrowfully he said, "We're supposed to fly out there tomorrow. I wanted to show him around. Marion too. She was never interested before."

"Better see that she doesn't let him know the wedding is off."

Kingship's eyes returned to the pamphlet. A moment passed. "He picked the wrong man," he said softly, still looking at the photograph of the smelter. "He should have picked on somebody else's daughters."

WAS THERE EVER SUCH a perfect day? Bud grinned at the plane, its compact body gleaming, the coppered KINGSHIP blazing in the early morning sun. He grinned at the ceramic blue of the sky, then stretched and pounded his chest happily, watching his breath plume upward. No, he decided judicially, there really never was such a perfect day.

Marion and her father were standing in the shade, having one of their tight-lipped arguments. "I'm going!" Marion insisted.

"What's the matter?" he smiled, coming up to them.

Kingship turned and walked away.

"Nothing's the matter," Marion said. "I don't feel well, so he doesn't want me to go." Her eyes were on the plane beyond him.

"Bridal nerves?"

"No. I just don't feel well, that's all."

"Oh," he said knowingly.

They stood in silence for a minute, and then he moved toward Kingship. Leave it to Marion to be off on a day like this. Well, it was probably all for the good; maybe she'd keep quiet for a change. "All set to go?" he asked.

"A few minutes," Kingship said. "We're waiting for Mr. Dettweiler."

"Who?"

"Mr. Dettweiler. His father is on the board of directors."

A few minutes later a blond young man in a pale blue overcoat approached from the direction of the commercial hangars. He nodded at Marion and came up to Kingship.

They shook hands. "I'd like you to meet my prospective son-in-law, Bud Corliss," Kingship said. "Bud, this is Gordon Dettweiler."

"How do you do."

"Well," Dettweiler said—he had a handshake like a mangle—"I've certainly been looking forward to meeting you. Yes sir, I certainly have." A character, Bud thought, or maybe he was trying to get in good with Kingship.

"Ready, sir?" a man asked from within the plane.

"Ready," Kingship said. Marion came forward. "Marion, I

honestly wish you wouldn't . . ." But she marched right past them and up the three-step platform into the plane. Dettweiler followed her in. Kingship said, "After you, Bud."

Bud jogged up the three steps and entered the plane. It was a six-seater, its interior done in light blue. He took the last seat on the right, behind the wing. Marion was across the aisle. Kingship took the front seat, across from Dettweiler.

When the engine coughed and roared to life, Bud fastened his seat belt. Son of a gun, if it didn't have a copper buckle! The plane began to roll forward. On the way . . .

Would Kingship be taking him to the smelter if he were still suspicious? Never!

Bud leaned over, tapped Marion's elbow and grinned at her. She smiled back, looking ill, all right, and returned to her window. Kingship and Dettweiler were speaking softly to each other over the aisle. Well, he hadn't wanted to talk to anyone anyway. He stared out the window, fingering the copper buckle. On the way to the smelter . . . The smelter! The fountainhead of wealth!

The plane roared forward.

HE WAS the first to see it; far ahead and below, a small black geometric cluster on the bed sheet of snow. Railroad tracks looped and encircled it; a freight train crawled along, its chain of open cars scintillating with salmon-colored glints.

The plane banked. The ground tilted, then leveled, and finally came slicing up under the wing.

There was a limousine waiting when they descended, a custom-built Packard, black and polished. Bud sat on a jump seat next to Dettweiler. He leaned forward, looking over the driver's shoulder.

Ahead, the smelter rose up. Brown structures merged into a crude pyramid, their belching smokestacks ranked around the largest one.

The limousine pulled up before a low brick building, at the door of which waited a lean, white-haired, smiling man, who turned out to be a Mr. Otto, the manager of the smelter.

AFTER A BRIEFING BY Mr. Otto, they left the brick office building and crossed the asphalt yard to the smelter itself. Bud walked slowly. The others hurried ahead, but he drifted behind, savoring the climactic sweetness of the moment. He gazed up at the monstrous brown form that filled more and more of the sky—a giant heart of American industry, drawing in bad blood, pumping out good! Standing so close to it, about to enter it, it was impossible not to share the surging of its power.

The others had vanished into a doorway at the base of the towering steel mass. Now Mr. Otto smiled within the doorway, beckoning. Bud moved forward less slowly, like a lover going to a long-awaited tryst.

A whistle screamed.

He went into the darkness of the doorway. The door closed after him. The whistle screamed again, piercingly, like a bird in a jungle.

HE STOOD on a chain-railed catwalk, staring in fascination at an army of huge cylindrical furnaces ranked before him in diminishing perspective like an ordered forest of giant redwood trunks. The air was hot and sulfurous.

"There are six hearths, one above the other, in each furnace," Mr. Otto lectured. "The ore is introduced at the top. It's moved steadily downward from hearth to hearth. The roasting removes excess sulfur from the ore."

Bud listened intently, nodding. He turned to the others to express his awe, but only Marion stood on his right, wooden-faced, as she had been all day. Kingship and that Dettweiler were gone. "Where'd your father and Dettweiler go?" he asked her.

"I don't know. Dad wanted to show him something."

"Oh." Bud turned back to the furnaces. "How many are there?" he asked Mr. Otto.

"Furnaces?" Mr. Otto dabbed perspiration from his upper lip with a folded handkerchief. "Fifty-four."

It was wonderful! He'd never been so interested in anything

in his whole life! He asked a thousand questions and Mr. Otto, visibly reacting to his fascination, answered them in detail, while Marion trailed unseeingly behind.

In another building there were more furnaces; brick-walled, flat, and over a hundred feet long. "The reverberatory furnaces," Mr. Otto said. "The ore that comes from the roasting furnaces is about ten percent copper. Here it's melted down. The lighter minerals flow off as slag. What's left is iron and copper—we call it matte—forty percent copper."

Bud shook his head, whistling between his teeth.

Mr. Otto smiled. "Impressed?" he asked as they moved on to the next building.

"It's wonderful," Bud said. "Wonderful."

"And now," Mr. Otto said, pushing his voice over a roaring tide of sound, "we come to the most spectacular part of the entire smelting process—the converters."

The building was a vast steel shell, percussant with the sustained thunder of machines and men. A murky haze obscured its far reaches, swimming around shafts of yellow sunlight that pillared down through crane tracks and catwalks from windows in the peaked roof dim and high above.

At the near end of the building, on either side, lay six massive dark cylindroid vessels, end to end, like giant steel barrels on their sides. Each vessel had an opening in its uppermost surface. Flames burst forth from these mouths—yellow, orange, red, blue—roaring up into funnellike hoods overhead.

One of the converters was rotating on the cogged rollers that supported it, so that its round mouth moved down to the side. Liquid fire rushed from the radiant throat, pouring down into an immense crucible on the floor. The molten flow, heavy and smoking, filled the steel container. The converter rolled back groaningly, its mouth dripping. The crucible now rose, pulled by cables, up to the underbelly of a grimy cab that hung from a single-railed track below the dimness of the roof. The cables contracted; the crucible rose until it was some twenty-five feet above the ground. Then cab, cables and crucible began to draw away, retreating toward the coppery haze at the northern end of the building.

The center of it all! The heart of the heart! With rapt eyes Bud followed the heat-shimmering column of air over the departing crucible.

"Slag," Mr. Otto said. They stood on an island of railed platform against the south wall, a few feet above the floor and midway between the two banks of converters. Mr. Otto touched his handkerchief to his forehead. "The molten matte from the reverberatory furnaces is poured into these converters. Silica is added, and then compressed air is blown in through pipes at the back. The impurities are oxidized; slag forms and is poured off, as you just saw. More matte is added, more slag forms, and so on. The copper keeps getting richer and richer until, after about five hours, it's ninety-nine percent pure. Then it's poured out in the same way as the slag."

"Will they be pouring copper soon?"

Mr. Otto nodded. "The converters are operated on a stagger system, so that there's a continuous output."

"I'd like to see them pour the copper," Bud said. He watched one of the converters on the right pouring off slag. "Why are the flames different colors?" he asked.

"The color changes as the process advances. That's how the operators tell what's going on inside."

Behind them a door closed. Bud turned. Kingship was standing beside Marion. Dettweiler leaned against a ladder that climbed the wall beside the door. "Are you enjoying the tour?" Kingship asked Bud over the thunder.

"It's wonderful! Overpowering!"

"They're going to pour copper over there," Mr. Otto shouted.

Before one of the converters on the left, a crane had lowered a steel vat with steep sides as high as a man. Its rim was seven feet across.

The mammoth cylinder of the converter began to turn, rumbling deeply. Blue flame flickered over its mouth. Then, as it rotated further, a volcanic radiance blasted from its interior, veils of white smoke arose, and a flood of racing incandescence came bursting out, spilling into the giant vat. The steady molten flow seemed motionless—a solid, shining shaft. Within the vat the liquid appeared, slowly rising, clouded by whorls of smoke. A bitter smell singed the air.

"What's the matter, Marion?" Bud heard Kingship ask.

"Matter?" Marion echoed.

"You look pale," Kingship said.

Bud turned around. Marion seemed no paler than usual. "I'm all right," she was saying.

"But you're pale," Kingship insisted, and Dettweiler nodded agreement.

"It must be the heat or something," Marion replied.

"The fumes," Kingship said. "Some people can't stand the fumes. Mr. Otto, why don't you take my daughter back to the administration building? We'll be along in a few minutes."

"Honestly, Dad," she said, "I feel—"

"No nonsense." Kingship smiled stiffly. "We'll be with you in a few minutes."

"But . . ." She hesitated a moment, looking annoyed, and then shrugged and turned to the door.

Mr. Otto followed her. He paused and turned back to Kingship. "I hope you'll show Mr. Corlis how we cast the anodes."

"Anodes?" Bud said.

"The slabs we send to an electrolytic refinery for further purification," Kingship explained.

"Very impressive," Mr. Otto said, and left, closing the door.

Kingship asked Bud, "Did Mr. Otto take you up on the catwalk?"

"No," Bud replied.

"You get a much better view from there," Kingship said.

Dettweiler, his back against the ladder, stepped aside. "After you." He smiled.

Bud went to the ladder and climbed the metal rungs which ran up the wall to the catwalk, some fifty feet above. Kingship and Dettweiler followed after him. As he emerged through the opening onto the ridged metal floor of the catwalk, he noticed that the thunder of the machines was diminished up here but that the air was hotter and the bitter smell stronger. The narrow catwalk, railed by heavy chain between iron stanchions, ended halfway down the building's length, where it was cut off by a broad steel partition that hung from roof to floor. Overhead, on either side, crane tracks paralleled the catwalk, passing clear of the partition and continuing into the northern half of the building.

To his right, twenty feet below and ten feet out from the catwalk, hung the vat of copper on its slow procession toward the far end of the building. Ghosts of smoke rose from the fiery orange of its surface. Bud's eyes climbed the vat's cables, six on either side, up to the cab a dozen feet above him.

He was nearing the steel partition, and now he saw that the catwalk didn't end there after all; instead it branched six feet to right and left, following the partition to its edges like the head of a long-stemmed T. He turned onto the left wing of the T. A three-foot chain swung across the catwalk's end. He leaned over it a bit and peered around the partition at the receding vat as it moved toward the other end of the building. "Where does it go now?" he called back.

Behind him Kingship said, "Refining furnaces. Then it's poured into molds."

Bud turned around. Kingship and Dettweiler faced him shoulder to shoulder. Their faces were oddly grim. He patted the partition on his left. "What's behind here?" he asked.

"The refining furnaces," Kingship said. "Any more questions?"

Bud shook his head.

"Then I've got one for you," Kingship said. His eyes were like blue marbles behind his glasses. "How did you get Dorothy to write that suicide note?"

EVERYTHING fell away; the catwalk, the smelter, the whole world; everything melted away like sand castles sucked into the sea, leaving him suspended in emptiness with two blue marbles staring at him and the sound of Kingship's question swelling and reverberating like being inside an iron bell. The floor of the cat-walk swayed anchorless and undulant beneath his feet, because his knees—oh, God!—were jelly, trembling and shaking. "What're you—" he started to say, but nothing came out. He swallowed air. "What're you . . . talking about?"

"Dorothy," Dettweiler told him. "You wanted to marry her. For the money. But then she was pregnant. You knew you wouldn't get the money. So you killed her."

Bud shook his head in confused protest. "No," he said. "No! She committed suicide! She sent a note to Ellen! You know that."

"You tricked her into writing it," Kingship said.

"How . . . how could I do that? How the hell could I do *that?*"

"That's what you're going to tell us," Dettweiler said.

"I hardly knew her!"

"You didn't know her at all," Kingship said. "That's what you told Marion."

"That's right! I didn't know her at all!"

"You just said you *hardly* knew her."

"I didn't know her *at all!*"

Kingship's fists clenched. "You sent for Kingship Copper publications in February 1950! Why?"

Bud stared, his left hand bracing tightly against the partition. The knob of the stanchion was damp under the grasp of his right. "What publications?" It was a whisper; he had to say it again. "What publications?"

Dettweiler said, "The pamphlets I found in the strongbox in your room in Menasset."

The catwalk dipped crazily. The strongbox! Oh, my God! The pamphlets and what else? The clippings about Dorothy? He'd thrown them out, thank God! The pamphlets . . . *and the list on Marion!* "Who are you?" he exploded to Dettweiler. "Where the hell do you come off breaking into a person's—"

"Stay back!" Dettweiler warned.

Withdrawing the single step he had advanced, Bud gripped the stanchion again. "Who are you?" he shouted.

"Gordon Gant," Dettweiler said.

Gant! The one on the Blue River radio—KBRI—The Discus Thrower! How the hell did he—

"I knew Ellen," Gant said. "I met her a few days before you killed her."

"I—" He felt the sweat running. "Crazy!" he shouted. "You're crazy! I never killed anybody!"

Gant said, "You killed Dorothy and Ellen and Dwight Powell!"

"And almost killed Marion," Kingship said. "When she saw that list . . ."

She saw the list! Oh, God almighty! "I never killed anybody! Dorrie committed suicide and Ellen and Powell were killed by a burglar!"

"Dorrie?" Gant snapped.

"I— Everybody called her Dorrie! I . . . I never killed anybody! Only a Jap, and that was in the army!"

"Why are your legs shaking?" Gant asked. "Why is sweat dripping down your cheek?"

He swiped at his cheek. He dragged a deep breath into his chest. . . . Slow up, slow up. . . . They can't prove a thing about— "You can't prove a thing," he said. "You're crazy, both of you." His hands wiped against his thighs. "Okay," he said, "I knew Dorrie. So did a dozen other guys. And I've had my eyes on the money all along the way. Where's the law against that? Okay, I'm probably better off poor than having a bastard like you for a father-in-law. Now get out of the way and let me pass."

They didn't move. They stood shoulder to shoulder six feet away, blocking the stem of the T.

"Move," he said.

"Look at the chain behind you," Kingship said.

He stared at Kingship's stonelike face for a moment and then turned slowly. The metal eye of the stanchion had been bent open into a loose C that barely engaged the first of the heavy links of the chain.

"We were up here when Otto was showing you around," Kingship said. "Touch it."

Bud's hand came forward, brushed the chain. It collapsed. The free end clanked to the floor; it slid rattlingly off and swung down, striking noisily against the partition. Fifty feet below, the cement floor seemed to sway. . . . He turned to face them, clutching the stanchion and the edge of the partition, trying not to think of the void behind his heels. "You wouldn't . . . dare," he heard himself saying.

"Don't I have reason enough?" Kingship asked. "You killed my daughters!"

"I didn't! I swear on the soul of my dead father . . ."

Kingship stared at him coldly.

Bud shifted his grip on the stanchion. It was slick with sweat. "You wouldn't do it," he said. "You'd never get away with it."

"Wouldn't I?" Kingship said. "Do you think you're the only one who can get away with it?" He pointed to the stanchion. "The jaws of the wrench were wrapped in cloth; there are no marks on the edge of that stanchion. An accident, a terrible accident; a piece of old iron weakens and bends when a man stumbles against the chain. And how can you prevent it? Yell? No one will hear you. Wave your arms? The men down there have jobs to attend to, and there's the haze and the distance. Attack us? One push and you're finished.

"Of course," Kingship continued after a moment, "I would rather hand you over to the police." He looked at his watch. "So I'll give you three minutes to talk. I want something that will convince a jury."

"Tell us where the gun is that killed Ellen and Dwight Powell," said Gant.

"How did you get Dorothy to write the note?" Kingship asked.

Bud's hands were so tight against the partition and the stanchion that they throbbed. "You're bluffing," he said. "You're trying to scare me into admitting—to something I never did."

Kingship shook his head slowly. He looked at the watch. "Two minutes and thirty seconds," he said.

143

Bud whirled to the right, catching the stanchion with his left hand and shouting to the men below at the converters. "Help!" he cried. "Help! Help!"—bellowing as loud as he could, waving his right arm furiously. "Help!"

The men might as well have been painted figures; their attention was centered on the molten copper.

Bud looked down desperately. Another vat, some two hundred feet away, was now full and smoking, its cables trailing slackly up to the cab above. The vat would be lifted; the cab would bear the vat forward, approaching along the track that passed behind and above him; and the man in the cab—a dozen feet up? four feet out?—would be able to hear! To see!

"One minute, thirty seconds," Kingship said.

Bud's eyes flicked back to the two men. He met their stares for a few seconds, and then risked a glance upward, cautiously, so that they should not guess his plan. (Yes, a plan! Even now, at this moment, a plan!) The boxlike cab was motionless under the track—and then it began to come forward slowly, bearing the vat, growing imperceptibly larger. So slowly! Oh, God, make it come faster!

"We aren't bluffing, Bud," Kingship said. "One minute."

If only they could be stalled until the cab was near enough! "Listen," Bud said frantically, "listen, I want to tell you something—something about Dorrie. She . . ." He groped for something to say—and then stopped, wide-eyed; there had been a flicker of movement in the dimness at the far end of the catwalk. Someone else was up here! Salvation!

"Help!" he cried, his arm semaphoring. "You! Come here! Help!"

The flicker of movement became a figure hurrying along the catwalk, speeding toward them.

Oh, dear God, thank you!

Then he saw that it was a woman.

Marion.

Kingship cried out, "Get out of here! For God's sake, Marion, go back down!"

She seemed not to hear him. She came up behind them, her face flushed and large-eyed.

Bud felt her gaze rake his face. "Marion," he pleaded, "stop them! They're crazy! They're trying to kill me! Stop them! They'll listen to you! I can explain about that list, I can explain everything! I love you! I swear to God I do! You know I wasn't lying about that!"

"*How* do I know?" she asked.

"I swear it!"

"You swore so many things. . . ." Her fingers appeared, curving over the men's shoulders; they seemed to be pushing.

"Marion! You wouldn't! Not when we . . . after we . . . Marion!" he begged futilely.

Suddenly he became aware of an added rumble. The cab! He wheeled, catching the stanchion with both hands. There it was! Not twenty feet away, grinding closer on the overhead track. Through the opening in its front end he could see a bent head in a visored gray cap. "You!" he bellowed. "You in the cab! Help! You!" The gray cap, coming closer, never lifted. *Deaf?* Was the stupid bastard *deaf?*

Kingship said, "The noisiest place in the smelter, up there in those cabs." As he said it, he took a step forward. Gant moved up beside him. Marion followed behind.

"Look," Bud said placatingly, clutching the partition in his left hand again. "Please . . ." He stared at their faces, masklike except for burning eyes, now another step closer.

The catwalk dipped and bucked like a shaken blanket. The baking heat on his right began extending itself across his back. They meant it! They were going to kill him! Moisture trickled all over him.

"All right!" he cried. "All right! Dorrie thought she was doing a Spanish translation! I wrote out the note in Spanish! I asked her to translate . . ." His voice faded and stopped.

What was the matter with them? Their faces . . . the masklike blankness was gone, warped into—into embarrassment and sick contempt, and they were looking down at . . .

He looked down. The front of his pants was dark with a spreading stain that ran down his trouser leg. Oh, God! The Jap . . . the Japanese soldier he had killed—that wretched, trembling, chattering caricature of a man—was that *him?* Was that *himself?*

The answer was in their faces.

"No!" he cried. He clapped his hands over his eyes, but their faces were still there. "No! I'm not like him!" He wheeled away from them. His foot slipped on wetness and kicked out from under him. His hands flew from his face and flailed the air. Falling, he saw a giant disk of molten metal sliding into place below; gaseous, restless, shimmering—

Hardness in his hands? The cables! The weight of his body swung down and around, pulling at his armpits and tearing his hands on protruding steel threads. His eyes stared at the frayed fibers that stabbed like needles into his hands. A chaos of sound; a whistle shrieking, a woman screaming, voices above, voices below . . . He squinted up at his hands—blood was trickling down the insides of his wrists.

The ovenlike heat was smothering—voices shouted to him—he saw his left hand starting to open. He was letting go because he wanted to, that's all, and everything was all right and his knees weren't shaking anymore. His knees weren't shaking anymore because he was in command again.

He hadn't noticed his right hand open but it must have, because he was dropping into the seething red of the vat and someone was screaming like Dorrie going down the shaft and Ellen when the first bullet wasn't enough—someone was screaming this god-awful scream and suddenly it was himself and he couldn't stop! Why was he screaming? Why on earth should he be—

The scream, which had knifed through the sudden stillness of the smelter, ended in a viscous splash. From the other side of the vat a sheet of red leaped up. Arcing, it sheared down to the floor, where it splattered in a million pools and droplets. They hissed softly on the cement and slowly turned from fiery red to copper.

KINGSHIP REMAINED AT the smelter. Gant accompanied Marion back to New York. In the plane they sat silent and immobile with the aisle between them.

After a while Marion took out a handkerchief and pressed it to her eyes. Gant turned to her, his face pale. "We only wanted him to confess," he said defensively. "And he *did* confess. What did he have to turn away like that for?"

The words took a long time to reach her. Almost inaudibly she said, "Don't . . ."

He looked at her downcast face. "You're crying," he told her gently.

She gazed at the handkerchief in her hands, saw the damp places in it. She folded it and turned to the window at her side. Quietly she said, "Not for him."

THEY went to the Kingship apartment. When the butler took Marion's coat—Gant kept his—he said, "Mrs. Corliss is in the living room."

"Oh, God," Marion said.

They went into the living room. In the late afternoon sunlight, Mrs. Corliss was standing by a curio cabinet looking at the underside of a porcelain figurine. She put it down and turned to them. "So soon?" She smiled. "Did you enjoy—" She squinted through the light at Gant. "Oh, I thought you were . . ." She came across the room, peering beyond them into the empty hallway.

Her eyes returned to Marion. Her eyebrows lifted and she smiled.

"Where's Bud?" she asked.

The King of the
Rainy Country

The King of the Rainy Country

A CONDENSATION OF
THE BOOK BY

Nicolas Freeling

ILLUSTRATED BY LEW McCANCE

Sole heir to the profits of Sopexique, a
shadowy conglomerate whose operations
stretched around the world, Jean-Claude
Marschal was one of the richest men in
Europe. And now he had disappeared. There
was no suspicion of foul play; so why did
the higher-ups in Amsterdam insist that
Inspector Van der Valk drop everything and
find the man?

The methodical Dutch policeman soon finds
himself a pawn in a fast-moving, jet-set game
involving Marschal; his stunning, headstrong
wife; a teenage German beauty queen; and
Canisius, the wily executive who really runs
Sopexique. As Van der Valk is drawn in
deeper and deeper, he realizes that the
"game" is really a subtle death scheme, and
that he too may be on the list of victims.

Called "intriguing, sensual, acid in its view
of the good life . . . a perfect blue-white
thirty-carat diamond," *The King of the Rainy
Country* is one of a series of Van der Valk
mysteries by British author Nicolas Freeling.

Van der Valk woke up. His mind was filled with confusion and there was a nasty taste in his mouth, like cheap Spanish brandy. Had he fallen asleep after drinking too much? In an overheated room with no window open? It felt like that. He had had horrible dreams too. And these blankets—he had thrashed about, gotten all wound up; obnoxious tangle. He gave a great kick and was astonished; nothing happened. Was he still dreaming? Surely he was not still asleep. It seemed his foot was. Something was wrong: he told his leg to kick but the leg refused. The whole leg seemed to be asleep, from the hip down. He must still be dreaming, because he remembered things about the dream—something to do with Biarritz. Ha, a holiday in Biarritz—a bit dear for the likes of him.

But no—not Biarritz. Something else beginning with a *B*. Bidassoa, Bidassoa; he felt triumphant at remembering. And his dream had had something to do with war. The Spanish border—the river Bidassoa. One of Napoleon's marshals—Soult, wasn't it?—had crossed the Bidassoa, going north. Marshal Soult was good at moving men but not much good at a fight. He would have to show the marshal how to fight.

Stop dreaming and wake up. Well, move an arm. He moved an arm, and the hand touched something very funny. A sort of coarse grass. And a stone, and it felt stony under his head too. He wasn't in bed at all; he had been drunk and had fallen asleep on the hill under the hot sun. He could smell the sun; baked grass and thyme. Then he suddenly recalled a most important thing. He had been shot.

The hillside spun around and around. Weeping with self-pity, he again reeled off to sleep.

When he woke up once more, there was a face that had not belonged to the dream. A round, youngish, muscular face, very French, with crew-cut hair and rimless glasses. Van der Valk moved his eyes and saw a white rolled-up shirt sleeve and a brown arm. Thin, delicate fingers were squirting the air bubble out of a hypodermic syringe; the needle turned in the air and pointed itself at him.

"Who are you?"

"Be a good boy and forget about Marshal Soult, will you? He's been dead for a hundred and twenty years. I'm going to put you to sleep now."

Van der Valk turned his eye with difficulty past the hand as it dipped out of sight. He was right enough about the hillside. On it stood a small, faded gray Citroën and a Peugeot 404 station wagon with a cross painted on it. *"I am like the king of a rainy country,"* Van der Valk said, *"rich—and impotent; young—and very old."*

"Really? Dear, dear, you've been in the sun much too long. We got you off Marshal Soult, and the first thing you do is quote Baudelaire at us. There, there, all gone, all these people. Sleepy-by now."

The next time he remembered waking it was better. Here was Arlette, his wife, her hair wild and matted, unusually blond and held back with a white bandeau, so that it almost looked as though they had been on holiday in Biarritz after all. He made a big effort to remember. Arlette . . . Napoleon's marshals.

"My poor boy," she said to him in French. He thought there

might have been a blank after that, for when he looked again there was the youngish man with the crew cut alongside Arlette, grinning down at him. Things began to slip into place; he remembered he was supposed to be a detective, and felt better.

"I've seen you before."

"That's right. Out on the hill—remember?"

"But who the hell are you?"

"I'm Dr. Capdouze. At your service. I will explain. Very briefly. You got shot. A man heard the shot and was curious about it, because there isn't much around here one shoots with a big rifle. He found you, which was just as well. He gave you some brandy, which bloody near killed you, and ran to get me. I'm the village doctor of Saint-Jean. We brought you away and you're not going to die this time. You're in Biarritz, in a nice clinic, not the clink, though there are some policemen who want to talk to you. In case you can't recall, you are Inspector Van der Valk of the Amsterdam police and this is your wife, Arlette.

"I have no idea what you were doing on the hill, but you are now surrounded by modern postoperative care, social security, nuns, me, Professor Gachassin, who is your surgeon, and your wife, who is a remarkably nice woman even if she does come from Provence. Okay? Nothing more to worry about; you're going to go on catching up with your sleep."

Van der Valk slept.

ARLETTE did not talk about the rifle shot, but Van der Valk stitched the information together. He had been shot somewhere near the right hip, with a high-speed Mauser cartridge—10.75 millimeter. The bullet had perforated the intestine, just missed the big artery, touched his spine, broken his pelvis, and popped out somewhere in his buttock, leaving a great deal of havoc. He would stay paralyzed quite a while, but they didn't think permanently. Dr. Capdouze was red-hot; doctors just didn't come any better—all the local people agreed on that. This Professor Gachassin was a big authority from Toulouse, and he had sworn that within a year Van der Valk would be walking again.

"We'll get him up on skis," they had said. Arlette thought the idea would amuse him and give him something to fight for.

He didn't much like the idea, though he did not tell her that. He had remembered the whole story by now. Skis came into it. Too much.

As soon as he felt lucid he himself had asked for the police. They turned out to be a man in a gray suit with a scrap of red cord in the lapel, who had short gray hair and was about fifty, brown and sun-dried as a Smyrna fig.

"My name is Lira. I'm the police commissioner. How are you?"

"I'm fine; though it seems there's a hole in my hip you could drive a truck through."

"I understand that you went after a maniac with a rifle for me," said Mr. Lira, "and I'm very grateful, because it might otherwise have been me lying there. Strasbourg, though, can't understand why the two of you came racing down here."

"There's a man called Canisius, a Dutch businessman. He was here. He went into Spain to look at houses he owns. He was coming back a little later. The idea was to pop him. Going into the hills was a suicide idea, I thought. That's why I followed. Was I right?"

Lira nodded. "We knew nothing, of course. Only that there was someone up on that hill with a rifle, who could use it too. We strung boys out with guns; we got a psychiatrist from Hendaye, and a loudspeaker. Useless. We went up when we heard the second shot. It was a toe job. No head left at that range. I have to make a report for the public prosecutor. I can't make sense of the story I got from Strasbourg; you know the story, it seems. If you can just tell me what you know."

"I'll tell you," said Van der Valk. "But not right now. I'm bloody tired. Can you come tomorrow?"

"Yes." Mr. Lira stood looking down at him. "Boy, did you have a close call. When you're better we'll drink to that."

Van der Valk spent twenty-four hours between waking and sleeping, thinking. This was the end of the story that had started: "Once upon a time, in a rainy country, there was a king. . . ."

The end had not happened in a rainy country but on a bone-dry Spanish hillside, a thousand feet from where Van der Valk had left a lot of blood, some splintered bone, a few fragments of gut, and a 10.75 Mauser rifle bullet. Only a few more hundred yards away was the spot where the last of the marshals, lying with a rifle in a patch of scrub, had waited for a businessman called Canisius to stop his car near the border.

It had been a cold day in early March. Van der Valk was in his office in Amsterdam, minding his own business, when Mr. Canisius was announced on the phone from the concierge's office downstairs.

"Wants to talk to someone in authority, he says."

"What's he look like?"

"Sort of a rich guy. His coat's got a fur collar."

"Send him up to me," said Van der Valk.

"Are you the duty inspector?" the man asked upon reaching the office.

"I am. Van der Valk is my name; would you like to sit down?"

Mr. Canisius would like to sit down; he seemed to be unathletic and there had been two flights of stairs. He did look rich. The fur collar on the overcoat was black and sleek; his gray worsted trousers were dark but expensive; his shoes were handmade. His gray trilby hat was lined with white silk and looked as though it had been bought ten minutes ago.

The face was big and bald, with a Roman nose and very black eyebrows, wide pale lips with a droop at the corners, drooping flesh under alert little dark eyes that did not droop. Mr. Canisius took his gloves off slowly to put in his hat, and at least three-quarters of a carat of diamond winked from a pale bun of a hand.

"I must ask you to listen to a slightly unusual tale," Mr. Canisius said. "I will develop the background briefly. You will have heard of the firm colloquially called Sopexique. It is a trading company with considerable interests in South and North America, and fewer, I am happy to say, in the Africa where it had its beginnings. The founder of this firm was called Marschal. The name is still represented by Sylvestre Marschal, who inherited and expanded a very great fortune. In fact, this is one of the largest fortunes in private hands anywhere. I say private, for it is distinct from the holdings of the company, which are themselves very considerable." A short pause to let all this sink in.

"Mr. Marschal is now over eighty years of age, but he visits the Paris office daily. Some few years ago he settled, for reasons I need not go into, a very large proportion of his wealth upon his only son, a man at present forty-two years old. Jean-Claude Marschal lives in Amsterdam, where the Sopex office is administered by me. He is head of public relations for the other European offices."

"That sounds quite impressive," said Van der Valk. "Is it?"

"I am pleased you asked; the question shows you to have some judgment. No, Inspector, it is not. Sopex is largely an investment trust, and where trade is still carried on, it is principally in raw materials. Our public relations are virtually nonexistent. Everybody has heard of us and nobody knows quite what it is we do, which is just the state of affairs we like. However, I do not wish to give you a notion that Mr. Marschal is an incompetent, tolerated because of his name. His work is largely meeting, entertaining and communicating with the men all over the world with whom the company does business. He draws an excellent salary. He also commands the very large fortune I have mentioned, income from which flows into balances held in banks throughout Europe, in many different names."

"And he's in trouble, is he?" It sounded banal. The spoiled child becomes the spoiled man. What had he done, knocked a pedestrian over while driving drunkenly?

"We do not know whether he is in any trouble. He has chosen to disappear. If there is trouble, naturally we wish to prevent it. We do not wish his father, an elderly gentleman in frail health, to know of it. We wish to safeguard a number of things. Health, property, good name."

"Has he any reason or motive to act purposely in a prejudicial way?" Van der Valk was making notes now.

"None."

"You sketch a man of no great talents, restricted to inconsequential activities in a company he owns, in a manner of speaking. He might feel slighted?"

"You have not quite the right picture." Mr. Canisius was unruffled. "I understand that such a conclusion might be drawn, but to say that Mr. Marschal has no great talents is inexact. He has unquestioned ability. Numerous positions of real responsibility have been open to him at all times and repeatedly offered. He has always rejected them. He has been content with the work he chose. I have only one criticism of him—that he preferred to use his charm rather than his mind."

"What are his interests? What engages his mind?"

"That is a puzzling question. I have asked it myself. When young, the usual amusements of a sportive nature. He was an excellent horseman, skier, aviator, racing-car driver. He played polo, sailed yachts—all the conventional pursuits. He was very gifted at all of them, I am told. I am also told that he lacked perseverance, and always loosened the rein at the moment he should have tightened. He did not sufficiently want to win. 'It is too easy for me!' he used to exclaim."

"He's married?"

"Yes. I will forestall you and state that it is not a stormy marriage and that there have been no upheavals or scandals."

"Does he chase women?"

"In a lackluster way."

"It comes down to this: he has vanished, without fuss or furor, quite simply, with no indication where or why."

"That is it exactly."

"And you simply want him found."

"Yes. It is puzzling, you understand. He has shown no evidence of emotional disturbance, is not given to extravagance or a parade of wealth, and is in perfect health."

"There is one thing I do not see, Mr. Canisius, and that is, why you come to me. You confirm that he has done nothing illegal. There is no suggestion of fraud or false pretense. He is just missing, and since there is a fortune involved, that is disturbing. But isn't this a job for a private detective?"

Mr. Canisius smiled then, very slightly, for the first time. He got up and straightened his coat. He picked up his hat and examined it for signs of contamination. Finding none, he put it on his head. He drew on a glove.

"I do not think I need answer that question, Mr. Van der Valk. I think, though, that you may receive an answer to it." He bowed slightly with perfect politeness, opened the door, and was gone.

Van der Valk shrugged. He scratched his jaw, then behind his ear, reading over the notes he had made. There were any number of possibilities. The man could have had a row with his wife. He could have done something to make himself the victim of a blackmail attempt. He could have just felt like getting away from it all for a while and not telling anyone. There were a million tensions or disturbances that might exist in the life of a very rich man to explain his taking off. None of them were of much interest to Van der Valk: his job was the detection and prevention of crime in the city of Amsterdam.

He shut the notebook and picked up a file he had been interrupted in reading. Suddenly the phone rang.

"Van der Valk."

"Chief commissioner here." It was an elderly, fussy tone, familiar to him. This was the head of the Amsterdam police, and his commander.

"Yes, sir."

"You have had a visit from a certain Mr. Canisius."

"Yes, sir. Missing person."

"You will act upon this request, Van der Valk. Yourself, personally, immediately. You are detached from your normal duties; your superiors will be notified. You will take steps to find this missing person.

"Ha-hm," the voice went on. "You are not permitted to use official transport or official channels. Your expenses will be allowed, within reason. You will work quietly, discreetly. Courtesy, Van der Valk, caution, tact—quiet. Is that clear?"

"Perfectly clear, sir."

"You may be called on to cross the frontier. You can begin at once. The subinspector will take over for you."

"Understood, sir."

The voice had a rasping, nagging note. "Mr. Canisius expects you at his office at two this afternoon."

"Very well, sir." The phone clanked crossly.

Mr. Canisius, or Sopexique, whichever way you cared to read it, possessed one hell of a lot of drag. They didn't need publicity; oh, dear, no. They picked up the telephone and asked for the top man. The press hadn't got this one.

He decided that the courtesy campaign had better begin with going home, having the best lunch he could lay his hands on, putting on a clean shirt, asking his wife to pack a weekend case, and immediately having a quick superdeluxe haircut. He would then put on his new suit, very dark brown, from Olde England— he didn't know whom he might be meeting.

THE tourist is told that what makes the city of Amsterdam notable is, first, twice as many waterways and bridges as Venice, and, second, the very fine seventeenth-century architecture. But he is inclined to be skeptical. For the city fathers have allowed the automobile and petty commerce full liberty to destroy practically all the beauty.

There had been a great deal of beauty. The moneygrubbing materialists of Amsterdam were among the world's foremost art patrons. They loved beauty and paid money for it. If artists died in the workhouse, or broke, like Hals, or sold pictures to pay the baker, like Vermeer, it was not altogether the fault of the money-grubbers, for these vulgar bankers and burgomasters built themselves superb houses and filled them with beauty.

The houses can still be seen, lying in a tight neat belt of four concentric semicircles around the heart of Amsterdam. The Singel, the Herengracht, the Keizersgracht, the Prinsengracht. But the beautiful houses are degraded and squalid, and nothing is left but the façades. In each house there are four or five cut-rate shops and businesses, and as many people crammed into the garrets, politely called flats. Sometimes a very important business has spread over a whole house, and embellished it with a reception hall in massive marble and mahogany and signs with curly bronze letters. But if there are two or three of these lovely houses in private ownership still, it is a little miracle.

Van der Valk arrived at the offices of Sopexique, which had, of course, a house to itself. There was a very small, very highly polished brass plate, and immediately inside the door, allowing room for one thin person to put his mouth somewhere near the concierge's forbidding peephole, there was another door, armorplated and massive, that would yield to nothing but a small button under the concierge's foot. Van der Valk showed his card, murmured, and waited humbly while checking went on over the telephone.

Mr. Canisius worked in an office like that found in many very rich businesses. It was clean, tidy and quiet, and had at least the merit of no pretensions at all.

"Sit down. I will tell you outright that I do not wish you to question the staff here. I have made very careful inquiries. No eccentricity, no irregularity whatever has been found."

"I will tell you something, equally outright, with your permission," said Van der Valk pleasantly and politely. "I will question whom I please, discreetly, according to my instructions, or I will go quietly and you can find someone else."

Mr. Canisius smiled very faintly. "I make no restriction outside this building. I will give you the addresses of Mrs. Marschal, a doctor, a lawyer, and a man named Libuda, the last person known to have spoken to Mr. Marschal. You must take my word for it that nobody in this office can help you."

"I'll take your word with pleasure right here and now. What I learn elsewhere may change my mind."

"In that case I will give you my home address. Telephone if you wish, come to see me if necessary—but do not, please, call or telephone here."

"Who had most to do with him here?"

"His personal secretary. Very well, she is a discreet person; I will allow the exception. Outside the office, please."

He picked up the telephone. "Twenty-three . . . Miss Kramer? I wish you to meet someone this evening for a short talk. Five thirty? Café Polen. . . . That suit you?"—to Van der Valk. Nod. "Take that as settled, Miss Kramer. Thank you."

Van der Valk stood up, took the piece-of paper handed to him with neat writing upon it, tucked it in his breast pocket, bowed, and opened the door.

"Telephone me from time to time, Mr. Van der Valk," came the polite murmur. "Shall we say at least once a week. Oftener, if you have anything of importance."

Van der Valk nodded and closed the door.

Mr. Canisius lived well outside the town, but all the other addresses, Van der Valk was pleased to see, were within a couple of hundred yards of where he stood.

At the lawyer's, he was let in right away, treated with freezing distaste, and told nothing whatever.

The doctor was a lot more difficult of access, but a great deal more communicative. Not that it helped.

"I gave him a routine checkup once a year, and apart from that he consulted me occasionally for something banal like laryngitis. Constitution of an athlete, lived a regular and pretty sober life, no weaknesses whatever. Sorry I can't help you. No physiological disability at all; heart, lungs and liver of a man of twenty. Psychological troubles . . ." Shrug.

"When was it you last saw him?"

The doctor flipped back through a file. "Last October, a little virus infection. August, renewal of vaccinations. February, a strep throat. Three calls in thirteen months."

"Many thanks."

"Many regrets."

Mrs. Marschal was only just across the road in the Keizersgracht. There are plenty of expensive flats there, but the Marschals had an entire house. He walked up steep stone steps, a bit awestruck in spite of himself, and found a bell with some difficulty, concealed in intricate but pure baroque wrought-iron work.

Nothing happened. He had nearly given up, and had turned his back to the door, when a soft voice surprised him.

"Monsieur wishes?"

Astonishment; there stood a majordomo, in full classic costume, striped yellow waistcoat and all.

"I should very much like to see madame if she is at home. Here is my card."

"I am sorry to disappoint you, sir, but madame cannot receive you unless she is expecting you."

The answer was, of course, to say "Police," but he had been told to be tactful. "I hope," he said, "that madame agrees when she looks at the card." On the back he had written "Canisius."

A smile, through the mask of courteous gravity. "I will certainly ask. Excuse my hesitation; my instructions have few exceptions. If monsieur will come in . . ."

Van der Valk was in a hall, tall and narrow, with a pinkish marble floor and painted walls, apple green and pale gold. Panels of white stuccowork; bunches of grapes and vine leaves in low relief. At the back of the hall was a door, more of that pure wrought iron repeating the vine pattern. Through this door vanished the butler. The house was absolutely noiseless, and noiseless too was the butler's return.

"Madame will be happy to receive you, sir. This way, please." He went through the doorway, and paused on the bottom step of a staircase. "Will monsieur wait a moment longer?"

Beyond the staircase was a small formal orangery. To his right, facing the foot of the stairs, was an alcove in which stood a small marble nude. He knew very little of such things: could it be a Rodin? There was a bronze boy at the foot of the stairs, that was supposed to be looked at from the orangery. Or one could climb the steps and look from above. Van der Valk was ten steps high, still openmouthed, wondering if the bronze could really possibly be a Donatello, and jumped when a voice spoke just behind him.

"You are quite right; they are there to be looked at, in just that way."

He turned, a scrap confused. A woman in a silk housecoat—narrow vertical stripes in two tones of green—was standing on the steps.

"Sorry, I was admiring them."

She had his card in her hand. She gave it back to him, with a careful slow look of appraisal, and they descended. "That does not matter in the least. Perhaps we will go in here, shall we?" She opened a door beyond the stairs and waited for him. "Please sit down, Mr. Van der Valk, and make yourself comfortable. Would you like some port?"

"Not just by myself."

She gave him a slight smile. "Oh, no. I like port." She did not ring for a footman, but went to pour it herself.

It was a small formal sitting room looking out on the orangery; a sort of morning room. Walnut furniture, grave, simple and pure, that was certainly English and he was fairly sure must be eighteenth century.

"Your good health," said Mrs. Marschal, sitting down.

He took a sip of port and thought furiously, Now why did that half-wit run away from this?

Perhaps it might be the woman; he studied her. Clear skin, clear classic features, a bit cold for some tastes. Dark hazel eyes, a lot of dark hair brushed into a frame around her face. Figure looked quite full; one couldn't tell in a housecoat. Manner polite, even warm. Lot of breeding. Sat very upright; convent trained.

"You liked the statues," she said reflectively. "How do you like this room?"

"Very much. English? Eighteenth century?"

"Hepplewhite. That piece there is William and Mary."

He drank his port, feeling slightly tipsy already.

"We are going to get along, I do believe," she said. "Did you know that the naked girl is by Rodin?"

"I didn't, but I thought it might be."

"We are going to get along. . . . You're plainly enjoying that; have some more. Get it yourself."

Pouring, he had a peep at the year. Nineteen forty-five!

"Mr. Van der Valk, what do you know about your errand in this house?"

"That your husband is missing. That I have been asked to find him. Beyond that, absolutely nothing."

"Was that really all Mr. Canisius had to say?"

"He gave me a superficial sketch of a life and a character."

She pushed her lower lip out a scrap. "He hasn't a high opinion of either, and he isn't necessarily right. He is only a business-man, after all."

"You want your husband back?"

"That is a fairly complex question. Since he has gone deliber-ately, I am not sure."

"Perhaps you could tell me more."

"I had decided that it would be a waste of time to tell any-body anything. Perhaps I am mistaken."

He was wide awake now, sharpened by the port, Rodin, and William and Mary. She didn't want him to look for her husband. She hadn't wanted to call the police and it hadn't been her idea. She plainly didn't like Canisius. Very likely that gentleman didn't care much for her. So why had Canisius called the police?

Van der Valk had a lot of understanding to do. A policeman, by the law of averages, gets his experience from ordinary people with ordinary jobs. But all this experience counts for nothing when you meet the very rich.

"I want to convey to you, simply, that this is not simple," she said slowly. "It is of very little use just asking me if I know where he went."

"Do you know where he went?"

The little half-secret smile again. "You want to tell me that you'll make up your own mind. It is your job, and you don't want a silly woman making things more difficult. Very well. I'll tell you whatever you ask, with nothing hidden, if you want it that way. Read into everything just what you please—conclude what you wish."

"Tell me about you."

"I live alone in this house. I have two children, both girls, who are away at school in Belgium. There are no more Marschals.

"I am Belgian. My name was De Meeus; my father was a baron. I used to be a ski champion. Champion means you are among the ten best. I met my husband at a time when he was also among the ten best. There was a lot of opposition from my family—all that money, and from pretty dubious sources. The old Marschal, Jean-Claude's grandfather, was a very nasty person, hand in glove, I imagine, with everything shady. They certainly saw me as something to increase their respectability. The old man, my father-in-law, is a very tough nut. It is very much his business. Canisius is just an accountant, an organization man. A nobody.

"The business, though, bores my husband stiff. Money to him is a tool like a hammer, to drive in nails with. It doesn't drive him. I don't pretend to understand him, you know. Not completely. But I can tell you that his whole life has been a ferocious pursuit of something that would satisfy. He is possessed by passionate enthusiasms every now and then. They absorb his whole life for three months, and then they are dropped. Crazes for sports, for arts, for exploring mountains or whatever. Never has it satisfied his thirst. How often I have sat with him on a terrace somewhere, watching a lot of people enjoy themselves, and heard him mutter, 'How do they do it, what is it they see, they feel?'— ready to scream with envy. He just utterly lacks the gift of being happy."

"Mr. Canisius told me he had sometimes pursued women 'in a lackluster way.' "

"I hadn't credited the 'grocer' with that much observation." She thought for a while, as though struggling with herself. "Come, I want to show you that I haven't anything to conceal and that I am not ashamed of being humiliated."

She was walking up the stairs; there was no sign of a servant— or were they trained to keep out of the way?

"How many servants have you?"

"Four, inside the house. The majordomo; the cook and my maid, who are sisters; and a housemaid."

"Any living in this house?"

"No. They all live in a house we bought for them and had made into flats. There is also a gardener, but he never comes inside. This is my bedroom." It was quite plain and unremarkable. She led him on without comment.

"This is my bathroom," she said colorlessly. Ah, they'd saved it up for in here.

It was twice the size of the bedroom. One long wall was all wardrobe, with sliding doors. The floor was a yellowish creamy marble with streaks of dark red in it.

The bath was a small sunken swimming pool, nine feet by fifteen. It was white marble, this time. There were steps at one side. At each end were fountains. One was rough and creviced and seemed very old. It was a moss garden, a fern garden, and Lord only knew what those plants down there were, probably South American orchids.

The other fountain was dull green bronze, a little slim naked figure, a Psyche. Mrs. Marschal must have turned a tap somewhere; two plumes of wavering water fanned out from the Psyche's upstretched hands; it was as though she strewed blessings, or light, or warmth—he didn't know.

Down the other side of the room ran a slight airy colonnade. There were more statues. The ceiling was marble too, a sort of cracked uneven paving—upside down! The whole thing, he was forced to admit, was beautiful.

"*Still they gazed, and still the wonder grew,*" he muttered.

"It kept him happy for a remarkable length of time," she answered. "You don't ask what it cost?" she added maliciously.

"If it didn't matter to him, it doesn't to me."

"For that you shall have a reward."

Jean-Claude's bedroom was on the far side. It told nothing at all; like his wife's, it was modern, tidy and without extravagance. There were plenty of things like clothes, hairbrushes and cuff links, simple and expensive, and he had left them all behind without a glance.

"Did he spend much time at home?"

"Yes. There might come a time when he was out every evening for a fortnight, and there came other fortnights when he never put a foot outside the door. He liked it here, and he liked me here. Peculiar as it may seem, he was very attached to his wife. She was, I say without any pride, the only woman who had any meaning for him. She failed, somewhere."

"Was there anything in his behavior at all that struck you, in the days—weeks, if you like—before he went?"

"No. He just went, silently. No scene, no edginess, no pointer at all. He was as he always is, and one morning he was not there. He took nothing."

"One stupid, obvious, rude question that I have to ask. Were you ever unfaithful to him?"

"No. I am, oddly, quite Spanish about such things."

"Thank you very much indeed."

"If you give your name on the telephone, this house will be open to you at any time."

"Again, thanks. May I ask your name?"

"Anne-Marie."

PROFESSIONAL skill at keeping appointments brought him to the Café Polen at precisely five thirty. Miss Kramer was not hard to recognize: a stocky woman of fifty, with graying fair hair and a tweed suit, standing just inside the doorway, clutching a huge secretarial handbag and a shopping bag containing the raw materials of the coming evening's supper.

"What will you have?" he asked.

"Might I have whiskey?" Just what he liked, a robust woman with no nonsense.

"Two whiskeys, please. . . . Well, you know what I'm after."

"I have thought and thought, but I can't recall anything the least unusual. He was always quiet and polite, not at all a difficult person to work for, once you knew his little ways."

"Do you remember at all what he talked about the last day? A person, a thing, a book, a play?"

"Nothing specific that I can recall. It was one of those very gray lowering afternoons, and I had to turn more lights on, and he said something about how dismal the town looked."

"What did you say?"

"Well, I come from Brabant, you see, and I said something about there, at least, one had the carnival at this time of year to cheer people up and give them some gaiety. I miss that here."

"What did he say to that?"

"Oh, just vaguely that yes, a carnival would enliven things."

"Do you know his wife at all?"

"Never even seen her. He never mentioned anything private. He wasn't the type to weep on his secretary's shoulder. I liked him; I miss him a lot."

"Who is doing his work?"

"I am, most of it. Not the dining and the wining."

"I won't hold you up. What have you got for supper?"

She laughed. "Scrambled eggs with frozen shrimps; pretty dull, I'm afraid."

"Good appetite."

HE STILL had to ring the Amstel Hotel. Mr. Libuda was back and could see him right away if he cared to come. Mr. Libuda was in the bar, and bought the whiskey.

"Yes, it was about this time of day—let's see, it was a week ago. We had dinner here; I had to go to Cologne the next day. Glad to be back, I can tell you. Carnival!"

Of course. Today was the last Monday before Lent. *Rosenmontag*—Rose Monday—in the Rhineland; high jinks in Cologne.

"Did you mention it while you were with him?"

"He reminded me, now that you mention it. I'd forgotten about it. I was groaning and he said he liked carnivals and I said rather he than me. Good grief, I left Rio to get away from all that Mardi Gras lark."

There was no more to be heard from Mr. Libuda, and it probably didn't mean anything at all. Still, it was a clue of sorts. It was the only one Van der Valk had.

At home there was ham omelet with spinach for supper, and

the television showed snips from the carnival gallivanting in various corners of Europe, including Cologne, Mainz and Munich. The Germans were all roaring about happily in cowboy suits, and the beer was going down *glug-glug-glug*.

He went to the office next morning and spent the day on the telephone, checking airline and ship bookings, car-rental firms, hotel registers.

"I hear you've got a nice soft job out of the private bin," said Chief Inspector Kan cattily, meeting him in the corridor. Van der Valk cursed halfheartedly.

Toward evening he got an idea. Jean-Claude Marschal had served during the war with a British army intelligence unit. Was there any corner of Europe where he had been parachuted or infiltrated or rowed ashore in a little rubber dinghy? Anything that might have given him a nostalgia for a time that had been less boring? Van der Valk phoned the War Office in London. They promised to send him a night letter.

Anne-Marie had promised him photographs, and on his way home that evening he picked them up. None was very recent, but the bony face with the sharp nose was not one that would change a great deal.

There was more jollification on TV that evening—climax of carnival, under a cold, dry, bitter, dusty northeast wind. Holland watched the goings-on with a confusion of disapproval and envy.

"Turn the rubbish off, it gets on my nerves," said Arlette. Van der Valk studied the map of Europe. Mr. Marschal had a French passport. If he were in Holland, he would surely have shown up by now.

If one went places to get away, to withdraw, to be alone, did one go to a place that held a special kind of memory? Why had Mr. Canisius been so insistent on bringing the police into it? Could there be any reason at all for suspecting a crime? Anne-Marie . . . complex woman.

Ash Wednesday. Arlette went to church to have her forehead marked and to be reminded that she was dust. He went to the office, with a gloomy feeling that a policeman was reminded daily that he was dust. But there was a reply for him from London.

Major Marschal had not done anything fancy. He had worked after the landings as a liaison officer between the British and General de Lattre. He had been at Colmar, Stuttgart, Ulm. Later, under the occupation, he had been de Lattre's contact man with the British commander in Cologne. Cologne again; strange, that. A superstitious person sometimes, especially when he had no facts to go on, Van der Valk was fascinated by the way the name kept cropping up. He had once been there himself, to arrest a gentleman working a check fraud. Van der Valk had made a friend too, of Heinz Stössel, the German policeman who had tidied up the case for him.

"Police Presidium, Cologne. . . . Hello? Any chance of finding Stössel in his office? . . . May not be gone yet? Let's try him. Put me through, please. . . . Hello? Heinz? How's your trade in missing persons?"

"Why d'you ask that? I have a very bad one, but it's not on your Teletype yet. You clairvoyant or something?" The voice sharpened suddenly. "You haven't found a girl, have you?"

"No. I've lost a man."

"You've come to the wrong address, son. We've lost a girl—and the press got it before we did."

"Yes, that's the worst sort."

"There's worse still—we've just found her clothes in some woods. You can see the headline: 'Naked Beauty Disappears!'"

"Any starting point?"

"Precious little. A barman saw her the night of Rose Monday with what is described as a handsome middle-aged man. Now you tell me your troubles. I haven't seen any signal."

"It isn't on the Teletype. It's one of those confidential jobs. The man's a millionaire."

A groan of disgust. "And I suppose he's middle-aged and handsome, is he?"

"I suppose he could be called that—by a barman. I'm not seriously suggesting it; I've got no clue at all. But the name of Cologne has come up three or four times in an oddly persistent way. The thing is that just before he ducked, my man was talking vaguely about the carnival."

"You got photos?" Stössel asked.

"In my pocket."

"Not much, though, is it? Handsome middle-aged man. You might as well say he had a glass of beer and a cowboy costume."

"I'm going to catch a plane."

"Are you serious?"

"My expenses are being paid."

He phoned the airport. There was a plane at noon. He went home to pick up his bag, already regretting the impulse a little.

He didn't believe Mr. Marschal was dead. He didn't believe a crime had been committed. Yet because he heard a nonsensical tale about a naked girl and a handsome middle-aged man, he went racing off to Cologne.

IN COLOGNE there was a message from Heinz. He had gone home to get some sleep. He would meet Van der Valk this evening at six on the Rhine Terrace. In the meantime, here was a transcript of the meager facts available.

The girl was seventeen. Her name was Dagmar Schwiewelbein, the kind of name a German sees nothing comic in. She was described as extremely pretty. Her parents were very quiet, simple, honest folk. The father was a clerk in an insurance office. There was an elder brother in the army; the girl had lived at home with her parents. They were utterly distraught, of course. They had brought their daughter up simply, innocently. She had not been an outstanding schoolgirl. Not bright enough to go on to a higher school. She had taken a job in a swanky shop as salesgirl, selling sports clothes. She had never been away from home till last year, when she had gone with two other girls on a wintersport holiday. Her hobby was gymnastics; she was mad about skiing. She had never had a regular boy friend, though she had been to the cinema with various young hopefuls. A good, quiet, innocent girl.

The parents had not liked her having a job. She had become

hard and flashy, "like all the other girls nowadays," and sometimes willful and cheeky with her mother.

Then last month a big event had come into her life. She had been chosen for the carnival as a *Tanzmariechen*.

This is a German phenomenon. The carnival prince has a troop of attendants, a sort of a bodyguard that goes about with him. These are the *Tanzmariechen,* twenty or so of the prettiest and longest-legged girls in the town. They wear a very fetching musical-comedy military costume: a sort of a hussar tunic, tights, high boots and a cossack-style fur hat. It is very becoming on a tall, slim girl.

The *Tanzmariechen* ride in the parade with the carnival prince on Rose Monday, and of course they appear at the great ball and banquet. This one hadn't. She had just disappeared. She had been seen that night having a drink with the so-called handsome man in a café. Nobody had ever seen her again. The costume—recognized by the sobbing mother—had been found in a neat pile in some woods a few miles outside the town. There was no sign of trampling or a struggle or anything else. Just a little pile of clothes. A presumably naked *Tanzmariechen* had disappeared into the cold March wind.

Van der Valk trudged through Cologne and got to the Rhine Terrace shortly before six. Ash Wednesday—a carnival hangover. The streets seemed empty, the people slow and depressed. Scarcely anyone was in the big glassed-in terrace. There was a view of a yellowish, clouded-over Rhine, the heavy current even dirtier and more sullen than usual.

Van der Valk sat in solitary state and waited for Inspector Stössel.

"Ha. Beer?"

"No beer. I've only just got up. Coffee." Everybody was drinking coffee in Cologne on Ash Wednesday.

"Black coffee for two," Van der Valk told the waitress, who was standing, bored, jingling the change in her apron pocket.

Heinz Stössel was like a large unsmoked ham, pale, solid, salted. Fat but firm and healthy. Without his reading glasses he looked dumb, and had deceived many people. When he put the glasses on, which he did to drink coffee, he looked like a wicked and intelligent Roman senator. He stirred his coffee and looked at the Rhine with distaste. "She's not in there, anyway. Nor in the woods. How serious are you about this?"

"She was seen with the man."

"Yes. Right here. Drinking *Sekt*. She was in her costume. The barman looked, because she's pretty, you see. The man is much vaguer—thin, ordinary clothes, described as elegant."

"Look," said Van der Valk. "I have a man. Exceedingly rich. Eccentric. A nervous type. He had gone, just gone like that. Supposing he was here. The vanishing of my man and the vanishing of your girl might be connected. Too much of a coincidence?"

Stössel sipped his coffee. "Yes, but what have we got to show any connection? Where are your photos? That barman is the one right there—that's why I brought you to this dump."

Van der Valk spread the photographs on the counter. The barman looked. "Well . . . I suppose it could have been. I didn't really look that close at him. Like him, all right. I couldn't honestly say for sure, though."

"What good is that?" asked Stössel heavily, back at the table.

"None at all. Just a crazy notion. There's something off-key all the same about the way this girl vanishes."

"You mean she's not quite the type. Neither is she the type to go running off with your millionaire."

"No."

"Come on," Heinz said, drinking some cold coffee. "Back to the shop."

"Assuming you're right"—sitting in an office a lot bigger, a chair more leather-padded, with a lot more ingenious machinery on the desk than in Van der Valk's office in Amsterdam, but with the same smell—"let's see if we can work out how. Planes are out. Taxis are out. Car rental is out. All too easy to trace. A train—maybe."

"Perhaps he bought a car."

"We'll try it," said Stössel. "What might he have had—traveler's checks, dollars—any idea?"

"A German check on a German bank is the likeliest, I think. How many cars, though, are bought on the spot for cash down and driven away?"

"All right. We'll make a composite photo and show it around. But I'm suppressing you in my report in any case; you've no official standing."

VAN der Valk could not take part in the hawking of a photo around the expensive showrooms where a man looking like Jean-Claude Marschal might have bought a car. So he went to see the parents of the *Tanzmariechen*. The mother was not much use—poor woman, she was a blur, like a watercolor left out in the rain. The father was more help. He was, thought Van der Valk, a man of surprising innocence. A kind man, a man of goodness, simplicity, a man who thought evil of nobody. The girl, thought Van der Valk, might have these characteristics too. Could that have struck Jean-Claude Marschal?

Later he went back to Stössel's office. Nobody had recognized the photo except one man, who thought it might have been someone he had sold a car to on Friday, just before carnival started. A silver Porsche Carrera 1900. A Mr. Alfred Kellermann.

Mr. Kellermann had spoken good German, but not like a Rhinelander. More like a southern German or an Austrian. The check was on a big bank. No information was forthcoming about the account without a court order.

Van der Valk was discouraged. "They're over the border long ago," he said. "Holed up in a winter-sport village somewhere. He was a good skier. She worked in a sports shop and liked skiing too."

"It's on the list," said Heinz briefly. His theory was that you can find anything and anyone with a routine, if that routine is only well enough coordinated. So he had made a list of everything he could imagine Mr. Marschal doing, had virtually every policeman in Germany working on it, and had every incoming report put on his Teletype. Every hour, with his red pencil, he went line by line through the reams of tape.

"I think there might be something here, though it's inconclusive. A large quantity of ski equipment and clothes, including some for a woman, was bought in Munich. The man does not follow our description particularly, but was tall, thin and assured. The only thing that really struck them was that at the end he signed a very large check without even checking the number of items on the bill. They said that another thing that struck them was being told to deliver everything to the luggage office at the station. The check was on a local bank. Munich looked for any more checks in the same name. They found one at a travel agency—two first-class tickets to Innsbruck."

"What's the name on the checks?"

"Funny name. Nay."

"Nay?" said Van der Valk. "N-a-y?"

"That's what it says on the tape. Nay."

"Call them up, Heinz. Call them up, tell them to check the spelling."

Slightly astonished, Stössel picked his phone up. "Munich one six seven, miss, please. . . . Hello? Hello? Schneegans? . . . Stössel here in Cologne. Those checks in the ski shop and travel agency. Did the operator get the name right? . . . Nay, yes. Check it, will you? . . . Yes? Okay, thanks."

He put the phone down. "How did you know? Easy slip to make; can't blame them really. An *e* instead of an *a*. Ney. I don't see it."

"Ney," said Van der Valk, grinning, "is the name—it's absurdly childish—of one of Napoleon's marshals. Born German, in the Saar. Kellermann was a marshal too. I've kept thinking and thinking what it was that was memorable about it."

"You mean this is him?"

"It can't be anyone else."

"Gone to Innsbruck by train. Looks like a risk, but it was safe really. Who the hell checks passports on the main line from Munich to Innsbruck? But what can have happened to the car?"

"I had every car checked—bought, rented, borrowed or stolen."

"You don't know a car's stolen, though, till someone reports it stolen."

"Yes, but—"

"What better way would there be of getting rid of a car you think might be recognized? Leave it on the street unlocked in a town that size; it'll be gone without trace in three hours. You simply never report its loss."

"What—a brand-new Porsche?" Heinz asked.

"We just haven't been keeping pace with this kind of mind. That brand-new Porsche means about as much to a fellow like this as a toy."

"I see. No wonder we missed him. . . . Anyway, we've got the two linked. We know now that he went off with the girl. Find him, and we find the girl. Or the other way round. I need to get the boss, now, to call up Innsbruck."

"No need. I'm going to go there myself."

"You've no authority, though."

"I don't need it. All I have to do is walk up to him and say the party's over. The whole drama will collapse and the girl will be returned home. What can it be, after all? Just a whim of a rich man? A romantic escapade. She'll have come to no harm. But he'll be watching the German papers, Heinz, amusing himself, I've no doubt."

It was like passing from one world into another, he thought, in the plane to Innsbruck. He hadn't been able to tell Stössel, but everything in Cologne had been out of key—the scenery and lighting false and melodramatic, the shadows exaggerated and distorted, the whole atmosphere wrong. If a girl disappears, there is a possible crime. There are distraught parents, the screaming press, hundreds of policemen—everything gets out of hand.

Van der Valk had to keep reminding himself that Jean-Claude Marschal had committed no crime. He had quite likely never even realized that the German police would take it all so seriously. To him, getting a girl to run away with him was a new experience. That was how it looked. Jean-Claude had run away. Had he guessed that he would be searched for? Really searched for? By the police? He had hidden himself cunningly. It had taken Heinz Stössel's fantastic routine, with threads from the whole of the Federal Republic twisted into a lasso by a Teletype, to find him. It hadn't caught him.

Marschal might have reckoned on Anne-Marie making no fuss. She hadn't wanted any police—she'd made that clear enough. He might have thought that Canisius also would be unperturbed. His absence made no difference to the business; he probably imagined that Canisius would be glad to have him gone, out of the way, forgotten even. And there he had made an error.

For not only had Canisius taken steps—he had taken very drastic steps. An inspector of the criminal brigade had been detached, with wide powers and all expenses guaranteed. As though there had been a crime.

Could Canisius have known or guessed something about the girl? That hardly seemed possible. Could he have known or guessed that Marschal might do something wild, something unstable? Had he known of some secret, some inner flaw in the man? Was that why Canisius had insisted on an inspector of the criminal brigade? And if that was the case, why hadn't Van der Valk been told?

Was Marschal unbalanced? Had he perhaps done something criminal in the past? Could this German girl be in any danger?

No, no. Van der Valk shook it off. The chief commissioner in Amsterdam would have satisfied himself that there was no crime. If there had been anything criminal, he would have followed the routine pattern—Interpol and all the rest—and he would not have departed from it for twenty millionaires. No, the chief had behaved in a way that was plausible enough. A millionaire with amnesia, who must not be chased or harried, who must be looked for very quietly and discreetly by a responsible, experienced officer—with all his expenses guaranteed; that magic phrase had been enough to quiet his highness' conscience, no doubt!

It was a grave mistake to get himself hot and bothered about motives, thought Van der Valk. He was, after all, simply a policeman, acting under orders. Orders to look for a man, find him, and report his whereabouts to Canisius. A little thread had brought him to Cologne, where Stössel, out of goodwill, had put a whole country's police apparatus in movement for him, and had gotten a positive result—a clue, inside of forty-eight hours, to where Marschal might be.

The next little thread, in Austria, might take a bit longer, but Van der Valk knew well enough that he would find his man. The frontiers were being watched; Stössel had sent a signal about the missing girl to the police of Innsbruck. Van der Valk would find Marschal easily enough, and that would be the end of it.

And Anne-Marie? Would she thank him for all that? She had not been any too enthusiastic about a policeman, however responsible, however tactful and discreet, running after her husband. She had yielded eventually, become more open, but she had not lost all suspicion. She had agreed that Marschal should be followed up, but she had made a clear hint that he was not an ordinary person. And she had made a clear appeal to Van der Valk to try to understand, not to accept everything he was told.

The plane bumped very slightly on concrete, taxied, turned, roared its engines, and relapsed into silence. Everybody hustled for the door. The air was stinging cold and there were mountains all around. This was Innsbruck.

First of all, Innsbruck was a great deal busier than he had thought. He got a hotel room, but not without a struggle. In a few days there would be the final big international competition of the ski season. The place was swarming with lookers-on and hangers-on, journalists and photographers. March or no March, there were sixteen inches of snow right here, and forty-eight on the slopes.

There he was too, deep in the sixteen inches, with town shoes, and a silly light overcoat that had looked perfectly all right in Cologne but was absurd here. Very well, Sopex was paying the expenses. He went into a shop in the Maximilianstrasse and bought himself a big pair of boots and a fur-lined loden jacket.

Once equipped, he had to make his routine call on the police. They weren't a bit interested. They said, "We've got all the hotel registrations, naturally, but the valley's full of chalets and houses that would take a year to check. People own a house. We know their name. They let it for a month; the tenants sublet; the sub-letter camps a dozen pals in the kitchen—do you think we know *their* names? We don't even get the tourist tax half the time."

The police commissioner's name was Bratfisch. He was rough and tough. Rough blond hair, a rough tweed jacket, and a pair of shoulders made to burst doors in. Van der Valk leaned back in his chair, with his hands in his pockets, and chewed on a matchstick.

"It isn't really my fault that they came here, though," he said softly.

"Ach, of course not. Just that this can't be done one-two-three. First, your birds could be in the Vorarlberg by now, or in the Engadine. Second, in Cologne they can get very worked up about a girl that's disappeared, but here these things are a daily ·occurrence. You know how many missing girls I've had here since the season started? I'll tell you—eighteen. They get seduced by ski bums and fall off the tree like cherries. Six weeks later they turn up at their consulates without a sou, asking for a ticket home."

Van der Valk did not mention Jean-Claude Marschal's real name. He knew what answer he would get. That a missing millionaire might be a great headache to some finance company, but that all the millions wouldn't put more than twenty-four hours in the day. However, Bratfisch obviously felt he had been a little too uncooperative. "I'll help you all I can, naturally. And next week it'll be different. These last few days are the worst. Blame it on the mountain air. The old women dress up as though they were twenty, leave money and jewels all over their hotel rooms, walk off a terrace leaving mink jackets on the backs of chairs. . . . Every man I have is up to his ears and short of sleep. By Monday the circus will be gone. Try me then, if you haven't found them yet."

"Thanks," said Van der Valk. He wasn't particularly bothered.

The reception desk was full of people writing picture post-cards. He asked for a telephone line to Amsterdam, was told there would be an hour's delay, and waited in the bar till the call came through.

"Mr. Canisius? Van der Valk here. Speaking from the Hotel Kandahar at Innsbruck. He's around here somewhere. He was in Germany. He went off with a girl. Yes, just picked up a young girl and seemingly talked her into leaving home without a word of warning. That got signaled, of course, by the German police. The two are here now. They'll find it very difficult to leave, because all the borders are on the lookout. I've no doubt I'll find them, but it's still very crowded with holidaymakers here, and it may take some days. Does this news surprise you?"

"Not at all," came Canisius' voice, dry, level, practiced at speaking over long-distance telephones. "It is exactly the kind of unbalanced act I had feared. A possible scandal looming. Now you know why I was emphatic about discretion. Do the local police know all this?"

"They know about the girl. That is the pretext for my inquiries. They don't know who he is."

"Good, good. Excellent. Call me again the moment you have any news. Good-by now."

Van der Valk had dinner. He was extremely sleepy from the mountain air, and his leg muscles were aching. He got some stuff from the porter to grease the stiff newness out of the snow boots, and put his legs in hot and cold water. But he was a little overtired and overtense when he went to bed.

He didn't understand a thing about Jean-Claude Marschal. To talk about being unbalanced . . . Running away suddenly with the *Tanzmariechen*—he was sure there was nothing premeditated about it—was that really unbalanced? What sort of fellow was he? Romantic, impetuous, contemptuous of consequence. There was something paradoxically schoolboyish about a millionaire who had private bank accounts in half the major towns in Europe, keeping them under the names of Napoleonic marshals. He was giving a romantic dash and sheen to that prosaic money.

He thought about the *Tanzmariechen*. Full of innocence, of courage, of trust. What pull could that exercise on Marschal? Did it really mean anything much to him?

He had had Anne-Marie's word that Jean-Claude had never found any woman but herself who really meant anything to him. Van der Valk hadn't thought she was lying, either.

If Marschal was behaving in a peculiar way, so was Canisius. Van der Valk had come around again to the old puzzle. Why was Canisius so anxious? Surely a more or less trivial escapade of the son of the family could not seriously worry the Sopex empire. How did it warrant siccing a criminal brigade inspector on his tracks?

Van der Valk didn't know. Right this minute he didn't much care. He turned on his stomach with a groan, pushed the pillow around a bit with his face, and fell instantly, heavily asleep.

He was still sound asleep when a tremendous bang at his door announced eight thirty, chambermaid and coffee. He sat up yawning and hungry. "Come in," he called. She was already gone when he noticed that there were two cups. Well, he could eat breakfast for two. With the commotion going on, probably Innsbruck chambermaids automatically brought breakfast for two! He was brushing his teeth when there was another bang. He turned around to find Anne-Marie Marschal, calmly sitting there pouring out coffee!

"Good morning. I hope you don't mind having a guest to breakfast. Black or milk?"

It took him some time to collect his scattered wits. "You a detective or something?"

"Canisius told me. I acted upon a sudden impulse. I discovered I could get a night connection, through Paris. My plane landed two hours ago."

It was all too much to grasp, when he hadn't even had coffee. She had, he supposed, a perfect right to come here, but wasn't it a bit drastic to appear like this with the coffee? Still, one had to admit it wasn't a disagreeable sight. She looked very young. In black trousers and sweater—she was even wearing ski boots—

he saw the girl of fifteen years back who had married Jean-Claude Marschal. He drank his coffee and felt less woolly.

"Canisius," she said calmly, eating brioche with apricot jam, "who thoroughly enjoys telling people things they might find disagreeable, said he had a girl with him. Who is it? Some rag doll of the ski slopes?"

"I don't know. She comes from Cologne. He met her there. She is seventeen years old, a shop assistant, very pretty, good at things like dancing and skating, and her name is Dagmar."

"You see? A rag doll," she said. "Jean-Claude must be out of his mind. There must be something wrong with him. That's why I came. You don't mind?"

"Madame, he's your husband. I've only been told to find him."

"It isn't a crime to run off with little girls in Cologne?"

"No. Unless he used violence of some sort. Which is extremely unlikely. I'm wondering whether your husband has ever committed any crime."

"Why should you think that?"

"Perhaps because I'm a policeman. I have to shave."

"Go ahead and shave. Don't mind me."

It was disconcerting. He felt oafish and provincial. This was really an infernal nuisance. Having this woman hanging about would not make things any easier.

"Is it impertinent to ask what you propose to do?" she asked.

He felt his jaw and put away his razor.

"Have a shower," he said, picking up his clothes. It must be because they are so rich. I don't belong in this league. In fact, I feel a bloody fool. I should be back in Amsterdam, writing reports in the office. I can't get used to waking up and finding a millionaire's wife by my bed pouring out coffee.

Still, the hint had been broad. She would have gone away, he hoped, rubbing his hair dry and feeling rather clearer.

She had gone away, but had come back again. On his bed lay a very gay, extremely luscious, appallingly expensive sweater—the kind of thing the exclusive sports shops display casually in their windows, knotted around a pair of ski poles.

"What's this?" he asked.

"A sweater. That V-necked thing you have is no good here. You need trousers too; I'll get you some. The boots will do." He stared at the sweater, which was extremely tempting.

"I have to tell you two things, Mrs. Marschal. First, I am a policeman and can't accept any sort of gift for obvious reasons. Second, I don't take things, even in private life, from women."

"You sound very stupid," she said calmly. "Put the sweater on. And don't talk that childish nonsense about gifts, since I know perfectly well that Canisius is paying your expenses."

Well, this was life with the rich. He picked up the sweater and started putting it on. While he had it over his head he was pulled over backward and held by hard and muscular arms that smelled good. The trouble was that this was not particularly disagreeable. He got the sweater over his head and took the biggest gulp of fresh air he could get. The arms let him go suddenly, and he straightened up. She leaned back on his bed and put her hands behind her head. In an absentminded sort of way she started doing leg lifts with her boots on, to strengthen her stomach muscles.

"I am a capricious, vexatious, nasty person," she said quietly. "I have been badly hurt. I hope I see this shopgirl, this dancing beauty. I hope I see her in the middle of the Olympic course. I'll knock her off her damn skis."

He brushed his hair and grinned. "Very nice sweater, this. I'm going to enjoy it. You're a downhill girl, aren't you?"

"Yes. When I schuss, I schuss. I don't just want to make pretty patterns."

"He could be anywhere in Austria, you know," Van der Valk observed.

"There's a competition starting today. The girls are going to run the Olympic course. Draw a big crowd."

"And you think it'll draw him?"

"He likes to watch the competition girls. Look over this year's crop. Of course, if you want to go running around Austria, that's your lookout. It would be a great waste of time. Loosen up, enjoy yourself; don't be so Dutch. This is all unimportant. Can't you see that?"

"Sure. Everything is unimportant."

"You're taking everything too seriously," she said impatiently. "It's all plain as daylight now. Jean-Claude went off in the mood for some amusement for a change. He picks up this ridiculous doll somewhere and goes off to do a bit of skiing. Can't you see that just knowing it is enough? There's no call any longer for all this pompous tracking performance. You're here now; very well, profit from the occasion. Amuse yourself."

"With you?" He grinned.

"Ach, pay no heed. That was just a little spat of jealousy on my part."

"You were once one of the competition girls, weren't you?"

"Yes. When it comes to a competition, I can go faster than this rag doll. What's her real name, anyway?"

"Dagmar Schwiewelbein."

"There you are. Call that a name?" She laughed.

"So you're thinking of just walking up and tapping him on the shoulder."

"Tell me, then, what would you have done if I weren't here to find him for you?"

"Oh, quite a boring long routine," he said, watching her. "Go through hotels, chalet-rental services, garages, shops. . . ."

"You see?" she said, shrugging. "It's perfectly imbecilic. Just as though he were a gangster or something. Forget you're a policeman."

"Very well," he said calmly. He would stick with her. There was truth enough in her tale to make it the right move.

HE WENT with Anne-Marie to watch the downhill competition, or rather the crowd. There was no sign of anyone that looked like either Jean-Claude or the *Tanzmariechen*.

He became quite interested in the skiing. It was the first time he had seen a competition, and he liked the way the girls hurtled around the curve, biting their skis in to grip the snow, leaning over against the centrifugal force, tucking their poles under their arms and hunching down for the long run in, rocking slightly to get the last scrap of speed from the slope. It was very fast, very graceful, very exciting.

There were perhaps ten thousand people in the huge white valley. The crowd was strung along the two and a half miles of the downhill course, and with a little patience one could look at everybody. Around the finish line at the bottom were perhaps no more than two thousand people; he had his binoculars on them.

There were still contestants coming down, but a ski competition is won and lost by the first dozen, and the fanatics, the ones who were interested only in the performance and not in the spectacle and the atmosphere, were already trickling down the slope at the bottom, back to their cars. He was looking at one pair in particular, perhaps four hundred yards away and fifty or forty yards below. They could perfectly well be Marschal and the *Tanzmariechen*. The girl, in a big white fur hat, was in the right clothes for the part. The man was loading skis onto the rack of a red station wagon. The glasses were suddenly snatched from him; Anne-Marie had noticed what he was doing. The red auto backed with a swirl and shot down the valley road. It was hidden at once by a clump of pines. The car had been a Fiat 2300.

Van der Valk glanced at Anne-Marie; she had put on an indifferent face. "I couldn't really see whether it was Jean-Claude or not," she said. "He was already stooping to get in—whoever he was." It was as obvious a lie as he had ever heard.

"The Austrian police can pick that car up in half an hour." He had no intention of telling the Austrian police, but he wanted to see how she would react.

"Don't be such an idiot," she said furiously. "If you call the police, the whole damn thing comes out in the open, just for that silly girl. Anyway, you don't need to. They'll be here tomorrow, for the slalom. You can watch for them—it'll be easy."

"It'll be even more easy to get them roped in right away. They could just as easily have seen us—you, I mean." He knew something would have to give now.

"You fool, you fool! Can't you see that's exactly what Canisius wants?" He was walking rapidly down the slope; she had to hurry to keep up with him. "Stop!" He stopped. The auto she had hired was parked in the crowd, perhaps fifty paces from where Jean-Claude had left in the red Fiat. "Please," she said. "Please come back in the car with me. I want to explain something to you. Will you just not do anything precipitate till you've heard what I have to say?"

"Very well."

She unlocked the car; there was the usual stuffy, tinny smell. It was an ordinary rental-agency Opel Rekord. Yesterday's fresh snow was lying thick on the whole valley, but they kept the road free and one could drive fairly fast. She was driving well, but a little too fast.

"Not much of a car, is it, by your standards?"

She shrugged. "They're all useless things. I've had them all, I know. You get there just as well on a scooter."

A downhill girl! Or no—Anne-Marie was really more of a slalom girl. There are two ways you can run a slalom. You can wildcat it, hoping you will hit nothing, or you can run it cunningly, taking damn good care you hit nothing. To Van der Valk, Anne-Marie was on a slalom course whose flags he could not see.

She stopped outside the Kaiserhof and jumped out. "Come on up to my room. I want to talk to you in quiet, and the place is full of gibbering journalists."

Upstairs, Anne-Marie kicked her boots off, flung her parka at a baroque gilded chair, and picked up the telephone. "Send up a bottle of whiskey and two glasses." She looked at him. "Sit down." She was abrupt. She walked about, and looked out the window; the snow was beginning to fall again. "I'm going to ask you to stop. To go home and forget Jean-Claude. I have a right to ask that. I'm his wife, after all. Don't bother about Canisius; I'll deal with him."

"I'm sorry. It's not quite that easy. Canisius didn't hire me like a private eye."

"But you can't arrest Jean-Claude. He's committed no crime."

"As to that, I haven't been told," he said dryly. "I'm a police officer, acting under instructions. Those instructions were to find him and establish if possible what he is proposing to do."

"And why do you think you were given those instructions?"

"I don't need to think about it. My superiors were satisfied that they were justified. We already have evidence that they were justified. Taking a girl away from her home sounds harmless enough. She's underage, though, and she comes under the care-and-protection statutes."

The whiskey was delivered. She poured out a big glass and drank it off, as though to fortify herself in a struggle against obstinate imbeciles. "Look, when I saw you in Amsterdam I could see you were not a foolish man. You don't believe all this claptrap. You know perfectly that it's a pretext."

"Certainly. From the moment I was handed this tale I began asking myself why the fact that a man is missing from home could justify sending an inspector of the criminal brigade to try and find him. Without any of the usual steps being taken. It's very unusual. In fact, I've never heard of such a thing being done before."

"And why do you think it was done?" Her voice was silky.

"I should say"—he spoke steadily—"that a very large quantity of money had something to do with the case. Mr. Canisius and his friends are perhaps nervous that your husband might do things that look irresponsible, in the eyes of the world."

"Have you sympathy with that point of view?"

"I don't have sympathies; I'm getting paid."

She shook her head over him sadly. "Try to understand."

He drank some whiskey; it was very good. "People who have a great deal of money—a very great deal—are not easy to understand," he said. "They do things that people like me find confusing. I am trying to see why a man like Mr. Marschal suddenly leaves his home without telling anyone. Why he goes to Cologne at carnival time and runs off with a pretty girl in a gay uniform. Why he then sails off to the winter sports and has no cares, apparently, but to look over this year's crop of ski girls."

"You are paid to have no sympathies," she said. "Here, have some more whiskey. Very well. I have, as you remark, a great deal of money. I will pay you to try and be less stupid."

She had already finished her second glass of whiskey. She picked up the bottle, brought it over with her, and bent over him to fill up his glass. Van der Valk understood at that moment that an extremely good-looking woman in ski clothes, drinking whiskey in a hotel bedroom with mountains outside the window, is a very tempting object. As tempting, perhaps, as a girl of seventeen at carnival time, dressed as a *Tanzmariechen*.

"Suppose I were to explain all this to you in bed?" she said gently in his ear. There was the smell of expensive wool from her sweater, of ski wax, of leather, of whiskey—together, the world's most seductive smell. "Canisius and the clan are very clever, you know. Take my clothes off."

"I can remember the same woman saying to me in Amsterdam, 'I am quite Spanish about such things.' Well, it just so happens . . . so am I," he answered.

"You think that Canisius has something on Jean-Claude—or on me. Don't you?" She was behind him now, with her arms around his neck. "You want me to tell you about it. I will show you how Spanish I am—if you like."

He loosened her arms and stood up. "Yes," he said. "I would like to know several things. I think that Mr. Marschal could tell me most of them. I want to meet him more than ever. If he's planning to go and see the girls slalom tomorrow, I'll be watching out for him. If he's not there, I'll turn the whole of Austria upside down and keep shaking till he pops out. The German police want this girl back. So do I. Going to bed with you would be very nice, and there's only one thing I want more. To talk to your husband. What Canisius thinks or does is of less interest to me than what Jean-Claude Marschal thinks—and does."

"Very well," she said after a moment. "Very well. You may be right. We'll see—tomorrow."

"I'll see you in the morning," he said easily. "Thanks for the whiskey."

At dinner that evening Van der Valk thought more about Anne-Marie's behavior. Yes, her slalom course was wickedly laid out. Why the sudden change of front? Why had she suddenly come racing over to Innsbruck? Why had she suddenly started heading him off after she had accepted the notion of his looking for her husband, back in Amsterdam?

Yes, Canisius had told her. It was normal that Canisius should phone her, reassuringly. We've got news of him; don't worry, whatever it is, we'll get it straightened out. But it hadn't been like that. Canisius, making malicious hints about Jean-Claude's being in Innsbruck with a pretty young German girl, had said something that had bitten her deeply.

It must have been a shock to her. He thought of her words: "I'm the only woman who had any meaning for him," and that little spat of jealousy she had shown over the coffee cups had not been mere pretense. But was it only jealousy? He wasn't so sure. She had made too abrupt an about-face, was now trying too crudely to head him off. What was so bad about his meeting Jean-Claude, talking to him, straightening out his *Tanzmariechen,* and sending her home to Mum? Surely Anne-Marie could have no objection to that!

Could her behavior have anything to do with Canisius? Something he had said, or hinted, or implied, or spoken about in a gloating kind of way? Van der Valk didn't know. He went to call up his wife before going to bed.

There was a terrific lineup for the ski lifts. A great many people were going up to look at the slalom course, which had been laid out in two halves along the slopes near the downhill track. The downhill course itself was open again to the public this morning, after having been closed for a week for the competition. Several people with skis on their shoulders were going up to see what they could do on the downhill run, excited and emboldened by the exploits of the girls yesterday. A goodly number of these were nowhere near skillful enough, nor experienced enough, to run a very fast and difficult course, and might pay well for biting off more than they could chew—with a broken leg or a dislocated shoulder! The Austrians were prepared for that, Van der Valk noticed cynically. They had a helicopter parked at the bottom of the course. If anybody had a real crash, they would use it to whisk the patient to the hospital.

Around the slalom course and thickest at the bottom, naturally, there was a large crowd and a lot of excitement. It was the last big competition of the season, and this run would decide the combination prize. The Austrian girls had fought for a tiny edge yesterday in the downhill run. Would the French girls steal it back with their better slalom technique? Everybody knew, and was busy explaining why to his neighbor. Van der Valk didn't know and didn't care. He had spotted a red Fiat station wagon parked in the lot below.

Anne-Marie, with her skis on her shoulder, was talking to one of the reporters whom she knew. She walked back toward Van der Valk. "Four inches fell during the night, but married well to the old stuff. Good powder, icy patches. Very fast course—they think it'll favor the French girls. I feel like having a go; I'm going up to the top."

"I'm staying here for the moment."

"Please yourself," she said.

He turned his glasses on the group climbing into the ski lift. A white fur hat caught his eye. The *Tanzmariechen* had worn just such a hat yesterday. It might be, and it might not be. There was a man with her. It might not be—and it might be; it was as simple as that. He ran toward the lift.

The crowd had thinned when he got there, and he did not have to wait long. The man and the woman were far up the slope. And Anne-Marie had gone on a bucket just a few places in front of him. How slowly the lift went—wobbling, vibrating. The sun came out suddenly, amazingly warm in the biting air.

As the lift reached the top, Van der Valk leaped off with no skis to wait for or encumber him and ran toward the top of the course. Yes, there was Anne-Marie, kneeling, doing something with the catch on her ski; he could see her flipping it as though

she were not quite satisfied with it. Half a dozen people were waiting for their turn to schuss. Van der Valk stumbled through the fresh snow. When he neared Anne-Marie she had her skis on, and as he came panting up she turned in his direction.

"So you did come. Watch me schuss." Then they both saw the fur hat. He gripped her sleeve. Two skiers positioned themselves gingerly at the top of the downhill course, leaning forward carefully, keeping their skis flat. She shrieked, "Jean-Claude! Jean-Claude!"

Marschal looked only for a second. He saw his wife, and his eyes rested for a fraction of a second on Van der Valk. He moved with no hesitation. He put a hand on the fur hat's back and launched her on the slope. Letting his skis down, he sideslipped, gathered his poles, hanging by the wrist loops, and went. With professional ease and speed; it was he, all right.

Anne-Marie, her poles planted, was tucking her hair under her cap, panting. "Go on, damn you, go. Catch up with them, do anything, stand on your head, but hold on to them. I have to talk to him, I must."

Marschal had caught up with the girl before the turn, swung well out to give her room, and passed her. She was going very carefully; it was too fast and steep for her, but she was skiing steadily. Anne-Marie went, with a long tearing sigh of the skis.

Van der Valk ran back madly toward the lift, stumbled, skated, and sprawled full length. He got up floundering, climbed clumsily into a lift bucket, muttering furiously, covered with snow, his shoulder hurting.

When he reached the end of his ride and tumbled out of the lift, there was no fur hat to be seen at the bottom of the downhill course. No Anne-Marie in black trousers and sweater, either. Where had the three of them gone? Three hundred yards farther on, the helicopter's motor coughed and roared. As Van der Valk looked, it tilted clumsily, lifted off, and turned, gaining height. Clouds of powder snow flew about wildly in the wind of the rotor. It soared directly over his head.

He saw Anne-Marie then, sliding down the last easy slope.

He ran over to her. "Where are they?" he asked stupidly. "How is it I'm ahead of you?"

"I had a fall," she said ruefully. "A royal one. I looked at the girl instead of the track. Served me right. I flew out at a curve. Lost both skis and all my breath. You had one too, by the look of you. Hurt your shoulder?"

A new commotion was growing on the slope below the crowd watching the finish of the slalom. A knot of people were gesticulating and shouting. A policeman in mountain boots was running heavily, yelling at another policeman below.

"Someone's pinched the bloody helicopter."

Anne-Marie laughed, a clear soft laugh with a silver edge of malice in it. Van der Valk would have laughed too, at any other moment. It was the sort of joke he appreciated. But with this mountain air he was out of breath. He rubbed his shoulder resignedly. To steal that helicopter, it took a combination of skill and cheek that comes from having a lot of money. And Jean-Claude had taken the girl with him.

Van der Valk went back alone to Innsbruck, rubbed liniment on his shoulder, changed, and had time to think what a fool he had made of himself. Floundering in snow . . .

Anne-Marie had shrieked. It had not been a cry of recognition, nor of astonishment, nor of anger. It had been a cry of warning. There was only one thing that she had not known, and that was Marschal's determination to keep the girl with him. Jean-Claude had seen that Van der Valk had no skis, but that his wife had. The girl had had perhaps thirty seconds' start—not enough for a skier as strong and experienced as Anne-Marie. By himself, Jean-Claude could have taken his red Fiat. He had chosen to wait for the girl. In those few seconds—perhaps a minute—he had made the extraordinarily reckless decision to fly off with a helicopter belonging to the Austrian government.

Van der Valk found a bar that was pleasantly dark and stuffy after the blinding white of the snowfields, and he ordered cognac gloomily. He had made a mess of this. But a lot of things were clearer than they had been, at least.

Jean-Claude Marschal was bored. There was not much that gave him pleasure. Not even vice, not even crime. To run off just because he was sick of everything was quite plausible.

But there was more to it. He had been afraid. The second he had seen Van der Valk he had guessed that Canisius had put the police on his track. He had recognized the menace. Perhaps Canisius had something on him. A crime? Maybe an escapade of years before. Suppose—as a hypothesis—he had once had a hit-and-run accident, or something of the sort.

Anne-Marie knew a good deal about it. She had not, at first, taken it very seriously. But when Canisius had phoned her and told her . . . He might have been a scrap premature with malicious triumph. When Van der Valk had phoned to tell him about the German police, he had been slightly too eager to imagine he had his young friend Jean-Claude Marschal over a barrel.

Van der Valk thought, I am in a predicament. Anne-Marie, who is badly frightened now that she has seen the light, has made a very crude panicky approach. She offered me money, lots of money; she offered to sleep with me—just to forget about Jean-Claude. And Canisius, for reasons I do not know, will press me all the harder to chase Jean-Claude, harry him, worry him into something still more imprudent, still more criminal.

The sensible thing to do is to go back to Amsterdam and make a very carefully worded report, stating just why I think we're being had, and why, at the very moment when I could undoubtedly take Mr. Marschal by the collar, I prefer to do no such thing. It's not only that I don't know enough.

There are several powerful arguments against this. First, it might look a little too much as though I had been sleeping with Anne-Marie—or worse. I have already committed the imprudence of taking a sweater she bought me.

Second, the bigger reason is the *Tanzmariechen*. Not only has she been charmed away from her home into what must seem to her a very romantic and glamorous adventure, but Marschal is, for some reason perhaps known only to him, not letting go.

Van der Valk could understand the attraction a girl like that might have for a man sick to death of expensive and sophisticated women. But how seriously did he take her? Was he aware that she was caught up in a tangle she could not possibly imagine? He was sacrificing an innocent girl on the altar of his own boredom.

That was the point: whatever Van der Valk did, he had to get little Dagmar Schwiewelbein back to her distracted parents in Cologne. Heinz Stössel was right. Marschal was of no importance. The central figure in this tale was not Jean-Claude, the millionaire, nor Anne-Marie De Meeus, ex–ski champion, nor Canisius, manager of one of the world's biggest financial trusts—but a seventeen-year-old shopgirl who had put on a fur hat and high boots to show off her pretty face and legs at carnival. Van der Valk drank his cognac and asked the waitress for a couple of coffee beans to chew.

MR. BRATFISCH was sitting at his desk telephoning. "Quite right. . . . No damage? Well, then, there's no more to worry about, is there? . . . Yes, of course, but that can wait. . . . Right you are." He put the phone down and grinned at Van der Valk.

"Well, found your millionaire yet?"

"Found your helicopter yet?"

Eyebrows went up. "So the wind lies there, does it?" Bratfisch rose and went to look out. "Clouding up, and we're going to get a warm wind. Make the snow sticky. Now, if that had happened yesterday, we'd have won that slalom."

"I was out there, but I had other things on my mind."

"So it was you. He ran away when he saw you?"

"He doesn't know me. He may have guessed what I am. His wife came here, supposedly to help find him. I was with her. She stupidly shouted when she saw him. We were at the top of the downhill course. He was on skis and I had to take the bucket down. He took a remarkably drastic means of getting away."

"That's of little enough consequence. We weren't worried. You can't hide a thing like a helicopter. We've just found it. Took us all of two hours' searching with another copter, though; it was quite cleverly hidden, at the top of a valley in a stand of pines."

"And?"

"Yes, I admit, this changes things. He has that girl with him—the one the Germans were flapping about?"

"Yes."

"Bit exaggerated, all this, isn't it? I mean I don't know why you're after him, but when he sees you he grabs our helicopter. For him to do a thing like that makes me think there's more in this than meets the eye."

Mr. Bratfisch might be casual, but he was not stupid.

"I don't know myself what he thinks I'm after," Van der Valk said. "My instructions were to find him and learn why he chose to vanish from his home. He has a young girl with him who is innocent of anything at all."

"Mm." Bratfisch tapped his strong white teeth. "We'd better go and look for them. And you must come, since you can recognize this chap. We've got no proper description. I may say I meant to sound lukewarm when you came to see me last time, because it all sounded a bit too trivial, and I had nothing on this chap. Still, I can act on the bulletin Cologne sent me about the girl. We'll see what we can do now." He led the way downstairs to his car, one of the old BMW sedans that are extremely solid and a great deal faster than they look.

After hunting in the valley below the spot where the helicopter had been found, they discovered the chalet where Marschal had been honeymooning with his *Tanzmariechen*. There was nobody there. It was furnished with the ordinary things one finds in all mountain chalets, but there were plenty of luxurious extras strewn about, from roses—flown into Innsbruck by plane at that time of year, and forced quite likely in Holland or Hyères, costing the earth—to a fancy Japanese camera which, alas, had no film in it. It was hard to say whether the couple had been back there or not. They had made little effort to take anything with them, and certainly no real luggage. The clothes that had been bought in Munich—and in Innsbruck—were lying about everywhere. A careful search failed to turn up anything remarkable.

"They'll try to get out of Austria now."

"Well, there aren't all that many ways of getting out," said Bratfisch comfortably. "We've picked up the red Fiat, so they'd have to get another car—and we've warned all garages and filling stations. They can't get a plane without us knowing, and I've got men on every train leaving Austria. He's got to follow the valleys, and what choice does that give him? Back toward Salzburg, or the other way into the Vorarlberg and over toward Constance, or up toward Germany to Mittenwald and Garmisch, or south over the Brenner Pass. That looks likeliest, but hell, it's easy enough to block the Brenner! Wait twenty-four hours and we'll have him in the bag, girl and all."

Van der Valk, feeling slightly curious, passed the Kaiserhof on his way back to supper. Anne-Marie was gone. She had packed her skis on top of her rented car and driven off earlier that afternoon, the porter said. No, she had been alone. No, she had had no messages or telephone calls, nor had she made any. No, she seemed quite calm and sunny.

It was easy enough to check further by telephone. Anne-Marie, alone, yes, quite alone, yes, they were quite sure, had passed the border at Füssen half an hour ago, still in the rented car with the skis on top. They had noticed her particularly—yes, naturally.

Where the hell was Füssen? After a minute's hunting on the map he found it, a little town just over the German border. It didn't have to mean anything. Anne-Marie had lost her taste for mountains and perhaps felt like a nice flat plain—Holland, for instance.

HE COULDN'T sleep. He was again overtired and overtense, and his shoulder was swollen, had stiffened, and was so painful that he could not lie on it. At midnight he was wandering about Innsbruck, but he was in no mood to join the skiers' postseason revelry. Finally he found a little bar where he could do some nice, neurotic solitary drinking.

Which way would the cat jump? Surely not Germany, with Heinz Stössel's high-powered machine, and every policeman there looking for the *Tanzmariechen*. The Yugoslav and Czech and Hungarian borders appeared unlikely for obvious reasons. No, it must surely be Switzerland or Italy. And trains would be out, for Marschal would certainly know that the passports on a train are easily controlled if anyone cares to take the trouble. The answer lay on the roads. Hiding on a truck or something. Naturally, but he had to consider Marschal's character as well as those huge packets of bank notes. Skulking like a refugee across the border wasn't his style. He would find it more in his nature to try something impudent, a gay piece of bluff, the riskier the better. If he was caught, then it would be time to try a bribe. He could see Marschal sailing across the Italian frontier in a huge Rolls-Royce, bowing slightly from side to side, with Ethiopian flags flying from the fenders. . . .

Van der Valk drank his cognac and meditated about passion. There are two kinds, he was thinking. There is the northern kind, that believes it is high on emotion and is only high on imagination. That is us. Me, the Germans, the Scandinavians, the English, the Americans. We weep buckets over passion, but we don't have it.

Real passion belongs to Latin peoples. Read the newspapers in France or Italy. There the crime of passion is commonplace. For a man to shoot his wife, and then himself, is a thing regarded as reasonable and psychologically probable. In northern Europe this sort of thing is extremely rare.

The interesting people are those with mixed blood. Jean-Claude Marschal had streaks of northern blood, and could weep, no doubt, with the best of them. And he had, quite undoubtedly, a strain of highly colored ancestry that was almost Corsican. He could be capable of a violent emotion. The *Tanzmariechen* might be, to him, nothing but a good theatrical gesture—and she might be intensely real and very important.

For several hours Van der Valk drank and meditated. After too much cognac, he had some coffee. It was still pitch-dark out, with blue and orange lights glaring livid through sleet, when he reeled off back to bed. He fell asleep instantly.

He woke at midday, and felt like being a detective. He was going to have a good lunch, and think about his immediate problem. If Jean-Claude Marschal wanted to get out of Austria, how would he go about it?

There was a very good, delicate sauerbraten, with almonds and raisins in it. There were nice feathery mashed potatoes, and there was red cabbage with a very faint flavor of cinnamon. Van der Valk felt much better. A good many tourists had left, and the hotel staff, with the end of the season in sight, were feeling light-hearted.

Marschal and the girl could have mixed with a crowd of tourists. It was possible, since nobody ever looked at tourists' passports; the most they did was to count and see if the number came out right. But those busloads were too obvious, and too many people would know, and the frontiers would not be quite as perfunctory as usual. Was there any other group where a person more or less, even two, would pass unnoticed?

Those gangs of skiers that had been making such an uproar in the Kaiserhof last night . . . There were various groups of characters that nobody thought about, accompanying a ski team. Families and friends, hangers-on as well as the technical boys, timekeepers and whatnot. And Jean-Claude had once been a competition skier.

Van der Valk hurried to the police station. Bratfisch was not there, but he found another man. "How do the ski teams travel? In a group, or do they scatter?"

"I suppose they just dribble off home by car in bits and scraps. The French have a caravan, as usual. Twenty or thirty autos, and of course their bus."

"Bus?"

"They shovel all their material, the skis and so on, into an ordinary touring bus. Stays with them through the season."

"Which way did they go?"

"Over the Arlberg, I suppose. Turn down toward the Saint Gotthard, Furka Valley, Rhone Valley, straight to France."

"Phone the Feldkirch frontier station for me, will you?"

Yes, the caravan had passed. Check the passports? Good grief, they were all piled like corpses after the big party. Why bother? Everybody knew the ski team; it spent half the year going to and fro between one end of the Alps and the other.

Switzerland confirmed that nobody would bother checking such well-known passport photographs, and Van der Valk felt he was getting warm. The Swiss had a detail or two to add. There had been two caravans, really. Another row of twelve or fifteen autos after the first. What? Yes, of course. Reporters, photographers and the French radio commentators.

"Yes, of course." The ski team was followed by its attendant circus of sports journalists. And that was certainly another crowd that would be familiar to Mr. Marschal. Indeed, now that he thought of it, ski competitors, managers and trainers followed one another in quick succession—no results, no contract—whereas those specialized journalists had often covered the same big meetings for twenty years.

It was so damn easy that he knew immediately Marschal would have loved the notion; it was so simple and impudent. No nerve-racking creeping around Germany or Switzerland. One fell asleep in Austria and woke up in Chamonix as fresh as though one had gone straight through by the Arlberg Express.

What did he risk? Van der Valk took the night train, and stepped out of it in the sharp bright morning in Chamonix, tipping his hat to the majestic, faintly boring silhouette of Mont Blanc. It was too early to go running about, so he sat comfortably in the warmth of the station buffet and had some coffee and a brioche, and read the *Figaro* of the day before, with its report from a "special correspondent in Innsbruck."

AN HOUR after a visit to the chamber of commerce, he was in a street on the outskirts of the town. The house he was looking for had a wrought-iron gate and a Gothic front door. An aluminum plaque said SERAILLER, JOURNALIST. He rang the bell.

A woman opened the door. "I've an idea he's still asleep, but it's high time he got up anyway. Who shall I say?"

He could be a policeman from Amsterdam or from Timbuktu; it was all in a day's work and left a journalist's wife indifferent. Van der Valk was put in the living room and given time to look around.

The big sunny room was untidy with souvenir dolls, outrageous ashtrays, stuffed animals and skiing trophies; there was a large and amazingly miscellaneous collection of books, and Van der Valk was glad he had come. Mr. Serailler seemed to be an amusing person. He was saved from further speculation by the door's opening and the man himself appearing, no more bothered by the police at nine in the morning than his wife had been.

A muscular forty-five, with a splendid mountain tan and the characteristic long fine wrinkles at the eyes. Short hair gone gray early, still wet from a comb held under the tap and run through it. Tight blue trousers that looked like denim but had cost a lot more money; a Mégève sweater whose sleeves he had tucked up above the elbows. Hand-knitted socks and no shoes. He padded over the smooth wooden floor and shook hands amiably.

"Really was high time I got out of bed."

"Just back from Innsbruck?"

"That's it. Long drive, but the roads weren't bad. What can I do for you?"

"You've been around the circuit a good many years—not many people you don't know," Van der Valk said.

"I suppose not. Used to be a skier myself."

"Ever come across a man named Marschal?"

"Probably; common enough name. Skier?"

"Playboy style but pretty good, I believe. Ten years, or more like fifteen years ago, might have been in the top twenty."

"Of course. Jean-Claude. Was fifth at Kitzbühel once when I was seventh. Sure, I remember. Didn't practice enough. Might have been a champion otherwise. Wonder what happened to him? Had lots of money—no need to work for his living like us."

The story had gone on too long; Van der Valk smiled a bit, secretly. It was all a little too casual.

"He was in Innsbruck last week."

"You don't say. Wonder why I didn't run into him."

"He was in Chamonix yesterday."

"Well, well. Old stamping ground. Nostalgic pilgrimage, perhaps. Why the interest?" It was still too casual.

"I just wondered whether it was you that gave him the lift."

The journalist felt in his trouser pocket, brought out a pair of horn-rimmed glasses, and put them on his nose. Gentian-blue eyes looked at Van der Valk curiously. "Whose business is it that you're making your business? I'm not quite clear. Mine?"

"No, his. I want to see him. I guessed he'd hitched a lift with the caravan."

"Is there anything illegal about that? You say you're from the police. He hasn't paid a parking fine or something?"

"Oh, nobody's worried about that helicopter."

A broad grin appeared. "Don't tell me it was Jean-Claude who pinched that helicopter? Just like him." A bark of laughter. "Hardly an extraditable offense, though."

"You got children?"

"One"—startled—"girl of twelve. Why?"

"Suppose your girl had gone to Innsbruck, say, and was suddenly missing. Nowhere to be seen. What would you do?"

"I know nothing about any girl missing."

"But that girl with Jean-Claude is missing. Her parents are terribly worried—do you blame them?"

"Of course not, but I don't see what all this has to do with me."

"Simply that if you'd known, you might not have been so quick to agree to giving Jean-Claude a lift. He must have said he wished to avoid anything looking like police. The frontier guards, for instance."

"Who said anything about my giving him or any girl a lift?"

"Ach, man, don't be childish. I don't care whether you did or not. You couldn't have known about anything serious. Probably he said the Austrian police were angry with him about the helicopter."

"Look. Jean-Claude is an old friend. We used to compete together. I gave him and his friend a lift—you can find that out easily enough, I suppose. And further than that I've nothing to say, not without better reasons than you've given me so far."

"I'll tell you frankly, there is something in all this that may be serious. The man is missing and there's nothing to show why. Why does he vanish from his own home and persuade some girl to vanish from hers? How well do you know him?"

"Fifteen years ago—nearer twenty—I knew him pretty well. I've seen him a couple of times since, winter sporting."

"Did you ever see anything in him out of the ordinary?"

"Everybody's out of the ordinary if you look deep enough," he said dryly.

"Sure. How was he on the road?" Van der Valk continued.

"Nothing unusual. We hardly talked, though. While I was driving, he was asleep, and when he drove, it was my turn. We'd both been at a party."

"The girl?"

"She was very quiet, and they were very affectionate with each other. Jean-Claude was gay and happy."

"Maybe because he was being clever and doing something exciting. The police of three countries are looking for him. I was looking for him in Holland, the German police are looking for their girl and know she's with him, and the Austrians want to talk to him about their helicopter. Furthermore, all the frontier posts are after him."

"I had no idea. I was driving when we crossed the frontier. I just showed the auto papers and my pass. They know us all, of course. We went right through."

"That was just what he was counting on. Where did he go?"

"He said he was going to catch a train."

"You know where he was headed?"

The gentian-blue eyes looked at Van der Valk for a long time before Serailler answered. "I have an idea"—slowly—"that he has a cottage or something in the Vosges."

"Know the address?"

"No."

"Phone number?"

"There isn't any phone."

"Whereabouts is it?"

"Fraid I don't know."

Van der Valk gave him a big homely grin. "How d'you know there's no phone, then?"

"You think he's a bit off the rails?" Serailler said suddenly.

"I don't know any damn thing. I'm a bit worried, though. I'd like to see this girl's parents knowing she was safe and happy. I'd like to talk to Marschal. There's nothing criminal against him, so I'm not going to arrest him or anything. He has a right to leave home anytime he wishes. But there are other people involved. He left his wife—she's anxious. He left his job—they're anxious. Obviously you thought it all a scrap queer too or you wouldn't have been so leery of me. It's better that you tell me."

"I have the phone number of a café," said Serailler thoughtfully. "He said they could give him a message."

"He gave you the number to call in case anybody came nosing around here after him?"

"I guess so," said Serailler a little unhappily.

"You see? Don't call the number—it might make things a lot worse. You noticed I'm not threatening you with anything, but if a criminal charge ever came out of this and the lawyers discovered that you'd helped him twice, once after I'd warned you, they might take a dim view. That's just a friendly remark."

Serailler got up, walked over to his table, and took a notebook from a drawer. He fluttered the leaves, tore one out, and gave it to Van der Valk. "There. What you do with it is your affair. Jean-Claude can't complain I've betrayed him. He should have told me I was taking a risk in taking him over the border."

THE telephone number was written hurriedly, slantways, as one might write while sitting in a car, holding the paper across the steering wheel. Somewhere in the Vosges . . . He went to a telephone, called the number, and got the address.

Half an hour later he was in a café, drinking cognac. He had bought a Michelin map of the Vosges, and after a bit of searching he had found the village. Tucked up in the foothills, between the high ground and the Alsace plain. It would be nice there, he thought. One is well away from the picturesque tourist country and the wine district, and the closely bunched villages of the plain have straggled out into the beech and pine woods.

It would be characteristic, of course, of Marschal to have a hideout and for it to be in a place like that. Van der Valk could easily believe that the man had even kept it secret from his wife. He might have had it some time, perhaps years. It would be a pleasant antidote to Canisius, and Sopex, and public relations, and maybe to Anne-Marie as well.

The train north from Chamonix to Strasbourg is a longish ride, but not dull, since the Alps give way to the Jura, and the Jura to the Belfort Gap, and from Belfort onward there are the Vosges on one's left. Van der Valk, watching the sunset, felt peaceful. He would catch up with Marschal here at his little hideaway, and give him a talking-to, and get this girl back, and what the fellow did then was his affair. Let Canisius worry about that; it wasn't police business. Van der Valk settled down to read a book he had bought.

He arrived in Strasbourg at dusk, and had a fairly unexciting dinner in an unexciting hotel near the station. Before going virtuously to bed, he phoned Arlette.

"I'm in Strasbourg. Nice here; we'll go together sometime."

"You're getting around, aren't you? How's the skiing?"

"Don't mention skiing. There's nothing at the moment I want to see more than Amsterdam on a rainy day. Nice and flat!"

"When d'you think you'll be home?"

"I might get finished tomorrow, with any luck. Storm in a teacup. Just that this fellow I'm supposed to be hunting for runs around like a rabbit. I've found out where the hole is now. I'll have a scene with this girl, no doubt, but that's only to be expected. All this has given me a strong taste for domesticity. You all right?"

"Yes, but getting sick of being widowed."

"I'll call you tomorrow; I ought to know something by then."

THE NEXT MORNING wet snow was falling heavily. He put on the serge trousers and the fur-lined jacket he had bought—on his expense account—in Innsbruck. And the mountain boots, and the sweater Anne-Marie had bought. It brought him back with a jolt. Why had Anne-Marie tried to seduce him? Why had she given that shriek of warning to Jean-Claude?

He rented a car, an old Renault, which gave him a bad time. The transmission was anything but sweet; the visibility was lousy; the heater was too hot; and he made several false turns.

He could not see the Vosges through the drizzling mass of low cloud till he was right on top of them. He lurched up a narrow foothill road off the highway and found his village, no more than a cluster around the four angles of a crossroad—a Romanesque church, a school, a French country town hall with grandiose pillars outside to support the dignity of the Republic.

The café was no trouble, either. There it was with farm buildings clumped behind it, and inside, a powerful French rural smell a hundred years old. Straw, denim overalls and dog. White wine and vegetable soup. Onions, smoked bacon and ironing. As usual, there was the mixture of the very old and the very new: the dented zinc that certainly dated from Napoleon III, and the espresso machine that glittered with chrome and winking red lights. A huge television set, gaudy as only the French make them, was flanked by classic decorative themes—a large china shepherd dog, and a stuffed otter with a stuffed trout in its mouth. There were a beefy man in blue overalls drinking wine, a thin man in a cap, and a stringy woman peeling carrots.

"Good morning."

"Moyng," came a triple grunt. Out of three pairs of eyes looked the glummest kind of peasant distrust.

"Soup smells good."

"Ugh."

"Cognac."

The man with the cap had to go to the cellar to hunt for a fresh bottle, which he did with poor grace, as though it were an unheard-of demand on his time and energy.

"Have one with me."

"I'll take a glass of white," he said in a grudging mutter.

The beefy man and the stringy woman seemed to be having an argument. It might have had something to do with potatoes, but the patois they talked was enigmatic.

"I'm looking for Mr. Marschal," Van der Valk said.

"Who's that?"

"He lives here."

"Yes."

"In the village?"

"Up the road."

"I'll go and knock on his door if you'll point out the house."

"Nobody there."

Oh, God, thought Van der Valk, not again.

"Is too," said the woman suddenly, violently. "Shutters were open yesterday."

"Closed today," said the thin man with relish. "Gone."

"I can always try," offered Van der Valk.

The beefy man now took a hand. "Car's there."

"Have a glass of wine," said Van der Valk hospitably. "What about you, madame?"

"Ugh. Gives me a sour stomach."

"Spot of gin?"

"Yes." The woman thawed. "You show'm th' way, Albert."

Albert seemed to be the beefy one. He was not at all easy to detach from his glass, but after taking off his beret twice to scratch, unwinding his scarf and putting it back again, he got unstuck.

Albert had a tractor outside. He climbed into the saddle, pointed up the side street with a finger, and said, "Can't miss'm. Got green shutters."

Van der Valk felt sure there were at least twenty houses with green shutters.

"Red house," Albert admitted, and turned the starter key.

There was a house built of Vosges sandstone, and it did have green shutters, and they were closed. It was not the isolated log cabin of fantasy, but a perfectly ordinary house in a village street, standing alone but crowded by bigger neighbors.

There was an oak front door with a narrow curtained porch window. He disregarded this for the moment and followed the wide paved path that led around to the backyard.

The back door obviously led to the kitchen. There was no sign of activity, but between the door and the shed stood an expensive auto. A black Lancia sedan. The showroom polish was still on it under the thin layer of snow, and the label of the Strasbourg garage was untarnished. Van der Valk had to grin a little. That Jean-Claude—he bought new cars and left them lying about the way you or I leave a half-empty box of matches. Van der Valk tapped on the door of the kitchen. Nothing happened. He went back around and rang the bell at the front. Nothing happened. He returned to the backyard, frowning, and tried the kitchen door. It yielded. He didn't like all this a bit.

It was perhaps the extreme ordinariness of the house that struck one most. It might have been any suburban kitchen he was standing in, with its very ordinary gas stove, refrigerator, white wood cupboards faced with Formica, and table to match. Everything was neat and tidy and, as far as he could see, clean. There was still some soup in a pot on the stove, onions in a metal rack. In the refrigerator were meat and milk, an opened packet of butter, half a can of tomato purée, a few slices of ham in greaseproof paper, a plastic box half full of grated cheese.

He went down to the cellar. Everything there also had a look of reassuring permanence, of a house lived in for many years, kept by a careful housewife. The furnace was slightly warm. He opened the door. It had not been raked and was full of ash. He felt the ash with his hand and drew the hand back quickly—gray and dead as it looked, it was still holding heat. That furnace had been stoked within fifteen hours; it was the type one makes up twice a day. Van der Valk trudged back up to street level.

Silence and a little dust lay on the polished furniture. Faded cheap carpets lay on the polished floorboards. Everything in the two downstairs rooms and the hall was old-fashioned and provincial. In one room was a cabinet with a glass front. Here Mother had kept the good dishes for visitors, the liqueur glasses, and the souvenirs brought home by soldier sons from Indochina. They were gone. In their place stood six porcelain figures. Van der Valk opened the door and took one out to handle it. He did not know much about such things, but they could be by Kaendler. In which case they were quite certainly worth five hundred pounds apiece.

When Van der Valk looked more closely at the other room, he saw that all the pieces in it had been bought from the kind of provincial dealer who specializes in ancient farmhouse and peasant furnishings. There was a sort of window seat that gleamed like water with age and loving handling. The wood was dark and had violent unexpected swirls and courses in it. On it stood a different kind of collection, to which he got down on his knees. Stones. Precious stones mounted on little bases of wood, bronze, iron or crystal. Opal matrix, rough turquoise, raw emerald.

Van der Valk straightened up with a sigh. In the hall there was a rifle on one of those ornate weapon stands beloved of French hunters, all deer antlers and carved wood. He looked at the rifle in passing. The weapon was a much heavier caliber than one usually finds in people's houses, he thought. Every Frenchman who lives in the country keeps a .22 for rats, cats, hooded crows, and the fox he always suspects may be after the chickens, but this was the kind of thing one took to shoot lions with. It was time to go upstairs. The wide shallow stairs of polished oak creaked under his feet, and he had the absurd shame one always has at making too much noise.

Light came through the wooden shutters in thin splinters and gave a dim unreal look to the bedroom. There were two people in the big bed. Real enough, even if they were dead. There was still a tiny trace of the sharp scent that comes from copper-jacketed 7.65 pistol cartridges.

He had to go and find the gendarmerie. He would have to explain who he was and what he was doing. They would have to

call the lieutenant, and the lieutenant, after listening to Van der Valk's ridiculous tale, would very likely decide he would have to phone Strasbourg.

IT ALL went off exactly as he had expected. While waiting back at the house again for the lieutenant, the doctor, the magistrate, the technical men and the ambulance, Van der Valk sat in the downstairs room with the precious stones. There were three or four books scattered about. Paperback thrillers, which he did not even glance at. A cheap edition of the poems of Baudelaire. Yes, he could understand that. Baudelaire was the kind of person who would appeal to Jean-Claude Marschal.

Wasn't it Sartre who called Baudelaire a deliberate failure, who had chosen a bad conscience, chosen to feel guilty, chosen sterility? Van der Valk started to read the poems; he had nothing else to do. Thinking would come later.

"Spleen"—now how did one interpret *spleen?* Depression? Too weak. Ennui? Too vague. Manic depression? Too forcible and too clinical. The answer was that it didn't need interpreting. Everybody understood it.

He read the poem with a fresh eye. He hadn't read it in years. It was a lot better than he had thought it.

I am like the king of a rainy country: rich—and impotent; young—and very old. Who despises the bowing down of his preceptors, is as bored with his dogs as with all his other creatures, whom nothing now, neither game nor falcon, can cheer. . . . A grotesque song from the favorite clown can no longer unwrinkle the forehead of this cruelly ill man.

The lieutenant of gendarmerie had read Baudelaire, perhaps, but had other things to think about and no time for poems. Since this was his district, he was mostly interested in what the two in the bed were doing here. They were dead, and there was nothing the police could do to help that, was there? He found a few stray facts to go on in the village. Mr. Marschal had owned this house for five years or more. He had not come here often. Seven or eight times a year, perhaps. Mostly for two or three days only. Always alone. An old woman in the village had had the keys. She had been very well paid to go there every second day or so, to keep things clean and in order.

Yes, she had seen him arrive with a young girl. No, that hadn't struck her. She had always thought he would turn up with a woman sooner or later. No, he had been laughing and joking. Not depressed a bit if you asked her. Like a couple in love rather than a couple having a furtive weekend.

The lieutenant was not happy with Van der Valk. This rigmarole of millionaires and winter sports had really nothing to do with him, he conveyed. There might be something odd about it, he agreed, but a double death had taken place on his territory, straightforward suicide pact, and he had a lot of forms to fill in now. He thought that Van der Valk had better repeat his tale to the criminal division in Strasbourg.

DIVISIONAL Commissioner Wollek was like an old gray wolf. His face, his voice, all his movements were as quiet as Chinese writing done on silk with a sable brush. Van der Valk liked him at once. He had the manners of a cardinal and thin delicate hands.

"Difficult for you, all this. But do tell me your story."

Van der Valk told it, leaving out nothing.

Wollek nodded. "Yes. A king in a rainy country. One wonders why he was there—he would have found Paris more congenial."

"The old gentleman, his father, is a tyrant, as I hear. He might have been very dictatorial," observed Van der Valk.

"The role of the wife is obscure."

"It's all obscure. Luckily we're not called on to understand it. Nothing now but to go back and tell them I've found him, and he's dead, under circumstances that almost look as though he had killed himself for fear I would find him."

"I don't understand why they were in such a hurry to find him," said Wollek. "The reason given was that he was an irresponsible person, as I understand, and might throw money about. Apparently he did throw money about. But with the amount of

217

money involved, that is only a drop. He couldn't have remained hidden for very long, after all. Why didn't they signal him as a missing person and wait till he was noticed somewhere?"

"I've wondered the same thing. His wife behaved more as though she didn't want him found. It's possible that when the old man heard about it, he issued an order that sonnyboy was to be traced and brought back to reason pretty damn quick."

"I think we'll have to find out," Wollek said slowly. "A French subject has died under obscure circumstances, on French soil. That means that I am responsible for any inquiry that may be made later. I'd better phone Paris. And perhaps you'd better notify the Germans, since you know these people in Cologne. And of course his wife. Both these people will have to be formally identified. Would you like to use my telephone?" He pushed it across the desk toward Van der Valk.

Van der Valk called Amsterdam. The majordomo was full of regret, but he had not seen or heard from Anne-Marie. It was peculiar, but since leaving Innsbruck, she seemed to have vanished.

Van der Valk phoned Canisius. A private secretary, as full of silky regrets as any majordomo, told him that Mr. Canisius was unfortunately away from home. They would be in communication with him that day; was there any message?

"No. Ask him to leave a number where I can reach him. It's extremely urgent."

They would do that. Would Mr. Van der Valk be kind enough to call again around five? That was extremely good of him.

"Police Presidium, Cologne. Herr Stössel, please. . . . Heinz? Van der Valk. I'm in Strasbourg. End of the trail, I'm afraid. They're both dead. Double suicide. You'll have to get hold of the father and bring him over here. Office of Commissioner Wollek in Strasbourg."

"I'll arrange that," came Stössel's distant, unemotional voice. "Peculiar thing. Your Mrs. Marschal is here. She turned up this morning. Said she wanted to see the girl's parents. She had a tale about persuading the girl to come back home as soon as she was found, and so forth."

"How did she strike you?"

"Rather shrill and emotional. She's staying here at the Park; she said she'd stay till I heard from you."

"Sorry, Heinz. You'd better bring her along as well. She'll have to identify her husband, and make the usual arrangements with the authorities here—funeral and so on."

"I'm just looking at the map. Frankfurt . . . mm . . . Karlsruhe. Looks as though it'll take about four hours on the road. You'd better expect me around six."

"Very well. I'll be waiting."

Mr. Wollek was nodding gently—every Strasbourgeois can follow German. "You'd better have lunch," he said. "Perhaps you'd like to come back with me here this afternoon."

"I don't feel much like lunch."

"Exactly, and that's just the time to have a good one. You know this town at all?" His voice was paternal. These young men, it seemed to say. Getting upset about a death and not eating properly. "I'll give you the address of a good place. I'd join you, but I'm afraid this has given me some extra work. Ask them for liver—it's still in season."

The old boy was perfectly right. What was the use of getting in an uproar? There was nothing left but the details of administration. The French would do that. And Heinz Stössel had a job to do that nobody liked—breaking the news. He himself had nothing to do at all. The lieutenant of the gendarmerie was filling in the forms. He just didn't know why he felt so uneasy. He would go and have a proper meal and plenty to drink.

There was fresh goose liver. Very simple, cut in slices and cooked in butter. Apples came with it, sliced too and cooked soft in a spoonful of white wine. Van der Valk read a newspaper, drank a bottle of champagne, and was shamefacedly surprised to find that it had done him a lot of good.

"You had a good lunch?" asked Wollek politely. He was sitting where Van der Valk had left him, in the same position.

"Very good. I'm more tired than I had realized."

"I can understand that. You were a little bit out of your depth, weren't you? Millionaires are not quite the same as other people, are they? Awkward kind of predicament. You were given ridiculous instructions too. Nothing clear-cut, nothing defined."

Van der Valk allowed himself to grin for the first time in days, it seemed.

"Well, I can add a bit to this picture. I phoned a colleague of mine in Paris, who has considerable experience of this financial set. I asked him about Marschal. He knew about him, all right. Said he was a bright and able fellow, but completely on the periphery of affairs. Quite frankly, his death wouldn't make the slightest difference to the business."

"But what about the old man?" asked Van der Valk. "This is his son, after all. Heir, what's more, to a terrific fortune. The old man has made over a tremendous amount of money to him already, to avoid the inheritance tax. It's salted away in God knows how many different banks. What happens to all this money?"

"Yes, that's exactly what I asked. Our man in Paris doesn't know, but he says he can probably find out. He knows this fellow Canisius who approached you, but only vaguely. He'll probably call me up this evening with whatever news he's managed to pick up."

"I've got to phone Canisius again anyway," said Van der Valk. "I might as well do it now, and see whether he can shed any light; they'll be here from Germany soon. Can I use your phone again?"

The secretary in Amsterdam was abominably suave. "Ah, Mr. Van der Valk. Thank you so much for calling. We have been in touch with Mr. Canisius since you called. Unfortunately he is tied up at present with some quite pressing business commitments. He will be back in Amsterdam on Monday. Perhaps you could be so good as to make personal contact with him then."

Van der Valk was irritated by all this creaminess. "Where is he, exactly? This situation needs his immediate attention."

"Oh, he realizes that; please reassure yourself. He particularly impressed upon me to make it clear that he quite understood the situation." The suavity had an unpleasant knowingness about it.

Van der Valk felt veins in his forehead swelling. "Where is he? Just tell me that. And where can I get hold of him if I need him? Police business, you hear?"

"Mr. Canisius has business in Spain," said the secretary very primly. "He generally stays on these occasions at the Prince de Galles in Biarritz."

Mr. Wollek, arms folded, had a faint smile as Van der Valk put the receiver back.

The telephone rang on the desk.

"Yes? . . . Send them up." Wollek wiped the amusement off his face. "Germany," he said quietly.

Heinz Stössel spoke slow, quite good French with an accent that did not make his impassive face any less formidable.

"This is Commissioner Wollek of the Strasbourg police," said Van der Valk formally.

"My sincere sympathies," said Mr. Wollek to Herr Schwiewelbein with equal formality, in the singsong German of Alsace.

Mr. Schwiewelbein was a man of fifty. His hair was brown and white in patches, both discolored. His clothes and hat were clerical and neutral, and he had a carefully neutral face, but there was even now a military look about him. The outward signs were shoulders that he had never let stoop or become rounded, and the heavy scar of a machine-gun bullet, which had plowed up one side of his jaw and mutilated his ear, and had healed roughly and never been prettified. It was a face that Van der Valk found strangely striking. There was a great deal of fortitude in that face. He had sat down without any fuss on the nearest chair, his hat on his knees, waiting for three senior police officers from three different countries to smash up his world for him.

Anne-Marie arrived. She was in street clothes, a suit that Van der Valk could see had cost a great deal. She noticed him studying it. "Nina Ricci," she said, with a touch of familiar sarcasm. She sat down in a chair, put her hands in her lap, shivered violently, controlled herself abruptly, and stayed quite still.

"I am very pleased," began Wollek gently in his fluent German, "to have the help of Herr Stössel and Mr. Van der Valk, who both know much more about these circumstances than I do. You understand that these formalities are demanded by the law and I am here to fulfill them. The facts are simple. Mr. Marschal was staying in a house he owned not far from here in the company of a young woman, and for reasons we do not know he put an end to both their lives. Both bodies have been brought to the city, and both will have to be formally identified, which is why your presence was necessary. It is now quite late, but it is good to get that done with. I don't doubt but that the public prosecutor will give the authorization to make whatever arrangements you wish tomorrow morning. Shall we go?"

There was a black Citroën in the cobbled courtyard, with a police driver. Mr. Wollek motioned to Anne-Marie and to Van der Valk, and got in himself. The two Germans got into Stössel's black Mercedes.

"Medico-Legal Institute," said Wollek.

The nasty part was conducted in a brisk way, though the attendant had a slight brassy smell of white wine about him.

"Will you formally identify the two persons found by you at the address named here?" Wollek intoned in the precise metallic French of the Republic's judicial forms.

"I recognize them both and I do so formally identify," said Van der Valk.

"Can you, madame, identify this man as Jean-Claude Marschal and as your husband?"

"I do identify him—as both." Anne-Marie's voice was as metallic as Wollek's, and much louder. It grated in the stillness.

"And can you, sir, identify the young woman as Fräulein Dagmar Schwiewelbein?"

"It is my daughter," said the man simply, very quietly.

"May I have your signatures, please?"

THEY were back in the office. Wollek brought several papers together on his desk, turned them on end, and tapped them to get the edges level.

"Copies of these documents, which you will need for your administration, Herr Stössel, will be made when we have the public prosecutor's signature of release. That should be done tomorrow morning." Heinz Stössel nodded.

"One more formality. Herr Schwiewelbein, the scene of this tragedy has been carefully examined by the lieutenant of gendarmerie and has been inspected by the deputy for the court, as French law requires. Some tests have been made by technicians, under my control. Your daughter did not kill herself. She was shot, and died instantly and painlessly at a moment when she was happy and peaceful. She may have been asleep. Immediately after, as far as can be judged, the man with her ended his own life." Wollek paused for a second, flicked his eyes at Anne-Marie, and went on smoothly.

"This kind of suicide is, in our experience, not altogether an act of despair. I would myself, speaking as a man as well as a police officer, call it an act of love. I hope that this will lighten, if only a very little, your sorrow."

That is a very clever man, thought Van der Valk. He too was looking at Anne-Marie, but she gave no sign, made no movement, said nothing.

"Thank you," said the German. There was the dignity in his voice that there was in his face. He hesitated briefly and then went on. "If I understood rightly, Herr Wollek, they were in bed together when they were found?"

Nod.

"They had been making love, then—when he shot her?"

"Yes," said Wollek with no hesitation.

"You think he loved her?"

Wollek glanced at Van der Valk. "There's no doubt of that."

"I don't think there's any doubt, either, that she loved him," said the German with an odd tranquillity. "I can feel, at the least, that it was not altogether a waste."

Anne-Marie still did not budge.

"I have been struck by your kindness, Herr Wollek," Schwiewelbein continued. "It confirms everything I had heard from

Herr Stössel, who, I had feared for a while, was inventing a romance to try and relieve my pain and to relieve his own painful embarrassment. You see, we spent four hours together in his car, coming here on an errand of despair. Herr Stössel spent much of that time explaining to me that he was certain my daughter had been happy." Everyone turned to Stössel, who did not move a muscle.

"She had a week's happiness," Schwiewelbein muttered. He looked like the kind of man whose highest pitch of emotion comes in finding that the quarterly accounts balance. "A wonderful holiday in the mountains, all kinds of clothes, the pleasure of skiing, which she loved, a shower of generous pleasures and presents, expensive cars—even the dodging about and running away must have seemed to her a very exciting adventure. A romantic slice of life—and a romantic death. What more could a girl of that age desire?"

None of them said anything. Wollek picked up his sheaf of papers and slid them gently into a manila envelope, busying himself unnecessarily with fastening it.

Herr Schwiewelbein got up. "I will remember—my wife and myself—the consideration shown me by the police of three countries." He walked out of the room slowly.

It was indeed a romantic death, Van der Valk was thinking. It is a very good thing to find beauty in that. There is just one thing. It was just a scrap too well timed. The stove was still warm when I got there. And the two of them had not been dead four hours. When I got to Strasbourg, Jean-Claude and his *Tanzmariechen* were still alive.

He turned his attention back to Anne-Marie. Death leveled everybody; the millionaire's wife, the sophisticated hostess of Amsterdam, had vanished. So had the gay siren of Innsbruck, the unaccountable downhill girl full of contradictions. One reached bedrock on these occasions. What sort of rock was at the base of Anne-Marie?

Wollek had become businesslike again. "You have heard what I said, madame. There is no reason for me to doubt the conclusions reached. Mr. Marschal shot the girl and himself. The deputy is satisfied, and so am I. We have, further, the experienced observation of Mr. Van der Valk. You have, of course, the right to query my findings, to see the doctor's report, anything. Do you wish to make any statement or pose any question before these papers go to the public prosecutor for his signature?"

"No," she said briefly. "I would like to see the house. I would like Mr. Van der Valk to show it to me."

Mr. Wollek considered this, taking his time answering.

"That is quite fair. It is good that Mr. Van der Valk accompanies you, since he knows a lot more about the attendant circumstances than I do. I will give the village gendarmerie a call, and ask them to give you the keys."

"I have my car," she said indifferently.

"Then I'll be with you in a moment or two," said Van der Valk.

"You wish to conspire together," she said with a sneer, putting on the coat he was holding for her. "Afraid I'll kill myself as well? I'll be in the courtyard; I want to stretch my legs anyhow."

Mr. Wollek looked at Van der Valk with a half smile.

"Is it really technically all aboveboard?" asked Van der Valk. "That wasn't just for poor old What's-his-name's benefit?"

"You find the death a little too pat, don't you?"

"Gunshot suicides are so easy to fake."

"That's why we always check them ve-r-y carefully. That lieutenant wasn't happy, either; that's why what you say doesn't surprise me." The smile widened. "But the technical crew did a thorough job. No hanky-panky. I'm satisfied; I can pass these papers to the public prosecutor tomorrow and he'll sign them, and the poor old chap can take his daughter home."

"I'll take Madame Marschal out there, then. It's true enough— she has the right to see."

"By the way, before you go, I found a message here when we got back from the institute. Our man in Paris. He says that he's seen one of the managerial types of Sopex. Your pal Canisius was there too, as a matter of fact. They didn't appear very perturbed about this death; just oh, how tragic, et cetera. One point of interest: the old man appears to have gone a bit balmy. It's being kept very dark, for the good of the firm and so on. He still trots into the office every morning, but apparently they have a whole façade erected for him to play with, to give him the illusion that he's still in command. Whereas in reality the inner ring makes all the decisions."

"There's certainly nothing left for me to do," said Van der Valk. "I can go back home tomorrow. You could perhaps send me on an extract of the relevant papers when they're all signed; I can turn that in with a written report. So long now and very many thanks. Anytime you're ever out our way . . ."

"Only sorry I didn't get the chance to show you a bit of hospitality here." Wollek smiled. "Good night."

They shook hands, and Van der Valk ran quickly down the echoing staircase.

It was the same rented car, the Opel Rekord, and her skis were still strapped on the roof. During the half hour's drive to the village from Strasbourg neither of them said a word. But he was conscious of her in a way so acutely sensitive as to be painful. She was sitting beside him in a loose, comfortable way, crowding in on him at corners. Her coat—it was the snobbish kind that has the mink on the inside—was thrown open and there was a pleasurable scent of warm delightful woman.

When they reached the village, he stopped at the police post and a yawning gendarme gave him the keys. The house was not far, and all the houses around it were dark and shuttered. They parked and went in.

It was miserable how the friendly little house had lost all warmth in that short space of time. It was icy cold now, disheveled by the police technicians. Anne-Marie looked about without curiosity.

"And you came here this morning? And found them dead?"

"Yes. Just too late. Everywhere I've been, it's been too late," Van der Valk said.

"How could a fool like you hope to understand?"

"I'm very often a fool, and I've learned that sometimes situations make one look even more foolish than one is."

"What a fool you are," she repeated cuttingly. "And how did you get to know he was here, you fool?"

"I guessed how he had got out of Austria. By following my nose I stumbled on the man who had helped him. The man was an old acquaintance. Jean-Claude had been a bit too clever. Asked my man to call up if any fools like me came sniffing about."

"You utter incompetent, ignorant imbecile. I told you to stop. I warned you that you were doing something you couldn't see the consequences of. Stupid lout. You went on blundering along and now you see the result. I offered you money. You could have had more money than you've ever earned in your life. I offered you myself. Do you think I'm the kind of woman to sleep with the first hayseed oaf she meets at a winter-sport resort? No. You had to play the honest, stupid copper, too virtuous to live."

Van der Valk sat down near the window seat. The stones glimmered on their bases. One looked a little like the knight in a set of chessmen. He picked it up. He hoped this was a good move for a knight.

"Your theory is that he killed himself because he knew I was after him, because he knew that he couldn't get away, because I would have barricades set up on all the main roads like after a bank holdup. So he killed himself just before I could get here?"

"No, fool, I don't believe that. He didn't kill himself. He was killed."

"Really? By whom?" inquired Van der Valk politely. "You?"

"Canisius, you blind imbecile. Canisius is sitting in Paris, finding it a fine joke."

"You don't believe in Mr. Wollek's hypothesis of suicide?"

"I suppose I have to tell you," she said in a suddenly dead, flat voice. "There's no other way for it now."

"Please do. I need to have things spelled out. That's exactly what I've needed since this began."

"Canisius has been looking for years for a good opportunity to blackmail him." Her voice was low and contained. "It happened when we were just married. Jean-Claude was much wilder then. We had been to the winter sports here in France, and Jean-Claude had a win. He was very gay and had had a lot to drink. He wasn't drunk, because he never was, but he was near it. We had a new sports car—you remember the first 300 SL, with the gull-wing doors.

"Outside the town where we stayed there was a straight stretch of road, a sort of avenue bordered by big plane trees. Jean-Claude got the idea of making the car slalom in and out of those trees. I had a stopwatch from that day's competitions; we made bets about the time he could make. I suppose you can guess what happened. It was night and the place was deserted, but there was a man walking there with a dog. We never saw him till too late. He must have got frightened, thought we were chasing him around the trees or something. Anyway, he lost his head and stepped out suddenly into the road. The car only touched him, but it threw him against the tree. It was the tree that killed him, really." She paused for a long sobbing breath.

"And what did the police do?"

"I don't know whether they did anything much. They must have taken it for pure accident. But the man left a widow, you see. Jean-Claude was a very honest, impulsive person, and he got the idea fixed in his head that he would go to her, admit frankly that it had been he, say it was pure accident, ask her to understand, and give her a lot of money to live on. Well, I was horrified at that, because I thought she would just blackmail him. I was very foolish myself, because I went to Canisius. He rushed straight to Jean-Claude, of course, told him he mustn't do anything so foolish, and that he himself would pay the woman off without ever letting her know where the money came from or even that it was blood money at all."

"I see. And why did the time come now, several years later, to use this piece of knowledge?"

"They've been fighting and plotting for years to get control of the business away from the Marschals. Well, they've succeeded. The old man has been getting potty. They can get him declared incompetent by a court. But the money all belongs to Jean-Claude, and there's a huge amount. Even the old man didn't know how much there was. They want desperately to get their hands on all that. Yes, you can say they control huge assets, and an enormous investment empire. But I happen to know they're not very liquid. They're hard up for ready cash, and this is how they planned to lay their hands on it."

"Aha. Most interesting. So Canisius puts the screw on Jean-Claude, who decamps. Canisius sends the police after him, thinking to harry him, make him lose his head, imagine that they are actually after him on a homicide charge. That's it, then?"

"But yes. Can't you see? That's why he was running away, in Innsbruck."

"And that's why you called after him, in Innsbruck? To try to warn him?"

"Now you're beginning to understand."

"You didn't know where he was yourself, so when you heard— from Canisius—that he was somewhere in Austria, you thought that you'd tag along and by sticking to me, find out where he was. When you saw that I was determined to get hold of him to find out what it was all about, you tried to seduce me. When that didn't work, all you could do was stay with me until I did find him, and then hope to be able to warn him before I could talk to him. Right?"

"Yes, that's right."

"You know what I think?"

"Is that very important?"

"Not to him anymore. To me it is. And to you maybe. I think you're a liar. Even a pretty bad liar, though you're quite a good actress."

She glared. She opened her mouth and made a sort of spitting sound. Then she thought better of it. She closed it again firmly and controlled herself into complete stillness.

"Perhaps you're quite a fair liar in the sense that there's quite an adroit mixture of fact and fiction in this ridiculous tale you've been telling me so convincingly. I think it's true that old Marschal is balmy. Mr. Wollek found that out this afternoon. I think it's true that Canisius and his pals would like to get hold of the money. About that liquidation story I wouldn't know and I doubt if you would, either. I think it simply burns them up to know that a huge sum of money is there and they can't get at it. I thought in the beginning of all this that Jean-Claude was simply a weak, unstable kind of person with a flawed character, who ran away because he couldn't stand up to Canisius. But I'm no longer convinced of that line of reasoning. I think money just didn't have any proper hold on him. I think that he just got sick of the squalid squabble; that he's been sick of it for years, but that he stuck to his life there in Amsterdam out of loyalty to you and a sort of loyalty to his name.

"I think that when you found out about your father-in-law you put a lot of pressure on your husband. To fight, to take his proper place, to get back control of the business, to be worthy of his father, to be worthy of you, and so on. I think that just disgusted him. He's always wanted to be free of the whole thing. He had bought this house several years ago. Every so often, when he could get away, after a trip and a business deal and some entertaining of important overseas customers, he came here, and pretended he was someone else for a few days.

"I think that he went to Cologne, perhaps out of sheer coincidence, though he seems to have been reminded that there was a carnival going on. I think he saw and fell into conversation with a young girl, herself with very simple, honest, unsophisticated standards, and suddenly decided that this was what he wanted. He must certainly have realized that she would be hunted for, and eventually traced. I imagine he just didn't think because he didn't want to think. He wanted to be free. His money could give him illusions of freedom, and this girl would supply him with more. He had seen every pleasure there was in life, and found them all pretty thin. He was like the king of the rainy country."

"The what?" Anne-Marie had not understood; how could she?

Van der Valk picked up the volume of Baudelaire's poems that he had found and that was still lying on the table.

"Sure. Here. A poem. He read it, he knew it, he liked Baudelaire; they had a lot in common. Great gifts, great sensitivity and a kind of tormented conscience. Baudelaire was always moaning about his bad luck, but he liked it, really. He enjoyed his bad conscience and the feeling he was a doomed and tormented person. Jean-Claude understood that and sympathized with it. Here, read the poem. He saw parallels there, all right."

Her eyes had narrowed and were watching attentively.

Van der Valk went on. "I don't believe a word of all that tale of slaloms and plane trees. It has a slick fabricated sound. I think you've just made it up to convince me that Canisius is the villain in this piece. You'd probably even like to convince yourself that it is so, and that he caused your husband's death. Because I'm pretty sure that was provoked by nobody but you."

She still wasn't saying anything, but she was looking at him with an oddly bright expectant look, her lips slightly parted. He picked up another of the stones, surprised at its weight. Even if he were certain that she had known about this house and had been in it, he could not prove it.

"My husband is dead," she said suddenly with something like hatred in the cold quiet voice, "and you sit there, doubtless very pleased with yourself, telling me I caused his death. To try to hide your own stupidity from yourself. You understand nothing. There is the same miserable meanness and narrowness in your thinking as all the other policemen show. Dutch, dim, obstinate, with your stupidly literal little mind. Get out of my sight! Find your own way back to Strasbourg. I don't have to listen to a fool like you trying to justify himself."

He sat quiet and looked at her smilingly. Froth, my dear, by all means, if it makes you feel better, he thought. She stood looking at him a moment with contempt, then turned abruptly and left the room, shutting the door with a bang. He listened to her climb the stairs. Overhead, she stood still a moment in the room of the two pistol shots. He was sorry for her, but there was nothing he could do. There was nothing he could do at all but get a carefully written report plotted out in his head. Heinz

Stössel, in Cologne, had a far more important and exacting piece of work. Since the sad thing was that nobody really cared about the Marschals. It was the little German shopgirl, who had happily put on the carnival costume, in which she looked so fine, who would, rightly, be mourned. Marschal had had nothing left to do in this world; that was why he had shot himself, surely? With nothing to take with him, he had left life. The girl had seen that, perhaps, dimly. She had wanted to go with him. She had offered. Marschal had yielded to that. It had been something to him that she, at least, had not wished to leave him.

As for Anne-Marie . . . Van der Valk could hear her now, coming down the stairs, looking around in the next room, taking leave of the pathetic remnant of Jean-Claude's deceptions. Then he heard the outer door slam shut. Well, well. There wasn't much he could do about that!

I am just a plodding Dutchman, he told himself. I was quite out of my depth. He felt the contour of the stone in his hand with his mouth and tongue, as though he were blind and trying to reach something with other senses. The stone was just a stone. None of its beauty and richness could be reached that way. He put it down with a sigh and reached in his inside pocket for his notebook and a ballpoint.

Canisius had been maneuvering to get the last of the Marschals into a position of impotence. That was not difficult, but to find a way to lay hands on all that money was more difficult. When Marschal had bolted he had seen an opening at once. Marschal was an irresponsible, reckless character, and might do or be led to do something unbalanced, and that might give Canisius a valuable handle. Naturally Canisius had been delighted to hear that Marschal had run off with a teenage girl in Germany. Nothing could have suited him better. And to confuse the situation further, he had maliciously told Anne-Marie. Her high-voltage emotions injected into the situation would doubtless tangle things even more. Astute. She would be maddened by Jean-Claude's stupidity and heedlessness in picking up the *Tanzmariechen*, and she would also be crudely and furiously jealous.

She had followed the turns of Canisius' mind without being able to realize that she herself was hopelessly enmeshed.

She might not ever have realized that in following her husband to this house—and Van der Valk was quite convinced she had followed him—she would precipitate a climax. He shook his head. He should have kept more of an eye upon her, instead of running so frenziedly off to Chamonix. He had been half seduced by Anne-Marie without realizing it, and had never managed to gain the grip on the situation he needed to keep in control of it. Throughout, a sort of trance, seductive and hypnotic.

He had better get out of this. He stood up to leave. The house was adding to his persistent sense of impotence. He snapped the light out and shut the door behind him.

There was something wrong about the hall. It struck him at once, but it took some minutes to find what was changed or missing. Then he noticed; it was the kind of thing that is so obvious one cannot understand why one had not seen it instantly. The rifle that had been hanging on that deer-antler weapon stand was no longer there.

Even then he had still been in his trance. With a kind of stiff slowness he had gone back to the police post to return the keys. They had phoned for a taxi to take him to Strasbourg.

By the time he was there he felt ready to believe he was making a fool of himself. Wollek's technical squad, finding a fire-arm death, had taken the rifle for examination: Van der Valk knew, of course, that this was ridiculous. Anybody with the flimsiest training in firearms could see that both deaths had been caused by the pistol found on the bed.

Though why on earth should Anne-Marie have taken the rifle? It certainly was not to commit suicide. First, suicide was not in her nature; second, women do not use a hunting rifle to kill themselves. He had better warn the police that Anne-Marie was loose somewhere with the rifle. Rather a dangerous weapon too; he had not looked closely at it, but it had been a much heavier caliber than an ordinary .22.

Van der Valk would get no thanks from the French police. If

he told them that he was certain Anne-Marie had been in that house before, had even provoked the double death, they would look at him in silence. He had no evidence of any such thing.

He called the unpretentious hotel where the two Germans were staying. Anne-Marie had not registered there. That was natural enough. She would choose the most palatial hotel in the town.

She had. She had also checked out again an hour ago. The porter had carried her expensive suitcase. He had driven her car around to the front for her. Yes, that was right, a gray Opel. Quite unmistakable—there was a bundle of skis on the rack, in one of those rainproof canvas sacks.

Van der Valk gave the porter a ten-franc note. Had she said or asked anything? Yes, she had asked for a main road toward the southwest. He had pointed out the Schirmeck road to her.

Van der Valk went off with a road map to think this over. Schirmeck . . . Saint-Dié. Yes, it went over the Vosges in a southwesterly direction toward Épinal. Now, what could be the point of that?

She couldn't be heading for Chamonix, could she, having known that was where he had gotten his information? And what would she do there anyway? He let his finger waver along the network of roads heading vaguely southwest. What along all these routes with their possible turnings could interest Anne-Marie? She couldn't be heading for Paris—she would have taken the Nancy road. He let his finger wander vaguely along the coast. La Rochelle? Down— He stopped suddenly. In the extreme southwestern corner, tucked in the angle formed by the French and Spanish coasts, his finger was resting on Biarritz. It was suddenly clear to Van der Valk what Anne-Marie was doing with a hunting rifle slid in between the skis on her car's roof. The more he thought about this the less he liked it.

He had a car too, didn't he? And she had only an hour's start.

WHAT was it Anne-Marie had called him? Slow and obstinate, mean and narrow, stupidly literal-minded, very Dutch. He sighed heavily. That was quite true. He couldn't help that. He had been born that way and trained that way. He was a professional. It is only in books that one finds the brilliant amateur detective. Real policemen are obstinate and hardheaded, are slow and literal-minded, are frequently mean and nearly always narrow. They have to be. They are part of the administrative machine, a tool of government.

But one needed amateurs too. Take this situation. What could a professional policeman do in these circumstances? His famous rules and procedures were all meaningless. Nobody had broken any laws. A professional policeman, if he had any sense, would have washed his hands of it at once.

Of course, the fatal mistake—going after Marschal at all—had been right at the start. The chief commissioner of police, a professional and a bureaucrat to his fingertips, had fallen headfirst, delightedly, into the pit the moment Canisius had stepped with his beautiful shoes on the concealed button that released the trapdoor.

A private detective, the beautiful unspoiled darling of a detective story, would have leaped straight into bed with Anne-Marie, given Canisius the old right hook straight to the shiny false teeth, beaten Marschal by two seconds flat on the Olympic downhill course at Innsbruck, had the *Tanzmariechen* fall in love with him instead, and been paid ten thousand pounds on the last page by grateful millionaires.

And here I am, thought Van der Valk ruefully. I've made every mistake I could have; I haven't been professional; I'm not clever enough, being much too Dutch, to be an amateur. A Dutch policeman was really good for only one thing, and that was filling in a form explaining how some other very wicked individual had filled in another form incorrectly.

A sensible policeman—a professional policeman—would have stopped several times on the road for solid provincial French meals, a good night's sleep between sheets. Actually, a professional policeman would never have embarked at all upon as ridiculous a goose chase as this one. He would have phoned Canisius. He would have phoned the gendarmerie of the department of Basses-Pyrénées and told them to stop a gray Opel Rekord with a bundle of skis on the roof. After all, from Strasbourg to Biarritz is just about six hundred miles by road. Twelve hours' driving. If you were very young and resilient, an excellent driver in a powerful car, and you had had a good night's peaceful rest, and you started at dawn, and had good weather and fairly uncrowded roads, you could do it in a day with a two-hour break for lunch.

Van der Valk was doing it because this was no place for a professional anymore. He had no evidence that Anne-Marie even had the gun. He had no evidence that she was even going to Biarritz. Nobody in the world would have believed him if he shouted at the top of his voice that she was heading for a professional financier in a fur-collared overcoat and a gray trilby hat, with the fixed idea of planting a bullet in him. Things like that do not happen, least of all in Biarritz, a pleasant town once favored by His Majesty the King of England and now thought highly of by the new French upper class.

The fact was that the cleavage between professionals and amateurs was here shown at its sharpest. The old Marschal had been a survivor of nineteenth-century banditry. A brilliant adventurer, like an American railroad king. Canisius was the modern professional financier, at home in modern circles of power and influence. The presence of the old man, that glaring anachronism, had stuck in his throat for years. But, senility and delusion helping, he had successfully set Sylvestre Marschal aside. There remained Jean-Claude. He would have liked to tip him overboard into the Atlantic, but financiers don't do such things.

Anne-Marie, and not her husband, was the last of the Marschals. It was ironic. She had a streak of buccaneer's blood that ran true to old Sylvestre's. And she had somewhere a confused feeling of loyalty to the Marschals. She had seen the direction behind the mortally slow and tortuous insinuations of Canisius and his tribe. She had seen the way the old man had been gradually trimmed by legal maneuvering. She had tried to whip up Jean-Claude and he had failed her. Who could tell what efforts she had made, what pressure she had put on the man before he bolted? He had bolted, and had promptly caved in utterly.

And now Anne-Marie was on her way to strike a last blow for the Marschals. With a rifle. God knew what she was thinking; quite possibly she imagined that that was what the old man would have done in similar circumstances.

Maybe she had known something about the little house in a Vosges village. The extraordinary performance Jean-Claude had put on at Innsbruck must have destroyed much of what balance she had left. For the man had not run away from Van der Valk, or from the police in general, or from Canisius. He had run away from his wife. She had gone to the little house for one last plea, perhaps. Jealousy had confused her ideas further. And Jean-Claude had reacted in a way she had not foreseen.

Van der Valk was tired. He had started at night, after a difficult day. For the sake of the shaky old man in Paris, for the sake of an innocent girl's parents, for the sake of Jean-Claude, who had made an effort for a scrap of peace and happiness, and yes, for the sake of Anne-Marie herself—he had liked her—he wasn't stirring up the whole French police apparatus. He was going up against a woman with a rifle—had she any idea how to use it?— with his bare hands. But he was too tired. If he went on this way, there would be an accident, and he was too much of a policeman not to know that, tired as he was, he was a menace. It was dawn; traffic would be thickening on the roads. He couldn't make the push to get into Biarritz that evening. Van der Valk pulled the Renault into a side road somewhere not far from Moulins—he had the difficult mountain roads of the central massif of France ahead of him—and slept while the day came up like thunder behind him in the east.

WHEN he awoke he looked at his watch and made a face to see how late it was. But Anne-Marie would have to rest too, somewhere. She might even be near him. There was, of course, no guarantee she was on the same road, and he had had no great hopes of catching the gray Opel. But she would not have reached

Biarritz before the middle of the night any more than he would. And Canisius would have spent the night in pleasant dreams in a luxury suite at the Prince de Galles.

Van der Valk had breakfast at the first place he came to; nothing particularly wonderful-looking, but the coffee was hot and strong. They cut him huge slices of ham, boiled three fresh eggs for him, and charged him a fortune. He didn't care: Marschal money. The only important thing was that Canisius should not know what efforts were being made on his behalf. Van der Valk knew that this was really why he had chosen not to warn the French police about the rifle in among the skis. If Canisius heard—and he would hear—that she was gunning for him, she was a dead duck. Nothing else stood between Canisius and all the bank accounts strewn about Europe. As long as Anne-Marie was not a criminal, she surely inherited the Marschal money.

Did she know Biarritz well? Did she know where Canisius would be staying, what his movements were, what his habits were? What sort of plan was she making, there somewhere ahead of him, in the rented Opel?

Van der Valk got in around one in the morning, and felt fairly safe. He parked the car in a quiet spot and slept until four.

Coffee in the station buffet—it was like Innsbruck all over again—where he struck up a variety of casual acquaintances, among others a customs man, who told him about the Spanish frontier. He found the bookstall woman too, and though her stall was not yet open, she let him have a Michelin, which he studied carefully. He did a good deal of driving around in the pale early sunlight, and decided that Biarritz was a nice place. Arlette would like it here. Be a fine place for a holiday, though the prices, even out of season, would make her shudder.

He got washed, shaved, drenched himself in eau de cologne, changed his slept-in suit, and felt human enough to risk the early morning snootiness of the Prince de Galles reception desk.

"I'm afraid that Mr. Canisius is not yet awake."

"When does he have his breakfast sent up?"

The pale creature consulted the Spirit of Tact, and balanced the results against the cherished principle of being as Rude as You Dare to Unknown Persons. "Eight o'clock."

"It's five to, now. Give him just a teeny buzz and tell him my name, will you?"

With reluctance this was done, in a hushed tone of respect. "Mr. Canisius asks you to be good enough to wait ten minutes. A page will take you."

"Thank you, young man," said Van der Valk in the tones of the Dowager Duchess.

A thin, elegant floor waiter was wheeling out a cart. There was a tinkle of silver and porcelain, a smell of hot chocolate— a whiff of after-shave—and over all, that indefinable hotel smell of old carpets. Mr. Canisius, cosseted and comfortable, was breaking bread on his little balcony in a nervous-looking way, as though a paper snake on a spring might suddenly come whizzing out.

Like all businessmen, Canisius looked utterly indecent in pajamas, though they were a restrained maroon color, with edgings of thin silver cord, quite correct. He was also considerably too grand to stand up or shake hands with policemen at breakfast, but he nodded amicably, patted his lip once or twice with a fringed napkin, and said, "Quite a surprise. How are you?" in his soft milky voice.

"Tired."

"Sit down. Have you had breakfast?"

Van der Valk sat in a rococo cane chair with buttoned cushions. "Yes, thanks."

"But how did you know I was here?"

"Your secretary told me." A slight frown disturbed the milky surface. "However, don't be hard on him; I had to twist his arm."

"Yes; there is some company property in Spain, certain investments in housing, and this is an old haunt of mine. So I combine a little necessary supervision with a little fresh air and exercise. Golf, you know."

"Ah, yes," Van der Valk said. "He mentioned that you had business in Spain, but no more."

Canisius nodded approval of this discretion. "I like to keep an eye on some building projects along the coast. In fact, I will have to ask you to excuse me very shortly, since I have arranged with two of my associates to pay a little visit this morning."

"Oh, it can wait till you get back," said Van der Valk. "Unless you happen to be coming back late."

"By no means. It is about fifty miles altogether and we shall be lunching at Irún, but I will be back at around three this afternoon. You wish to give me all the details?"

"Yes. It is a fairly complex business and I thought it right to come and see you personally, right away."

"Excellent, excellent. I am most appreciative, believe me, of the zeal you have shown throughout this unhappy business. Pity that you weren't in time to prevent that very sad death." There was something about these words, mouthed by a businessman in maroon pajamas drinking chocolate, that irritated Van der Valk.

"The truth about the very sad death will not appear in the written report I will make to my superiors."

"You're being rather enigmatic. I'm afraid that I know nothing but the bare fact of the death, and that I only learned in quite a roundabout way from the police in Paris."

"Oh, there's nothing doubtful about the death itself. That's plain sailing from the administrative angle. Indeed, the authorities there in Strasbourg cut the formalities to a minimum in order to spare unnecessary pain to the girl's parents."

"Ah, of course. I recall your telling me about this girl—a German girl?" Canisius asked.

"Quite right. For similar reasons, I left a variety of things unsaid in my dealings with the police, and I will do the same in my own report at home. That is why I thought it better to have a conversation with you before going back to Amsterdam."

"I begin to follow." Canisius had finished breakfast. He was in less of a hurry now to get rid of Van der Valk. "I am pleased," he said carefully, "that you have shown the very qualities of discretion that were needed. If the press had chosen to make a drama of this affair, it might have been most unfortunate."

"I'm only a policeman, and I don't have much experience with millionaires. I've seen quite a bit of Mrs. Marschal."

"Very sensitive, highly strung woman," said Canisius gravely. "You had to break the news to her, of course; a most disagreeable duty, I'm afraid. She took it badly?"

"She was quite calm. But she behaved oddly."

"I see it all." Canisius broke into a warm, friendly smile. "She feels that her husband's death should be blamed on someone, isn't that it?" He had gotten up and was walking around the table with a kind of jerky animation. "Quite possibly she has made meaningful hints as to some malign influence I had upon her husband, who I'm afraid had rather a weak character. Something like that, hey?"

"Yes, various remarks have been made. Nothing substantial."

"Well, well, that's all quite easily explained. An explanation is certainly due you after all the pains you have taken. Now, why don't you pass a quiet day here—all your expenses continue to fall to my charge, naturally—and may I suggest then that you come to dinner with me tonight. We'll straighten all this out, and you can go back to Amsterdam and write your report, because I'll tell you quite frankly that your superior officer has no more information than you had yourself at the start. But yes, we'll discuss all that tonight, shall we?"

"Sure." I hope we can both of us count on this evening appointment, thought Van der Valk.

"I'm afraid I must interrupt our visit, interesting though it is, since my car will be waiting for me in just half an hour. This evening, then? Perhaps seven thirty, in the bar here? Splendid, splendid."

Van der Valk, who hated elevators, walked down two broad flights of ambassadorial stairway contentedly. He wasn't sure that splendid was the right word. But Mr. Canisius had talked much too much. From viewing Van der Valk's sudden appearance in Biarritz with a lack of enthusiasm, he had suddenly become that gentleman's very closest friend. Endearing of him.

Van der Valk walked about the public rooms with nonchalance, staring out the windows a good deal. There was no sign of Anne-Marie. Was he imagining the whole thing? Tired as he was, he still had two sides to his head, he hoped.

Jean-Claude Marschal was primarily the northern type he had thought about that night, drinking cognac in a little bar in Innsbruck. The theatrical type who commits crimes, such as suicide, theft of a government helicopter, or abduction of a minor of the female sex, with a flourish and a bow to the audience. Anne-Marie was not like that at all. Lying in wait for somebody with a gun was no stranger to her than it was to a Corsican farmer whose sister-in-law has an assignation with the farmer over the hill. There was nothing, he had thought and still thought, intrinsically improbable about this at all.

There was no need for her to hang about a hotel entrance waiting for Canisius to show himself. She almost certainly knew Biarritz well. She might also know all about Canisius' business in Irún. It was possible that, once knowing that Canisius was in Biarritz, she would know which route he would take to the border.

Knowledge like that made this one of the easiest kinds of assassination going; as everybody in the world knows since the day Mr. Kennedy took a ride in an open car through Dallas. Nor was there anything odd about a woman getting the idea. A rifle, one tends to think, is essentially a man's weapon. But any woman can learn to shoot. It is simply a question of the right position, and then looking along the sights. Lying down, a woman can shoot as well as a man. A high-powered rifle has a big kick from the recoil—but that is after the shot.

Anne-Marie, an ex–ski champion, was not going to be either scared of the bang or disconcerted at any technical difficulty such as loading, adjusting the sight, getting the safety off.

Canisius coming out of a hotel door would make an ideal target. But there was no square or anything with handy windows. Opposite the Prince de Galles was nothing except the pompous avenue de l'Impératrice and the still, silky Atlantic. No perspective and no cover.

Somewhere along the road, where there were little hills, patches of greenery and shrubbery, clumps of trees? But the car would be moving at thirty-five miles an hour. Unless one was dead in line, the sights nearly parallel to the road, the shot was impossible. Where, then, would the car slow down? At the frontier, obviously, to show the papers. But he had understood from the customs man with whom he had gossiped at the station that morning that the frontier was in Hendaye, where National Ten ran straight out of the little town, across the bridge over the Bidassoa River, slap into Spain. It would be tricky to find cover there too, but he would see. He intended to be close by when Canisius went sailing over that bridge. If Anne-Marie saw him, and realized he had guessed her move, she would be disconcerted. She might not be put off, but the bare fact of seeing him would be grit in the wheels. It might, for instance, spoil her aim.

There came Canisius, talking to two other financial fellows, one an echo of himself, probably from the Paris office of Sopex. The other was more sunburned, and much more wrapped up—a local man, in a tweed jacket. The contractor or supervisor in charge of the building work, or possibly the architect. Canisius made a marvelous target, thought Van der Valk gloomily. Cream silk suit. And a Panama hat!

And the car! One of the gigantic six-liter Mercedes battleships that are longer than a Cadillac—and the top down! A chauffeur in riding boots and a peaked hat was holding doors open, and the porter of the Prince de Galles was making dignified fluttering movements.

The Mercedes rippled off with a noise like a woman's fingers smoothing a satin evening skirt, and Van der Valk climbed into the hired Renault, which made a noise like a dockhand stacking empty oil drums, but the employees of the Prince de Galles were far too distinguished to look.

Keeping up was easy: the huge black car was very sedate. They slid through Saint-Jean-de-Luz without as much as a toot, Van der Valk the regulation hundred yards in the rear, in his shirt sleeves. But instead of sailing on along the coast to Hendaye, the Mercedes suddenly swung abruptly to the left at a main road junction, and Van der Valk grabbed at the Michelin on the seat beside him. Oho! There was another road, damn it, that skirted Hendaye and crossed the Bidassoa half a mile farther up. The type of road described by guidebooks as a "picturesque stretch." Which it was. Here the foothills of the Pyrenees came down toward the narrow coastal strip where one squeezes through to Irún. A thick Mediterranean vegetation, with cork oaks and umbrella pines, was looking very springlike in the hot sunshine, though at about three thousand feet the snow looked waist-deep still. As the Mercedes slowed for the frontier post, Van der Valk was realizing uneasily that the shooting cover was perfect. Nothing had happened, and nothing happened now. Yet instead of a vaguely troubling theory, he had a sudden wave of fierce feverish certainty. Somewhere, somehow, there had been eyes along that road. Eyes along a gun barrel.

He stopped the car before the frontier. Here the hills took a dip into the valley of the Bidassoa, and the river, swollen by the melting snow, passed under the bridge that formed the frontier.

There was gooseflesh on his bare arms; he wondered whether it came from the chilly little breaths of air, or from that terrifying feeling of complete certainty. He was very tired and was not certain whether his judgment was good. He tried to think coldly.

All along the road there were flat patches, a mixture of gravel, old pine needles and a thin sprinkling of earth with coarse grass. In the summer, people parked their cars there and climbed up to one of the ledges for a picnic. At the curves the road had been cut into the hillsides, and the shoulders were revetted with stone.

He was not impressed by the possibility of a shot at a car stopping for the frontier. It was a long shot, and blocked from too many angles. He was trying to see how he would have done it himself. Suppose I were looking for a good place . . .

There was time in front of him. Canisius would not be back for several hours and one would have leisure to find a good spot. But he knew obscurely that the good spot had been found. It was not only the feeling of eyes somewhere; he knew that these plans could not be carried out spontaneously. They needed rehearsal. If he had been behind the gun, he knew he would have let the big Mercedes pass unhindered too. The important thing was to get a good notion of how fast it went, what sort of target was presented, whether any unforeseen factor blocked the view and the shot. The woman was a skier. She knew something about terrain, about slopes and dips and humps of ground. She had the right blend of cold judgment to add to her boiling fury.

He let the motor turn, and swung the boxy little Renault back the way he had come. The melting snow coursing down steep slopes that were almost vertical in places could cause accidents. The falling water brought away loose stones and pebbles, bits of dead branch; occasionally even a tree might come down.

There! As he drove up a slope and turned around a sharp bend, a large stone suddenly crashed on the roadway in front of him at a spot where the hill went up abruptly in a tangle of thin undergrowth. He braked and stopped. A stone the size of his two fists. If that stone had landed on his hood . . . He got out and went to look at the slope. It ran up for some fifteen yards over his head, with little flat heathery bushes. The terrain was perfectly sound, not crumbling or insecure-looking in any way.

The stone had not fallen; it had been thrown.

He stood still a long moment. Anne-Marie Marschal could have been watching where the road forked outside of Saint-Jean. She could have followed at her leisure. She would have seen the little Renault behind the whalelike Mercedes, but had not looked at it. There were ten thousand such in France. There was nothing to connect him with it. When he had accompanied her it had always been in her car. When it had come back along the road it had meant nothing, either. The stone had been a rehearsal.

But he had gotten out, and she had certainly seen him. The plan had been a good one. To throw a stone in front of the Mercedes— not big enough to cause a revolution, but enough to cause comment. Curiosity. Anybody would stop, slightly indignant, a little frightened. The chauffeur too would walk up and look in a puzzled way to see where it could possibly have come from, before tossing it over, off the road, so as not to endanger other people. It had been well thought out. There would be a delay of two minutes. Enough to lie down, take a careful unhurried sight—and send a bullet straight into Mr. Canisius' cream silk bosom.

A sudden cold anger flamed in him. She had seen him—and he was the last person she wanted to see. The last person she would have chucked a stone at. Very well. The yokel, the clod, the Dutch peasant, the illiterate snoop from the police was going to climb that slope.

He got into the car, backed it, with a grind and a tearing noise of little stones, and let it go till he reached a patch where he could get if off the road altogether. He took his binoculars and started to walk forward, looking for a good place to climb.

It was not difficult to find her place; all he had to do was to keep looking back till he saw the road from exactly the right height and distance. Near enough to toss a stone weighing a couple of pounds, far enough back to have a comfortable shot; the range was not more than about forty yards. There were three more biggish stones collected, so that his was not, probably, the last rehearsal.

The pine needles had been scuffed, a twig broken. There was a handy branch to rest the gun barrel on. Sitting would be the best shot; one cannot lie well pointing downhill. A naughty little boy might have made the signs he found; a naughty little boy with a slingshot. But he knew it was she.

She must have gone uphill; there was no way back onto the road, or he would have noticed. She had had a good head start. He looked at his watch; it was after eleven already. Canisius would be back about three.

"Anne-Marie," he shouted. "Anne-Marie. It's useless. You won't get anything done this way." His voice sounded thin and impotent, and higher up it might not even be heard. He went on climbing, stopping to use his binoculars wherever he had a patch of open ground to look across. It was warmer up here, where the sun was not filtered through trees, and at the same time colder. The breeze was blowing straight off the snow line.

He never saw her at all. It was a wink of sudden intense light that caught his eye. It might have been metal, but it was more likely the lens on the telescopic sight that caught the sun for an instant and caused a reflection like a mirror. When the shot came, it took him by surprise in a way he would never have thought possible. There was the physical surprise, if you can call it a surprise when something like a huge iron hand from nowhere takes you full swing in the middle of your body and sends you crashing down the slope, in a huddle of limp clothes, with no breath or feeling left in you. Yet before he lost consciousness he had time to register the mental surprise of being shot. She's shot me, he told himself in a querulous, old-maidish voice. The stupid, stupid bitch. He felt pain from a graze on his nose and forehead—he had scraped himself falling.

Little idiot, he thought. What will she do when she realizes she's killed me? She won't go back to her hideout to wait for Canisius now. Probably she'll give herself up to the police. I don't particularly mind being killed, since it had to come sometime. But it is very stupid. Nobody knows but me.

He went under.

"How do you feel?" asked Mr. Lira. He had been taking Van der Valk over one point after another, never in a hurry, never surprised, never critical, writing slowly in longhand in a school exercise book.

"I feel all right. It's not disagreeable—like being a baby all over again. I just wonder how long it all goes on."

"I had a colleague of yours in to see me. They're very filled with concern. They were agitated at your having come running down here, so I had to tell them a few things, which fluttered their pigeons a bit. They'll get a nice long report from me too. They won't be able to say you exceeded your instructions—they simply won't dare. I've also explained the facts of life to your financial friend."

"Canisius?"

"Canisius. You never really got it clear, did you? How he'd worked it out. Why he insisted on you, or someone like you."

"No."

"I read my notes over and thought I saw it. So I made myself a bit scary—rattled chains at him a good deal. I got it out of him. He'd been told to hold himself at the disposition of the examining magistrate, and I sent him a summons. Showed him the bullet—the one we got out of the hillside below you. The one that went through Mrs. Marschal," said Lira dryly, "we left where it was. I put the bullet on the desk, and asked him if he realized how easily it could have made a hole in him. Have you ever noticed? You can't scare the ones with lawbooks—he knew all the law backward; he'd done nothing the least illegal—but if you can frighten them physically, they melt. He got like ice cream in a hot sun."

Van der Valk was entranced. "I mustn't laugh, because it hurts, but tell me."

"Ah. Well, hearing all your tale, reading the report Strasbourg made, getting some dope on this Sopexique from Paris, there were a few points that struck me. The same things that worried you, the same things that bothered Strasbourg. Why was Canisius so insistent on getting a professional policeman? Why was he in such a hurry, when the chap would certainly turn up sooner or later? And so on.

"You've got to see it as a question of character. Canisius understood that couple pretty well. He caused as much friction as possible. From one side, he bored and irritated Marschal as much as he could with all the little petty trickeries and mean expedients the business involved. If a competitor had to be attacked, he brought Marschal into it. If a supplier had to be bribed, he got Marschal to do it. And on the other side, he tickled the woman every way he could, knowing that she would be nagging at Marschal continually to stand up for himself, to fight, to work at the business and get some control of it, instead of standing passive and watching Canisius get the whole thing between his hands. He even let the wife know that the old man in Paris was losing his grip and that it was only a question of time before he and his pals had absolute control.

"Sooner or later Marschal would just turn his back and walk away; the wife knew that too. Neither of them would have been very surprised when it happened. The idea of stirring up the police was simply a move to keep up the pressure on Marschal. The woman, I think, couldn't make it out, not at first, anyhow."

"She was undecided," said Van der Valk, thinking about Anne-Marie in the house in Amsterdam. "She would have liked to put a stop to it, but she couldn't very well. Too official."

"That was just the point. One reason why Canisius went to your boss. He wanted a pompous, official, rigid reaction. Another reason may have been that a professional from the criminal brigade would—just by nature of his training—imagine that there was more to this than he had been told. He would go after Marschal wondering whether he was going to find something fishy. When your bird really ran off with this girl from Germany, it must have been a success past Canisius' wildest dreams. Not only was Marschal behaving in a reckless way, without foresight or judgment, but he even did something technically criminal and stirred up all the police in Germany. Then, I reckon, Canisius was so confident he had it all in the bag, he couldn't resist calling the wife up and taunting her with it."

"No doubt about that. She went haywire," Van der Valk said. "Jealousy as well—she was badly upset by the German girl. When I saw her at first in Austria she was more wild at that than anything else. Then she realized that I was more of a menace than she'd thought. Originally she'd counted on me to find Marschal and get him to come home. Then she started to see me as an ally of Canisius', as a threat. She'd hoped I would lead her to Marschal, where she could talk to him, work on him, patch it all up. She tried to get me to go to bed with her—did I tell you that? When she realized that all she'd done was to make me more curious and more determined to find out what the hell was going on, she lost her head and yelled at him. I think when Marschal saw her at the top of the ski slope it was unexpected, and I think he was a lot more upset at seeing her than at seeing me."

"Her tragedy was that he thought of her as an enemy as great as Canisius," said Mr. Lira. "That was why she shot herself, in the long run. Why she shot you. Everything she touched turned to ashes. Finding that he'd killed himself in bed with that girl was a shock that put her completely off the rails. You know what I thought? Sounds crazy to you, perhaps, coming from someone like me. I think she didn't forgive his not killing himself in bed with her."

"No," said Van der Valk slowly. "I don't find that crazy. Not that there's any explanation needed. They were both doomed. In this world of ours, it's the types like Canisius who win."

"Canisius," said Mr. Lira, with a little smile as he thought about that gentleman. "I really scared him badly. And I got the reaction you'd expect from a type like that. You took his bullet. He's overflowing with conscience money. Not that the flow of generosity will last long," Lira added dryly.

"I couldn't care less about him. Let him arrange all the funerals; pleasant job for him."

"You're wrong, my boy. I know how you feel, but you're wrong. I've talked to your wife. And I've taken the liberty of doing a bit of bargaining on your behalf. Your social security pays your hospital bill, but it doesn't pay you for the pain. Maybe you have a bit of a disability. You get a pension payment— No, no, don't quarrel with me; I'm a policeman myself, I know how these things go. Say they shove you out on pension. How old are you, forty? Have you even twenty years' service? What would you get? Your wife told me. So don't get mad at me; I screwed your Mr. Canisius a bit. The Marschal estate—I have this in writing— will triple any payment made you or your wife."

"What are they saying about me? Total disability?"

"They can't honestly say. They tell me they're eighty percent certain they'll put you on your feet as good as new—or nearly. I know the surgeon pretty well. If he said that, he meant it. It's good—but it isn't quite good enough."

Van der Valk started to grin. "All the same, how the hell did you manage to get a thing like that out of Canisius? He's tough; he can't have been that frightened."

Mr. Lira started to grin too. "Not of me. It was your wife who did it. Nice woman, your wife. I'd asked her to the office when he was there." His grin broadened. "She did fine."

"What did she say?" Van der Valk knew that Arlette, in the push, was capable of anything. Not unlike Anne-Marie Marschal.

"She walked straight up to him," Lira related with great enjoyment, "and said that for two pins she'd shoot him herself. And, what's more, he saw that she meant it. I tell you there's nothing like a bit of physical fear to cut those types down to size."

Van der Valk started to laugh. It hurt so much he had to stop, but it was worth it. "How does it strike you, finally? I made a mess of it. I make a hell of a fool of myself; look where it puts me—in a plaster coffin."

Mr. Lira tucked his exercise book under his arm and shook his head. "Nothing strikes me. What does one ever do, knowing it to be the right thing?" He shook hands. The door opened and he looked up. It was Arlette. "Hello, madame, how are you? No, no, I'm just going. All finished. When you're up"—to Van der Valk—"we'll go fishing." He stopped at the door and snapped his fingers. "There's a phrase I'm trying to remember. La Bruyère. The one they give to tease the philosophy students."

Van der Valk looked blank.

"I know it," said Arlette with a laugh. She had come over to the bed to give him a kiss. "You don't know it, my poor wolf, you're too Dutch. '*Tout est dit—*' "

"Everything is said and we come too late. . . ."

Van der Valk began to laugh again. "We'll drink to that, the three of us. The moment I'm on one foot."

"Shouldn't we invite Canisius?" asked Arlette maliciously.

Five Passengers
From Lisbon

Five Passengers From Lisbon

A CONDENSATION OF
THE BOOK BY

Mignon G. Eberhart

ILLUSTRATED BY BEN WOHLBERG

Death stalks the pitiful survivors of a
shipwreck at sea. First it claims the officer in
the lifeboat with a knife in his back. Then,
after a miraculous rescue by a hospital ship, a
second crewman is found with his throat cut.
A third victim is beaten into unconsciousness
and later shot. And whenever death makes
a move on the fog-shrouded hospital ship,
the man with the bandaged face is lurking in
the background. But he is a badly burned
sailor coming home from Europe after World
War II. What possible connection could he
have with the three crew members from the
ill-fated ship and the five passengers
fleeing war-torn Europe from Lisbon?

Slowly the pieces fit together, revealing a
pattern of deceit and betrayal, telling a story,
by one of America's leading mystery writers,
of men and women pushed far beyond their
limits by the unbearable pressures of war.

Chapter 1

THE three women sat miserably in the cramped stateroom and waited for orders to abandon ship. The stateroom creaked, and the ship creaked and strained and came down in the trough of a wave with a shaking, trembling series of shudders so strong that Marcia held her breath, listening, thinking, Now—now the ship will be torn apart; this time it will go. Its rotten timbers cannot hold together; its rusted bolts must pull apart.

Marcia knew that the others shared her thought. Daisy Belle's thin, fine-drawn, overcivilized face wore a listening look too; and Gili's enormous green eyes slanted to one side warily, like a cat which senses danger. They were three days and two nights out from Lisbon, on the broad, dark Atlantic, and there was no help anywhere.

The stateroom was small and in frantic disorder; bags and boxes were open, with clothing strewn about; they'd had to select quickly the articles they could take on the lifeboat with them. Nobody had taken much, naturally—passports, such money as they had. Daisy Belle had pinned a chamois bag full of jewels inside her brassiere and now sat in sweater, slacks and a mink coat, her thin hair tied up in a woolen scarf, smoking a small cigar.

She had put brandy in the pocket of her mink coat, and more cigars. Gili had given her own battered box one contemptuous look and taken nothing from it; she too wore slacks, and a fur coat which Daisy Belle had given her—another mink.

Only Daisy Belle Cates, thought Marcia, could emerge from five years of warring Europe with two mink coats. And only Daisy Belle would have presented one, casually like that, to Gili. "You may as well take it," she'd said ten minutes ago. "It'll go down with the ship."

Gili was delighted. She gave Daisy Belle one of her avid, darting looks and then snatched the coat and put it on, looking down at herself and stroking the fur, her long yellow hair hanging over her face. "Suppose the ship doesn't go down. Suppose somebody picks us up. Will you want it back?"

A queer expression flickered over Daisy Belle's face. "Then you can keep it," she said, her long, thin fingers working at the bag of jewels inside her brassiere.

"Oh," said Gili, twisting around to get a glimpse of herself in the small mirror over the washbasin. "Of course, if we ever get out of this, you'll have all the fur coats you want."

Daisy Belle's mouth tightened. "I doubt it."

Gili, exactly like a cat, seemed almost to lick her full lips. But then you couldn't really blame her, thought Marcia wearily. In all probability she had actually scavenged for food and clothes. Gili had not talked of her past; she might have sprung into being just as she appeared at the dock there at Lisbon—brightly blond, luxuriantly curved, with a handsome face and bright green eyes. Her blond hair had been dyed and was getting rapidly darker at the part; her eyebrows and lashes were darkened. She had a certain strength that was rather attractive in a queer way, for it went with the frank predatoriness of some small hunted animal. Nobody could enjoy food or warmth or clothing as Gili obviously did, who had not had to go without them. But then Daisy Belle Cates, with all her money and her internationally famous society name, probably had had to scrounge for food too while France was occupied.

Marcia wore slacks and two sweaters and heavy seaman's shoes. If the lifeboat swamped, she wouldn't have a chance with all that clothing, and nothing about the *Lerida*—the tiny Portuguese cargo ship in which they had set out from Lisbon for Buenos Aires—led Marcia to think that the lifeboats would be either adequate or in good condition. But there wasn't a chance to keep afloat, swimming, in a stormy sea. If the lifeboat didn't turn over while they launched it, if it didn't capsize at the first wave, they might drift for days before they were picked up. Or they might never be picked up.

Well, there was no use thinking of that. She went to the mirror and tied her thick red scarf around her neck. The ship lurched and she steadied herself against the washbasin. It brought her very near her own reflection in the mirror and she looked at it with a kind of objective interest. Her face, that she had lived with nearly twenty-five years. She reached for lipstick, pretending she wasn't afraid. How many times had she lipsticked the mouth she saw now in the mirror!

It was a good mouth, warm and sweetly curved. It was a good face, as a matter of fact, very tanned, so her blue eyes with their black heavy lashes looked intensely blue. Her hair was black, smoothly drawn to a chignon at the back of her neck; she wore a snug black beret. She didn't look frightened; she looked puzzled, the black slender arches of her eyebrows drawn together.

Marcia lurched to the bunk and put on her fur coat. She caught a glimpse of the label: Revillon Frères, London, Paris, New York. How queer it was to see that label, proclaiming the existence of another world, incredibly remote. She remembered when she'd bought that coat. It was a crisp fall day in Paris, and she had met Mickey later in the cocktail bar of the George V. They'd gone for a walk in the Bois de Boulogne, with the trees a hazy pinkish bronze, and he'd bought her violets. The Maginot Line was still standing, and outwardly Paris was unchanged. By the time the next fall came around, the Germans were in Paris and Mickey was in a concentration camp and she was in the cold little villa near Marseilles.

MICKEY SUDDENLY opened the door of the stateroom, and as he did so, the ship plunged down into the trough of a wave. Nobody moved until that terrible shuddering and straining ceased. Sluggishly, as if with a great effort, the ship began to climb another wave. Mickey said loudly, "Are you ready?"

Marcia felt a sudden surge of pity for him, he looked so white. It was all wrong that his stubborn struggle for life should have come at last to this. The day—almost a month ago now—that he'd come to her in Marseilles, he had worn a hunted look as if the Nazis were still after him. They weren't, of course; he'd escaped, and now the Americans were in Marseilles and the war was over, but Mickey couldn't comprehend it physically. He knew it in his mind, but his tortured body still cringed. Even in Lisbon he would not believe in his own safety; he still walked close to buildings, listening nervously behind him, his blond head bent, his shoulders slumped and his eyes darting quick glances this way and that. It had made her heart ache to contrast this war-scarred Mickey with the Mickey she had once known—who walked so confidently, smiling and easy upon a concert stage; who bent so effortlessly and yet so full of power over the keyboard. And his hands! She couldn't bear to think of those beautiful, strong, square-fingered musician's hands, now so scarred and mangled.

She went to him, staggering as the ship staggered. Gili slid down from the upper bunk and lurched toward Mickey and seized his lapels in her strong hands. "This is horrible," she cried. "I don't want to leave the ship. I'm afraid."

It was queer how receptive to small impressions one's mind could be in a moment of danger. Marcia thought swiftly that Mickey had learned patience; he had been patient, even kind, with Gili ever since she had joined their small party. Luther and Daisy Belle Cates, herself and Mickey, Gili—all trying to get away from Europe—joining forces in Lisbon because they got passage together on this small, dirty cargo boat, which was now going down.

Mickey said patiently, looking down at Gili, "We've got to leave the ship. The captain says she's going down. Come on."

Daisy Belle put out her cigar as carefully as if she intended to return. "Where is Luther?"

"He's on deck. Hurry."

"I hope he's wrapped himself up. He's had pneumonia twice. And with his heart . . ."

There were sounds from the passageway and somebody ran past, shouting something in Portuguese. Mickey dragged Gili's clutching hands away and shouted above the tumult, "Come on, they're waiting."

Marcia followed Mickey down the dark, narrow passages, Gili followed her, and Daisy Belle came last. They got on deck, and wind and spray and darkness flung themselves upon their faces, so they leaned against the nearest bulkhead. "Keep together!" Mickey called out.

There was no sign of the ship's captain. Voices were shouting all around them; moving figures were blurs of blackness. Marcia felt Mickey's hand and reached backward for Daisy Belle, but Luther came out of the chaos, his thin, bony face vaguely white. "Where's Daisy Belle?" he cried. Daisy Belle's voice rose shrilly, telling Luther not to leave her. There was a clatter as of chains and something bumped hard against the ship. Then seamen were lifting Marcia through the chaos. She landed abruptly in the lifeboat.

She moved over on the seat; Daisy Belle was beside her. Other dim shapes with blurred white faces were in the boat too. Two of them, seamen apparently, were yelling at each other in Portuguese, their voices rough with terror.

"She's going down," screamed Luther in a high, shrill voice. "For God's sake, hurry."

The lights of the ship were tilted crazily; perhaps they themselves were tilted; the whole world resolved itself into an insane pattern of noise, darkness, spray and cold. Daisy Belle said, panting, "Now if they can pull away quick . . . Luther, I'll take an oar."

Mickey was there; quite suddenly he came, lurching, from the roar and crazy quilt of motion. "It's okay," he was shouting. "It's okay. . . ." But they dropped down, down, down, as if there was never any end of that drop; a wave broke; there was salty cold water everywhere. Then some force seemed to come up under the little boat and there was air again in their faces. "We made it," said Daisy Belle harshly.

Nobody knew when the ship went down. If other lifeboats were successfully lowered, they did not know that, either. Their only preoccupation was the darkness, the waves, the cold, the sickening glides down, then the equally sickening thrusts upward. Existence became a matter of clinging to the boat, huddling together, trying to row, trying to bail out seawater. At first, spasmodically, the women tried to help; soon they could only cling to the boat, to each other, fight for air, for life.

This went on through the night. Marcia did not know when she became aware of others in the lifeboat. Alfred Castiogne was there and giving orders about rowing and bailing; he was one of the ship's officers. A sudden flirtation had sprung up between him and Gili on the ship; but probably he was with them not because of Gili but because he was in charge of that lifeboat. He was behind Marcia, at the rudder; she could hear his shouts above the crash of the waves. There were herself and Mickey, Gili, and Luther and Daisy Belle Cates. There were two other crewmen. It was a small boat, but it was not full. She wondered vaguely why more people from the *Lerida* had not accompanied them; but they were the only passengers, so she supposed that the rest of the seamen and officers had taken other lifeboats.

Once there was a sort of lull and Daisy Belle made them drink from her flask of brandy. Marcia's hands were so numb she could scarcely feel the flask. They passed it around from one fumbling hand to another. From time to time the men changed places.

Marcia could just barely see Mickey. How horribly tired he looked! Other shapes were beginning to emerge dimly from the blackness. One of the two seamen, bending over an oar, made a short, thick outline; the other looked thin and wizened and wore a stocking cap. Daisy Belle had taken another turn at rowing and then crawled back to a place near Marcia. Her nose and chin were sharp and gray and haggard. Gili was huddled ahead of them, her head down in her arms. It was getting to be morning; there was a faint gray light showing at the rim of the world. The waves seemed to be abating in violence.

Gradually the darkness was broken into by a faintly red glow way ahead, like a distant fire or the late reflection of a crimson sunset. Only it was toward the east.

It was Luther who first said it was a ship; and then they shifted about confusedly, all of them searching in the dim gray light for rockets. They found them in a small locker and Mickey sent them up. Long streaks of flame curled up above the lifeboat. Sometime about then Alfred Castiogne collapsed; he lay in the stern and Luther and one of the seamen moved him. Luther again took an oar, while one of the seamen, the one with the thick, strong silhouette, huddled over in the dim light and worked on Castiogne to revive him. After a while he gave up and went back to rowing. The ship lay dead ahead and had a strange rosy radiance all about her now, but it was not fire.

Daisy Belle said in a faraway, hoarse voice that mumbled the words, "It's a hospital ship. See the red cross on the side."

Mickey was then just ahead of them. He jerked around toward Daisy Belle. His face looked queer, stony and drawn. His mouth was stiff from cold; his words were barely intelligible. "American? Is she American?"

Marcia could have told him yes. She knew the hospital ships; she'd seen them often at Marseilles. Words stirred faintly in her consciousness, but not strongly enough to induce numbed muscles and nerves to speech. When they were picked up thirty minutes later, Marcia was only vaguely aware of it. She knew when she was slung over a shoulder and carried up a swaying ladder. She knew when they lifted her from a litter to a warm bunk.

The others were in various stages of shock from exposure and cold, except for Alfred Castiogne, who was dead.

He had not, however, died of exposure.

"This man," said the doctor who examined him, looking at the knife wound in his back, "was murdered."

Chapter 2

MARCIA opened her eyes and inspected the small, cheerful cabin. There were double-deck bunks accommodating four people, chintz-covered chairs, a door leading to the passageway, and another, open, to a tiny bathroom; there were two portholes and the light was on, so it must be night again. Then she saw a slipper, shabby, high-heeled, rimy from seawater, lying on the floor. It was Gili's slipper. Then she remembered everything and sat up. Every muscle ached, but she was alive and warm. The miracle had happened; she was still Marcia Colfax, breathing, thinking.

The two bunks directly opposite had been slept in and were still not made up. A tray with empty dishes and a coffeepot stood on the table. Someone had placed a crimson bathrobe across the foot of her own bunk. She was wearing, she discovered, pale gray flannel pajamas which smelled of soap. She reached for the crimson robe, and as she did so, the door opened and a young nurse looked in, smiled and came into the cabin. She was in uniform, beige and white striped seersucker which looked very crisp and clean, and she carried some clothes over her arm.

"Awake?" she said. "I'm Lieutenant Stoddard. How do you feel? I've brought you some clothes."

"I feel wonderful," said Marcia. Her voice sounded hoarse and weak. "I can't believe it. It really is a miracle."

"Not at all," said Lieutenant Stoddard. "People are rescued every day." She put down the clothes, depositing a pair of brown oxfords on the floor. "I'll just make sure you are all right," she said, and came to Marcia and put her fingers on her wrist. "Well, no double pneumonia here. I'd better take your temperature, though."

"Where are the others? Is everybody all right? Is Mickey . . . ?" She suddenly remembered that on the *Lerida* she had had to address Mickey as André in order to square with the papers he was using; but that didn't matter now. If they were on an American boat headed for home, they could tell the truth, explain why he was using a false name and false papers, explain everything and everything would be all right.

The nurse put the thermometer in her mouth and said, "No double pneumonia anywhere. We got you just in time, I imagine."

She must have thought that Marcia's eyes were questioning, for she went on pleasantly. "I expect you don't even know where you are. It's a hospital ship, the *Magnolia*. We are on our way home with wounded and sick soldiers. We picked you up just about dawn; you were unconscious, I think. We put you and Mrs. Cates and the other young lady in this cabin. Neither of them seems to be suffering any ill effects."

"The others . . . ?" said Marcia around the thermometer.

"Quite all right, I believe. We gave everybody treatment for shock. Mr. Cates was the worst off; he had to have digitalis and I don't know what all, but he's all right now except for a cold. Mr. Messac is up and about too. He looks quite all right." She removed the thermometer, glanced at it and said, "Perfectly normal. Now then, I'll get you something to eat."

She gave a little nod and went quickly away. Marcia lay back luxuriously on the pillow. Mickey was all right, then; everybody, she thought comfortably, was all right, and she slipped into a dreamy state which was not quite sleep but near it, so it seemed only a moment before the crisp, pleasant young nurse came back.

It was not until she'd had hot food, the incredible luxury of a hot bath and was dressed—in a nurse's uniform, which luckily fit—that she had any warning that everything was actually all wrong. But even then she did not know that Alfred Castiogne was dead. The nurse only said that the ship's captain wanted to see her.

She had been thinking, naturally, of seeing Mickey. "The ship's captain?"

"Captain Svendsen." The nurse hesitated. "I think it is rather important." Something in the nurse's manner and voice seemed to be evasive.

Five years in warring Europe had given Marcia an awareness of the very breath of danger. She looked quickly at the nurse.

"What is wrong? What has happened? Is it André? André Messac? Is anything wrong?"

"Oh, no, no. Mr. Messac is quite all right. It's only— They'd like to ask you some questions, I think."

Questions? She considered it slowly; but naturally there would be questions: her name, her destination, matters of record.

The nurse continued. "I brought you a nurse's coat, Miss Colfax. I'm afraid yours is ruined with seawater. I guessed at size twelve." She held up the brown, trimly tailored coat with its gay scarlet lining, slipped it around Marcia's shoulders and ushered her into the narrow, gray, glistening passage.

The air was fresh and warm and there was an inviting, floating fragrance of coffee and the clean smell of antiseptics. Doors were open here and there, giving glimpses of other cabins, of a glittering little diet kitchen; then they emerged into a transverse corridor and climbed up a stairway. There were people—corpsmen in white, two medical officers in uniform talking to a transport corps officer. Marcia had a quick view of a sick ward with its rows of double bunks and lights and several soldiers also in crimson bathrobes helping put up a screen for movies. Over and above everything was an indescribable sense of warmth. It struck Marcia with a poignancy that was like a comforting hand. An American ship, a mercy ship, and she and Mickey were on it, safe and cared for and going home.

They reached another deck. Everywhere, above and below, she saw people in uniform going quickly and quietly about their business. "It's a floating hospital," Lieutenant Stoddard said. "We have everything—laboratories, X-ray rooms, three operating rooms. Up this way."

Again they walked along a shining gray passageway, with the motion of the ship seeming to push a little stronger against their feet as they approached the bow and the captain's quarters. The door at the end of the passageway was closed. Lieutenant Stoddard knocked and it opened. The nurse said, "This is Miss Colfax, sir," and a slim young major said, "Thank you, Lieutenant," and held the door wider for Marcia to enter.

It was a small room, paneled, with built-in wooden cabinets; there were deep red leather-covered chairs and a sofa, a rack of pipes, a solid table built crosswise below the square windows opposite and laden with papers and books, photographs and lamps. An open door at the left showed a bunk neatly made up. There were three men in the room and Mickey was one of them. He came to her at once, taking her hand.

"Marcia! Are you all right? They said it was better for you to sleep. I've been worried about you." He was wearing an olive-drab Army uniform, without insignia; he looked white and drawn, but was clean-shaven and obviously rested. "Something pretty bad has happened, Marcia. They want to—"

"If you don't mind, Mr. Messac," someone behind him said rather sharply. A man had risen from a chair beside the table; he was in blue uniform, with the four gold stripes denoting his rank across his sleeve. He was stocky, with yellow hair, eyebrows that were white and heavy, a red, weathered face and narrow, intensely sharp blue eyes. He said, "I am Captain Svendsen, Miss Colfax. This is Major Williams." The young major who had opened the door bowed briefly. Captain Svendsen indicated one of the red chairs. "Will you sit down?" He resumed his own seat and said, "Miss Colfax, did you know the third officer on the *Lerida?*"

"The third officer . . ." began Marcia, puzzled, looking to Mickey for enlightenment, and Mickey said quickly, "Castiogne. I told them, of course, that you had never seen him before we got on the Portuguese ship."

"Mr. Messac," the captain snapped, "I am master of this ship. The responsibility for this is altogether mine."

"You are making it unnecessarily hard for Miss Colfax."

"That is all, Mr. Messac," said the captain. "I'll talk to Miss Colfax alone. Major . . ." He nodded toward the door. The slim young major opened it.

Mickey said, "Oh, nonsense. I'm going to stay. Miss Colfax and I are to be married as soon as we get to America. I have a right to stay."

"You have no right that supersedes mine on my ship, Mr. Messac," said the captain.

Mickey shrugged, started to speak, stopped, finally said, "I beg your pardon."

The captain leaned back in his chair. "I've no objection to your remaining, Mr. Messac, if you'll be so good as to keep quiet. Answer my question, please, Miss Colfax. Did you know Alfred Castiogne?"

"He was on the lifeboat."

"Did you know him before you left Lisbon?"

"I had never seen him before."

"You know, of course, exactly who was in the lifeboat?"

"Why, I— Yes, of course. Myself and—" She had started to say Mickey but quickly substituted, "and André. Mrs. Cates and her husband. Gili—that is, Gili Duvrey. This man, Alfred Castiogne. I think two seamen, but I don't remember their faces and I don't know their names. That's all."

"Who of them knew Castiogne best?"

Suddenly she remembered Gili's flirtation with the third officer. "I think Miss Duvrey saw something of him on the ship. We were only three days out when the storm struck. She couldn't have known him well. If you'll tell me, Captain Svendsen, why you are asking . . ."

The captain leaned forward. "It is no secret, Miss Colfax. This third officer, Alfred Castiogne, was murdered."

It had no reality. She repeated, "Murdered," almost politely, as if she had not heard it rightly.

"He was stabbed," said the captain slowly. "He died of hemorrhage from a knife wound in his back." He frowned and said, "Obviously he was murdered in the lifeboat."

But that, thought Marcia, was the thing they had left behind. Murder. And violence, terror and betrayal. Her hands were digging into the red arms of her chair. Mickey stared silently at the carpet. Mickey, who had seen so much of the blood and horror of Nazism.

"But I don't understand." A small blurred memory of the night returned to her. She cried, "He was rowing! He was directing everybody."

"When did Castiogne collapse?"

"I don't know exactly. I believe I noticed that he had collapsed about the time we sent up rockets."

The captain turned to Mickey. "Is that as you remember it?"

Mickey shrugged. "It's as I told you. I remember thinking that he'd collapsed, and somebody tried to revive him, one of the other seamen, I think. It was about the time we sighted your ship. But everything was very confused."

The captain looked again at Marcia. "Miss Colfax, I want you to tell me everything you can remember of the lifeboat; everything that happened. Start with abandoning the ship. Who put you in the lifeboat? Who sat beside you? Who in front of you? What was said and done? Who saw the *Magnolia* first? Everything."

"I didn't know Castiogne was dead. I didn't see anything."

Captain Svendsen sighed and began again. "Who sat nearest you?"

His questioning, though, had few results beyond the small details Marcia remembered from the night. She told how they had left the *Lerida*; how they had rowed and bailed and hung on to life; the way they had huddled in the boat. She had sat for the most part beside Mrs. Cates, but there had been moving about and change as the men shifted places.

"After you sighted us?"

She thought back as one tries to pierce the convolutions of a long and shifting dream. "Yes. We hunted for rockets. Everybody seemed to shift and move about."

"Castiogne too?"

"I don't remember."

"But it was after that when he collapsed?"

She corrected him. "It was after that when I saw he had collapsed. One of the seamen tried to help him."

"Which one?"

"I don't know their names. He was short and thick."

"Go on."

They had sent up rockets. They had rowed and looked for the red glow that was the *Magnolia*. Somebody—Mrs. Cates, she thought—had said it was a hospital ship. She remembered being carried upward, aboard the *Magnolia*. That was all.

The small sounds of the ship, the rush of distant water, the ticking of a clock on the table, were the only sounds in the cabin. Mickey did not move; his eyes, as clear and gray as the sea, looked straight ahead. The young major stood by the door, his face without expression.

The captain leaned back in his chair again. "Your name is Marcia Colfax. Right? You claim to be a United States citizen?"

"I am an American citizen. My passport—"

"I have it here." He pulled open the deep drawer of the table beside him and then, as if he did not need to refresh his memory after all, closed it again. "You came to Lisbon from where?"

"From Marseilles."

Captain Svendsen reached for a pipe and began to fill it carefully. "How long had you been in Marseilles?"

"Since the first summer of the war. I had gone from New York to France—to Paris—the summer before the war began. I stayed on in Paris that winter. Then when the Germans occupied Paris I went to the south of France. To a villa outside Marseilles."

"You were there all that time?"

"Yes, until about three weeks ago when I went to Lisbon."

"Where is your present home in the United States?" he asked as he lighted the pipe.

She thought of home. It was a flashing picture of the big old house with the wisteria and maples, a picture that had haunted her through those grim and troubled years. She thought of the pleasant high apartment overlooking the park. She said, "Maryland and New York City."

"Why didn't you go directly to the United States? Why did you set out for Buenos Aires?"

"Because we could get passage to Buenos Aires; we would have had to wait to get directly to the United States."

"We?" said Captain Svendsen. "You mean yourself and Mr. Messac?"

Mickey said suddenly, "I've told you all this, Captain. We were going home to be married." He looked at Marcia and she could see he was trying to tell her something, but what was it?

The captain turned toward the table, wrote quickly on a memorandum pad, tore off the paper and held it toward Major Williams. "Thank you, Mr. Messac. I'll not require your further presence," said the captain as the young major took the paper, read the scribbled note briefly and turned toward the door. "Oh, Major, take Mr. Messac to the officers' lounge, if you please. Or his own quarters, if he prefers it."

Mickey, looking white again and strained, said, "But I'd like to stay, Captain. I'll not interfere."

"Please remain here, Miss Colfax." The captain nodded toward Major Williams, who waited for Mickey.

"Very well," said Mickey. He stopped beside Marcia. "Don't let them upset you, Marcia. Castiogne was nothing to you and me. I promise you, darling, as sure as my name is André Messac, that all our trouble is in the past. Forever." He smiled, but his eyes were intent.

She saw then what he'd been trying to tell her. He had been André Messac on the Portuguese ship; he was still using that name, the name on his passport, and wished her to do so. She said quickly, to show him that she understood, "Yes, André, I'll see you when the captain is finished."

As the door closed, Captain Svendsen said, "I don't think you have quite understood the situation, Miss Colfax. There were only a handful of people in that lifeboat. One of you murdered that man. Which one was it?"

Chapter 3

SHE heard everything he said; she did not think beyond the incomprehensible fact of murder. It wasn't possible that during the horror of those hours in the lifeboat another horror had added itself quietly to the night. But murder, if it had existed, was in the lifeboat, not the hospital ship. The seeds of that murder had been sown on the Portuguese ship. She said suddenly, "The two seamen . . ."

The captain rose abruptly, paced across the cabin and back again and stopped before her, looking down. "Almost any one of the people in that boat could, I believe, have managed to stab Castiogne without being seen. You were all confused, preoccupied. Why did you mention the two seamen?"

"Because they knew him; they must have known him. There may have been some . . . oh, some grudge, some quarrel. The rest of us were passengers only."

"In other words, you are deliberately blaming one or both of these men?"

"No, I didn't say that."

"Listen, Miss Colfax, every one of the passengers in that lifeboat has suggested that solution. It is so unanimous a belief on the part of the five of you that one might be inclined to think that you actually knew of the murder and mutually agreed to blame the seamen."

"No, no, you are wrong. Don't you see, Captain Svendsen, how confusing it is, how terribly shocking and—"

He interrupted. "How long have you known the Cates couple?"

"I met them in Lisbon for the first time. That is, of course, I'd heard of them. I knew their name; everybody knows that, I suppose. They were always in the papers."

"Where in Lisbon did you meet?"

"At the hotel, while we were waiting to get some sort of passage."

"What about Gili Duvrey? How long have you known her?"

"She was at the hotel too. I saw her here and there, in the cocktail lounge or the lobby."

The captain lighted his pipe again, with slow deliberate puffs, watching her closely with those bright blue eyes. He smoked for a moment and said simply, "I am the master of this ship. I am particularly responsible because of the load I carry—hundreds of sick and wounded men. It is my job now to see to them. There are two things I can do. I can put you all under arrest and in confinement until we reach home. Or I can induce you to tell me who murdered Alfred Castiogne. I don't propose to let a murderer run at large on my ship. Do you understand me? Now then, why did you not return to America before now?"

Her thoughts went swiftly back over those war years that had seemed so long and so ugly, so filled with terror and despair, so tenuous with hope that Mickey would escape and would come to her—as eventually he did. In fact, of course, it was a very brief story, and not unusual.

"I hoped that—" She caught herself; she must say André Messac, not Mickey Banet; she must remember that. She went on. "I hoped that André would return. He was taken to a concentration camp when the Germans occupied Paris." She paused. So many memories. Marcia's mind went swiftly back five years, to the great gray ship, the *Normandie*, pulling away from the pier on one of her last trips. Marcia's father, on the pier, waving and laughing. It was actually her last glimpse of him. That day had launched the gay holiday voyage during which she had met Mickey. London and humid July weather and Mickey. Paris and August and Mickey. September and war, and Mickey telling her he loved her.

After that, naturally, she remained in France, in spite of the war, in spite of the frantic cables from her father. And then there was the first autumn of the war. She had walked with Mickey, lunched with Mickey, dined with Mickey; listened to Mickey practice at the great piano in his apartment for hours on end, and listened to Mickey and his friends talk of the war. She herself had been lulled as Paris was lulled that winter; but not Mickey, and not a small select nucleus of his friends. All over Paris there were men who believed that they could see ahead; already that winter the seeds of the French resistance were sown.

She had not known actually, however, that Mickey was a part of that beginning movement. Up to then his only interest had been music; he was on the beginning wave of what would certainly have been a great career; he had played in London and New York with brilliant press notices; he was, in fact, returning from a series of American concerts when Marcia met him on the ship. He was then a slender, gay young man, with a tanned face, light sun-streaked hair and gray eyes, which Marcia had always thought were exactly the color of the sea, as deep, as clear, as changeable.

The war had brought the bright world of the 1930s crashing to an end. And it had ended his career. In June the Germans entered Paris; Mickey and three other men Marcia had known were arrested.

Captain Svendsen was tapping the pipe lightly and precisely. He said, lifting it, "You were in Paris, then, when the war began? And you went to Marseilles?"

"I went to Marseilles that summer, after the Germans occupied Paris. I was with a friend—Madame Renal. She had a car and we drove to her villa. It was on a hill just outside Marseilles," Marcia said.

She remembered that flight from Paris. They had all intended to go together. She and Mickey and Madame Renal—the kind, stout old Frenchwoman her father had cabled her to get in touch with. Madame Renal had a car and gasoline, and a villa near Marseilles; she was old and ill and she could not make the journey alone. Otherwise, Marcia would not have gone with her, for at the last Mickey did not come. She would never forget and she did not want to remember that day in Paris, the day of frantic confusion while she tried to find Mickey and in the end gave up and went with Madame Renal. Mickey would find them; he knew where they were going; he knew the address—so Madame Renal assured her over and over again. When they reached the villa, cold with its stone floors, Mickey was not there. A month later she learned that he had been arrested and sent to Germany.

"André finally escaped, just at the end of the war; he knew where I'd be, of course, and came to me as soon as he could."

"Wouldn't it have been better to wait in Lisbon until you could get passage directly home? If your people are there . . ."

It seemed to Marcia for an instant that the man sitting opposite her was bent upon touching all the sore and poignant scars of the past years. She said, "My father died while I was in Marseilles. I learned of it months later through the Red Cross."

There was a slight pause, then the captain said, "I'm sorry, Miss Colfax. Go on, please."

Go on? Oh, yes. Why had they taken passage on the little Portuguese ship bound for Buenos Aires instead of home? But how could she tell him or describe to him her anxiety about Mickey, the urgency of her wish for him to leave Europe. New surroundings, any new surroundings, a fresh start, a different place—these things Mickey had to have, for his soul's sake. His eyes were alight and his face looked young and gay again when he had brought her another man's passport and the news of the possibility of a Lisbon sailing.

She said slowly, "André had suffered greatly; I wanted him to be away from Europe as soon as possible." She hesitated; the passport situation would have to remain as it was—at least until she talked to Mickey and they decided together to tell the truth of it—but there was no harm in telling Mickey's profession. "André, as he may have told you, was a musician, a pianist. Perhaps the Germans knew that; perhaps it was merely one of their unspeakable forms of torture. In any case, you've seen his hands—his fingernails and the ends of his fingers." Her throat grew tense, so she stopped.

The captain nodded, his face hard. "I saw them. I've seen several such."

"I want to get him to a plastic surgeon. I don't think he can ever play again, but there may be some hope. It seemed important to get him home, by any means, as soon as possible."

"I see. Yes, I see that. There may be some hope. Miss Colfax, you are being quite frank with me?"

Mickey's passport was not Mickey's; she had not told him that. There had been, however, no other evasion. "Yes."

Someone knocked, and Captain Svendsen said, "Yes? Oh, Colonel Morgan. Will you come in?"

A tall, well-built man—a patient obviously, for he wore a long crimson dressing gown—came into the room, followed by Major Williams, who closed the door again behind him. Captain Svendsen said, "Miss Colfax, this is Colonel Josh Morgan."

The tall man in the dressing gown turned to her. She caught a flash of intent blue-gray eyes before he bowed and then took the hand she held out—took it, however, with his left hand, as his right arm was in a sling. "How do you do, Miss Colfax."

Captain Svendsen said, "You haven't met before, I take it."

"Why, no. . . ." Colonel Morgan hesitated, looked at Marcia again directly, and said, "Or have we?"

She had met, casually, many Americans in Paris before the war, and in Marseilles after the Americans came. But she would have remembered this man, she thought suddenly; his black hair, the curve of his mouth, his quick, direct look. There was some spark, some extra bit of electricity in the air between them; it was curious, a small and unimportant fact, but a fact. She knew that she'd have remembered him. She said slowly, "No, no, I'm sure we've not met," and Colonel Morgan said, "No, of course not. I'd have remembered you," and smiled briefly.

It was merely a conventional compliment, but it startled her a little because it was so near her own thought. She met his eyes for an instant that suddenly seemed a long time, as if she had met that deep and direct look, unguarded, with no barriers, many times before. Which was nonsense! She turned abruptly toward Captain Svendsen, who said, "Colonel Morgan was a newspaperman in civilian life. He spent considerable time in Paris before the war. I thought you might have met."

Marcia thought swiftly, He is trying to check my story, my identity. Why?

Josh Morgan said shortly, "Paris is a big place."

"Yes," said Captain Svendsen heavily. "Yes. Still, the American colony was not large. There were some other Americans on the lifeboat we picked up, Colonel."

"Oh, is Miss Colfax one of the *Lerida* survivors?"

Captain Svendsen nodded. "There were five passengers," he

said. "And two seamen, besides the man who was killed. The passengers were"—Captain Svendsen's blue eyes watched Colonel Morgan sharply—"Mr. and Mrs. Cates, Americans. Gili Duvrey, French. Miss Colfax, here. And André Messac, French also."

It seemed to Marcia that a flash of something like surprise came into Colonel Morgan's eyes. When he spoke, however, his voice was flat and impersonal. "*The* Cateses?" he asked. "The famous Cateses? I think his name is Luther."

"Yes. Do you know them?"

Colonel Morgan reached for cigarettes and with his free hand managed to extract one. "I know of them. It's a famous name. Tons of money, patrons of the arts, fashionable, smart. Rather decent as I remember. But I never knew them."

The captain sighed and rose. "I won't trouble you further just now, Miss Colfax."

She said, "I haven't thanked you, Captain."

He would have none of that. "Part of my job. Fortunate we happened upon you and saw your rocket. Unfortunately, once we'd rescued you we cast the lifeboat adrift. That was before we knew about Castiogne. So, if there were any clues in that boat, they are gone. Well, that's all, Miss Colfax. Thank you."

Major Williams opened the door. Colonel Morgan made a motion toward her, stopped and said, "I hope we'll meet again."

The door closed behind her and she walked along the narrow gray passage. It was still impossible, really, to comprehend it. Who would have wanted to murder Alfred Castiogne? Who cared, just then, about anything in the world but the next wave, the next pulse of life? She reached the central passageway and Mickey was waiting for her, lounging against a bulkhead, smoking and talking to Luther Cates. Mickey sprang forward.

"Okay, Marcia? Let's get out on deck. Better put on that coat. It's still cold."

Luther looked tired and old, as if the previous night had added years. His face was drawn and gray; there were deep pouches under his pale blue, rather bewildered eyes, but he was freshly shaved and the thin gray hair over his temples was plastered down neatly. He too wore an Army uniform from which the insignia had been removed. He took Marcia's hand in his. "How are you, my dear? I suppose they've been questioning you about this man Castiogne. Well, well, it's a queer thing, of course. I can't understand it myself. I don't remember anything at all that is suggestive; I had no idea he was dead. But obviously one of the two seamen did it. Nobody else would have had a motive."

"How is Daisy Belle?"

"Oh, she's all right. She always says she has the constitution of a horse. More than I've got." Luther coughed a little, and waved to them as they turned toward the deck.

Suddenly the air was fresh and cold on her face. It was night and the sea was black, but the ship was glowing with light. The red crosses painted on her sides and on her smokestack were brilliantly outlined with red lights; portholes all along the decks were lighted; floodlights shone down to give further illumination to the enormous red crosses, those symbols of mercy which had been the ship's protection.

Marcia slipped her arm through Mickey's and they crossed the slippery deck and stopped to lean over the railing. The radiance of the lighted red crosses on the ship touched the black water so that they seemed to move in a glittering track of red and gold light. Mickey said suddenly, "What did the captain say? Did you tell him that I am using André Messac's name?"

"No. No, but, Mickey, we've got to tell them your real name."

He sighed and took out a package of cigarettes. He had never got used to having cigarettes, plenty of cigarettes, all he wanted. He said now again, as he had said so many times in the past weeks, "Cigarettes! Think of it! Real cigarettes! Have one?"

She took it and bent to the small flame in his cupped hands. As she did so, she saw the mangled, twisted scar tissue of the fingers. She wanted to put her lips upon them; she mustn't do that and wound his pride, or let him know how terribly that sight wrenched at her heart. He said, "I wanted a chance to talk to you before the captain did and simply couldn't make one. The first I knew of the murder was when they got me up there in the captain's quarters and I couldn't get away to warn you not to tell them that I'm using a borrowed passport."

"But, Mickey, we've got to tell the truth."

"Tell them who I really am? Why? The passport is all right. They'll never question it."

"No, no, it's not that! It's because— Oh, there are so many reasons, Mickey. For one thing it's— Well, it's the truth."

He smoked for an instant. "You agreed to my idea of using that passport when I suggested it," he said finally.

"Yes, it seemed convenient and much quicker than waiting. It didn't seem important so long as we were not going directly home. I thought that later, at Buenos Aires, when we applied for your visa, we could simply tell the consul exactly why and what happened. But now we are going directly home. The only thing to do, I think, is to tell the truth and make an appeal to the State Department."

"They'll send me back to Europe."

Would they? She wished desperately that she knew more of law. Had they been not only mistaken but criminally wrong as well? She said slowly, "I shouldn't have let you do it, Mickey. You weren't well, you weren't yourself. All that—"

"Listen, Marcia," said Mickey suddenly. "Everybody thinks that Michel Banet, the concert pianist, is dead. Well, then he's going to be dead. I am André Messac from now on. Marcia, for God's sake, pride is the only thing left to me. I *can't* let people know the truth! If you tell them who I am, there'll be nothing but pity and curiosity and failure for me. Michel Banet, they'll say; he could have been the world's greatest pianist. Look at him now. And look at his hands." He spread them out pitilessly as he flung away his cigarette, a tiny red rocket, into the sea.

Chapter 4

MICKEY, Marcia now realized, had intended all along to keep the name of André Messac. Never would anyone really know what had happened to Michel Banet; a new name, a new personality were to be his shield. Knowing Mickey as he had been before the war, and knowing him now, she could not fail to comprehend it. She said out of the silence, "Who was André Messac?"

Mickey lighted another cigarette and squinted at the smoke clouds floating off into the night. "He was one of us," he said. "He was arrested at the same time that I was. He died . . . later. I never knew exactly how or when. But I saw his mother in Paris; she still had his clothes and papers. To make it short, she gave the passport to me, and I knew somebody who could fix it all up with my photograph and visas and so forth. You learn things like that." He paused and then said deliberately, "I never intended to resume my own name. You may as well know that now."

It was, then, as she had guessed. She waited for a moment, seeking words, seeking arguments, and finding none that would avail against that long and stubborn scheme.

"But, Mickey, it isn't practical. People will recognize you. You've appeared in concerts."

"People in an audience never remember the face of a pianist. Nonsense!"

"All your friends, all the people who knew you . . ."

"Marcia, you don't understand. I'll never play again. I knew a very small group of people. Well, all those people are out of my life. I'm André Messac now. When I found you in Marseilles, I didn't want anything except to see you again. I'd thought of you all those years of horror. There were times when I could keep alive only by thinking as hard as I could about you. Well, that's in the past, my darling. I want everything new for us. Everything on a clean slate. No clutter from the past, and no echoes of what I might have become."

"We ought to have gone to America while we still could. I thought of that, so many, many times I thought of that."

"How could I?" asked Mickey simply. "I'm a Frenchman. How could I have gone?"

It had been his argument then. She shivered a little and pulled the thick brown coat tighter around her. And suddenly for a queer, illogical second she wished she could talk over the situation with the tall man in the crimson dressing gown she had met in the captain's cabin—Colonel Josh Morgan.

She was tired; that was the explanation. She felt the need to lean upon someone, and until Mickey was better, she could not lean upon him. Contrarily, she must make herself strong and certain, so that Mickey now, while he needed it, could derive some strength from her. Obviously she could only agree to his plan, fall in with it, until Mickey himself had regained confidence and assurance and his grip upon reality.

She said, however, with odd feminine tenacity, "I think we should tell Captain Svendsen—no one else. I liked him. I believe he'd understand and . . . and help."

Mickey whirled around toward her. "No, Marcia! He'd have to tell. He has to do whatever his duty is. He couldn't conceal my real name; he'd have to report it. You can't say anything to him that would induce him to swerve an inch from his job; that's the kind of man he is. If you tell him who I am, Marcia, everybody will know it." He stopped and searched her eyes almost incredulously. "Does my only chance for a new life mean so little to you?"

"Oh, no, no, Mickey. I love you." She put her hands upon his then, but his hands were cold. His eyes were those of a stranger for an instant, so she seemed to be reaching out toward someone who was not there.

"Well, then call me André, not Mickey. You will, won't you, Marcia—" He broke off as someone else came out on deck.

"There you are," said Daisy Belle Cates. Marcia turned; Daisy Belle and Gili came toward them, both in nurses' uniforms and coats like the one Marcia was wearing.

Gili stopped beside Mickey. Her long golden hair was twisted into a heavy knot on top of her head; her face was without makeup, except for her full mouth, which was deeply crimson with lipstick she had managed to borrow. She said, "What about the murder, André? Do they suspect any of us? Do they think we did it?"

"You saw something of Castiogne on the *Lerida*, Gili," Daisy Belle said. "What do *you* think of it?"

"I know nothing of it!" cried Gili vehemently, her eyes flashing toward Daisy Belle. "Nothing at all. Oh, I talked to him a little on the ship." She shrugged. "He was a man. He talked; I listened. He was nothing to me. Nothing." She paused, appeared to consider her words and then turned to Mickey, linking her arm through his and looking up confidingly and appealingly into his face. "You see, don't you, André? It was— Well, call it a tiny bit of a flirtation; that's all. He was nothing to me. You understand?" She pressed one cheek against Mickey's shoulder and moved it softly back and forth, like a cat rubbing its head, purring and begging for something.

It was, thought Marcia, an instinctive gesture on Gili's part to enlist Mickey's sympathy. Probably in the world she had known she had never been able to put her faith in women's friendship. It was men who ruled everything, and men could be cajoled, men could protect her. All the same, Marcia wished Mickey would move away from Gili. Which was silly; that golden head meant nothing to him. Besides, Mickey was an attractive man; certainly Marcia did not intend to go through life having twinges of jealousy every time another woman looked at him.

Mickey said, "Did he tell you anything about himself, Gili?"

"Nothing at all," she cried. "There really wasn't anything. He talked . . . oh, nonsense mostly." She gave a shrug that this time was more like a shiver and said in a low voice, "I wish I'd never seen him. It's horrible."

Mickey said, "I'm going to talk to the captain again."

"I'll go inside too." Gili hunched up her shoulders. "I'm cold. The sea frightens me. I was sure last night that we'd all be drowned. I'm going inside where it's warm and lighted." She turned with Mickey, still clinging to his arm.

Mickey said, "See you here when I've finished, Marcia."

They vanished into the lighted passageway. And after a moment Daisy Belle said dryly, "A man's woman."

"She can't help it."

"No. Actually she can't," Daisy Belle said. "She was born that way. But I think she'll manage. And there was more to that little affair with Castiogne than she pretends!" She laughed shortly and added, "Not that I think she murdered him. It's merely instinct for her to cling to some man, the way she's clinging to André. But André, if I may say so, is eminently clingable."

Marcia laughed. Daisy Belle's crispness and directness, the very sound of her flat, dry voice seemed to dispel an annoying little cloud. How much did Daisy Belle know about her and about Mickey? How much had those sophisticated, knowledgeable eyes seen and stored away? She said on an impulse, "You've never asked a question, Daisy Belle."

The older woman glanced at her rather sharply. "About you and André? Why should I?"

"Well, but— There we were, dumped down at that grisly little hotel in Lisbon. Traveling together . . ."

"My dear child, I've seen something of the world. You are obviously what you are—a decent American girl who's been having rather a rough time of it. André is obviously what he is too— a man who has had his own share of war and horror. You are both anxious to get away from Europe, to get home, to straighten out your lives. There you are—and I like you. What else is there to know? And if it comes to that, what do you know of me and Luther?"

"Everybody knows about you!"

Daisy Belle's fine profile suddenly looked a little grim against the night. She did not speak for a moment. Then she said, "You mean, it is rumored that Luther and Daisy Belle Cates, well-known members of the so-called international set, are about to buy a house or sell a house, or back a horse, or get a divorce, or—or any damned bit of nonsense anybody can think up? That sort of thing?"

"Well, yes. Only it doesn't seem to fit you, now that I've known you."

"You can't imagine me being one of the ten best-dressed women, can you? Well, as a matter of fact, I wasn't. I only had big dressmakers' bills. Not that any of that matters now. The point is, how did we get here? Well, we were in Paris when the

Germans came. We went to the Riviera. After a while the Germans came there too. They were everywhere." Her elegant, straight shoulders made a little movement of distaste. "Luther was very ill for a long time. We stayed with a . . . a friend, in a château in the hills back of Nice. Eventually the war was over and we decided to go to Buenos Aires. So here we are."

She stopped. It struck Marcia that there was something expectant in her deliberate pause.

Marcia said, "It will be good to be at home."

"Will it?" said Daisy Belle. "I'm sure I hope so. Well—" She stopped again and then said abruptly, "I'm going to find Luther. I do think that this Castiogne person took a very inconvenient time to get himself murdered. But one of the seamen will eventually confess and that will be the end of that." She patted Marcia's shoulder and walked briskly away.

Marcia started to follow her, remembered that Mickey would expect to find her somewhere on deck, and after leaning against the railing for a few moments, she turned and strolled slowly forward. The lighted deck, roped off in sections in the daytime to provide specified spaces for patients, was now clear, so she could walk entirely around the ship.

She crossed the bow and emerged on the port side, and another long strip of brightly lighted, clean white deck stretched ahead of her. About midway along it she paused to lean against the railing and watch the red and gold glitter of light reflected from the shiny black waves. Engrossed in her own thoughts, she did not hear the footsteps coming along the deck aft until they had almost reached her. Then she whirled, thinking it was Mickey.

It was Colonel Morgan. He paused beside her at the railing and fumbled in a pocket with his uninjured hand and drew out a package of cigarettes. "I think I'll have another smoke before turning in," he said. "Will you join me? I'd like to talk to you for a moment, if you don't mind."

He was wearing a uniform with Air Corps insignia. His long Army overcoat was flung loosely around his shoulders. His face was shaded somewhat by his cap, but she caught the brief smile.

"I'm not supposed to be here. I'm a patient, you know. And at this hour every patient is tucked away and accounted for. But they give me a little extra leeway because I drew a two-bunk cabin and the other bunk is empty. Or rather my eagles drew it— the rank, not the man. And then I'm what is called ambulatory. That is, I can walk around and don't require a nurse's care." He glanced down at her, leaned against the railing and said, "Looks as if we're running into fog after the storm. A good thing it wasn't last night. Your rockets might never have been seen."

It was curious how familiar he seemed to her, yet she was sure she had not known him. She found herself leaning against the railing too, companionably, smoking the cigarette he had lighted for her. He added quickly, as if he regretted introducing a topic which must inevitably hold horror for her, "But that's luckily in the past. I assumed from what Captain Svendsen said that you lived in Paris for some time."

Had Captain Svendsen sent him to question her, spy out any secrets she had? If so, he'd find nothing. She said, "Yes, that's true. I was there when the war began."

He smoked for a long moment, staring out toward the black sea and sky. Finally he said, "I was in Paris then. Who were some of the people you knew best? Americans, I mean."

"Why, I . . ." She hesitated; yet probably it was actually quite in order, and quite American; the old business of finding mutual friends. "Not many, really. The war began so soon and most of the Americans went home. Of course there were some people." Slowly she dredged names and faces out of her memory, casual acquaintances, all but forgotten in the intervening time. He listened to each name intently, and again the thought crossed her mind that Captain Svendsen might have asked him to question her. But he was not doing it very expertly or very objectively. It was more as if he had some obscure personal motive.

When she'd finished the unimportant little roll call, he said merely, "The good old business of it's a small world doesn't seem to fit in this case, does it?" He put his cigarette to his lips. "André Messac is not a common name."

Mickey must have returned to the deck by now. She glanced over Josh Morgan's shoulder, but the deck was empty and white. She replied, "It is not an uncommon name."

"No? Well." He smoked for a moment, then added, "Was he around Paris that first winter?"

"Yes. But then the Germans came."

He seemed to be waiting for her to say something more. When she didn't, he said finally, "It's queer, really, to accept the fact that the war in Europe is over. I can't, yet. I know it with my mind, but I feel . . ." Again he paused, looking out into the darkness beyond the rim of light close to the ship, and then said in a harsher voice, "I feel as if there are still things to do." His mouth looked stern and hard; the one hand that lay on the railing had doubled up suddenly into a fist.

"I don't know what you mean," she said. "The war in Europe *is* over."

"Yes, yes, of course. You realize that Captain Svendsen asked me to come to his quarters in order to discover whether or not I knew you."

"Yes. That is, I supposed so. Because of the murder."

Colonel Morgan's shoulders lifted in a quick, easy shrug. "He probably hoped to check your account of yourself. I know about the murder—it isn't supposed to be known, of course—but that's due to my eagles. Later I— Well, I got to thinking we *had* met somewhere. But no, I must be wrong."

Mickey would be waiting. She'd better return to the other side of the deck, to the place where he had left her and would expect to find her again. She moved away from the railing and Colonel Morgan fell into place beside her. They reached the bow, and as they turned, with the sea air strong in their faces, an unexpected small thing happened. The ship thrust into a wave with a sudden heavy motion. Marcia made an unsteady step, wavered, reached for a bulkhead which was too far to touch and Colonel Morgan caught her in his free arm. His hard, warm cheek brushed her own; his arm was tight and strong, so he seemed to be, just for that fraction of time, the only safe and unmovable thing in the night. Then he laughed a little and said rather unevenly, "Okay?"

"Quite. Thanks." Her own voice was uneven too. She pulled herself away, although his arm held her lightly until she was steady and balanced.

He said, "It's always tough going around the bow. Better hang on to my arm."

She slid her arm through his; she felt a little confused, which was silly. Neither of them spoke. It was darker as they rounded the bow, and as so often in the night at sea, there was the strong sense of being alone and very small in an immensity of darkness. They emerged onto the other side of the deck and Mickey was not there. They reached the door into the main lobby and Colonel Morgan said rather abruptly, "I'd better get back to my quarters before I'm sent back. Coming in?"

"Not just yet. I'm waiting for André."

Something flickered in his face, under the bright floodlights; yet there was no definable change in expression. "Well, I'll see you again, I hope. Good night, Miss Colfax." He smiled, touched his cap in a friendly salute and disappeared into the lighted passageway of the ship.

The fog was perceptible now. Gray wreaths floated at the edge of the area of light surrounding the ship and reflected a wavering red and gold haze as the *Magnolia* plowed sturdily ahead through the heavy waves. Marcia could not be sure, but as the mist thickened, it seemed to her that the ship's pace slackened a little—a safety measure, no doubt, in this low visibility. She'd give Mickey three more minutes, then she'd go down to the cabin. She walked slowly along, this time aft.

She passed another, smaller doorway, and strolled into a thick bank of shadow below a rank of lifeboats. It was unexpectedly dark just there; her eyes were adjusted to lights. But she saw then a deeper shadow huddled against the bulkhead near her and stopped abruptly.

The outline became clearer. It was a man sagging down upon the deck. His head was bare, his hand outflung limply. She was on her knees beside him, and it was Mickey.

"Mickey, Mickey."

He didn't answer; his head drooped limply as she moved him. "Mickey," she cried despairingly, and remembered Alfred Castiogne, who was murdered in the lifeboat the night before with a knife in his back.

But Mickey was not dead. His heart was beating; there was a faint pulse at his wrist. "Mickey," she whispered, and thought, I must get help. I must hurry. She lowered his head gently to the deck, turned toward the nearest doorway into the ship and was instantly lost.

Passageways stretched forward and aft and across; there were lights and doors everywhere. She went to the right and hurried along. Which way were the wards? There would be nurses there and corpsmen. She came on a bisecting passage and turned again and found herself among laboratories and storerooms. She doubled back, pushed open a door and found herself on deck. But this time she was on the port side. She'd go back to the starboard side of the ship and Mickey. She ran along the deck and entered the heavy, sudden shadow around the stern.

She groped for a bulkhead to guide her. The fog, cold and misty on her face, was like a curtain further obscuring the shadowy curve of the deck ahead. And very near, there was a curious regularity about the whisper and rush of the waves. Like someone breathing heavily.

She stopped.

Then, with indescribable suddenness, the black water seemed to roar and crash upon her ears, engulfing her, dragging her down across the slippery deck into its own blackness and chaos. Her fighting hands brushed the middle railing, caught at it, missed and caught again, and then there was nothing but darkness.

Chapter 5

GRADUALLY the throb of the engines emerged from darkness and the rush of water and began to beat against Marcia's ears. Light cut through the darkness too and beat upon her eyes. Someone was holding her; she was taking great gulps of air that stung her throat and burned her lungs, and her heart was louder than the engines. Someone was rubbing her hands, saying something she could not understand. She opened her eyes and the light was not half as bright as it had seemed.

A man held her and bent over her. He was in uniform; the coat hung like a cape over his shoulders, so it fell around her too. His cap shaded his eyes, but she knew the face and she knew the voice. Only she couldn't just then say to whom the face and voice belonged, or how she knew. She felt, however, an enormous sense of safety, as if she had been awakened from the chill horror of a nightmare. She closed her eyes again.

He held her against him and said, "Do you hear me? Marcia . . ." It seemed odd somehow that this voice should speak to her just like that, call her Marcia. He said more urgently, "Can you walk? I'll help you. Try to walk." Of course she could walk. She was on her feet, leaning against this man she knew so well and yet somehow could not name.

The light was diffused, coming from misty halos. All around the ship fog lay in thick curtains and reflected the radiance of the red crosses on her sides and on her smokestack, so it touched everything with a soft rosy glow, like firelight. It touched the face of the man beside her. She looked up at the strongly curved mouth and broad chin. The shadow cast by the visor of his cap fell over his eyes. She said in a husky voice, "Colonel Morgan. That's who it is."

"In this way," he said, and held open a door, and suddenly they had left the deck and were in a warm, dry, brightly lighted passage. And she remembered the nightmare.

"I caught the railing. I caught the railing and missed and caught again and someone—"

"Don't talk. I'll get a doctor. It's only a little farther."

They were at a door which was open; she was still half dazed by the warmth and the lights. A man in officer's uniform got up inquiringly from a desk chair and came toward them. Colonel Morgan said rapidly, "There's been an accident."

And another memory of the nightmare came to her. "*Mickey,*" she cried. "He is hurt. He's on deck."

She was on a small white couch; the man in uniform was leaning over her. Colonel Morgan had disappeared. "These slippery decks," said the doctor. "Here, let me look at you. Anything broken?"

She tried to tell him. "He is out there. I tried to get help. Someone was there."

He was busy at a table across the room; he came back toward her with a glass of water and something in his hand. "Take this."

"You don't understand."

"Take this." He held her head up so she could swallow the little pill. He pulled a blanket over her. "Now then, just don't move for a minute. I'll send a nurse in to you. Don't worry." Then he too disappeared, closing the door firmly behind him.

But her mind was clearer; by snatches the whole nightmare was revealed and it was not a nightmare; it was a murderous attack upon her. As it had been upon Mickey. But why? What had they brought from that sinister, harried little lifeboat onto this ship?

She sat up and was pushing away the blanket when the door opened and a nurse came into the room. More time than she had realized must have passed while she groped backward into the blackness of the nightmare. The nurse knew everything. She came to Marcia and said quickly, "Your friend slipped on the deck and was hurt, but not seriously. The doctor who was here took him to the other dispensary to dress his wound. He struck his head against the bulkhead, but it is nothing serious. Do you understand?"

"Someone was there . . . by the lifeboats, in the shadow. I heard something move. I felt it."

"You're not to talk." The nurse smiled. Her face was young and pretty; her eyes were firm. She pulled up the blanket again. "I'm going to sit here by you. Don't talk." Drowsiness and calm seemed to enter the shining room. Marcia's eyes closed heavily against the light and she slept.

When she suddenly was aroused, there was a small, green-shaded desk light on the table at the opposite side of the room. Drowsy from the pill the doctor had given her, she had a confused sense of much time having passed. The nurse was beside her, saying quietly, "Miss Colfax. Miss Colfax."

She sat up, blinking. There were other people in the room. Captain Svendsen was removing an oilskin coat glistening with moisture. Josh Morgan was there too, still in uniform, and another man also in Army uniform—a tall, thin man, forty or so, with a thin face and very intelligent, quick brown eyes, who came over to the cot to put his hand on her wrist. He wore a lieutenant colonel's insignia and the medical caduceus. She had not seen him before, but there was an air of authority about him which was instantly recognizable. He said, "Miss Colfax, I am Colonel Wells. I'm sorry I haven't had a chance to see you before. I've been busy." His fingers were delicate and sure on her wrist. He said, "Pulse seems to be steady enough."

The nurse glanced down at Marcia. "Colonel Wells is our medical commanding officer, Miss Colfax."

Captain Svendsen sighed and sat down. Josh Morgan leaned against an examining table. Colonel Wells said quietly, "Miss Colfax, Captain Svendsen wishes you to tell us what happened to you." He looked at the captain. "I think she's able to talk, Captain. She's had a bit of a shock, I imagine, but that's all."

Marcia glanced at Josh Morgan, who was looking at her soberly, his eyes very intent yet somehow encouraging.

Captain Svendsen ran his hand over his thick yellow hair impatiently. "Now then, Miss Colfax. Colonel Morgan says he found you on the deck, and then found Messac, knocked unconscious. Messac says he slipped and hit his head on the bulkhead. But Colonel Morgan said that you claimed somebody tried to put you overboard. What exactly do you mean?"

She could still feel the movement of a presence in the shadow near her. She could still hear the rushing of the black water in the wake of the ship, far below. She must keep her voice even, tell them briefly and quietly what had happened.

She tried to do so. She had found André—she remembered to say André—unconscious on deck; she had gone for help and become confused; she had come out on the port side of the deck, opposite the way she had entered, had decided to go back to André, had hurried along the deck and, just as she entered the shadow around the stern, had been caught and forced toward the railing.

There was a short silence while Captain Svendsen frowned at her. "Do you mean somebody attacked you? Who was it?"

"I don't know. I couldn't see anything. It happened so suddenly."

"But that would be a deliberate attempt to murder you."

Put like that, in the slow, hard voice of the captain, it was not conceivable; it could not have happened. Yet it was not conceivable, either, that murder had struck in that small, plunging lifeboat. She met the captain's cold blue eyes without speaking.

He said, "See here, Miss Colfax, I cannot believe that any of the ship's staff or personnel, or any of our patients, could have tried to murder you. It is extremely unlikely that anyone of the *Magnolia* should attack you. You do understand this?"

"Yes. Yes, but—"

"In view of the fact that you had a very painful and exhausting experience in the lifeboat, and also that the man Alfred Castiogne was murdered, don't you think it possible that you are only nervous and frightened? Perhaps you slipped, perhaps you struck something there on deck."

"No," said Marcia. She thought of the black water so near it seemed to beat in her ears. "*No.* There was somebody, Captain. It was horrible."

Again there was a small, tense silence. Then Captain Svendsen turned to Colonel Morgan. "You say you didn't see anybody near her when you found her?"

"No. Of course, it was very dark there. I only saw Miss Colfax; or rather I only saw that somebody was there on the deck. I ran to her and picked her up. I thought she'd slipped and hurt herself. The deck is very slippery with the fog."

"You came from which side of the deck?"

"The port side. I thought I'd have a last cigarette before going to bed."

The medical commanding officer gave him a brief, cool glance. "Of course you know you're not supposed to be on deck at this hour, Colonel."

"I know that, Colonel."

For an odd, fleeting instant their punctiliousness seemed too polite and too formal. Then Marcia caught the fractional grins they exchanged. Ranking officers probably conceded certain privileges to each other. Captain Svendsen rubbed his forehead impatiently. He said, "If anybody had been there, Colonel Morgan, is it possible he could have heard you coming along the deck from that direction?"

"I suppose so, sir. Or he could have seen me. I was silhouetted, I imagine, against the lighted portion of the deck. The fog made everything rather hazy." Then he said suddenly, "By the way, Colonel, I suppose you took a look at Miss Colfax. If she was struck . . ."

Colonel Wells looked up quickly. "An excellent suggestion," he said, and came to Marcia. "If you don't mind," he said kindly, and tipped her head back, turning her so the light from the green-shaded lamp fell strongly upon her. Josh Morgan had taken a quick step or two nearer and was looking down into her face. Colonel Wells touched her chin and temples lightly. "Does that hurt? Did you strike your head here . . . here . . . ?"

She could remember only that swift knowledge of motion somewhere near her, and then a crash and roar as if of water, and blackness. "I don't know. I don't know. . . . No, it doesn't hurt."

His sensitive professional hands explored deftly, pushing back her hair, tilting her head again so he could observe her throat. He folded the crisp collar of the nurse's uniform away from her throat and looked for a long moment. Finally he said, "It's hard to tell. Were you wearing a coat?"

"Yes."

"Does this hurt . . . or this . . . ?" Again his deft fingers moved delicately over her.

"No . . . no. . . ."

"The sedative would have dulled any pain. The coat would have protected the flesh." With a queer, thoughtful look on his thin face, Colonel Wells turned to Captain Svendsen. He said, "I think Miss Colfax might take another sedative." He glanced at the nurse. "Will you see to it, Lieutenant? And please see her to her cabin." The nurse nodded. "I'll go with you to the bridge, if you don't mind, Captain. I know you're anxious to get back."

"I'll turn in too, I think, sir," Josh said. "Do you mind if I stroll along with Miss Colfax and the lieutenant?"

Captain Svendsen got heavily to his feet and picked up his oil-skins. "We'll have some coffee sent up," he said. "I've got to stay on the bridge the rest of the night. I've not run into a fog like this since the summer of 1936."

Colonel Wells glanced back from the doorway. "Good night, Miss Colfax. Try to sleep. If you need anything, the lieutenant will be glad to help you."

He disappeared behind the captain. The lieutenant turned on a faucet across the room. Josh Morgan waited without speaking as the nurse came back and held the glass and another small white pill toward Marcia. She swallowed the pill, then handed the glass to the nurse. She said to Josh, "There are marks on my throat."

Josh glanced at the nurse, who quickly said, "Now, now, Miss Colfax, don't try to talk. We want you to get some rest."

Marcia got up unsteadily as the ship rolled, so Josh, who was nearest, put out his good arm to support her. The nurse, her uniform rustling crisply, bent to pick up the red-lined coat, then went to the door.

"Would you be kind enough to pick up my cap?" Josh asked the lieutenant, nodding toward the sling around his right arm. "I'll help Miss Colfax."

His brown cap lay on the examining table. The nurse took it up, waited for them to go into the hall, straightened the blanket over the cot, turned out the light and followed them, closing the door and trying it to be sure she had locked it.

All that took a few seconds. They were perhaps ten paces ahead of her along the passageway when she emerged. Josh, holding Marcia steady with his left arm, said in a low voice which the nurse could not possibly have heard, "There's a queer contagion about murder. Perhaps it is terror of being discovered; perhaps it's . . . something else. The man last night was murdered. You were in the lifeboat when he was killed. If somebody tried to kill you tonight—" He stopped, and they could hear the click of the latch behind them as the nurse tried it. "Don't take any chances. If anybody tried to kill you tonight, he'll try again."

Nothing that had happened since the storm began seemed real; perhaps nothing that had happened since the war began seemed real. Yet all of it had happened. If the attack upon her was connected with the tiny, sinister lifeboat from the Lerida and its occupants, then what about Mickey?

She said, "I have to see André. Now."

The nurse was coming nearer. All around them lay the hushed ship; they neared a bisecting passage. Josh said in a low tone, "Messac was given a stateroom on the deck above your cabin and forward, on the port side—three doors this side of the officers' lounge."

Chapter 6

THE nurse led them along intersecting passages, through doors, across an entrance to a ward, into another passage and another, stopped before one of the closed doors and opened it briskly. The interior of the cabin was dark.

Josh said briefly, "Sleep well," took his cap from the nurse and went away.

The nurse put the coat over Marcia's arm. "Are you sure you're all right, Miss Colfax? Or shall I stay?"

"No, no. Thank you. You've been very good. I'm keeping you from other things."

"I'm on night watch. So I'll go along and get my supper before I go back to my ward. If you're sure there's nothing I can do for you . . ."

"No, thank you." Marcia entered the cabin and closed the door. She'd wait until the nurse was out of sight and then find her way to Mickey's cabin.

Where were the lights? The other nurse had said that Gili and Daisy Belle Cates shared the cabin with her. It occurred to her that they must be already in their bunks in the tiny room and already asleep, for neither of them spoke to her.

It would be better simply to wait for a few minutes until she was quite sure the nurse had gone and then slip out again without turning on the light. She wondered what time it was. Something about the ship, the hushed atmosphere, the quiet, empty stretches of corridors and closed doors had given her a sense of lateness. The nurse had spoken of supper. That would be, she supposed, about midnight, as in a hospital.

She waited, her hand on the round knob of the door, listening and counting. In two minutes, when she had counted twice sixty seconds, it would be safe to leave the cabin without being observed by the nurse. She had reached thirty when an odd thing happened. She had heard no footstep in the corridor outside, but the handle of the door turned under her fingers.

It turned very quietly and very steadily. Unconsciously, her own hand tightened, resisting the pressure. For an instant there was a queer, small combat, one pressure against the other. Then, as suddenly and as silently as it had begun, that stealthy pressure stopped. Her heart was pounding so heavily that she could hear nothing else.

"If anybody tried to kill you tonight, he'll try again." Josh had said that only a few minutes ago. But she was safe here inside the ship, with all its lights, with all the nurses and corpsmen and doctors awake and going about their tasks. With Daisy Belle and Gili in the cabin, so she could call them.

Were they in the cabin? Her fingers still gripped the handle of the door, as if frozen. She scrabbled along the wall with her other hand and touched a switch and the cabin sprang into light and nobody was there.

The bunks were made up, flat and neat. Nightclothes borrowed from the wards—men's pajamas and men's crimson bathrobes—lay across each bunk above the neatly folded blankets.

Where was Gili, then? Where was Daisy Belle? And who had turned that handle so silently and so stealthily and then, aware of her resisting hand, had stopped?

If it had been Gili or Daisy Belle, she'd have knocked or called out. Either of them had a right to enter the cabin openly. Marcia felt she must look into the corridor quickly. Already seconds had passed. She took a long breath and opened the door.

The passage was lighted and perfectly empty. No one moved anywhere along it; no one stepped furtively out of sight into some doorway; there was no sly flicker of motion anywhere.

She would go to Mickey. She dropped the coat on a chair and then, leaving the lights on, closed the door quietly behind her and started along the passage to the right, in the direction of the main corridor and the nearest stairs.

The ship seemed very large after the tiny Portuguese vessel, and again, very bewildering. She knew that she was now in the forward portion of the ship and that when she had entered from the deck to find help for Mickey, she had been aft. She came out into a lobby, and there were bulletin boards, a divan, a door opening upon a lounge, heavy doors at each side leading to the deck. From some office came the subdued sound of a machine—a typewriter or a Teletype. It was a heartening, small sound, indicating the presence of other people.

She climbed some stairs. The port side, Josh had said, and forward. She turned, moving very quietly, as one does in a hospital at night. Through an opening she caught a glimpse of a night-lighted ward. Two corpsmen in white were standing in a doorway, drinking coffee. Marcia turned again, crossed to the left, found a narrow lighted passage there and went along it.

There were rows of closed doors, and at the very end of the passage an open doorway and a lighted room beyond, showing red lounge chairs and a table stacked with magazines. This must be the officers' lounge, so Mickey's cabin was very near. She walked on, and then Josh appeared in the doorway of the officers' lounge and came toward her. He'd changed to pajamas and the crimson bathrobe in which she had first seen him; one sleeve of the bathrobe hung empty. "I was waiting for you," he said. "Messac's room is here." He knocked at one of the narrow gray doors.

Marcia sensed a sudden stillness within the cabin. Josh knocked again, more firmly. There was the sound of quick movement and Mickey opened the door. He was still in the uniform that had been lent him; there was a white gauze dressing across his temple.

"Marcia!" He gave a surprised glance at Josh and said, "Come in," and stood aside so they could enter. Gili was just sitting down on the bunk opposite, perfectly composed, her slanting green eyes bright and curious.

"I expect you don't remember me," Josh said to Mickey. "You were in a pretty dazed condition. The doctor and I helped you to the dispensary."

"Oh, of course, Colonel Morgan. The doctor told me." Mickey closed the door. "Gili—Miss Duvrey, Colonel Morgan."

Gili's eyes were suddenly very luminous and warm. She tossed back a lock of her long golden hair and smiled slowly and leaned forward to put her hand in Colonel Morgan's. He said rather briskly, "How do you do," and let go her hand. "Are you fixed up, Messac?" he inquired of Mickey. "The doctor was just starting to work on you when I left."

Mickey's scarred fingers touched the dressing on his face. "Oh, yes, I'm okay. I've only got a thumping headache. Stupid of me! I was looking for you, Marcia. I got back to the deck where I'd left you. The captain was busy and I couldn't bother him just then, so I wasn't gone very long, really. You weren't there and— Do sit down. Here's a chair."

"There's room here. Sit by me, Colonel Morgan," said Gili. She put her hand invitingly on the bunk beside her.

Josh sat down, leaning forward to miss the upper bunk. Marcia took the chair Mickey had pulled out. She said, "I had walked around to the port side. I met Colonel Morgan and we talked awhile. Then I came back and you weren't there. After a few minutes I walked aft and found you."

"I don't see how I could give myself such a knockout blow. I certainly wasn't tight," said Mickey with a shrug. "It's as if somebody hit me."

The ceiling light cast a white illumination directly down upon them, so every face and every detail was very clear and sharp. Gili was sitting crouched forward a little too, but relaxed and graceful, with her long legs stretched out and one hand spread out on the bunk backward so as to support her. Her hair fell over her shoulders, bright gold at the ends and darker along the part. She was at ease, yet, as always with Gili, there was a suggestion of latent power, of muscles able to spring at an instant's notice, as with a slumberous cat. She was watching now and listening—and shifted just then, gracefully and deliberately, a little nearer Josh.

"*Did* anybody hit you, Messac?" Josh asked.

Mickey's face showed the sharp lines those war years had brought, the hollows around his gray eyes. He went to sit on the edge of the opposite bunk and said slowly, "I don't know. I was walking along the deck. I just suddenly knew I was falling, that I'd hit my head, that everything was black and confused and . . . that's all."

"Didn't you see anybody?"

Mickey shook his head. "I tell you there was nothing." He brooded for a moment and said, "I fainted once or twice. Maybe more. I mean while I was in prison." His words and voice were matter-of-fact and even. His hands, as if they had a secret, frightened life of their own, went out of sight behind him, holding to the mattress. "Everybody did, for various reasons. That's in the past. But that's the way it seemed to me there on deck tonight. I simply blanked out."

Marcia linked her hands on her knee and said steadily, "André, there was someone on the deck—"

Josh cut in. "Miss Colfax had rather a bad experience, Messac. She came inside to get help and then decided to return to you, and on her way around the deck she either crashed into something in the darkness or there was someone on deck who seems to have tried to . . . well, to push her overboard."

Gili gave a queer, small scream and clapped her hand over her mouth. Mickey jumped up and stared down at Marcia. "What happened? Who was it? Marcia, tell me." He put his hand hard on her shoulder. His face was white and drawn.

Josh said quickly, "Oh, she's all right. The doctor looked her over. But it was rather a shock. The point is, if somebody tried to kill her, it was somebody from the lifeboat. At least nobody else on the ship would have a motive. Or so the captain says."

Gili slid out of the bunk in one long, sinuous movement. Her face was glistening queerly and so white that it had a greenish tinge around the shadows of mouth and nose. Her eyes were bright. She cried jerkily, "It is the murderer. None of us is safe! None of— He was killed. Alfred. He was big and strong and . . . then he was killed. Just like that. In a moment, under our eyes, he was killed. We are not safe. We—" Her eyes darted around and around the cabin, her head moved to and fro like a panther's seeking a way out of its cage. "I know who killed him," she said, still gasping and hoarse. "I know why—"

Josh rose suddenly and Mickey said, "Gili, what are you saying? What do you know?"

"What do I . . . ?" Gili's searching eyes reached him and stopped and she caught her full lower lip in strong white teeth and held it so hard there was a tiny smudge of blood suddenly upon it.

Josh said, "Go on. Who killed him?"

"That . . . that American woman did it. The Cates woman. She was afraid of him. She was a friend of the Nazis. Alfred knew it. She's rich. He'd have got money from her. She killed him."

Josh said, "You'd better explain that, Miss Duvrey. How do you know that Mrs. Cates was a friend of the Nazis?"

"Because"—she eyed him sulkily now—"because she was. And he knew it. Alfred Castiogne."

"How did he know?"

Gili bit her lip again, but this time in a perplexed way, as if arranging certain events in her own mind and choosing her words. Then she said, "I was with him. With Alfred, I mean. We heard them talking. It was on the other ship." She looked at the floor. "It was at night." The lines on her face were deeply etched and her skin shone with faint dampness. "If you must know, we were sitting in a lifeboat! They didn't know that we were there; they thought themselves alone."

Mickey said impatiently, "You've told nobody about this before now. This is a very serious accusation. You don't realize how serious. If I were you, I'd keep it to myself."

"Perhaps you are right," she said unexpectedly. "Yes, I'm sure, but it can do no harm. I mean if they *are* Nazis . . ."

"They?" said Josh.

"The Cates two. The husband and wife. They were talking." Her voice sounded reluctant.

Josh said abruptly, "What exactly did they say?"

Gili looked at her hands. "They . . . well, they said at last they were on a ship. One said to Buenos Aires. The other said yes, and they might better stay there forever than return to the United States. Then he said quite clearly, 'We were collaborationists; we were friends of the Nazis; nobody will ever forget it. We can never go home.' And after a long time she said, oh, so softly, 'No one need ever know!'" Gili stopped and examined one fingernail closely. "Then I think they saw us. Alfred made some movement. He understood English, you see; he heard the word Nazi. They were standing by the railing. They were very still for a moment and then they seemed to whisper and they walked away. But I think they knew it was Alfred. So I think they killed him. For fear of . . . of . . ." She hesitated, fumbling for a word.

"Blackmail?" said Josh Morgan.

"Blackmail. Yes, yes. Money from her to keep silent."

"Did he ask them for money?"

Gili's face clouded. "I don't know. I think he meant to."

"Why do you think that?"

"He said they were very rich. And he said to himself, as if he were thinking aloud, something about money; he used the word money. He said they'd never miss it. Then he thought of me, I suppose, and laughed and talked of something else. But that is what happened. She killed him. The husband wouldn't have the courage to do it. He is a mouse, that man."

She hesitated, and then said very rapidly, "So I was frightened when you said someone tried to push Marcia into the sea." She turned to Marcia, flinging out her hands, speaking theatrically, so her words took on a falseness they had not previously had. "I am afraid. Of the Cates woman. She killed him. She did it when she saw this was an American ship. She knew it was going to the United States. If their friends know they were Nazis, if it is in the papers, if anyone tells . . . well, they are finished. Do you see?"

It did not square with anything Marcia had perceived or felt instinctively about Daisy Belle Cates or about Luther. Yet it was consistent with certain other small facts. Daisy Belle had given the extra coat to Gili, and when Gili had said, 'But then, you'll have all the coats you want,' or something of the kind, Daisy Belle had replied with a bleak look on her face that she doubted it. Yet theirs was one of the famous moneyed families and had been for generations. Did she doubt that they would be permitted to claim that money?

There was the care Daisy Belle took of her jewels; not, somehow, as if she liked them as ornaments, but rather as if they might represent the necessities of life. And there was Daisy Belle's solicitude about Luther. She loved him, obviously, and cared for him; but there was something else, something dimly felt that suggested trouble and anxiety.

But mainly there was the fact that they had worked so hard to get passage on the ship to Buenos Aires. With their money and connections, it would have been reasonable to expect them to stay on in Lisbon until their passage directly home and in comfort could have been arranged. Marcia realized suddenly that there had always been to her something a little mysterious about their presence on that ship bound for Buenos Aires.

All those things bore out Gili's accusation in a way that had a certain ugly authority. Yet, to offset that, there was Marcia's belief in Daisy Belle. She turned to Mickey. "Daisy Belle is honest. She couldn't have been a Nazi. Ever."

Gili said with quick anger, "I heard it. That is what I heard. You don't believe me."

. "Oh, yes," said Mickey, his face taut. "We believe you. But"—he moved restively—"accusations, threats, all that. If only there were a little peace somewhere."

"The man was murdered, Messac," said Josh. "Someone attacked Miss Colfax; someone may have attacked you."

Mickey rubbed his face wearily. "I don't really think anyone attacked me. I think I slipped. And as for the Cates couple, I—Well, I think Gili's mistaken; she may have got things confused."

"I didn't," said Gili furiously. "I'm telling the truth."

Mickey said quickly and peaceably, "I didn't say you were lying. I only meant it's better not to do anything hastily."

Gili subsided with another sulky flash of her green eyes.

Josh said, "If whoever murdered Castiogne thinks that you saw it, Messac, or have evidence against him, he might attack you, or Miss Colfax, for the same reason. Don't you think we should tell Captain Svendsen Miss Duvrey's story?"

"No," cried Gili, rousing abruptly and changing her mind again. "No, I won't. I'm afraid to. You made me tell you, but I won't tell the captain. I won't tell anybody. I'll deny it if you do."

"Please wait," Marcia said to Josh. "We can't do anything to-night anyway."

"What about the two seamen?" Josh asked. "Who are they? Where are they? There were two seamen in the lifeboat, isn't that right?"

"Oh, yes." Mickey looked at the Air Force colonel somberly. "I asked Captain Svendsen about the two seamen. Their names are Para and Urdiola. The captain questioned them first. He arranged quarters for them with the seamen of the *Magnolia*."

"Still at liberty, then," said Josh.

"Yes," said Mickey. "I suppose so."

Josh started toward the door. "We'd better all go to bed," he said coolly. "It's very late. As to the Cates couple, I don't know. There may be some mistake. Let's wait."

Mickey put his arm lightly around Marcia, who was now standing. "I feel sure you are right about Luther and Daisy Belle," he said. "Besides, anything you say is right with me."

Gili gave a short, hard little sound very much like a snort and flounced out of the cabin. Josh said, "Good night, Messac. By the way, doesn't Cates share this cabin with you?"

"Yes," said Mickey. "I don't know where he is. I suppose he'll be along soon."

"It's odd that he is not here," Josh said slowly. "I mean, the decks were searched. He wasn't in the officers' lounge when I was there just now."

"Oh, he's somewhere around," said Mickey. "We've all got a Cates bee in our bonnets."

"Maybe," said Josh. "But there aren't really many places to go on a ship." At the door he said, "I'll stroll down to your cabin with you, Miss Colfax. I'm going that way."

He wasn't, of course. His stateroom was in quite another section of the ship. But he had found her, as Mickey had not found her, there on the black and foggy deck. He was at least partially convinced, as Mickey was not, that someone had been there, that someone had meant to murder her.

Marcia said good night to Mickey and went along with Josh.

Gili had gone on ahead. The skirt of her uniform fluttered swiftly around the end of the passage. Why had she been in Mickey's cabin? How long had she been there? And where was Luther? And Daisy Belle?

They reached the central passage and a bell sounded clearly, yet far away somehow, as if striking against the curtain of fog. Josh said, "One o'clock. It seems later."

When they reached the deck below, a typewriter was still clacking busily away in some office. "Who shares your cabin?" Josh asked. "The luscious blonde? Anyone else?"

"Mrs. Cates."

"Oh." They crossed the main passage and entered the narrow one. This time she counted and recognized her own door. He paused just before they reached it. "Look here," he said, his eyes very direct and intent. "You're going to be okay, you know. Only remember what I said. If anything, anything at all, seems wrong to you or the least bit odd, run. Run and yell like hell. There are always people around."

He hesitated, and added, "I hope you don't mind my asking, but you and Messac are to be married, is that right?"

Marcia said rather stiffly, with an odd sense of crossing some boundary, "Yes. We— That's why we were going home."

"By way of Buenos Aires?"

"Yes. We could get passage; otherwise we'd have had to wait."

"Of course," he said after a moment. "I see. Well, here we are." They reached the door to the cabin. He said good-night pleasantly and impersonally, and turned quickly away.

The cabin was still lighted. Daisy Belle Cates, in gray pajamas, lay in her upper bunk, smoking thoughtfully. Her thin red-gray hair was done up in little tight wads of curls and tied with a piece of white gauze dressing. Any other woman would have looked ugly and grotesque; Daisy Belle even then had an irresistible air of elegance and dignity. Gili was in a corner, undressing furiously, flinging off her clothes, her face sulky and angry.

Daisy Belle said, "Oh, there you are. I was beginning to worry. I turned in ages ago, right after I talked to you up on deck. Did my hair and went straight to sleep." She yawned. "I don't think I'll ever quite catch up with sleep."

Marcia thought with a kind of sick stab, But you weren't here, Daisy Belle; you weren't here when I came back and you weren't asleep and you're lying. Why?

She could not question her just then. It was Gili who, hurling out the words jerkily, told Daisy Belle what had happened. But in the telling, Gili, either intentionally or unintentionally, gave an account of her own actions during the two or three hours just past.

"I was in the nurses' lounge," she said. "I was there all evening. That is"—she bent to strip off a stocking—"for an hour or so. Then

I strolled around to André's cabin. He wasn't there and I waited.
I didn't know anything about it until he came with his head bandaged. It was terrible."

Daisy Belle, sitting up, her face shocked, cried, "*Marcia!* I
can't believe it! Are you sure it really *was* somebody? I mean,
well, not just nerves and imagination?"

Marcia said yes, she was sure. She turned to hang up her coat
beside Daisy Belle's in the shallow closet. Daisy Belle's coat was
damp and dark around the shoulders, as if wet with fog.

They did not talk much after that. Gili crawled into pajamas
and then into the bunk opposite Marcia's. Marcia undressed
quickly too and turned out the lights. In the silence the ship came
to life, sighing, throbbing, steadily forging ahead.

Just before she went to sleep, a memory of the night, a small
thing unnoticed at the time, came floating out into Marcia's consciousness. When Josh Morgan had found her there in the fog,
he had called her Marcia. "Do you hear me, Marcia?" he had
asked, and held her. It was as if he had known her, somewhere,
for a long time. It was as if the sense of security in his arms was
an old and familiar one too.

But that, she thought suddenly and sharply, was like disloyalty
to Mickey. She loved Mickey; she was to marry Mickey, not Josh.
She turned on her side and fell into a deep sleep.

Chapter 7

THE fog entered the ship.

It was kept out of the sick wards—lights and warmth and activity kept it at bay. That morning was, so far as the wards were
concerned, exactly like any other. The nurses in their crisp beige
and white striped uniforms went briskly and quickly about their
routines. Breakfast trays, which hooked neatly onto the sides of
the bunks; charts, baths, the doctors' rounds; jokes and good
spirits on the part of the patients.

But the rest of the ship was at the mercy of the fog. It crept
into the main passageways, it darkened the day, it permeated

everything. The decks were gray and slick with moisture. The *Magnolia* proceeded slowly, through a gray wall which ever yielded and yet ever enclosed. That morning the foghorn began to sound at long intervals. It woke Marcia.

It was late, and Daisy Belle and Gili had apparently dressed already and left the cabin. By the time Marcia had had a shower with all the fragrant soap she wanted and had dressed in clothes that were fresh and attractive, she began to doubt things that were not sensible, that were outrageously out of place. If Castiogne had been murdered, one of the seamen had done it and, by then perhaps, had confessed. Daisy Belle was no more a Nazi than she was a man-eating tigress. The hand that had silently turned the doorknob had belonged to somebody mistaking that cabin for another. Gili had been in Mickey's cabin simply because she was Gili and she'd wanted to talk to Mickey and had done so.

Marcia was even ready to accept Mickey's accident as an accident, and nothing more. And if the attack upon her had been what it seemed, then it was obviously one of the seamen, afraid for some unfathomable reason that she had seen him kill Alfred Castiogne. She combed her dark hair back to a smooth roll, low on her neck; she put on lipstick, a gay, soft red which made her blue eyes seem more deeply blue. She caught up the nurse's coat again and went down to breakfast. Everything was going to be all right.

The mess hall was a large, low-ceilinged pleasant room—white walls, white ceiling and red chairs. The nurses ate at two long tables at one end, the officers at two round tables at the other end. A mess boy brought her orange juice, and pancakes with butter, and all the milk and coffee she wanted. She was finishing when Major Williams, the young officer who had been present when the captain first interviewed her, came into the room, saw her and came forward. The captain, he said, would like to see her again. But she must finish her breakfast, he added politely.

The sense of well-being still held good. She smiled at the young major, finished her coffee and went with him.

The captain was waiting for them and he looked tired. His

ruddy face had a grayish tinge; there were deep pockets around his eyes. "Please sit down, Miss Colfax," he said. "Bring in the two men, Major."

Major Williams ushered in two men. They were small, dark and active-looking, with suspicious eyes. One was thin and wizened, like an elderly monkey; the other very short, thick and sturdy. Their swarthy faces were faintly familiar to her, but only that. She stared and they stared.

"These men were in the *Lerida* lifeboat," said Captain Svendsen. "Their names are Manuel Para and José Urdiola. Now then, was it either of these two men last night?"

The two men shifted uneasily. She felt embarrassed under their dark scrutiny, but she looked at them, thinking back, trying to dredge up some distinguishing mark, some sound, some clue. She shook her head. "I can't tell. There was nothing I can remember. But someone—"

The captain cut in. "You told me that one of them tried apparently to revive Castiogne." He glanced at the sturdy-looking man and said shortly, "Para, step forward."

He did so quickly. "Yes, sir."

"Was it this one, Miss Colfax?"

"I think so. I could not see his face."

Para burst out in fluent and vehement English, "But, sir, I told you. I tried to revive him, yes. I did not know he was dead. I thought exhaustion, yes. A collapse. I told you—"

"That's enough," said the captain curtly. He nodded at Major Williams and said, "Take them away." Para, looking worried and angry, followed the other, who had said nothing. Major Williams closed the door smartly after them. Then the captain said to Marcia, "What do you know of the Cates couple?"

She stiffened. Had someone already told him Gili's story? She replied warily, "I met them in Lisbon while we were waiting for a passage."

"What do you know of them before they reached Lisbon?"

Suddenly and disconcertingly she remembered Daisy Belle's words: "We stayed with a . . . a friend, in a château in the hills back of Nice." What friend? *And why had Daisy Belle lied,* apparently so pointlessly, the night before?

For an instant she felt that the captain could read her thoughts. She said quickly and firmly, "They were caught in France and remained there. He was ill. I think they lived somewhere along the Riviera."

He leaned forward, resting his elbows on the table, his blue eyes impatient. "Look here, Miss Colfax. I've no time for evasions. I want you and everybody else on the lifeboat to help, not hinder, my investigation." He shoved back his chair and got to his feet. He was reaching for his oilskins. "I'm going back to the bridge," he said. "I'm risking my ticket to leave it for a moment in a fog like this. Think it over, Miss Colfax. Try to remember details— about the Cateses or anyone else." He held the door open for her, then walked faster than she along the passage and disappeared around a corner.

Thinking again of Daisy Belle Cates, it seemed unfair to give her no chance to defend herself against the nagging little questions in Marcia's mind. There could be a dozen reasons for Daisy Belle's absence from the cabin the previous night, a dozen reasons for the damp coat, a dozen reasons for a misstatement—all of them innocent.

She came to the main lobby. No sign of Daisy Belle. Marcia wanted to talk to Mickey too; probably he would be on deck outside. She put on her nurse's coat and climbed the stairs again to the lobby of the boat deck. Still she saw none of the *Lerida* survivors. She went out, and instantly it seemed to her she entered a remote and secret world. The fog was everywhere; the ship seemed to lie still in it, unmoving. The railings were beaded with moisture. She could scarcely see beyond them. Gili was standing at the railing. She too wore a nurse's thick, warm coat. Her golden head was bare and looked rather lank and wet. She turned and saw Marcia.

"Oh," she said. A flash of expectancy in her face changed to quite frank and open disappointment. "Oh, it's you."

Marcia said, "Have you seen André? Or Mrs. Cates?"

"No." Gili's voice was sullen. She tugged at a pocket, got out a cigarette case and clicked it open. She held it out to Marcia. "Cigarette?"

"Thank you, I—" Marcia stopped.

The case was Mickey's. She knew it and remembered it well— the thin, plain gold, the design around the edge. She stared at it and saw, besides the case, tables in restaurants with rose-shaded lamps, tables along the walks, below the bronze-leaved trees of the Bois. She could almost hear the squawking taxis and smell liqueurs and coffee.

She said stiffly, "Where did you get that?"

Gili licked her lips and said, "Oh, that. The case. I . . . I borrowed it. It belongs to Mickey." The fog was so close it seemed to drift between them. How odd, Marcia thought. She knows his real name. Mickey.

Then Gili's green eyes changed, and Marcia could see the change. Gili shrugged and looked away. Marcia said, in a voice so queer and hard she did not recognize it as her own, "Where did you know him? How long?"

Gili shot a sideways glance at Marcia. She said, "All right. We may as well understand each other, you and I. I knew it would have to be sometime. Mickey belongs to me. He only came back to you for your money. We wanted to leave Europe, you see, and we have no money." She smiled. "He knew he could get enough for both of us from you."

Someone came rapidly along the deck behind Marcia. She heard the quick, hard tread and saw the flash of relief in Gili's face. "Why, Colonel Morgan," cried Gili. "How nice." Her voice was eager, her face alight, but her eyes avoided Marcia's. Josh stopped beside them.

"Hello," he said, looking at Marcia and then at Gili.

Gili said quickly with a nervous giggle, "I'm going inside. The fog is too cold. See you later." She hunched her coat up around her neck and slid away across the deck and inside the ship.

"Now what's all that for?" said Josh. "She's scuttling away like a scared cat. What's she done?"

Marcia moved so she avoided his eyes, so he could not see her face. She was conscious only of a deep inner stillness, as if everything about her had stopped.

It wasn't true; it couldn't be true! Gili was lying. She had to be lying. Mickey loved *her,* Marcia.

The man beside her said gently, "Come and walk with me, will you? Have you had lunch? It's past time, you know."

"I had a late breakfast," she replied automatically. The railing was wet and cold under her hands, but it seemed just then the only fixed point in her life.

Josh put his hand over hers. "Look at me. What's that woman done to you?"

She stared down at his hand. It was big and warm and well shaped, with a small seal ring on the little finger. Then she thought of Mickey's hands—fine and square, with their pitiful scarred fingertips, fingertips that had once been so strong and fine, the fingers of a musician. Gili had lied.

Josh took her hands from the railing and tucked one of them under his arm. "I've got to have a walk. Come along." She could feel the texture of his sleeve, the hard warmth of flesh and muscle below it. She moved along beside him, as if he had wound her up and set her in motion. They reached a sheltered spot beside a projecting bulkhead where there was a steamer chair. "Come on," he said, "sit here."

She said stiffly, "I've got to talk to Mickey."

"All right, all right. Anything you like. I'll get him for you. Only just for a minute or two, stay here. Are you warm?"

She was in the chair. He leaned over to tuck her coat around her chin, then sat down on the foot of the chair. "Don't talk if you don't want to. I'll do the talking. How about my life story? Let me see. Well, I was born in California, I went to school in Massachusetts, studied law at Columbia and got a job writing for a newspaper. Then I went to Paris and got another job. . . . You're not listening to me. Well, it isn't very interesting, really. Listen, Marcia, that woman's a little wharf rat. Don't let her hurt you like that." He leaned over suddenly, quite near. "I can't bear it," he said. He put his arm around her, holding her close, as one might gather up a child. Only then he kissed her, turning her face with his hard cheek, feeling for her lips. His mouth moved away a little but she could still feel its warmth and tenderness, and he kissed her again.

After a long time, time enough for the world to be remade, he lifted his face. The long, deep blast of the foghorn sounded, prolonging the moment, holding them both suspended in time and space as they searched each other's eyes.

The last echoes dwindled in the fog. He said slowly, "I didn't know I was going to do that. I didn't mean—" He broke off abruptly, then said, "That's not true. I did mean it. I meant it since I saw you there in the captain's cabin. I meant it since—" Again he stopped; this time he released her so she lay back against the chair. Her breath was uneven; all the stillness inside her had been driven away. "So you see, I can't let anyone hurt you like that. Besides, I don't think he's worth it. I mean Mickey, André"— he paused, and added quite slowly, quite deliberately—"or whoever he really is."

She had said Mickey. She remembered it clearly. "Did I call him Mickey? It's a . . . a nickname."

"I see," he said. "Do you want me to find him now? Shall I tell him to come here?"

Now? she thought. Face Mickey now, ask him about Gili, hear what he might say? She took a long breath. "Yes, please."

He waited a moment, as if to give her a chance to change her mind, then briskly he got up. "All right. I'll not be long." He walked rapidly away along the deck, turned abruptly at some door and went inside without looking back.

The fog, after he'd gone, seemed to come closer. It was extremely quiet there on the deserted deck. The white planks were slippery and wet, the brass and metal glistened with moisture.

She wondered where Josh would find Mickey and what she would say and why she had let Josh undertake such an errand. When she heard footsteps coming slowly along the deck, she looked up quickly, thinking it was Mickey.

It was, however, Luther Cates strolling along toward her, his hands in the pockets of an Army overcoat which was much too large for him, a black beret pulled over his forehead. He looked tired and ill, with heavy pouches under his faded blue eyes, but he smiled when he saw that she was looking at him.

"Hello," he said. "I hear there was some excitement last night. I got back to my cabin just after you'd gone. Found André all bandaged up. It seems so inexplicable, somehow. I don't understand why anybody would want to attack you. Do you have any possible explanation for it?"

She shook her head and he answered for her. "No, I'm sure you can't have. But who was it? Who was it that knocked out André, and why? Of course, he says he's not sure whether anybody hit him or not. But it seems reasonable to think that somebody did. I suppose he might know more than he's admitting. . . ."

There was a question in his hesitation. Marcia said quickly, "He doesn't know what happened. He thinks he may have slipped. I'm sure if he knew anything about it he'd tell the captain."

"Well," said Luther, rubbing his eyes wearily, "I think so too. The captain, naturally, thinks it was somebody from the *Lerida*, if it was anybody. I mean"—he amended it quickly—"I believe you; I know you. He seems a little skeptical, however. He had me up this morning to question me. I think I convinced him that I hadn't gone around all night bopping my friends." He laughed, and Marcia, unwillingly yet irresistibly driven by some impulse she would not have wished to name, said, "How did you convince him?"

"By being in the engine room with his first officer all the time the ruckus was taking place," said Luther. "Daisy Belle prowled the ship, she says, looking for me. She thought I ought to have been in bed. But it was warm down there and I'm crazy about engines. Always have been. I might have done something about it if I hadn't had so much money. Well, well, I'll just go along and get a bit of exercise before Daisy Belle catches me and sends me inside." His tone warmed, as it always did, when he spoke of Daisy Belle. He gave a thin chuckle, which turned into a cough, and started back along the deck again. Marcia watched him go. So Daisy Belle had prowled the ship looking for him.

It explained the dampness on her coat. It gave her an alibi which, to Marcia at least, was a very real and complete alibi, for Daisy Belle cared for Luther as if he were a child. And in speaking to Marcia, obviously, she had simply never thought of mentioning so usual and probably so brief an errand. Marcia's own short return to their cabin had happened to coincide with Daisy Belle's search for Luther. That was all. It might not have satisfied the captain; it did satisfy Marcia.

She would put everything else out of her mind, including Gili's story. Gili's words were merely words, without a basis of any sort of fact. Everything about what she said was absurd and confused and—and all wrong.

At least something, somewhere, was wrong. Something outside emotion; something within another province, as if a small segment of a familiar picture had been turned askew, placed inaccurately, so all at once the whole picture was rather puzzling and strange. She tried to seek out that obscure wrong piece, pin it down, decide exactly how it was wrong, but she could not.

The fog seemed thicker and darker; even the sky seemed to press down blackly, smothering the ship. The foghorn sounded again, isolating the ship in sound as she was already isolated in fog. Mickey did not come. Josh did not come back. Considerable time must have passed. And suddenly Marcia didn't like the empty, cold deck and the fog. Inside the busy ship were lights and warmth and people; she rose and then saw that someone was standing on the deck, leaning against the railing—a patient, obviously, for he was wearing a crimson bathrobe. The decks were forbidden to patients that day owing to the fog, she thought.

Apparently he had only then come out on deck. She'd have to pass him to reenter the ship by the same door from which she had come. She looked along the deck in the other direction, orienting herself.

She was on the upper boat deck, on the same level as the

captain's quarters. To reach her own cabin she'd have to go to the next deck below. Only a short distance away from her, toward the right, was a stairway which must lead downward to that deck. She glanced again at the man in the bathrobe, and as she did so, he turned a little and she could see the glimmer of white bandages about his head. She did not wish to meet his look; she did not wish to pass him. She turned abruptly toward the open stairway leading to the deck below.

The foghorn sounded and its clashing echoes died away. The small thud of her heels seemed very loud in the silence that followed. She felt that the man at the railing was watching her. Without definable reason, she hastened her steps so as to pass quickly out of his range of vision.

She reached the last wet black step on the deck below and stopped, holding the railing. The deck was horribly inhabited. The foghorn began again, shaking the ship and the impenetrable gray world about her with dreadful tumult. It kept on sounding while Marcia stood looking down at the dark, swarthy little man who lay with his eyes no longer suspicious but closed in death. He was Manuel Para and his throat had been cut.

A very long time seemed to have passed when suddenly she knew that someone was coming down the stairway immediately above her. She looked up. It was the man in the crimson bathrobe. He had no face, only white bandages, with slits for eyes and mouth.

And it was strange, she thought in some remote level of awareness, that there was something familiar about the way he moved down the steps toward her. It was almost as if she knew him.

Chapter 8

THE foghorn stopped. The patient in the crimson bathrobe had, in a swift second or two, come nearer. Marcia turned and ran. She screamed too, without intending to do so, but no one could hear, for the foghorn started again.

She reached a companionway and whirled into the lighted ship.

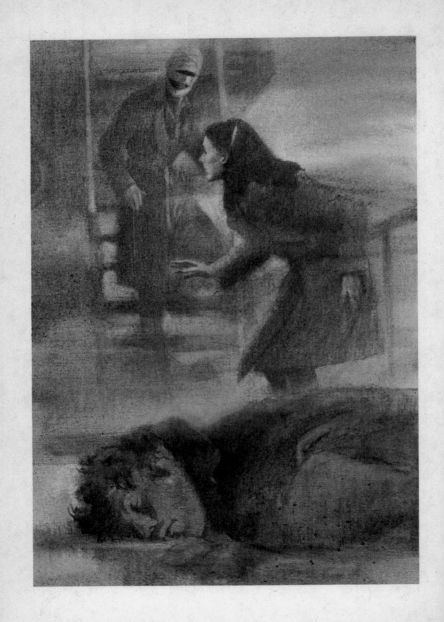

Two nurses in smart little caps seemed to float out of the lights. They said things to her and instantly there were people and voices everywhere.

The scene dissolved and shifted like a dream. She was in a small office, in an armchair with chintz cushions. A nurse with a captain's bars on her collar was beside her, saying, "Now, now, it's all right." But it wasn't all right, because someone came to the door and whispered to the nurse. Marcia watched her pretty young face lose its color, turn pinched and white. She cried, "Who was it? It can't be! *Murder* . . ." The nurse closed the door and said stiffly, "One of the seamen was killed, Manuel Para. He was in the lifeboat with you. I have to go check the wards. I'll send someone to you." Suddenly she was gone.

Why was Manuel Para murdered?

Marcia closed her eyes and immediately it was as if she were in the pitching lifeboat again, with a dead man, with Manuel Para and the other seaman, with herself and Daisy Belle, Gili and Luther and Mickey, dim shapes in the night, huddled together.

A long time must have passed when the door opened at last, and it was Josh Morgan. He lifted her up and held her against him. "Marcia, Marcia . . ." He was real too, like the neat little office, like the homely pleasant details of living, except this reality was much better. She was alive and warm and safe. She clung to Josh and could not talk.

He seemed to know that. He put his cheek down against her face and held her until her breath came evenly, until the warmth of his embrace had shut out the cold of the lifeboat.

"All right now?" he said at last. "I ought not to have left you alone."

He had gone to find Mickey. Suddenly she remembered that, and Gili and everything that had gone before. She could see Gili's slanting, triumphant green eyes and smiling red lips, and the soft golden shimmer of Mickey's cigarette case.

Josh said, "I didn't find André. He wasn't in his cabin. I looked and— Marcia, what happened? Was anyone with you when you found him?"

321

"No. Except the patient. He was there by the railing. He followed me down the stairs."

"*Who* followed you down the stairs? Tell me everything."

But there was not much, really, to tell. A patient leaning against a railing; a dead man on the deck below; the patient descending the steps above her. She hesitated, and added, "I thought for a moment that I knew him. But I couldn't have known him. And I screamed and ran."

He held her suddenly tighter. "That was what I told you to do. Run and yell like hell and— Listen, Marcia, what was there about him that you recognized?"

"Not anything, really. There couldn't have been! His face and head were bandaged. It was all so quick and confused. I can't be sure of anything."

"But it was a man? You are sure it wasn't— Well, Gili? Or Daisy Belle Cates?"

She hadn't thought of that.

Josh looked gray. He said, "We'll go to the captain." They left the little office and hurried through the ship—a ship that was vastly different. The news had spread like wildfire, and there was already a hubbub of swift and controlled activity. Groups of armed men were searching, leaving no inch of hiding place unexplored.

Marcia and Josh reached the door of the captain's quarters. It opened and Mickey started out, saw them and stopped.

"Marcia!" He was pale and excited; he took her hand and drew her toward him. "Marcia, where have you been? Are you all right? I tried to find you."

Behind him Captain Svendsen said, "Come in, Colonel Morgan. You too, Miss Colfax."

Colonel Wells, the medical officer in command, was there too. The room was shadowy, except for a light on the desk which threw the captain's weary face into sharp relief. "I was about to send for you, Miss Colfax," he said. "Tell me exactly what happened." So again she told her story. When she had finished, the captain and Colonel Wells exchanged a long look.

"There is a patient with a bandaged face on this trip, isn't there, Colonel?"

Colonel Wells cleared his throat. "Right. He's Navy, an enlisted man. If I remember the case correctly, his face is burned. He was on a destroyer which was torpedoed. He got the burns—bad facial burns and paralyzed throat muscles—swimming through oil that was on fire."

"I think I've seen him on deck."

"He's ambulatory; nothing the matter with him except his face and throat. He'll eventually have plastic surgery and skin grafts. However, he shouldn't have been on deck today. No deck privileges were granted, owing to the fog." Colonel Wells cleared his throat again. "Besides, it may not have been him. There are hundreds of red bathrobes—every patient has one. And I suppose anyone could get hold of some gauze and wrap up his face. It would be an excellent disguise for a man or for a woman."

The captain's eyes were like pins of light, impaling Marcia. "Was it a man or was it a woman?"

"I thought then that it was a man. I suppose it could have been a woman."

"Was there anything familiar about him? His height? The way he walked? The way he carried his arms?"

"I don't know. I don't know anything about him. Except that he was there."

"Have you seen the patient Colonel Wells mentioned?"

She had seen hundreds of patients, but she could not remember any whose face was bandaged, except the figure on the stairway. She said so quickly. Colonel Wells moved to the telephone. "I'll check on this man," he said. They listened to his terse questions. He said finally, "Tell him to report to the captain's quarters at once. Send his records along with him."

He hung up the receiver and turned toward them. "His name is Jacob Heinzer. He's not in a ward, he's in one of the cabins. Ambulatory, as I said, and perfectly able to take care of himself. Matter of fact, I've never even seen his face. The present bandages won't be removed until he gets to the surgeon."

The captain's bleached eyebrows were drawn somberly together. "What about the knife? No weapon was found; it was doubtless thrown in the sea."

"From the wound, I'd say it was a sizable knife. Not a pocketknife. But it could not have been taken from any of the surgeries or dispensaries," said Colonel Wells flatly. "That is impossible. The cases are sterile and locked."

The captain looked thoughtfully at his red, strong hands. "We'll have to try to establish the approximate time of the murder, try to investigate from that basis. You examined the body, Colonel?"

"Right. But I can't say to the minute when he was murdered, Captain. At the time I looked at the body, I'd say he'd been dead more than half an hour but not much over an hour. There were no other wounds, no marks of struggle. I'd say the murderer took him by surprise."

"That's an hour's leeway," said the captain. "It's a wide margin of time on a ship, with people coming and going constantly." He turned again to Marcia. "How long were you on the boat deck before you found Para?"

"I don't know exactly. I went there directly from here."

He glanced at his watch. "That must have been about two hours ago. It has been nearly an hour since the murder was reported. According to Colonel Wells, then, Para might have been murdered during the time you were on the boat deck. Surely Para could call for help; surely he would struggle. It seems incredible, Miss Colfax, that you, sitting on the deck directly above, heard nothing."

"There was the foghorn," said Josh suddenly. "It drowned out every other sound. I was on the boat deck too, talking to Miss Colfax."

"When?" said the captain.

Josh told him. He wasn't sure about the time. But he had met Miss Colfax and Miss Duvrey. Miss Duvrey had gone inside. He and Miss Colfax had strolled aft and talked awhile.

"Where did you go then?"

"Inside. I was in the lounge when I heard of the murder."

The captain eyed him thoughtfully for a moment and then turned back to Marcia. "You talked to Miss Duvrey while on deck and to Colonel Morgan. Anyone else?"

"No. That is . . ." She'd forgotten Luther; she amended it. "Luther came along."

The captain seized upon it instantly. "Luther Cates? Where had he come from? The deck below?"

"He was walking around the boat deck. I saw him come toward me."

"From what direction?"

"Forward."

"How long did he talk to you?"

"A few minutes. Five or ten."

"Where did he go?"

"Along the deck aft."

"How long was this before you discovered Para?"

"Perhaps twenty minutes. I wasn't thinking of the time. It may have been longer."

The captain reached impatiently for the telephone. "I want Mr. Luther Cates. Announce it over the PA. Yes, here in my quarters."

Colonel Wells said, "We'll have to investigate everybody's movements for at least an hour, Captain, if we hope to establish any alibis. Frankly it seems to me an impossible undertaking. Anybody could have done it and escaped notice. To attempt to establish alibis for nearly a thousand people seems to me"—he shrugged—"a monumental task."

"Six," said the captain bluntly, "would satisfy me."

Marcia's thought touched them all, listing them: herself and Mickey, Gili, Luther and Daisy Belle Cates. And the remaining Portuguese seaman, Urdiola. Perhaps everyone in the room counted with her, but only the colonel spoke. "That's right," he said, avoiding Marcia's eyes, avoiding Mickey's, looking only at the captain. "Six."

Someone knocked on the door, and it was a patient in a crimson bathrobe, with bandages over his face and head, concealing them entirely. A nurse was with him.

There was a moment of silence in the cabin. Then the captain said, "Come in, Heinzer. Come in. Now then, Miss Colfax, can you identify this man?"

The nurse gave the patient a little push forward and he walked slowly into the middle of the cabin and stood there, surveying them all with that hidden, shadowed gaze. Marcia, her heart hammering, watched him. What had the captain asked—his height, the way he walked, the way he carried his arms?

There was nothing. He could have been the figure on the stairway; he could have been anybody and anything. He was completely anonymous. She met the captain's waiting eyes and shook her head. "I can't tell. There's nothing . . ."

"All right," the captain said. "Take him away. Will you question him outside, Colonel?"

The colonel held out his hand for the thick envelope which contained the patient's record. The nurse gave it to him and then put her hand on the arm of the tall figure in crimson. They reached the door, the little procession of nurse, patient, doctor, and suddenly the patient seemed to try to speak. There was a hoarse, rasping whisper of sound; his hands moved. The nurse urged him into the passage and the door closed behind them. I can't tell, Marcia thought sickly; I don't know. And if it wasn't this man, then it was one of us.

For a moment the captain sat hunched forward, staring thoughtfully at his hands. "There's only one course for me to follow," he said. "I cannot take chances with lives under my protection. But as much for the safety of the *Lerida* survivors as for other reasons, I'm putting every person who was on the *Lerida* lifeboat under guard."

He reached for the telephone, but Marcia did not hear his orders, for she was thinking again of the inexorable link of circumstance that seemed to hold the survivors of the ill-fated little Portuguese ship together. It was like a chain; it was like a rope from which one of them might hang.

Colonel Wells returned as the captain put down the receiver. He closed the door and advanced briskly into the cabin. "His name is Jacob Heinzer. He's a naturalized American citizen, thirty years old, born in Argentina of French parents, living in New York since he was twenty." He put the patient's record down on the table near the captain. "He says he knew nobody from the *Lerida*. He only knew that some survivors had been picked up. He says he was not on deck at any time during the day. He says he was alone in his cabin and knew nothing of the murder until I told him. Here's his record if you want to look at it."

The captain glanced at the envelope and then up at the colonel. "Do you believe him?"

The colonel shrugged. "I don't know. I have no reason not to believe him."

"That is not an alibi," said Mickey suddenly. He had been silent so long that everyone turned quickly toward him.

"No," said the captain. "That's not an alibi. Do you know anybody by that name?"

Mickey shook his head. "Not to my knowledge. Certainly he would have had no motive in attacking me and Marcia. Unless it's a case of war nerves, something like that."

"Is that possible, Colonel?" asked the captain.

Again Colonel Wells shrugged. "Anything's possible. He seems all right to me, however. Except for his wounds."

"How about you, Miss Colfax?" the captain asked Marcia. "Ever heard that name before?"

"Not so far as I know. Certainly I cannot think of any motive that anybody might have for trying to murder me."

Josh stirred suddenly. "Captain," he said, "if I may interrupt. Obviously the person on the stairway either wished to be seen and thus reported by Miss Colfax, or intended to murder her. If the former, it was obviously a disguise. If the latter, she is in very definite danger."

The colonel said slowly, "So she would report it. So that a man in a red bathrobe and bandages would be suspected, you mean, Colonel Morgan, instead of the real murderer."

There was a knock at the door and the captain said impatiently, "Come in, come in."

It was Luther, his faded eyes anxious. "Somebody said you wanted to see me, Captain."

"Close the door. Now then, one of the *Lerida* seamen, Manuel Para, has been murdered."

"Yes, I know." Luther glanced at Marcia and smoothed his scant hair nervously. "It must have happened about the time we were talking. Do you know who did it, Captain?"

"That," said the captain bluntly, "is why I sent for you. You were on deck about that time. Did you see Para?"

"No," he said soberly. "After I spoke to Miss Colfax, I walked on around the deck and then inside the ship. I was lounging around the lobby of the upper deck—which I suppose you call the boat deck—when I heard of the murder." He hesitated, and then lifted his stooped shoulders in a brief shrug. "I have no alibi, Captain, if that is what you want."

"It would help," said Captain Svendsen dourly. "I'll have to have statements from each of you." And again there was a knock on the door. This time it was Major Williams, followed by three other officers.

The captain, with Colonel Wells's assistance, gave them quick directions. The *Lerida* passengers were to be placed under guard. The decks were to be searched again, the patients carefully checked. Inquiries were to be made about a patient with a bandaged face having been seen about the ship. Inquiries were to be made about Manuel Para—who had seen him, where, when.

The group around the captain broke apart. An officer went to Mickey and Luther and all three moved toward the door. The captain went quickly away too, adjusting his oilskins with impatient hands. A young lieutenant said curtly, "Will you come with me, Miss Colfax?"

So she went along the narrow gray passageways again, with the lieutenant at her elbow. When they reached her cabin, a seaman with a revolver strapped at his waist already stood in the passageway. "I've searched the cabin, sir," he said quickly to the lieutenant. "I did not find any sort of knife. No gauze, either. But there are three red bathrobes."

"Thank you. I'll report it."

The young lieutenant opened the door, motioned Marcia to enter and closed the door firmly behind her. Daisy Belle was already in the cabin, pacing up and down its narrow length, smoking nervously. "Marcia!" She came quickly and put her hand on Marcia's shoulder. "Is it true? Did you find him? They made me come here. I was in the nurses' lounge and they sent a seaman to find me. He searched the cabin." She caught her breath. "Who did it? Who killed him? What did you see?"

Daisy Belle took Marcia to the bunk, drew up blankets around her, asked the guard for hot coffee and got it very quickly. Marcia, staring at the gray underside of the bunk close above her head, told again that short and ugly story.

"*Was* it the patient?" asked Daisy Belle.

"I don't know. I couldn't possibly say."

"Heinzer," said Daisy Belle blankly. "Heinzer. I never knew anybody by that name."

Gili flounced into the cabin, her face both angry and frightened. She flung herself into a chair with a furious and baffled look at a young officer who had escorted her there, and who now settled his blouse around his shoulders with a suggestion of relief and left hurriedly. She saw the coffee and helped herself to it, looking at Daisy Belle and at Marcia over the edge of the cup.

The rest of that day passed in waiting and inactivity, except that Daisy Belle and then Gili were questioned by the captain, who came with Major Williams to their cabin. The captain told them he had questioned the others—the three men and Marcia.

"Tell me, please, exactly what you did today," he said to Daisy Belle. "Where you were, who talked to you, everything."

"I see," said Daisy Belle after a moment. "We are all suspect. Very well. I'll try to remember." She had had breakfast early. She had gone on deck for a cigarette or two, found it cold and dismal, drifted back through the ship and eventually to the nurses' lounge, where she had found some magazines and read. She had gone to lunch, had looked for Marcia there and didn't find her.

Neither the captain nor Daisy Belle glanced at Marcia, yet

somehow, irresistibly, she had to explain. "I was on deck," she said. "I'd had breakfast late. I did not go to lunch."

Daisy Belle had returned to the lounge after lunch and read again until a young officer came to find her. He told her of the murder and the captain's orders for her to return to the cabin. She paused, and then added, "Any number of nurses were in and out during the time. Some of them must remember seeing me."

Gili's green eyes flashed. She cried, "Oh, you are afraid! That is a . . . what do you call it . . . ? It is legal. A legal word . . ."

Daisy Belle gave Gili a fraction of a glance and said coolly, "Never mind. You know what it means, all right."

The captain's blond head jerked around toward Gili. "What about you? What's your story?"

Gili replied with unaccustomed meekness. "I didn't do anything, really, all day. I went on deck and walked and then I had breakfast. A nurse took me down to the salon. And then I . . . oh, I went around over the ship, looking at things, talking to"—she lifted one shoulder in a ghost of a shrug—"talking to this one or that one. Nothing much. They all seemed very"—a shade of discomfiture crossed her face—"very busy," she said somewhat regretfully. "So many handsome men too."

Daisy Belle's mouth twitched. The captain said, "Continue, please. Where were you when the murder occurred?"

"I don't know when that was. I know nothing."

"When you heard of it then?"

Gili glanced at Marcia. "I had met you on the deck. You remember?"

"I remember," said Marcia.

Gili went on rather hurriedly. "And then . . . you remember, the handsome officer, the colonel, came. And I . . . oh, I thought you might wish to be together, you and he. So I . . . I went into the ship. And in a few minutes I . . ." She hesitated. Her eyes slid to Marcia and then away. She caught her lower lip in her teeth for a second, then said, "I met André and we went on deck, that is, on the other side, the . . . the left—"

"Port," said the captain automatically.

"We were there smoking and talking for an hour or longer. A long time. Then, well . . ." She shrugged. "People were running. We heard about the murder."

Daisy Belle said dryly, "The word is alibi, Gili. I felt sure you understood it." And Marcia thought, So Gili went straight to Mickey after making the claims she had made. What had they talked of, there in the fog, for an hour or more?

Major Williams said, "That agrees with André Messac's statement, sir."

"I know." The captain turned to Marcia. "Does that square with your opinion about the length of time that passed while you were on deck and after you spoke to Miss Duvrey?"

"Yes. That is, I wasn't thinking of time. It seems about right."

The captain went on. "Since it is not likely that two murderers are on this ship, I have to conclude that the person who tried to kill Miss Colfax, and who attacked Monsieur Messac a few minutes earlier that same night, is the person who succeeded in killing Castiogne and, today, Para. So far I can find no motive linking you together. If any of you knows of anything of the kind, it is your duty to tell me. Now." He paused then, and the silence in the little cabin seemed fraught with things untold.

Yet there was nothing more that Marcia could tell him, except, of course, Mickey's real name and identity, and that had nothing to do with the two murders, or with the attack upon Mickey and herself. She looked at Daisy Belle, whose fine-drawn face was lifted frankly and openly, but who also did not speak. She looked at Gili, who was equally still, but whose look suddenly to Marcia seemed secretive and listening. She thought swiftly, Why is she listening; what does she expect me or Daisy Belle to say? And then Marcia knew.

Gili had accused Daisy Belle and Luther of being Nazis. To Marcia, at least, it was an impossible story to accept. She thought that Mickey and Josh found it equally difficult to credit. Certainly all three of them had tried to persuade Gili to tell no one else; certainly, so far, Gili had let herself be persuaded.

But suddenly that very acquiescence seemed somehow wrong.

It was not like Gili. It was as if something in a familiar picture had swung suddenly awry. And that thought brought her to another. Sometime not long ago (just before she'd walked down the stairs, wasn't it, and found Para?) something else had suddenly and obscurely seemed wrong. For a moment there had been that same troubling sensation of some very small thing that was askew. Whatever it was, it had eluded her. She could not pin it down and identify it.

She could, however, with Gili now. It would have fitted the picture of Gili if, under pressure of the investigation into murder, she had blurted out her accusation of the Cateses again. She did not do it and that was wrong. It was not so easy, though, to understand why.

The pause had lengthened. Captain Svendsen's bleached eyebrows were drawn heavily together. Suddenly he whirled around and walked out of the cabin without another word. Major Williams gave them a worried glance, mumbled something and followed the captain. The door closed and they heard the click of the lock.

Night came early, due to the fog. It was curious, thought Marcia, to realize that all around them the busy life of the hospital ship went on. But in the cabin there were only the faraway throb of the ship's engines, the feeling of motion and the distant sound of the foghorn. And the three women, shut up together, each thinking her own thoughts.

Eventually, speaking only at intervals and then saying nothing, they got into the three narrow bunks. Daisy Belle turned out the light and there was only the soft shaft of faintly crimson light coming from the porthole opposite the door. For Marcia the darkness, the wail of the foghorn, the lap and rush of water outside, all merely served to heighten and sharpen the questions that seemed to fill the cabin as if they had substance.

Morning dawned gray and chilly, with the fog, if anything, heavier and the foghorn sounding at three-minute intervals.

It was that morning early that Urdiola was charged with murder and the other *Lerida* survivors were released.

Mickey came to the women's cabin when they were having breakfast. His eyes were bright and eager, going from one to the other of the three. He said, "Urdiola killed them both. He's arrested and"—his clear, light gray eyes fastened on Daisy Belle—"he's got your diamond, Daisy Belle."

Daisy Belle stared at Mickey and, forgetting her tray, jumped up. The tray clattered to the floor, and Daisy Belle cried above the clash of china, "But Castiogne had my diamond!"

Chapter 9

DAISY Belle sat down on Gili's bunk. Her face was gray, her eyes blank. She said, "I gave it to Castiogne. That is, Luther gave it to him. It was to pay for our passage. It was a bribe."

Mickey, bending over the spilled dishes, said, "Yes, of course. That's what Luther told them. He recognized it at once. And after due consideration we were all released. They just haven't got around to informing you three yet."

Daisy Belle said, "Tell me what happened. Tell me."

Mickey sat down on Marcia's bunk, directly opposite Daisy Belle, and drew Marcia down beside him. "Well, it's a short story," he said, "but a convincing one. Naturally it looked from the first as if Castiogne's death and then Para's were actually the result of some sort of private feud among the three *Lerida* crewmen. They questioned Urdiola at length yesterday. He said he hadn't even seen Para since early yesterday morning, but they weren't satisfied. They searched his bunk and found the diamond."

"Did Luther"—Daisy Belle was gripping her hands hard—"did Luther identify it?"

"Of course, right away. Urdiola broke down immediately and said that Para had given it to him."

"Para gave it to him!" cried Daisy Belle. "But it was Castiogne . . ."

"He said that Para, yesterday morning early, had given him a little packet and told him to hold it for him, and if anything should happen, to send it to Para's wife. The captain asked why

Para did that, why did he think he was in danger, and Urdiola said he didn't know. Oh, his story is very thin."

"Do you mean"—Daisy Belle was leaning forward, her face an anxious, lined mask—"do you mean that the captain believes he murdered both Castiogne and Para for the diamond? *My* diamond," she said in a tone of horror.

"There's nothing else to think," said Mickey. "Urdiola is a stupid fellow. Only a stupid fellow would try to get away with a story like that." Looking searchingly at Daisy Belle, Mickey went on. "It is a very large and very fine gem. I had a look at it. The captain sent for me and Luther immediately to ask us if we knew anything of it. What's only a trinket to you, Daisy Belle, is a lifetime of ease to a man like Urdiola. It's a sound motive for murder, all right."

She moved her lips but did not speak. Mickey continued. "They believe that Para murdered Castiogne for the diamond and that Urdiola knew it and in his turn murdered Para for the same reason. Either that, or Urdiola murdered Castiogne for the stone and Para knew it and wanted to split with him—threatened him maybe with disclosure unless Urdiola came across with part of the proceeds. Of course, Urdiola insists that all three of them were the best of friends. Particularly Castiogne and Para. He says they were boyhood pals, inseparable."

"Has he"—Daisy Belle wet her lips—"has he confessed?"

"Oh, no. He has barely the wit to stick to his story and deny murder. He'll keep on denying it, I suppose. He just stands there and shakes his head."

"Where is Luther?" said Daisy Belle.

"Still with the captain, I imagine."

Daisy Belle picked up the nurse's coat, flung it around her shoulders and turned to Mickey. "Are we really free? Will the guard stop me?"

"I don't think so."

The guard didn't stop her. Perhaps he had, as they talked, received orders to let them go. Daisy Belle's coat flashed through the door and she was gone.

Then Gili, who had not spoken, got up, hung her coat around her shoulders and gave Mickey a swift glance. "I'm going out to get some fresh air," she said. "I've been shut up in this hole too long." She put her hand on the door and paused, as if she were waiting, her green eyes holding Mickey's.

But Mickey leaned back against the bulkhead and shoved his hands in his pockets. "It's foggy out," he said.

For an instant Gili waited. Then, as Mickey did not move, she said, "I'll be on the boat deck," and left the cabin, closing the door hard behind her.

Marcia said, "Mickey, she wanted you to go with her!"

"Nonsense," said Mickey, lounging back and staring absently at the bulkhead.

"But she . . . she almost demanded it. As if—" She was about to say, As if she had a right to demand it. She stopped the words on her lips.

And Mickey said in an absent, careless tone, "Oh, Gili's always that way."

Something was in Marcia's throat, swelling and beating. She waited for a moment, looking at Mickey, who still stared absently at the bulkhead.

"*Always?*" said Marcia finally.

And Mickey said, "Always quick-tempered. Always going off on tangents. Hard to manage—" He stopped abruptly and his clear gray eyes focused and sharpened. He turned to Marcia quickly. "That is," he said, "she seems so to me."

Marcia said, "How long have you known her, Mickey?"

"But you know. She was in Lisbon. What do you mean?"

She swallowed hard. "Tell me the truth, Mickey. She has your cigarette case. She called you Mickey."

"Don't be a fool! I don't know Gili at all, except on that damned little ship, and before that I saw her around the bars in Lisbon. If she's got my cigarette case, she—" He got up and stood above her, his hands thrust in his pockets. "She may have taken it, borrowed it, I don't know. I don't remember. If she knows my name, you told her."

"No, no, Mickey, I didn't."

"What did she say? Did she call me Mickey? Then she's heard you call me Mickey. I've begged you not to."

"She said—" Her voice sounded tight and harsh; she made herself go on. "She said that you came back to me because I had some money, enough for you and her."

His eyes were suddenly bright and fixed with anger. He did not speak for a moment, only stood there looking down with that angry brightness. Then he cried, "You believed her! Marcia, how could you? Have you questioned her?"

"This is between you and me, not Gili."

His face cleared. He cried, "You are right, darling! You are always right. Gili doesn't matter."

She said slowly, "Mickey, you spoke as if you'd known her a long time. As if the things she said could have been true."

"Marcia, listen to me. You've known me for five years, Gili about five days. And you'd take her word against mine?"

She put back her head and met his eyes. She said directly, "Are you in love with her?"

"In love with Gili!" cried Mickey, and then laughed. He took her hands and kissed them lightly. "You're jealous. You know that I love you. I came back to you." He looked straight down into her eyes with his own clear, gray gaze and said, "I'll get Gili. I'll make her take back whatever silly things she has told you."

"No." Marcia got up and faced him directly and angrily. "No. If I believe you, Mickey, I believe you. I don't want to talk to her. If we've been released, let's get out on deck. I feel as if I'd been in this cabin for a month."

"Right," he said. "It's a relief to have the thing settled. I mean Urdiola."

She found her coat and he took it from her hands. "Suppose he didn't do it," she said unexpectedly.

Mickey frowned. "Don't suppose any such thing. Besides, there's no doubt of his guilt. That diamond is a huge and, I should say, a very valuable stone. Shall we go?"

He held open the door. The seaman on guard had gone. It

suddenly seemed extraordinarily pleasant to be walking along, free to come and go without restraint. They emerged on deck and it was still foggy and cold and the foghorn smote raucously upon their ears. It stopped and Mickey said, "Of course, I can't help remembering that other nonsensical story Gili told us. You know, about the Cateses being Nazis. But undoubtedly that was just another of her notions. You—" He reached for cigarettes and held the package toward her and did not finish until he had held a match too for her light. Then he said, "You didn't tell anyone about it, did you?"

"No. I didn't believe it."

He smiled and gave her a glance of reproach. "Yet you believed Gili when she told you all that stuff about me! Marcia, Marcia!" He shook his head gaily. "Nevertheless, it flatters me. But you were right about the Cateses. An accusation like that is a very unpleasant one; it sticks. Denial never catches up with accusation. I never knew them, but I knew *of* them. Everybody knows of them. I don't believe that they were Nazis. I think that we should just forget Gili's little story. Never tell anybody." He took a long breath of smoke and added, "And, darling, remember too, will you, *not* to call me Mickey?"

She turned to him swiftly. "Mickey, we've got to tell the truth about that. We're going home. We can't enter America with a false name and false passport."

Unconsciously she had placed her hands on his arm. With a brusque motion he shook them off. His eyes were blazing suddenly, his face white. "*No*," he cried. "*No*."

"But you—"

"Marcia, you've got to promise me never to tell anyone that I'm Michel Banet. Promise me now."

"Mickey, I can't."

He waited a moment while the foghorn sounded again, its desolate, dreary wail coming back at them in echoes from the surrounding fog. She looked up into his angry face. Naturally he felt bitter. Naturally he was nervous and quick to anger. Yet something inside her insisted stubbornly that she was right. She tried to speak and the foghorn blared again and suddenly Mickey took her hands and held them quickly to his lips, then whirled around, left her standing at the railing and disappeared quickly into the ship.

She started after him, to reason with him, to do anything that would make peace between them. But after the first step or two she stopped. He'd get over his anger; he'd come back; he'd talk to her, reasonably and quietly.

She told herself that and did not quite believe it. She glanced along the deck, the same deck where, the previous day, she had found the body of Manuel Para near the stairway. Now the deck was deserted. She did not wish, however, to pass the place where Para had sprawled so horribly, so she turned in the opposite direction, toward the bow. And then she saw Josh. He was leaning against the railing. She wondered how much of the scene between herself and Mickey he had seen. As she thought that, he turned abruptly, called, "Hello," and came toward her.

They met at a sheltered turn of the deck. Josh's face looked white in the fog, his eyes very grave and dark. Without a word he put his arm around her and held her close against him. And Marcia, as if another woman had got into her body, moved closer within his embrace and turned her face upward so his mouth met her own.

She must draw away. This was a man she scarcely knew; a man she did not love. Except his mouth was so warm and strong upon her own that she could not move, she could not think, and her body was charged with a newness and strangeness too bewildering just then to conquer.

Josh drew away first. He looked down at her and laughed a little. "I love you, Marcia. And I remember now where I saw you. For I did see you, you know. So I've loved you really for five years. Only I didn't know it was you."

Marcia leaned against him, looked up into his eyes and said, half whispering, "I never saw you before. I'd have remembered you."

"We didn't meet. But I remember now. It was at a concert in

Paris. You were with some people. I saw you and I watched you. It was in October. It had been a warm, sunny day. That night was starlit and cold. I know because I walked home thinking about you, and I sat on the little balcony outside my room and looked at the stars and kept on thinking about you."

"There in the captain's cabin, you didn't know me. You didn't recognize me."

"No, I didn't. But a lot of things have happened to me and to everybody since then. I never knew your name. I never saw you again. I never knew anything about you. And about that time I got involved in . . . well, never mind that. You had your hair done up high that night. You wore a white dress, sort of thin and long." He held her again so her head came against his shoulder. "How was I to recognize you in a nurse's uniform, in the middle of the Atlantic, after a night spent in a lifeboat? Then last night I realized it was you. The girl I'd been in love with all that time."

"You can't have been! You—"

"Well, I wanted to be in love with you! I think I was, really. Marcia, I'm talking a lot of nonsense, but I do love you. Five years ago doesn't really have much to do with it, except that I liked you the first instant I saw you, standing there at the concert. It's been a long time and in some ways I suppose we are different people. But that doesn't matter. The only thing that matters is you and me and the people we are now."

That sunny, long-ago October in Paris, concerts on chill fall nights—and Mickey.

Mickey, the man she'd waited for and loved. Loved? she thought suddenly. But that had nothing to do with love! That was— Well, what? And it didn't matter; she couldn't analyze it, for now she knew all in a minute about love and the quality of love. The new Marcia had informed her; every drop of blood in her body, hammering in her pulses, had informed her.

And she was to marry Mickey.

He saw the change in her face. "What is it? What's wrong? Tell me." And then he guessed. "You've remembered André."

She must have made some gesture of assent, for his face

changed subtly; it became older, harder. He took his arm away and got out cigarettes. "Help me light this blasted thing, will you? I can manage, but . . ." She took the lighter and held it for him until the cigarette between his lips showed red. "Thanks," he said, and took the lighter and dropped it in his pocket. "This crazy arm of mine."

She glanced at the white sling supporting his right arm. "You were in combat?"

"Yes." His voice was remote and impersonal. "I stayed around Paris that first winter. It was a busy winter. One way and another. Then in the spring, when the Germans came . . ." He paused; there was a hiatus in his story, for he said finally, "I eventually got home by way of England and into uniform. I was sent back to England and then to Brittany. From there my story is just the same as everybody's, except I didn't get a scratch until just before the war was over. Then I got a piece of shrapnel in my shoulder. They dug it out and it is healing." Without a change in face or voice, he said, "What are you going to do about this . . . André?"

Mickey, not André. Mickey, who needed her, who had come back to her.

She moved away from Josh, not realizing she had moved. The deck under her feet was real. The railing, wet and cold under her fingers, was real too. Not this world she had so bewilderingly discovered in the embrace of the man who followed her now and leaned against the railing.

Josh said again, but as if a long time had elapsed, as if something had changed since he had spoken, "What are you going to do about André?"

She would not look at him. "I'm going to marry André."

"Why?" said Josh quietly.

"Because—" She stopped. It was as if the memory of Josh's kiss had the power to press upon her lips, silencing them.

Josh said evenly, "You were going to say because you love him. Do you?"

"I've told you," she said unsteadily, staring down at the black water rushing away from the ship. "We were to be married. Then he was sent to a German concentration camp. I stayed in France, waiting . . . hoping. Then finally he came back. As you see him. His hands . . . You heard what he said."

"I've heard," said Josh rather grimly, "what a lot of men have said and experienced. Is that why you are marrying him? From pity, I mean?"

Pity? After a moment she said stiffly, "He came back to me. I'm the only thing he has left from a life of—" She checked herself, on the verge of telling Josh of Mickey, and of all the glow and triumph that life had given him and promised him before the Nazis took it away.

And Josh said coolly, "What about Gili?"

"That was nothing."

"Don't try to lie to me, Marcia. What exactly did she do to you yesterday? It was something about André, wasn't it? Had she staked out a claim upon him?"

"No. That is, it was not true. She happened to be at the same hotel in Lisbon while we were waiting for a passage on the *Lerida*. He never saw her before that."

"I gather that Gili claimed to have come to Lisbon in order to join André."

"Yes, but . . ."

"How did she happen to tell you? Exactly what brought it on?"

"She had borrowed his cigarette case. I saw it and recognized it. It was very silly, really."

"Go on," said Josh inexorably. "What did she say about André?"

She did not want to tell him but she had to. "She said that he had come back to me because I had some money, and that he needed money for himself and, she said, for her. It was stupid of me to listen to her."

"Well," said Josh reflectively, "she could be serious, or she could be simply malicious and stupid, trying to make trouble between you. The point is, do you believe André?"

"Yes. He loves me; he needs me. It sounds trite. . . ."

"Very," said Josh, suddenly irritable. "You're being childish.

You're seeing yourself as the heroine of some play. Either you love him or you don't."

She thought of Mickey and the way he had looked when he came to her in Marseilles, and said quickly, "I love him." Then she felt the almost sickening shock of irrevocability. Words once said cannot be unsaid, no matter how swift, how defiant or how false they may be.

But even if she had tried to take back the hasty words she had spoken, she could not, for Josh said abruptly, "All right. That's that. We'll get on to another subject. And God knows there are several other subjects at hand. You've heard about Urdiola? What do you think of it? Seems reasonable, doesn't it, that he did it?"

She nodded and Josh looked out into the fog and said, "Too damned reasonable. A quarrel among the three Portuguese over a diamond; two murders because of it. Oh, yes, it's reasonable. I was there when Luther identified the diamond. He did so right away, took one look at it and got very red and told the captain he'd got it from his wife to give to Castiogne for arranging their passage. Did you bribe Castiogne for a passage?"

"No. That is, if André had done so, he'd have told me. He arranged everything."

Josh said reflectively, "Luther said they had nothing with them now but Daisy Belle's jewelry. They've been selling it, he said, piece by piece. He said he'd wondered why the diamond was not found on Castiogne, but supposed he had sold it and banked the money in Lisbon or something of the kind. Naturally he wasn't anxious to tell it, so he didn't volunteer the information. But then when he saw the diamond there on the table in the captain's cabin he didn't hesitate. I'll say that for him. And the fact of its turning up in Urdiola's possession right after Para's murder does sound bad. I've been thinking. Suppose Para murdered Castiogne in the lifeboat. Would that have been possible?"

She thought back again to the nightmare hours on the *Lerida* lifeboat. "Yes. I remember that he bent over Castiogne. I thought he was trying to revive him."

Josh was looking at her quietly and thoughtfully. "Para could have killed him then and removed the diamond, if he knew that Castiogne had it. Or he could merely have removed the diamond after somebody else murdered him. Is that right?"

She shivered and pulled her coat more closely about her. "Anything could have happened that night in that boat, anything."

Josh paused and then said, "Marcia, was it Urdiola who tried to murder you on deck here?"

"I don't know. It was dark and so sudden and dreadful. I don't know."

"I've got to ask you this, Marcia. Please answer me quite honestly. Have there been any other attempts? Besides the man in the red bathrobe yesterday?"

She hesitated, not wanting to acknowledge it and thus somehow mark its authenticity. But she told him. "Someone tried the handle of the cabin door the same night, perhaps fifteen minutes before I met you on my way to André's cabin. That was all that happened," she added quickly. "I opened the door to the corridor as soon as I could make myself do it. Nobody was there. It probably was nothing. In any case, we are safe now, all of us."

"Yes," said Josh. "Well, I wouldn't count too much on that."

"What do you mean?"

He would not meet her eyes. "I don't know. Anything, nothing. Only . . . listen, Marcia. Once before, twice before, I've said you were in danger. Well, I still think so."

"But Urdiola is locked up!"

"In spite of that. In spite of everything. I think that you have been in danger ever since an American ship came into view from the lifeboat."

"Josh—" But the foghorn began again, harshly checking her question.

Then it stopped and he turned to her. "Now then, we'd better go inside. Your hair's all misted."

"You must explain. There's something you know or guess."

"Marcia," he said abruptly, "is there anything *you* guess or know that you've not told me?"

"There's nothing I know. But I . . ." She hesitated, trying to put a very nebulous impression into words. "Twice I've had an odd sort of feeling that something was wrong somehow. I mean, not what I'd have expected it to be. One time it was with Gili. When she was talking to the captain. Somehow I'd have expected her to tell the captain the same story about the Cateses being Nazis that she told us."

"And she didn't?"

"No. She looked very secretive and didn't mention it."

He thought for a moment or two, watching her, and finally said, "It's just as well. I didn't believe it. What else was there, Marcia?"

"It happened just after you had talked to me on deck and then gone inside. I was lying back in the chair, thinking about Gili and the things she had said to me about André. All at once I felt as if I were looking at a picture I knew, but that something in the picture was crooked and wrong. Oh, I know that makes no sense—" She broke off.

Josh's face was very thoughtful. He repeated, "Something wrong in the picture. Something . . ." He stopped.

For minutes he just stood there motionless, as if he'd forgotten her existence. And then quite suddenly he looked at her with bright, intent eyes. He took her arm. "I think I see what you mean," he said, and whirled her around. "You'll have to go inside. You're cold. Your hair's all wet." They reached the lobby and everywhere was warmth and cheer and people. He said, "Now mind what I told you, Marcia. I'll see you later."

He vanished so abruptly toward the stairway that she stared after him, puzzled. Then she turned toward her cabin, thinking over the long conversation she'd had with him. The long and somehow very final conversation. For he had accepted her decision about Mickey completely; there was no doubt of that. It was in his manner, in his impersonally friendly tone, in everything about him.

She reached the little cabin, which was empty, the bunks neatly made up. She went to the porthole and gazed out for a long time into the fleecy gray; it was as if the ship made no progress, as if life itself had stopped.

Only it hadn't, she realized presently. It would go on and on and on. But forever without Josh. Forever without another moment of the real kind of life she had touched for an instant on the deserted deck in Josh's embrace.

She did not know exactly when she realized that someone had entered the shadowy cabin behind her. Quite gradually, however, the fact telegraphed itself to her senses. Someone was in the cabin; someone stood between her and the door; someone who had entered very softly, very stealthily, without her knowledge.

Chapter 10

THE hard, terrible hands that had gripped her at the railing on the dark deck seemed to reach out again toward her. She could not move, she could not turn, she could not speak. Her mind was racing. It seemed important not to let whoever stood behind her know that she was aware of that furtive presence. Only thus could she hope to avoid a physical struggle which could have only one conclusion. And she must think of some way to escape.

The thing she did was quick and impulsive. She spoke. She called out clearly and evenly, "Daisy Belle, did I leave my toothbrush in the bathroom? Look, will you?"

Daisy Belle, of course, was not in the bathroom. Nobody was there. The door was slightly ajar. But if whoever stood in that cabin with her could not quite see into the bathroom, if whoever was there believed that someone else was near, that she was not alone . . . Her heart, her breath, everything about her seemed to have stopped.

And then there was nothing. No rustle, no sound, no door closing, no motion of any kind. When that silence and feeling of emptiness had persisted long enough, she turned.

No one was there.

But a small hump of something white lay on the floor. Her heart beating hard again, she walked toward it and stared down.

It was a gauze bandage, twisted and turned so it made a crude sort of helmet such as the patient with the bandaged face and slits for eyes might have worn. Only it was not a real bandage. It had not been a patient.

She locked the cabin door. Then she sat down in the chair under the porthole and looked at the twisted tangle of white gauze. Urdiola was locked up and charged with murder. Who, then, could have worn that disguising helmet, and why?

She was still there when much later Daisy Belle and Gili returned to the cabin together. She heard their voices as one of them tried the door and then knocked. On her way to the door she picked up the gauze helmet, rolled it tightly, hating the touch of the thin material, put it in the pocket of her coat which still hung over her shoulders and opened the door.

"Why did you lock the door?" said Daisy Belle, more as an exclamation than a question. She snapped on the lights abruptly and the cabin leaped from its dim gray shadow to light under which Daisy Belle looked tired and old. Gili crossed to her bunk, stretched out and said nothing, but only gazed at the bunk above her with narrowed green eyes. She said nothing, in fact, until Daisy Belle said briskly that it was time for lunch and she'd wash up first. She disappeared into the bathroom. Gili swung her long, handsome legs around and sat up.

She said, "You talked to Mickey!" She shook back the blond lock of hair that hung over her face. "You with your fine lady ways. And your money. Don't answer. I don't care. Why do you suppose Mickey wanted you if it wasn't for the money he could get out of you!" Her hands curled hard around the mattress, and she leaned forward, her eyes furious. "Listen. I could tell you that I heard you call him Mickey; that that's how I knew his real name. I could tell you that I borrowed his cigarette case, that I saw it and picked it up and used it. I could tell you that everything I said was just to tease you. Or to make you angry with Mickey so you'd give him up. I could tell you anything like that. And you'd believe me." Drawing her mouth back from her teeth, she cried, "But I'm not going to. Do you understand? I'm not

347

going to give him up to you. He doesn't need you now. He's got everything he wants from you. He's through with you. He belongs to me."

Mickey had said, "Do you believe me or Gili?" Marcia remembered that clearly. She said, "I don't believe you."

"You think I'm lying!" Gili put back her head and laughed. "Lying! About Mickey and me!" She stopped laughing. She sprang across the room and her hands were reaching out like strong white claws toward Marcia and Marcia slapped her face. Hard.

Gili stopped. Marcia's hand tingled. Daisy Belle was in the bathroom doorway, staring.

Gili's hand went slowly to her jaw. She said, "I didn't think you had it in you."

Marcia looked at Gili's reddened cheek without a twinge of apology. Daisy Belle said briskly, "Best thing in the world for hysterics! Now then, let's go to lunch." She put her hand on Marcia's shoulder and turned her toward the door. She said to Gili, "You'd better come too. Pin up your hair. We'll wait. Hurry." She was like a schoolmistress, making quick order of childish chaos. And, like a child, Gili sulkily obeyed.

It was difficult to sit over a long lunch, listening to the pleasant, animated talk of the nurses, knowing that Gili sat on the other side of Daisy Belle. The officers' tables at the other end of the room were vacant. Marcia did not see Mickey, Josh or Luther.

After lunch the three women started back to the cabin together, Gili swishing along ahead with a look of latent fury in every motion she made. Daisy Belle stopped for a moment in the nurses' lounge and came out with an armload of magazines. "There's nothing else to do," she said, answering Marcia's glance. "And, my dear, don't talk to Gili now. Don't talk to André just yet. Wait. Time."

Daisy Belle, of course, had heard everything Gili had said. But she did not know of the crumpled roll of gauze in Marcia's pocket. So Marcia left Daisy Belle at the door of the cabin. She said something about going on deck for exercise.

Walking slowly along the warm, brightly lighted passageways, Marcia looked for Josh. He was not in any of the lounges, nor was he in his cabin, for she asked a young sergeant to take her there, then knocked on the door and opened it. She could not find him, and not wanting to see Gili again, she went to the nurses' lounge and sat there pretending to read.

The gauze, of course, was evidence. Since she could not find Josh, the obvious course was to give it to Captain Svendsen.

It was later than she had realized. The lights were on now everywhere and the fog was creeping again into the ship. She'd not wait longer for Josh. She looked for him, nevertheless, as she went back through the lobby and up the stairs. When she knocked on Captain Svendsen's door and Colonel Wells opened it, Josh was there.

"Hello," Josh said in a matter-of-fact tone. Colonel Wells smiled politely. The captain said courteously, "Come in, come in."

The captain went on. "I'm glad you came, Miss Colfax. Colonel Morgan has been trying to make me believe that you are in danger. But, as you know, the thing is over. We've got Urdiola and a sound case against him. You know all about that?"

She moved her head in acknowledgment, started to speak, stopped and pulled the gauze helmet from her pocket.

Josh understood first, took the roll of gauze from her hand and held it so they could see it. Then he put it on the captain's desk. "Tell us what happened. Tell us. Hurry."

But she had not realized how unsubstantial a story it was until she told it and saw the captain's face, fixed and hard as granite. Colonel Wells came over to the desk, picked up the gauze, looked at it, said, "Inexpertly made. No nurse or doctor made that," and put it down again.

The captain said, "Urdiola is locked up. The patient Jacob Heinzer is naturally not under guard, but I expect we can check on his whereabouts. I'll try. In the meantime, though, are you perfectly sure anyone was really there?"

Before she could reply, Josh said, "Captain, I'm afraid I'm guilty of withholding some evidence."

"What's that, Colonel?" The captain's bleached eyebrows were suddenly heavy and threatening.

"The fact is, sir, the Cateses have been accused of collaboration with the Nazis. If the story is right, Castiogne knew it."

"Castiogne! You mean that you think he tried to blackmail Cates? But Cates said he gave him the diamond as a bribe for their passage. Cates said—"

"Right, sir."

"Wait." The captain touched a bell and gave quick orders to the boy who appeared. "Get hold of Mr. Cates and his wife. Get them both here. Now then, Colonel Morgan, exactly what *do* you mean?"

Josh stared very intently at the end of his cigarette while he told Gili's story almost word for word exactly as she had told it. As he finished, the captain began to pace the cabin angrily. "Why didn't you tell me before now?"

"Because I didn't believe it."

"And you do believe it now?" The captain shot him an angry and troubled look.

"I believe that Marcia is in grave danger," said Josh obliquely.

As he spoke, the boy ushered Daisy Belle and Luther into the room. Marcia immediately thought they guessed; and that, therefore, incredible though it was, it was true.

Daisy Belle did not look at Marcia. She said quite clearly to Luther, looking up into his tired, pale face, "I was right, Luther. I was right." She took his hand in her own and suddenly her face crumpled and she began soundlessly to cry. Josh brought her a chair.

The captain said, "Look here, Cates, why did you give that diamond to Castiogne?"

Luther took a long breath, put his hand on his wife's shoulder and said steadily, "I gave the diamond to Castiogne to pay him for securing our passage, as I told you. But there is something else—something my wife and I ought to have told you, perhaps. But we had hoped to forget it. It is not pleasant."

Daisy Belle patted the hand on her shoulder and Luther went

on. "You see, my wife and I, during the years when France was occupied, were"—he swallowed hard, but his faded blue eyes did not waver—"we were what you could call Nazis. What everybody will call Nazis. We lived in the home of someone who proved to be a Nazi. An old acquaintance who offered us a refuge. We did not then know what he was; we had already taken food and shelter. But circumstances were such that, even after we suspected, we continued to take what we thought we had to have. There is no excuse for us. We realize that."

Daisy Belle cried suddenly, "It was not your fault, Luther. It was mine. You had to have drugs; you had to have digitalis. I thought you were dying."

"Don't, my dear." His thin hand pressed down upon her shoulder. "Since Castiogne's death, we began to think that, in some possible way, the fact could have a connection with the murders. So we had talked of telling you the truth. And it does not matter, you see, because," said Luther with sudden dignity, "we can never forgive ourselves, never forget that we've taken food and lodging and medicine from bloody hands."

There was a long silence in the cabin. Finally the captain said, "Why do you think it had a connection with the murders?"

"I don't know," said Luther simply.

"According to the story I've heard, Castiogne knew that you had done this. Did he try to blackmail you?" asked the captain bluntly.

"No. As we told you, the diamond was . . . well, a bribe. We saw him in Lisbon. He said he could arrange it for money. We had no money, so we gave him the diamond. And he got our passage."

There was another silence; then the captain said suddenly, "Thank you. You may go."

With unbroken dignity they left. Daisy Belle, passing Marcia, stopped for an instant beside her chair and touched her lightly with her hand. "My dear," she said. "Don't look like that. It's all right."

The door closed upon them and Josh said suddenly, "There's one more thing, sir. The man traveling with Miss Colfax is not

André Messac. I knew André Messac. He was my close friend. This man is a former concert pianist. I have heard him play many times. His name is Michel Banet." Josh's voice went on as hard and harsh as iron. "His hands show marks of torture which he says he received in a German prison. In fact, however, I believe him to be a fleeing Nazi war criminal."

The cabin seemed to Marcia to darken and tilt. The captain's face, purple and swollen-looking, seemed to tilt with it. She heard him shout, "Why haven't you told me this before?"

She heard Josh's answer too, quite steady and firm. "For a good reason, sir. A good reason . . ."

Even in the crazily tilting room she heard them giving orders to bring in André Messac. But they meant Mickey Banet . . . Mickey Banet . . . Mickey Banet . . . The name droned through her senses like a hammer, over and over and over.

It was, however, too late to ask questions of Mickey Banet. He was found on deck, in the shadow of the lifeboats, unconscious. He had been shot, and died shortly after an emergency operation, although everything possible was done to save him.

Before he died he rallied briefly and made a curious and terrible statement. A woman, he said, had shot him, and he would explain later. It was the last thing he said.

It was about that time that a young lieutenant, a member of one of the armed searching parties, reported to his superior that he had lost the revolver which had been issued to him.

Chapter 11

THE *Lerida* passengers, at the captain's orders, waited together in the officers' lounge. Eventually Josh and Colonel Wells came to tell them briefly that Mickey had died. However, neither told them then what Mickey's last statement had been. They stayed only a moment and went away again.

Among the four people in the lounge there was very little expression, either of relief or regret. Gili sat huddled on a sofa, her long streaked hair shading her face, and neither moved nor spoke.

Luther, looking ill and tired to death himself, put his drawn face in his hands and kept it there so long that Daisy Belle went to him with an anxious inquiry in her eyes.

"Are you all right?"

"Oh, yes." He lifted his face reassuringly, but she put her fingers on his wrist for a moment nevertheless.

Marcia thought, This is not possible; Mickey cannot have died like this. But she knew it was true.

There was after that another long and horrible wait; a corpsman came about midnight with sandwiches and hot cocoa in thick cups on a tray. Marcia drank slowly, holding the cup in both her cold hands. There is a state of shock that is almost like an anesthetic; fortunately, under an anesthetic one has no feeling. Marcia stared into the cocoa, remembering Mickey's candid, clear gray eyes, his smile, the things he had said. Also she recalled the things that Josh had said which precipitated the search for Mickey. A Nazi war criminal, trying to escape a Europe which was too dangerous for him now that the Americans had come. Mickey with his hands maimed by those same Nazis.

She was strongly aware all the time of Gili's presence, and perhaps Gili was as strongly aware of hers. Their eyes did not meet until Josh returned. He came into the room quickly and everyone looked up with a jerk. The ship had been by that time thoroughly searched, he told them tersely. No revolver was found and nothing leading to evidence concerning Mickey Banet's murder had been discovered.

"What are they going to do?" asked Luther, his face ashen under the brilliant light.

"Investigate as best they can," said Josh. "Hope, I suppose, that somebody saw something and will come forward to say so. They are making an urgent appeal. Anybody who knows of anything at all suspicious is asked to go to the captain at once."

"Do you think that will come to anything?" asked Luther after a pause.

"I don't know," replied Josh, "but I'm sure the captain will tell us if he's learned anything. He said he'd be here in a few minutes."

There was a silence and then Daisy Belle said abruptly, "To ask us if one of us murdered him?"

"Yes," said Josh quietly. "I suppose he'll ask that."

It was then that Marcia became aware of Gili's eyes, bright and fixed, staring at her thoughtfully. She did not speak, however, but only sat there, her hair hanging lankly about her face, her eyes fastened upon Marcia in that thoughtful way. Before anyone else spoke, the captain and Colonel Wells came into the room.

They looked terribly tired. It was Colonel Wells who had operated on Mickey. He came to Marcia directly. "I'm sorry," he said. "I did what I could. Whatever he was, or wasn't, I'm sorry." But there was also a sharp and cold question in his eyes.

Captain Svendsen, however, swiftly took matters into his own hands. They all knew, he said, what had happened. If any of them knew anything of the murder, or suspected anything, they must tell it. He did not wait for anyone to speak but went on. "Shortly before he was found injured, a question of his identity arose." He turned directly to Marcia. "You were engaged to marry him. You must have known the truth. Colonel Morgan says that he was really a man by the name of Banet, a concert pianist. Is that right?"

"Yes."

"Why was he using a false passport? And a false name?"

She told him. It had seemed best to leave Europe as quickly as possible. Mickey had decided to use a passport which had belonged to a friend, André Messac. He had his own photograph substituted.

"Why didn't he use his own passport?"

"He said he had none. He had nothing, no personal possessions. It would take time to secure a passport of his own."

"If he had turned Nazi, he would not have dared to apply for one. He would have been afraid to let his identity be known anywhere in France, wouldn't he?"

"I suppose so. Yes."

"And you subscribed to his plan to use a false passport. Why? You must have known that that is a criminal offense."

At the time it had seemed the only course which might help to restore Mickey to himself quickly. Now it seemed futile to try to explain it. She replied, "It seemed right then. We intended to do something about it in Buenos Aires, go to the American consul and tell him the whole story. But then he determined to keep the name of André Messac."

"Why?" the captain asked.

She told him that too. Mickey had been on the threshold of a great career. It had been taken from him. He had wished, he said, to save his pride and never again to be known as Michel Banet.

There was a short silence and they could hear the throb of the ship's engines driving the ship on and on through the fog.

"When did he tell you that?" asked the captain suddenly. "On the *Lerida*? On the *Magnolia*?"

"The night after we were taken aboard the *Magnolia*."

"And you agreed to keep his real identity a secret?"

She had neither the wish nor the strength to defend herself. "For the time being. Yes."

Captain Svendsen turned to Josh. "Will you tell Miss Colfax exactly what you told me while Colonel Wells was operating."

Josh looked at Marcia and crossed to pull up a small chair near her. He sat down and leaned forward to take her hand. "Marcia, André Messac was murdered by the Nazis." He looked down at her hand for an instant, his face set and grave.

Captain Svendsen said impatiently, "Colonel Morgan, during the first fall of the war, joined a group of French resistance men. André Messac was one of them. So was Michel Banet. André Messac was arrested suddenly by the Germans and shot. Colonel Morgan was always of the opinion that he was betrayed by one of his own men. He thinks that man was the man who came on this ship using André Messac's name. He thinks it was Michel Banet. What do you know about it?"

"He could not have been a Nazi. Mickey was arrested by the Nazis. He was tortured by the Nazis."

Josh looked up into her eyes. "Not everybody who was tortured," he said, "was a hero. One stands torture, another does not. The Germans knew that; that was why they tortured. They wanted information about other people. They had a double lever with Michel Banet; pain and the maiming of his fingers which meant his whole life. I think he gave in. I think he turned Nazi within a day or two of his imprisonment and torture. Unfortunately for him, it was already too late to save his hands, but he could save his life, and did. By telling everything he knew.

"I've always thought that André Messac was betrayed by one of a very small group. André had a genius for organization. He realized how unsafe it would be for us to know too much of each other and he arranged it so we knew the fewest possible names, the fewest possible men who were allied to us. Michel Banet was one of the few who knew André Messac was our leader. I knew it. Perhaps a few others. But Michel Banet was arrested, and almost immediately André was arrested and shot. I did not know that Michel Banet had betrayed. I only knew that André must have been betrayed. Banet had disappeared. The rumor was that he was killed too.

"The Germans were in Paris. War between the United States and Germany seemed inevitable. I got back home, as I told you, and into the Army. But you don't forget people like André. Well, when I knew that a man had turned up on this ship using that name, when I saw that man and knew it was not his name and that he was a man I had known to be taken by the Germans only a day or so before André was murdered, I"—he stared down again at his hand still holding hers—"I had to find out the truth."

The captain said, "Why didn't you tell me?"

Josh lifted his head; his face was very white. "Because I had to kill him with my own hands," he said.

There was a long silence in the lounge. Then the captain cried, "But he said a woman did it!" Everyone looked at Marcia, except Josh. With his dark head bent, he stared down at her hand and his own, locked together.

Suddenly Marcia took in the sense of the captain's words. "Mickey said a woman shot him?" she cried.

And Josh told her, "Before Banet died, he was conscious for a minute or two and made a sort of statement. He said that a woman had shot him and he'd explain later. But he died shortly afterward."

To somebody in that room, Marcia thought suddenly, there had been a second of terror when Josh quoted Mickey's words and then paused before he added that Mickey had said no more. Somebody had waited for a name. Somebody? All of them. She glanced swiftly around the room and everybody else was doing the same thing—covertly, swiftly, eyes searching and speculative, bright with suspicion.

Then the captain said heavily and point-blank, "If you killed him, Miss Colfax, it would be better for you to say so now."

"No, no, I didn't."

Colonel Wells said slowly, "Whoever killed him must have made two attempts: the first one, that night on the deck when Banet was knocked out. Miss Colfax couldn't have done that, for she was attacked the same night, about the same time as Banet. Certainly by the same person who attacked Banet, so—"

"Oh, no," cried Josh. He got up. "Oh, no! I did that. I hit Banet."

"You?" began the captain, his great fist doubling up. "That was you?"

"I told you that I wanted to kill him with my own hands."

"You didn't tell me that you had tried," said the captain grimly. "Did you shoot him?"

"No, I didn't," said Josh. "But I wanted to. When I heard there was an André Messac on board, among the *Lerida* survivors, I wanted to see the man using that name. So I looked for him on deck that night. It was dark where I stood. He passed under a light and then came toward me. I recognized him instantly. I'd heard him play many times. And I saw red. There was Michel Banet, using André's name and passport. So I hit him, just slammed out at him. I didn't say anything. I suppose I didn't know what I was doing. Except that it was what I'd wanted to do for five years—"

The captain broke in harshly. "You'd wanted to kill Michel Banet?"

"I'd wanted to kill whoever it was who'd betrayed André Messac to the Germans."

"Then you killed him tonight?"

"No," said Josh soberly, "I didn't."

"But you—"

The captain's face was swelling with rage and Colonel Wells stepped in peaceably. "What did you do?" he asked Josh. "Why didn't you report it?"

Josh paused for a moment, thinking. He said finally, "After I hit him I . . . well, came to. I realized how stupid it was. He seemed to be knocked out but not really hurt. I didn't think he'd seen me. And he'd never known me in the Paris days. Later that night I went to his cabin and then I was sure that he didn't recognize me, and I think that he was honestly puzzled as to just what had happened."

For a moment no one spoke or moved. Then Josh went on. "I decided to keep quiet and find out everything I could about him. If he was guilty, I'd prove it. But I"—he looked again at the captain and said stubbornly—"I had to do it myself. André was my friend. It was . . . I had to."

"What did you do then?" asked Colonel Wells.

"I walked on around the deck, thinking. He was a fake. But why? Then I met Marcia and questioned her about him. But I didn't get very far."

"You ought to have told me about Banet!" the captain cried, and Josh replied obstinately, "I did not believe that Michel Banet had anything to do with the murder of the two Portuguese."

"You still required a private revenge?" asked Colonel Wells.

"In a sense, yes. But there were other reasons. For one thing, Miss Colfax was engaged to be married to him; consequently she had to know that he was using another man's name and she had to know the reason for it. So that was an argument in favor of Banet. I had a certain"—he hesitated—"faith in Miss Colfax's own faith in him. Besides, it was a very serious charge I had to make. It was based on nothing but my own imaginings, really, and it was a charge that would stick to him all the rest of his life, and

359

to his wife." He shrugged and finished in a very quiet tone. "So naturally I had to be sure that my suspicions had more than a grain of fact before I reported them."

"You said you believed him to be a Nazi war criminal. Why?" asked the captain.

"Because he was so frantically determined to escape Europe. I think he may have been used in some minor way by the Nazis. I think he was afraid of revenge—perhaps by someone whose relative he had injured; certainly he was afraid of being caught by the Americans."

"But did you get any proof?" asked Luther suddenly.

Josh looked at Marcia. "I'm afraid I've hurt you very much, Marcia. I'm afraid I've got to hurt you more," he said, and turned to Gili. "Where is the cigarette case?"

She wasn't going to answer. For a moment the decision, sullen and unmistakable, was in her face. Josh said, "We know you have it. It was Banet's. Where is it?"

With a sulky gesture Gili pulled the case from the pocket of her uniform. She said, half muttering, eyeing Josh, "I borrowed it. I . . . borrowed it."

He took the thin gold case which flashed in the light. Again Marcia had a swift and fleeting memory of that case and dappled sunlight on a table and Mickey's smiling gray eyes.

Josh said to the captain, "This case belonged to Michel Banet. How could an expensive trinket like this have been permitted to remain in the possession of a prisoner in a German concentration camp for five years?"

The captain took the case in his hand and looked at it and said judicially, "Well, it couldn't." He looked at Marcia. "Did Banet own this before the war?"

"Yes." Her voice was almost a whisper.

The captain weighed the case in his hand. "No," he said thoughtfully. "They wouldn't have let a prisoner keep a trinket like this." He looked at Josh. "But it's not proof, you know."

Josh turned to Gili. "You knew him in Germany," he said. "You came to Lisbon to wait for him. You were both getting out of

Germany as fast as you could. But you couldn't use German money. So you had to get money. You planned the whole deception with him."

Gili leaped to her feet and stood there, trembling and white, shrieking, "You are lying. That's not true. They said a woman killed him. It was Marcia. She did it because she thought he loved me. We quarreled and she struck me. She was beside herself. And you"—she whirled around to Daisy Belle—"you saw it. You heard it. You know I'm telling the truth. She murdered him. Mickey said it was a woman. Why don't you arrest her?"

Chapter 12

CURIOUSLY, it was almost in the very moment that Gili spoke— so wildly and yet with at least one ingredient of truth—that Marcia perceived a change taking place in the relationship between Josh and the two ship's officers. When she saw the long look that the captain and Colonel Wells exchanged—they pointedly excluded Josh Morgan—she felt something very like fright. Josh was now one of the suspects.

But then she was suspect too. *If* Mickey had spoken the truth, *if* a woman had shot him, then there were only herself and Gili and Daisy Belle who could conceivably have had a motive for doing so.

And immediately Daisy Belle came to Marcia's defense. "Captain," she said, "there was nothing about that so-called quarrel that was serious or that would give rise to murder. It was like a hysterical explosion between two schoolgirls." She drew herself up, a dignified, poised and experienced woman. "It was nothing."

The captain looked at Marcia. "But you did quarrel? You did strike her? What did you quarrel about?"

Josh said suddenly, "I expect Mrs. Cates knows."

Daisy Belle gave him a flicker of approval and said quickly, "I do indeed. I'll tell you exactly. Gili said that this Banet person had only wanted money from Marcia and that Gili wouldn't give him up. That, I believe, was the main theme of her declaration."

"Did she say," asked Captain Svendsen, "that she had known him anywhere else?"

Daisy Belle thought for an instant. "I'm not sure she said exactly that. It was a very strong implication. I mean the few days on the *Lerida* and the *Magnolia* could scarcely have given her the . . . well, proprietary rights she seemed to feel she had."

"What did you think of it?"

"I thought what was undoubtedly the truth. This Banet person had deceived Marcia. He had pretended not to know Gili beyond the casual acquaintance all of us had there in Lisbon and on the *Lerida*. He was using Marcia; and Gili, through jealousy or bad temper, told Marcia the truth. In any case, I felt perfectly certain that what Gili said was the truth. She knew all about him. Ask her."

"I didn't," said Gili defiantly. "That is not true. I knew nothing of him. I . . . I said all that because I . . . I liked him. And I hate Marcia. She thought she owned him. He didn't love her. I could see that. I thought I might make a quarrel between them."

"Why were you on the *Lerida?*" asked Josh.

She caught her breath, eyed him smolderingly for an instant and said, "Because I wanted to go to Buenos Aires, of course."

"Why?"

"Because . . ." She bit her lip. Then with a flash of her eyes she turned to the captain. "I've done nothing. Marcia killed him. She was furious. She struck me. She stole the revolver and shot him. Mickey said it was a woman."

Josh turned to Captain Svendsen. "This was not the first time she told Marcia all this. The first time, though, she was more specific. Marcia, tell them what she said to you."

Marcia told the ugly little story quickly. "She said they wanted to leave Europe, that they had no money. That he came back to me in order to get money for both of them."

"Did you question Banet about it?" asked Colonel Wells.

"Yes. He said it was not true."

The captain then questioned Gili bluntly. It was a curious, dogged struggle between them and for the moment Gili won.

"I've told you everything I know. Everything," Gili said.

"Was Banet a Nazi?"

"I don't know."

"Where did you know him?"

"In Lisbon. And on the *Lerida*. That's all."

"But he was a Nazi?"

"I don't know." And then she added, "Ask her. Ask Marcia. She killed him."

Colonel Wells said, "As Colonel Morgan points out, today is not the first time Miss Duvrey made her claims about Banet to Miss Colfax."

Josh picked it up quickly. "So if Marcia had been going to shoot him, she'd have done it then. Not now."

The captain said doubtfully, "Perhaps only today she was convinced." He looked at his watch. "I've got to get back to the bridge."

Colonel Wells said, "I beg your pardon, Captain. The patient with the bandaged face. I inquired about him. He spent the entire day in one of the wards playing bridge with three other boys. He went to mess with two of them who are also ambulatory. They'll all swear to it. He is out as a suspect."

"He was never in," said the captain bluntly. "Now then, there's something that you people may not know about a ship. I am no detective. I wouldn't know what to do with a fingerprint if I had one. But on a ship, no matter what happens or when, sometime, somewhere, an eyewitness turns up. And I might add that I have wired home a full report together with an urgent request for all available information about every *Lerida* passenger I picked up. I did this the day we rescued you. I have already reported Banet's real name and murder. I should very soon begin to receive any facts which the State Department or the FBI or any other source is able to secure."

Gili rose from the corner of the sofa in one swift motion and moved across the lounge to the captain. "Will you promise me protection?"

"So you're going to confess?" said the captain.

"No, no!" she cried. "But if you've wired for information—" She stopped and sucked in her lower lip and, her eyes sullen but frightened, cried, "I didn't mean to be a Nazi. I couldn't help it. I had to be a Nazi to . . . to live!"

"That is what they all say," said the captain. "What about Banet? Tell me anything you know."

She talked rapidly, loudly, repeating herself, disclaiming responsibility—a torrent of words so frankly designed to ingratiate herself by accusing Mickey that even Daisy Belle, with her civilized tolerance for human frailty, looked rather sickened.

Mickey had been a Nazi. He had turned Nazi immediately, and to convince his torturers of his sincerity had betrayed André Messac and others. Gili knew that. He had boasted of it. Gradually he had worked into a position of small eminence among the Nazis in a branch of the Gestapo. His business was that of informer. He was bitter about his hands, but apparently had no thought of revenge. Instead, he seized every opportunity to solidify his standing with the Nazis—probably he believed that if he had a future, it lay now with them. He was by no means a major war criminal. Still, he had achieved enough importance in a small way that when the war was over, somebody was sure to inform the Americans.

So he had to hide his identity and escape. It was an added touch of cold cruelty that he really had got André's passport from his mother, who believed Mickey as Marcia had believed him. And he had to have money. "He made me come too. He loved me," said Gili with a sidelong glance of triumph at Marcia.

The captain accused her flatly. "You murdered Banet," he said. "You were jealous, you were afraid he'd leave you."

Gili laughed harshly. "Murder the man who was going to provide me with . . . with food, and a home and clothes? What can I do in America? I worked in a barbershop in Berlin. That's where I met him. I didn't love him, but he loved me. He would have taken care of me. Murder *him!*" said Gili, and laughed again.

The captain gave up. He turned to Colonel Wells. "Colonel, will you see to the disposition of these people that we discussed?

Thank you. Colonel Morgan, I have to tell you that your movements about the ship are now restricted."

"You mean I'm a suspect?"

"You had a strong motive—a comprehensible motive," the captain said. "By your own admission you tried once to kill Banet. But I do not believe that a dying man would attempt to deceive. I believe that a woman shot him."

Daisy Belle got up and stood with dignity under the harsh light. "You mean one of us."

"I don't know who else," said the captain plainly, and he went away, tired and angry, hurrying back to the bridge.

Colonel Wells said wearily, "He'll question you further tomorrow. I do beg you to consider what he says. If anybody knows anything at all, it would be better in the long run to tell us."

Luther got up wearily too. He looked gray with fatigue. "Maybe an eyewitness will turn up. Somebody must have seen something."

"Apparently," said Colonel Wells, "nobody did. Now then . . ." He went on quickly to explain that their cabins were to be changed. The *Lerida* survivors were to be separated. He would show them.

Marcia, probably by mere chance, was allotted the same cabin which the three women had formerly shared. Already Gili's and Daisy Belle's few clothes and cosmetics had been removed. She did not see to what cabins Gili and Daisy Belle were taken. She had an impression that Luther remained alone in the cabin he and Mickey had shared.

As Marcia settled down for the night the ship seemed to stand still. It had, in fact, slowed almost to a stop, owing to the extraordinary thickness of the fog, and the foghorn had resumed its monotonous wail. Yet murder still walked these slippery decks.

Along toward morning the ship suddenly hove to. Marcia did not hear the cries of "Man overboard!" and she knew nothing of the launching of the boats and the searchlights which strove vainly to pierce the fog.

A wakeful patient had seen a man go past a porthole near him.

He had given the alarm. The ship was stopped and the crew got out boats. A quick check of wards and passengers was made. Luther Cates was missing.

The probability was that even if he were still alive he would not be found. True, the ship had been traveling at a very slow speed and the alarm had been given instantly. Even so, the *Magnolia* moved some distance before she could stop and before the small boats could be launched. The fog, too, seriously hindered the search.

It was still dark, in spite of approaching dawn, when Josh came to Marcia. She was awake and knew that the ship had stopped. She had heard the subdued echoes of commotion, but did not know the reason for it or for the brief visit of Major Williams, who, while checking the whereabouts of the *Lerida* passengers, had knocked on the door and called to her. When she replied he hurried away.

When Josh knocked she was wrapped in a bathrobe, standing at the porthole and watching the misty flares in the fog. The searchlights were gleaming this way and that from small boats. "It's me," he called. She opened the door, which she had bolted.

He stood, white-faced, in the passageway. His head was bare and his dark hair shone with moisture. His overcoat shoulders were damp. He came in quickly. "It's a man overboard. Luther. So far they've not found him."

"Luther! What happened?"

"Nobody knows," Josh said. "They'll never find him in a fog like this."

"Luther," she whispered. "Why?"

Josh looked into her eyes. "I wanted to talk to you last night, Marcia," he said gravely. "I'm sorry."

"You mean about Mickey."

"Yes. Even to you, Marcia, the cigarette case must have raised a question. Do you remember telling me that something seemed wrong to you—out of the picture? Wasn't that it? Subconsciously, it seemed wrong to you as it did to me."

There were other things, she thought suddenly, excuses she had made in her mind for Mickey, things he had said and done, the way, even with the war over, he had seemed nervous and too wary; his insistence on taking passage on the *Lerida* to Buenos Aires, not home; his determination to use a false name.

She said slowly, staring out into the drifting fog, "There were always explanations—always reasons. . . ." She pulled the over-size bathrobe closer around her throat.

"Marcia, I had to tell them about Mickey to save your life. It was Banet who tried to murder you."

"*Mickey!*" She turned to him in bewildered disbelief. "*Mickey* tried to murder me? Oh, no, Josh! There's no reason."

"Oh, my dear, my dear. Don't you see that there was a very strong reason? Mickey never intended to let anyone know he was Michel Banet the traitor, the Nazi. But you insisted on telling the truth."

"Josh, he couldn't have tried to kill me that first night on the *Magnolia*. He was unconscious. You saw him."

"Wait. Listen to me. Go back to the moment when you sighted an American ship from the lifeboat. Don't you see that you were Banet's danger? He could never hide his identity so long as you were with him. Castiogne's murder suggested the whole thing, perhaps. That, with the fact that Banet knew in the end you would insist upon telling the truth. Did you insist?"

"Yes, yes," she whispered. "But it couldn't have been Mickey that first night on deck," she repeated. "He was unconscious."

"Oh, was he?" said Josh, and shook his head. "I don't think so. I think I did knock him out. Just for a minute or two. I think he came to, just about when you found him. He didn't know what had happened. At any rate, he must have thought, Here's an alibi. Unconsciousness. And there you were. When he saw you come out on the port side of the deck, he ran quickly around the stern. And you came that way as he hoped, and in the shadow it was easy. He tried to kill you and heard me coming."

"I can't believe it was Mickey," she whispered. But she did believe it.

Josh said, "Then he ran back to the starboard side to the spot where you'd left him—there to be found later, still apparently unconscious. It wasn't actually an alibi for the time of the attack upon you, but it had all the effect of one. Both of you presumably were attacked at almost the same part of the ship and almost at the same time. Anybody would conclude that it was the same person who did it, and certainly it would be linked with the murder of Castiogne. I think too that on his way back to his cabin from the dispensary he tried the door to your cabin, just on the chance of finding you there. He need not have returned to his cabin where Gili was waiting for him more than a minute or two before you and I reached it."

Marcia turned to the porthole and opened it. The air was cold and misty on her face and the distant voices of men searching through the fog and darkness for the body of a man overboard drifted eerily to their ears.

Josh stared out into the graying fog and said slowly, "I think that it was Mickey who came to your cabin yesterday in another attempt to kill you. Those gauze bandages around his face made a simple and easy disguise. I've inquired about the gauze. Almost anybody could have managed to snag that from some supply closet or dressing tray. But when you came to the captain with that horribly twisted thing, I knew beyond all doubt that Banet would kill you if he could."

"But who killed him?"

"I don't know."

"He said a woman."

"If it was a woman, there's only Gili and Daisy Belle. I don't think it was Gili for the reasons she gave. She needs food and clothing and shelter and just at that moment Mickey was her only hope of getting any of them. And Daisy Belle had no motive. Even if Banet was trying to blackmail her on account of the Nazi business that Gili told us about, that threat was spiked when they confessed. I simply don't know why he was killed, Marcia, unless somehow he was linked up with Castiogne and Para and the diamond. Originally, Luther could have had the same motive as Daisy Belle, but since they've come out with the truth, he too lacks a motive. And nothing accounts for Luther's murder."

He turned from the porthole, put his hand thoughtfully under Marcia's chin and said, "My darling, no matter what happens, you are safe. Nothing can hurt you now. Do you want to go to Daisy Belle? She's in the captain's cabin. I think she needs you."

She didn't want him to leave. There was so much she had to say, and yet she had no words.

"Wrap yourself up if you go on deck," he said matter-of-factly. "It's damned cold." He touched her cheek lightly and walked out of the cabin and closed the door.

For a long time Marcia did not move. She stood huddled in the long crimson bathrobe, gradually aware of the chill and the stealthy fingers of fog. Presently she sat down on the edge of the bunk, staring at nothing.

She roused herself finally with a sharp realization that some time had passed since Josh had gone. He had said that Daisy Belle would need her. She'd better go.

She had on gray pajamas—men's pajamas—too big for her, like the bathrobe. She'd not wait, though, to dress. She'd wrap herself in the thick nurse's coat that lay over a chair. As she went to get it, she heard the door open. Someone entered the cabin quickly, and she turned, saying, "Josh—" Her voice died in a gasp, as if hands had already caught her throat.

She had a glimpse of the tall figure in the doorway—a figure in a crimson bathrobe, with white bandages over its face. Then the light switch clicked and the cabin was in darkness.

There was a soft rustle of motion. And then, in the thick silence, an unintelligible choking whisper which said nothing, which merely made sounds.

Chapter 13

BUT Mickey was dead. He had once come to her cabin, masked and fearfully anonymous like that, but he was dead.

The whisper had stopped. There was a listening quality in the silence. Marcia was listening too, every nerve in her body strained to hear, for there were shouts from the fog, shouts from the darkness and the black sea, shouts of "Found . . . found." She knew then that something—a man, Luther, alive or dead?—had been found.

Yet it seemed unimportant; it was part of another world. It had nothing to do with the small, horribly limited, black world around her just then. And Mickey said it was a woman. Gili—or Daisy Belle? If it was Gili, she would fight. If it was Daisy Belle, she would reason with her.

She cried, summoning strength and voice and will from desperation, *"Daisy Belle, you must listen to me. Daisy Belle . . ."* Her voice was unexpectedly loud, strained and harsh and clear in the small space around her.

Daisy Belle did not answer.

Suddenly, and as clearly almost as her own voice sounded upon her ears, an intangible but positive emptiness sounded upon her senses. She had heard no move. If the door had opened upon the lighted corridor outside, she had not seen it.

But the sense of emptiness was so convincing in a queer and primitive way that her breath of its own accord began to come more freely. She knew that she was alone.

There was something she'd been about to do. She'd been reaching for her coat; she'd been going to Daisy Belle. As she thought that, suddenly the door swung open and Josh's figure was outlined against the light of the corridor.

"Marcia," he cried. "Marcia."

The light streamed into the cabin. Nobody else was there, but she still could not move. She said stiffly, "Turn on the light—beside you—there by the door."

"Marcia, they've found him. He's still alive. They've found him." He snapped on the light and she blinked and looked. Only she and Josh stood in the small cabin. Josh came quickly to her. "Don't look so . . . so white and terrified, my darling. Everything is all right now."

"Everything . . ."

"My darling." He put his arm around her and made her sit beside him on the edge of the bunk and said excitedly, "The captain and Colonel Wells talked to Urdiola again. They think he may be telling the truth. And . . . Marcia, listen. Why would Mickey Banet say that it was a woman who shot him? I mean, if it wasn't a woman, if it really was a man, why would he say it was a woman? Unless he wanted to protect that man. And why would he protect the man who shot him unless he wanted something from him?"

"But Mickey was dying."

"No, that's it. He was dying, but *he didn't know it;* he didn't think so; he was under drugs; he had a false sense of security; he thought he was going to live. He tried to protect whoever it was that shot him. Exactly as he did when I hit him, and he didn't know who it was that hit him. Yet he came out with that vague story about having slipped or fainted. No, we ought to have known then that it was somebody whose *continued* life was important to Banet. We ought to have known it all along. There were only you and Gili and Daisy Belle and Luther Cates and the mysterious patient—"

"Josh," she cried, "he was here! He went away just before you came."

"Here!" He jumped up. "Here! What do you mean?"

She told him quickly.

He stood, however, for a long moment without speaking. And then suddenly he began to speak in a queerly measured way.

"Mickey," he said, "hoped to make a living for the rest of his life. Gili, when she told him what she and Castiogne had overheard, provided him the way. That, you see, is why he was through with you. He could now blackmail Luther Cates and get much more money than you could supply. Much more."

She did not understand the listening look on his face. It was as if he were talking not to her but to somebody else. Somebody invisible, who was not there and yet might hear him. He went on. "Castiogne had hoped to do that too, but he was fobbed off with a diamond, then killed. Para was Castiogne's confidant and partner. When Castiogne was killed, Para was afraid; so he gave Urdiola the diamond to keep for him to send his wife. He knew he was in danger, but he had by then another partner and that partner was Mickey Banet, who had invited himself into the game and was going to stay in."

He looked at the door of the little bathroom and said, "Come out."

There was no one there; the patient had gone—only he hadn't. Unbelievably, the narrow gray door swung slowly open. A red, thin figure, masked in white, stood in the doorway.

Josh said gravely, "It's all over, Cates. You haven't got a chance. They found Jacob Heinzer and got him back; he's still alive. He told them exactly what happened—how he'd slipped out on deck and you came along and offered him a cigarette and, as he took it, slugged him. The next thing he knew he was in the water. It was sheer luck for him that one of the boys in the ward had seen him go past the porthole and gave the alarm—sheer luck that he was found. But bad luck for you."

The figure did not move. Josh said, "What exactly did you do for the Nazis? Or rather, how much money did you turn over to them?"

There was a sort of whisper from the tall figure. Then it swayed a little queerly. The ship was moving again, gathering speed, steady upon her course. The familiar motions and creaks of the ship were louder. Josh said, "Why did you come to this cabin?"

Luther's voice from those bandages said wearily, "I came to see Daisy Belle. I thought she'd be here in this cabin. I didn't know that only Marcia was here. I had the gauze hidden under a cushion in the officers' lounge. I had seen Heinzer. I had to disguise myself in order to approach Para, for he knew I'd killed Castiogne and he knew I'd kill him if I could. But I didn't come here to kill Marcia. I thought Daisy Belle was in this cabin. I had to tell her my plans. I had to. And then I heard them shout from the boats out there that they'd found him—Heinzer. So I knew then there was no escape for me. I couldn't leave this cabin. I couldn't . . ."

Josh said, "You'd better get to a doctor . . ." and suddenly sprang forward as the thin figure wavered and crumpled against the door.

"Get a doctor, Marcia. Hurry. Go on."

Luther Cates had a bad heart attack. He lived until the next morning. He did not make any further statement.

It was not necessary.

A few hours later replies to wired inquiries which the captain had sent began to clatter into the ship's receiving sets. All the great wealth that Luther Cates had banked in Switzerland before the war was gone. It had gone without any question to the Nazi cause. The captain summoned the *Lerida* survivors to his quarters.

The news was a surprise to Daisy Belle. She had not dreamed that Luther's collaboration had been so expensive, so positive and so appalling. "My own," she said brokenly to the captain, "seemed so great. It was as if we shared a dreadful burden of guilt. I never dreamed that there was anything worse. So much worse. I knew there was a shortage of cash; we used my jewels for everything. I didn't know why. I thought it had something to do with war conditions, with getting funds—" She stopped, and after a moment continued very slowly. "I think he did it because he thought they were going to win."

The captain said, "The diamond he gave Castiogne was not a passage bribe, then?"

She had thought the whole thing through. She said steadily, "I think it was the first payment for silence to Castiogne. Luther came to me on the *Lerida* the day of the storm and said it was to pay Castiogne for getting us a passage. Actually it must have been shortly after Gili and Castiogne heard us talking. Castiogne must have seen his way to blackmail and undertaken it immediately. He must have come to Luther for money. And then . . . then Mickey Banet heard the tale from Gili. And he thought, as Castiogne did, that here was his chance to bleed Luther. Were they partners, he and Castiogne?"

Gili was questioned. She still said that she didn't know, but admitted that when she had accused the Cateses, there in

Mickey's cabin the first night on the *Magnolia,* she had been afraid of Mickey. "I knew then that he didn't want me to talk of the Cates couple and of what Castiogne and I had heard them say. I knew Mickey was trying to make me stop talking about it. So I stopped. I didn't know why he wanted me to stop. I never knew why." She paused there, and presently added sullenly, "I knew Mickey. I knew when not to question him."

He had tried, too, to ensure that Marcia would keep the potentially valuable secret by playing on her loyalty to Daisy Belle. "An accusation like that is a very unpleasant one," he had said. "It sticks. Never tell anybody." And Marcia had been only too glad to agree.

Josh said now, thoughtfully, "Gili told him what she'd heard and what she thought Castiogne would do. To Banet it was like the discovery of a gold mine. He suggested to Castiogne that they become partners. Castiogne had to agree. But Castiogne must have already confided in Para. Perhaps Para was to be the strong man. I think that Castiogne had not told Mickey that Para was his partner. But Para knew that Mickey was one of them and told Cates later, on the *Magnolia.* So there were three people in a conspiracy against Luther. He did not know that at first. He thought it was only Castiogne and killed him when he saw that an American ship was about to pick you up.

"He realized that if he let Castiogne leave the lifeboat alive he'd be at his mercy forever. But Para took the diamond from Castiogne while he pretended to revive him. Then Para came to Luther on the *Magnolia.* So Luther, disguised as the patient Heinzer, killed Para. He made sure that Miss Colfax would see him, to direct suspicion away from the *Lerida* people. Then Banet had to be murdered. Probably up to that point Cates had had a difficulty about weapons. The knife from the locker in the lifeboat? A knife stolen from the galley? We'll never know about that. But this time he had a revolver. He killed Banet. There wasn't anything else to do."

Colonel Wells said, "He might have succeeded in passing himself off as Jacob Heinzer until they got him to the hospital. Once ashore, he must have thought he could contrive some way to escape. If he'd sat tight and said nothing, he'd never have got away. He knew it. We'd have kept after them, all of them, until the truth came out about the money. Cates was on deck and Heinzer came along and suddenly there was a chance. And he seized it."

The captain took up a thick sheaf of papers from his table and said, "Here is my report to my superiors. I wish you to listen and, insofar as you can do so, verify the details." He read in a precise, deliberate way. The succinct phrases took on a quality of fate and of irrevocability as the grim and twisted strands of the story picked themselves out, stripped of anything but fact. When he was finished he stopped, as if struck by a thought. He looked hard at the paper. Finally he took up a pencil and wrote, reading the interpolation as he wrote it: "Cates and Banet were Nazis. They destroyed each other. This was their destiny."

VERY early one morning the ship came into Charleston harbor. Josh and Marcia stood at the railing and watched as the *Magnolia* went on slowly along the broad and gracious river, past the lovely old city, her houses dimly outlined in the dawning light.

The sun came up and the river turned to gold. They drew evenly up to a long pier, and the sun glittered upon the shining instruments of the welcoming bands. Lines of ambulances and buses stood waiting. Companies of medical corpsmen were at attention. Music burst upon the ship like a warm embrace.

Josh said suddenly, "I'm going to kiss you." He held her for a long time. "I love you," he said. "I'll always love you."

The band played and the sun shone. A boy on the gangway threw his cap in the air and gave a loud shout of happiness. "Home," he yelled. "Home."

And Marcia thought, But this is home, close to Josh, like this forever.

The
Moving Target

The
Moving Target

A CONDENSATION OF
THE BOOK BY

Ross
Macdonald

ILLUSTRATED BY HOWARD ROGERS

An oil millionaire is missing, and private eye Lew Archer is hired to track him down in the bizarre underworld of southern California.

The trail leads first to an aging starlet and her ruthless chorus-boy husband, then to a guru in a mountaintop sanctuary, to a blues pianist fighting a cocaine habit, and finally to a fortune-hunting attorney. They are all linked in a web of evil, but before Archer can figure out how, the disappearance turns into a multiple murder, with the wrong man making the last killing for the wrong reasons. Through it all drifts the spoiled young daughter of the millionaire, pursuing a dreamlike "moving target" unaware that she herself is exactly that for at least one desperate man.

Lew Archer, based on Raymond Chandler's archetypal tough private eye, Philip Marlowe, is the hero of numerous mysteries by Ross Macdonald, among them *The Goodbye Look* and *The Way Some People Die*.

1

THE cab turned off U.S. 101 in the direction of the sea. The road looped around the base of a brown hill into a canyon lined with scrub oak.

"This is Cabrillo Canyon," the driver said.

There weren't any houses in sight. "The people live in caves?"

"Not on your life. The estates are down by the ocean."

A minute later I started to smell the sea. We rounded another curve and entered its zone of coolness. A sign beside the road said PRIVATE PROPERTY: PERMISSION TO PASS OVER REVOCABLE AT ANY TIME.

The scrub oak gave way to ordered palms and Monterey cypress hedges. I caught glimpses of lawns effervescent with sprinklers, deep white porches, roofs of red tile and green copper. A Rolls with a doll at the wheel went by us like a gust of wind, and I felt unreal.

We turned up a drive between sentinel yews, cruised around in a private highway network for a while, and came out above the sea stretching deep and wide to Hawaii. The Sampson house stood partway down the shoulder of the bluff, with its back to the canyon. It was long and low. Through screens of shrubbery I caught the bright glare of tennis courts, the blue-green shimmer of a pool.

The driver stopped beside the garages. "This is where the cavemen live. You want the service entrance?"

"I'm not proud."

A heavy woman in a blue linen smock came onto the service porch and watched me climb out of the cab. "Mr. Archer?"

"Yes. Mrs. Sampson?"

"Mrs. Kromberg. I'm the housekeeper."

I paid the driver and got my bag out of the back. I felt a little embarrassed with it in my hand. I didn't know whether the job would last an hour or a month.

"I'll put your bag in the storeroom," the housekeeper said. "I don't think you'll be needing it."

She led me through a chrome and porcelain kitchen, down a hall that was vaulted like a cloister, and into an elevator. She pressed the button for the second floor.

"All the modern conveniences," I said to her back.

"They had to put it in when Mrs. Sampson hurt her legs. It cost seven thousand five hundred dollars."

If that was supposed to silence me, it did. She knocked on a door across the hall from the elevator. Nobody answered. After knocking again, she opened the door on a high white bedroom.

"Mrs. Sampson!" the housekeeper called.

A cool voice answered her, "I'm on the sun deck. What do you want?"

"Mr. Archer's here—the man you sent the wire to."

"Tell him to come out."

Mrs. Sampson was lying on a chaise longue with her back to the late morning sun when I stepped out through the French windows. There was a wheelchair standing beside her, but she didn't look like an invalid. She was lean and brown, tanned so dark that her flesh seemed hard, carved from mahogany. Her hair was bleached, and curled tightly. Her age was hard to tell.

"Sit down, Mr. Archer. You must be wondering why I sent for you. Or don't you wonder about your clients?"

I sat on a deck chair beside the chaise. "I wonder. I even conjecture. Most of my work is divorce."

"You don't talk like a detective. I'm glad you mentioned divorce. I want to make it clear at the start that divorce is not what I want. I want my marriage to last. I can't use my legs anymore, but I'm twenty years younger than my husband is, and I'm going to survive him." Bitterness had come into her voice, buzzing like a wasp.

"You mentioned Albert Graves in your telegram."

"He recommended you. He's one of Ralph's lawyers."

"He isn't DA anymore?"

"Not since the war."

"I did some work for him in '40 and '41. I haven't seen him since."

"He told me. He told me you were good at finding people."

"Your husband's missing?"

"Not exactly. Just gone off by himself, or in company."

"I see. You want me to find him and identify the company. And what then?"

"Just tell me where he is, and with whom. I'll do the rest."

"When did he go away?"

"Yesterday. He was in Las Vegas—we have a desert place near there—and he flew to Los Angeles yesterday afternoon with Alan. Alan's his pilot. Ralph gave him the slip at the airport. I suppose he was drunk." Her red mouth curved contemptuously. "Alan said he'd been drinking."

"Does he often go off on a binge?"

"Not often, but totally. He loses his inhibitions about money when he drinks. He tied one on a few months ago and gave away a mountain, complete with hunting lodge."

"To a woman?"

"I almost wish he had. He gave it to a Los Angeles holy man with a long gray beard."

"He sounds like a soft touch."

"Ralph? He'd go stark-staring mad if you called him that to his face. He started out as a wildcat oil operator. You know the type—half man, half alligator, with a piggy bank where his heart should be. That's when he's sober. But alcohol softens him up, at least it has the last few years. A few drinks, and he wants to be a little boy again."

"And you want me to find him before he gives away another mountain?"

"Yes, and if he's with a woman, naturally I'll be interested."

"Have you any particular woman in mind?"

"Ralph doesn't confide in me—he's much closer to his daughter, Miranda—and I'm not equipped to spy on him. That's why I'm hiring you."

I got up and walked to the seaward end of the sun deck. Below it the terraces descended in long green steps to the edge of the bluff, which fell sharply down to the shore.

I heard a splash around the corner of the house and leaned over the railing. A girl and a boy were playing tag in the pool, cutting the water like seals. The girl was chasing the boy. He let her catch him.

Then they were a man and a woman, and the scene froze in the sun. Only the water moved, and the girl's hands. She was standing behind him with her arms around his waist. Her fingers slid over his ribs gently as a harpist's. Her face was hidden against his back. His face held pride and anger like a blind bronze.

He pushed her hands down and stepped away. Her face was naked then and terribly vulnerable. Her arms hung down as if they had lost their purpose. Drops fell off the tips of her hair like tears.

Mrs. Sampson called me by name. "You haven't had lunch?"

"No."

"Lunch for three in the patio, then, Felix," she said to a Filipino houseboy who had appeared at the open French windows. "I'll eat up here alone as usual."

Felix bowed slightly and started away. She called him back. "Bring the photo of Mr. Sampson from my dressing room. You'll need it, won't you, Mr. Archer?"

The face in the leather frame was fat, with thin gray hair and a troubled mouth. The smile that folded the puffed eyelids and creased the sagging cheeks was fixed and forced.

"A poor thing, but mine own," said Mrs. Sampson.

THE young man I had seen in the pool was there in the patio when Felix led me out for lunch. He had laid away his anger and his pride, changed to a fresh light suit, and looked at ease. He was tall enough when he stood up to make me feel slightly undersized—six feet three or four.

"Alan Taggert's my name. I pilot Sampson's plane." His grip was hard. He rotated a small drink in his left hand. "What are you drinking?"

"Milk."

"No kidding? I thought you were a detective." He had a pleasant white smile. "Mine's gin and bitters. I picked up the habit at Port Moresby."

"Done a good deal of flying?"

"Fifty-five missions. And a couple of thousand hours."

"Where?"

"Mostly in the Carolines. I had a P-38."

The girl came out then, wearing a beige skirt and a light top. Her dark red hair, brushed and dried, bubbled around her head. Her wide green eyes were dazzling and strange in her brown face, like light eyes in an Indian.

Taggert introduced her. She was Sampson's daughter, Miranda. She was about twenty-one, a little too old to be Mrs. Sampson's daughter. I watched her over my salmon mayonnaise; a tall girl whose movements had a certain awkward charm, the kind of girl who developed slowly and was worth waiting for.

"My stepmother," she said, "is always going to extremes."

"Do you mean hiring me, Miss Sampson?"

"Not you, especially. Everything she does is extreme. Other people fall off horses without being paralyzed from the waist down. But not Elaine. I think it's psychological. She isn't the raving beauty she used to be, so she retired from competition. For all I know, she deliberately fell off the horse."

Taggert laughed shortly. "Come off it, Miranda. You've been reading a book."

The Filipino servant moved unobtrusively across the patio. Felix's steady smile was a mask behind which his personality waited in isolation.

Taggert changed the subject abruptly. "I don't think I ever met a real-life detective before."

"I'd give you my autograph, only I sign it with an X," I said. "Let's see, you were with Mr. Sampson when he dropped out of sight. When was this exactly?"

"About three thirty—when we landed at Burbank yesterday afternoon. While I was putting the plane away, Mr. Sampson went to call the Valerio to send out a limousine."

"The hotel off Wilshire?"

"Ralph keeps a bungalow there," Miranda said.

"When I got out to the main entrance of the airport," Taggert continued, "Mr. Sampson was gone. I didn't think much about it. He'd been drinking pretty hard, but he could still look after himself. It made me a little sore, though. There I was stranded in Burbank, simply because he couldn't wait a few minutes."

He glanced at Miranda to see if he was saying too much. "Anyway, I took a bus to the hotel. And he wasn't there, hadn't been there at all. I waited till nearly dark and then flew home."

"Did he say anything about his plans?"

"He was going to spend the night at the Valerio."

"Maybe he's there now."

"No," Miranda put in. "Elaine's been phoning every hour on the hour."

"Did he carry any luggage?"

"He kept whatever he needed in his bungalow at the Valerio."

I turned back to Taggert. "How long was he by himself while you were parking the plane?"

"Fifteen minutes or so."

"The limousine from the Valerio would've had to get there pretty fast. He may never have called the hotel at all. Did he have many friends in Los Angeles?"

"Business acquaintances mostly," Miranda said. "You can ask his lawyer, Albert Graves, about them. I'll call his office in Santa Teresa and tell him you're coming. Felix will drive you in. And then I suppose you'll go back to Los Angeles?"

"It looks like the logical place to start."

"Alan can fly you." She stood up and looked down at him imperiously.

"Glad to," he said. "It'll keep me from getting bored."

She switch-tailed angrily into the house.

"Give her a break," I said.

He stood up and overshadowed me. "What do you mean?"

He had a trace of high school arrogance, and I needled it. "She needs a tall man. You'd make a handsome pair."

"Sure, sure." He wagged his head from side to side. "I'm interested in somebody else. More people jump to conclusions about me and Miranda. I eat with the family, but I'm a servant when the chips are down. A bloody flying chauffeur."

"It's an easy enough job, isn't it?"

"I like the flying. What I don't like is being the old guy's keeper. Last week in the desert you'd think he was trying to drink himself to death. A quart and a pint a day. When he drinks like that he gets delusions of grandeur. He wants to adopt me and buy an airline for me." His voice went harsh and loose, in satiric mimicry of a drunken old man's. " 'I'll look after you, Alan boy. You'll get your airline.' But he doesn't give anything away when he's sober. Not a thin dime."

"What makes him like that?" I said.

"I wouldn't know for sure. That woman upstairs would drive anybody crazy. Then he lost a son in the war. That's where I come in, I guess. Bob Sampson was a flier, too. Shot down over Sakishima. Miranda thinks that's what broke the old man up."

"How does Miranda get along with him?"

"Pretty well, but they've been feuding lately. Sampson's been trying to make her get married."

"To anybody in particular?"

"Albert Graves." He said it deadpan, neither pro nor con.

2

THE highway entered Santa Teresa near the sea. Felix drove the Cadillac through a mile of slums where children played in the dust. Nearer the main street there were a few tourist hotels and a series of shabby taverns. After Cabrillo Canyon I felt like a man from another planet.

Felix turned left at the main street, away from the sea. The street changed as we went higher. Men in seersucker suits and women in bright-colored slacks moved in and out of California Spanish shops and offices.

Taggert had been sitting in silence, his handsome face a blank. "How do you like it?" he asked me.

"I don't have to like it. How about you?"

"It's pretty dead for my money. People come here to die, like elephants."

"You should have seen it before the war," I said. "There was nothing but rich old ladies clipping coupons."

"I didn't know you knew the town."

"I worked on a couple of cases with Bert Graves—when he was district attorney."

Felix parked in front of a yellow stucco office building. "I'll wait out here," Taggert said.

Graves's office was a contrast to the grimy cubicle in the courthouse where he used to prepare his cases. The waiting room was finished in cool green cloth and bleached wood. A blond receptionist with cool green eyes completed the color scheme.

I gave her my name and sat down in an overstuffed chair. I was still feeling unreal, hired to look for a man I couldn't quite imagine. An oil tycoon who consorted with holy men and was drinking himself to death. I pulled his photograph out of my pocket and looked at it again.

The inner door opened, and an old lady backed out bobbing and chortling. Graves followed her. She was telling him how very clever he was. When he saw me he winked.

"It's good to see you, Lew," he said when he came back from the door.

His grip was as hard as ever, but the years had changed him. His hairline was creeping back at the temples; his small gray eyes peered out from a network of little wrinkles. He wasn't five years older than I was, but Graves had come up the hard way, and that was an aging process.

"It must be six or seven years," he said.

"All of that. You're not prosecuting anymore."

"I couldn't afford to. How's Sue?"

"Ask her lawyer. She didn't like the company I kept." I changed the subject. "Doing much trial work?"

"Not since the war. It doesn't pay off in a town like this."

"Something must." I looked around the room.

"This is just my front. I'm still a struggling attorney. But I'm learning how to talk to the old ladies." His smile was wry. "Come inside, Lew."

The inner office was bigger, cooler, more heavily furnished. "You talked to Mrs. Sampson?"

"I did. But I don't quite get the point of this job. Do you?"

"Sampson may need protection. A man with five million dollars shouldn't take the chances he does. He's an alcoholic, Lew. He's been getting worse since his boy was killed, and sometimes I'm afraid he's losing his mind. Did Mrs. Sampson tell you about Claude, the character he gave the hunting lodge to?"

"Yeah. The holy man."

"Claude seems to be harmless, but the next one might not be. Los Angeles isn't safe for an elderly lush by himself."

"Mrs. Sampson seemed to think that he's off on a round of pleasures."

"I encouraged her to think that. Otherwise she wouldn't spend the money to protect him."

"How much is she good for?"

"Whatever you say. Fifty a day and expenses?"

"Make it seventy-five. I don't like the imponderables in this. There may not even be a case. Sampson could be with friends."

"I've tried them. He doesn't have many friends here. His real friends are in Texas, where he made his money."

"You're taking this pretty seriously," I said. "Why don't you go to the police?"

"If the police found him for me, he'd fire me in a minute. And I can't be sure he isn't with a woman. Last year I found him in a fifty-dollar house in San Francisco."

"This smells more and more like divorce," I said. "But Mrs. Sampson insisted that isn't it. I still don't get it—or her."

"She has a few dominant motives, like greed and vanity. But she doesn't want a divorce. She'd rather wait and inherit all his money—or half of it. Miranda gets the other half."

"How long has she been married to Sampson?"

"Six years. She tried to have a career before that: dancing, painting, dress designing. No talent. She was Sampson's mistress for a while, and finally she married him as a last resort."

"And what happened to her legs?"

"She fell off a horse she was trying to train, and hit her head on a stone. She hasn't walked since."

"Miranda thinks she doesn't want to walk."

"Were you talking to Miranda?" His face lit up. "Isn't she a marvelous kid?"

"She certainly is." I stood up. "Congratulations."

He blushed and said nothing. I felt slightly embarrassed.

"She's a marvelous kid," he repeated on the way out with me. At forty he was drunk on love.

He sobered up in a hurry when we reached the car. Miranda was in the back seat with Alan Taggert. "I followed you in," she said to me. "I decided to fly down to Los Angeles with you."

Graves gave her a hurt look. She was looking at Taggert. Taggert was looking nowhere in particular. It was a triangle, but not an equilateral one.

WE ROSE into the offshore wind sweeping across the airport. Then the plane leaned gradually and turned out over the sea. I was in the back of the four-seater. Miranda was in front on Taggert's right. We hit a downdraft and her left hand grasped his knee. He let it stay there. What was obvious to me must have been obvious to Albert Graves. Miranda was Taggert's if he wanted her.

Graves was building himself up to a very nasty letdown. Miranda was everything he'd dreamed about—money, youth, beauty. He'd set his mind on her and had to have her. All his life he'd been setting his mind on things—and getting them.

He was a farmer's son from Ohio. When he was fourteen or fifteen, his father lost his farm and died soon after. Bert supported his mother by making tires in a rubber factory. After she died, he put himself through college and came out a Phi Beta Kappa. Before he was thirty he had taken his law degree at the University of Michigan. He had come west and settled in Santa Teresa because he had never seen mountains or swum in the sea. His father had always intended to retire in California, and Bert had inherited the midwestern dream—which, for him, now included the daughter of a Texas oil millionaire.

The dream was still unfulfilled. He'd worked too hard to have any time for women. Deputy DA, City Attorney, DA. He prepared his cases as if he were laying the foundations of society. I knew, because I'd helped him.

Taggert shook his leg like a horse frightening flies. Miranda removed her hand. With a little angry flush spreading to his ears, he pulled the wheel back and climbed—climbed as if he could leave her behind and be all alone in the heart of the sky.

After a few minutes we turned left toward the white smudge of Los Angeles and began the descent to Burbank.

The taxi starter at the Burbank airport remembered Sampson when I showed him the photograph.

"Yeah, he was here yesterday. I noticed him because he was a little under the weather. Not blotto—just a couple of drinks too many."

"Sure," I said. "Was anybody with him?"

"Not that I saw."

"How did he leave?"

"By car—a plain black limousine."

"You know the driver?"

"Naw. A little guy, I think, kind of pale."

The starter didn't remember the make of the car or the license number. I gave him a dollar anyway.

I went upstairs to the cocktail bar, where Miranda and Taggert were sitting like strangers thrown together by accident.

"I called the Valerio," Taggert said. "The limousine should be here any minute."

The limousine, when it came, was driven by a pale little man in a shiny blue serge suit. The taxi starter said he wasn't the man who had picked up Sampson.

I got into the front seat with the driver. "Were you on duty yesterday afternoon?"

"Yes, sir." He shifted gears.

"Did you have any calls to the Burbank airport?"

"No, sir." A worried expression was creeping into his eyes.

"You know Ralph Sampson?"

"At the Valerio? Yes, sir. Indeed I do, sir."

"Have you seen him lately?"

"No, sir. Not for several weeks."

"Tell me, who takes the calls for you?"

"The switchboard operator at the Valerio."

All the rest of the way he drove in tight-mouthed silence.

"I'd like to look at the bungalow," I told Miranda when we pulled up to the hotel. "But first I want to talk to the switchboard operator."

"I'll get the key and wait for you."

The operator was a frozen virgin who dreamed about men at night and hated them in the daytime. "Yes?"

"Yesterday afternoon you had a call for a limousine from the Burbank airport."

Her eyes were small and hard. "We do not answer questions of that nature. I'll have to call the manager."

"All right. I work for Mr. Sampson."

"Mr. *Ralph* Sampson?" she trilled.

"That's correct."

"But he was the one that made the call!"

"What happened to it?"

"He canceled it almost immediately, before I had an opportunity to tell the driver."

"You're sure it was him both times?"

"Oh, yes," she said. "I know Mr. Sampson well. He's been coming here for years." Then she turned to the switchboard, which had three red lights on it.

Miranda stood up when I went into the lobby. "Ralph hasn't been here for nearly a month. We got the key from the assistant manager, and Alan's gone to open the bungalow."

I followed her down a corridor that ended in a wrought-iron door. The grounds back of the main building were laid out in little avenues, with bungalows on either side, set among terraced lawns and flower beds, tennis courts and a swimming pool.

The door of Sampson's bungalow was standing open. We passed through it into a hall cluttered with uncomfortable-looking Spanish chairs before entering a big living room with a high oak-beamed ceiling. It had that mass-produced and impersonal look, like most hotel rooms.

On the chesterfield in front of the fireplace Taggert was hunched over the telephone. "I thought I'd call a buddy of mine." He looked up at Miranda with a half smile. "Since I have to hang around anyway."

"Where does your father keep his things?" I asked Miranda.

"In his bedroom. He doesn't keep much here. A few changes of clothes."

She opened a door across the hall and switched on the light.

"What on earth has he done to it?" she said. "It didn't used to be like this."

The room was twelve-sided and windowless. The indirect lights were red. The walls were covered with thick red stuff that hung in folds from the ceiling to the floor. A heavy armchair and the bed in the center were covered with the same dark red material.

"No wonder he took to drink, if he had to sleep in here," I said. I moved around the room. Each of the twelve panels was embroidered in gold with one of the twelve signs of the zodiac.

"Is your father interested in astrology?"

"Yes, he is," Miranda said. "He went off the deep end when Bob died. I had no idea he'd gone so far, though."

I found the entrance to the closet behind a curtain. It was stuffed with suits and shirts and shoes of all sorts, from golf clothes to evening dress. In the breast pocket of a jacket I found a wallet that held a mass of twenties and a single photograph.

I held the picture up to the bulb that lit the closet. It showed a black-haired woman with dark and mournful eyes and a full drooping mouth. She had written on it, "To Ralph from Fay with Blessings." I replaced the wallet in Sampson's jacket and added the picture to my photographic collection of one.

"Look," Miranda said, when I stepped back into the room. She was lying on the bed with her skirt above her knees. Her up-turned face was closed and dead. And her slender body was burning up in the rosy light, like a sacrifice on an altar. She closed her eyes. "What does this mad room make you think of?"

I crossed the room and put my hand on her shoulder. "Open your eyes."

She opened them. "You saw it, didn't you?" she asked. "The sacrifice on the heathen altar—like Salammbô."

"You read too many books," I said.

My hand was still on her shoulder, conscious of young flesh. She turned toward me and pulled me down. Her lips were hot on my face.

"What goes on?" Taggert asked from the doorway. He was smiling in the red light. The incident amused him.

I stood up and straightened my coat. I was not amused. Miranda was the freshest thing I'd touched in many a day. But she had been using me to stir up Taggert, and it made me angry. The red room made me angry. It was like the inside of a sick brain.

I pulled out the dark woman's picture and showed it to both

of them. "Did you ever see her before? She signs herself 'Fay.'"

"I never did," said Taggert.

"No," said Miranda. She was smiling at him side-eyed and secretly, as if she had won a point.

3

Morris Cramm was night legman for a gossip columnist and worked from seven in the evening to five in the morning. Now, at three thirty in the afternoon, he was at the kitchen table in his apartment eating breakfast, a dark little man with sharp black eyes behind thick spectacles. Behind the glasses was a card-index brain that contained the vital statistics of all Los Angeles.

"Morning, Lew," he said, without getting up.

I sat down opposite him. "It's late afternoon."

"It's morning to me. Which lobe of my brain do you want to pick this morning?"

I showed him the picture signed "Fay." "Do you know the face? I have a hunch I've seen it before."

He studied the photograph. "Superannuated vampire. Forty-ish, but the picture's maybe ten years old. Fay Estabrook."

"You know her?"

"I've seen her around."

"What does she do for a living?"

"Nothing much. Lives quietly. Does some bit parts for Tele-pictures."

"She wouldn't be an astrologist on the side?"

"Could be. I got no file on her, Lew. She isn't that important anymore. But she must have some income. She makes a moderate splash at Chasen's. I've seen her there more than once with an English-remittance-man type."

"Description?"

"Do I get paid for wearying my lobes?"

"Five bucks," I said. "I'm on an expense account."

"White hair, premature, eyes blue or gray. Middle-sized and wiry. Well dressed. Handsome, if you like an aging chorus boy."

"You know I do. Anybody else?"

"One at least. She had late supper with a fat tourist type dressed in ten-dollar bills. He was so squiffed he had to be helped to the door. That was several months ago. I haven't seen her since."

"And you don't know where she lives?"

"Somewhere out of town. It's off my beat. Anyway, I've given you five bucks' worth." I handed him his money. He kissed it and pretended to use it to light a cigarette.

I took a taxi home and went to work on the telephone directories. There was no Fay Estabrook listed.

I called Telepictures in Universal City and asked for Fay Estabrook.

"Miss Estabrook is here," the operator said. "But she's working just now. Is there a message?"

"I'll come out. What stage is she on?"

"Number three."

I parked in a residential block around the corner from Universal City and walked to the main entrance of the studio. There were ten or twelve people outside the casting office, trying to look sought after and complacent, the usual assortment of displaced actors—fat, thin, bearded, shaven, tuxedoed, sombreroed—sitting there with great dignity, waiting for nothing.

I went down a dingy hall to a swinging gate. A middle-aged man in a blue uniform was sitting beside it. The guards at the major studios asked for passports and visas and did everything but probe the body cavities for concealed hand grenades. The independents were more lax, and the guard pushed open the gate and waved me through.

I emerged in a concrete alley and lost myself among anonymous buildings before turning down a dirt road with a sign that said WESTERN MAIN STREET. I went up to a couple of workmen who were painting the weather-warped front of a saloon and asked, "Stage three?"

"Turn right, then left at the first turn. You'll see the sign across the street from New York Tenement."

The false fronts looked so real from a distance, so ugly and thin close up, that they made me feel suspicious of my own reality. I felt like going into Continental Hotel for an imitation drink with the other ghosts.

When I reached stage three, the red light was off, and a herd of chorus girls in bunny costumes were coming out through the soundproof doors. I held the door for the last pair and stepped inside.

The interior of the sound stage was a reproduction of a theater, with red plush orchestra seats and boxes, and gilt decorations. The stage was bare, but there was a small audience grouped in the first few rows. A baby spot illuminated the heads of a dark-haired woman and a gray-mustached man sitting in the center of the first row. I moved down the side aisle and recognized Fay Estabrook.

A buzzer sounded, and there was a heavy silence in the room. It was broken by Fay's voice. "Isn't he marvelous?"

She turned to the man beside her and gently shook his arm. He smiled and nodded.

"Cut!" A tired-looking little man got up from behind the camera and leaned toward Fay. "Look, you're his mother. He's up there on the stage singing his heart out. This is his big chance; it's what you've hoped and prayed for all these years."

He was so emotional that I glanced at the stage involuntarily. It was still empty.

"More heart, my dear Fay. Pour out your mother love to your son singing so gloriously up there. Try again."

"Isn't he marvelous?" Fay said throatily.

"Much, much better," said the little man. He called for lights and camera.

"Isn't he marvelous?" she said again. The gray-mustached man smiled and nodded some more.

"Cut!"

The lights went out. "You may go, Fay," the little director called. "Tomorrow at eight. And try to get a good night's sleep, darling." The way he said it sounded very unpleasant.

I was waiting outside the main entrance with my motor idling when Fay came out. Half a block up the sidewalk she stopped by a black Buick sedan, unlocked it, and got in. I eased out into the traffic and let her slide into the lane ahead of me. Fay cut in and out of the flow, driving furiously and well. On the long, looping grade sloping down to Pacific Palisades I almost lost her. I caught her again a minute before she turned off the boulevard to the right.

I followed her up a road marked WOODLAWN LANE. A hundred yards ahead of me she swung wide and turned into a driveway. I stopped my car where I was and parked.

Through a japonica hedge I saw her climb the steps to the door of a two-storied white house, set far back from the street among trees, with an attached garage. It was a handsome house for a woman on her way out.

After a while I got tired of watching the front door. I took off my coat and tie and rolled up my sleeves. There was a long-spouted oilcan in the trunk, and I took it with me. I walked straight up the driveway past the Buick and through the open door of the garage.

The garage was enormous, big enough to hold a two-ton truck with space to spare for the Buick. The queer thing was that it looked as if a heavy truck had recently been there. There were wide tire marks on the concrete floor and thick oil drippings.

A small window in the rear of the garage looked out on the backyard. A heavy-shouldered man in a scarlet silk sport shirt was sitting in a canvas deck chair with his back to me. He leaned sideways, the crooked fingers of his large hand groping for a bottle of beer. Then he turned his head, and I saw the side of his face. It wasn't Ralph Sampson's, and it wasn't the face the man in the scarlet shirt had started out with. It was a stone face hacked out by a primitive sculptor. It told a very common twentieth-century story: too many fights, not enough brains.

I returned to the tire marks and went down on my knees to examine them. Too late to hide, I heard shuffling footsteps on the driveway.

The man in the scarlet shirt said from the door, "What business you got messing around in here?"

I inverted the oilcan and squirted a stream of oil at the wall. "Get out of my light, please."

"What's that?" he said laboriously.

He wasn't as wide as the door, but he gave that impression. He made me nervous, the way you feel talking to a strange bulldog on his master's property.

"Yes," I said. "You certainly got them, brother."

"What do you mean, we got them?" I didn't like the way he moved toward me. "We ain't got nothing."

"Termites," I said rapidly. "The tiny animals that eat wood." I squirted more oil at the wall.

"What you got in that there can?"

"It's termite killer," I said. "They eat it and die. You tell Mrs. Goldsmith she's got them, all right."

"I don't know no Mrs. Goldsmith."

"The lady of the house. She called up Killabug headquarters for an inspection."

"Oh!" He was puzzling over the words. "Yeah. But we got no Mrs. Goldsmith here."

"Isn't this Eucalyptus Lane?"

"Naw, this is Woodlawn Lane. You got the wrong address, bud." He smiled widely at my ridiculous mistake.

"I'd better be going, then. Mrs. Goldsmith will be looking for me."

"Yeah. Only wait a minute."

His left hand came out fast and took me by the collar. "Don't come messing around in here no more. You got no business messing around in here."

His face filled with angry blood. His eyes were hot and wild. A punchy fighter was less predictable than a bulldog, and twice as dangerous.

"Look." I raised the oilcan. "This stuff will blind you."

I squirted oil in his eyes. He let out a howl of agony. I jerked sideways and didn't look back. I ducked out of the garage and kept running, circling the block. When I came back, the garage door was closed, but the Buick was still standing in the drive. The white house looked very peaceful and innocent in the early evening light.

It was nearly dark when Fay Estabrook came out in a spotted ocelot coat. I drove past her driveway before the Buick backed out, and waited for it on Sunset Boulevard. She drove with great fury all the way back to Hollywood.

Near the corner of Hollywood and Vine, Fay nosed into a parking lot and left her car. I double-parked in the street till I saw her enter Swift's. Then I went home and changed my shirt.

The gun in my closet tempted me, but I didn't put it on. I compromised by taking it out of the holster and putting it in the glove compartment of my car.

4

THE back room of Swift's was paneled in black oak that glowed dimly under the polished brass chandeliers. Fay Estabrook was in a booth at the rear. Her companion on the opposite side of the table was almost completely hidden by the partition.

I went to the bar and ordered a beer, leaning forward to look in the mirror behind the bar. I caught a three-quarter view of Fay Estabrook's face. It was earnest and intense. The mouth was moving rapidly. Just then her companion stood up.

He was the kind who was usually in the company of younger women, the aging chorus boy Morris Cramm had described. His blue jacket fitted him too well. A white silk scarf at his throat set off his silver hair.

He had stood up to shake hands with a red-haired man standing by the booth. I recognized the red-haired man when he wandered back to his own table. He was a contract writer for Metro named Russell Hunt.

The silver-haired man waved good-by to Fay and set his course for the door. He walked efficiently and neatly, looking straight ahead, as if the place were deserted. When he went out, a few heads turned, a couple of eyebrows were elevated. Fay was left in her booth by herself.

I carried my glass to Russell Hunt's table. An ex-reporter from Chicago who had sold his first novel to Metro and never written another, Hunt was turning from a hopeful kid into a nasty old man with migraine. I had helped him lose his second wife to make way for his third, who was no improvement.

"How's the word business, Russell?"

"Sit down, sit down," he said, when I didn't go away.

I slid into a chair. "Who was that you were just shaking hands with?"

"The elegant lad in the scarf? That was Fay Estabrook's husband, Dwight Troy."

"What does he do?"

"I don't know for sure. Fay says he's an importer."

"Do you know Fay Estabrook?"

"A little. I passed her on the way up a few years ago. A few more years, and I'll pass her on the way down."

"Introduce me to her. I've always wanted to meet her."

"I don't get it, Lew. She's old enough to be your wife."

"I have a sentimental regard for her, stemming from the dear dead days beyond recall."

Russell got up laboriously, as if the top of his red head supported the ceiling. I picked up my drink and steered him across the room. "Don't tell her my business," I said in his ear.

Fay Estabrook looked up at us with eyes like dark searchlights.

"This is Lew Archer, Fay. He's an old admirer of yours."

"How nice!" she said. "Won't you sit down?"

"Thank you." I sat down in the leather seat opposite her.

"Excuse me," Russell said. "I have to wage war with the waiter." He went away, lost in his private maze.

"It's nice to be remembered occasionally," the woman said. "Most of my friends are gone. Helene and Florence and Mae—all gone and forgotten."

I took my cue from her winy sentimentality. "Helene Chadwick was a great player in her day. But you're still carrying on."

"I try to keep my hand in, Archer. The life has gone out of the town, though. We used to care about picture-making—it wasn't the money we worked for."

"*The play's the thing.*" It was less embarrassing to quote.

"The play *was* the thing. It isn't like that anymore. The town has lost its sincerity." She poured the final ounce from her half bottle of sherry.

"You're doing all right." I let my glance slide down the heavy body half revealed by the open fur coat. It was good for her age, alive, with a subtly persistent female power.

"I like you, Archer. You're sympathetic. Tell me, when is your birthday?"

"The second of June."

"Really? I didn't expect you to be Geminian. Geminis have no heart. They're double-souled like the Twins, and they lead a double life." She leaned toward me with wide, unfocused eyes. "Do you believe in the stars?"

"Do you?"

"Of course I do. When you look at the evidence, you simply can't deny it. I'm Cancer, for example, and anybody can see that I'm the Cancer type. I'm sensitive and imaginative; I can't do without love. But I've been unlucky in marriage, like so many other Cancerians. Are you married, Archer?"

"Not now."

"That means you were. You'll marry again. Gemini always does. And he often marries an older woman, did you know that?"

"No." Her insistent voice was pushing me slightly off-balance. "You're very convincing. You should do this professionally. There's a lot of money in it."

Her eyes narrowed to two dark slits. She studied me through them, made a tactical decision, and opened them wide again. "Oh, no," she said. "I never do this professionally. It's a talent I have, a gift, and I feel it's my duty to use it. But not for money— only for my friends."

"You're lucky to have an independent income."

"That's Gemini for you," she said. "Always looking for facts."

She'd fired at random and hit the target by accident. "I didn't mean to be curious," I said.

"Oh, I know that." She moved suddenly. "Let's get out of here, Archer. Let's go someplace we can talk."

She left a bill on the table and walked out with heavy dignity. I followed her, feeling a little like a male spider about to be eaten by a female spider.

In the Hollywood Roosevelt bar she complained of the air and said she felt wretched and old. Nonsense, I told her, but we moved to the Zebra Room. In the Zebra Room she accused a man at the next table of looking at her contemptuously. I suggested more air. She drove to the Ambassador as if she were trying to break through into another dimension. I had to park the Buick for her. I'd left my car at Swift's. She quarreled with the Ambassador barman on the grounds that he laughed at her when he turned his back. Fay was pale as a corpse by then, but she was vertical, able to see, talk, drink, and possibly even think.

I was steering her in the direction of the Valerio. A few more drinks, and I could take the risk of suggesting it. I wanted her far enough gone to say whatever came into her head. Archer the midwife to oblivion. I looked at my face in the mirror behind the bar and didn't like it too well. I caught myself wondering how it looked to Miranda Sampson.

Fay leaned forward over the bar with her chin in her hands. She was tasting the bitterness at the bottom of her life, droning out elegies. "He had the body of a wrestler and the head of an Indian chief. One sweet guy, a real one-woman man, the last I ever seen. He got TB and went off in one summer. It broke me up. He was the only man I ever loved."

She drained her glass and stood up. "Take me home, Archer."

I slid off my stool with gigolo alacrity and took her by the arm. "You need another drink to snap you back."

"You're nice." My skin was thin enough to feel the irony. "Only I can't take this place. It's a morgue."

"There's a good bar next street up," I said.

"The Valerio?"

"I think that's it."

"All right. One more drink, then I got to go home."

The bartender in the Valerio cantina came all the way around from behind the bar to say hello to her and to ask after Mr. Sampson.

"He's still in Nevada," she said. I was watching her face, and she caught my look. "A very good friend of mine. He stops here when he's in town."

"A great old guy," the bartender said. "We sure miss him around here."

"Ralph's a wonderful, wonderful man," Fay said.

The bartender took our order and went away.

"Have you cast his horoscope?" I said. "This friend of yours?"

"Now, how did you know? He's Capricorn. One sweet guy, but a very dominant type. He's had tragedy in his life, though. His only boy was killed in the war." She leaned toward me confidentially. "I wish I could show you the room I redecorated for him. It's in one of the bungalows here."

The bartender brought our drinks, and I sipped mine. A door in the wall beside a silent grand piano opened into the lobby. Alan Taggert and Miranda came through the door together.

"Excuse me," I said to Fay.

Miranda saw me when I stood up, and started forward. I put a finger to my mouth and waved her back with the other hand. She moved away with a bewildered look.

Alan was quicker. He took her arm and hustled her out the door. I followed them.

Miranda turned on me. "I don't understand this. You're supposed to be looking for Ralph."

"I'm working on a contact. Go away, please."

"But I've been trying to get in touch with you." She was strained to the point of tears.

I said to Taggert, "Take her away from here before she spoils my night's work."

"But Mrs. Sampson's been phoning for you," he said.

"She's heard from Ralph." Miranda's eyes glowed amber. "A special-delivery letter. He wants her to get a hundred thousand dollars in cash ready for him."

"Say that again."

"He wants her to cash a hundred thousand dollars' worth of bonds."

"Does she have that much?"

"*She* hasn't, but she can get it. Bert Graves has Ralph's power of attorney."

"What's she supposed to do with the money?"

"He said we'll hear from him or he'll send a messenger for it."

"Does he say where he is?"

"No, but the letter's postmarked Santa Maria. He must have been there today."

"Not necessarily. What does Mrs. Sampson want me to do?"

"She didn't say. I suppose she wants your advice."

"All right. Tell her to have the money ready, but not to hand it over to anybody without proof that your father's alive."

"You think he's dead?" Miranda's hand plucked at her neckline.

"I can't afford to guess." I turned to Taggert. "Can you fly Miranda up tonight?"

"I just phoned Santa Teresa. The airport's fogged in. First thing in the morning, though."

"Then tell Mrs. Sampson over the phone. Graves had better contact the police, quietly. Both the local police and the Los Angeles police. And the FBI."

"The FBI?" Miranda whispered.

"Yes," I said. "Kidnapping is a federal offense."

WHEN I went back to the bar, a young Mexican with a guitar was leaning against the grand piano, singing a Spanish bullfighting song. His fingers marched thunderously in the strings. Fay Estabrook was watching him and barely noticed me when I sat down.

She clapped loudly when the song was over. "It's Ralph's favorite," she said.

"About this friend of yours—Ralph. He wouldn't object to your being here with me?"

She laughed harshly. "Didn't I tell you I had a husband? But you don't have to worry about *him*. It's purely a business proposition." She laughed again. "Anyway, my friendship with Ralph is on a different level. You know, more spiritual." She was sobering up on me. I held up two fingers to a waitress.

The second drink fixed her. Her face went to pieces as if by its own weight. Her eyes went dull, and she whispered, "I don't feel so good."

"I'll take you home."

"You're nice."

I helped her to her feet. The waitress held the door open, with a sharp glance at me. I held Fay up on her anesthetized legs, and we made it to her car. I headed it toward Pacific Palisades.

"Got to climb on the treadmill in the morning. I should weep if I get thrown out of pictures. I got independent means."

"You look like a businesswoman," I said encouragingly.

"You're nice, Archer, taking care of an old hag like me. You wouldn't like me if I told you where I got my money." Her laugh was ugly and loose.

She passed out. At least she said nothing more. She'd told me a number of things about herself, but not what I wanted to know, and I was too sick of her to probe deeper. The one sure thing I knew about her was that she was bad company for Sampson or any incautious man. Her playmates were dangerous—one rough, one smooth.

She woke up when I parked in front of her house. "Put the car in the drive. Would you, honey?"

I backed across the road and took the car up the driveway. She needed help to climb the steps to the door, and handed me the key to open it. "You come in. I been trying to think of something I want to drink."

I followed her into the hallway. I felt my way after her into a room to the left, where she switched on a lamp.

The room was nothing like the insane red room she had made

for Ralph Sampson. It was big and cheerful, a solid middle-class room with Postimpressionist reproductions on the walls, built-in bookshelves, a glazed brick fireplace with a heavy sectional sofa curved in front of it.

She was at a portable bar in the corner beside the fireplace. "What are you drinking?"

"Whiskey and water."

She brought me my glass. Half of its contents slopped out en route, leaving a trail of dark splotches across the light green carpet.

She sat down. Her eyes closed. Her body subsided on the cushions of the sofa, and she began to snore. To make certain that she was sound asleep, I gently raised one of her eyelids. The marbled eyeball stared whitely at nothing.

I went into the next room, closed the door behind me, and turned on the light. It shone down from the ceiling on a bleached mahogany table with artificial flowers in the center, a china cabinet at one side, and six heavy chairs ranged around the wall. I turned off the light and went into the kitchen, which was neat and well equipped.

I wondered for an instant if I had misjudged the woman. There were honest astrologists—and plenty of harmless drunks. Her house was like thousands of others in Los Angeles. Except for the huge garage and the ex-prizefighter who guarded it.

The bathroom cabinet was stuffed with creams and paints and powders, Luminal, Nembutal, Veronal. The clothes in the hamper were female. There was only one toothbrush in the holder. A razor but no shaving cream, nor any other trace of a man.

The bedroom next to the bathroom was flowered and prettied in pink. The undergarments in the chest of drawers were peach and baby blue and black lace. I looked under the mass of stockings in the second drawer and found the core of strangeness in the house. It was a row of narrow packages held together with elastic bands. The packages contained money, all in old bills, ones and fives and tens. If all the packages assayed like the one I examined, the bottom of the drawer was lined with eight or ten thousand dollars. A bedroom drawer was hardly a good place to keep it. But it was safer than a bank for people who couldn't declare their income.

The burring ring of a telephone cut the silence like a dentist's drill. I shut the drawer before I went into the hall where the telephone was. There was no sound from Fay in the living room.

I muffled my voice with my tie. "Hello."

"Mr. Troy?" It was a woman.

"Yes."

"Is Fay there?" Her speech was rapid and clipped. "This is Betty."

"No."

"Listen, Mr. Troy. Fay was fried in the Valerio about an hour ago. The man she was with could be plainclothes. You wouldn't want him around when the truck goes through. And you know Fay when she's oiled."

"Yes," I said, and risked: "Where are you now?"

"The Piano, of course."

"Is Ralph Sampson there?"

Her answer was a hiccup of surprise. At the other end of the line I could hear the murmur of people, the clatter of dishes. Probably a restaurant.

She recovered her voice. "Why ask me? I haven't seen him lately."

"Where is he?"

"I don't know. Who is this talking? Mr. Troy?"

"Yes. I'll attend to Fay." I hung up.

The cut-glass knob of the front door rattled slightly behind me. The door swung open suddenly, and Dwight Troy stood in the opening. His silver head was hatless. He stepped inside like an actor coming onstage, shutting the door neatly with his left hand. His right hand was in the pocket of his topcoat. The pocket was pointed at me.

"Who are you?" He became more peremptory. "I asked you a simple question, old chap. Give me a simple answer." His voice held a trace of an English accent.

"The name is Archer," I said. "I brought Fay home. I was just going to call a taxi for myself. I left my car at Swift's."

"Perhaps you had better do that now," he said.

I picked up the receiver and called a Yellow Cab. He moved toward me lightly. His left hand palpated my chest and armpits, moved down my hips. I was glad I'd left my gun in the car.

He stepped back and showed me his gun, a nickel-plated revolver, .32 or .38 caliber. "Now turn around."

He jammed the gun into my back above the kidneys. "Into the bedroom."

He marched me into the lighted bedroom and turned me to face the door. I heard his feet cross the room, a drawer open and shut. The gun came back to my kidneys.

"What were you doing in here?"

"I wasn't in here. Fay turned on the light."

"Where is she now?"

"In the front room."

He walked me into the room where Fay Estabrook was lying, hidden by the back of the sofa. Her mouth was open, but she was no longer snoring.

He looked at her with contempt. "She never could hold her liquor."

"We were pub-crawling," I said. "We had a wizard do."

He looked at me sharply. "I'm not a jealous man, Mr. Archer, but I must warn you to keep away from my wife. She has her own small circle of associates, and you simply wouldn't fit in. Fay's very tolerant, of course. But some of her associates aren't tolerant in the least."

"Are they all as wordy as you?"

He showed his small, regular teeth and subtly changed his posture. The gun twirled on his finger like a silver wheel and came to rest pointed at my heart. "They have other ways of expressing themselves. Do I make myself clear?"

"It's a simple idea to grasp." The sweat was cold on my back.

A car honked in the street. He went to the door and held it open for me. It was warmer outside.

412

"I'M GLAD I called in," the driver said. "Saves me a dry run. I had a long haul out to Malibu." He slowed for the stop sign at Sunset. "Going back to town?"

"Do you know of a place called the Piano?"

"The Wild Piano?" he said. "In West Hollywood. Sort of a bottle joint. You want to go there?"

"Why not?" I said. "The night is young." I was lying. The night was old and chilly, with a slow heartbeat. The tires whined like starved cats on the fog-sprinkled blacktop. The neons along the Strip glared with insomnia.

The Wild Piano was on a badly lit side street among a row of old duplexes. I handed my hat to a hatcheck girl in a cubbyhole and asked for a table near a low platform where a woman was playing the piano. The pianist looked unreal through the smoke, a mechanical doll with clever hands and a rigid, immovable back.

A waiter skidded ahead of me, his napkin fluttering like a pennon, trying to create the illusion that business was brisk. It wasn't. Two thirds of the tables were empty. The rest were occupied by the offscouring of the better bars, putting off going home. Fat and thin, they were fish-faced in the blue aquarium light that emanated from the walls, fish-faced and oyster-eyed.

"Scotch or bourbon, sir?" the waiter said.

"Bourbon and water. I'll mix it."

"Yes, sir. We have sandwiches."

I remembered that I was hungry. "Cheese."

"Very good, sir."

I looked at the pianist again. Her tense, bare shoulders were thin and shapely. Her hair poured down on them like tar, hiding her face. I signaled the waiter and ordered a drink for her.

The waiter pointed me out when he set down her drink, and she turned to look. Her face was oval, so small and delicately modeled it looked pinched. She made no effort to smile. I raised my chin by way of invitation. Her head jerked negatively and bent over the keyboard again.

Her left hand drummed and rolled in the bass, while her right hand elaborated a blues melody. She began to sing in a hard, sibilant voice, frayed at the edges but somehow moving:

> "Brain's in my stomach,
> Heart's in my mouth,
> Want to go north—
> My feet point south."

She deserved a better audience than the chattering room behind me. I clapped when she finished and ordered her another drink.

She brought it to my table and sat down. She had a small and perfect body, poised somewhere between twenty and thirty. "You like my music," she stated. She inclined her forehead and looked up at me from under it, the mannerism of a woman proud of her eyes. Their brown-flecked irises were centerless and disturbing.

"You should be on Fifty-second Street."

"Don't think I wasn't. Got a cigarette?"

I lit it for her, and she inhaled deeply. The rims of her nostrils were bloodless, as white as snow. "My name is Lew," I said. "I must have heard of you."

"I'm Betty Fraley." The name didn't mean anything to me.

"I remember you." I lied more boldly. "You got a tough break, Betty." All snowbirds wore stigmata of bad luck.

"You can say it twice. Two years in a white cell, and no piano. They wanted publicity, and my name was known. It isn't anymore, and if I ever kick the habit, it won't be with the help of the feds." Her red mouth twisted over the wet red end of the cigarette. "Two years without a piano."

"You do nicely for a girl that's out of practice."

"You think so? You should have heard me in Chicago when I was at my peak. You heard my records, maybe."

"Marvelous! I'm crazy about them."

But I'd picked the wrong words or overdone my praise. The bitterness of her mouth spread to her eyes and voice. "I don't believe you. Name one."

"It's been a long time."

"Did you like my 'Gin Mill Blues'?"

"I did," I said with relief. "You do it better than Sullivan."

"You're a liar, Lew. I never recorded that number." She looked intently into my face. "You could be a cop, you know. You got cop's eyes—they want to see people hurt."

"Take it easy, Betty. You're only half psychic. I don't like to see people hurt, but I am a cop."

"Narcotics?" Her face was brushed by terror.

"Nothing like that. A private cop. I don't want anything from you. I just happen to like your music."

"You lie." Her voice was a dry rustle. "You're the one that answered Fay's phone and said you were Troy. What are you after?"

"A man called Sampson."

She leaned toward me, projecting hatred like a magnetic field. "Get out of here and stay out."

She stood up and went to the door behind the piano. "Puddler!" Every head in the room jerked up.

The door sprang open, and Fay's watchdog in the scarlet shirt came out. His small eyes moved from side to side, looking for trouble.

She pointed a finger at me. "Take him out and work him over. He's a peeper, trying to pump me."

I went to meet him and took the sucker punch. The scarred head rolled away easily. I tried with my right. He caught it on the forearm and moved in.

His dull eyes shifted. One fist came into my stomach. I dropped my guard. The other came into my neck below the ear.

My legs were caught by the edge of the platform. I fell against the piano. Consciousness went out in jangling discord.

A TALL shadow appeared at the mouth of the alley, stood one-legged like a stork for an instant, then limped grotesquely toward us. Puddler was too absorbed in punching me to notice. The shadow straightened up behind him and swung one arm high in the air. The arm came down with a dark object swinging at the end of it. It made a sound like cracking walnuts on the back of Puddler's head.

Alan Taggert put his shoe on and squatted beside me. "We better get out of here. I didn't hit him very hard."

My lips felt puffed. My legs were like remote and rebellious colonies of my body. I established mandates over them and got to my feet.

Taggert took my arm and pulled me toward the mouth of the alley. A taxi was standing at the curb. Across the street the entrance of the Wild Piano was deserted. He pushed me into the cab and got in after me.

"Where do you want to go?"

"Home, but I'm not going. Swift's on Hollywood Boulevard."

"They're closed," the driver said.

"My car's in their parking lot." And my gun was in the car. We were halfway there before my brain caught up with my tongue. "Where in hell did you come from?" I said to Taggert.

"I was looking for Sampson at the Wild Piano. He took me there once, and I thought I'd ask them about him."

"That's what I was doing."

"I saw you coming out," he said. "I waited in the taxi to see what gave. When the bruiser took you into the alley I came in after you."

"I haven't thanked you," I said.

"Don't bother." He leaned toward me and said in an earnest whisper, "You really think Sampson's been kidnapped?"

"It's one idea I had."

"Who would have kidnapped him?"

"There's a woman named Estabrook," I said, "and a man named Troy. Ever meet him?"

"No, but I've heard of the Estabrook woman. She was with Sampson in Nevada a couple of months ago. I never got to see her, but Sampson mentioned her. I think she's a sidekick of this holy man Claude."

"You should have told me before. That was her picture I showed you and Miranda."

"I didn't know that."

"She was the woman I was with in the Valerio. I'm going to pay her another visit now. And I could use some help. Her household is a rather violent one."

My reactions were still slow, and after we picked up my car, I let him drive. The Estabrook house was dark when we got there. The Buick was gone from the driveway, and the garage was empty. I knocked on the front door with the muzzle of my gun. No answer.

"We'll break in," I said. But the door was bolted and too strong for our shoulders.

We went around to the back. Taggert flung himself against the kitchen door. When we pushed together it splintered at the lock and gave. We went through the kitchen into the dark hall.

"You're not carrying a gun?" I said.

"No."

I handed him my automatic. "Make do with this." I went to the front door, pulled back the bolt, and opened it a crack. "If anybody comes, let me know. Don't show yourself."

He took up his position with great solemnity, like a new sentry at Buckingham Palace. I went the rounds of the living room, dining room, kitchen, and bathroom. They were as I had seen them last. The bedroom was slightly different.

The difference was that the second drawer had nothing but stockings in it, and a used envelope, torn and empty. The envelope was addressed to Fay Estabrook. Someone had scrawled some words and figures in pencil on the back:

Avge. gross $2000. Avge. expense (Max) $500. Avge. net $1500.

May—1500 × 31—46,500 less 6,500 (emerg.)—40,000 $\frac{40,000}{2} =$ 20,000

It looked like a crude prospectus for a remarkably profitable business. I turned the envelope over again. It was dated April 30, a week before, and postmarked Santa Maria. While that was sinking in, I heard a heavy motor growling in the road. I put the envelope in my pocket, snapped off the light, and moved into the hall. A wave of light poured in at the crack of the door where Taggert was standing. "Archer!" he whispered hoarsely.

Then he did a bold and foolish thing. He stepped out onto the front steps, in the full white glare, and fired the gun in his hand.

"Hold it," I said, too late. The bullet rapped metal and whined away in ricochet.

I elbowed past him and plunged down the steps. A blue truck with a closed van was backing out of the drive in a hurry. I sprinted across the lawn and caught the truck in the road before it could pick up speed. The window was open on the right side of the cab. I hooked my arm through it and braced one foot on the fender. A thin white face with a peaked cap turned toward me. The truck stopped as if it had struck a stone wall. I lost my grip and fell in the road.

The truck backed away, changed gears with a grinding clash, and came toward me while I was still on my knees. I flung myself sideways and rolled to the curb. The truck passed ponderously over the place where I had been and roared on up the street.

When I reached my car, Taggert had started the engine. I pushed him out of the driver's seat and followed the truck. It was out of sight when we reached Sunset.

I turned to Taggert, who was sitting rather forlornly with the gun in his lap. "Hold your fire when I tell you to."

"It was too late when you told me. I aimed over the driver's head, anyway, to force him out of the cab." He handed me the gun, butt foremost.

"He tried to run me down. He wouldn't have got away if you could be trusted with firearms." He was silent after that.

I dropped Taggert at the Valerio and went home. A quart of milk was waiting on my doorstep. I took it in for company. The electric clock in the kitchen said twenty after four. I undressed and got into bed without looking at the empty twin bed on the other side of the room. In a way it was a relief not to have to explain to anyone what I had been doing all night.

IT WAS ten in the morning before I got downtown to Peter Colton's office. He had been my colonel in army intelligence and was now a senior investigator in the DA's office. When I opened the ground-glass door, he glanced up sharply from a pile of police reports, then lowered his eyes immediately to show that I wasn't welcome. I made myself uncomfortable on a hard-backed chair against the wall.

After a while he looked up at me again. "What happened to your face?"

"I got into an argument."

His smile dragged down the corners of his mouth. "All right, spill it. You want something for nothing again."

"I'm giving you something. It could grow up to be the biggest thing in your life."

"And of course you want something in return."

"A little something," I admitted.

"Let's see the color of your story."

"My client's husband left Burbank airport day before yesterday in a black limousine, ownership unknown. He hasn't been seen since. Yesterday she got a letter in his handwriting asking for a hundred grand in bills. What does it suggest to you?"

"Kidnapping?" he said absently.

"It smells like a snatch to me. What does the hot sheet say?"

He took a sheaf of mimeographed sheets from the upper left-hand drawer of his desk and scanned them. "No black limousines in the last seventy-two hours. People with limousines look after them. Day before yesterday, you say. What time?"

I gave him the details.

"It would help if you gave me your client's name."

"This isn't for publication. My client doesn't know I'm here. Besides, I want the guy back alive."

"It's too big to sit on, Lew." He was up and walking, back and forth like a caged bear, between the window and the door.

"Can I trust you?"

"Some. Further than you can see me."

"The name is Sampson," I said. "Ralph Sampson is missing."

"I've heard of him. I guess your client could have a hundred grand in bills."

"You'll be getting the report through official channels soon. In the meantime you can be doing something."

"For you?"

"For yourself. Start checking the car-rental agencies. That's number one. Number two is the Wild Piano—"

He turned on me suddenly. "Is Dwight Troy in this?"

"I'd like to know myself. Tell me about him."

"Poison in a small package. He runs the Wild Piano," said Colton. "We've been trying to get him for years. He's smooth and versatile. He goes just so far in a racket, then he shifts to something else. He rode high in the early 1930s, running liquor from Baja until that petered out. He had a gambling pitch in Nevada for a while, but the syndicate forced him out. His pickings have been slender lately, I hear, but we're still waiting to take him."

"While you're waiting," I said, with heavy irony, "you could close the Wild Piano."

"We close it every six months," he snapped. "You should have seen it before the last raid, when it was the Rhinestone. A woman by the name of Estabrook ran it then."

He moved toward me unexpectedly and put a heavy hand on my shoulder. "If you meet Troy again, don't try to take his gun. It's been tried."

"Not by me."

"No," he said. "The men that tried it are dead."

It was a two-hour drive at sixty from Los Angeles to Santa Teresa. When I reached the Sampson house, Felix admitted me and led me to the living room.

Mrs. Sampson was propped in a padded chair beside a giant window. She was dressed in lime-colored silk jersey. Her gold-shod feet rested on a footstool. The metal wheelchair was beside the door.

"You've taken your time about coming." The voice of the still mahogany face was petulant.

"I can't apologize. I've been working hard on your case, and I relayed my advice to you. Have you taken it?"

"In part. Bert Graves is attending to the money now. Come closer, Mr. Archer, and sit down. I'm perfectly harmless, really." She indicated an armchair facing her own. "You'd better read the letter."

She picked up an envelope from the coffee table beside her and tossed it to me. I took out the envelope I'd found in Fay Estabrook's drawer and compared the two. The only similarity was in the Santa Maria postmark.

"What time did you get it?"

"About nine o'clock last night. It's special delivery, as you can see. Read it."

The letter was a single sheet of plain white typewriter paper covered on one side with a blue ink scrawl:

Dear Elaine:

I am involved in a deal which came up suddenly, and I need some cash in a hurry. There are a number of negotiable bonds in our joint safe-deposit box at the Bank of America. Albert Graves can arrange to have them cashed to the value of one hundred thousand dollars. I want no bills larger than fifties and hundreds. Do not permit the bank to mark them or record the numbers, since the deal I mentioned is confidential and highly important. Keep the money in my safe at home until you hear from me again, as you shortly will.

You will have to take Bert Graves into your confidence, of course, but it is of the outmost importance that you should not tell anyone else about this business. If you do, I stand to lose a very large profit and might even find myself on the wrong side of the law. That is why I am asking you to obtain the money for me, instead of going directly to my bank. I will be finished with this business within the week, and will see you soon.

My best love, and don't worry.
Ralph

"It's carefully done," I said, "but not convincing. Are you absolutely certain this is your husband's writing?"

"There's no doubt about that. And did you notice the spelling of 'utmost'? He always misspells it. He even pronounces it 'outmost.' Ralph isn't a cultivated man."

"The question is, is he a living one?"

Her level blue eyes turned to me with dislike. "Do you really think it's as serious as that, Mr. Archer?"

"I don't know, but this is my guess: your husband is being held for ransom. He wrote this letter from dictation with a gun at his head. If it was really a business deal, he'd have no reason to write to you. Graves has his power of attorney. But kidnappers prefer to deal with the victim's wife. It makes things easier for them."

"What am I going to do?" she said in a strained voice.

"Follow instructions, except that you should let Graves bring in the police, so they'll be standing by. You see, Mrs. Sampson, the easy way for kidnappers to dispose of a victim, after the money's been collected, is to blow his brains out and leave him. He's got to be found before that happens, and I can't do it alone."

"You seem very sure he's been kidnapped. Have you found out anything you haven't told me?"

"Quite a few things. They add up to the fact that your husband's been keeping bad company—as bad as there is in Los Angeles."

"He's always had a taste for low companions—" She broke off suddenly, raising her eyes to the door behind me.

Miranda was standing there. Her eyes were wide with fury, and her words came out in a rush.

"You dare to say that about my father! He may be dying, and all you care about is proving something against him." Miranda strode toward us. She was standing over her stepmother, with her back to me. Even in anger her body had the grace of a young cat. She showed her claws. "My father wouldn't be God knows where if you'd given him any love. You made him come out here to California, away from all his friends, and now you've driven him away from his own house."

"Nonsense!" But Mrs. Sampson was showing the strain. "You've hated me from the beginning and sided against me whether I was right or wrong. Your brother was fairer to me—"

"You leave Bob out of this. You had him under your thumb, but it's no credit to you. It pleased your vanity, didn't it, to have your stepson dancing attendance?"

"That's enough, you wretched girl," Mrs. Sampson said hoarsely.

Miranda fell silent. She was too young and vulnerable to stand the quarrel for long. I turned in my chair and looked out the window at the shifting colors of the ocean: green and white where the surf began, sage-honey-colored in the kelp zone farther out, then deep-water blue to the horizon.

My eye was caught by an unexpected movement beyond the belt of white water where the waves began to break. A little black disk skimmed out along the surface, skipped from wave to wave, and then sank out of sight. Another followed it a moment later. The source of the skimming objects was near the shore, hidden by the steep fall of the cliff. When six or seven had skipped along the water and disappeared, there were no more. Unwillingly I turned back to the silent room.

Miranda was still standing above the other woman's chair, but her posture had altered. Her body had come unstarched. "I'm sorry, Elaine." She walked over to a far corner of the room and sat down with her face averted.

"All this must have been very instructive to Mr. Archer," Mrs. Sampson said. "I'm dreadfully tired. I'm going upstairs."

She lifted a silver handbell from the table beside her. Its sudden peal was like the bell at the end of a round. "You've seen us at our worst," Mrs. Sampson said to me. "Please don't judge us by it. I've decided to do as you say. I'll have Bert Graves call the police. He's familiar with all the Santa Teresa authorities. He should be here any minute."

Mrs. Kromberg, the housekeeper, entered the room and pushed the wheelchair across the carpet. Almost effortlessly she raised Mrs. Sampson in her arms and placed her in the chair. They left the room in silence.

I sat down beside Miranda on the divan in the corner of the

room. She refused to look at me. "You must think we're terrible people," she said. "To fight like that."

"You seem to have something to fight about."

"I don't really know. Elaine has always hated me, I think. Bob was her pet. He was everything I'm not. Strong and controlled and good at everything he tried. Our family's been quite different since he died. Father's gone to pieces, and Elaine's come up with this fake paralysis, and I'm all mixed up. And now something's happened to Father."

"We'll get him back," I said. "Anyway, you have other friends. Alan and Bert, for example."

"Alan doesn't really care for me. I thought he did once—no, I don't want to talk about him. And Bert Graves isn't my friend. He wants to marry me, and that's quite different."

"He loves you, by all the signs."

"I know he does." She raised her round, proud chin. "That's why he bores me."

"You're asking for a hell of a lot, Miranda." And I was talking a hell of a lot. "Things never work out quite perfectly, no matter how hard you push them. You're romantic, and you're an egotist. Someday you'll come down to earth so hard you'll probably break your neck. Or fracture your ego, anyway, I hope."

"Is there any charge for the diagnosis?" she said, too lightly.

"Don't go arrogant on me now. You already have once."

She opened her eyes very wide in demure parody. "Kissing you yesterday?"

"I won't pretend I didn't like it. I did. But it made me mad. You should be able to think of better ways to fascinate Taggert."

"Leave him out of this." Her tone was sharp, but then she softened. "Did it make you very mad?"

"This mad."

I took hold of her shoulders with my hands, of her mouth with mine. She didn't struggle. Neither did she respond.

"Did you get any satisfaction out of that?" she said, when I released her.

I looked into her wide green eyes. They were candid and

steady, but they had murky depths. I wondered what went on in those sea depths, and how long it had been going on.

"It salved my ego."

She laughed. "It salved your lips, at least. There's lipstick on them."

I wiped my mouth with my handkerchief. "How old are you?"

"Twenty. I know. I shouldn't fling myself around. I'm sorry for making you mad." She leaned toward me suddenly and kissed my cheek very lightly.

I felt a letdown, because it was the kind of kiss a niece might give to an uncle.

There was the sound of a car in the drive. "That must be Bert," she said.

We were standing well apart when he entered the room. But he gave me a single glance, questioning and hurt, before he found control of his face. He looked as if he hadn't slept. But he moved with speed and decision, cat-footed for a heavy man.

"Did you get the money?" I asked him.

He unlocked his briefcase and dumped its contents on the coffee table—a dozen or more oblong packages wrapped in brown bank paper and tied together with red tape.

"One hundred thousand dollars," he said. "A thousand fifties and five hundred hundreds. What'll we do with it?"

"Put it in the safe for now. There's one here, isn't there?"

"Yes," Miranda said. "In Father's study. The combination's in his desk."

"And another thing. You need protection for this money and the people in this house."

Graves turned to me. "What about you?"

"I'm not going to be here. Get one of the sheriff's deputies to come out. It's what they're for. And for God's sake see them in person, Bert."

"Why?"

"Because," I said, "this has some of the earmarks of an inside job. Somebody in this house could be interested in a telephone conversation."

"I see what you mean. But where are you going to be?"

"This envelope is postmarked Santa Maria." I didn't bother telling him about the other envelope in my pocket. "There's a chance Sampson may be there."

"Have you tried the ranch?" Miranda said to Graves.

"I called the superintendent this morning. They haven't heard from him."

"What ranch is that?" I said.

"Father has a vegetable ranch on the other side of Bakersfield. He wouldn't be likely to go there now, though, on account of the trouble."

"The field workers are out on strike," Graves said. "They've been out for a couple of months, and there's been some violence. It's a nasty situation."

"Could it have anything to do with this one?"

"I doubt it."

"You know," Miranda said, "he may be at the Temple. When he was there before, his letters came through Santa Maria."

"The Temple?"

"The Temple in the Clouds, the place he gave to Claude. Father spent a couple of days there in the early spring. It's in the mountains near Santa Maria."

"And who," I said, "is Claude?"

"I told you about him," Graves said. "The holy man he gave the mountain to."

"Have you been up to the Temple?" I asked Miranda.

"I drove Ralph up, but I left when Claude started to talk. I couldn't bear him. He's a dirty old goat with nasty eyes."

"How about taking me there now?"

"All right. I'll put on a sweater."

Graves watched her anxiously as she left the room. Then he moved toward me with his fists clenched.

"Listen to me, Archer," he said in a monotone. "Wipe the lipstick off your cheek or I'll wipe it off for you."

I rubbed my left cheek where Miranda had left her mark. "Don't get her wrong—"

"I suppose it was Mrs. Sampson you were playing kissing games with?" He uttered a small, heartbroken laugh.

"Miranda was feeling low and I talked to her and she kissed me once. It was purely filial."

"I'd like to believe you," he said uncertainly. "You know how I feel about Miranda."

"Take it easy," I said. "I'm no threat to your love life, and while I'm being blunt, I don't think Taggert is either. He simply isn't interested."

"Thanks," he said. He wasn't the kind of man who went in for intimate confessions, but he added miserably, "She's so much younger than I am. Taggert has youth and looks."

There was a soft plopping of feet in the outside hall, and Taggert appeared in the doorway as if on cue. "Did somebody take my name in vain?"

He was naked except for wet bathing trunks—wide-shouldered, narrow-waisted, and long-legged. With the wet dark hair curling on his small skull, the lazy smile on his face, he could have posed for the Greeks as a youthful god.

Bert Graves looked him over with dislike and said slowly, "I was just telling Archer how handsome I thought you were."

Alan's smile contracted slightly but stayed on his face. "That sounds like a left-handed compliment, but what the hell! Hello, Archer, anything new?"

"No," I said. "And I was telling Graves that you're not interested in Miranda."

"Right you are," he answered airily. "She's a nice girl but not for me. Now if you'll excuse me, I'll put on some clothes."

I called him back. "Wait a minute. Do you have a gun?"

"A pair of target pistols. Thirty-twos."

"Load one and keep it on you, eh? Stick around the house and keep your eyes open. Try not to be trigger-happy."

"I learned my lesson," he said cheerfully. "Do you expect something to break?"

"No, but if something does, you'll want to be ready. Will you do what I said?"

"I sure will."

"He's not a bad kid," Graves said, when Taggert was gone, "but I can't stand the sight of him. It's funny; I've never been jealous before."

"Ever been in love before?"

"Not until now," he said. "Tell me, what was Miranda feeling low about? This business of her father?"

"Partly that. She feels the family's been going to pieces. She needs some sort of steady backing."

"I know she does. It's one reason I want to marry her. There are other reasons, of course."

I risked a candid question. "Is money one of them?"

He glanced at me sharply. "Miranda has no money of her own."

"She will have, though."

"She will have, naturally, when her father dies. I don't object to the money"—he smiled wryly—"but I'm not a fortune hunter, if that's what you mean."

"It isn't. But she might come into that money sooner than you think. The old man's been running in some funny circles in L.A. Did he ever mention a Fay Estabrook? Or a man called Troy?"

"Sampson introduced me to Troy in Las Vegas a couple of months ago. The three of us went the rounds, and all the croupiers knew him, if that's a recommendation."

"It isn't. And I don't think kidnapping would be beneath Troy's dignity. How did he happen to be with Sampson?"

"I got the impression that he worked for Sampson, but I couldn't be sure. He's a queer fish—he gives me the creeps." He broke off short when Miranda entered the room.

"Ready?" she said. "Don't worry about me, Bert."

She pressed his shoulder with her hand. Her bright face slanted toward him like a challenge.

He kissed her cheek lightly and tenderly. I felt sorry for him. He was a strong, intelligent man, but he looked a little stuffy beside her in his blue pin-striped business suit. A little weary and old to tame a filly like Miranda.

THE pass road climbed through sloping fields of dust-colored chaparral and raw red cutbacks, then looped around into mountain wilderness, grayed and chilled suddenly by the clouds in the pass. The fog grew denser, limiting my vision to twenty-five or thirty feet. I took the last hairpin curves in second. Then the road straightened and we came out of the cloud. From the summit of the pass we could see the valley filled with sunlight and the mountains clear and sharp on the other side.

Miranda was silent for a while. The road cut straight and flat now through the green-and-yellow checkerboard valley. With no one in sight but the Mexican braceros in the fields, I floorboarded. The speedometer needle stuck halfway between eighty-five and ninety.

"Tell me," she said, "why do you do your kind of work? Because you like danger?"

"It's as good a reason as any. It wouldn't be true, though."

"Why, then?"

"I inherited the job from another man."

"Your father?"

"No. Myself when I was younger. I used to think the world was divided into good people and bad people, that you could pin responsibility for evil on certain specific people and punish the guilty. I'm still going through all the motions. And talking too much."

"Don't stop."

"I'll take it from the beginning. When I went into police work in 1935, I believed that evil was a quality some people were born with. A cop's job was to find those people and put them away. But evil isn't so simple. Everybody has it in him, and whether it comes out in his actions depends on a number of things—environment, opportunity, economic pressure, a piece of bad luck, a wrong friend."

"And you find evil in everybody?"

"Just about. Either I'm getting sharper or people are getting worse. And that could be. War and inflation always raise a crop of stinkers, and a lot of them have settled in California."

"You wouldn't be talking about our family?" she said. "You can't blame Ralph on the war—not entirely. He's always been a bit of a stinker."

"I didn't know you felt that way about him."

"I've tried to understand him," she said. "He started out with nothing. His father was a tenant farmer who never had land of his own. You'd think he'd be more sympathetic to poor people, because he was poor himself. The strikers on the ranch, for instance. Their living conditions are awful, and their wages aren't decent, but he's been doing everything he can to starve them out and break the strike. He can't seem to see that Mexican field workers are people."

"It's easier to gouge people if you don't admit they're human."

"Are you judging me like you've judged Ralph?" she asked me after a pause.

"Provisionally. The evidence isn't in."

"You're a strange man," she said softly. "And do you judge yourself?"

"I did last night. I was feeding alcohol to an alcoholic, and I saw my face in the mirror."

"What was the verdict?"

"The judge gave me a tongue-lashing."

"And that's why you drive so fast?"

"Maybe it is."

"I do it when I'm bored. I've done a hundred and five on this road in the Caddie. I pretend to myself I'm going to meet something—something utterly new. Something naked and bright, a moving target in the road."

My obscure resentment came out as fatherly advice. "You'll meet something new if you do it often. A smashed head and oblivion."

"Damn you!" she cried. "You're as stuffy as Bert Graves. I suppose you think a woman's place is in the home, too?"

"Not my home."

The road began to rise. I let the gradient brake the car. At fifty we had nothing to say to each other.

Apart from the road, the country we were coming into looked as if no one had ever been there. A valley dotted with boulders and evergreen opened below us as we crawled over the rim of the mountain. At a height that made me conscious of my breathing we came to a new gravel road, barred by a wooden gate. A metal mailbox on the gatepost bore the name "Claude" in stenciled white letters. I got out and opened the gate, and Miranda drove the car through.

"It's another mile," she said. "Do you trust me?"

"No, but I want to look at the scenery."

In the center of the mesa below, the Temple in the Clouds stood hidden from everyone but hawks and airmen. It was a square one-storied structure of white-painted stone and adobe, built around a central court. There were a few outbuildings inside a wire fence that formed a kind of stockade around it.

On the flat roof of the main building an old man was rising with majestic slowness, a huge leather-brown figure. With tangles of gray hair and beard standing out from his head, he looked like the rayed sun in an old map. He stooped to pick up a piece of cloth, which he wound around his naked middle. He raised one arm as if to tell us to be patient, and descended into the inner court.

Its ironbound door creaked open. He emerged and unlocked the wire gate. I saw his eyes for the first time. They were milky blue, bland, and conscienceless. In spite of his great sun-blacked shoulders and heavy beard, he had a womanish air.

"Greetings, greetings, my friends. Any traveler who comes to my out-of-the-way doorstep is welcome to share my fare."

"Thanks. Do we drive in?"

"Please leave the automobile outside the fence, my friend. Even the outer circle should not be sullied by the trappings of a mechanical civilization."

When we came nearer, his blue-white eyes peered at Miranda.

"Hello, Claude," she said crisply.

"Why, Miss Sampson! I was not looking for a visit from youth and beauty today. Such youth! Such beauty!"

I looked at his feet to check his age. Shod in sandals with thongs between the toes, they were gnarled and swollen: sixty-year-old feet.

"Thank you," she said. "I came to see Ralph, if he's here."

"But he isn't, Miss Sampson. I am alone here. I have sent my disciples away for the present." He smiled vaguely. "I am an old eagle communing with the mountains and the sun."

"An old vulture!" Miranda said. "Has Ralph been here?"

"Not for several months. He has promised me, but he has not yet come." He turned to me. "Who is this young man?"

"Mr. Archer. He's helping me look for Ralph."

"I see. I'm afraid you must take my word that he is not here, Mr. Archer. I cannot permit you to enter the inner circle, since you have not submitted to the rite of purification."

Miranda stepped between us. "All this is nonsense. We're going in to look. I wouldn't take your word for anything, Claude."

He bowed his shaggy head. "As you will, Miss Sampson. The sacrilege will rest upon you."

She brushed past him disdainfully. I followed her through the arched doorway into the inner court. Claude mounted a stone staircase inside the door and disappeared onto the roof.

The stone-paved court was empty. Its walls were lined with closed wooden doors. I pressed the latch of the nearest. It opened into an oak-raftered room that contained a built-in bed covered with dirty blankets; a scarred iron trunk, and a cheap cardboard wardrobe.

"Your father actually gave this place to Claude?"

"I don't know if he deeded it to him. I suppose he'll take it back sometime, if he ever gets over this religious lunacy of his."

"It's a queer sort of hunting lodge," I said.

"It's not really a hunting lodge. It dates from Ralph's pre-religious phase. He was convinced another war was just around the corner. This was going to be his sanctuary if we were invaded. But he got over the fear last year, before they started work on the bomb shelter. He took refuge in astrology instead."

"I didn't use the word 'lunacy,' " I said. "You did."

She smiled a little bleakly. "Ralph doesn't seem so crazy if you understand him. He felt guilty, I think, because he made money out of the war. And then there was Bob's death. Guilt can cause all sorts of irrational fears."

"You read another book," I said. "This time it was a psychology textbook."

Her reaction was surprising. "You make me sick, Archer. Don't you get bored with yourself playing the dumb detective?"

"Sure I get bored. I need something naked and bright. A moving target in the road."

She flushed and turned away.

We went from room to room, opening and closing the doors. Most of the rooms had beds in them and very little else. In the big living room at the end there were five or six straw pallets on the floor. It was narrow-windowed and thick-walled like a fortress, and it smelled like the tank of a county jail.

"Did you see any of the disciples when you were here before?"

"No. But I didn't come inside."

We finished our circuit of the court without seeing anyone and crossed the gravel yard to an adobe outbuilding with a smoking chimney. I looked in through the open door. A girl with a shawl over her head was sitting on her heels in front of a glowing fireplace, stirring a five-gallon pot full of beans.

"It looks as if the disciples are coming for supper." Without moving her shoulders the girl turned her head. The whites of her eyes shone like porcelain in the clay-colored Indian face.

"Have you seen an old man?" I asked her in Spanish. "One who is beardless, fat, and rich. His name is Señor Sampson."

She shrugged both shoulders and turned back to her steaming pot. Claude's sandals crunched in the gravel behind us. "I am not wholly alone, as you can see. This is my handmaiden. If you have done with us, perhaps you will permit me to return to my meditation. Sunset is approaching, and I must pay my respects to the departing god."

Beside the adobe there was a galvanized-iron shed with a padlocked door. "Before you go, open the shed."

Sighing, he took some keys from the folds of his body cloth. The shed contained a pile of empty bags and cartons, several sacks of beans, a case of condensed milk, and some overalls and work boots.

Claude stood in the doorway watching me. "My disciples sometimes work in the valley by the day. Such work in the vegetable fields is a form of worship."

He moved back to let me out. I noticed the imprint of a wide truck tire in the clay at the edge of the gravel. I'd seen the herringbone pattern of the tread before. "I thought you didn't let mechanical trappings come inside the fence?"

He peered at the ground and came up smiling. "Only when necessary. A truck delivered some provisions the other day."

"I hope and trust it was purified?"

"The driver has been purified, yes." With a backward glance at the declining sun he returned to his perch on the roof.

BEFORE we reached the valley the red sun had plunged behind the clouds over the coastal range. The shadowed fields were empty. We passed a dozen truckloads of field workers returning to their bunkhouses on the ranches. Crammed like cattle in the rattling vans, they stood in patient silence, men, women, and children, waiting for food and sleep and the next day's sunrise.

The clouds flowed in the pass on the other side of the valley like a torrent of milk and preceded us down the mountain all the way to U.S. 101. While I was waiting at the stop sign for a break in the highway traffic, a pair of headlights came up fast from the direction of Santa Teresa. The speeding car suddenly swung toward us, trying to turn into the pass road. Its brakes screamed, its tires skittered and snarled.

"Head down!" I said to Miranda.

The driver straightened out, roared into second gear at forty-five or fifty, spun in front of my bumper, and passed on my right in the space between me and the stop sign. I caught a flashing glimpse of the driver's thin, pale face under a peaked leather cap. His car was a dark limousine.

I backed and turned and started after it, but the blacktop was slick from the wet, and I was slow in getting under way. The red rear lights hightailing up the road were swallowed by the fog. It was no use anyway. The driver could turn off onto any of the county roads that paralleled the highway. And perhaps the best thing I could do for Sampson was to let the limousine go.

"He's reckless, but he drives very well," Miranda said.

"Yeah, he's a moving target I'd like to hit sometime."

She looked at me curiously. "You're looking grim, Archer. Have I made you angry again?"

"Not you," I said. "It's waiting for a break in this case that does it. I prefer direct action."

The break was a white envelope stuck in the mailbox at the entrance to Sampson's drive.

Miranda noticed it first. "Stop the car."

"Wait," I said. "Let me handle it."

I took the envelope by one corner and wrapped it in a clean handkerchief. "There may be fingerprints."

"How do you know it's from Father?"

"I don't. You drive up to the house."

In the kitchen, I slit one end of the unmarked envelope and drew out a folded sheet with my fingernails.

My heart dropped when I saw the printed letters pasted on the paper. In the classic tradition of kidnapping, the letters had been cut out individually and arranged in words:

Mr. Sampson is well put one hunderd thousan dollars in plain paper parsel put parsel on grass in middle of road at south end of highway divider oposite Fryers Road one mile south of Santa Teresa do this at nine oclock tonite after you leave parsel drive away imediately north direction Santa Teresa do not attent pollice ambush if you value Sampsons life he will come home tomorrow if no ambush no attent to chase no marked bills

                              too bad for Sampson if you dont
                              freind of the family

"Go and see if Graves is around," I said to Miranda.

I leaned over the sheet of paper on the enameled kitchen table and examined the cutout letters. They varied widely in size and type, and were printed on smooth paper, probably cut from the advertising pages of a big-circulation magazine. The spelling pointed at semiliteracy, but it might have been faked.

I had memorized the letter when Graves came into the kitchen, with Taggert and Miranda trailing behind. I pointed to the table. "That was in the mailbox. It may have been dropped a few minutes ago by a car that passed me on the highway."

Graves leaned over the letter and read it aloud. He raised his head. "This is it. I'll get the deputy. He's in the study with the money. And I'll call the sheriff."

"Has he got a fingerprint man?"

"The DA's is better."

"Call him, too. They're probably too smart to leave fresh prints, but there may be latent ones."

"Right. Now what was that about a car that passed you?"

"Keep it to yourself for now. I'll handle that end. I'm not getting Sampson bumped off if I can help it."

"That's what's worrying me," he said, and left the room on piston-quick legs.

I glanced at Miranda. She looked ready to drop. "Make her eat something, Taggert."

"I couldn't possibly eat," she said. "Do you think he's alive?"

"Yes. But I thought you barely liked him."

"This letter makes it so real. It wasn't real before."

"It's too damned real! Now go away. Go and lie down." She wandered out of the room.

The deputy sheriff came in. He was a heavy, dark man in his thirties, wearing brown store clothes that didn't quite fit.

"What goes on out here?" he said with tentative belligerence.

"Nothing much. Kidnapping and extortion."

"What's this?" He reached for the letter on the table. I had to take hold of his wrist to keep him from touching it.

He glared dully into my face. "Who do you think you are?"

"The name is Archer. Settle down, Officer. You have an evidence case?"

"Yeah, in the car."

"Get it, eh? We'll hold this for the fingerprint men."

He went out and came back with a black metal box. I dropped the letter into it, and he locked it. He left the room with the box under his arm.

Taggert was standing by the open refrigerator with a half-eaten turkey leg in his fingers. "What do we do now?" he asked me between bites.

"Stick around. You may see a little excitement. Got your gun?"

"Sure thing!" He patted the pocket of his jacket.

"Where's a phone?"

"There's one in the butler's pantry. Right through here." He opened a door at the end of the kitchen.

It was a small room with a wall telephone by the door. I called Peter Colton in the DA's office in Los Angeles. He answered the phone himself.

"Lew speaking. It's a snatch. We got the ransom note a few minutes ago. You better talk to the DA. It probably happened in your territory when Sampson left the Burbank airport day before yesterday. Did you get anything on the black limousine?"

"Too much. There were twelve of them rented that day. All but two came back to the agencies the same day. The other two were taken for a week, paid in advance."

"Descriptions?"

"Number one—a Mrs. Ruth Dickson, blond dame, around forty, living at the Beverly Hills Hotel. Number two was a guy on his way to San Francisco. He hasn't turned in the car at that end; but it's only two days, and he has it for a week. Name of Lawrence Becker, a little thin guy, not too well dressed—"

"That may be our man. Did you get the number?"

"Wait a minute, I have it here—62 S 895. It's a 1940 Lincoln."

"Agency?"

"The Deluxe in Pasadena. Why the sudden enthusiasm, Lew?"

"I saw a man on the highway here who could fit your description. He passed me in a long black car about the time the ransom note was dropped. And the same man tried to run me down with a blue truck in Pacific Palisades this morning."

"Why didn't you put the arm on him?"

"The same reason you're not going to. We don't know where Sampson is, and if we throw our weight around, we'll never find out. Put out the word for tailing purposes only."

"Any more helpful hints?"

"Plant a man in the Wild Piano when it opens."

"I've already assigned him. Is that all?"

"Have your office contact the Santa Teresa DA. I'm turning the ransom note over to them for fingerprinting. Good night and thanks."

He hung up, and the connection was broken. I kept the receiver to my ear, listening to the dead line. In the middle of the conversation there had been a click and crackle on the wire. It could have been a receiver being lifted on another extension.

A full minute passed before I heard the faint, metallic rustle of a receiver's being replaced somewhere in the house.

8

Mrs. Kromberg was in the kitchen. She jumped when I opened the door of the pantry.

"I was using the phone," I said.

Mrs. Kromberg managed a smile. "I didn't hear you in there."

"How many phones are there in the house?"

"Five. Two upstairs, three down."

I gave up the idea of checking the phones. Too many people had access to them. "Where is everybody?"

"Mr. Graves called the staff together in the front room. He wanted to know if anybody saw the car that left the note."

As I went out, three other servants passed me in the hallway—two young Mexicans in gardeners' clothes, walking in single file with their heads down, and Felix bringing up the rear. Felix's eyes were glittering like lumps of coal.

Graves was in front of the fireplace in the living room.

"What's the matter with the servants?" I asked him.

"They seem to think they're under suspicion. I asked them if they'd seen the car. What I really wanted, of course, was a look at their faces before they could close them up."

"You think it's an inside job, Bert?"

"Whoever put together that letter is too well posted. How did he know, for example, that the money would be ready for a nine-o'clock deadline?" He glanced at his watch. "Seventy minutes from now."

"Did anyone see the car?"

"Mrs. Kromberg heard it. The others played dumb, or are. These Mexicans and Filipinos are hard to read." He was careful to add, "Not that I've any reason to suspect the gardeners, or Felix either."

"What about Sampson himself? If he pays an eighty percent income tax, he could make eighty grand by staging this. It has been done."

"But in Sampson's case it's fantastic."

"Don't tell me he's honest."

"Not by everybody's standards. But he doesn't need the money. A hundred thousand dollars is small change to Sampson. This kidnapping is the real thing, Lew. You can't get around it."

"I'd like to," I said. "So many kidnappings end up in murder."

"This one doesn't have to," he said in a deep, growling voice. "We'll pay them their money, and if they don't come through with Sampson, we'll hunt them down."

"I'm with you." But it was easier said than done. "Who delivers the money?"

"Why not you?"

"For one thing, they may know me. And I have something else to do. You do it, Bert. And you'd better take Taggert along. He's a sharp kid, and he's not afraid of a gun."

"All right—if you say so."

"I say so."

Mrs. Kromberg appeared in the hall doorway. "I wish you'd

talk to Miranda, Mr. Graves. I tried to take her up something to eat, and she wouldn't unlock the door, wouldn't even answer."

"She'll be all right. Leave her alone for now. Ask Mr. Taggert to meet me in the study, will you? And ask him to bring his pistols—loaded."

"Yes, sir." She was on the point of tears as she went away.

When Graves turned from the door, I saw that she had communicated some of her anxiety to him.

"Miranda's probably feeling guilty," he said, half to himself. "She's watched the old man going downhill, and she probably feels he wouldn't have gone down so far if she had been closer to him."

"She isn't his wife," I said. "What's Mrs. Sampson's reaction?"

"She's taking it very nicely. Reading a novel, in fact. How do you like that?"

"I don't. Maybe she's the one that should be feeling guilty."

Straw-yellow fog lamps brushed the side of the house, and a moment later a car door slammed. "That must be the sheriff," Graves said. "It took him a hell of a long time."

The sheriff was a big man in a business suit, carrying a wide-brimmed rancher's hat. Like his clothes, his face was hybrid, half cop and half politician.

He thrust out his hand to Graves. "I would have been here sooner, but you asked me to pick up Humphreys."

The other man, who had followed him quietly into the room, was wearing a tuxedo. "I was at a party," he said. "How are you, Bert?"

Graves introduced me. The sheriff's name was Spanner. Humphreys was the district attorney. He was tall and balding, with the lean face and haunted eyes of an intellectual sharpshooter. He and Graves didn't shake hands. They were too close for that. Humphreys had been deputy prosecutor when Graves was district attorney.

I stood back and let Graves do the talking. When he had finished, the sheriff said, "The letter orders you to drive away in a northern direction. That means he'll be making his getaway south, toward Los Angeles. Now if we set up a roadblock down the highway, we should be able to catch him."

"If we do that, we can kiss Sampson good-by," I said. "Even if we obey instructions, there's a better than fifty-fifty chance that he won't come out alive. The best thing you can do is get on the wires. Let Graves handle the business at this end."

Spanner's face was mottled with anger. "But if we catch the kidnapper, we can make him talk—"

Humphreys cut him off. "Hold it, Joe. We've got to assume that there are more than one. If we knock off one of them, the other or others will knock off Sampson. The thing is to save Sampson's life." He stood up. "What say we get back to town now?" The sheriff followed him out.

"Can we trust Spanner not to make his own arrangements?"

"I think so," Graves said slowly. "Humphreys will keep an eye on him." He glanced at his watch. It was nearly eight thirty. "Time to get on our horse."

Alan Taggert was in the study, in a tan trench coat that made his shoulders look huge. He brought his hands out of his pockets with a gun in each fist. Graves took one, and Taggert kept the other. They were .32 target pistols with slender bluesteel snouts and prominent sights.

"Remember," I said, for Taggert's benefit, "no shooting unless you're shot at."

"Aren't you coming along?"

"No." I said to Graves, "You know the corner at Fryers Road?"

"Yes."

"There's no cover around?"

"Not a thing. The open beach on one side and a steep slope on the other."

"There wouldn't be. You go ahead in your car. I'll tag along behind and park a mile or so down the highway."

"You're not going to try a fast one?"

"Not me. I just want to see him go by. I'll meet you at the filling station at the city limits afterward. The Last Chance."

"Right." Graves twirled the knobs of the wall safe.

FROM THE CITY LIMITS to Fryers Road the highway was a four-lane shelf cut into the bluffs that stood along the shore. It was divided in the middle by a strip of curbed turf. At the intersection with Fryers Road, the turf ended and the highway narrowed to three lanes. Graves's Studebaker had made a U-turn at the intersection and parked on the shoulder of the highway heading north.

It was a good place for the purpose, a bare corner rimmed on the right by a line of white posts. There wasn't a house in sight, or a tree.

It was ten minutes to nine by my dashboard clock as I waved to Taggert and Graves and drove on past them. It was seven tenths of a mile to the next side road. Two hundred yards beyond this side road was a parking space for sightseers on the beach side of the highway. I turned off there and parked with the lights out. The fog closed around the car when it stopped. At two minutes after nine, rushing headlights came around the curve from the direction of Fryers Road.

The plunging car wheeled sharply before it reached me and turned left up the side road. I couldn't see its color or shape, but I heard it losing rubber. The driver's technique seemed familiar.

Leaving my lights out, I drove across the highway and along its shoulder toward the side road. Before I reached it I heard three sounds, remote and muffled in the fog: the banshee wail of brakes, the sound of a shot, the ascending roar of a motor picking up speed.

When I was a few feet short of the side road, a car came out of it and turned left in front of me toward Los Angeles. It was a long-nosed convertible painted light cream. I couldn't see clearly through the fog, but I thought I saw a dark mass of a woman's hair.

I switched on my fog lamps and turned up the side road. A few hundred yards from the highway, a car was standing with two of its wheels in the ditch. I parked behind it and got out with the gun in my hand. It was a black prewar Lincoln limousine. The engine was idling and the lights were on. The license number was 62 S 895. I opened the front door with my left hand, my gun cocked in my right.

A little man leaned toward me, peering into the fog with intent dead eyes. There was a round hole in the peaked leather cap above his left ear. I caught him before he fell out.

Holding him up in the seat with one hand, I went through his pockets with the other. The side pockets of his Windbreaker contained a windproof lighter, a cheap case half full of cigarettes, and a four-inch spring knife. There was a worn sharkskin wallet in the hip pocket of his Levi's, containing eighteen dollars in small bills and a California driver's license recently issued to one Lawrence Becker. The address on the license was a Los Angeles hotel on the edge of skid row. It wouldn't be his address, and Lawrence Becker wouldn't be his name.

The left side pocket of the Levi's held a dirty comb in a plastic case. The other pocket held a heavy bunch of car keys and a half-used book of matches labeled THE CORNER, COCKTAILS AND STEAKS, HIGHWAY 101 SOUTH OF BUENAVISTA. The rest of the car was as clean as a whistle.

I put the things back in his pockets and propped him up in the seat, slamming the door to hold him. I looked back once before I got into my car. The lights of the Lincoln were still burning, the idling motor still sending out a steady trickle of vapor from the exhaust. The dead man hunched at the wheel looked ready to start on a long, fast trip to another part of the country.

Graves's Studebaker was parked by the pumps at the Last Chance filling station. Graves and Taggert were standing beside it and came running when I drove up.

"It was a black limousine," Graves said. "We drove away slow and saw him stop at the corner. I couldn't see his face, but he was wearing a peaked cap."

"Did you see him pass you?" Taggert's voice was tense.

"He turned off before he got to me. He's sitting in his car on the next side road with a bullet in his head."

"Good God!" Graves cried. "You didn't shoot him, Lew?"

"Somebody else did. A cream convertible came out of the side road a minute after the shot. I think a woman was driving. She headed for L.A. Now, are you sure he got the money?"

"I saw him pick it up."

"He hasn't got it anymore; so one of two things happened. It was a heist, or his partners double-crossed him. If he was hijacked, his partners don't get the hundred grand. If they double-crossed him, they'll double-cross us. Either way it's bad for Sampson."

"What do we do now?" Taggert said.

Graves answered him. "We take the wraps off the case. Give the police the go-ahead. Post a reward. I'll see Mrs. Sampson about it."

"You better start with the sheriff," I said. "Then the highway patrol and the FBI. Get as many men on it as you can."

I released my brakes and let the car roll a few inches. Graves backed away from the window. "Where do you think you're going?" he said.

"On a wild-goose chase."

It took me down the highway fifty miles to Buenavista, where the highway doubled as the main street. I stopped in the middle of the town, in front of an overgrown cigar store. Two dozen Mexican boys with ducktail haircuts were swarming in and out, drawn two ways, by the pinball machines in the back of the store and the girls who went by on the street, in ribbons and paints, cutting the air with their bosoms.

I called one of the boys to the curb and asked him where The Corner was. He pointed south. "Straight ahead, about five miles, where the road goes down to White Beach. There's a big sign. You can't miss it."

I thanked him. He bowed and smiled and nodded as if I had done him a favor.

The sign spelled out The Corner in red neon script on the roof of a long, low building to the right of the highway. At the intersection beyond it another sign pointed to White Beach. I parked in the asphalt parking lot beside the building.

To the left as I went in was a long bar, totally empty. The dining room and dance floor were to the right. There weren't enough dancers to bring the big room to life.

I stood at the entrance as if I were looking for somebody. The solitary waitress came up to me. "You want a table, sir?"

"Thanks, I'll sit in the bar. You may be able to help me, though. I'm looking for a man I met at a baseball game."

"What's his name?"

"That's the trouble—I don't know his name. I owe him money on a bet, and he said he'd meet me here. He's a little fellow, about thirty-five, wears a Windbreaker and a leather cap. Blue eyes, sharp nose."

"I think I know who you mean. His name's Eddie something. He comes in for a drink sometimes, but he hasn't been in to-night."

"He said he'd meet me here. When does he usually come in?"

"Around midnight. He drives a truck, don't he?"

"Yeah, a blue truck."

"That's the one," she said. "I seen it in the parking lot. He was in a couple of nights ago, used our phone for a long-distance telephone call. Three nights ago, it was. The boss didn't like it, but Eddie said he'd reverse the charges, so the boss let him go ahead. How much do you owe him?"

"Plenty. You don't know where he was calling?"

"No. It's none of my business, anyway. Is it any of yours?"

"I want to get in touch with him so I can send him his money."

"You can leave it with the boss if you want to."

"Where's he?"

"Chico, behind the bar."

The bartender's face, from receding hairline to slack jaw, was terribly long and thin. His night of presiding at an empty bar made it seem even longer. "What'll it be?"

"A beer," I said. "I'm looking for a guy called Eddie. The one that phoned me long-distance the other night."

"You from Las Vegas?"

"Just came from there."

"What were you looking for him for?"

"I owe him some money. Does he live around here?"

"Yeah, I think he does. He come in once or twice with a blond dame. He might come in tonight for all I know. Stick around."

"Thanks, I will."

I took my beer to a table beside the window, from which I could watch the parking lot and the main entrance. While I was drinking the beer a black sedan rolled into the parking lot, a black Ford sedan with a red police beacon sticking out like a sore thumb.

The man who got out wore plain clothes as obvious as a baseball umpire's suit. I saw his face when he came into the circle of light from the entrance. It was the deputy sheriff from Santa Teresa. I got up quickly and went through the door at the end of the bar into the men's lavatory, locking the door behind me. I lowered the top of the toilet seat and sat down to brood over my lack of foresight. I shouldn't have left the book matches in Eddie something's pocket.

In a few minutes there was a metallic pounding on the door. "Open up," the deputy said. "I know you're in there."

I slipped the bolt and pulled the door wide open. "You in a hurry, Officer?"

"I thought maybe it was you." His black eyes were bulging with satisfaction. He had a gun in his hand.

"This is the guy," the bartender said, at his shoulder. "He said Eddie phoned him in Las Vegas."

"What you got to say to that?" the deputy demanded. He waggled the gun in my face.

"Come in and close the door."

"Then put your hands on your head." The gun poked into my solar plexus. "You carrying a gun?" He started to frisk me with his other hand.

I stepped back out of his reach. "You can't have it."

He moved toward me again. The door swung closed behind him. "You know what you're doing, eh? Resisting an officer in performance of his duty. I got a good mind to put you under arrest."

"Hold it," I said. "Don't lay a finger on me."

Our glances met and deadlocked. "Now put your gun away," I said. "I don't like being threatened."

"Nobody asked you what you liked," he said, but his fire had gone out.

"I came here for the same reason you did—Officer." The word came hard, but I managed to get it out. "I found the book matches in Eddie's pocket—"

"How come you know his name?" he said alertly.

"The waitress told me."

"Yeah? The bartender said he phoned you in Las Vegas."

"I was trying to pump the bartender. Get it? It was a gag. I was trying to be subtle."

"Well, what did you find out?"

"The dead man's name is Eddie, and he drove a truck. He came in here for drinks sometimes. Three nights ago he phoned Las Vegas from here. Sampson was in Las Vegas three nights ago."

"It all fits in, don't it?" he said.

"I never thought of that," I said. "Thank you very much for pointing it out to me."

He gave me a queer look, but he put away his gun.

I DROVE half a mile down the highway, turned, drove back again, and parked at the intersection diagonally across from The Corner. The deputy's car was still in the lot.

The fog was lifting, dissolving into the sky like milk in water. The expanding horizon only reminded me that Ralph Sampson could be anywhere at all—starving to death in a mountain cabin, drowned at the bottom of the sea, or wearing a hole in the head like Eddie.

A truck came up from the south and passed me slowly. It wheeled into the parking lot of The Corner. The truck was blue and had a closed van. A man jumped down from the cab and shuffled across the asphalt. In the light from the entrance I recognized his face. A savage sculptor had hacked it out of stone.

He stopped with a jerk when he saw the deputy's black police car. Stopped and turned and ran back to the blue truck. It backed out with a grinding of gears and moved down the road toward White Beach. When its taillight had dwindled to a red spark, I followed it. The road changed from blacktop to gravel, and finally to sand.

Where the road came down to the beach between two bluffs, another road crossed it. The lights of the truck turned left and climbed the slope. When they were over the rise and out of sight, I followed slowly with my lights out. There was a traveling moon in the clouds, which were drifting out to sea.

Before I knew it I was abreast of the truck. It was standing in a lane off the road. I kept going until the road ended abruptly at the bottom of the hill. I turned my car in the dead end and climbed the hill on foot. A row of trees edged the lane where the truck was standing The ground was uneven, dotted with clumps of grass. I stumbled more than once. Then space fell open in front of me, and I nearly walked off the edge of a bluff.

To the right below me there was a white square of light. I slid down the side of the hill, holding on to the grass to keep from falling. A small white cottage took shape around the light.

The unblinded window gave me a full view of the single room. I felt for the gun in my holster and approached the window on my hands and knees.

Puddler was wedged into a chair, his broken profile toward me, a bottle of beer in his fist. He was facing a woman on an unmade bed against the wall. The gasoline lamp that hung from a rafter in the unplastered ceiling threw a hard white light on her streaked blond hair and her thin, harried face.

The clapboard walls were so thin that I could hear Puddler's voice. "I can't wait here all night, can I? I got a job to get back to. And I don't like that police car up there at The Corner."

"That car don't mean anything."

"I should of been back at the Piano already; you know that. Mr. Troy was mad when Eddie didn't show."

"If he don't like the way Eddie does the job, he can stick it." The woman's voice was sharp and thin like her face.

"You ain't in no position to talk like that, Marcie." Puddler looked from side to side of the room. "You didn't talk like that when Eddie come sucking around for a job when he got out of the pen."

"You shut your yap about Eddie and the pen." Her voice bit like a thin knife blade. "How many jails you seen the inside of, dim brain?"

His scarred face gathered in folds of hurt surprise. "Lay off me, hear?"

"All right, then, lay off Eddie."

"Where the hell is Eddie, anyway?"

"I don't know where he is, but I know he's got a reason."

"It better be good when he talks to Mr. Troy."

"*Mister* Troy, *Mister* Troy. He's sure got you hypnotized."

His small eyes peered at her. "Listen, Marcie," he said after a pause. "You can drive the truck."

"The hell you say! I want no part of that racket."

"You're awful fancy since Eddie took you off the street."

"Shut up or you'll be sorry!" she said. "The trouble with you is you're yellow. You see a patrol car and you try to get a woman to take your rap, like any other pimp."

He stood up suddenly, brandishing the bottle. "Lay off me, hear? You was a man, I spoil your face." The beer foamed out on the floor and over Marcie's knees.

She answered very coolly. "Sit down, Puddler. Everybody knows you're a powerful battler. I'll get you another beer."

She got up and moved across the room. Taking a towel from a nail beside the sink, she dabbed at her beer-stained bathrobe.

"You drive the truck?" Puddler said hopefully.

"Do I have to say everything twice? I'm not driving the truck. If you're afraid, let one of them drive."

"Naw, I can't do that. They don't know the road."

"You're wasting time, then, aren't you?"

"Yeah, I guess so."

I left the window and started up the hill. Before I reached the top, a door swung open, then closed. Puddler's shadow came out of the pool of shadows behind the house. He went up the steep lane toward the truck.

I had to choose between him and Marcie. I chose Puddler. Marcie could wait. She'd wait forever before Eddie something came back.

9

A FEW miles north of Buenavista the blue truck left the highway, turning off to the right. I let it get well ahead. Before I turned up after it I switched to my fog lamps. The fog had blown out to sea, but I didn't want Puddler to see the same headlights behind him all the way.

All the way was close to seventy miles, two hours of rough driving through mountains. We were coming by a different route into the valley Miranda and I had crossed in the afternoon. On the straight valley road I turned out my car lights entirely and drove by the light of the moon.

On the other side of the valley the truck climbed again, up the twisting blacktop which led to the Temple in the Clouds. When I reached Claude's mailbox, the wooden gate beside it had been closed. The truck was far above me, a glowworm crawling up the mountain.

So far as I knew, besides the holy man's "handmaiden," there were only the two of them there, Puddler and Claude. I had a gun—and the advantage of surprise.

I opened the gate and drove up the winding lane to the rim of the mesa, and down toward the Temple. Above its white mass there was a faint glow from an interior light. The truck was standing inside the open wire gate, its back doors swinging wide. I parked at the gate and got out.

There was nothing inside the truck but a wooden bench padded with burlap along each side, and the pungent odor of men and sweat.

The ironbound door of the Temple creaked open then. Claude came out, a moonlit caricature of a Roman senator. "Who is that?" he said.

"Archer. Remember me?"

I moved from behind the truck and let him see me. He had an electric lantern in his hand. It shone on the gun in mine.

"What are you doing here?" His voice was steady.

"Still looking for Sampson," I said.

As I approached, he backed toward the door. "You know he is not here. Was one sacrilege not enough for you?"

"Skip the mumbo jumbo, Claude. Did it ever fool anybody?"

"Come in if you must, then," he said. "And I see you must."

He held the door for me and closed it after me. Puddler was standing in the center of the court.

"Get over there with Puddler," I said to Claude.

But Puddler came toward me in a shuffling run. I shot once at his feet. The bullet made a white scar in the stone in front of him and whined into the adobe wall on the other side of the court. Puddler stood still and looked at me.

"Come here," I said. "I want to talk to you."

He stayed where he was. Claude cried out in a Spanish dialect I didn't understand. A door sprang open on the other side of the court. A dozen men came out. They were small and brown, moving quickly toward me. They came on silently, and I was afraid of them. Because of that, or something else, I held my fire. They looked at my gun and came on anyway.

I clubbed the gun and waited. The first two got bloody scalps. Then they swarmed over me, hung on my arms, kicked my legs from under me, kicked consciousness out of my head.

When I came to, my arms were pinned, my raw mouth kissing cement. My arms were tied behind me, my legs bent up and tied to my waist. All I could do was rock a little and beat the side of my head against cement. I decided against this policy.

I tried yelling. I couldn't hear my voice above the roar in my skull. Then the real pain began, pounding my temples in syncopated rhythm. I was grateful for any interruption, even Claude.

"The wrath of the god is heavy," he said, above and behind me.

"Stop gabbling," I said to the cement. "You'll be up against two kidnapping raps instead of one."

By straining my neck I could see his gnarled sandaled feet on the floor near my head. "You misunderstand the situation," he said. "You invaded our retreat by armed force, assaulted me, attacked my friends and disciples—"

"Is Puddler one of your disciples? He's a very spiritual type."

"Listen to me, Mr. Archer. We might with perfect justification have killed you in self-defense. Your life is still our gift." He stamped with his heel in my side, just above the kidney. My mouth opened and my teeth ground on the cement.

"Think about it," he said.

The light receded and a door slammed. The pain in my head and body pulsated like the tip of a restless drill. With my arms roped tight behind me, my heels pressed into my buttocks, I slid over the threshold of consciousness.

Light against my eyelids brought me back. I heard a voice above me and kept my eyes closed. It was Troy's soft purr.

"You've made a serious error, Claude. I know this chap, you see. Now why didn't you tell me about his earlier visit?"

"I didn't think it was important. He was looking for Sampson, that was all. Sampson's daughter was with him." Claude was speaking naturally for the first time.

"You didn't think it was important, eh? I'll tell you just how important it is for you. It means that your usefulness is ended. You can take your so-called handmaiden and get out."

"This is my place! Sampson said I could live here. You can't order me out."

"I've already done so, Claude. You've bungled your piece of the line and you're finished. Probably the whole thing is finished. We're clearing out of the Temple."

"But where can I go? What can I do?"

"Open another storefront church. What you do is no concern of mine."

"Fay won't like this," Claude said hesitantly.

"I don't propose to consult her. And we'll have no more argument, because I have one more job for you."

"What is it?" Claude's voice tried to sound eager.

"You can complete the delivery of the current truckload. I'm not at all sure you're competent even for that, but I must risk it. The foreman will meet you at the southeast entrance of the ranch to give them safe-conduct. When you've unloaded, drive the truck back to Bakersfield and lose it. Don't try to sell it. Leave it in a parking lot, and disappear. Can I trust you to do that?"

"Yes, Mr. Troy. But I have no money."

"Here's a hundred."

"Only a hundred?"

"You're lucky to get that, Claude. You can start now. Tell Puddler I want him when he's finished eating."

Claude's sandals scraped away. This time the light remained. Something pulled at the rope that held my wrists. My hands and forearms were numb, but I could feel the strain in my shoulders. "Lay off!" The movement of my jaw set off a fit of chattering.

"You'll be perfectly all right in a jiffy," Troy said. "They've trussed you up like a fowl for market, haven't they?"

I heard a knife whisper through fiber. The tension in my arms and legs was released. They thudded on the cement like pieces of wood.

"Do get up, old fellow."

"I like it here." Sense was returning to my arms and legs, burning like a slow fire.

"I warned you once about my associates, Mr. Archer. If they've dealt with you rather violently, you must admit that you asked for it." Troy stepped back. "The gun in my hand is aimed at the back of your head. You may get up slowly, if you feel able."

I forced my body off the pavement. The room spun and lurched to rest. It was one of the bare cells off the court of the Temple. An electric lantern stood on a bench against one wall. Troy was beside it, as dapper and well groomed as ever.

"I gave you the benefit of the doubt last night," he said. "You've rather disappointed me."

"I'm doing my job."

He moved the gun in his hand. "Just what exactly is your job, old man?"

"I'm looking for Ralph Sampson."

"Is Sampson missing?"

I looked into his impassive face, trying to judge how much he knew. "Rhetorical questions bore me, Troy. The point is that you won't gain anything by pulling a second snatch on top of the first. It will pay you to let me go."

"Are you offering me a deal, my dear fellow? You're rather low on bargaining power, aren't you?"

"I'm not working alone," I said. "The cops are in the Piano tonight. They're watching Fay's. Miranda Sampson will be bringing them here today. No matter what you do to me, your racket is finished. Shoot me, and you're finished."

"Perhaps you overestimate your importance." He smiled carefully. "You wouldn't be considering a percentage of tonight's gross?"

"Wouldn't I?" I was trying to think my way around his gun.

"Consider my position," Troy said. "A small-time private eye blunders into my business, not once, but twice in rapid succession. I grin and bear it. Instead of killing you, I offer you a one-third cut of tonight's gross. Seven hundred dollars, Mr. Archer."

"A one-third cut of tonight's gross is thirty-three grand."

"What?" He was startled, but he recovered his poise immediately. "That's a rather grandiose estimate."

"One third of a hundred thousand is thirty-three thousand and change."

"What kind of a shakedown are you trying to pull?" His voice was anxious.

"Forget it," I said. "I wouldn't touch your money."

"But I don't understand," he said earnestly. "You mustn't talk in riddles. It makes me jumpy. It makes my hands nervous." The gun moved in illustration.

"Don't you know what goes on, Troy? I thought you knew the angles."

"Assume that I don't know anything." He raised the gun and let me look into its eye. "Tell me about the hundred grand. And talk fast."

"Why should I tell you your business? You kidnapped Sampson two days ago."

"Go on."

"Your driver picked up the hundred grand a few hours ago."

"Puddler did that?" His impassivity had vanished for good. He went to the door and opened it, holding the gun between us. "Puddler!" His voice rose high and cracked.

"The other driver," I said. "Eddie."

"You're lying, Archer."

"Wait for the cops to come and tell you. They know by now who Eddie was working for."

"Eddie hasn't the brains."

"Enough brains for a fall guy. Eddie's in the morgue."

"Who killed him? Coppers?"

"Maybe you did," I said slowly. "A hundred grand is a lot of money to a small-timer."

He let it pass. "What happened to the money?"

"Somebody shot Eddie and took it away. Somebody in a cream-colored convertible."

Those three words hit him behind the eyes and turned them blank for an instant. I moved to my right and swatted his gun with the palm of my left hand. It spun to the floor and slid to the open door.

Puddler was in at the door and on the gun before me. I backed away.

"Do I let him have it, Mr. Troy?"

Troy was shaking his injured hand. "Not now," he said. "We've got to clear out of here. Take him to the pier on the Rincon. Use his car. Hold him there until I send word. You follow me?"

"I get it, Mr. Troy. Where are you going to be?"

"I don't quite know. Is Betty at the Piano tonight?"

"Not when I left."

"Do you know where she lives?"

"Naw—she moved the last couple weeks. Somebody lent her a cabin somewheres, I don't know where—"

"Is she driving the same car?"

"The convertible? Yeah."

"I see," Troy said. "I'm surrounded by fools and knaves as usual."

They marched me out to my car. The black Buick was standing beside it. The truck was gone, and so were Claude and the brown men.

Puddler brought a coil of rope from the shack beside the adobe.

"Put your hands behind you," Troy said to me.

"If you push me around some more, I'll have a grudge against you," I said.

"You talk a great fight," Troy said. "Quiet him, Puddler."

Puddler's fist struck the nape of my neck. Pain whistled through my body, and the night fell on me solidly again.

When I came to I was wedged on the floor of my car between the front and back seats. The floor was vibrating with motion, and the pain in my head kept time. My hands were bound behind me again. Puddler was in the front seat, outlined by the reflection of the headlights.

By dark, untraveled roads we came down out of the mountains and back to the sea. Puddler parked the car under a tarpaulin stretched on poles. As soon as the engine died I could hear the waves below us beating on the sand. He lifted me out by my coat collar and set me on my feet. I noticed that he pocketed my ignition key.

"Don't make no noise," he said, "unless you want it again." He pushed me out from under the tarpaulin.

I was at the shore end of a long pier built out over the water. There were oil derricks on the skyline behind me, but no lights. We walked in single file, with Puddler at the rear. The planks of the footwalk were warped. Black water gleamed in the cracks.

When we were about a hundred yards from shore, I made out an oil pump at the end of the pier, rising and falling like a mechanical teeter-totter. There was a toolshed beside it.

457

Puddler unlocked the door of the shed, lifted a lantern off a nail, and lit it.

"Sit down, punk." He swung the lantern toward a heavy bench that stood against the wall. There were a few tools scattered along it: pincers, wrenches of various sizes, a rusty file.

I sat down on a clear space. Puddler shut the door and set the lantern on an oil drum. Lit from below by the yellow flaring light, his face was low-browed like a Neanderthal's, heavy, forlorn, and without thought.

"You're in a rather unusual position," I said.

He didn't answer. He leaned against the door, blocking my way. I listened to the thump and creak of the pump outside, the water lapping below against the piling. And I thought over the things I knew about Puddler.

"You're in a rather unusual position," I said again. "Acting as jailer, I mean. It's usually the other way around, isn't it? You sit in the cell while somebody else watches you."

"Button your lip."

"How many jails you seen the inside of, dim brain?"

"I warned you." He slouched toward me.

"It takes a lot of guts," I said, "to threaten a man when his hands are tied behind him."

His open hand stung my face.

"The trouble with you is you're yellow," I said. "Just like Marcie said. You're even afraid of Marcie, aren't you, Puddler?"

He stood there blinking, overshadowing me. "I kill you, hear, you talk like that to me." The words came out disjointed, moving too fast for his laboring mouth. A bubble of saliva formed at one corner.

"You fifth-rate bum," I said. "You has-been. Down-and-outer. Hit a man when he's tied—it's all you're good for."

He took a clasp knife out of his pocket and opened it. His little eyes were red and shining.

"Stand up," he said. "I show you who's a bum."

I turned my back to him. He cut the ropes on my wrists and snapped the knife shut. Then he whirled me toward him and met me with a quick right cross that took away the feeling from my face. I knew I was no match for him. I kicked him in the stomach, and he went to the other side of the room.

While he was coming back I picked up the file from the bench. Its point was blunt, but it would do. I clinched with him. Holding the file in my right hand, I cut him across the forehead from temple to temple. He backed away from me. "You cut me," he said incredulously.

"Pretty soon you won't be able to see, Puddler." A Finnish sailor on the San Pedro docks had taught me how Baltic knife fighters blind their opponents.

"I kill you yet." He came at me like a bull.

I made for the door. He came after me and caught me in the opening. We staggered the width of the pier and fell into space. I took a quick breath before we struck water. We went down together. Puddler fought me violently, but his blows were cushioned by the water. I hooked my fingers in his belt and held on.

He threshed and kicked like a terrified animal. I saw his air come out, the silver bubbles rising through the black water to the surface. I held on to him. My lungs were straining for air, the contents of my head were slowing and thickening. And Puddler wasn't struggling anymore.

I had to let go of him to reach the surface in time. One deep breath, and I went back down through strata of cold until my ears were aching with pressure. Puddler was out of reach and out of sight. I tried six times before I gave him up. The key to my car was in his trouser pocket.

When I swam to shore, my legs wouldn't hold me up. I had to crawl out of reach of the surf. It was partly physical exhaustion and partly fear. I was afraid of what was behind me in the cold water. I lay in the sand until my heartbeat slowed.

Finally I got to my feet and climbed the bank to the tarpaulin shelter where my car was. I found a piece of copper wire attached to one of the poles that held the tarpaulin. I pulled it loose and wired my ignition terminals under the dash. The engine started on the first try.

10

THE sun was over the mountains when I reached Santa Teresa. From the canyon road the Sampson house looked like a toy villa built of sugar cubes. Closer up I could feel its massive silence when I stopped the car. I had to unwire the ignition to cut the motor.

Félix came to the service entrance when I knocked. "Were you in an accident, Mr. Archer?"

"Apparently. Is my bag still in the storeroom?" I had fresh clothes in it and a duplicate set of car keys.

"Yes, sir. There are contusions on your face, Mr. Archer. Should I call a doctor?"

"Don't bother. I could do with a shower, though, if there's one handy."

"Yes, sir. I have a shower over the garage." He led me to his quarters and brought my bag. I showered and shaved in the dinky bathroom, and changed my sea-sodden clothes.

When I returned to the kitchen, he was setting a tray with a silver breakfast set. "Do you want something to eat, sir?"

"Bacon and eggs, if possible."

"So soon as I have finished with Miss Sampson's tray, sir."

"Is she all right?"

"I do not know, sir. It was past midnight when she came home."

"From where?"

"I do not know, sir. She left at the same time as you and Mr. Graves."

"What car did she take?"

"The Packard convertible."

"Let's see, that's the cream one, isn't it?"

"No, sir. It is red. Bright scarlet. She drove over two hundred miles in the time she was gone."

"You keep a pretty close watch on the family, don't you, Felix?"

He smiled blandly. "It is one of my duties to check the cars for gas and oil, sir, since we have no regular chauffeur."

"Do they give you a rough time, Felix?"

"No, sir. But my family is well known on Samar. I have come to the United States to attend college when I am able to. I resent Mr. Graves's assumption that I am automatically suspect because of the color of my skin."

"I don't think Mr. Graves meant it that way."

Felix smiled again.

"Is Mr. Graves here now?"

"No, sir. He is at the sheriff's office, I think. If you will excuse me, sir?" He hoisted the tray to his shoulder.

I dialed the sheriff's office from the butler's pantry and asked for Graves. A sleepy deputy called him.

"Where in God's name have you been?" His voice was hoarse and tired.

"I'll tell you later. Any trace of Sampson?"

"Not yet, but we've made some progress. I'm working with a major case squad from the FBI. We wired the dead man's prints to Washington and got an answer about an hour ago. He's in the FBI files with a long record. Name's Eddie Lassiter."

"I'll be over as soon as I eat. I'm at the Sampson place."

"Perhaps you'd better not." He lowered his voice. "The sheriff's peeved at you for running out last night. I'll come there." He hung up, and I opened the door to the kitchen.

Bacon was making cheerful noises in a pan. Felix transferred it to a warming dish and poured me a cup of coffee from a steaming pot.

I sat down at the kitchen table and gulped the scalding coffee. "Are all the phones in the house on the same line?"

"No, sir. The phones in the front of the house are on a different line from the servants' phones. Do you wish your eggs turned over, Mr. Archer?"

"I'll take them the way they are. Which ones are connected with the phone in the pantry?"

"The one in the linen closet and the one in the guest cottage up on the hill. Mr. Taggert's cottage."

Between mouthfuls I asked him, "Is Mr. Taggert there now?"

"I do not know, sir. I think I heard him drive in during the night."

"Go and make sure, will you?"

"Yes, sir." He left the kitchen by the back door.

A car drove up a minute later, and Graves came in. He still moved quickly, but his eyes were red-rimmed.

"You look like hell, Lew."

"I just came from there. Did you bring the dope on Lassiter?"

"Yeah."

He handed me a Teletype flimsy:

Children's Court, New York, March 29, 1923, truancy. . . . Brooklyn Special Sessions Court, January 9, 1928, bicycle theft. Suspended sentence and probation. . . . Arrested May 17, 1932, possession of stolen money order. Case dismissed for lack of evidence. . . . Arrested for car theft October 5, 1936, sentenced to 3 years in Sing Sing. . . . Arrested with sister Betty Lassiter by U.S. Narcotics Bureau, April 23, 1943. Convicted of selling one ounce of cocaine, May 2, 1943, sentenced to year and a day in Leavenworth. . . . Arrested August 3, 1944, for holdup of General Electric payroll truck. Pleaded guilty, sentenced to 5 to 10 years in Sing Sing. Released on parole September 18, 1947. Broke parole and disappeared, December 1947.

Those were the high points that marked Eddie's course from a delinquent childhood to a violent death.

Felix said at my shoulder, "Mr. Taggert is in his cottage, sir. He is dressing."

"How about some breakfast?" Graves said.

"Yes, sir."

Graves turned to me. "Is there anything we can use in that Teletype?"

"Just one thing, and it isn't nailed down. Lassiter had a sister named Betty who was arrested with him on a narcotics charge. There's a woman named Betty in Los Angeles with narcotics in her rap sheet, a pianist in Troy's clip joint. She calls herself Betty Fraley."

"Betty Fraley!" Felix said from the stove.

"This doesn't concern you," Graves told him unpleasantly.

"Wait a minute," I said. "What about Betty Fraley, Felix? Do you know her?"

"I do not know her, no, but I have seen her records, in Mr. Taggert's cottage. I have noticed the name when I dusted there."

"Are you telling the truth?" Graves said.

"Why should I lie, sir?"

"We'll see what Taggert has to say about that." Graves got to his feet.

"Wait a minute, Bert." I put my hand on his arm, which was hard with tension. "Bulldozing won't get us anywhere. Even if he has the woman's records, it doesn't have to mean anything. We're not even certain she's Lassiter's sister. And maybe Taggert's a collector."

"He has quite a large collection," Felix said.

Graves was stubborn. "I think we should take a look."

"Not now. Wait until Taggert isn't there. Then I'll look over his records."

Graves let me pull him back into his seat. He stroked his closed eyelids with his fingertips. "This case is the wildest mess I've ever seen or heard of," he said.

"Is the general alarm out for Sampson?" I asked.

"Since ten o'clock last night. We've alerted the highway patrol, the FBI, and every police department between here and San Diego."

"You'd better get on the phone," I said, "and put out another alarm. This time for Betty Fraley. If we don't get to her fast, there'll be somebody there ahead of us. Dwight Troy is gunning for her."

Graves gave me a curious look. "Where do you get your information, Lew?"

"I got that the hard way. I talked to Troy himself last night."

"He is mixed up in this, then?"

"He is now. I think he wants the hundred grand for himself, and I think he knows who has it."

"Betty Fraley?" He took a notebook out of his pocket.

"That's my guess. Black hair, green eyes, regular features, five foot two or three, between twenty-five and thirty, probable cocaine addict, thin but well stacked, and pretty if you like to play with reptiles. Wanted on suspicion of the murder of Eddie Lassiter."

He glanced up sharply from his writing. "Is that another guess, Lew?"

"Call it that. Will you put it on the wires?"

"Right away." He started across the room to the butler's pantry.

"Not that phone, Bert. It's connected with the one in Taggert's cottage."

He stopped and turned his face to me. "You seem pretty sure that Taggert's our man."

"Would it break your heart if he was?"

"Not mine," he said.

I WAITED in the hall at the front of the house until Felix came to tell me that Taggert was eating breakfast in the kitchen. Felix then led me around the back of the garages, up a path to the one-story white frame guest cottage.

I opened the unlocked door and went in without him. The pine-paneled living room was furnished with easy chairs, a radio-phonograph, a large table covered with *Jazz Record* and *Down Beat* magazines, and piles of records.

I went through the records and albums one by one. There were many names I had heard of—Fats Waller, Red Nichols, Mary Lou Williams—but no Betty Fraley.

I was on my way to talk to Felix again when I remembered the black disks skipping out to sea the day before. Avoiding the house, I headed for the shore. From a glassed-in pergola on the edge of the bluff a long flight of concrete steps descended to the beach. There was a bathhouse at the foot of the steps. In it I found a diving mask and snorkel hanging on a nail. I stripped to my shorts and adjusted the mask to my head.

I waded slowly into the surf, pulled the mask down over my

face, and pushed off. About fifty yards from shore I surface-dived and breaststroked to the bottom.

It was pure white sand broken by long brown ribs of stone. I zigzagged forty or fifty feet along the bottom and found nothing but a couple of undersized abalones clinging to a rock. I kicked off and went to the surface for air.

When I raised the mask I saw that a man was watching me from the cliff. He ducked behind the pergola, but not before I had recognized Taggert. I took several deep breaths and dived again. When I came up, Taggert had disappeared.

On the third dive I found what I was looking for: an unbroken black disk, half buried in the sand on the bottom. Holding the record against my chest, I turned on my back and kicked myself to shore. I took it into the shower and washed it. I dried it with tender care as I was getting dressed.

Taggert was sitting on the veranda when I came out of the dressing rooms. He gave me a boyish grin that didn't touch his eyes. "Hello there, Archer. Have a nice swim?"

"Not bad. The water's a little cold."

"You should have used the pool. It's always warmer."

"I prefer the ocean. You never know what you're going to find. I found this."

He looked at the record in my hands as if he were noticing it for the first time. "What is that?"

"A record. Somebody seems to have scraped the labels off and thrown it in the sea. I wonder why."

He got up and took a step toward me. "Let me see it."

I jerked it out of his reach. "You might break it."

He stood and looked at me for ten long seconds. The boyish charm was very slow in coming. "I'd like to know what's on the bloody thing."

"So would I."

"Let's play it, then. There's a portable player here." He opened a square fiber box on a table in the center of the veranda and then sat down again, stretching his legs in front of him.

I placed the record on the turntable. Taggert was smiling expectantly. I stood and watched him, waiting for a sign, a wrong move. The handsome boy didn't fit into the system of fears I had. He didn't fit into any pattern I knew.

The record was scratched and tired. A single piano began to beat, half drowned in surface noise. Three or four hackneyed boogie chords were laid down and multiplied. Then the right hand wove through them, twisting them alive, moving across them and back again like something being chased.

"You like it?" Taggert said.

"Within limits."

The record ended, and I turned off the machine. "You seem to be interested in boogie-woogie. You wouldn't know who made this record?"

"I wouldn't, no. The style could be Lux Lewis."

"It sounds more like a woman's playing."

He frowned in elaborate concentration. "I don't know of any woman who can play like that."

"I know of one. I heard her in the Wild Piano night before last. Betty Fraley."

"I never heard of her," he said.

"This is one of her records. You should know. You tossed it in the sea. Now why would you do that?"

"I wouldn't dream of throwing good records away."

"I think you dream a great deal, Taggert. I think you've been dreaming about a hundred thousand dollars."

He shifted slightly in his chair. His stretched-out pose had stiffened and lost its air of casualness. "Are you suggesting that I kidnapped Sampson?"

"I'm suggesting that you conspired to do it—with Betty Fraley and her brother, Eddie Lassiter."

"Now just a minute," he said. "You're going too fast for me. Is this because I threw those records away?"

"This is your record, then?"

"Sure." His voice was vibrantly frank. "I admit I had some of Betty Fraley's records. I got rid of them last night when I heard you talking to the police about the Wild Piano."

"You also listen to other people's telephone conversations?"

"It was purely accidental. I overheard you when I was trying to make a phone call of my own."

"To Betty Fraley?"

"I told you I don't know her."

"I thought perhaps you phoned her last night to give her the green light on the murder of Eddie Lassiter."

"But I don't know anything about these people. I'd heard of her, that's all. I knew she played at the Wild Piano."

"Don't try to kid me the way you've kidded yourself," I said. "An innocent man would never have thought of throwing those records away. And it happens that you threw them in the sea a good many hours before you heard my phone call—before Betty was ever mentioned in connection with this case. So let's forget about the records and talk about something important." I sat down in a wicker chair across the veranda from him.

"What do you want to talk about?" His puzzled smile was natural, and his voice was easy. Only his muscles gave him away, bunched at the shoulders, quivering in the thighs.

"Kidnapping," I said. "We'll leave the murder till later. I'd have seen everything sooner if I hadn't happened to like you. You had more opportunity than anyone. You resented Sampson's treatment of you. You resented all the money he had. You hadn't much yourself—"

"Still haven't," he said.

"You should be well-fixed for the present. Half of the hundred thousand is fifty thousand."

He spread his hands humorously. "Am I carrying it with me?"

"You've acted like a rube, Taggert," I said. "The city slickers sucked you in and used you. You'll probably never see your half of the hundred grand."

"Let's hear your story," he said smoothly.

I showed him my best card. "Eddie Lassiter phoned you the night before you flew Sampson out of Las Vegas."

There was a new white line around Taggert's mouth. "Don't tell me you're psychic, Archer."

"I'm psychic enough to tell you what you said to Eddie. You told him you'd be flying into Burbank about three o'clock the next day. You told him to rent a black limousine and wait for your phone call from the Burbank airport. When Sampson phoned the Valerio for a limousine, you canceled the call and sent for Eddie instead. The operator at the Valerio thought it was Sampson calling back. You do a pretty good imitation of him, don't you?"

"Go on," he said. "I've always been fond of fantasy."

"When Eddie turned up at the front of the airport in the rented car, Sampson got in as a matter of course. He had no reason to suspect anything.

"That canceled telephone call was important, Taggert. It was the thing that tied you into the story in the first place. Nobody else could have known that Sampson was going to phone the Valerio. Nobody else knew when Sampson was going to fly in from Nevada. Nobody else was in a position to give Eddie the tip-off the night before. Nobody else could have made all the arrangements and run them off on schedule."

"I never denied I was at the airport with Sampson. You're hipped on circumstantial evidence, like any other cop. And this business of the phonograph records isn't even circumstantial evidence. You haven't got anything on Betty Fraley, and you haven't proved any connection between us. Hundreds of collectors have her records."

His voice was still cool and clear, bright with candor, but he was worried. His body was hunched and tense, as if I had forced him into a narrow space. And his mouth was turning ugly.

"It shouldn't be hard to prove a connection," I said. "Wasn't it you that called her the other night when you saw me in the Valerio with Fay Estabrook? You weren't really looking for Sampson at the Wild Piano, were you? You were going to see Betty Fraley. You put me off when you pulled Puddler out of my hair. I thought you were on my side. So much so that I put it down to stupidity when you fired at the blue truck. But you were warning Eddie off, weren't you, Taggert?"

"Now we'll get down to business," Taggert said.

His hand came up from beside him with a gun. It was one of his .32 target pistols, a light gun, but heavy enough to make my stomach crawl.

"I didn't think you'd give up so easily."

"I haven't given up. I'm simply guaranteeing my freedom of action."

"Shooting me won't guarantee it. It'll guarantee death by gas. Put your gun away and we'll talk this over."

"There's nothing to talk over." Now that the gun was in his hand, ready for violence, his face was smooth and relaxed.

"I'm trying to find Sampson," I said. "If I can get him back, nothing else counts."

"You've forgotten what you said last night: if anything happens to the people that kidnapped Sampson, it's the end of him."

"Nothing has happened to you—yet. You have your money. Let him go."

"I intended to, Archer. I was going to turn him loose today. But that will have to be postponed—indefinitely. If anything happens to me, it's good-by Sampson."

"We can reach an understanding."

"No," he said. "Don't you see that you've spoiled it now? You have the power to spoil things, but you haven't the power to guarantee that we'll get clear. There's nothing I can do with you but this."

He glanced down at the gun, which was pointed at the middle of my body, then casually back at me. Any second he could shoot, without preparation, without anger.

"Wait," I said. My throat was tight.

"We don't want to stretch this out." He stood up and moved toward me.

I shifted the weight of my body in the chair. As I drew back my feet I talked rapidly. "If you'll give me Sampson, I can guarantee that I won't try to hold you and I won't talk."

His rigid arm came up with the gun at the end like a hollow blue finger. I looked sideways, away from the direction I was going to move in. I was halfway out of the chair when the gun went off. Taggert was listless when I got to him. The gun slid out of his hand.

Another gun had spoken. Albert Graves was in the doorway with the twin of Taggert's pistol in his hand.

"Too bad," he said, "but it had to be done."

Taggert's dark eyes were open and glistening. They didn't react to the touch of my fingertips. The round hole in his right temple was bloodless.

Graves was standing over me. "He's dead?"

"He didn't fall down in a fit. You did a quick, neat job."

"It was you or Taggert," he said.

"I don't like to quibble," I said. "But I wish you'd shot the gun out of his hand or smashed his elbow."

His mouth twisted wryly. "You're a carping son of a bitch, Lew. I save your life, and you criticize the method."

"Did you hear what he said?"

"Enough. He kidnapped Sampson."

"But he wasn't alone. His friends aren't going to like this. They'll take it out on Sampson."

"Who are these others?"

"Eddie Lassiter was one. Betty Fraley is another. There may be more. You'll be calling the police about this shooting?"

"Naturally."

"Tell them to keep it quiet."

"I'm not ashamed of it, Lew," he told me sharply, "though you seem to think I should be."

"Look at it from Betty Fraley's point of view. When she hears what you've done to her sidekick she'll beeline for Sampson and make a hole in *his* head. Why should she bother keeping him alive? She's got the money—"

"You're right," he said, and after a pause, "I wonder how Miranda's going to take it."

"Pretty hard. She liked him, didn't she?"

"She had a crush on him. Taggert had things she thought she wanted, youth and good looks and a hell of a combat record. This thing is going to shock her."

"I don't shock easily," I said, "but it took me by surprise. I thought he was a pretty sound kid, a little self-centered, but solid."

Graves looked down at the corpse on the floor. Its eyes were still open, gazing up through the roof at the empty sky. I bent down and closed them. "We're becoming very elegiac," I said. "Let's get out of here."

"In a minute." He laid his hand on my arm. "I want you to do me a favor, Lew."

"What is it?"

He spoke with diffidence. "I'm afraid if I tell Miranda, she won't see it the way it happened. You know what I mean—she might blame me."

"You want me to tell her?"

"I'd appreciate it."

"I can do that," I said. "I suppose you did save my life."

Mrs. Kromberg was running a vacuum cleaner in the big front room. She glanced up when I entered, and switched it off. "Mr. Graves find you all right?"

"He found me. Do you know where Miranda is?"

"She was in the morning room a few minutes ago."

She led me through the house and left me at the door of a sun-filled room. Miranda was standing at a window that overlooked the patio. She had daffodils in her hands and was arranging them in a bowl.

"Good morning," she said. The flesh around her eyes was swollen and faintly blue.

"I have some moderately good news for you. I talked to one of your father's kidnappers—"

The daffodils fell to the floor, and she came at me headlong, clutching at my arm. "What did he say to you?"

"That your father is alive."

Her hand released my arm and took hold of her other hand. "But you can't trust what they say. They'd naturally claim he's alive. What did they want? Did they phone you?"

"It was just one of them I talked to. Face to face."

"You saw him and let him go?"

"I didn't let him go. He's dead. His name is Alan Taggert."

"But that's impossible. I—"

"Why is it impossible?" I said.

"He couldn't do it. He was decent. He was always honest with me—with us."

"Until the big chance came. Then he wanted money more than anything else. He was ready to murder to get it."

A question formed in her eyes. "You said Ralph was alive?"

"Taggert didn't murder your father. He tried to murder me. Albert Graves shot him."

"Albert?" Her giggle passed back and forth like a quick spark between laughter and hysteria. "Albert did that?"

"He's a dead shot—we used to do a lot of target shooting together," I said. "If he wasn't, I wouldn't be here with you now."

"I want to see Albert," she said. "Where is he?"

"In the bathhouse, where it happened. Taggert's there, too."

"Take me to Albert."

We found him on the veranda, sitting over the dead man. Sheriff Spanner and District Attorney Humphreys were looking at Taggert and listening to Graves's story. All three stood up for Miranda.

She had to step over Taggert to reach Albert Graves. She did this without a downward glance at the uncovered face.

"I'll marry you now," she said.

11

For half a minute nobody spoke.

"We'd better get out of here, Miranda," Graves said finally. He glanced at the district attorney. "If you'll excuse us? Mrs. Sampson will have to be told about this."

"Go ahead, Bert," Humphreys said.

While a man from his office took notes, and another photographed the body on the floor, Humphreys questioned me. Sheriff Spanner listened restlessly, biting a cigar to shreds.

"Unfortunately this shooting leaves us worse off than before," Humphreys said. "We have practically no leads."

"You're forgetting Betty Fraley," I said.

"We haven't caught her yet, and even if we do, we can't be certain that she knows where Sampson is."

"And the hundred thousand dollars," Spanner said. His gray eyes shifted to me. "If you're finished with Archer here, Humphreys, I want to have a talk with him."

"Take him," Humphreys said coldly. "I've got to get back to town." He took the body with him.

When we were alone, the sheriff got up heavily and stood over me. "You didn't tell me everything you should of last night. I heard from your friend Colton this morning. He told me about the limousine this Lassiter was driving; it came from a car rental in Pasadena, and you knew it." He raised his voice suddenly. "You didn't tell me you saw it before, when the ransom note was delivered. If you had, we could have taken him. We could have stopped the shooting and saved the money—"

"But not Sampson," I said.

"You're not the judge of that." His face was bursting at the seams with angry blood. "You took things in your own hands. You withheld information. Right after Lassiter got shot, you disappeared. You were the only witness, and you disappeared. A hundred thousand dollars disappeared at the same time."

"I don't like the implication." I stood up. He was a big man, and our eyes were level.

"I'm not saying you took the money—I'm saying you could have. I want your gun, and I want to know what you were doing when my deputy caught up with you down south at The Corner. And I want to know what you were doing after that."

"I was looking for Sampson."

"You were looking for Sampson," he said, with heavy irony. "You expect me to take your word for that." He leaned toward me. "If I wanted to be ugly, I could put you away this minute."

My patience broke. "Don't look now," I said, "but you are ugly."

"Do you know who you're talking to?"

"A sheriff. A sheriff with a tough case on his hands, and no ideas. So you're looking for a goat."

The blood went out of his face, leaving it haggard with rage. "They'll hear about this in Sacramento," he stuttered. "When your detective's license comes up—"

I sat down and crossed my legs. "Take it easy, Sheriff. Sit down and relax. We've got some things to talk over."

He wrinkled up his eyelids in an effort to look shrewd, and succeeded in looking puzzled.

"Sit down," I said again. "I didn't find what I was looking for last night, but I found something else. It should make you and the immigrant inspectors very happy. I'm offering it to you as a free gift, no strings."

He lowered his haunches into a canvas chair. Curiosity had taken the place of anger. "It better be good."

I told him about the closed blue truck, the brown men at the Temple, Troy and Eddie and Claude. "Troy is the head of the gang. The others work for him. They've been running an underground railway on a regular schedule between the Mexican border and the Bakersfield area. The southern end is probably at Calexico."

"Yeah," Spanner said. "That's an easy place to cross. All they got to do is crawl through a wire fence."

"And Troy's truck would be waiting to pick them up. They used the Temple in the Clouds as a receiving station for illegal immigrants. God knows how many have passed through its gate. There were twelve or more last night."

"Jesus!" Spanner said. "If they brought over twelve a night, that's three hundred and sixty a month. If they're charging a hundred bucks apiece, this Troy has been making big money. Do you know where he hangs out in Los Angeles?"

"He runs a place called the Wild Piano, but he won't be showing there. I've told you what I know." With two exceptions: the man I had killed, and the blond woman who would still be waiting for Eddie.

"You seem to be on the level," the sheriff said slowly. "But if this turns out to be a song and dance, I'll remember it."

I hadn't expected to be thanked, and I wasn't disappointed.

I PARKED IN THE lane above Marcie's cottage. Farther down was a rusty green Ford sedan. On the registration card taped to its steering wheel shaft I read the name, "Mrs. Marcella Finch."

The white cottage was ugly and dilapidated in the noon sun, a dingy blot against the blue field of the sea. Nothing in sight moved. I felt for my gun butt.

The door creaked partly open when I knocked.

A woman's voice said dully, "Who's that?"

I stood aside and waited, in case she had a gun. She raised her voice. "Is somebody there?"

"Eddie," I whispered. Eddie had no further use for his name, but it was a hard thing to say.

"Eddie?" A hushed and wondering word.

I waited. Before I could see her face, her right hand grasped the edge of the door. Under the peeling scarlet polish her fingernails were dirty. I took hold of her hand.

"Eddie!" The face that looked around the door was blind with a desperate hopefulness. When she saw I wasn't Eddie, she squawked like a parrot. "Dirty liar!"

I caught her other wrist and forced her back into the house, slamming the door with my heel. She tried to knee me, then to bite my neck. I pushed her down on the bed.

"I don't want to hurt you, Marcie."

She flung herself sideways, burrowing under the covers. Her body moved in rhythmic grief.

She sat up after a while and lit a cigarette, dragging deep.

The voice that came out with the smoke was contemptuous. "I should stage a crying jag to give a copper his kicks." She looked at me with cold interest. "How low can you bastards get? You blow Eddie down, then you come and tell me you're Eddie at the door. For a minute you make me think the newscast was wrong. Can you get any lower than that?"

"I'm no copper," I said. "I thought you might have a gun."

"I got no gun. I never carried a gun, nor Eddie neither."

"Be quiet for a minute. Listen to me. You must have been in on it, Marcie. You knew what Eddie was doing?"

"He had a job driving a truck. He trucked beans from the Imperial Valley." She stood up suddenly. "Take me down to headquarters and get it over."

"Sit down," I said. "We're not going anywhere. I don't belong to headquarters. I'm a private cop hired to find Ralph Sampson. He's all I want—do you understand? If you can give him to me, I'll keep you in the clear."

"I wouldn't trust a cop, private or any other kind. Anyway, I don't know where Sampson is." She sat down on the bed. "I don't know a damn thing."

"Eddie didn't do it by himself. He must have had a partner." I sat down and lit a cigarette. "I'll tell you a funny thing. I was there when Eddie was shot. He stopped on a side road to pass the money to another car. It was a cream-colored convertible. It had a woman in it. She shot him. Where is that woman now?"

Her eyes were glistening like wet brown pebbles. The red tip of her tongue moved across her upper lip.

"Are you going to sit and take it, Marcie? Where is she?"

"I don't know who you're talking about."

"Betty Fraley," I said.

After a long silence she repeated, "I don't know who you're talking about."

I left her sitting on the bed and drove back to The Corner. I parked in the parking lot and lowered the sun visor on my side. She knew my face but not my car.

For half an hour the road from White Beach was empty. Then a cloud of dust appeared in the distance, towed by the rusty green Ford sedan. Before the car turned south toward Los Angeles I caught a glimpse of a highly painted face and an aggressively tilted hat with a bright blue feather. Cosmetics and half an hour alone had done a lot for Marcie.

The Ford's top speed was under fifty, and it was easy to keep in sight. Marcie left the highway at Sunset Boulevard and went through Pacific Palisades. The Ford labored and trailed dark blue oil smoke on the hills below the Santa Monica Mountains. On the edge of Beverly Hills it left the boulevard suddenly.

I followed it up a winding road lined on both sides with hedges. Marcie parked behind a laurel hedge in the entrance to a gravel drive. In the instant of passing I saw her crossing the lawn toward a deep brick porch screened with oleanders. She seemed to be hustled along by a deadly energy.

I turned and parked on the shoulder beyond the next drive. I had the car door open and one foot in the road when an engine roared. I drew in my leg and crouched down behind the wheel. Troy's black Buick backed out of the drive. A man I didn't know was driving. Marcie was beside him in the front seat. Gray hearselike curtains were drawn over the rear windows.

At the boulevard the Buick turned back toward the sea. I followed as closely as I dared. Between Brentwood and Pacific Palisades it went off to the right, up a climbing road into a canyon. I accelerated on the downhill grade, crossed a narrow stone bridge that spanned a dry barranca, and climbed the hill after it. It was moving slowly down the other side, like a heavy black beetle feeling its way in unfamiliar territory. Then it paused and followed a rutted lane off to the right.

I parked on the hill behind a tree, which screened my car from below. The Buick stopped in front of a matchbox house. A woman with black hair came out. Two men and two women got out of the car and surrounded her. All five went into the house like a single insect with many legs.

I left my car and climbed down through the underbrush to the bottom of the canyon until I was directly behind the house. It was an unpainted wooden shack with its rear end resting on short fieldstone columns.

Inside it a woman screamed, very loudly, again and again. The screams raked at my nerves, but they covered the noises I made crawling under the house. The screaming died away after a while. I lay flat and listened to scrabbling movements on the floor.

A soft voice began to talk over my head. "You seem to feel that our motive is simple revenge. My point is, Betty, that you've acted very badly. You went into business for yourself, a thing I seldom approve in my employees. To make matters worse, you failed in it.

Furthermore, you chose a valuable associate of mine as the victim of your wretched little plot. And to cap the climax you showed yourself devoid not only of esprit de corps but of sisterly affection. You shot and killed your brother, Eddie Lassiter."

"We know you swallowed the dictionary." I recognized Fay Estabrook's voice. "Get on with it, Troy."

"I didn't kill him." The whine of a hurt cat.

"You're a liar," yapped Marcie.

Troy raised his voice. "Be quiet, all of you. We have a chance to recoup, which brings us to the occasion of this little party. I don't know where the money is, but of course I intend to find out. You might as well come clean, Betty. Otherwise you'll suffer rather terribly. You may never walk again."

"I'm not talking."

"If you cooperate, Betty," Troy went on smoothly, "I'm sure the group will be glad to help you. We'll take you out of the country tonight. You know Luis and I can do that for you."

"You wouldn't do it," she said. "I know you, Troy."

"Take off her other shoe, Luis."

A dropped shoe rapped the floorboards. I calculated my chances of ending it now. But there were too many for one gun. And Betty Fraley had to come out alive.

Troy said, "We'll test the plantar reflex, I think it's called."

"I don't like this," Fay said.

"Neither do I, my dear. But Betty is being most obdurate."

A moment of silence, then the screaming began again.

"Your plantar reaction is very fine," Troy said. "It's a pity that your tongue doesn't work so well."

"Will you let me go if I give you the money?"

"You have my word."

"Your word!" She sighed horribly. "Let me up, then. Let me sit up."

"Of course, my dear."

"It's in a locker in the bus station in Buenavista. The key is in my handbag."

As soon as I was out of sight of the house I began to run. I backed my car down the hill to the stone bridge and halfway up the grade on the other side. I waited for the Buick with one foot on the clutch and the other on the brake.

After a while I heard its motor whining up the other side of the hill. Moving ahead in low, I held the middle of the road and met it on the bridge. Brakes screeched, and the Buick came to a stop five feet from my bumper. I was out of my seat before it stopped rolling.

The man called Luis glared at me over the wheel, his fat face twisted with anger. I opened the door on his side and showed him my gun. Beside him Fay Estabrook cried out in fury.

"Out!" I said. "Hands on your head." Luis raised his hands and stepped into the road.

"You, too, Fay. This side."

She came out, teetering on her high heels.

"Now turn around."

They rotated cautiously, watching me over their shoulders. I clubbed the gun and swung it to the base of Luis' skull. He went down on his knees and collapsed softly on his face. Fay cowered away with her arms protecting her head.

"Put him in the back seat," I said. "Hurry."

"I can't lift him."

"You have to." I took a step toward her.

She stooped awkwardly over the fallen man. With her hands in his armpits she raised the upper part of his body and dragged him to the car. I opened the door, and together we slung him into the back seat.

"Now give me the key to the locker, Fay."

"What key? I haven't got any key." But her gaze had flickered almost imperceptibly toward the front seat of the Buick.

There was a black suede purse on the seat. The key was in it. I transferred it to my wallet.

"Get in," I said. "On the driver's side. You do the driving."

She did as I said, and I got in behind her. Luis was slumped in the far corner of the back seat. His eyes were partly open, but the pupils were turned up out of sight.

"I can't get past your car," Fay said petulantly.

"You're backing up the hill."

She cursed me, but she backed cautiously up the hill and down the other side. At the entrance to the lane I told her to turn and drive down to the cottage.

"Slow and careful, Fay. No leaning on the horn. You wouldn't be any good without a spinal column." I touched the back of her neck with the muzzle of my gun.

"Stop in front of the door," I said. "Then set the emergency."

I lowered the rear window as the door of the cottage began to open inward. I ducked my head. When I raised it again, Troy was in the doorway, with his right hand resting on the edge of the frame. I sighted and fired. At twenty feet I could see the fat red mark the bullet made on the knuckles of his hand.

He was immobile for an instant. Long enough for me to reach him and use the gun butt again. He sat down on the doorstep, rolled out of the doorway, and curled on the shallow porch, perfectly still.

I pulled Fay out of the Buick by the shoulders. She tried to spit at me and slobbered on her chin.

"We'll go inside," I said. "You first." She walked almost drunkenly, stumbling on her heels.

The odor of burned flesh was still in the room. Betty Fraley was on the floor, with Marcie at her throat. I pulled her off and motioned to Fay with the gun to stand in the corner beside her.

Betty Fraley sat up, the breath whistling in her throat. Across one side of her face, from hairline to jawbone, four parallel scratches dripped blood.

"You're a pretty picture," I said.

"Who are you?" Her voice was a flat caw.

"It doesn't matter. Let's get out of here before I have to kill these people."

"That would be pleasant work," she said. She tried to stand up and fell forward on hands and knees. "I can't walk."

I lifted her and carried her out to the car and sat her in the front seat. I opened the back door, laid Luis out on the ground.

There were suds on his thick blue lips, blown in and out by his shallow breathing.

"Thank you," Betty said, as I climbed behind the wheel. "You saved my life, if that's worth anything."

"It isn't worth much, but you're going to pay me for it. The price is a hundred thousand—and Ralph Sampson."

I PARKED the Buick in the road at the entrance to the stone bridge and kept the ignition key. As I lifted Betty Fraley out of the seat and into my car her right arm slipped around my shoulders. I could feel her small fingers on the nape of my neck.

"You're very strong," she said. "You're Archer, aren't you?" She looked up at me with a sly and feline innocence.

"It's time you remembered me. Take your hand off me, or I'll drop you."

She lowered her eyelids. When I started to back my car, she cried out suddenly, "What about them? You're going to let them get away?"

"We don't have room for them."

"We've got to go back. They've got something of mine!"

"No," I said. "I have it, and it isn't yours anymore."

"The key?"

"The key."

I turned the car toward Sunset Boulevard. She slumped down in the seat as if her spine had melted. "You can't let them go," she said sullenly. "You let Troy run loose, and he'll get you for today."

"I don't think so," I said. "Forget about them and start worrying about yourself."

"I haven't got a future to worry about. Have I?"

"I want to see Sampson first. Then I'll decide."

"I'll take you to him. He's in a place on the beach about forty miles from Santa Teresa."

"This is straight?"

"The straight stuff, Archer. But you won't let me go. You won't take money, will you?"

"Not from you."

"Why should you?" she said nastily. "You've got my hundred grand."

"I'm working for the Sampsons. They'll get it back."

"They don't need the money. Why don't you get smart, Archer? There's another person in this with me. Why don't you let me go, keep the money, and split it with this other person?"

She didn't know Taggert was dead, and it wasn't the time to tell her. "You still haven't told me exactly where Sampson is. The longer it takes, the less I'll feel like doing anything for you."

"He's in a place on the beach about ten miles north of Buena-vista, in the dressing room of a beach club that folded."

"And he's alive?"

"He was yesterday. The first day he was sick from the chloroform, but he's all right now."

"He was yesterday, you mean. Is he tied up?"

"I haven't seen him. Eddie was the one."

"I suppose you left him there to starve to death."

"I couldn't go there. He knew me by sight. Eddie was the one he didn't know."

"And Eddie died by an act of God."

"No, I killed him." She said it almost smugly. "You'll never be able to prove it, though. I wasn't thinking of Sampson when I shot Eddie."

"You were thinking of money, weren't you? A two-way cut instead of a three-way cut."

"It was partly that, but only partly. Eddie pushed me around all the time I was a kid. When I finally got on my feet and was heading places, he sang me into the pen. I was using the stuff, but he was selling it. He helped the feds hang conspiracy on me, and got off with a light sentence himself. He didn't know I knew that, but I promised myself to get him. Maybe he wasn't surprised. He told Marcie where to find me if anything went wrong."

I turned onto the boulevard and stopped at the first gas station I came to. She watched me remove the ignition key.

"What are you going to do?"

"Phone help for Sampson. He may be dying, and it's going to

take us an hour and a half to get there. Has the place got a name?"

"It used to be the Sunland Beach Club. It's a long green building. You can see it from the road, out near the end of a point."

For the first time I was sure she was telling the truth. I called Santa Teresa from the station's pay telephone while the attendant filled the tank of my car.

Felix answered the phone. "This is the Sampson residence."

"Archer speaking. Is Mr. Graves there?"

"Yes, sir. I will call him."

Graves came to the phone. "Where the hell are you?"

"Los Angeles. Sampson is alive, or at least he was yesterday. He's locked up in the dressing room of a beach club called the Sunland. Know it?"

"I know where it is, north of Buenavista on the highway."

"See how fast you can get there with first aid and food. And you better bring a doctor and the sheriff."

"Is he in bad shape?"

"I don't know. He's been alone since yesterday. I'll be there as soon as I can." I hung up on Graves and called Peter Colton. He was still on duty.

"I've got something for you," I said. "Partly for you and partly for the Department of Justice."

"Another migraine headache, no doubt." He didn't sound glad to hear from me. "This Sampson case is the mess of the century."

"It was. I'm closing it today. I know where Sampson is, and I've got the last of the kidnap gang with me now."

"Don't be coy, for Christ's sake! Where is he?"

"Out of your territory, in Santa Teresa County. The Santa Teresa sheriff is on his way to him now."

"I thought you had something for me and the Department of Justice."

"I have, but not the kidnapping. The case has by-products. There's a canyon feeding into Sunset between Brentwood and Pacific Palisades. The road that leads into it is Hopkins Lane. About five miles in, there's a black Buick sedan in the road; past that, a lane leading down to an unpainted shack. There are four people there. One of them is Troy. Whether it knows it or not, the Department of Justice wants them for smuggling illegal immigrants. Have I said enough?"

"For the present," he said.

Betty Fraley looked at me blankly when I went back to the car. "What now?" she said.

"I did you a favor. I called the police to pick up Troy and the others."

"The smuggling rap?"

"Right. Troy disappointed me. Trucking in Mexicans is a pretty low-grade racket for a gentleman crook."

"He made it pay off double," she said. "He took the poor creeps' money for the ride, then turned them over to the ranches at so much a head. The Mexicans didn't know it, but they were being used as strikebreakers. That way Troy got protection from the local cops. Luis greased the Mexicans at the other end."

"Was Sampson buying strikebreakers from Troy?"

"He was, but you'd never prove it. Sampson was very careful to keep himself in the clear."

"He wasn't careful enough," I said. She was silent after that.

I turned north on the highway. After a pause she tried again. "You could still let me go and keep the money yourself. You'll never have another crack at a hundred grand."

"Neither will you, Betty—and neither will Alan Taggert."

She uttered a groan of surprise. "You've been kidding me. What do you know about Taggert?"

"What he told me."

"I don't believe you. He doesn't know anything to tell."

"He did."

"Did something happen to him?"

"Death happened to him. He's got a hole in the head like Eddie."

She started to say something, but the words were broken by a high drawn-out whimper that gave way to steady sobs. After a long time she whispered, "Why didn't you tell me he was dead?"

"You didn't ask me. Why did you drag him into this?"

"I didn't drag him in. He wanted to do it. We were going to go away together."

"And live happily ever after?"

"Keep your cheap cracks to yourself."

"I won't buy love's young dream from you, Betty. He was a boy, and you're an old woman, as experience goes. I think you sucked him in."

"That's not the way it was." Her voice was surprisingly gentle. "We've been together for half a year. He came into the Piano with Sampson the week after I opened. I fell, and it was the same with him. But neither of us had anything. We had to have money to make a clean break."

"And Sampson was the obvious source. Why didn't you blackmail him? That would be more your line."

"We thought of that. We knew plenty about him, but he was too big for us to handle and he has the best lawyers in the state." Her voice cracked. It was humble and small when she spoke again. "I didn't do Alan any good. I know that. But I couldn't help myself, and neither could he. How did he die, Archer?"

"He got into a tight corner and tried to push out with a gun. Somebody else shot first. A man called Graves."

"Where is Alan now?"

"In the morgue in Santa Teresa."

"I wish I could see him—once more." The words came softly out of a dark dream. In the silence that followed, the dream spread beyond her mind and cast a shadow as long as the shadows thrown by the setting sun.

12

When I slowed down for Buenavista, the lights were going on along the main street. I noticed the neon greyhound at the bus station but didn't stop. A few miles beyond the town the highway converged with the shoreline again, winding along the bluffs above the beaches.

"This is it," Betty Fraley said. She had been so still I'd almost forgotten she was in the seat beside me.

I stopped on the asphalt shoulder of the highway. On the ocean side a road slanted down to the beach. I could see the old beach club two hundred yards below the highway, long, low, and faded against the glimmering whiteness of the surf.

"You can't drive down," she said. "The road's washed out."

"I thought you hadn't been down there."

"Not since last week. I looked it over with Eddie when he found it. Sampson's in one of the little rooms on the men's side of the dressing rooms."

I took my flashlight from the glove compartment, pocketed the ignition key, and left Betty in the car. As I went down, the road narrowed to a clay pathway with deeply eroded ditches on both sides. The wooden platform in front of the building was warped. The windows were high under the eaves, and dark.

I turned my flashlight on the twin doors in the middle, and saw the stenciled signs: GENTLEMEN on one, LADIES on the other. The one on the right, for gentlemen, was hanging partly open. I pulled it wide, but not very hopefully. The place seemed empty and dead.

I looked at my watch, which said a quarter to seven. It was well over an hour since I'd called Graves. He'd had plenty of time to drive the forty-five miles from Cabrillo Canyon. I wondered what had happened to him and the sheriff.

I shot my flashlight beam across the floor. Opposite me was a row of closed doors in a plywood partition. I took a step toward the row of doors. The movement behind me was so lizard-quick I had no time to turn. Ambush was the last word that flashed across my consciousness before it faded out.

Sucker was the first word when consciousness returned. The eye of an electric lantern stared down at me. My first impulse was to get up and fight. The deep voice of Albert Graves inhibited the impulse. "What happened to you?"

"Turn the lantern away." Its light went through my eye sockets like swords. "You're late."

"I had some trouble finding the place in the dark."

"Where's the sheriff? Couldn't you find him either?"

"He was out on a case, committing a paranoiac to the county hospital. I left word for him to follow me down and bring a doctor. I didn't want to waste time."

"It looks to me as if you've wasted a lot of time."

"I thought I knew the place, but I must have missed it. I drove on nearly to Buenavista before I realized it. Then when I came back, I couldn't find it."

"Didn't you see my car?"

"Where?"

I sat up. A swaying sickness moved back and forth like a pendulum in my head. "At the corner just above here."

"That's where I parked. I didn't see your car."

I felt for my car keys. They were in my pocket. "You're sure? They didn't take my car keys."

"Your car isn't there, Lew. Who are they?"

"Betty Fraley and whoever sapped me. There must have been a fourth member of the gang guarding Sampson." I told him how I had come there.

"It wasn't smart to leave her in the car," he said.

"Three sappings in two days are making Jack a dull boy."

I got to my feet and found that my legs were weak. Graves offered his shoulder for me to lean on. I leaned against the wall.

I picked up my flashlight and crossed to the row of doors. Sampson was waiting behind the second one, a fat old man slumped on a bench against the rear wall of the cubicle. His head was wedged upright in the corner. His open eyes were suffused with blood.

Graves crowded in behind me and said, "God!"

I handed him the flashlight and bent over Sampson. His hands and ankles were bound together with quarter-inch rope, one end of which was strung through a staple in the wall. The other end of the rope was sunk in Sampson's neck and tied under his left ear in a hard knot. I reached behind the body for his wrist. It wasn't cold, but the pulse was gone.

Graves's breath came out. "Is he dead?"

"Yes. But he must have been alive when I got here. How long was I out?"

"It's a quarter after seven now."

"I got here about a quarter to. They've had a half hour's start. We've got to move."

"And leave Sampson here?"

"Yes. The police will want him this way."

We left him in the dark. I drew on my last reserve to get up the hill to Graves's car.

"Which way?" he said as he climbed behind the wheel.

"Buenavista. We'll go to the highway patrol."

I looked in my wallet, expecting the locker key to be gone. But it was there, tucked in the card compartment. Whoever sapped me hadn't had a chance to compare notes with Betty Fraley.

I said to Graves as we passed the town limits, "Drop me at the bus station." I told him why, and added, "If the money isn't there, it probably means they came this way and broke open the locker. You go to the highway patrol and pick me up later."

He let me out in front of the bus station. I stood outside the glass door and looked into the big square waiting room. None of the people showed the tension I was looking for. They were waiting for ordinary things: supper, a bus, Saturday night.

I pushed the glass door open and crossed the butt-strewn floor to the green metal lockers to the right of a doughnut counter. The number I wanted was stamped on the key: twenty-eight. As I pushed the key into the lock I glanced around the room. A fat woman at the doughnut counter was watching me incuriously. Nobody else seemed to notice.

There was a red canvas beach bag in the locker. I sat down on the nearest empty bench and unzipped it. The brown paper packages it contained were torn open at one end. I felt the edges of the stiff new bills with my fingers. I tucked the bag under my arm, went to the doughnut counter, and ordered coffee.

Graves appeared in the doorway, gesticulating violently. I set down my cup and followed him out. "They just wrecked your car," he told me on the sidewalk. "About fifteen miles north of here. One of them was killed."

"What happened to the other?"

"The highway patrol doesn't know yet. All they had was the first radio report."

We covered the fifteen miles in less than fifteen minutes. The place was marked by a line of standing cars and a crowd of human figures like animated cutouts in the headlights. Graves pulled up short of a policeman who was trying to wave us on with a red flashlight.

My car was there beyond the line of cars, its nose crumpled into the bank. Jumping out of the Studebaker, I took off at a run and elbowed my way through the crowd around the wreck. A highway patrolman with a seamed brown face put his hand on my arm. I shook it off. "This is my car."

His eyes narrowed. "What's your name?"

"Archer."

"That's who she's registered to all right." He called out to a young patrolman standing by a motorcycle, "Come here, Ollie! It's this guy's car."

I saw a blanket-covered figure on the ground beside the smashed car. I lifted one end of the blanket. The object underneath wasn't recognizably human, but I knew it by its clothes.

My stomach revolted. The two patrolmen waited until I was able to talk.

"This woman steal your car?" the older one said.

"Yes. Her name is Betty Fraley."

"The office said they had a bulletin on her—"

"That's right. But what happened to the other one?"

"What other one?"

"There was a man with her."

"Not when she wrecked the car," the young patrolman said. "I saw it happen. I was responsible in a way."

"Naw, naw, Ollie." The older man put his hand on Ollie's

shoulder. "You did exactly the right thing. Nobody's going to blame you."

"What did happen?" I asked him sharply.

"I was tooling along about fifty a few miles south of here, heading north. This dame passed me as if I was standing still, and I gave chase. I was traveling around ninety before I started to pull up on her. Even when I was abreast of her, she went right on gunning down the road. She didn't pay any attention when I signaled to pull over, so I cut in ahead. She swerved and tried to pass me on the right and lost control of the car. It skidded a couple of hundred feet and piled up in the bank. When I pulled her out of it, she was dead."

"You're absolutely sure there was nobody else in the car?"

"Unless they went up in smoke— It's a funny thing," he added in a high, nervous voice, "there was no fire, but the soles of her feet were blistered. And I couldn't find her shoes. She was in her bare feet."

"That is funny," I said. "Extremely funny."

Albert Graves had forced his way through the crowd. "They must have had another car."

"Then why would she bother with mine?" I reached inside the wreck, under the warped and bloody dash, and felt the ignition wires. The terminals had been reconnected with the copper wire I had left there in the morning. "She had to rewire my ignition to start the engine."

"That's more like a man's work, isn't it?"

"Not necessarily. She could have picked it up from her brother. Every car thief knows the trick."

Sheriff Spanner arrived in a radio car. "What's been happening?" He looked from me to Graves with moist, suspicious eyes.

I let Graves tell him. When he had heard that Sampson was dead, Spanner turned back to me.

"You see what's come of your meddling, Archer. I warned you to work under my supervision."

I wasn't in the mood to take it quietly. "Supervision, hell! If you'd gotten to Sampson soon enough, he might be alive now."

"You knew where he was, and you didn't tell me about it," he yammered. "You're going to suffer for that, Archer."

"I sent you a message a couple of hours ago. Why were you out at the county hospital committing a loony when the case was breaking wide open?"

"I haven't been out at the hospital since yesterday," he said. "What are you talking about?"

"Didn't you get my message about Sampson?"

"There was no message. You can't cover yourself that way."

I looked at Graves. His eyes avoided mine.

GRAVES drove very slowly back to Santa Teresa. My thoughts were poor company. He looked at me curiously as we entered the city. "I wouldn't give up hope, Lew. The police have a good chance to catch him."

"Who do you mean?"

"The murderer, of course. The other man."

"I'm not sure there was another man."

His knuckles tightened on the wheel. "But somebody killed Sampson."

"Yes," I said. "Somebody did."

I watched his eyes as they turned slowly to meet mine. He looked at me coldly for a long moment.

"Watch your driving, Graves. Watch everything."

He turned his face to the road again, but not before I had caught its look of shame. Where the highway crossed the main street of Santa Teresa, he stopped for a red light. "Where do we go from here?"

"Where do you want to go?"

"It doesn't matter to me."

"We'll go to the Sampson place," I said. "I want to talk to Mrs. Sampson."

"Do you have to do it now?"

"I'm working for her. I owe her a report."

The light changed. Nothing more was said until we turned up the drive to the Sampson house.

"I don't want to see Miranda if it can be helped," he said. "We were married this afternoon."

"Didn't you jump the gun a little?"

"What do you mean by that? I've been carrying the license for months."

"You might have waited until her father was home. Or decently laid away."

"She wanted it done today," he said. "We were married in the courthouse."

"You'll probably be spending your wedding night there. The jail's in the same building, isn't it?" He didn't answer.

When he stopped the car by the garages, I leaned forward to look into his face. He had swallowed the shame. Nothing was left but a gambler's resignation.

"Do you expect me to leave you out here by yourself?"

"Why not?"

"I can't trust you. You were the one man I thought I could trust—" I couldn't find the words to end the sentence.

"You can trust me, Lew. I've got a gun in my pocket, but I'm not going to use it. I'm sick of violence."

"You should be sick, with two murders on your stomach."

"Why did you say two murders, Lew? I shot Taggert in good faith. I admit I wasn't sorry to have him out of the way on account of Miranda," he said. "But the reason I shot him was to save you."

"I don't believe you." I sat there in cold anger. "You're a dead shot, Graves. You didn't have to kill him."

He answered me harshly. "Taggert deserved to die. He got what was coming to him."

"But not at the right time. You must have heard enough of what he said to me to know he was one of the kidnappers. Probably enough to be pretty sure that if Taggert died, his partners would kill Sampson."

"I heard very little. I saw he was going to shoot you, and I shot him instead." The iron returned to his voice. "Evidently I made a mistake."

"You made several mistakes. The first was killing Taggert— that's what started it all, isn't it? It wasn't really Taggert you wanted dead. It was Sampson himself. You never wanted Sampson to come home alive, and you thought that by killing Taggert you'd arranged that. But Betty Fraley, Taggert's surviving partner, had no chance to kill Sampson. So you had to murder him for yourself."

Shame, and what looked like uncertainty, pulled at his face again. He shook them off. "Sampson's no loss to anybody."

"You're taking murder more lightly than you used to," I said. "You've sent men to the gas chamber for murder. Has it occurred to you that that's where you're probably headed?"

He managed to smile. The smile made deep and ugly lines around his mouth. "You have no proof against me. You haven't even enough to bring me to trial."

"It isn't my job to do that. You know where you stand, better than I do. I don't know why you had to murder Sampson."

He was silent for some time. When he spoke, his voice was candid and somehow young, the voice of the man I had known years ago. "It's strange that you should say that I had to, Lew. That was how I felt. I hadn't made up my mind until I found Sampson there by himself in the dressing room. I didn't even speak to him. I saw what could be done, and once I'd seen it, I had to do it."

"Aren't you being a little easy on yourself? Your motives were more obvious. You'd gotten married this afternoon to a girl who was potentially very rich. After my phone call you arranged to be alone with Sampson to finish the job that Taggert's partners had failed to do for you. Don't tell me you're not aware that you and your bride have been worth five million dollars for the last couple of hours?"

"I know it well enough," he said. "But it's not five million. Mrs. Sampson gets half."

"I forgot about her. Why didn't you kill her, too? Weren't you being a piker, Graves? Or were you planning to murder Mrs. Sampson and Miranda later on?"

"You know that isn't true," he said tonelessly. "What do you think I am?"

"You're a man who married a girl and killed her father the same day to convert her into an heiress."

I left him sitting in the car. My back was to him as I crossed the gravel drive to the house. He had a gun in his pocket, but I didn't look back. I believed him when he said he was sick of violence.

The lights were on in the kitchen, but nobody answered my knock. I went through the house to the elevator. Mrs. Kromberg was in the upstairs hall when I stepped out. "I have to see Mrs. Sampson," I told her.

"I'll see if she's asleep," she said. She went to the closed door of Mrs. Sampson's room and opened it quietly.

A light switched on. Mrs. Sampson leaned on her elbows, blinking. Her brown face was drugged and sodden with sleep or the hope of sleep.

I shut the door behind me. "Your husband is dead."

"Dead," she repeated after me.

"You don't seem surprised."

"Should I be surprised? You don't know the dreams I've been having about him."

"Your husband was murdered two hours ago, Mrs. Sampson."

"I knew I was going to outlive him."

"Is that all it means to you?"

"What more should it mean?" Her voice was blurred and empty of feeling. "When Bob was killed, I cried for days. I'm not going to grieve for his father. I wanted him to die."

"You have your wish, then."

"Not all of my wish. If Miranda had married the other one, Ralph would have changed his will and I'd have had it all for myself." She looked up at me slyly. "I know what you must be thinking, Mr. Archer. That I'm an evil woman. But I'm not evil, really. I have so little, don't you see?"

"Half of five million dollars," I said.

"It's not the money. It's the power it gives you. I needed it so badly. Now Miranda will go away and leave me all alone. Come and sit beside me for a minute. I have such terrible fears before I go to sleep. Do you think I'll have to see his face every night before I go to sleep?"

"I don't know, Mrs. Sampson." I felt pity for her, but the other feelings were stronger. I went to the door and shut it on her.

Mrs. Kromberg was still in the hall. "I heard you say that Mr. Sampson is dead."

"He is. Mrs. Sampson is too far gone to talk. Do you know where Miranda is?"

"Someplace downstairs, I think."

I found her in the living room, hugging her legs on a hassock beside the fireplace.

She looked up when I entered the room, but she didn't rise to greet me. "Is that you, Archer?"

"Yes. I have some things to tell you."

"Have you found him?" A glowing log in the fireplace lit up her head and neck with a fitful rosiness.

"Yes. He's dead."

"I knew that he'd be dead. He's been dead from the beginning, hasn't he?"

"I wish I could tell you that he had."

"What do you mean?"

I put off explaining what I meant. "I recovered the money."

"The money?"

"This." I tossed the bag at her feet. "The hundred thousand."

"I don't care about it. Where did you find him?"

"Listen to me, Miranda. You're on your own."

"Not entirely," she said. "I married Albert this afternoon."

"I know. He told me. But you've got to get out of this house and look after yourself. The first thing you've got to do is put that money away. I went to a lot of trouble to get it back, and you may be needing it."

"I'm sorry. Where shall I put it?"

"The safe in the study, until you can get to a bank."

"All right." She rose with a sudden decisiveness and led the way into the study. While she was opening the safe I heard a car go down the drive. She turned to me with an awkward movement more appealing than grace. "Who was that?"

"Albert Graves. He drove me out here."

"Why on earth didn't he come in?"

I gathered the remnants of my courage together and told her. "He killed your father tonight."

Her mouth moved breathlessly and then forced out words. "You're joking, aren't you? He couldn't have."

"He did." I took refuge in facts. "I found out this afternoon where your father was being held. I phoned Graves from Los Angeles and told him to get there as soon as he could. When I arrived, there was no sign of him. He'd parked his car somewhere out of sight and was inside the building with your father. When I went in, he hit me from behind and knocked me out. When I came to, he pretended he'd just arrived. Your father was dead. His body was still warm."

"I can't believe Albert did it." She sat down limply in a leather armchair. "So many people have died. Father and Alan—"

"Graves killed them both."

"But he killed Alan to save you. You told me—"

"He didn't have to kill Taggert," I said. "He's a good shot. He could have wounded him. But he wanted Taggert dead. He had his reasons."

"What possible reasons?"

"I think you know of one."

She raised her face in the light. "Yes, I do. I was in love with Alan."

"But you were planning to marry Graves."

"I hadn't made up my mind until today. I was going to marry someone, and he seemed to be the one."

"He gambled on you, and won. But the other thing he had gambled on didn't happen. Taggert's partner failed to kill your father. So Graves strangled your father himself."

She spread one hand over her eyes and forehead. "It's incredibly ugly," she said. "I can't understand why he did it."

"He did it for money."

"But he's never cared for money. It's one of the things I admired in him." She removed her hand from her face, and I saw she was smiling bitterly. "I wonder what happened to him."

"There may have been a time when Graves didn't care about money. There may be places where he could have stayed that way. Santa Teresa isn't one of them. Money is lifeblood in this town. If you don't have it, you're only half alive. It must have galled him to work for millionaires and handle their money and have nothing of his own. Suddenly he saw his chance to be a millionaire himself. He realized that he wanted money more than anything else on earth."

"I thought I knew him well. Now I'm uncertain—about everything. I'm not even sure I have to go on living."

"Don't go romantic on me," I said harshly. "Self-pity isn't your way out. You've had terrible luck with two men. I think you're a strong enough girl to take it. You've got a life to make. You're on your own."

She inclined toward me. Her mouth was soft. "I don't know how to begin. What shall I do?"

"Come with me."

"With you? You want me to go with you?"

"Come with me, and we'll talk to the DA. We'll let him decide what to do."

"Very well. We'll go to Humphreys. He's always been close to Albert."

She drove me up a winding road to the mesa that overlooked the city. When she stopped in front of Humphreys' redwood bungalow, another car was standing in the drive.

"That's Albert's car," she said. "Please go in alone. I don't want to see him."

I left her in the car and climbed the stone steps to the terrace. Humphreys opened the door before I could reach the knocker.

He stepped out on the terrace and closed the door behind him. "Graves is here," he said. "He came a few minutes ago. He told me he murdered Sampson. I've called the sheriff. He's on his way over." He ran his fingers through his thinning hair. His gestures, like his voice, were light and distant, as if reality had moved back out of his reach. "This is a tragic thing. I believed that Albert Graves was a good man."

"Crime often spreads out like that," I said. "It's epidemic. You've seen it happen before."

"Not to one of my friends." He was silent.

I went back to Miranda. "You weren't entirely wrong about Graves. He decided to do the right thing."

"Confessed?"

"He was too honest to bluff it through. If nobody had suspected him, he might have. But he knew that I knew. He went to Humphreys and told his story."

"I'm glad he did." A moment later, deep shaking sobs bowed her over the wheel.

I lifted her over and drove myself. As we rolled down the hill, I could see all the lights of the city. They didn't seem quite real. The stars and the house lights were firefly gleams, sparks of cold fire suspended in the black void. The real thing in my world was the girl beside me, warm and shuddering and lost.

I could have put my arms around her and taken her over. She was that lost, that vulnerable. But if I had, she'd have hated me in a week. I kept my hands to myself and let her lick her wounds. She used my shoulder to cry on as she would have used anyone's.

Her crying was settling down to a steady rhythm. The sheriff's radio car passed us at the foot of the hill and turned up toward the house where Graves was waiting.

Strangers
on a Train

Strangers on a Train

A CONDENSATION OF
THE BOOK BY

Patricia Highsmith

ILLUSTRATED BY TOM HALL

It was a long, boring train ride, and as the two young men sat talking and drinking late into the night, they confided in each other about their troubles—an unfaithful wife who wouldn't grant a divorce, a tyrant of a father who had twisted the other man into a lonely, aimless playboy. Suddenly something clicks and there is a plan.

"We murder for each other, see?" says the playboy, Charles Bruno. "I kill your wife and you kill my father! We meet on the train, see, and nobody knows we know each other! Perfect alibis!"

It is unthinkable, of course, but ten days later Guy Haines's unfaithful wife is found strangled on a secluded island in an amusement park . . . and a nightmare begins. As Bruno insinuates himself more and more into Guy Haines's life, Guy realizes he will never be free of Bruno until he carries out his part of the bargain.

A tense psychological drama, *Strangers on a Train* became one of Alfred Hitchcock's most powerful films. Patricia Highsmith is also the author of *Ripley's Game* and *Edith's Diary*.

1

THE train tore along with an angry, irregular rhythm. It was having to stop at smaller and more frequent stations, where it would wait impatiently for a moment, then attack the prairie again. But progress was imperceptible. The prairie only undulated, like a vast, pink-tan blanket being casually shaken. The faster the train went, the more buoyant and taunting the undulations.

Guy took his eyes from the window and hitched himself back against the seat of the Pullman car.

Miriam would delay the divorce at best, he thought. She might not even want a divorce, only money. Would there really ever be a divorce from her?

He could sense Miriam ahead of him, not much farther now, pink and tan-freckled, and radiating a kind of unhealthful heat, like the prairie out the window. Sullen and cruel.

He reached for a cigarette, tapped it twice on the face of his wristwatch, read the time, five twelve, and fitted the cigarette into the corner of his mouth. Then he lighted it and smoked in slow, steady pulls. Again and again his brown eyes looked out the window. In the reflection the dusk had started to create in the window's glass, the rise of his black hair and the slope of his long nose gave him a look of intense purpose and forward motion. From the front, though, his heavy, horizontal brows and mouth imposed a stillness and reserve. He wore flannel trousers that needed pressing, a dark jacket that slacked over his slight body, and a conservative woolen tie, carelessly knotted.

He did not think Miriam would be having a child unless she wanted it. Which should mean the lover intended to marry her. But why had she sent for him? She didn't need him to get a divorce. And why did he go over the same dull ground he had four days ago when he had gotten her letter? The five or six lines in Miriam's round handwriting had said only that she was going to have a child and wanted to see him. That she was pregnant guaranteed the divorce, he reasoned, so why was he nervous?

There was so much to look forward to now. His divorce, the work in Florida—it was practically certain the board would pass on his drawings, and he would learn this week—and then there was Anne. He and Anne could begin to plan now. He felt a pleasant explosion of happiness inside him as he mashed his cigarette stub and threw it away, and he relaxed in the corner of the plush seat. For the last three years he had been waiting for this to happen so he would be free. He could have bought a divorce, of course, but he hadn't ever amassed that much spare money. Starting a career as an architect in New York, without benefit of a job with a firm, had not been easy and still wasn't. Miriam had never asked for an income. Occasionally she wrote him from Metcalf for money, small but irritating amounts which he let her have because it would be so easy, so natural, for her to start a campaign in Metcalf against him, and his mother was there.

A tall blond young man in a rust-brown suit dropped into the empty seat opposite Guy and, smiling with a vague friendliness, slid over into the corner. Guy glanced at his pallid, undersized face, then looked out the window again.

The young man seemed to debate whether to start a conversation or take a nap. His elbow kept sliding along the windowsill, and whenever his stubby lashes came open, the gray bloodshot eyes were looking at Guy and the soft smile came back. He might have been slightly drunk.

Guy opened his book, but his mind wandered after half a page. He looked up and let his eyes travel to the monogram that trembled on a thin gold chain across the tie of the young man opposite him. The monogram was CAB, and the tie was of green silk, hand-painted with offensively orange-colored palm trees. The long rust-brown body was sprawled vulnerably now, the head thrown back. It was an interesting face, though Guy did not know why. It looked neither young nor old, neither intelligent nor entirely stupid. Between the narrow bulging forehead and the lantern jaw, it scooped degenerately—deep where the mouth lay in a fine line, deepest in the blue hollows that held his eyes. The skin was smooth as a girl's and waxenly clear.

For a few moments Guy read again. The words began to lift his anxiety. But what good will Plato do you with Miriam? an inner voice asked him. He looked out the window and, seeing his own image, straightened his curling collar. He shifted his position, accidentally touched the outstretched foot of the young man asleep, and watched fascinatedly as the lashes twitched and came open.

"Sorry," Guy murmured.

"'S all right," the other said. He sat up and shook his head sharply. "Where are we?"

"Getting into Texas."

The blond young man brought a gold flask from his inside pocket, opened it, and extended it amiably.

"No, thanks," Guy said.

"Where you bound?" The smile was a thin wet crescent now.

"Metcalf," Guy said.

"Oh. Nice town, Metcalf. Down on business?"

"Yes."

"What business?"

Guy answered reluctantly, "Architect."

"Oh," with wistful interest. "Build houses and things?"

"Yes."

"I don't think I've introduced myself." The young man half stood up. "Bruno, Charles Anthony Bruno."

Guy shook his hand briefly. "Guy Haines."

"Glad to meet you. You live in New York?"

"Yes."

"I live on Long Island. Going to El Paso and then to Santa Fe for a little vacation. Ever been to Santa Fe?"

Guy shook his head.

"Great town to relax in." He smiled, showing poor teeth. "Mostly Indian architecture there, I guess."

A conductor stopped in the aisle, thumbing through tickets. "That your seat?" he asked Bruno.

Bruno leaned possessively into his corner. "Drawing room three, next car."

The conductor went on.

Guy went back to his book, but the other's obtrusive boredom kept him from concentrating. The train was slowing down. When Bruno looked as if he were going to speak, Guy got up, retreated toward the next car, and ran down the steps to the crunchy ground as the train stopped.

There was a smell of dusty, sun-warm gravel, of oil and hot metal. He was hungry and lingered near the dining car, pacing in slow strides with his hands in his pockets. Yesterday Anne might have come this route, he thought, on her way to Mexico. She had wanted him to come with her as far as Metcalf. He might have asked her to stay over a day and meet his mother, if it had not been for Miriam. He had told Anne about Miriam, about almost all of it, but he could not bear the thought of their meeting. He had wanted to travel alone on the train in order to think.

The conductor's voice shouted a warning, and Guy swung himself aboard and went to the dining car. The waiter had just taken his order when the blond young man appeared in the doorway of the car, swaying, looking a little truculent with a short cigarette in his mouth. Guy had put him quite out of mind and now his tall rust-brown figure was like a vaguely unpleasant memory. Guy saw him smile as he sighted him.

"Thought you might have missed the train," Bruno said cheerfully, pulling out a chair.

"If you don't mind, Mr. Bruno, I'd like some privacy for a while. I have some things to think over."

Bruno stabbed out the cigarette that was burning his fingers and looked at him blankly. "We could have privacy in my place. We could have dinner there. How about it?"

"Thanks, I'd rather stay here."

"Oh, but I insist. Waiter!" Bruno clapped his hands. "Would you have this gentleman's order sent to drawing room three and bring me a steak, medium rare, with french fries and apple pie? And two Scotch and sodas fast as you can, huh?" He looked at Guy and smiled, the soft wistful smile. "Okay?"

Guy debated, then got up and went with him. What did it matter after all? And wasn't he utterly sick of himself?

There was no need for the Scotches except to provide glasses and ice. The four yellow-labeled bottles of Scotch lined up on an alligator suitcase were the one neat unit of the little room. Suitcases and wardrobe trunks were piled everywhere, and on top of them were strewn sports clothes and equipment, tennis rackets, a bag of golf clubs, a couple of cameras, a wicker basket of fruit and wine bedded in fuchsia paper. A splay of current magazines, comic books, and novels covered the seat by the window.

"Looks kind of athletic, I guess," Bruno said, suddenly apologetic.

"It's fine." Guy smiled. The room amused him and gave him a welcome sense of seclusion. With the smile his dark brows relaxed, transforming his expression. His eyes looked outward now, examining things like a curious cat.

"Brand-new. Never felt a ball," Bruno said, holding out a tennis racket for him to feel. "My mother makes me take all this stuff, hoping it'll keep me out of bars. Good to hock if I run out, anyway. I like Scotch when I travel. It enhances things, don't you think?" The drinks arrived, and Bruno strengthened them from one of his bottles.

There was an awkward several minutes when they had nothing to say to each other. Guy took a swallow of the drink that seemed to be all Scotch, and looked down at the littered floor. Bruno had odd feet, Guy noticed, or maybe it was the shoes. Small, light tan shoes with a long plain toe cap shaped like Bruno's lantern chin. Somehow old-fashioned–looking.

"I hope you weren't annoyed," Bruno said cautiously, "when I came into the diner. I felt lonely. You know."

Guy said something about its being lonely traveling in a drawing room alone. He was conscious of Bruno's shy stare. He was going to be bored, of course. Why had he come? Then the waiter arrived with a pewter-covered tray and snapped up a table. The smell of charcoal-broiled meat cheered Guy. Bruno insisted so desperately on paying the check that Guy gave it up. Bruno had a big mushroom-covered steak. Guy had ordered a hamburger.

"What're you building in Metcalf?"

"Nothing," Guy said. "My mother lives there."

"Oh," Bruno said interestedly. "That where you're from?"

"Yes. Born there."

"You don't look much like a Texan." Bruno shot catsup all over his steak and french fries. "How long since you been home?"

"About two years."

"Your father there, too?"

"My father's dead."

"Oh. Get along with your mother okay?"

Guy said he did. The taste of Scotch was pleasant, because it reminded him of Anne. She drank Scotch, when she drank. It was like her, golden, full of light, made with careful art. "Where do you live on Long Island?"

"Great Neck."

Anne lived much farther out on Long Island.

"In a house I call the Doghouse," Bruno went on. "Everybody in it's in some kind of doghouse, down to the chauffeur." He laughed with real pleasure and bent again over his food.

"Why?" Guy asked.

"Account of my father. Bastard. I get on okay with my mother though. She's coming out to Santa Fe in a couple of days."

"That's nice."

"We have a lot of fun together—sitting around, playing golf. We even go to parties together." Bruno laughed, half ashamed, half proud, and suddenly uncertain and young. "You think that's funny?"

"No," said Guy.

"I just wish I had my own dough. See, my income was supposed to start this year, only my father won't let me have it. He's deflecting it into his own exchequer. I have to ask for a hundred dollars now and then from my mother."

"I wish you had let me pay the check."

"A-aw, no!" Bruno protested. "I just mean it's a hell of a thing, isn't it, when your own father robs you. It isn't even his money, it's my mother's family's money."

"Hasn't your mother any say about it?"

"My father got the money put in his name when I was a kid!" Bruno shouted hoarsely. He brought his hands up in a hopeless shrug. "I said he was a bastard, didn't I? He robs everyone he can. He thinks my mother and I have too good a time as it is. He's always scheming up ways to cut in."

Guy could see him and his mother, a youngish Long Island society woman who used too much mascara. "Where'd you go to college?"

"Harvard. Busted out sophomore year. Drinking and gambling." He shrugged again. "Not like you, huh? Okay, I'm a bum, so what?" He poured more Scotch for both of them.

"Who said you were?"

"My father says so. He should've had a nice quiet son like you, then everybody would've been happy."

"What makes you think I'm nice and quiet?"

"I mean you're serious and you chose a profession. Like architecture. Me, I don't feel like working. I don't have to work, see? Is there any reason a person should work if they don't have to?

My father still has hopes I'll enter his hardware business. I tell him all business is legalized throat-cutting. Am I right?"

Guy looked at him wryly and sprinkled salt on the french fried potato on his fork. He was eating slowly, enjoying his meal. It had just occurred to him that, if he got through with Miriam quickly, he could fly to Mexico to see Anne, and then fly from there to Palm Beach. It hadn't occurred to him before because he couldn't afford it. But if the Palm Beach contract came through, he could.

"Can you imagine anything more insulting? Locking the garage where my own car is?" Bruno's voice had cracked and was stuck at a shrieking pitch.

"Why?" Guy asked.

"Just because he knew I needed it bad that night! My friends picked me up finally."

"But what's he got against you?"

"Against me and my mother, too! He's different from us or any other *human!* He doesn't like anybody. He doesn't like anything but money. He cut enough throats to make a lot of money, that's all. Sure he's smart! Okay! But his conscience is eating him now! That's why he wants me to go into his business, so I'll cut throats and feel as lousy as he does!"

"Can't you leave home if you want to?"

Bruno didn't seem to understand his question at first, then he answered calmly, "Sure, only I like to be with my mother."

And his mother stayed because of the money, Guy supposed. "Cigarette?"

Bruno took one. "You know," he went on, smiling, "the night he locked the garage, I was sore enough to kill him. Ever feel like murdering somebody?"

"No."

"I do. I'm sure sometimes I could kill my father." He looked down at his plate with a bemused smile. "You mind if I ask you how old you are?"

"Twenty-nine."

"Yeah? I would've said older. How old you think I look?"

Guy studied him politely. "Maybe twenty-four or five."

"Yeah, I am. Twenty-five. In Santa Fe," Bruno went on, "I want everything there is. Wine, women, and song. Hah! I got a theory a person ought to do everything it's possible to do before he dies, and maybe die trying to do something that's really impossible."

Something in Guy responded with a leap, then cautiously drew back. He asked softly, "Like what?"

"Like a trip to the moon in a rocket. Setting a speed record in a car—blindfolded. I did that once. Didn't set a record, but I went up to a hundred sixty."

"Blindfolded?"

"Sure. And I did a robbery." Bruno stared at Guy rigidly. "Good one. Out of an apartment."

An incredulous smile started on Guy's lips, though actually he believed Bruno. Bruno could be violent. He could be insane, too. Despair, Guy thought, not insanity. The desperate boredom of the wealthy.

"Not to get anything," Bruno went on. "I didn't want what I took. I especially took what I didn't want."

"What did you take?"

"Cigarette lighter. And a statue off the mantel." Bruno shrugged. "You're the only one knows about it. I don't talk much. Guess you think I do." He smiled.

Guy drew on his cigarette. "How'd you go about it?"

"Watched an apartment house in Astoria till I got the time right, then just walked in the window. Down the fire escape. Sort of easy."

Guy looked at the stiff, shaky hands that had stolen, at the nails bitten below the quick. The hands played clumsily with a matchbook cover and dropped it onto the ash-sprinkled steak. Who would know from Bruno's hands, or his ugly wistful face, that he had stolen?

"Tell me about you," Bruno said pleasantly.

"Nothing to tell." Guy took a pipe from his jacket pocket, banged it on his heel, looked down at the ashes on the carpet, and then forgot them. The tingling of the alcohol sank deeper into his flesh. He thought, If the Palm Beach contract came through, the two weeks before work began would pass quickly. A divorce needn't take long. He felt immensely secure suddenly, and blessed.

"What kind of houses you build?" Bruno asked.

"Oh—what's known as modern. I've done a couple of stores and a small office building." Guy smiled.

"You married?"

"No. Well, I am, yes. Separated."

"Oh. Why?"

"Incompatible," Guy replied.

"How long you been separated?"

"Three years."

"You don't want a divorce?"

Guy hesitated, frowning.

"Is she in Texas, too?"

"Yes."

"Going to see her?"

"I'll see her. We're going to arrange the divorce now." His teeth set. Why had he said it?

"What kind of girl's your wife?"

"Rather pretty," Guy said cautiously. "Red hair. Plump."

"What's her name?"

"Miriam. Miriam Joyce."

"Hm-m. Smart or dumb?"

"She's not an intellectual. I didn't want to marry an intellectual," Guy said.

"And you loved her like hell, huh?"

"Why do you say that?"

"You're a nice guy. You take everything serious. You take women the hard way, too, don't you?"

Guy felt a rush of affection for Bruno because Bruno had said what he thought about him. Most people he knew didn't say what they thought about him.

"What's the hard way?" Guy asked.

"All out, with a lot of high hopes. Then you get kicked in the teeth, right?" Bruno said.

"Not entirely." A throb of self-pity piqued Guy, however.

Bruno kept staring at him, one foot dangling at the end of the crossed leg, flicking his finger again and again on the cigarette he held over his plate.

"What happened with your wife? She start sleeping around?" Bruno's accuracy irritated him. "No. That's all past, anyway."

"But you're still married to her. Couldn't you get a divorce before now?"

"She just decided she wanted one. I think she's going to have a child."

"Oh. She's been sleeping around for three years and finally landed somebody?"

Just what had happened, of course, and probably it had taken the baby to do it. How did Bruno know? Guy turned to the window. He could feel his heartbeats shaking his body, perhaps because he had never told anyone so much about Miriam. He had never told Anne as much as Bruno knew already. Except that Miriam had once been different—sweet, loyal, lonely, terribly in need of him and of freedom from her family. Failure overwhelmed him suddenly.

"What happened with your marriage?" Bruno's voice asked gently. "I'm really very interested, as a friend. How old was she?"

"Eighteen."

"She start sleeping around right away?"

Guy looked away, annoyed and fascinated at the same time. "Yes." How ugly the words sounded, hissing in his ears!

"I know that southern redhead type," Bruno said, looking down at his apple pie with coy amusement. "Marriage," he sighed. "What happened? You don't mind telling me, do you? I'm interested."

Steve had happened. Guy picked up his drink. He saw an image, gray and black now, like a photograph, of the afternoon he had found them in the apartment. He wanted to tell everything to Bruno, the stranger on the train who would listen, commiserate, and forget. And Steve wasn't the first betrayal, only the surprise ending that made the rest fall into place. It was Guy's twenty-six-year-old pride that had finally exploded that afternoon.

"I expected too much of her," he said casually, "without any right to. She happened to like attention. She'll probably flirt all her life, no matter whom she's with."

"I know." Bruno waved his hand. "The eternal high school type. Can't even pretend to belong to one guy, ever."

Guy looked at him. Miriam had, of course, once.

Abruptly he abandoned his idea of telling Bruno, ashamed that he had nearly begun.

"Women like that draw men," Bruno mumbled, "like garbage draws flies."

The shock of Bruno's words detached him from himself. "You must have had some unpleasant experiences yourself," Guy remarked casually.

"Oh, my father had one like that. Redhead, too. Named Carlotta." He looked up, and the hatred for his father penetrated his fuzziness like a barb. "Fine, isn't it? It's men like my father keep 'em in business."

Carlotta. Guy felt he understood now why Bruno loathed Miriam. It seemed the key to Bruno's whole personality, to the hatred of his father and to his retarded adolescence. "What about your mother?"

"I never seen another woman like my mother," Bruno declared. "I never seen a woman take so much. She's good-looking, too, lots of men friends, but she doesn't fool around with them."

Silence. Guy tapped another cigarette on his watch and saw it was ten thirty. He must go in a moment. "Tell me what else you want to do before you die."

"Die? Who said anything about dying? I got a few foolproof rackets doped out. And I got a lot of ideas for perfect murders. Didn't you ever feel you wanted to kill somebody? You must have. Everybody feels those things."

"No," Guy said.

Bruno hesitated. "But you've had people in your life you'd have liked out of the way, haven't you?"

"No." He suddenly remembered Steve. Once he had thought of murdering him.

Bruno cocked his head. "Sure you have. I see it. Why don't you admit it?"

"I may have had fleeting ideas, but I'd never have done anything about them. I'm not that kind of person."

"That's exactly where you're wrong! Any kind of person can murder. People get so far—and it takes just the least little thing to push them over the brink. I know!"

"I don't happen to agree," Guy said tersely.

"I tell you I came near murdering my father a thousand times! Who'd you ever feel like murdering? The guys with your wife?"

"One of them," Guy murmured.

"How near did you come?"

"Not near at all. I merely thought of it." Guy remembered the hundreds of sleepless nights and how he had despaired of peace unless he could avenge himself. "You read too many detective stories," he said.

"They're good. They show that all kinds of people can murder."

"I've always thought that's exactly why they're bad."

"Wrong again!" Bruno said indignantly. "Do you know what percentage of murders get put in the papers?"

"I don't know and I don't care."

"One-twelfth. One-twelfth! Just imagine! Who do you think the other eleven-twelfths are? A lot of little people that don't matter. All the people the cops know they'll never catch." He started to pour more Scotch, found the bottle empty, and dragged himself up. A gold penknife flashed out of his trouser pocket on a gold chain fine as a string. It pleased Guy aesthetically, as a beautiful piece of jewelry might have. And he found himself thinking, as he watched Bruno slash around the top of a Scotch bottle, that Bruno might murder one day with the little penknife, that he would probably go quite free, simply because he wouldn't much care whether he were caught or not.

Bruno turned, grinning, with the new bottle of Scotch. "Come to Santa Fe with me, huh? Relax for a couple days."

"Thanks, I can't."

"I got plenty of dough. Be my guest, huh?" He spilled Scotch on the table. "I got nothing to do till my mother comes. We could have a swell time."

"Pick up somebody else."

"Cheeses, Guy, what d'you think I do, go around picking up traveling companions? I like you, so I ask you to come with me. One day even. I could cut right over with you from Metcalf to Santa Fe and not even go to El Paso. I'm supposed to stop off there and see Carlsbad Caverns, but I could skip that."

"Thanks, I've got a job as soon as I finish in Metcalf."

"Oh." The wistful, admiring smile again. "Building something?"

"Yes, a country club. The new Palmyra in Palm Beach."

Bruno had heard of the Palmyra Club. It was the biggest in Palm Beach. "You designed it?" He looked at Guy like a hero-worshipping little boy. "You're gonna be famous, huh? Maybe you're famous now."

They hadn't passed on his sketches yet, Guy reminded himself, but he was sure they would. And so was Mr. Brillhart, the manager of the Palmyra Club. The biggest commission of his life.

"I might be famous after this," Guy said. "It's the kind of thing they publicize."

Bruno took a deep breath. "If your wife made a stink now about the divorce— Say she fought about it while you were in Palm Beach and made them fire you, wouldn't that be motive enough to murder her?"

"No," Guy said. But the question disturbed him.

"When she was two-timing you, didn't you feel like murdering her?" Bruno asked.

"No. Can't you get off the subject?" For an instant Guy saw both halves of his life, his marriage and his career, side by side as he felt he had never seen them before. He glanced at Bruno, who still stared at him, and, feeling slightly befuddled, set his glass on the table.

"You must have wanted to once," Bruno said with gentle, drunken persistence.

"No." Guy wanted to get out and take a walk, but the train kept on and on like something that would never stop.

Bruno was smiling. "Shall I tell you one of my ideas for murdering my father?"

"No," Guy said. He put his hand over the glass Bruno was about to refill.

"Which do you want, the busted light socket in the bathroom or the carbon monoxide in the garage?"

"Do it and stop talking about it!"

"I'll do it, don't think I won't! Know what else I'll do someday? Commit suicide if I happen to feel like committing suicide, and fix it so it looks like my worst enemy murdered me."

Guy looked at him in disgust. Bruno seemed to be growing indefinite at the edges, as if by some dissolving process. He seemed only a voice and a spirit now, the spirit of evil.

"Want me to dope out a perfect murder of your wife for you? You might want to use it sometime." Bruno squirmed with self-consciousness under Guy's scrutiny.

Guy stood up. "I want to take a walk."

Bruno slammed his palms together. "Hey! Cheeses, what an idea! We murder for each other, see? I kill your wife and you kill my father! We meet on the train, see, and nobody knows we know each other! Perfect alibis! Catch?"

The wall before Guy's eyes pulsed rhythmically, as if it were about to spring apart. *Murder*. The word sickened him, terrified him. He wanted to break away from Bruno, get out of the room, but a nightmarish heaviness held him.

Bruno's tobacco-stained hands jumped and trembled on his knees. "Airtight alibis!" he shrieked. "It's the idea of my life! Don't you get it? I could do it sometime when you're out of town and you could do it when I was out of town."

Guy understood. No one could ever, possibly, find out.

"It would give me great pleasure to stop a career like Miriam's and to further a career like yours." Bruno giggled. "Don't you agree she ought to be stopped before she ruins a lot of other people?"

She hasn't ruined me, Guy wanted to remind him, but Bruno gave him no time.

"You could tell me all about where she lived, you know, and I could do the same for you, as good as if you lived there. We could leave fingerprints all over and drive the police batty!" He snickered. "Months apart, of course, and strictly no communication. It's a cinch!" He stood up and nearly toppled.

Shut up with your damned theories, Guy wanted to shout back, but instead his voice was a whisper. "I'm sick of this."

"Okay. I still say it's a good idea and we got the absolutely perfect setup right here. It's the idea I'll use. With somebody else, of course. Where you going?"

"I'm going to bed," Guy said.

"Don't forget to call me in the morning," Bruno said. "I'll leave the door unlocked. If I don't answer, come on in, huh?"

Guy lurched against the walls of green curtains as he made his way to his berth. Habit made him think of his book as he lay down. He had left it in Bruno's room. His Plato. He didn't like the idea of Bruno's touching it and opening it.

2

Guy had called Miriam immediately, and she had arranged to meet him at the high school, which lay between their houses.

Now he stood in a corner of the asphalt game field, waiting. She would be late, of course.

He walked through the wide gate between the crisscross wire fence and looked up College Avenue again. Then he saw her, under the yellow-green trees that bordered the sidewalk. She walked at her usual rather stolid pace, taking her time. She gave him a relaxed wave, and Guy pulled a hand out of his pocket, returned it, and went back into the game field, suddenly tense and shy as a boy.

"Hello, Guy," Miriam said, coming up to him.

"How are you, Miriam?" Involuntarily he glanced at her figure, plump but not pregnant-looking.

She sat down primly on the one stone bench that was in the shade. "In January," she spoke in a flat voice. "In January the child's due."

It was about two months advanced then. "I suppose you want to marry him."

She turned her head slightly and looked down. "Not right now. See, there're complications. We might not be able to marry as soon as we'd like to."

"Oh." *We.* He knew what he would look like, tall and dark, with a long face, like Steve. The type Miriam had always been attracted to. "That needn't delay the divorce though, I suppose."

"Well, I didn't think so—until a couple of days ago. I thought Owen would be free to marry this month."

"Who?"

"Owen. Owen Markman."

"Oh. He's married now?"

"Yeah, he's married," she said with a little sigh.

Guy looked down in vague embarrassment and paced a slow step or two on the asphalt. He had suspected the man would be married and would have no intention of divorcing and remarrying unless he were forced to. "Where is he? Here?"

"He's in Houston," she replied. "Don't you want to sit down?"

"No."

"You still have your ring."

"Yes." His class ring that Miriam had always admired because it meant he was a college man. She was staring at the ring with a self-conscious smile. He put his hands in his pockets. "As long as I'm here, I'd like to settle it this week."

"I want to wait, Guy," she said. "Would you mind? Just a while?"

"I should think you'd mind. Does he intend to marry you or not?" Guy asked.

"He could marry me in September. He'd be free then, but—"

"But what?" In her silence, in the childlike lick of her tongue on her upper lip, he saw the trap she was in. She wanted this child so much, she would sacrifice herself in Metcalf by waiting until four months before it was born to marry its father. In spite of himself, he felt a certain pity for her.

"I'm tired of staying here, Guy. I want to go away with you." The dreaminess in her gray-green eyes was dispersing like a mist. "Your mother said you were going to Palm Beach."

"I might be going there. To work." He thought of the Palmyra with a twinge of peril. He was going to live in Palm Beach several months, and he would be expected to keep on a social par with the directors. Miriam could lose him the commission.

"Take me with you, Guy? It's the last thing I'll ask you. If I could stay with you till after January, then get the divorce—"

"Oh," he said quietly, but something throbbed in his chest, like the breaking of his heart. She disgusted him suddenly. Another man's child. Go away with her, be her husband until she gave birth to another man's child. In Palm Beach!

"If you don't take me, I'll come anyway."

"Miriam, I could get that divorce now. I don't have to wait to see the child. The law doesn't—" His voice shook.

"You wouldn't do that to me," Miriam replied.

And she was right. He wouldn't divorce her now. But it was not because he still loved her, but because he pitied her and because he remembered he had once loved her. "I won't take the job if you come out there," he said. "There'd be no use taking it."

"I don't think you'd give up a job like that," she challenged.

He turned away from her twisted smile of triumph. Be calm, he told himself. What could anger accomplish? "I haven't even got the job yet, you know," he said. "I'll simply send them a telegram saying I don't want it."

"And then what?"

"A lot of things. But you won't know about them."

"Running away?" she taunted. "Cheapest way out."

He paced slowly again, and turned. He felt strangely resigned because he was with Miriam, the symbol of his youthful failure. There was inside him, like a flaw in a jewel, not visible on the surface, a fear and anticipation of failure that he had never been able to mend. At times failure was a possibility that fascinated him, as when in school he had allowed himself to fail exams he might have passed, as when he married Miriam against the will of both their families and all their friends. Hadn't he known it couldn't succeed? And now he considered giving up his biggest commission without a murmur. He would go to Mexico and have a few days with Anne. It would take all his money, but why not? Could he possibly go back to New York and work without having seen Anne first?

"Is there anything else?" he asked.

"I've said it," she told him.

He walked back to his mother's home slowly, approaching Ambrose Street through Travis, which was shaded and still. He felt quiet, resigned, and even rather happy. Strange how re-mote—how foreign—Miriam seemed five minutes after talking with her, how unimportant, really, everything seemed.

"Not bad, Mama," he said with a smile when he came home.

His mother had greeted him with an anxious lift of her eye-brows. "I'm glad to hear that," she said.

She pulled a rocker around and sat down to listen. She was a small woman with light brown hair and a pretty, rather fine, straight-nosed profile. And she was almost always cheerful. Guy liked to nurse his griefs, discover all he could about them, while his mother counseled him to forget. "What did she say? You cer-tainly weren't gone very long. I thought you might have had lunch with her."

"No, Mama." He sighed and sank down on the brocade sofa. "Everything's all right, but I'll probably not take the Palmyra job."

"Oh, Guy. Why not? Is she— Is it true she's pregnant?"

"It's true," he said, and let his head go back until he felt the cool of the sofa's wooden frame against the back of his neck. His mother would be disappointed about the Palmyra job, Guy thought. He was glad she didn't know what the job really meant. He thought of the gulf that separated his life from his mother's.

His mother, who kept herself busy with her big house and her garden and her pleasant, loyal friends in Metcalf—what could she understand of a total malice like Miriam's?

"Now what's Palm Beach got to do with Miriam?" she asked finally.

"Miriam wants to go there with me. Protection for a time. And I couldn't bear it." Guy clenched his hand. He had a sudden vision of Miriam in Palm Beach, Miriam meeting Clarence Brillhart and the directors of the Palmyra Club. Yet it was not the vision of Brillhart's shock beneath his calm, unvarying courtesy, Guy knew, but his own revulsion that made it impossible. He simply couldn't bear having Miriam anywhere near him on a project like this one.

He got up and took his mother's soft face in his hands. "Mama, I don't care a bit," he said, kissing her forehead. "I really don't care a row of beans."

"I don't believe you do care. Why don't you?"

He crossed the room to the upright piano. "Because I'm going to Mexico to see Anne."

"Oh, are you?" She smiled gaily. "Aren't you the gadabout!"

"Want to come to Mexico?" He smiled over his shoulder. He began to play a saraband that he had learned as a child.

"Mexico!" his mother said in mock horror. "Wild horses wouldn't get me to Mexico. Maybe you can bring Anne to see me on your way back."

"Maybe."

She went over and laid her hands shyly on his shoulders. "Sometimes, Guy, I feel you're happy again. At the funniest times."

Guy telegraphed Anne that he would fly down Sunday for several days. He also sent a telegram to Clarence Brillhart:

OWING TO CIRCUMSTANCES IMPOSSIBLE FOR ME TO TAKE COMMISSION. DEEPEST REGRETS AND THANKS FOR YOUR CHAMPIONING AND CONSTANT ENCOURAGEMENT.

Because there was Anne, he did not bother to wonder how many months it would be, how many years, perhaps, before another job as big as the Palmyra would come within his reach.

SATURDAY evening Charles Anthony Bruno was lying on his back in an El Paso hotel room. He was too restless to go to sleep, not energetic enough to go down to one of the bars in the neighborhood and look things over. He had looked things over all afternoon, and he did not think much of them in El Paso. He did not think much of Carlsbad Caverns either. He thought more of the idea that had come to him night before last on the train. A pity Guy hadn't awakened him that morning. Not that Guy was the kind of fellow to plan a murder with, but he liked him, as a person. Besides, Guy had left his book, and he could have given it back.

He sat up on the edge of the bed and reached for the telephone. "Gimme long distance." He looked blankly at a smudge of dirt his shoe had put on the white counterpane. "Great Neck, Long Island. Great Neck 4-1662." He waited. "In *New York*, lunk, ever hear of it?"

In less than a minute he had his mother.

"Yeah, I'm in El Paso. You still leaving tomorrow? Good. . . . Yeah, I seen the caverns. . . . How's things with you?"

He began to laugh. He pushed off his shoes and rolled back on the bed with the telephone, laughing. She was telling him about coming home to find his father entertaining two of her friends— two men she had met the night before—who had dropped in, thought he was her father, and proceeded to say all the wrong things.

PROPPED on his elbow in bed, Guy stared at the letter addressed to him in pencil. There was also one from Palm Beach.

"Guess I'll have only one more time to wake you for another good long while," his mother said. She leaned over and needlessly tucked in the foot of his bed.

"Maybe not so long, Mama."

Guy picked up the letter from Palm Beach. It was from Mr. Brillhart. He had been given the commission.

"I've got some good strong coffee this morning," his mother said from the threshold. "Like breakfast in bed?"

Guy smiled at her. "Would I!"

He reread Mr. Brillhart's letter carefully, put it back in its envelope, and slowly tore it up. Then he opened the other letter. It was one page, scrawled in pencil. The signature with the heavy flourish below it made him smile again: Charles A. Bruno.

Dear Guy:

This is your train friend, remember? You left your book in my room last night & I found a Texas address in it which I trust is still right. Am mailing book to you.

A great pleasure dining with you last night & hope I may list you among my friends. It would be fine to see you in Santa Fe & if you change your mind, address is: Hotel La Fonda, Santa Fe, New Mex. for next two weeks at least.

I keep thinking about that idea we had for a couple of murders. It could be done, I am sure. I cannot express to you my supremest confidence in the idea! Though I know subject does not interest you.

What's what with your wife as that was very interesting? Please write me soon.

Your friend,
Charles A. Bruno

The letter pleased him somehow. It was pleasant to think of Bruno's freedom.

"Grits!" he said happily to his mother. "Never get grits with my fried eggs up north!"

He put on a favorite old robe and sat back in bed with the Metcalf *Star* and the teetery-legged bed tray that held his breakfast. Afterward he showered and dressed as if there were something he had to do that day, but there wasn't. Guy lighted a cigarette. Tonight his uncle, and probably some friends of his mother's would be dropping over.

A sudden impulse to write to Bruno made him sit down at his worktable, but, with his pen in his hand, he realized he had nothing to say. He could see Bruno in his rust-brown suit, camera strap over his shoulder, plodding up some dry hill in Santa Fe. Bruno with a thousand easy dollars in his pocket, sitting in a bar, waiting for his mother. What did he have to say to Bruno? He tossed his pen back on the table.

Why hadn't he left for Mexico today? The next idle twenty-four hours were going to be miserable, he knew.

That evening, while he sat with his uncle and his uncle's wife and two cousins in the living room, the telephone rang. His mother answered it, then came in and called him.

"It's long distance," his mother said.

Guy nodded. It would be Brillhart, of course, asking for explanations. Guy had answered his letter that day.

"Hello, Guy," the voice said. "Charley."

"Charley who?"

"Charley Bruno."

"Oh! How are you? Thanks for the book."

"I didn't send it yet but I will," Bruno said with the drunken cheer Guy remembered from the train. "Are you coming out to Santa Fe?"

"I'm afraid I can't."

"What about Palm Beach? Can I visit you there?"

"Sorry, that's all off. I've changed my mind."

"Account of your wife?"

"N-no." Guy felt vaguely irritated.

"She wants you to stay with her?"

"Yes. Sort of."

"Miriam wants to come out to Palm Beach?"

Guy was surprised he remembered her name.

"Yes, *I'm* paying for this call!" Bruno shouted to someone disgustedly. "Listen, Guy, you gave up that job account of her?"

"Not exactly. It doesn't matter. It's finished. . . . I can't talk any longer, Charley. We've got guests here tonight."

"Oh." Bruno sounded lost now. Then the voice again, with

sullen intimacy, "Listen, Guy, if you want anything done, you know, all you have to do is give a sign."

Guy frowned. A question took form in his mind, and immediately he knew the answer. He remembered Bruno's idea for a murder.

"Good-by, Charley," Guy said. It annoyed him that Bruno had his address. Guy ran his hand hard across his hair and went back into the living room.

ALL of what he had just told her of Miriam, Guy thought, did not matter so much as the fact he and Anne were together in Mexico City. He took her hand as they walked, and he gazed around at a scene in which every object was foreign—a broad level avenue bordered with giant trees, military statues on pedestals, and beyond, buildings he did not know.

Their shoulders brushed, and Anne turned to him with a smile. "You couldn't have borne it, Guy?"

"No. Don't ask me why. I couldn't." He noticed that her smile stayed, tinged with perplexity, perhaps annoyance.

"It's such a big thing to give up."

It vexed him now. He felt done with it. "I simply loathe her," he said quietly. "She has no decency, no conscience. She's the type who goes to bad movies, reads love-story magazines, lives in a bungalow, and whips her husband into earning more money this year so they can buy on the installment plan next year, breaks up her neighbor's marriage—"

"Stop it, Guy! You're talking like a child!"

"And the fact I once loved her," Guy added, "loved all of it, makes me ill."

"Sometimes I believe you're still in love with her," Anne said, in that distant, expressionless tone that terrified him, because he felt she might abandon him and never come back.

He smiled, and she softened. "I'm sorry," he said.

"Oh, Guy!" She put out her hand, and he took it. "If you'd only grow up!"

He wanted to ask her why everything was so much easier and

simpler when he was with her, but the question would have been unanswerable by Anne in words, because the answer was simply Anne.

"I know you have it in you, Guy," she said suddenly, "the capacity to be terribly happy."

Guy nodded quickly. He felt somehow ashamed. Anne had the capacity to be happy, and it was only he, his problems, that ever seemed to daunt her happiness for an instant. He would be happy, too, when he lived with Anne. He had told her so, but he could not bear to tell her again now.

That evening Guy and Anne went with her parents to a concert at the Bellas Artes, then had a late supper at a restaurant across the street from the Ritz. Mrs. Faulkner was a thin, nervously energetic woman, tall as Anne, and for her age as attractive. Guy had come to be devoted to her, because she was devoted to him.

The Faulkners were sorry he wouldn't be able to continue on with them to Acapulco. Anne's father, an importer, intended to build a warehouse there.

"We can't expect to interest him in a warehouse if he's building a whole country club," Mrs. Faulkner said.

Guy said nothing. He couldn't look at Anne. He had asked her not to tell her parents about Palm Beach until after he left.

Mrs. Faulkner laid her hand on his arm and laughed. "He wouldn't smile if he got all New York to build over, would you, Guy?"

He hadn't been listening. He wanted Anne to take a walk with him later, but she insisted on his coming up to their suite at the Ritz to see the silk dressing gown she had bought for her cousin Teddy, before she sent it off. And then, of course, it was too late for a walk.

He was staying at the Hotel Montecarlo, about ten blocks from the Ritz, a great shabby building that looked like the former residence of a military general. One entered a huge dark lobby, paved in black and white tile. There was a grottolike barroom and a restaurant that was always empty. Guy had liked the place instantly, though the Faulkners, including Anne, chaffed him about his choice.

His cheap little room in a back corner was crammed with pink and brown painted furniture, had a bed like a fallen cake, and a bath down the hall. Somewhere down in the patio water dripped continuously, and the sporadic flush of toilets sounded torrential.

What was it that he liked? he wondered. To immerse himself in ugly, uncomfortable, undignified living so that he gained new power to fight it in his work? Or was it a sense of hiding from Miriam? He would be harder to find here than at the Ritz.

Anne telephoned him the next morning to say that a telegram had come for him. "I just happened to hear them paging you," she said. "They were about to give it up."

"Would you read it to me, Anne?"

Anne read, "'Miriam suffered miscarriage yesterday. Upset and asking to see you. Can you come home? Mama.' Oh, Guy!"

He felt sick of it all. "She did it herself," he murmured.

"You don't know, Guy."

"I know." His fingers tightened on the telephone. "I'll get the Palmyra back, anyway," he said.

He wired Mr. Brillhart, asking if he might be reconsidered for the job.

Of course he would be, he thought, but how asinine it made him seem. Because of Miriam. He wrote to her:

> This changes both our plans, of course. Regardless of yours, I mean to get the divorce now. I shall be in Texas in a few days. I hope you will be well by then, but if not, I can manage whatever is necessary alone.
>
> Again my wishes for your quick recovery.
>
> Guy

He sent the letter airmail special delivery. Then he called Anne. He wanted to take her to the best restaurant in the city that night. But to start with, he wanted the most exotic cocktails in the Ritz bar.

"You really feel happy?" Anne asked, laughing, as if she couldn't quite believe him.

"Happy and—strange."

"Why?"

"Because I didn't think it was fated. I didn't think it was part of my destiny. The Palmyra, I mean."

"I did. Miriam won't follow you now, will she?"

"This time next week," Guy said, "she won't have a single claim on me."

3

AT HER dressing table in Hotel La Fonda, Santa Fe, Elsie Bruno leaned closer to the mirror to examine the little mesh of wrinkles below her lids and the laugh lines that curved from the base of her nose. Though her chin was somewhat recessive, the lower part of her face projected, thrusting her full lips forward in a manner quite different from her son's face. Santa Fe, she thought, was the only place she could see the laugh lines in the mirror.

"This light around here—might as well be an X ray," she said.

Bruno, slumped in his pajamas in a rawhide chair, cast a puffy eye over at the window. He was too tired to go and pull the shade down. "You look good, Mom," he croaked.

He frowned thoughtfully. Like an enormous walnut in feeble, jittery squirrel hands, an idea, bigger than any idea he had ever known, had been revolving in his mind for several days. When his mother left town, he intended to crack open the idea and start thinking in earnest. His idea was to go and get Miriam. The time was ripe, and Guy needed it now. Very soon it might be too late for the Palm Beach thing, and then he wouldn't need it.

Elsie picked up her shower cap and turned to Charles with her quick broad smile that had no variations. "Darling," coaxingly.

"Umm-m?"

"You won't do anything you shouldn't while I'm gone?" She looked at a long narrow red nail, then reached for an emery board.

"No, Ma."

Bruno closed his eyes, thinking contentedly of last night. That was when he had decided yes. He had been thinking about it ever since Saturday, when he talked to Guy, and here it was Saturday again, and it was tomorrow or never, after his mother left for California. Something kept telling him that the time, the circumstances, would never be better. A pure murder, without personal motives! He didn't consider the possibility of Guy's murdering his father a motive, because he didn't count on it. Maybe Guy could be persuaded, maybe not. He'd called Guy's house again last night to make sure he still wasn't back from Mexico. Guy had been in Mexico since Sunday, his mother said.

"You won't change your mind and come with me?" Elsie asked, getting up. "If you did, I'd go up to Reno. Helen's there now and so's George Kennedy."

"Only one reason I'd like to see you in Reno, Mom."

"Charley—" She tipped her head to one side and back again. "Have patience. If it weren't for your father, we wouldn't be here."

"Sure we would."

She sat down on the arm of his chair and laid the cool backs of her fingers against his forehead. "Don't do anything too awful, darling, because I haven't got the money just now to throw around cleaning up after you."

"Stick him for some more. Get me a thousand, too."

"You won't change your mind, darling? I'll miss you."

"I'll be there day after tomorrow probably."

She tweaked the thin dangling hair over his forehead and went on into the bathroom.

Bruno jumped up and shouted against the roar of her running bath, "Ma, I got money to pay my bill here!"

"What, angel?"

He went closer and repeated it, then sank back in the chair, exhausted with the effort. He did not want his mother to know about the long-distance calls to Metcalf. If she didn't, everything would work out fine. Bruno dragged himself up, feeling a desire rising in him to tell his mother he was staying on in Santa Fe for the biggest experience of his life. He wanted to say, Ma, life's going to be a lot better for both of us soon, because this is the beginning of getting rid of Sam Bruno. Whether Guy came through with his part of the deal or not, if he himself were successful with Miriam, he would have proved a point. A perfect murder. Someday another person he didn't know yet would turn up and some kind of a deal could be made. Bruno bent his chin down to his chest in sudden anguish. How could he tell his mother? Murder and his mother didn't go together. "How gruesome!" she would say. He looked at the bathroom door with a hurt, distant expression. It dawned on him that he couldn't tell anyone, ever. Except Guy. He sat down again.

"Sleepyhead!"

He blinked when she clapped her hands. Then he smiled with a wistful realization that much would happen before he saw her again. He watched his mother's legs flex as she tightened her stockings. The slim lines of her legs always gave him a lift, made him proud. His mother had the best-looking legs he had ever seen on anyone, no matter what age. Ziegfeld had picked her, and hadn't Ziegfeld known his stuff? But she had married right back into the kind of life she had run away from. He was going to liberate her soon, and she didn't know it.

HE STUMBLED on a cobblestone, then drew himself up pridefully and tried to straighten his shirt in his trousers. Good thing he had passed out in an alley and not on a street, or the cops might have picked him up and he'd have missed the train. He stopped and fumbled for his wallet. His hands shook so, he could hardly read the railroad ticket. It was eight ten, and the train left at ten twenty. On top of a bad hangover, he ached now from sleeping on the damned cobblestones. Why had he drunk so much? he wondered, almost tearfully. Today he'd be in Metcalf, and he'd have to be sharp.

"Any mail?" he asked mechanically at the hotel desk, but there wasn't any.

He bathed solemnly and ordered hot tea, then went to the closet and stood a long while, wondering vaguely what to wear. He decided on the rust-brown suit in honor of Guy. It was rather inconspicuous, too, he noticed when he had it on.

Suddenly he began to shake all over in his haste to get his things and leave. What things? He didn't need anything really. Just the paper on which he had written everything he knew about Miriam. He got it from the back pocket of his suitcase and stuck it into the inside pocket of his jacket. He put a white handkerchief into his breast pocket, then left the room and locked the door. He figured he could be back tomorrow night, sooner if he could possibly do it tonight and catch a sleeper back.

Tonight! He could hardly believe it as he walked toward the Santa Fe bus station where one caught the bus for Lamy, the railroad terminal. He had thought he would be so happy and excited, and he wasn't at all. He frowned suddenly. Was something going to take the fun out of it after all? Maybe it was the hangover that had made him doubt. He went into a bar and bought a fifth from the barman, filled his flask, and asked for an empty pint bottle to put the rest in. The barman looked, but he didn't have one.

At Lamy, Bruno went on to the station, carrying nothing but the half-empty bottle in a paper bag, not even a weapon. He hadn't planned yet, he kept reminding himself, but a lot of planning didn't always mean a murder was a success. He boarded the train casually, and it began to move before he found his seat.

When he awakened from a nap, the world seemed quite changed. The train was speeding through cool bluish mountain-land. Dark green valleys were full of shadows. The sky was gray. The air-conditioned car and the cool look of things outside were as refreshing as an ice pack. And he was hungry. In the dining car, he had a delicious lunch of lamb chops, french fries, salad, and fresh peach pie, washed down with two Scotch and sodas. Afterward he strolled back to his seat feeling like a million dollars.

A sense of purpose, strange and sweet to him, carried him along on an irresistible current. Merely in gazing out the window, he felt a new coordination of mind and eye. He began to realize what he intended to do. He was on his way to commit a murder which not only would fulfill a desire of years but would benefit a friend. It made Bruno very happy to do things for his friends. And his victim deserved her fate.

He took out the paper about Miriam and studied it earnestly. "Miriam Joyce Haines, about twenty-two," said his handwriting in precise, inked characters, for this was his third copy. "Rather pretty. Red hair. Plump, not very tall. Noisy, social type. Probably flashy dressed." He might have to go through the whole list of Joyces and Haineses to find her. He thought she'd be living with her family probably. Once he saw her, he was sure he would recognize her. The little bitch! He hated her.

"She's going to have a child," Guy's voice had said. The little floozy! Women who slept around made him furious, made him ill, like the mistresses his father used to have.

When Bruno finally replaced the paper in his pocket and sat back with legs comfortably crossed, anyone seeing him would have judged him a young man of responsibility and character, probably with a promising future. He did not look in the pink of health, to be sure, but he did reflect poise and an inner happiness seen in few faces, and in Bruno's never before.

In Metcalf, he went immediately to a telephone book and checked on the Haineses. No Miriam Haines, but there were seven Joyces. Bruno scribbled a list of them on a piece of paper. Three were at the same address, 1235 Magnolia Street, and one of them there was Mrs. M. J. Joyce. Bruno's pointed tongue curled speculatively over his upper lip. Certainly a good bet. Maybe her mother's name was Miriam, too. He hurried toward a yellow taxi parked at the curb.

IT WAS almost nine o'clock. The long dusk was sliding steeply into night, and the residential blocks of small, flimsy-looking wooden houses were mostly dark, except for a glow here and there on a front porch where people sat in swings and on their front steps.

"Lemme out here, this is okay," Bruno said to the driver. Magnolia Street and College Avenue, and this was the one-thousand block. He began walking.

On some houses Bruno couldn't find a number. Suppose he couldn't find 1235?

But when he came to it, 1235 was very legible in tin numerals over the front porch. The sight of the house brought a slow, pleasant thrill. It was a small house like all the others on the block, only its yellow-tan clapboards were more in need of paint. It had a driveway at the side, a scraggly lawn, and an old Chevy sedan sitting at the curb. A light showed at a downstairs window and one in a back corner window upstairs that Bruno thought might be Miriam's room.

Nervously Bruno crossed the street and went back a little the way he had come. He turned and stared at the house, biting his lip. Then his eyes slid alertly to the next-door front porch as a man and woman came out. The woman sat down in the swing, and the man went down the walk. Bruno backed into the niche of a projecting garage front.

"Pistachio if they haven't got peach, Don," the woman called.

"I'll take vanilla," Bruno murmured, and drank some whisky out of his flask.

He stared quizzically at the yellow-tan house, put a foot up behind him to lean on, and felt something hard against his thigh: the knife he had bought in the station when the train stopped at Big Spring, a hunting knife with a six-inch blade in a sheath. He did not want to use a knife if he could avoid it. Knives sickened him in a funny way. And a gun made noise. How would he do it? Seeing her would suggest a way. Or would it? Quickly he took another drink. He mustn't start to worry; that would spoil everything.

A preference for attacking her outdoors had taken root in his mind on the train, so all his ideas began from a simple physical approach to her. He preferred to use his bare hands, or to hit her over the head with something. Now and then it crossed his mind how happy Guy would be when it was done.

He heard a man's voice, and a laugh, he was sure from the lighted upstairs room in 1235, then a girl's voice: "Stop that! Please? Plee-ee-ease?" Maybe Miriam's voice.

The light blinked out and Bruno's eyes fastened on the dark window. Then the porch light flashed on and two men and a girl—*Miriam*—came out. It was her, all right. Bruno held his breath. He could see the red in her hair. The bigger fellow was redheaded, too—maybe her brother. Bruno's eyes caught a hundred details at once, the chunky compactness of her figure, the flat shoes, the easy way she swung around to look up at one of the men.

"Think we ought to call her, Dick?" she asked in a thin voice. "It's kinda late."

A corner of the shade in the front window lifted. "Miriam? Don't be out too long!"

"No, Mom."

They were going to take the car at the curb.

Bruno moved toward the corner, looking for a taxi. He ran. He hadn't run in months, but he felt fit as an athlete. "Taxi!" He didn't even see a taxi, then he did and dove for it.

He made the driver circle and come into Magnolia Street in the direction the Chevy had been pointed. The Chevy was gone. Darkness had closed in tight. Far away he saw a red taillight blinking under some trees.

"Keep going!"

When the taillight stopped for a red light, the taxi closed some of the distance, and Bruno saw it was the Chevy.

"Where do you want to go?" asked the driver.

"Keep going!" Then as the Chevy swung into a big avenue, "Turn right."

"Who're the people's names you want to go to?" the driver asked. "Maybe I know 'em."

"Just a minute, just a minute," Bruno said, pretending to search through the papers he had dragged from his inside pocket, among them the paper about Miriam. He snickered suddenly, feeling very amused, very safe. Now he was pretending to be the dopey guy from out of town, who had even misplaced the address of where he wanted to go. He bent his head so the driver could not see him laughing, and reached automatically for his flask.

"Need a light?"

"Nope, nope, thank you." He took a hot swallow. "Keep going."

"Where?"

"Keep going and shut up!" Bruno shouted, his voice falsetto with anxiety.

The driver shook his head and made a click with his tongue. Twice Bruno lost sight of the Chevy, but each time it reappeared. They passed road stands and drive-in movies, then darkness put up a wall on either side. Bruno began to worry. He couldn't tail them out of town or down a country road. Then a big arch of lights appeared over the road. WELCOME TO LAKE METCALF'S KINGDOM OF FUN, it said, and the Chevy drove under it and into a parking lot. There were all kinds of lights ahead in the woods and the jingle of merry-go-round music. An amusement park! Bruno was delighted.

"Four bucks," said the driver sourly, and Bruno poked a five through the front window.

He hung back until Miriam and the two men and a new girl they had picked up had gone through the turnstile, then he followed them. He stretched his eyes wide for a good look at Miriam under the lights. She was cute in a plump sort of way, but definitely second-rate, Bruno judged. Her red socks and red sandals infuriated him. How could Guy have married such a thing?

She stood in front of a sideshow where a Gypsy woman was dropping things into a big fishbowl. The other girl started laughing, leaning all over the redheaded fellow.

Miriam went across to the frozen-custard stand. They all bought frozen custards. Bruno smiled and waited, looking up at the Ferris wheel's arc of lights and the tiny people swinging in benches up there in the black sky. The merry-go-round played *Casey would waltz with a strawberry blonde*. Grinning, Bruno turned to Miriam's red hair, and their eyes met, but hers moved on and he was sure she hadn't noticed him. Miriam didn't look at all smart, he decided. He could see why Guy would loathe her. He loathed her, too, with all his guts! Maybe she was lying to Guy about having a baby. And Guy was so honest himself, he believed her. Bitch!

Miriam and her friends entered a big lighted section at the bottom of the Ferris wheel, where several concessions and side-shows were located. The roller coaster made a *tat-tat-tat-tat-tat* like a machine gun over their heads. There was a clang and a roar as someone sent the red arrow all the way to the top with a sledgehammer. He wouldn't mind killing Miriam with a sledge-hammer, he thought.

Bruno examined Miriam and each of the three to see if any of them seemed aware of him, but he was sure they weren't. This was his night. He liked Texas, Guy's state! Everybody looked happy and full of energy. He let Miriam's group blend into a crowd while he took another gulp from his flask. Then he loped after them. They were looking at the Ferris wheel, and he hoped they would decide to ride it.

"Ralph, how 'bout it?" Miriam squealed, poking the last of the frozen-custard cone into her mouth.

"Aw, 's ain't no fun. H'bout the merry-go-round?"

And they all went. The merry-go-round was like a lighted city in the dark woods, a forest of nickel-plated poles crammed with zebras, horses, goats, bulls, and camels, all plunging down or leaping upward, some with necks arched out over the platform, waiting desperately for riders.

People were choosing mounts. And Miriam and her friends were eating again, Miriam diving into a popcorn bag Dick held for her. The pigs! Bruno was hungry, too. He bought a frank-furter, and when he looked again, they were boarding the merry-go-round. He scrambled for coins and ran. He got the horse he had wanted, a royal-blue one with an upreared head and an open mouth, and as luck would have it, Miriam and her friends kept weaving back through the poles toward him. Miriam and Dick took the horses right in front of him. Luck was with him tonight! Tonight he should be gambling.

They started off slowly and militantly to "The Washington Post" march. Up, up, up he went and down, down, down went Miriam on her horse. The world beyond the merry-go-round vanished in a light-streaked blur. Bruno held the reins in one hand and ate the frankfurter with the other.

"Yeeee-hooo!" yelled the redheaded fellow.

"Casey would waltz with a strawberry blonde, while the band . . . played . . . aaaawn!" Miriam's date sang out with vehemence.

They all joined in, Bruno with them. The whole merry-go-round was singing.

"Hi, Casey!" Miriam cooed to Dick, opening her mouth to catch the popcorn he was trying to throw into it.

Miriam looked ugly and stupid with her mouth open, as if she were being strangled and had turned pink and bloated. He could not bear to look at her and, still grinning, turned his eyes away. The merry-go-round slowed to a stop and they all got off. Bruno watched the four link arms and begin to walk toward the twinkling lights on the water. He paused under the trees for another little nip from his flask.

They were taking a rowboat. The prospect of a cool row was delightful to Bruno. He engaged a boat, too, and got close enough to see that the redheaded fellow was doing the rowing in Miriam's boat, and that Miriam and Dick were squeezing each other and giggling in the back seat. Bruno bent for three deep strokes that carried him past them, then let his oars trail.

"Want to go to the island or loaf around?" the redheaded fellow asked.

Petulantly Bruno slumped sideways on the seat, waiting for them to make up their minds. In the dark nooks along the shore he heard murmurs, soft radios, laughter. He tipped his nearly empty flask and drained it.

He waited until they had paddled past, then followed leisurely. A black mass drew closer, pricked here and there with the spark of a match. The island looked like a neckers' paradise. Maybe Miriam would be at it again tonight, Bruno thought, giggling.

When Miriam's boat landed, he rowed a few yards to one side and climbed ashore, and set his boat's nose up on a little log so it would be easy to recognize from the others. The sense of purpose filled him once more, stronger and more imminent than on the train. He pressed the knife against him through his trousers. If he could just get her alone and clap his hand over her mouth—or would she be able to bite? He squirmed with disgust at the thought of her wet mouth on his hand.

Slowly he followed their steps, up rough ground where the trees were close.

"We can't sit here, the ground's wet," whined the other girl, who was called Katie. They turned around right in Bruno's face, so he had to move off to one side. He got tangled in some thorny underbrush and occupied himself getting free of it while they passed him. Then he followed, downward.

Miriam stood on slightly higher ground, not three yards away from him now, and the others slid down the bank toward the water. Bruno inched closer. The lights on the water silhouetted her head and shoulders. Never had he been so close!

"Hey!" Bruno whispered, and saw her turn. "Say, isn't your name Miriam?"

She faced him, but he knew she could barely see him. "Yeah. Who're you?"

He came a step nearer. "Haven't I met you somewhere before?" he asked cynically. Then he sprang with such concentrated aim that the wrists of his spread hands touched.

"Say, what d'you—"

His hands captured her throat on the last word, stifling its abortive uplift of surprise. He shook her. His body seemed to harden like rock, and she made a grating sound in her throat, but he had her too tight for a scream. With his leg behind her, he wrenched her backward, and they fell to the ground together, with no sound but of a brush of leaves. He sank his fingers deeper, enduring the distasteful pressure of her body under his

so her writhing would not get them both up. Her throat felt hotter and fatter. Stop, stop, stop! He willed it. And the head stopped turning. He was sure he had held her long enough, but he did not lessen his grip. He hitched himself onto his knees, pressing her with a force he thought would break his thumbs. All the power in him poured out through his hands. She was still and limp now.

"Miriam?" called the girl's voice.

Bruno sprang up and stumbled straight away toward the center of the island, then turned left to bring himself out near his boat. He was thinking! He felt great! It was done!

"Mi-ri-am!" with lazy impatience.

But what if he hadn't finished her, if she were sitting up and talking now? The thought shot him forward and he almost toppled down the bank. He didn't see his boat. He started to take any boat, changed his mind, then a couple of yards farther to the left found it, perched on the little log.

"Hey, she's fainted!"

Bruno shoved off, quickly, but not hurrying.

"Help, somebody!" said the girl's half gasp, half scream.

"Huh-*help!*"

The panic in the voice panicked Bruno. He rowed for several choppy strokes, then abruptly stopped and let the boat glide over the dark water. What was he getting scared about? Not a sign of anyone chasing him.

"Hey!"

"F'God's sake, she's *dead!* Call somebody!"

A girl's scream was a long arc in the silence. A beautiful scream, Bruno thought with a queer, serene admiration. He approached the dock easily, behind another boat.

Slowly, as slowly as he had ever done anything, he paid the boatkeeper.

"On the island!" said another excited voice from a boat. "Girl's dead, they said!"

"Somebody call the cops!"

Bruno idled toward the gates of the park. Thank God he was

so tight or hung over that he could move so slowly! But a fluttering, unfightable terror rose in him as he passed through the turnstile. Then it ebbed quickly.

To steady himself, he concentrated on finding a drink. There was a place up the road with red lights that looked like a bar, and he went straight toward it.

"I want a Scotch," he said to the barman.

"Can't get no hard liquor round here, man, just beer and wine."

"I'll have a beer, then," said Bruno.

Police sirens sounded, coming closer.

A man came in the door.

"What happened? Accident?" somebody asked him.

"I didn't see anything," the man said unconcernedly.

Bruno looked the man over, but it didn't seem the thing to do to go over and talk to him.

He felt fine. He noticed a streak on his hand, got out his handkerchief, and calmly wiped between his thumb and forefinger. It was a smear of Miriam's orange lipstick. He thanked the barman and strolled out into the darkness. A bus passed, and he ran for it. He enjoyed its bright interior, and read all the placards.

At the railroad terminal, he got an upper berth on a sleeper leaving at one thirty, which gave him an hour and a half to kill. Everything was perfect and he felt terribly happy. He wanted a woman now more than ever before in his life, and that he did pleased him greatly. One of the taxi drivers outside would be the fellow to ask.

"Ah don' know," said the blank, freckle-faced driver leaning against his fender.

"What d'you mean, you don't know?"

"Don' know, that's all."

Bruno left him in disgust.

Another driver was more obliging. He wrote Bruno an address and a name on the back of a company card, though it was so close by, he didn't even have to drive him there.

4

Guy leaned against the wall by his bed in the Montecarlo, watching Anne turn the pages of the family album he had brought from Metcalf. These had been wonderful days, his last two with Anne. Tomorrow he would leave for Metcalf. And then Florida. A telegram had come from Mr. Brillhart, saying the commission was still his. There was a stretch of six months' work ahead, and in December the commencement of the house they were planning to build in Connecticut. He had the money for it now. And the money for the divorce.

He leaned over the album with her, identifying the people that she asked about, watching amusedly as she examined the double page of his pictures that his mother had collected, from Guy's babyhood to about twenty. He was smiling in every one of them.

"Do I look happy enough there?" he asked.

She winked at him. "And very handsome. Any of Miriam?"

"No," Guy said.

"I'm awfully glad you brought this."

"It's the most humane way of meeting families," he said.

"Guy, did I put you through much?"

He smiled at her plaintive tone. "No! I never minded a bit!" He sat down on the bed and pulled her back with him. He had met all of Anne's relatives, by twos and threes, by dozens at the Faulkners' Sunday suppers and parties. It was a family joke how many there were, all living in New York or on Long Island. "I'm thinking about the house, Anne," he said suddenly.

"You want it big."

He smiled. "Yes."

"Let's have it big." She relaxed in his arms. They both sighed, like one person, as he wrapped her closer.

He could see the house shining white and sharp against the brown bureau across the room. It projected from a certain white rock he had seen near a town called Alton in lower Connecticut.

The house was long, low, and flat-roofed, as if alchemy had created it from the rock itself, like a crystal.

Guy felt rather giddy, as if he had taken some mildly euphoriant drug. It was the altitude, Anne said, that made people feel that way in Mexico City. "I feel as if I could call up Miriam tonight and talk to her and everything would be all right," Guy said slowly, "as if I could say just the right thing."

He'd hardly finished speaking when the telephone rang, in nervous, insistent rings.

Guy answered it. He heard a voice talking distantly to an operator. Then the voice came louder, his mother's voice. "Hello?"

"Hello, Mama."

"Guy, something's happened."

"What's the matter?"

"It's Miriam."

"What about her?" Guy pressed the receiver against his ear. He turned to Anne, and saw her face change as she looked at him.

"She's been murdered, Guy. Last night—" She broke off.

"Murdered!"

"Guy, *what?*" Anne asked, getting up.

"Last night at the lake. They don't know anything."

"You're—"

"Can you come home, Guy?"

"Yes, Mama. What happened?" he asked stupidly.

"Strangled." The one word, then silence.

"I'll be home as fast as I can, Mama. Tonight. Don't worry. I'll see you very soon." He hung up slowly and turned to Anne. "It's Miriam. Miriam's been killed."

"Do they know who?"

"No. I've got to go tonight."

He looked at Anne, standing motionless in front of him. "I've got to go tonight," he said again, dazedly. Anne went to the telephone to call for a plane reservation, talking rapidly in Spanish.

He began to pack. It seemed to take hours getting his few possessions into his suitcase. He stared at the brown bureau, wondering if he had already looked through it to see if everything was out of its drawers. Now, where he had seen the vision of the white house, a laughing face appeared, first the crescent mouth, then the face—Bruno's face. The tongue curved lewdly over the upper lip, and then the silent, convulsed laughter came again, shaking the stringy hair over the forehead.

Suppose Bruno had done it? He couldn't have, of course, but just suppose he had? And if they caught him, would Bruno say the murder was a plan of theirs? Guy could easily imagine Bruno hysterical, saying anything.

On the plane, Guy searched his hazy memory of the conversation on the train and tried to recall if he had said anything that might have been taken as a consent to Bruno's insane idea. He hadn't. Against this negative weighed Bruno's letter, which he remembered word for word: . . . *that idea we had for a couple of murders. It could be done, I am sure. I cannot express to you my supremest confidence* . . .

Toward dawn he fell asleep, yielding to the shaking roar of the motors that seemed bent on tearing the plane apart, tearing his mind apart, and scattering the pieces in the sky. He awakened to a gray overcast morning, and a new thought: Miriam's lover had killed her. It was so obvious, so likely. He had killed her in a quarrel. One read such cases frequently in the newspapers; the victims were so often women like Miriam.

A plainclothesman met him at the Metcalf airport and asked if he would answer a few questions.

"Have they found the murderer?" Guy asked him.

"No." The plainclothesman looked tired, as if he had been up all night. They got into a taxi together and drove down to police headquarters.

"Guy Daniel Haines, 717 Ambrose Street, Metcalf. . . . When did you leave Metcalf? . . . And when did you get to Mexico City?"

Chairs scraped. A noiseless typewriter started bumping after them.

Another plainclothesman strolled closer. "Why did you go to Mexico?"

"To visit some friends."

"Who?"

"The Faulkners. Alex Faulkner of New York."

"You sent your wife a letter asking for a divorce. What did she reply?"

"That she wanted to talk with me."

"But you didn't care to talk with her anymore, did you?" asked a clear tenor voice.

Guy looked at the young police officer, and said nothing.

"Didn't you want a divorce pretty badly, Mr. Haines?"

"Are you in love with Anne Faulkner?"

"You know your wife had a lover, Mr. Haines. Were you jealous?"

"That's all!" someone said.

On the ride home, he read the double column on the front page of the Metcalf *Star*:

QUEST CONTINUES FOR GIRL'S SLAYER

June 13—The quest continues for the slayer of Mrs. Miriam Joyce Haines of this city, victim of strangulation by an unknown assailant on Metcalf Island Sunday night.

Two fingerprint experts arrived today who will endeavor to establish classifications of fingerprints taken from several oars and rowboats of the Lake Metcalf rowboat docks. Authorities yesterday afternoon expressed the opinion that the crime might have been the act of a maniac. Apart from dubious fingerprints and several heelprints around the scene of the attack, police officials have not yet uncovered any vital clue.

Most important testimony at the inquest, it is believed, will come from Owen Markman, 30, longshoreman of Houston, and a close friend of the murdered woman.

Guy lighted a cigarette from the end of another. His hands were still shaking from the police questioning, but he felt vaguely better. He hadn't thought of the possibility of a maniac. A maniac reduced it to a kind of horrible accident.

His mother sat in her rocker in the living room with a handkerchief pressed to her temple, waiting for him, though she did not get up when he came in. Guy embraced her and kissed her cheek, relieved to see she hadn't been crying.

"I spent yesterday with Mrs. Joyce," she said, "but I just can't go to the funeral."

"There isn't any need to, Mama."

Upstairs on his bureau he found a letter and a small square package with a Santa Fe store label. The package contained a narrow belt of braided lizardskin with a silver buckle formed like an H.

A note enclosed said, "Lost your Plato book on way to post office. I hope this will help make up. Charley."

Guy picked up the penciled envelope from the Santa Fe hotel. There was only a small card inside. On the card's back was written, "Nice town Metcalf." Turning the card, he read mechanically:

24 HOUR
DONOVAN TAXI SERVICE
RAIN OR SHINE
Call 2-3333

SAFE   FAST   COURTEOUS

Something had been erased beneath the message on the back. Guy held the card to the light and made out one word: Ginnie. It was a Metcalf taxi company's card, but it had been mailed from Santa Fe. It doesn't prove anything, he thought. But he crushed the card and the envelope and the package wrappings into his wastebasket.

He loathed Bruno, he realized. He threw the box in the wastebasket, and the belt, too. It was a handsome belt, but he happened to loathe lizard and snakeskin.

Anne telephoned him that night from Mexico City. She wanted to know everything that had happened, and he told her what he knew.

"Don't they have any suspicion who did it?" she asked.

"They don't seem to." He couldn't tell her now about Bruno.

His mother had said that a man had called twice, wanting to talk to him, and Guy had no doubt who it was.

"We've just sent those affidavits, darling. You know, about your being here with us?"

He had wired her for them after talking to the police. "Everything'll be all right after the inquest," he said.

"Not more than seven yards and not less than five," the grave young man in the chair replied. "No, I did not see anyone."

"I think about fifteen feet," said the wide-eyed girl, Katherine Smith, who looked as frightened as if it had just happened.

"About thirty feet. I was the first one down at the boat," said Ralph Joyce, Miriam's brother. His red hair was like Miriam's, and he had the same gray-green eyes, but his heavy square jaw took away the resemblance. "I wouldn't say she had any enemy. Not enough to do something like this."

"I didn't hear one thing," Katherine Smith said earnestly, shaking her head.

Ralph Joyce said he hadn't heard anything, and Dick Schuyler's positive statement ended it. "There weren't any sounds."

The facts repeated and repeated lost their horror and even their drama for Guy. The nearness of the three others was almost unbelievable. Only a maniac would have dared come so close.

"Were you the father of the child Mrs. Haines lost?"

"Yes." Owen Markman slouched forward over his locked fingers. A glum, hangdog manner spoiled his dashing good looks.

"Do you know who might have wanted Mrs. Haines to die?"

"Yes." Markman pointed at Guy. "Him."

People turned to look at him. Guy sat tensely, frowning straight at Markman, for the first time really suspecting him.

"Why?"

Owen Markman hesitated a long while, mumbled something, then brought out one word: "Jealousy."

Guy's lawyer chuckled. He had in his hand the affidavits from the Faulkners that clearly established Guy's alibi.

The coroner suggested in his summation that the murder would seem to have been committed by a maniac unknown to the victim and the other parties. A verdict was brought in of "person or persons unknown," and the case was turned over to the police.

A telegram arrived the next day, just as Guy was leaving his mother's house.

ALL GOOD WISHES FROM THE GOLDEN WEST. UNSIGNED.

"From the Faulkners," he said quickly to his mother.

She smiled. "Tell Anne to take good care of my boy." She pulled him down gently by his ear and kissed his cheek.

Guy struggled to find a definite answer about Bruno—had he or hadn't he?—and then gave it up. Wasn't it far more likely that a maniac had done it, as the coroner and everyone else believed?

When he got to Palm Beach, he finally closed his mind to Metcalf, to Miriam, and to Bruno, and began concentrating on the work for the new country club. And the more he immersed himself in the new effort, the more he felt at peace.

Most evenings Guy read or wrote long letters to Anne. She was working in the design department of a textile company in Manhattan. In the fall she planned to go into partnership in a studio with another woman designer she had met. Some nights he merely went to bed, for he was always up by five and often worked all day at the construction site with a blowtorch or mortar and trowel. He knew almost all the workmen by name. He liked to judge the temperament of each man, and to know how it contributed or did not contribute to the spirit of his buildings.

Then one evening a letter from Bruno arrived. It was from Los Angeles, forwarded by Guy's mother from Metcalf. It congratulated him on his work in Palm Beach, wished him success, and begged for just a word from him. The postscript said:

Hope you are not annoyed at this letter. Have written many letters and not mailed them. Phoned your mother for your address, but she wouldn't give it to me. Guy, honestly there is nothing to worry about or I wouldn't have written. Don't you know I'd be the first one to be careful? Write soon. Your friend and admirer. C.A.B.

A slow ache fell through him to his feet. He could not bear to be alone in his room. He went out to a bar, and almost before he knew what he was doing, had two ryes and then a third. In the mirror behind the bar he saw his sunburned face, and it struck him that his eyes looked dishonest and furtive. *Bruno had done it*. It came thundering down with a weight that left no possibility of doubt any longer.

5

"CHARLEY, what're all these clippings?"

"Friend of mine, Ma!" Bruno shouted through the bathroom door. He turned the water on harder, leaned on the basin, and concentrated on the bright nickel-plated drainstop. After a moment he reached for the Scotch bottle he kept under towels in the clothes hamper. He felt less shaky with the glass of Scotch and water in his hand. In the mirror he saw a framed portrait of a young man of leisure, of reckless and mysterious adventure, a young man of humor and depth, power and gentleness—a young man with two lives. He drank to himself.

"Charley?"

"Minute, Mom!"

He cast a wild eye about the bathroom. Lately it happened about twice a week. Half an hour or so after he got up he felt as if someone were kneeling on his chest and stifling him. He closed his eyes and dragged air in and out of his lungs as fast as he could. Then the liquor took. It quieted his leaping nerves like a hand passing down his body. He straightened up and opened the door.

His mother was in tennis shorts and a halter, bending over his unmade bed, where the clippings were strewn. "Who was she?"

"Wife of a fellow I met on the train coming down from New

York. Guy Haines." Bruno smiled. He liked to say Guy's name. "Interesting, isn't it? They haven't caught the murderer yet."

"Probably a maniac," she sighed.

Bruno's face sobered. "Oh, I doubt it. Circumstances are too complicated."

Elsie stood up and slid her thumb inside her belt. The bulge just below her belt disappeared, and for a moment she looked as trim as a twenty-year-old, down to her thin ankles. "Your friend Guy's got a nice face."

"Nicest fellow you ever saw. It's a shame he's dragged in on it. He told me on the train he hadn't seen his wife in a couple of years. Guy's no more a murderer than I am!" Bruno smiled at his inadvertent joke, then nodded toward the bed. "Did you read all that?" he asked.

"No, not all that. How many drinks this morning?"

"One."

"I smell two."

"All right, Mom, I had two."

"Darling, won't you watch the morning drinks? Morning drinks are the end." Bruno frowned. "Sammie Franklin's coming over this morning," she continued. "Why don't you get dressed and come down and keep score for us?"

"Sammie gives me ulcers."

She walked to the door as gaily as if she had not heard. "Promise me you'll get some sun today anyway. You're too pale."

He nodded and moistened his dry lips. He did not return her smile as she closed the door, because he felt as if a black lid had fallen on him suddenly, as if he had to escape something before it was too late. He had to see *Guy* before it was too late! He had to get rid of his father before it was too late! He had things to do! He did not want to be here, in his grandmother's house, furnished just like his father's house in Louis Quinze, eternal Louis Quinze! But he did not know where else he wanted to be. He was not happy if long away from his mother, was he?

The telephone . . .

Bruno had been staring at it. Every telephone suggested Guy, but a call might annoy him. A letter should come any day now, because Guy must have gotten his letter the end of last week.

"Charley?" called the high, sweet voice of his grandmother. "I'm going into town this morning. I thought you might like to come with me."

"Yeah, I'd like that, Grannie," he said good-naturedly.

Bruno enjoyed the day, helping her in and out of the car, piloting her around the shops.

Sammie was still at the house when they came home, staying for dinner. Bruno's eyebrows drew together at the first sight of him. What had Sammie and his mother been doing all day? They'd played tennis, then gone to a movie, they said. And there was a letter for him in his room.

Bruno ran upstairs. The letter was from Florida. He tore it open with shaking hands. He had never wanted a letter so badly, not even at camp, when he had waited for letters from his mother.

September 6

Dear Charles,

I do not understand your message to me, or for that matter your great interest in me. I know you very slightly, but enough to assure me that we have nothing in common on which to base a friendship. May I ask you please not to telephone my mother again or communicate with me?

Thank you for trying to return the book to me. Its loss is of no importance.

Guy Haines

Bruno brought it up closer and read it again, his eyes lingering incredulously on a word here and there. He felt shorn. It was a feeling like grief, or like a death. Worse! Then the pain centered in his chest, and he began to cry.

In the month after Guy returned to New York, his restlessness, his dissatisfaction with himself, with his work, with Anne, had focused gradually on Bruno. It was Bruno who made him hate to look at pictures of the Palmyra now, Bruno who was the real cause of the anxiety which he had blamed on the dearth of commissions since he had come back from Palm Beach, Bruno who had made him argue so senselessly with Anne the other evening about not getting a better office, Bruno who had made him tell Anne he did not consider himself a success, that the Palmyra meant nothing.

He fretted about everything and about nothing, but chiefly about his work. Anne told him to be patient. Anne reminded him that he had already proven himself in Florida. More than ever, she offered him tenderness and reassurance, yet he found that he could not always accept them.

One morning in December the telephone rang as Guy sat idly studying his drawings of their Connecticut house.

"Hello, Guy. This is Charley."

Guy felt his muscles tensing.

"How are you?" Bruno asked with smiling warmth. "Merry Christmas."

Slowly Guy put the telephone back in its cradle. It rang again.

"I'd like to see you, Guy," Bruno said.

"Sorry. I don't care to see you."

"What's the matter?" Bruno forced a little laugh. "Are you nervous, Guy?"

"I just don't care to see you."

"Oh. Okay," said Bruno, hoarse with hurt.

Guy waited, determined not to retreat first, and finally Bruno hung up.

On a snowy evening a few days later, as he and Anne came down the brownstone steps of his West Fifty-third Street apartment house, Guy saw a tall bareheaded figure standing on the sidewalk gazing up at them. Involuntarily his hand tightened on Anne's arm.

"Hello," Bruno said, his voice soft with melancholy. His face was barely visible in the dusk.

"Hello," Guy replied, as if to a stranger, and walked on.

"Guy!"

Guy and Anne turned at the same time. Bruno came toward them, hands in the pockets of his overcoat.

"What is it?" Guy asked.

"Just wanted to say hello. Ask how you are." Bruno stared at Anne with a kind of perplexed, smiling resentment.

"I'm fine," Guy said quietly. He turned away, drawing Anne with him.

"Who is he?" Anne whispered.

"He's a fellow who came around looking for work last week."

"You can't do anything for him?"

"No. He's an alcoholic."

As they walked to a movie Guy began to talk about their house, because there was nothing else he could talk about now and possibly sound normal. He had bought the land, and the foundations were being laid. After New Year's he was going up to Alton and stay for several days.

At the movie, Guy sat with his fists clenched and speculated as to how he could shake Bruno off.

But what did Bruno want with him?

THE fact that Guy would not see him was torture for Bruno. To blot out his pain and depression he drank a great deal at home in Great Neck during the next ten days. And to occupy himself he measured the house and the grounds in paces, and measured his father's room with tailor's tape.

In mid-January he left for Haiti with his mother, her friend Alice Leffingwell, and a crew of four. They sailed on the yacht *Fairy Prince*, which Alice had spent months wresting from her most recent husband. The trip was a celebration of her third divorce, and she had invited Bruno and his mother to come along.

On shipboard he detailed three plans for the murder of his father—one with gun in his father's bedroom, one with knife and two choices of escape, and one with either gun, knife, or strangulation in the garage where his father put his car every evening at six thirty. He could all but hear in his ears the efficient *click-click* of his plans' operations. He was eternally making drawings and tearing them up. The sea was strewn with the subdivided seeds of his ideas when the *Fairy Prince* rounded Cape Maisí bound for Port-au-Prince.

As important as the plans, of course, was the person for the job. He would do it himself, he thought, if not for the fact that Gerard, his father's private detective, would nail him no matter how carefully he planned it. Besides, he wanted to put his no-motivation scheme to the test again.

Suddenly he hated Guy! He had killed for him, dodged police for him, kept quiet when he asked him to, and Guy didn't even want to see him! Guy spent his time with that girl he had seen near Guy's apartment house in New York! If he had her here, he would kill her just like he had killed Miriam!

Guy would marry again and never have time for him. He'd been seeing her in Mexico, not just visiting friends. No wonder he'd wanted Miriam out of the way! And he hadn't even mentioned Anne on the train! Guy had used him. Maybe Guy would kill his father whether he liked it or not. Anybody can do a murder.

"Have a drink with me," Bruno said. He had appeared out of nowhere, in the middle of the sidewalk.

"I don't care to see you."

Bruno's eyes were wary. "Come across the street. Ten minutes."

Now is the time, Guy thought. Here he is. Call the police. Jump him, throw him down to the sidewalk. But Guy only stood rigidly.

"Ten minutes," Bruno said, luring him with his tentative smile.

Guy hadn't heard a word from Bruno in weeks. He tried to summon back his anger so that he could turn Bruno over to the police.

This was the critical moment. Guy went with him. They walked into a bar on Sixth Avenue and took a back booth.

Bruno's smile grew wider. "What're you scared about, Guy?"

"Not a thing."

"Are you happy?"

Guy sat stiffly on the edge of his seat. He was sitting opposite a murderer, he thought.

"Listen, Guy, why didn't you tell me about Anne?"

"What about Anne?"

"I'd like to have known about her, that's all. On the train, I mean."

"This is our last meeting, Bruno."

"Why? I just want to be friends, Guy."

"I'm going to turn you over to the police."

"Why didn't you do that in Metcalf?" Bruno asked impersonally, sadly, yet with triumph.

"Because I wasn't sure enough. But I can still turn you over for investigation."

"No, you can't. They've got more on you than on me." Bruno shrugged. "If I wanted to say you paid me for it, the pieces would sure fit!" He frowned self-righteously.

"You're insane!" Guy was suddenly furious.

"Face it, Guy! You're not making any sense!" Bruno's voice rose hysterically over the jukebox that had started up near them. He pushed his hand flat across the table toward Guy, then closed it in a fist. "I like you, Guy, I swear. We shouldn't be talking like this!"

Guy did not move. The edge of the bench cut against the back of his legs. "I don't want to be liked by you."

"You didn't turn me in in Metcalf because you like me, Guy. You like me in a way."

"I don't like you in the least."

"But you're not going to turn me in, are you?"

"No," Guy said between his teeth. Bruno's calm amazed him. Bruno was not afraid of him at all. "Don't order me another drink. I'm leaving."

"Wait a minute." Bruno got money from his wallet and gave it to the waiter.

Guy sat on, held by a sense of inconclusiveness.

"Good-looking suit." Bruno smiled, nodding toward Guy's chest.

His new gray flannel chalk-striped suit, Guy thought. Bought with the Palmyra money, like his new shoes and the new brief-case beside him on the seat. "What's your game, Bruno?" he said.

"You know," Bruno said quietly. "What we talked about on the train. The exchange of victims. You're going to kill my father."

Guy made a sound of contempt. He had known it before Bruno said it, had suspected it since Miriam's death. He stared into Bruno's eyes, fascinated by their cool insanity.

"I told you I could arrange every detail." Bruno sounded amused, apologetic. "It'd be very simple."

He hates me, Guy thought suddenly. He'd love to kill me, too.

"You know what I'll do if you don't." Bruno made a gesture of snapping his fingers. "I'll just put the police on to you."

Ignore him, Guy thought, ignore him! "You don't frighten me. It'd be the easiest thing in the world to prove you insane."

"I'm no more insane than you are!"

It was Bruno who ended the interview a moment later. He had a seven-o'clock appointment with his mother, he said.

For two weeks there was hardly an evening when Bruno was not standing on the sidewalk across the street from Guy's office building. Or if not there, standing across the street from where he lived. There was never a word now, never a sign, only the tall figure with the hands in the pockets of the long, rather military overcoat. Then the first letter came.

It was two sheets of paper: the first a map of Bruno's house and the grounds and roads around it and the course Guy would take, neatly drawn with dotted and ruled ink lines; and the second a typed, closely written letter lucidly setting forth the plan for the murder of Bruno's father. Guy tore it up, then immediately regretted it. He should have kept it as evidence against Bruno. He kept the pieces.

But there was no need to have kept them. He received such a letter every two or three days. They were all mailed from Great

Neck, as if Bruno stayed out there now—writing perhaps on his father's typewriter, sometimes when he was drunk. It showed in the typing mistakes and in the emotional bursts of the last paragraphs. If he was sober, the last paragraph was affectionate and reassuring as to the ease of the murder. If he was drunk, the paragraph was either a gush of brotherly love or a threat to haunt Guy all his life and ruin his career.

After the shock of the first letter, the next few bothered Guy hardly at all. Then as the tenth, twelfth, fifteenth appeared in his mailbox, he felt they hammered at his consciousness or his nerves in a manner that he could not analyze.

The twenty-first letter mentioned Anne. "You wouldn't like Anne to know your part in Miriam's murder, would you? What girl would marry a murderer? Certainly not Anne. The time is getting short. The first two weeks in March is my deadline."

Then the gun came. It was handed him by his landlady, a big package in brown paper. Guy gave a short laugh when the black gun toppled out. It was a big shiny Luger.

Some impulse made Guy take his own little revolver from the back of his top drawer, made him heft his own beautiful pearl-handled gun over his bed where the Luger lay. He smiled at his action, then brought his gun up closer to his eyes and studied it. He had seen it in a glutted pawnshop window on lower Main Street in Metcalf when he was fifteen, and had bought it with money from his paper route, not because it was a gun but because it was beautiful.

Guy put his own gun back into its lavender flannel bag and replaced it in the drawer. But how should he get rid of the Luger? Drop it over an embankment into the river? Into some ashcan? Everything he thought of seemed either suspect or melodramatic.

He decided to slip the gun under his socks and underwear in a bottom drawer until something better occurred to him. He thought suddenly of Samuel Bruno, for the first time as a person. Here in his room was the complete picture of the man and his life, according to his son, the plan for his murder—and the gun with which he was supposed to kill him. Guy got one of Charley Bruno's recent letters from among a few he had kept in the bottom drawer.

Samuel Bruno is the finest example of the worst that America produces. He comes of low-class peasants in Hungary. He picked a wife of good family, with his usual greed, once he could afford her. All this time my mother quietly bore his unfaithfulness, having some concept of the sacredness of the marriage contract. I wish I could kill him myself but I have explained to you that due to Gerard, his private detective, it is impossible. Samuel Bruno would be your personal enemy, too. He is the kind of man who thinks all your ideas about architecture as beauty and about adequate houses for everyone are idiotic & doesn't care what kind of factory he has as long as the roof doesn't leak and ruin his machinery. It may interest you to know his employees are on strike now. See *N.Y. Times* last Thurs. p. 31 bottom left. They are striking for a living wage. . . .

Guy burned the letter, then hurried to get ready for Long Island.

He and Anne were going to spend the day at her parents' home, riding around, walking in the woods, then drive up to Alton the following day. Their house would be finished by the end of March, which would give them a leisurely two months before the wedding to furnish it. Guy smiled as he gazed out the train window. On the back of an envelope he began sketching the twenty-story office building he had learned last week he had a good chance of being commissioned for. He had been saving that as a surprise for Anne.

Running down the platform steps, he saw Anne in the little crowd by the station door.

"Anne!" He put his arm around her and kissed her cheek.

She took his hand and they ran across the lane toward her car. "I've got a surprise!"

"So have I. What's yours?"

"Sold five designs yesterday on my own."

Guy shook his head. "I can't beat that. I've just got one office building. Maybe." .

She smiled and her eyebrows went up. "Maybe? Yes!"

"Yes, yes, yes!" he said, and kissed her again.

That evening, standing on the little wooden bridge over the stream back of Anne's house, Guy started to say, "Do you know what Bruno sent me today? A gun." Then the remoteness of Bruno and his connection with Anne's life shocked him with a terrible realization. Bruno, the name that haunted him, would mean nothing to Anne.

"What is it, Guy?"

"Nothing." She knew there was something, he thought.

He followed her as she turned and walked toward the house. The night had blackened the earth, made the snowy ground hardly distinguishable from woods and sky. Guy felt a growing sense of hostility. Before him, the kitchen door spilled a warm yellow light.

"I'll walk around again," he said.

Anne went in, and he turned back. He wanted to see if the sensation was stronger or weaker when Anne was not with him. He tried to feel rather than see. It was still there, faint and evasive.

The dull snap of a twig focused his consciousness at a point where the darkness deepened at the baseline of the woods. He sprinted toward it. A crackling of bushes now, and a moving black figure in the darkness. Guy released all his muscles in a long dive, caught the figure, and recognized the hoarse intake of breath as Bruno's. Bruno writhed in his arms like a great powerful fish underwater, twisted, and hit him an agonizing blow on the cheekbone. Clasping each other, they fell, fighting as if they both fought death. Bruno's fingers scratched at Guy's throat.

Bruno's breath hissed in and out between drawn-back lips. "Guy!" he burst out indignantly.

Guy caught him by the front of his collar. Suddenly they both stopped fighting.

"You knew it was me!" Bruno said in a fury. "Dirty bastard!"

"What're you doing here?" Guy pulled him to his feet.

"Okay, kill me if you want to! You can say it's self-defense!" Bruno whined.

Guy glanced toward the house. They had struggled a long way into the woods. "I don't want to kill you. I'll kill you next time I find you here. Clear out."

Bruno laughed, the single victorious clap. "You ready to do that job in two weeks?"

"Get someone else for your dirty work," Guy muttered.

"Look who's talking! I want you and I've got you! Okay!" A laugh. "I'll start. I'll tell your girl friend all about it. I'll write her tonight." Bruno lurched away, tripped, and staggered on.

Guy told Anne he had fought with a prowler in the woods. He suffered only a reddened eye from the battle, but he saw no way to stay on at the house, not go to Alton tomorrow, except by feigning injury. He had been hit in the stomach, he said. He didn't feel well. Mr. and Mrs. Faulkner were alarmed, and insisted to the officer who came to look over the grounds that they have a police guard for the next few nights. But a guard was not enough. If Bruno came back, Guy wanted to be there himself. Anne suggested that he stay on Monday, so he would have someone to look after him in case he were sick. Guy did stay on. He was ashamed that he felt the need to stay, ashamed that on Monday morning, after Anne left for her design studio in New York, he looked on her writing table where the maid put her mail to see if Bruno had written. He hadn't.

Guy stayed until Tuesday morning, when there was still no letter from Bruno, and then he went in to Manhattan. Work had piled up. A thousand things nettled him. The contract with the Shaw Realty Company for the new office building still had not been settled. He felt his life disorganized, chaotic.

Thursday evening, when Guy got back from a meeting at an architectural club, his landlady, Mrs. McCausland, said he had had three calls. The telephone rang as they stood in the hall. It was Bruno, sullen and drunk. He asked if Guy was ready to talk sense.

Guy started to reply, but Bruno cut him off. "I didn't think so," he said. "I've written Anne." And he hung up.

On Saturday afternoon Guy was supposed to meet Anne in Hempstead, Long Island, to see a dog show. If Bruno had written the letter, Anne would have gotten it by Saturday morning, Guy thought. But obviously she hadn't. He could tell from her wave to him from the car where she sat waiting for him.

He tried desperately to think of something to say as they walked along the rows of dog cages.

"Have you heard anything from the Shaw people?" Anne asked.

"No." He stared at a nervous dachshund and tried to listen to Anne.

She didn't know yet, Guy thought, but it would be only a matter of time until she did get the letter.

"Anne," he began. He had to prepare her, he thought. And he had to *know*. "If someone were to accuse me of having had a part in Miriam's death, what would you . . . ? Would you—"

She stopped and looked at him. The whole world seemed to stop moving.

"Had a part? What do you mean, Guy?"

"Just accused me," Guy answered. "I just want to know. Accused me for no reason. It wouldn't matter, would it?" Would she still marry him? he wanted to ask, but it was such a pitiful, begging question, he could not ask it.

"Guy, *has* someone accused you?"

"No!" he protested. He felt awkward and vexed. "But if someone tried to make out a strong case against me—"

Anne looked at him with that flash of disappointment, of surprise and mistrust, that he had seen before when he said or did something that she did not approve. "Do you expect someone to?" she asked.

"I just want to know!" He was in a hurry and it seemed so simple!

"At times like this," she said quietly, "you make me feel we're complete strangers."

"I'm sorry," he murmured. He felt she had cut an invisible bond between them.

"I don't think you're sorry, or you wouldn't keep on doing this!" She looked straight at him, keeping her voice low, though her eyes had filled with tears. "But yes—since you ask me, I think it would make a difference if someone accused you. I'd want to ask why you expected it. Why do you?"

"I don't!"

She brushed a tear from the corner of her eye quickly. "Just one thing, Guy. Will you stop expecting the worst—about everything?"

"Yes," he said. "God, yes."

"Let's go back to the car."

He spent the day with Anne, and they had dinner that evening at her house. There had been no letter from Bruno. Guy put the possibility from his mind, as if he had passed a crisis.

On Monday evening at about eight she telephoned.

"Darling—I guess I'm a little upset."

"What's the matter?" He knew what was the matter.

"I got a letter. In this morning's mail. About what you were talking about Saturday. It's typewritten, and it's not signed."

"What does it say? Read it to me."

Anne read shakily, but in her distinct speech, " 'Dear Miss Faulkner, It may interest you to know that Guy Haines had more to do with his wife's murder than the law thinks at present. But the truth will out. This writer knows that Guy Haines will not remain a free man much longer.' Signed, 'A friend.' "

Guy closed his eyes.

"Guy, do you know who it could be? Guy? Hello?"

He knew from her voice she was merely frightened, that she believed in him, was afraid only for him. "I don't know, Anne."

"Is that true, Guy?" she asked anxiously. "You should know. Something should be done."

"I don't know," Guy repeated, frowning. His mind seemed tied in an inextricable knot.

"You must know. *Think*, Guy. Someone you might call an enemy?"

"What's the postmark?"

"Grand Central. It's perfectly plain paper. You can't tell a thing from that."

"Save it for me."

"Of course, Guy. And I won't tell anyone. The family, I mean." A pause. "There *must* be someone, Guy. You suspected someone Saturday—didn't you?"

"I didn't." His throat closed up. "Sometimes these things happen, you know, after a trial."

"Well, I can mail you the letter. Special delivery."

It came the next morning, along with another of Bruno's letters with an affectionate but exhorting last paragraph in which he mentioned the letter to Anne and promised more.

6

GUY sat on the edge of his bed and covered his face in his hands. If he told Anne the story, wouldn't she consider he had been partially guilty? Marry him? How could she? What sort of beast was he that he could sit in a room where a bottom drawer held plans for a murder and the gun to do it with?

Should he dress and go out for a walk or try to sleep? His step on the carpet was light, unconsciously avoiding the spot by the armchair where the floor squeaked. *You would skip these squeaking steps just for safety*, Bruno's letters said. *My father's door is just to the right, as you know. I have gone over everything and there is no room for a hitch anywhere. See on map where the butler's (Herbert's) room is. The hall floor squeaks there where I marked X.* He flung himself on the bed. *You should not try to get rid of the Luger between the house and the RR station no matter what happens.* He knew it all by heart, knew the sound of the kitchen door and the color of the hall carpet.

If Bruno should get someone else to kill his father, he would have ample evidence in these letters to convict Bruno. He could avenge himself for what Bruno had done to him. It would be only a matter of time until Bruno got someone. If he could weather Bruno's threats only a while longer, it would all be over and he could sleep. If he did it, he thought, he wouldn't use the big Luger, he would use the little revolver—

Guy pulled himself up from the bed, aching, angry, and frightened by the words that had just passed through his mind.

"*Mr. Haines!*"

Startled, Guy went to the door.

"Phone call for you," the landlady called up.

"Hello, Guy. Are you ready yet?" asked the voice on the telephone, lewd in the early morning. "Want some more?"

"You don't bother me."

Bruno laughed.

Guy hung up, trembling.

The shock lingered through the day, tremulous and traumatic. He took a long walk up Riverside Drive to tire himself, but slept badly nevertheless, and had a series of unpleasant dreams. It would be different, Guy thought, once the Shaw contract was signed, once he could go ahead on his work.

Douglas Frear of the Shaw Realty Company called the next morning.

"Mr. Haines," said his slow, hoarse voice, "we've received a most peculiar letter concerning you."

"What? What kind of a letter?"

"Concerning your wife. I didn't know— Shall I read it to you?"

"Please."

" 'To whom it may concern: No doubt it will interest you to learn that Guy Daniel Haines, whose wife was murdered last June, had more of a role in the deed than the courts know. This is from one who knows, and who knows also that there will be a retrial soon which will show his real part in the crime.' I trust it's a crank letter, Mr. Haines. I just thought you should know about it."

"Of course."

"I think I heard about—uh—the tragedy last year. There's no question of a retrial, is there?"

"Certainly not. That is, I've heard nothing about it." Guy cursed his confusion. Mr. Frear wanted only to know if he would be free to work.

"Sorry we haven't quite made up our minds on that contract, Mr. Haines."

The Shaw Realty Company waited until the following morning to tell him they weren't entirely satisfied with his drawings. In fact, they were interested in the work of another architect.

How had Bruno found out about the building? Guy wondered. But there were any number of ways. It had been mentioned in the papers, as had the Palmyra Club, and Bruno obviously kept himself informed on architectural news.

It would be only a matter of time until Bruno informed the next client, and the next. This was his threat to ruin Guy's career.

Guy thought of Anne with a flash of pain. It seemed to him that he was forgetting for long intervals that he loved her. He felt Bruno was destroying his courage to love. Disgusted with himself, Guy went out in the middle of the day and drank martinis in a Madison Avenue bar. He was to have had lunch with Anne, but she had called and broken the appointment, he could not remember why. She certainly hadn't said she was going shopping for something for the house, or he would have remembered it. Or would he have? Nothing in the world made sense except to escape from Bruno. But there was no way of doing it that made sense.

Guy glanced again at the row of brownstones across the street, sure he had seen Bruno. His eyes smarted and swam, fighting the dusk. He *had* seen him, there by the black iron gate, where he was not. Guy turned and ran up his steps. He had tickets to take Anne to a Verdi opera tonight. He didn't feel like seeing her, didn't want her kind of cheering, didn't want to exhaust himself pretending he felt better than he did.

Mrs. McCausland gave him a number he was supposed to call.

He thought it looked like that of one of Anne's aunts. He hoped Anne might be busy tonight.

"Guy, I don't see how I can make it," Anne said. "These two people Aunt Julie wanted me to meet aren't coming until after dinner. And I can't duck out on it."

"It's perfectly all right."

"I *am* sorry. Do you know I haven't seen you since Saturday?"

Guy bit the end of his tongue. He felt an actual repulsion against her clinging, her concern, even her clear, gentle voice.

"Yes, I know."

"I do love you. You won't forget that, will you?"

"No, Anne."

He fled upstairs to his room, hung up his coat, washed, and then combed his hair. Suddenly there was nothing to do, and he wanted Anne.

His room seemed filled with palpable, suspenseful silence. He glanced at the low bookshelves he had built around the walls, at the ivy plants Mrs. McCausland had given him, at the empty red plush chair by the reading lamp, at the monk's-cloth curtains that concealed his kitchenette. Almost casually he went and moved the curtains aside and looked behind them. He had a definite feeling that someone was waiting for him in the room, though he was not in the least frightened.

A few moments later he was in a bar drinking a martini. He had to sleep, he reasoned, even if it meant drinking alone, which he despised. He walked down to Times Square, got a haircut, and on the way home bought a quart of milk and a couple of tabloids. After he wrote a letter to his mother, he thought, he would drink some milk, read the papers, and go to bed.

Guy awakened to Bruno's presence in the dark, though he heard nothing. After the first small start at the suddenness, he felt no surprise at all. Was it *really* Bruno? Yes. Guy saw the end of his cigarette now, over by the bureau.

"Bruno?"

"Hi," Bruno said softly. "I got in with a skeleton key. You're ready now, aren't you?" Bruno sounded calm and tired.

Guy raised himself to one elbow. "Yes," he said. It undid the knot in his head so suddenly that it hurt him. It was what he had been waiting to say, what the silence in the room had been waiting to hear.

Bruno sat down on the side of the bed and gripped both his arms above the elbows. "Guy, I'll never see you again."

"No." Bruno smelled abominably of cigarettes and sweet brilliantine, of the sourness of drink, but Guy did not draw back.

"I tried to be nice to him these last couple days," Bruno said. "Not nice, just decent. He said something tonight to my mother, just before we went out—"

"I don't want to hear it!" Guy said.

They were both silent for several seconds, then Bruno snuffled with a disgusting rattle. "We're going to Maine tomorrow, starting by noon positively. My mother and me and the chauffeur. Tomorrow night is a good night. Anytime after eleven."

He kept talking, repeating what Guy already knew, and Guy did not stop him, because he knew he was going to enter the house and it would all come true.

"I broke the lock on the back door two days ago, slamming it when I was tight. They're too busy to get it fixed. But if they do—" He pressed a key into Guy's hand. "And I brought you these gloves—ladies' gloves, but they'll stretch." Bruno laughed.

Guy felt the thin cotton gloves.

"You got the gun, huh? Where is it?"

"In the bottom drawer."

Guy heard him stumble against the bureau and heard the drawer pull out. The light came on, and Bruno stood there huge and tall, in black trousers with a thin stripe, and a new polo coat so pale it was nearly white. A white silk muffler hung long around his neck.

Guy examined him from his small brown shoes to his stringy hair, as if from his physical appearance alone he could discover what had caused his own change of feeling, or even what the feeling was. It was familiarity and something more, something brotherly. Bruno clicked the gun shut and turned to him. His gray eyes looked bigger with his tears and rather golden. He gazed at Guy as if he were trying to find words, as if he were pleading with Guy to find them. Then he moistened his thin parted lips, shook his head, and reached an arm out toward the lamp. The light went out and he was gone.

A gray glaring afternoon light filled the room when Guy awakened. He remembered that he had gotten up and telephoned his office that morning to say he didn't feel well enough to come in. He lay there thinking that tonight he was going to do it, and after tonight it would all be over. Then he got up and slowly went about his routine of shaving, showering, and dressing, aware that nothing he did mattered at all until the hour between eleven and midnight. He felt he moved on certain definite tracks now, and that he could not have stopped himself or gotten off them even if he had wanted to.

There was plenty of time, so much that he wandered about his room absently for a while. Should he bother to wear crepe-soled shoes? Should he wear a hat? He got the Luger out of the bottom drawer and laid it on the bureau. He got the cotton gloves from the table by his bed. A small yellow card fluttered from them. It was a ticket to Great Neck.

He stared at the black Luger, which more than before struck him as outrageously large. He got his own little revolver from the top drawer. Its pearl handle gleamed with a discreet beauty.

For a moment he was utterly confused. Take the Luger, of course, the Luger was in the plan. He put the Luger in his overcoat pocket. His hand moved for the gloves on the bureau top. The gloves were purple and the flannel bag of his revolver was lavender.

Suddenly it seemed fitting he should take the small revolver, because of the similar colors, so he put the Luger back in the bottom drawer and dropped the little revolver into his pocket. A cup of coffee might make him more alert, he thought. He would get one at the station.

There was a moment on the train, when a man bumped his

shoulder, when his nerves seemed to go quivering up and up to a pitch at which he thought something *must* happen. *It's not really a gun in my pocket. I've never thought of it as a gun. I didn't buy it because it was a gun.* And immediately he felt easier, because he knew he was going to kill with it. He was like Bruno. Hadn't he known Bruno was like himself? Or why had he liked Bruno? He loved Bruno. Bruno had prepared every inch of the way for him, and everything would go well because everything always went well for Bruno.

It was drizzling in a fine, directionless mist as he stepped off the train. Guy walked straight to the row of buses Bruno had described. The bus moved out of the lighted community center and into a darker road with houses along both sides. At the Grant Street stop, he stood up automatically, and the feeling of moving on established tracks returned to comfort him.

His step had a moist elastic sound on the dirt road. There was the vacant lot with the solitary tree, and off to the left, darkness and the woods. The streetlamp Bruno had put in all his maps wore an oily blue and gold halo.

He came upon the house suddenly, and it was as if a curtain had lifted on a stage scene he knew already: the long seven-foot-high wall of white plaster in the foreground, darkened here and there by a cherry tree that overhung it, and beyond, the triangle of white housetop. The Doghouse. He crossed the street. He walked fifteen paces beside the wall, sprang up, gripped its cornice, and scrambled astride it. Almost directly below him, he saw the pale form of the milk crate Bruno had said in one of his letters that he had flung near the wall. He jumped down.

When he moved toward the house, a limb took his hat off. He rammed the hat in the front of his overcoat and put his hand in the pocket where the key was. He took a breath and moved across the lawn in a gait between running and walking, light and quick as a cat. He hesitated at the edge of the grass, glanced at the garage, then went up the six steps. The back door opened, heavy and smooth. He moved diagonally toward the back stairs, counting off his steps.

Twelve steps up first, skip seven, Bruno had written. *Then two little flights after the turn. . . . Skip four, skip three, step wide at the top. You can remember it, it's got a syncopated rhythm.* He skipped the right steps as he went up, and made no sound. Ten feet ahead on his left was the butler's door.

The floor gave the tiniest wail of complaint, and Guy resiliently withdrew his foot, waited, and stepped around the spot. *My father's door is just to the right.* The tracks were still under him.

He took the knob in his left hand, and his right moved automatically to the gun in his pocket. He felt like a machine, beyond danger and invulnerable. Suppose the old man saw him first? *The night-light on the front porch lights the room a little bit*—but the bed was over in the opposite corner. He closed the door—*the wind might blow the door*—then faced the corner.

The gun was in his hand already, aimed at the bed that looked empty however he peered at it.

He frowned at the bed, and then with a terrible thrill made out the form of the head lying near the wall side, tipped sideways as if it regarded him with a kind of gay disdain. The face was darker than the hair, which blended with the pillow.

One should shoot the chest. Obediently the gun pointed at the chest. Guy slid his feet nearer the bed. There was no sound of breathing. One would not think he was alive. That was what one must think, that the figure was merely a target. And that, because he did not know the target, it was like killing in war.

He pulled the trigger. It made a mere click. He pulled again and it clicked. It was a trick! It was all false and didn't even exist! Not even his standing here! He pulled the trigger again. The room tore up with a roar. His fingers tightened in terror. The roar came again, as if the crust of the world had burst.

"*Kagh!*" said the figure on the bed. The gray face moved upward, showing the line of head and shoulders.

Guy was on the porch roof, falling. The sensation awakened him like the fall at the end of a nightmare. By a miracle an awning bar slid into one of his hands, and he fell downward again, onto hands and knees. He jumped off the porch edge, ran along

the side of the house, then cut across the lawn, straight for the place where the milk crate was.

"Hey!" a voice called.

The butler was after him, just as he had anticipated. He felt the butler was right behind him. The nightmare!

"Hey! Hey, there!"

Guy turned under the cherry trees and stood with his fist drawn back. The butler was not just behind him. He was a long way off, but he had seen him. Guy jumped for the wall.

Darkness ran up higher and higher about him. He dodged a little tree, leaped over what looked like a ditch, and ran on. Then suddenly he was lying face down and pain was spreading from the middle of him in all directions, rooting him to the ground.

Damn! He knew where he was now, in the field west of the house that in Bruno's plans was never to be used! He felt as if he had been shattered apart with the explosion of the gun, that he could never gather the energy to move again, and that he really didn't care. But suddenly his arms and legs scrambled under him and he was running across the field.

A strange sound made him stop—a low musical moan that seemed to come from all sides.

Police sirens, of course. He ran on blindly, away from the sirens that were over his left shoulder now, knowing that he should veer left to find the little dirt road that Bruno had said he should take. He started to cut left to cross the main road that surely lay in that direction, when he realized the sirens were coming up the road. He would either have to wait— He couldn't wait. He ran on, parallel to the cars. Then something caught his foot, and cursing, he fell again. He lay in a kind of ditch with his arms outspread. Frustration maddened him to a petulant sob.

Close on his right, a siren shrieked in triumph as if it had found him. A rectangle of light sprang up in front of him, and he turned and fled from it. A window. He had nearly run into a house. The whole world was awake! And he *had* to cross the road!

The police car passed him with a blink of headlights. Another siren moaned to his left, where the house must be, and droned away to silence. Stooping, Guy crossed the road not far behind the car and entered deeper darkness. No matter where the little road was now, he could run farther from the house in this direction. *There's sort of unlighted woods all around to the south, easy to hide in in case you have to get off the little road.*

Something had caught him and was holding him. He fought it automatically with his fists, and found it was bushes, twigs, briers. He kept fighting and hurling his body through, because the sirens were still behind him and this was the only direction to go.

He concentrated on the enemy ahead of him, and on both sides and even behind him, that caught at him with thousands of sharp tiny hands. He spent his strength joyfully against them, relishing their clean, straight battle against him.

He awakened at the edge of a woods, face down on a downward sloping hill. Had he awakened, or had he fallen only a moment ago? But there was grayness in the sky in front of him, the beginning of dawn, and when he stood up, his flickering vision told him he had been unconscious.

Below, the sparse lights of a little town glowed like stars at dusk. Mechanically Guy got out a handkerchief and wrapped it tight around the base of his thumb, where a cut had oozed black-looking blood. He moved toward a tree and leaned against it. His eyes searched the town and the road below. There was not a moving thing. He wanted water. On the dirt road that edged the town he saw a filling station. He made his way down toward it.

There was an old-fashioned pump beside the filling station. He held his head under it. His face stung like a mask of cuts. Slowly his mind grew clearer. He couldn't be more than two miles from Great Neck. He removed his right glove and put it in his pocket. Where was the other? Had he left it in the woods? He searched his overcoat pockets, opened his overcoat and searched his trouser pockets. Then he found what was left of the glove inside his left sleeve, nothing more than the hem at the top that had circled his wrist. He pocketed it with an abstract happiness. He decided to walk south, catch a bus, and ride until he came to a railroad station.

Then daylight made a sudden thrust at the night, and cracked the whole horizon on his left. A silver line ran around the top of a hill, and the hill became mauve and green and tan, as if it were opening its eyes.

7

FOR the hundredth time he examined his face in the bathroom mirror and patiently touched every scratch with the styptic pencil. He went back and fell down on his bed. There was the rest of today, and tomorrow, Sunday. He needn't see anyone, now that he'd been out for the newspaper. Except for his scratched hands, he might have believed it all a dream. Because he had not wanted to do it, he thought, it had not been his will. It had been Bruno's will, working through him. He wanted to curse Bruno, curse him aloud, but he simply had not the energy now. The curious thing was that he felt no guilt, and it seemed to him now that the fact Bruno's will had motivated him was the explanation. But what was this thing, guilt, that he had felt more after Miriam's death than now?

The newspaper had a long account, with a silhouette of the murderer, composed from the butler's description, of a man six feet one, weighing about one hundred and seventy to eighty pounds, wearing a dark overcoat and hat. Guy read it with mild surprise, as if it might not have been about him; he was only five nine and weighed about a hundred and forty. And he had not been wearing a hat. He skipped the part of the story that told who Samuel Bruno was, and read with greatest interest the speculation about the murderer's flight. North along Newhope Road, it said, where it was believed he lost himself in the town of Great Neck, "perhaps taking the 12:18 a.m. train." Actually he had gone southeast.

He felt suddenly relieved, safe. The coolness of the murderer was stressed, and the fact that it seemed to be an inside job. No fingerprints, no clue except some shoe prints, size nine and a half, and the smudge of a black shoe on the white plaster wall. It was odd they overestimated his shoe size, Guy thought, with the ground so wet. "An unusually small caliber of bullet," the paper said. He must get rid of his revolver, too. He felt a little wrench of grief. He would hate that! He pulled himself up and got more ice for the towel he was holding against his head.

Anne telephoned him in the late afternoon to ask him to go to a party with her Sunday night in Manhattan.

"Helen Heyburn's party. You know, I told you about it. And I'll spend the night with her."

Guy's voice came evenly, "I guess I don't quite feel like a party, Anne."

Her words seemed distant, irrelevant. He listened to himself saying the right things, not even caring that Anne might notice any difference.

"Why don't I bring in some delicatessen things Sunday afternoon," Anne said, "and we'll have a snack together?"

"I thought I might go out Sunday, Anne. Sketching."

"Oh. I'm sorry. I had something to tell you."

"What?"

"Something I think you'll like. Well—some other time."

Guy crept up the stairs, alert for Mrs. McCausland. Anne was cool to him, he thought. The next time she saw him, she would know and she would hate him. Anne was through, Anne was through. He kept chanting it until he fell asleep.

He slept until the following noon, then lay in bed the rest of the day in a torpor that made it agony even to cross the room to refill his towel with ice. He felt he would never sleep enough to get back his strength.

On Monday morning the lobby doorbell rang. The police are downstairs, he thought. And he didn't care. He would make a complete confession. He would blurt it all out at once!

He leaned on the release button, then went to his apartment door and listened.

Light, quick steps ran up. Anne's steps. Rather the police than

Anne! He turned completely around and stupidly drew his shade.

"Me," Anne whispered as she slipped in. "I walked over from Helen's. It's a wonderful morning!" She saw his bandage, and the elation left her face. "What happened to your hand?"

He stepped back in the shadow near his bureau. "I got into a fight."

"When? Last night? And your face, Guy!"

"Yes." He had to have her, had to keep her with him, he thought. He would perish without her.

"Where, Guy? Who was it?"

"A man I don't even know," he said tonelessly. "In a bar."

"In a bar?"

"I don't know how it happened. Suddenly."

"Someone you'd never seen before?"

"Yes."

"I don't believe you." She spoke slowly. "How can I? And I don't believe you about the man you fought with in the woods. Was it the same one?"

"No."

"You're keeping something from me, Guy."

Then she softened, but each simple word seemed to attack him. "What is it, darling? You know I want to help you. But you've got to tell me."

"I've told you," he said, and set his teeth. If he could keep Anne now, he thought, he could survive.

He looked at the straight, pale curtain of her hair, and put out his hand to touch it, but she drew back.

"I don't see how we can go on like this, Guy. We can't. You once said I made you happy," she said slowly, "or that I could in spite of anything. I don't see it anymore."

Certainly he did not make her happy. But if she could still love him now, how he would try to make her happy! How he would worship and serve her! "You do make me happy, Anne. I have nothing else." He bent lower with sudden sobs, shameless, racking sobs that did not begin to cease until Anne touched his shoulder.

"I DON'T GIVE A damn what you think!" Bruno said, his foot planted in his chair. He looked at Gerard like a golden, thin-haired tiger driven to madness.

"Didn't say I thought anything," Gerard replied with a shrug of hunched shoulders, "did I?"

"You implied."

"I did not imply." The round shoulders shook twice with his laugh. "You mistake me, Charles. I didn't mean you told anyone on purpose you were leaving. You let it drop by accident."

Bruno stared at him. Gerard had just implied that it was an in-side job and that Bruno and his mother must have had something to do with it. Gerard knew that he and his mother had decided only Thursday afternoon to leave Friday. Gerard didn't have anything, and he couldn't fool him by pretending that he had.

"Mind if I shove off?" Bruno asked.

"In a minute. Have a drink."

"No, thanks." Bruno was dying for a drink, but not from Gerard.

"How's your mother?"

"You asked me that." His mother wasn't well, wasn't sleeping, and that was the main reason he wanted to get home. A hot re-sentment came over him again at Gerard's friend-of-the-family attitude. "By the way, we're not hiring you for this, you know."

Gerard looked up with a smile on his round, faintly pink-and-purple–mottled face. "I'd work on this case for nothing, Charles. That's how interesting I think it is." Arthur Gerard didn't even look like the kind of a detective who was not supposed to look like a detective. In spite of his record, Bruno found it impossible to believe that Gerard was a top-notch detective.

"Your father was a very fine man, Charles. A pity you didn't know him better," Gerard said.

"I knew him well," said Bruno.

"You hated your father, didn't you?"

"He hated me."

"But he didn't. That's where you didn't know him."

Heat rose up the sides of Bruno's neck. The next few weeks

would be terrible on his mother, and Gerard would make it worse because he was an enemy of both of them. Bruno stood up and tossed his raincoat over one arm.

"Now I want you to try to think once more"—Gerard wagged a finger at him—"just where you went and whom you saw Thursday night. You left your mother and Mr. Templeton and Mr. Russo in front of the Blue Angel at two forty-five that morning. Where did you go?"

"Hamburger Hearth," Bruno sighed.

"Didn't see anyone you knew there?"

"Who should I know there, the cat?"

"Then where'd you go?" Gerard checked on his notes.

"Maybe I went straight home, I don't know. What about all the people my mother and I talked to Friday morning? We called up a lot of people to say good-by."

"Oh, we're covering those. But seriously, Charles"—Gerard leaned back and concentrated on puffing his cigar to life—"you wouldn't leave your mother and her friends just to get a hamburger and go straight home by yourself, would you?"

"Maybe. Maybe it sobered me up."

"Why're you so vague? You must think yourself it's funny your father was killed the night of the same day you left."

"I didn't see anyone. I invite you to check up on everyone I know and ask them."

"Oh, we'll do that. Meanwhile, I'll be around. Yes, you can go now, Charles." Gerard made a careless gesture.

Bruno lingered a moment, trying to think of something to say, and not being able to, went out. He walked back through the shabby, depressing corridor of the Confidential Detective Bureau. How gaily he had come in an hour ago, determined not to let Gerard rile him, and now— He could never control his temper when Gerard made cracks about him and his mother, and he might as well admit it. So what? So what did they have on him? Nothing!

Guy! Bruno smiled going down in the elevator. Not once had Guy crossed his mind in Gerard's office! Not one flicker even when Gerard had asked him about Thursday night! Guy! Guy and himself! Who else was like them? He longed for Guy to be with him now. He would clasp Guy's hand, and to hell with the rest of the world! Their feats were unparalleled!

At about the same time the next day, Bruno was sitting in a beach chair on the terrace of his house in Great Neck, in a mood of content quite new and pleasant to him. A few hours earlier, a check had arrived for twenty thousand for his mother. There would be a lot more when the lawyers and the insurance people stopped yapping. At lunch he and his mother had talked about going to Capri. And tonight they were going out to dinner for the first time, at their favorite little *intime* restaurant not far from Great Neck.

Casually he turned the pages of the address book in his lap. He had noticed it this morning, and he wanted to make sure there wasn't anything about Guy in it before Gerard found it.

"Dan 8:15 Hotel Astor," he found in the memos at the back of the book. He didn't even remember Dan. "Get $ from Father by June 1."

The next page sent a little chill down his spine: "Item for Guy $25." He tore the perforated page out. That Santa Fe belt for Guy. Why had he even put it down?

Gerard's big black car purred into the driveway.

Bruno forced himself to sit there and finish checking the memos. Then he slipped the address book in his pocket and poked the torn-out page into his mouth.

Gerard strolled onto the flagstones with a cigar in his mouth.

"Anything new?" Bruno asked.

"Few things."

Bruno's jaw moved casually on the little wad of paper, as if he chewed gum. "Such as what?" he asked.

"Such as the fact that the murderer didn't cut back to town." Gerard gestured like a country-store proprietor pointing out a road. "He cut through those woods over there and must have had a pretty rough time. We found these."

Bruno got up and looked at a piece of the purple gloves and

a shred of dark blue material, like Guy's overcoat. "Gosh. You sure they're off the murderer?"

"Reasonably sure. One's off an overcoat. The other—probably a glove."

"Pretty fancy gloves."

"Ladies' gloves." Gerard looked up with a twinkle.

Bruno gave an amused smirk, and stopped contritely.

"I first thought he was a professional killer," Gerard said with a sigh. "He certainly knew the house. But I don't think a professional killer would have lost his head and tried to get through those woods at the point he did."

"Hm-m," said Bruno with interest.

"He knew the right road to take, too. The right road was only ten yards away."

"How do you know that?"

"Because this whole thing was carefully planned, Charles. The broken lock on the back door, the milk crate by the wall . . ."

Bruno was silent. Herbert had told Gerard that he, Bruno, broke the lock. Herbert had probably also told him he put the milk crate there.

"Purple gloves!" Gerard chuckled, as gaily as Bruno had ever heard him chuckle. "What does the color matter as long as they keep fingerprints off things, eh?"

"Yeah," Bruno said.

Gerard entered the house through the terrace door.

Bruno followed him after a moment. Gerard went back to the kitchen, and Bruno climbed the stairs.

He opened his mother's door carefully. She was lying on her bed with the pink satin comforter drawn up to her chin and her eyes open.

"Gerard's here again, Mom."

"I know."

"If you don't want to be disturbed, I'll tell him."

"Darling, don't be silly."

Bruno wandered about the room. He wanted to sound off about Gerard now, but his mother wouldn't understand. She insisted on their continuing to hire him, because he was supposed to be the best. They were not working together, his mother and he. His mother might say something else to Gerard—like the fact they'd decided only Thursday to leave Friday—of terrible importance and not mention it to him at all!

Gerard knocked a few minutes later. Bruno opened the door for him and then went to his own room. Slowly he mixed himself a short drink, downed it, then went softly back down the hall and heard Gerard talking to his mother.

"Didn't seem in high or low spirits, eh?"

"He's a very moody boy, you know. I doubt if I'd have noticed," his mother said.

"Too bad, because I'd like more cooperation from him."

"Do you think he's withholding anything, Arthur?"

"I don't know. Do you?"

"Of course, I don't think he is."

"You want me to get at the truth, don't you, Elsie?" Gerard asked, like a movie detective. "He's hazy about what he did Thursday night after leaving you. He's got some pretty shady acquaintances. One might have been a hireling of a business enemy's of Sam's, or something like that. And Charles could have mentioned that you and he were leaving the next day—"

"What're you getting at, Arthur, that Charles knows something about this?"

"Elsie, I wouldn't be surprised. Would you, really?"

"Damn him!" Bruno murmured. Damn him for saying that to his *mother!*

"I'll certainly tell you everything he tells me."

Bruno drifted toward the stairway. Her submissiveness shocked him. Suppose she began to suspect? Murder was something she wouldn't be able to take. Hadn't he realized it in Santa Fe?

And if she remembered Guy, remembered that he had talked about him in Los Angeles? If Gerard found Guy in the next two weeks, he might have scratches on him from getting through those woods, or a bruise or a cut that might raise suspicion. Bruno heard Herbert's soft tread in the downstairs hall. He retreated to his own room, took a big drink, then lay down and tried to fall asleep.

MOMENTARILY and faintly, as one reexperiences a remembered sensation, Guy felt secure and self-sufficient as he sat down at his worktable where he had his books and notes for the hospital he had been commissioned to plan.

The newspapers had stopped mentioning the murder six weeks ago. He had taken care of every clue—the purple gloves cut up and flushed down the toilet, the overcoat and the trousers torn in pieces and disposed of gradually in the garbage. And the Luger dropped off the Manhattan Bridge, his shoes off another.

In his bureau was his little revolver. It was the one clue he had not disposed of, and all the clue they needed if they found him. He knew exactly why he kept the revolver: it was *his*, a part of himself, with its mechanical, absolute logic, the third hand that had done the murder.

If Bruno dared to contact him again, he would kill him, too. Guy was sure that he could. Bruno would know it, too. Bruno had always been able to read him. Guy and Bruno. Each was what the other had not chosen to be, the cast-off self, what he thought he hated but perhaps in reality loved.

GUY slammed his foot on the brake pedal, but the car leaped, screaming, toward the child. There was a tinny clatter of the bicycle falling. Guy got out, ran around the car, and dragged the child up by his shoulders.

"I'm okay," the little boy said.

"Is he all right, Guy?" Anne ran up, white as the child.

"I think so."

Guy gripped the bicycle's front wheel with his knees and straightened the handlebars, feeling the child's curious eyes on his own violently trembling hands.

"Thanks," said the boy.

Guy watched him mount the bicycle and pedal off as if he

watched a miracle. He looked at Anne and said quietly, with a shuddering sigh, "I can't drive any more today."

"All right," she replied, as quietly as he, but there was a suspicion in her eyes, Guy knew, as she turned to go around to the driver's seat.

Guy apologized to the Faulkners as he got back into the car, and they murmured something about such things happening to every driver now and then. But Guy felt their real silence behind him, a silence of shock and horror. He had seen the boy coming down the side road. The boy had stopped for him, but Guy swerved the car toward him as if he had intended to hit him. Had he? Tremulously he lighted a cigarette. Nothing but bad coordination, he told himself; he had seen it a hundred times in the past two weeks—collisions with revolving doors, his inability even to hold a pen against a ruler, and so often the feeling he wasn't *here*, doing what he was doing. Grimly he reestablished what he was doing now, riding in Anne's car up to Alton to see the new house. The house was finished. Anne and her mother had put the drapes up last week.

It was Sunday, nearly noon. "If anybody's hungry, speak up now," Anne said. "This little store's the last place for miles."

But no one was hungry.

"I expect to be asked for dinner at least once a year, Anne," her father said. "Maybe a brace of ducks or some quail. I hear there's good hunting around here. Any good with a gun, Guy?"

Anne turned the car into the road that led to the house.

"Fair, sir," Guy said finally, stammering twice. He wished he could have a brandy or something.

Mrs. Faulkner walked beside him across the new lawn. "It's simply beautiful, Guy. I hope you're proud of it."

Guy nodded. It was only a month until their marriage now. Four more Friday nights, and Anne would sit in the big square green chair by the fireplace, her voice would call to him from the kitchen, they would work together in the studio upstairs. But what right had he to imprison her with himself? He stood staring at their bedroom, vaguely aware that it seemed cluttered, because Anne had said she wanted their bedroom "not modern."

"Don't forget to thank Mother for the furniture, will you?" she whispered to him. "Mother gave it to us, you know."

The cherry bedroom set, of course. He remembered her telling him that morning at breakfast. But when he should have said something about the furniture, he didn't, and then it seemed too late. They must know something is the matter, he felt. Everyone in the world must know. He was somehow being reprieved, being saved for some weight to fall upon him and annihilate him.

"Thinking about a new job, Guy?" Mr. Faulkner asked.

Guy had not seen his figure there when he stepped onto the side porch. With a sense of justifying himself, he pulled a folded sketch from his pocket and showed it to him. Mr. Faulkner's bushy gray and brown eyebrows came down thoughtfully.

"A new hospital, eh? Funny, Anne didn't say anything to me about it," Mr. Faulkner said.

"I'm saving it."

"Oh." Mr. Faulkner chuckled. "A wedding present?"

Later the Faulkners took the car and went back for sandwiches from the little store. Guy was tired of the house. He wanted Anne to walk with him up the rock hill.

"In a minute," she said. "Come here." She stood in front of the tall stone fireplace. She put her hands on his shoulders and looked into his face, a little apprehensive. "Those are getting deeper, you know," she told him, drawing her fingertip down the hollow in his cheek. "I'm going to make you eat."

"Maybe need a little sleep," he murmured. He had told her that lately his work demanded long hours. He had told her, of all things, that he was doing some hack jobs to earn some money.

"Darling, we're—we're well off. What's troubling you?"

She had asked him half a dozen times if it was the wedding, if he wanted not to marry her. If she asked him again, he might say yes, but he knew she would not ask it now, in front of their fireplace. "Nothing's troubling me," he said quickly.

"Then will you please not work so hard?" she begged him; then spontaneously, out of her own joy, she hugged him to her.

GUY CROSSED THE Faulkners' kitchen and turned at the back door. "Awfully thoughtless of me to invite myself on the cook's night out."

"What's thoughtless about it? You'll just fare as we do on Thursday nights, that's all." Mrs. Faulkner brought him a piece of the celery she was washing at the sink. "But Hazel's going to be disappointed she wasn't here to make shortcake for you."

Guy went out. The afternoon was still bright with sun, though the picket fence cast long oblique bars of shadow over the flower beds. He could just see Anne's tied-back hair and the pale green of her sweater as she gathered mint and watercress from the stream that flowed out of the woods where he had fought Bruno. Bruno is past, he reminded himself, gone, vanished.

What was he doing here, Guy asked himself, where he deceived everyone, even the cook who liked to make shortcake for him because—once, perhaps—he had praised her dessert? If he should step out of Anne's life, what difference would it make to her? He began to walk toward her.

"I'm almost done," she said to him as he came up to her.

A sprig of watercress was floating away on the stream, and he sprang to rescue it. "I think I'll take a job soon, Anne," he said.

She looked up, astounded. "A job? You mean with a firm?"

It was a phrase to be used about other architects—"a job with a firm." He nodded, not looking at her. "I feel like it. Something steady with a good salary."

"But why?"

"I feel like it!"

"Why do you feel like it? Why do you want to be a martyr?" He said nothing. "Guy, I'm sorry," she said. She came closer to him. "I think I know what it is."

"What do you mean?"

She waited a long while. "Listen, Guy," Anne said softly, "maybe you don't want the wedding as much as you think you do. If you think that's part of it, say it, because I can take that a lot easier than this job idea. If you want to wait, or if you want to break it off entirely, I can bear it."

Her mind was made up, and had been for a long while. He could feel it at the very center of her calmness. He could give her up at this moment. The pain of that would cancel out the pain of guilt.

"What do you say, Guy?"

His tongue pressed the top of his mouth. He thought, She is the sun in my dark forest. But he couldn't say it. He could only say, "I can't say. . . ."

"Well, I want you now more than ever, because you need me now more than ever." She pressed the mint and watercress into his hand. "Do you want to take this to Dad? And have a drink with him. I have to change." She turned and went off toward the house.

Guy drank several mint juleps. Anne's father made them the old-fashioned way, letting the sugar and bourbon and mint stand in a dozen glasses all day, getting colder and more frosted. Guy could feel the precise degree to which his tension lessened, but it was impossible for him to become drunk.

There was a moment after dusk, on the terrace with Anne, when he suddenly felt a tremendous, joyous longing for her. Then he remembered the house in Alton awaiting them after the wedding, and all the happiness he had known already with Anne rushed back to him. He wanted to protect her, to achieve some impossible goal that would please her. It seemed the most positive, the happiest ambition he had ever known. There was a way out, then, if he could feel like this. It was only a part of himself he had to cope with, not his whole self, not Bruno, or his work. He had merely to crush the other part of himself, and live in the self he was now.

8

BUT there were too many points at which the other self could invade the self he wanted to preserve. The wedding so elaborately prepared for, so festive, so pure with white lace and linen, seemed the worst act of treachery he could commit, and the closer it drew, the more frantically he debated canceling it. Up to the last hour, he wanted simply to flee.

Bob Treacher, a close friend of his from Chicago, was now living in Montreal. Guy telephoned and asked him to be his best man. The Sunday morning of the wedding, walking in slow circles around Bob Treacher in the vestry of the church, Guy clung to his memory of the hospital drawings as to a single last shred of hope, the single proof that he still existed. He had done an excellent job. Bob Treacher, his friend, had praised him. He had proved to himself that he could still create.

"You didn't by any chance bring a bottle?"

Bob jumped up. "I certainly did. It's weighing me down." He set the bottle on the table and waited for Guy to take it. Bob was about forty-five, with the indelible stamp of contented bachelorhood and of complete absorption in his profession. "After you," he prompted Guy. "I want to drink a private toast to Anne. She's very beautiful, Guy."

The door opened, and Peter Wriggs's thin figure slipped in. Guy introduced him to Treacher. Peter, who had grown up with Guy in Metcalf, had come all the way from New Orleans to be at his wedding. There was gray at Peter's temples now, though his lean face still grinned like a sixteen-year-old's. Guy returned his quick embrace, feeling that he moved automatically now, on rails as he had on that Friday night.

"It's time, Guy," Bob said, opening the door.

Guy walked beside him. It was twelve steps to the altar. The accusing faces, Guy thought. They were silent with horror, as the Faulkners had been in the back of the car. When were they going to interfere and stop it all?

"Guy!" somebody whispered.

Six, Guy counted, seven.

"Guy!" Faint and direct, from among the faces. Guy glanced left, followed the gaze of two women who looked over their shoulders, and saw Bruno's face.

Guy looked straight again. Was it Bruno or a vision? The face had been smiling eagerly, the gray eyes sharp as pins. Ten, eleven, he counted. *Twelve steps up, skip seven. . . . You can remember it, it's got a syncopated rhythm.* His scalp tingled. He prayed, Lord, don't let me faint. Better you fainted than married! an inner voice shouted.

He was standing beside Anne, and Bruno was here with them; not an event, not a moment, but a condition. Something that had always been and always would be. Bruno, himself, Anne. And the moving on the tracks. The lifetime of moving on the tracks until death do us part, for that was the punishment.

Faces bobbed and smiled all around him, and Guy felt himself aping them like an idiot. They were in the Sail and Racquet Club. There was a buffet breakfast, and champagne. Then Mrs. Faulkner put an arm around his neck and kissed his cheek, and over her shoulder he saw Bruno thrusting himself through the door with the same smile, the same pinlike eyes that had already found him. Bruno came straight toward him and stopped, rocking on his feet.

"My best—best wishes, Guy. You didn't mind if I looked in, did you? It's a happy occasion!"

"Get out. Get out of here fast."

Bruno's smile faded hesitantly. "I just got back from Capri," he said. He wore a new dark royal-blue gabardine suit with broad lapels. "I just wanted to wish you well."

"Get out," Guy said again. "The door's behind you." He mustn't say any more, he thought. He would lose control.

"Call a truce, Guy. I want to meet the bride."

Guy let himself be drawn away by two middle-aged women, one on either arm. Though he did not see him, he knew that Bruno had retreated, with a hurt, impatient smile, to the buffet table.

"Bearing up, Guy?" Mr. Faulkner took his half-empty glass from his hand. "Let's get something better at the bar."

Guy had half a glassful of Scotch. He talked without knowing what he was saying. He was sure he had said, Stop it all, tell everyone to go. But he hadn't, or Mr. Faulkner wouldn't be roaring with laughter.

Bruno came up to Anne. "I think I met you somewhere before. Are you any relation to Teddy Faulkner?"

Guy watched their hands meet. He had thought he wouldn't be able to bear it, but he was bearing it, without making a move.

"He's my cousin," Anne said with her easy smile.

Bruno nodded. "I played golf with him a couple of times."

Guy felt a hand on his shoulder.

"Got a minute, Guy?" It was Peter Wriggs. "I'd—"

"I haven't." Guy started after Bruno and Anne. He closed his fingers around Anne's left hand.

Bruno sauntered on the other side of her, very erect, very much at ease. "I'm an old friend of Guy's. An old acquaintance." Bruno winked at him behind Anne's head.

"Really? Where'd you two know each other?"

"In school. Old school friends." Bruno grinned. "You know, you're the most beautiful bride I've seen in years, Mrs. Haines. I'm certainly glad to have met you," he said, with emphatic conviction.

"Very glad to have met *you*," Anne replied, smiling.

"I hope I'll be seeing you both. Where're you going to live?"

"In Connecticut," Anne said.

"Nice state, Connecticut," Bruno said with another wink at Guy, and left them with a graceful bow.

"He's a friend of Teddy's?" Guy asked Anne. "Did Teddy invite him?"

"Don't look so worried, darling!" Anne laughed at him. "We'll leave soon."

Guy turned, looking for Bruno, and saw him helping himself to shirred eggs, talking gaily to two young men who smiled at him as if under the spell of a devil.

Then they were on their way out to Montauk Point. One of Anne's relatives had lent them her cottage for their honeymoon. The honeymoon was only three days, because he was to start work at Horton, Horton and Keese, Architects, in less than a month, and he would have to work on the double to get the detailed drawings for the hospital under way before he began.

"Did the man in the blue suit go to college with you?" Anne asked as they drove.

"No, the institute. For a while." But why did he fall in with Bruno's lie?

"Interesting face he has," Anne said.

"Interesting?" Guy asked.

"I don't mean attractive. Just intense."

Guy set his teeth. Intense? Couldn't she see he was insane? Morbidly insane? Couldn't everyone see it?

THE receptionist at Horton, Horton and Keese, Architects, handed him a message that Charles Bruno had called and left his number. It was the Great Neck number.

"Thank you," Guy said, and went on across the lobby.

Suppose the firm kept records of telephone messages. They didn't, but supposed they did. Suppose Bruno dropped in one day.

Guy went into the big skylighted, leather-upholstered lounge and lighted a cigarette. Mainwaring and Williams, two of the firm's first-string architects, sat in big leather armchairs, reading company reports. Guy felt their eyes on him as he stared out the window.

They were always watching him, because he was supposed to be something special—a genius, the junior Horton had assured everyone. So what was he doing here? He might be broker than everybody thought, of course, and he had just gotten married, but quite apart from that and from the Bronx hospital, he was obviously nervous. Guy gazed down onto the dirty jumble of Manhattan roofs and streets. When he turned around, Mainwaring dropped his eyes like a schoolboy.

Guy spent the morning dawdling over a job that he had been on for several days. Take your time, they told him. All he had to do was give the client what he wanted and sign his name to it. This job was a department store for an opulent little community in Westchester, and the client wanted something like an old mansion, in keeping with the town, only sort of modern, too, see? And he had asked especially for Guy Daniel Haines. Guy could have tossed it off, but the fact it was really going to be a department store kept intruding certain functional demands. He erased and sharpened pencils all morning, and figured it would take him well into next week before he had even a rough idea to show the client.

"CHARLEY Bruno's coming tonight, too," Anne called that evening from the kitchen.

"What?" Guy had come to the doorway.

"Isn't that his name? The young man we saw at the wedding." Anne was cutting chives on a wooden board.

"You invited him?"

"He seems to have heard about the housewarming, so he called up and sort of invited himself," Anne replied, so casually that a wild suspicion she might be testing him sent a faint chill up his spine. "Do you mind his coming, Guy?"

"Not at all, but he's no friend of mine, you know." How could he stop him?

"You do mind," Anne said with a smile.

"I think he's sort of a bounder, that's all."

"It's bad luck to turn anyone away from a housewarming. Don't you know that?"

Bruno's eyes were bloodshot when he arrived. He stepped down into the brick-red and forest-green living room as if he lived there, Guy thought as he introduced him around the room. Bruno focused a grinning, excited expression on Guy and Anne.

"How's every little thing?" he asked Guy after he had gotten himself a drink.

"Fine. Very fine." Guy was determined to be calm, even if he had to anesthetize himself. He had already had two or three straight shots in the kitchen. But he found himself walking away, retreating toward the perpendicular spiral stairway in the corner of the living room.

He ran upstairs and into the bedroom, to be alone for a few minutes, just to get his bearings.

Bruno and Anne were on the right-angled sofa by the fireplace when he came down. The glass Bruno wobbled casually on the sofa back had made dark green splotches on the cloth.

"He's telling me all about Capri, Guy." Anne looked up at him. "I've always wanted us to go there."

"The thing to do is to take a whole house," Bruno went on, ignoring Guy, "take a castle, the bigger the better. My mother and I lived in a castle so big we never walked to the other end of it."

Deeply conscious of Bruno's avid, shyly flirtatious gaze at Anne, Guy busied himself with a cigarette.

"Guy and I once talked about traveling," Bruno's voice said distinctly.

Guy jabbed his cigarette into an ashtray. "How about seeing our game room?" he said to Bruno.

"Sure." Bruno got up. "What kind of games you play?"

Guy pushed him into a small room lined with red and closed the door behind them. "What's the idea of telling everyone we're old friends?"

"Didn't tell everyone. I told Anne."

"What's the idea of telling her or anyone? What's the idea of coming here?"

"Quiet, Guy! Sh—sh—sh-h-h!" Bruno swung his drink casually in one hand.

"The police are still watching your friends, aren't they?"

"Not enough to worry me."

"Get out. Get out now." His voice shook with his effort to control it.

Bruno looked at him and sighed. "I think Anne's beautiful," he remarked pleasantly.

"If I see you talking with her again, I'll kill you."

Bruno's smile went slack, then came back even broader. "Is that a threat, Guy?"

"That's a promise."

Half an hour later Bruno passed out behind the sofa where he and Anne had been sitting. He looked extremely long on the floor, and his head tiny on the big hearthstone. Three men

picked him up, but then they didn't know what to do with him.

"Take him . . . I suppose to the guest room," Anne said.

"That's a good omen, Anne." Helen Heyburn laughed. "Somebody's supposed to stay overnight at every housewarming, you know. First guest!"

Guy climbed the steps to the studio and closed the door. On his worktable lay the unfinished sketch of the cockeyed department store that conscience had made him take home to complete that weekend. The familiar lines, blurred now with drinking, almost made him sick. He took a blank sheet of paper and began to draw the building they wanted.

HE KNEW exactly what they wanted for their department store, and when the drawings were finished they were accepted and highly praised, first by the Hortons and then by the client. Guy rewarded himself by spending the rest of the day in his office thumbing through a morocco-bound copy of Sir Thomas Browne's meditations that he had just bought to give Anne on her birthday. What atrocity would he be asked to do next? he wondered. Another thing like the department store would be unbearable. He got up from the drawing table, went to his typewriter, and began his letter of resignation.

Anne insisted they go out and celebrate that evening. She was so glad about his resignation, so overflowing with gladness that Guy felt his own spirits lifting a little, uncertainly, as a kite tries to lift itself from the ground on a still day.

"And Guy, can't we make the cruise now?" she asked as they came down into the living room.

Anne still had her heart set on the cruise down the coast in their boat, *India*, the honeymoon trip they had put off. Guy had intended to give all his time to the drafting offices that were working on his hospital drawings, but he couldn't refuse Anne now.

"How soon do you think we can leave? Five days? A week?"

"Maybe five days."

"Oh, I just remembered." She sighed. "I've got to stay till the twenty-third. There's a man coming in from California who's interested in all our cotton stuff."

He waited while she pulled the hood of her coat up about her head, amused at the thought of her driving a hard bargain with the man from California next week. Then he saw the long-stemmed orange flowers on the coffee table for the first time. "Where'd these come from?" he asked.

"Charley Bruno. With a note apologizing for passing out Friday night." She laughed. "I think it's rather sweet."

Guy stared at them. "What kind are they?"

"African daisies." She held the front door open for him, and they went on out to the car.

She was flattered by the flowers, Guy thought. But her opinion of Bruno, he also knew, had gone down since the night of the party. Guy thought again of how bound up they were now, he and Bruno, by the score of people at the party. The police might investigate him any day.

During the next idle days he was compelled to spend at Horton, Horton and Keese to launch the drawings of the department store interior, he even asked himself whether he could be mentally deranged, if some subtle madness had not taken possession of him. He remembered the week or so after that Friday night, when his safety, his existence, had seemed to hang in a delicate balance that a failure of nerve might upset in a second. Now he felt none of that. Yet he still dreamed of Bruno invading his room. If he woke at dawn, he could still see himself standing in that room with the gun. He still felt that he must, and very soon, find some atonement for what he had done. He felt rather like two people, one of whom could create—and feel in harmony with God when he created—and the other who could murder. "Any kind of person can murder," Bruno had said on the train. At the time Guy had hotly disagreed, but the man who had glanced into the mirror just last night had seen for one instant the murderer, like a secret brother.

And how could he sit at his desk thinking of murder, when in less than ten days he and Anne would be off on their delayed honeymoon on the *India?* Why had he been given Anne, or the power to love her? And had he agreed so readily to the cruise only because he wanted to be free of Bruno for three weeks? Bruno, if he wanted to, could take Anne from him. He had realized that for a long time. Since he had seen them together, since the day of the wedding, the possibility had become a specific terror.

He got up and put on his hat to go out to lunch. He heard the switchboard buzz as he crossed the lobby. Then the girl called to him, "Take it from here if you like, Mr. Haines."

Guy picked up the telephone, knowing it was Bruno, knowing he would agree to Bruno's seeing him sometime today. Bruno asked him to have lunch, and Guy promised to meet him at Mario's Villa d'Este in ten minutes.

Bruno spotted him from the bar and slid off his stool with a grin. "Hi, Guy. I've got a table at the end of this row."

Bruno was wearing his old rust-brown suit. Guy thought of the first time he had followed the long legs down the swaying train to the compartment, but the memory brought no remorse now. He felt, in fact, strangely well-disposed toward Bruno.

Bruno ordered the cocktails and the lunch. He ordered broiled liver for himself—because of his new diet, he said—and eggs Benedict for Guy, because he knew Guy liked them. Waiters scurried zealously. Could it all be a show created and enacted by madmen, he and Bruno the main characters, and the maddest of all?

"Here's to the trip," Bruno said, lifting his glass.

Bruno had spoken to Anne this morning on the telephone, and Anne had mentioned the cruise, he said. Bruno kept telling him, wistfully, how wonderful he thought Anne was.

"She's so pure-looking. You certainly don't see a—a *kind*-looking girl like that very often. You must be awfully happy, Guy." He wanted very much to put his hand over Guy's fist, resting lightly on the edge of the table, just for a moment, as a brother might, but he restrained himself.

"What does she like to do outside of designing? Does she like to cook? Things like that?" Bruno watched Guy pick up his martini and drain it in three swallows. "You know. I just like to know the kind of things you do together. Like take walks or work crossword puzzles."

"We do things like that."

"What do you do in the evenings?"

"Anne sometimes works in the evenings." His mind slid easily, as it never had before with Bruno, to the upstairs studio where he and Anne often worked in the evenings. When she dabbled her paintbrush fast in a glass of water, the sound was like laughter.

"I saw her picture in *Harper's Bazaar* a couple months ago with some other designers. She's pretty good, isn't she?"

"Very good."

"I"—Bruno laid his forearms on the table—"I sure am glad you're happy with her."

Why was he sitting here with Bruno, eating at the same table with him? He wanted to fight Bruno and he wanted to weep. But all at once he felt his curses dissolve in a flood of pity. Bruno did not know how to love, and that was all he needed. Bruno was too lost, too blind to love or to inspire love. It seemed all at once tragic.

"You've never even been in love, Bruno?" Guy watched a restive, unfamiliar expression come into Bruno's eyes.

Bruno signaled for another drink. "No, not really in love, I guess." He moistened his lips. Not only hadn't he ever fallen in love, but he didn't care too much about sleeping with women.

Guy looked at Bruno, and Bruno lowered his eyes. "Do you know the greatest wisdom in the world, Bruno?"

"I know a lot of wisdoms." Bruno smirked. "Which do you mean?"

"That everything has its opposite close beside it."

"Opposites attract?"

"That's too simple. I mean—you invited me to lunch. But it also occurred to me you might have the police waiting for me here."

"F'God's sake, Guy, you're my *friend!*" Bruno said quickly, suddenly frantic. "I like you!"

I like you, I don't hate you, Guy thought. But he could foresee a balance of positive and negative will that would paralyze every action before he began it. He jumped up, and the glasses trembled on the cloth.

Bruno stared at him in terrified surprise. "Guy, what's the matter?" Bruno followed him. "Guy, wait! You don't think I'd do a thing like that, do you? I wouldn't in a million years!"

"Don't touch me!"

"*Guy!*" Bruno was almost crying. On the sidewalk, he shouted, "Not in a million years! Not for a million dollars! Trust me, Guy!"

Guy pushed his hand into Bruno's chest and closed the taxi door. Bruno would not in a million years betray him, he knew. But if everything was as ambiguous as he believed, how could he really be sure?

9

"WHAT's your connection with Mrs. Guy Haines?"

Bruno had expected it. Gerard had his latest charge accounts, including the bill for the flowers he had sent Anne. "Friend. Friend of her husband."

"Oh. Friend?"

"Acquaintance." Bruno shrugged.

"Known him long?"

"Not long." From his horizontal slump in his easy chair, Bruno reached for his lighter.

"How'd you happen to send flowers?"

"Feeling good, I guess. I was going to a party there."

"Do you know him that well?"

Bruno shrugged again. "He was one of the architects we thought of when we were talking about building a house."

"Matt Levine. Let's get back to him." Gerard was leafing through Bruno's address book.

Bruno sighed. Skipping Guy, maybe because he was out of town, maybe just skipping him. Now Matt Levine—they didn't come any shadier, and he might be useful, without realizing it.

He had seen a lot of Matt before the murder. "What about him?"

"How is it you saw him the twenty-fourth, twenty-eighth, and thirtieth of April, the second, fifth, sixth, seventh of March, and two days before the murder?"

"Did I?" He smiled. "He was interested in buying my car."

"And you were interested in selling it? Why, because you thought you'd get a new one soon?"

"Wanted to sell it to get a little car."

Gerard smiled. "What was the matter? Couldn't you two come to terms?"

"About the car?"

"Charles," Gerard said patiently.

"I'm not saying anything." Bruno looked at his bitten nails, and thought again how well Matt matched Herbert's description of the murderer.

BAREFOOT, in white duck trousers, Guy sat cross-legged on the *India*'s forward deck. Long Island had just come in sight. The gently rolling movement of the yacht rocked him pleasantly and familiarly, like something he had always known. The day he had last seen Bruno, in the restaurant, seemed a day of madness. Surely he had been going insane.

The three weeks at sea had given Guy a peace and resignation that a month ago he would have declared foreign to him. He had come to feel that his atonement, whatever it might be, was a part of his destiny, and, like the rest of his destiny, would find him without his seeking. He had always trusted his sense of destiny. As a boy he had known that he would create famous buildings, that his name would take its proper place in architecture, and finally—it had always seemed to him the crowning achievement—that he would build a bridge. It would be a white bridge with a span like an angel's wing, he had thought as a boy.

It was a kind of arrogance, perhaps, to believe so in one's destiny. The murder that had seemed an outrageous departure, a sin against himself, he believed now might have been a part of his destiny, too. And if it were so, he would be given a way to make his atonement, and given the strength to make it. And if death by law overtook him first, he would be given the strength to meet that also.

He turned so that he could see Anne as she leaned against the mainmast. There was a faint smile on her lips as she gazed down at him, a half-repressed, prideful smile like that of a mother, Guy thought, who had brought her child safely through an illness. He and Anne had never been closer, their lives never more like one harmonious life, than during these three weeks at sea, and he marveled that she could be his.

BRUNO telephoned a few evenings later. He was in the neighborhood, he said, and wanted to come by. He sounded very sober, and a little dejected.

Guy told him no. He told him calmly and firmly that neither he nor Anne wanted to see him again.

Guy sounded so cold, Bruno could not bring himself to tell him that Gerard had gotten his name, that he might be interviewed, or that he himself intended to see Guy only secretly from now on—no more parties or even lunches—if Guy would only let him.

"Okay," Bruno said mutedly, and hung up.

Then the telephone rang again. Frowning, Guy put out the cigarette he had just lighted, and answered it.

"Hello. This is Arthur Gerard of the Confidential Detective Bureau." Gerard asked if he could come over.

Guy went upstairs to tell Anne.

"A private detective?" Anne asked, surprised. "What's it about?"

Guy hesitated an instant. There were so many, many places where he might hesitate too long! Damn Bruno! Damn him for dogging him! "I don't know."

Gerard arrived promptly. He fairly bowed over Anne's hand, and made polite conversation about the house. Guy stared at him in some astonishment. Gerard looked dull, tired, and vaguely untidy. Then, as Gerard settled himself with a cigar and a drink,

Guy caught the shrewdness in the light hazel eyes and the energy in the chunky hands. Guy felt uneasy then. Gerard looked unpredictable.

"You're a friend of Charles Bruno, Mr. Haines?"

"Yes. I know him."

"His father was murdered last March, as you probably know, and the murderer has not been found."

"I didn't know that!" Anne said.

Gerard's eyes moved slowly from her back to Guy.

"I didn't know either," said Guy.

"You don't know him that well?"

"I know him very slightly."

"When and where did you meet?"

"At"—Guy glanced at Anne—"the Parker Art Institute, I think around last December."

Gerard regarded him, Guy thought, as if he didn't believe a word of it. Why hadn't Bruno warned him about Gerard? Why hadn't they *settled* on a story?

"And when did you see him again?" Gerard asked finally.

"Well—not until my wedding in June." He felt himself assuming the puzzled expression of a man who does not yet know his inquisitor's object. "We didn't invite him," Guy added.

"He just came?" Gerard looked as if he understood. "But you did invite him to the party you gave in July?"

"He called up," Anne told him, "and asked if he could come."

Gerard then asked if Bruno knew about the party through any friends of his who were coming, and Guy said possibly.

Gerard leaned back. "Do you like him?" He smiled.

"Well enough," Anne replied finally, politely.

"All right," Guy said, because Gerard was waiting. "He seems a bit pushing." The right side of his face was in shadow. Guy wondered if Gerard would notice the scar in his eyebrow.

Gerard smiled, but the smile no longer looked genuine, or perhaps it never had. "Sorry to bother you with these questions, Mr. Haines."

Five minutes later he was gone.

"What does it mean?" Anne asked. "Does he suspect Charles?"

Guy bolted the door, then came back. "He might think Charles knows something, because he hated his father so. Or so Charles told me."

"Do you think Charles might know?"

"There's no telling. Is there?" Guy took a cigarette.

"Good Lord." Anne stood looking at the corner of the sofa, as if she still saw Bruno where he had sat the night of the party. She whispered, "Amazing what goes on in people's lives!"

"Listen," Guy said tensely into the receiver. "Listen, Bruno!" Bruno was drunker than Guy had ever heard him, but he was determined to penetrate to the muddled brain. "I told Gerard we met at the Parker Art Institute."

Bruno mumbled something drunken. He wanted to come over. Guy felt it was even more imperative to break completely with Bruno than to arrange a story with him that would tally. What annoyed him most was that he couldn't tell from Bruno's driveling what had happened to him, or even what kind of mood he was in.

Guy was upstairs in the studio with Anne when the door chimes rang. He opened the door only slightly, but Bruno bumped it wide, stumbled across the living room, and collapsed on the sofa. Guy stopped short in front of him, speechless first with anger, then disgust. Bruno's fat, flushed neck bulged over his collar. He seemed more bloated than drunk, as if an edema of death had inflated his entire body. Bruno stared up at him. Guy went to the telephone to call a taxi.

"Guy, who is it?" Anne whispered down the stairway.

"Charles Bruno. He's drunk."

"Not drunk!" Bruno protested suddenly.

Anne came halfway down the stairs and saw him. "Shouldn't we just put him upstairs?"

"I don't want him here." Guy was looking in the telephone book, trying to find a taxi company's number.

"Yes-s-s!" Bruno hissed, like a deflating tire.

Guy turned. Bruno was muttering something, rhythmically.

"What's he saying?" Anne stood closer to Guy.

Guy went to Bruno and caught him by the shirtfront. "Get up and get out!" Then he heard it.

"I'll *tell* her, I'll *tell* her—I'll *tell* her, I'll *tell* her," Bruno chanted. "Don't send me away, I'll *tell* her—I'll—"

Guy released him in abhorrence.

"What's the matter, Guy? What's he saying?"

"I'll put him upstairs," Guy said.

Guy tried with all his strength to get Bruno over his shoulder, but the flaccid deadweight defeated him. Finally Guy stretched him out across the sofa. Bruno slept noiselessly, and Guy sat up watching him.

Bruno awakened about three o'clock in the morning, and had a couple of drinks to steady himself. After a few moments, except for the bloatedness, he looked almost normal. He was very happy at finding himself in Guy's house, and had no recollection of arriving. "I had another round with Gerard." He smiled. "Three days. Been seeing the papers?"

"No."

"You're a fine one, don't even look at the papers!" Bruno said softly. "Gerard's hot on a bum scent. This crook friend of mine, Matt Levine. He doesn't have an alibi for that night. Herbert thinks it could be him. I been talking with all three of them for three days. Matt might take the rap for it. He's got two or three killings on him now. The cops're glad to have him." Bruno shuddered and finished his drink.

Guy wanted to pick up the big ashtray in front of him and smash Bruno's bloated head. He caught Bruno's shoulders hard in both hands. "Will you get out? I swear this is the last time!"

"No," Bruno said quietly, without any movement of resistance, and Guy saw the old indifference to pain, to death, that he had seen when he had fought him in the woods.

Guy put his hands over his own face, and felt its contortion against his palms. "If this Matt gets blamed," he whispered, "I'll tell them the whole story."

"Oh, he won't. They won't have enough. It's a joke, son!" Bruno grinned. "Matt's the right character with the wrong evidence. You're the wrong character with the right evidence."

Guy looked down at him. "There's no reason for you to see me. Why do you do it?"

But Guy knew. Because his life with Anne fascinated Bruno. Because he himself derived something from seeing Bruno, some torture that perversely eased him.

Bruno watched him as if he knew everything that passed through his mind. "I like you, Guy, but remember—they've got a lot more against you than against me. I could wiggle out if you turned me in, but you couldn't. There's the fact Herbert might remember you. And Anne might remember you were acting funny around that time. And the scratches and the scar. And all the little clues they'd shove in front of you, like the revolver, and the glove pieces. . . ." Bruno recited them slowly and fondly, like old memories. "With me against you, you'd crack up, I bet."

A few days later, on the *India*, Guy pulled the revolver from the pocket of his jacket and let it drop over the side. He watched it disappear.

Bruno hesitated about the drink. The bathroom walls had that look of breaking up in little pieces, as if the walls might not really have been there, or he might not really have been here.

"Ma!" But the frightened bleat shamed him, and he drank his drink.

He tiptoed into his mother's room and awakened her with a press of the button by her bed, which signaled to Herbert in the kitchen that she was ready for her breakfast.

"Oh-h," she yawned, then smiled. "And how are you?" She patted his arm. "We're supposed to see that travel agent this afternoon. You'd better feel like going in with me."

Bruno nodded and sat down. It was about the trip they might make to Europe. It had no charm this morning. He might like to go on a trip with Guy.

Herbert knocked on the door and came in.

"Good morning, madam. Good morning, sir," he said, without looking at either of them.

With his chin in his hand, Bruno frowned down at Herbert's polished, turned-out shoes. Herbert's insolence lately was intolerable! Gerard had made him think he was the key to the whole case. Everyone said how brave he was to have chased the murderer. And his father had left Herbert twenty thousand in his will.

"Does madam know if there'll be six or seven for dinner?"

"Oh, dear, I haven't called yet, Herbert, but I think seven."

"Very good, madam."

Rutledge Overbeck II, Bruno thought. He had known his mother would end up inviting him, though she pretended to be doubtful because he would make an odd number. Rutledge Overbeck was madly in love with his mother, or pretending to be.

"You know, I'm dying to make the trip," she said through a bite of toast. She had propped a map up against her coffeepot.

He stood up. "Ma," he said, "I don't feel so hot."

She frowned at him concernedly. "What's the matter, darling?"

He hurried to his own room, feeling he was going to be sick. His mother followed him. "What, Charley? What is it?"

"Feel like I'm dying!"

"Lie down, darling. How about some—some hot tea?"

Bruno tore off his robe, then his pajama top. He was suffocating. He had to pant to breathe. He *did* feel as if he were dying!

She brought him a wet towel. "Is it your stomach?"

"Everything." He kicked off his slippers and went to the window to open it, but it was already open. He turned, sweating. "Ma, maybe I'm dying. You think I'm dying?"

"I'll get you a drink!"

"No, get the doctor!" he shrieked. "Get me a drink, too!" What was it? Not just the shakes. He was too weak to shake. Even his hands were weak and tingly. He held them up. The fingers were curved inward. He couldn't open them. "Ma, somp'n's the matter with my hands! Look, Ma, what is it, what is it?"

"Drink this!"

He heard the bottle chatter on the rim of the glass. He couldn't wait for it. He trotted into the hall, stooped with terror, staring at his limp, curling hands. The two middle fingers on each hand were curving in, almost touching the palms.

"Darling, put your robe on!" she urged.

"Get the doctor!" A robe! She talked about a robe! "Ma, don't let 'em take me away!" He plucked at her as she stood at the telephone. "Lock all the doors! You know what they do?" He spoke fast and confidentially, because the numbness was working up and he knew what was the matter now. He was a case! He was going to be like this all his life! "Know what they do, Ma, they put you in a straitjacket, without a drop, and it'll kill me!"

Bruno screamed. "Massom—" He gasped. He couldn't talk, couldn't move his tongue.

"Charles!"

Bruno gestured toward his mouth with his crazy hands. He trotted to the closet mirror. His face was white, flat around the mouth as if someone had hit him with a board, his lips drawn horribly back from his teeth.

"Drink this!"

Yes, liquor, liquor. He tried to catch it all in his stiff lips. It burned his face and ran down his chest. He motioned for more. He let Herbert and his mother push him onto the bed.

He twisted his mother's dressing gown and nearly pulled her down on top of him. But at least he could hold on to something now. "Dome tehmeh way!" he gasped, and she assured him she wouldn't.

Gerard, he thought. Gerard was working against him, and he would keep on and on and on. Not only Gerard but a whole army of people, checking and snooping, hammering typewriters, running out and running back with more pieces, and one day Gerard might put them together right. One day Gerard might come in and find him like this morning, and ask him and he would tell everything. He had killed someone. They killed *you* for killing someone. Maybe he couldn't cope.

The cruel jab of the hypodermic needle shocked him to sharper consciousness.

The doctor was talking to his mother in a corner of the darkened room. But he felt better. They wouldn't take him away now. He had just been panicky. Cautiously, just under the top of the sheet, he watched his fingers flex. "Guy," he whispered. His tongue was still thick, but he could talk. Then he saw the doctor go out.

"Ma, I don't want to go to Europe!" he said in a monotone as his mother came over.

"All right, darling, we won't go." She sat down gently on the side of the bed, and immediately he felt better.

He touched the shoulder of his mother's dressing gown, but he thought of Rutledge Overbeck at dinner tonight, and let his hand drop. He was sure his mother was having an affair with him. She went to see him too much at his studio, and she stayed too long. It was the first affair, and his father was dead, so why shouldn't she, but why did she have to pick such a jerk? She hadn't improved since the days after his father's death. She was going to be like this, Bruno realized now, stay like this, never be young again the way he liked her.

"Don't look so sad, Mom."

"Darling, will you promise me you'll cut down? The doctor said this is the beginning of the end. This morning was a warning, don't you see? Nature's warning."

He closed his eyes tight shut. If he promised, he would be lying. "Hell, I didn't get the d.t.'s, did I? I never had 'em."

"But this is worse. I talked with the doctor. It's destroying your nerve tissue, he said, and it can kill you. Doesn't that mean anything to you?"

"Yes, Ma."

"Promise me?" She watched his eyelids flutter shut again, and heard him sigh. The tragedy was not this morning, she thought, but years ago when he had taken his first drink by himself. And hard as she tried, she could never discover why it began, because Charley had always been given everything, and both she and Sam had done their best to encourage him in anything he had ever shown interest in. She got up, needing a drink herself.

Bruno opened his eyes tentatively. He felt deliciously heavy with sleep. He turned on his side, smiling. That travel agent wouldn't see them today or any other day. Home was a hell of a lot more comfortable than Europe. And Guy was here.

He went back to sleep and dreamed that Gerard was chasing him through a forest. Gerard already had Guy, who was tied up, his hand bleeding fast.

"Guy!" But his voice sounded feeble.

With all his power, Bruno struggled to sit up. The nightmare slid from his brain like heavy slabs of rock.

Gerard! There he was!

"What's the matter? Bad dream?"

The purply pink hands touched him, and Bruno whirled himself off the bed onto the floor.

Gerard laughed. "Woke you just in time, eh?"

Bruno set his teeth hard enough to break them. He bolted to the bathroom and took a drink with the door wide open. In the mirror his face looked like a battlefield in hell.

"Sorry to intrude, but I found something new," Gerard said in the tense, high-pitched voice that meant he had scored a little victory. "About your friend Guy Haines. The one you were just dreaming about, weren't you?"

He staggered back to bed.

"When did you meet him, Charles? Not last December." Gerard leaned against the chest of drawers, lighting a cigar. "Didn't you meet him about a year and a half ago? Didn't you go with him on the train down to Santa Fe?" Gerard pulled something from under his arm and tossed it on the bed. "Remember that?"

It was Guy's Plato book from Santa Fe. "Sure, I remember it." Bruno pushed it away. "I lost it going to the post office."

"Hotel La Fonda had it right on the shelf. How'd you happen to borrow a book of Plato?"

"I found it on the train." Bruno looked up. "It had Guy's address in it, so I meant to mail it. Found it in the dining car, matter of fact." He looked straight at Gerard, who was watching him with his sharp, steady little eyes.

"When did you meet him, Charley?" Gerard asked again, with the patient air of one questioning a child he knows is lying.

"In December."

"You know about his wife's murder, of course."

"Sure, I read about it. Then I read about him building the Palmyra Club."

"And you thought, how interesting, because you had found a book six months before that belonged to him."

Bruno hesitated. "Yeah."

Gerard grunted, and looked down with a little smile of disgust. "And you made all those calls to Metcalf not even knowing Guy Haines." Gerard picked up the book.

"What calls?"

"Several calls."

"Maybe one when I was tight."

"Several. About what?"

"About the book. And maybe I called when I heard his wife got murdered."

Gerard shook his head. "You called before she was murdered."

"So what? Maybe I did."

"So what? I'll have to ask Mr. Haines. Considering your interest in murder, it's remarkable you didn't call him after the murder, isn't it?"

"I'm sick of murder!" Bruno shouted.

"Oh, I believe it, Charles, I believe it!" Gerard sauntered out, and down the hall toward Mrs. Bruno's room.

A few moments later that morning, Guy walked through the drafting room at Hanson and Knapp, happier than he had felt in weeks. The firm was copying the last of the hospital drawings, the last okays had come through on the building materials, and he had gotten a telegram early that morning from Bob Treacher that made Guy rejoice. Bob had been appointed to an advisory committee of engineers for the new Alberta bridge in Canada, and he wanted Guy to design it.

One of the draftsmen came up to him. "Mr. Haines? There's a telephone call."

Guy hoped it wouldn't be long, because he was to meet Anne for lunch in ten minutes. He took the call in an empty office off the drafting room.

"Hello, Guy? Listen, Gerard found that Plato book. . . . Yeah, in Santa Fe. Now, listen, it doesn't change anything."

Five minutes had passed before Guy was back at the elevators. He had always known the Plato might be found. Not a chance, Bruno had said. Bruno could be wrong. Bruno could be caught, therefore. And somehow it had been incredible, until now.

Momentarily, as he came out into the sunlight, he clenched his fist in frustration. "I found the book on the train, see?" Bruno had said. "If I called you in Metcalf, it was on account of the book. But I didn't meet you until December." The voice more clipped and anxious than Guy had ever heard it before—so alert, so harried, it hardly seemed Bruno's voice. Guy went over the fabrication Bruno had just given him as if it were something that didn't belong to him, as if it were a swatch of material he indifferently considered for a suit. No, there were no holes in it, but it wouldn't necessarily wear. Not if someone remembered seeing them on the train. The waiter, for instance, who had served them in Bruno's compartment.

He tried to slow his breathing, tried to slow his pace. He looked up at the small disk of the autumn sun. He felt suddenly inadequate and dull-witted, helpless. Death had insinuated itself into his brain. It enveloped him. He had breathed its air so long, perhaps, he had grown quite used to it. Well, then, he was not afraid. He squared his shoulders superfluously.

Anne had not arrived when he got to the restaurant. Then he remembered she had said she was going to pick up the snapshots they had made Sunday at the house.

Guy pulled Bob Treacher's telegram from his pocket and read it again and again:

JUST APPOINTED TO ALBERTA COMMITTEE. HAVE RECOMMENDED YOU FOR THE BRIDGE. GET FREE AS SOON AS POSSIBLE. ACCEPTANCE GUARANTEED. LETTER COMING. BOB.

Acceptance guaranteed. Regardless of how he engineered his life, his ability to engineer a bridge was beyond question. Guy sipped his martini thoughtfully, holding the surface perfectly steady.

10

"I've wandered into another case," Gerard murmured pleasantly, gazing at the typewritten report on his desk. He had not looked at Bruno since the young man had come in. "Murder of Guy Haines's first wife. Never been solved."

"Yeah, I know."

"I thought you'd know quite a lot about it. Now tell me everything you know." Gerard settled himself.

Bruno could tell he had gone all the way into it since Monday, when he had the Plato book. "Nothing," Bruno said. "Nobody knows. Do they?"

"What do you think? You must have talked a great deal with Guy about it."

"Not particularly. Not at all. Why?"

"Because murder interests you so much."

"What do you mean, murder interests me so much?"

"Oh, come, Charles, if I didn't know from you, I'd know from your father!" Gerard said in a rare burst of impatience.

Bruno started to reach for a cigarette and stopped. "I talked with Guy about it," he said quietly, respectfully. "He doesn't know anything."

"Who do you think did it? Did you ever think Mr. Haines might have arranged it? Were you interested maybe in how he'd done it and gotten away with it?" At his ease again, Gerard leaned back with his hands behind his head, as if they were talking about the good weather that day.

"Of course I don't think he arranged it," Bruno replied. "You don't seem to realize the caliber of the person you're talking about."

"The only caliber ever worth considering is the gun's, Charles." Gerard picked up his telephone. "Have Mr. Haines come in."

Bruno jumped a little, and Gerard saw it. Bruno told himself he had expected Gerard would do this. So what, so what, so what?

Guy looked nervous, Bruno thought. He spoke to Gerard and nodded to Bruno.

Gerard offered him his remaining chair, a straight one. "My whole purpose in asking you to come down here, Mr. Haines, is to ask you a very simple question. What does Charles talk with you about most of the time?"

Bruno saw Guy's eyebrows draw together with the look of irritation that was exactly appropriate. "He's talked to me now and then about the Palmyra Club," Guy replied.

"And about your wife's murder?"

"Yes."

"How does he talk to you about it?" Gerard asked kindly.

Guy felt his face flush. He glanced at Bruno. "He often asked if I knew who might have done it."

"And do you?"

"No."

"Do you like Charles?" Gerard's fat fingers began playing with a matchbook cover on his desk blotter.

"Yes, I like him," Guy answered puzzledly.

"Hasn't he thrust himself on you many times?"

"I don't think so," Guy said.

"Were you annoyed when he came to your wedding?"

"No."

"Did Charles ever tell you that he hated his father?"

"Yes, he did."

"Did he ever tell you he'd like to kill him?"

"No," he replied in the same matter-of-fact tone.

Gerard got a book from a desk drawer. "Charles meant to mail this to you. Sorry I can't let you have it just now, because I may need it. How did Charles happen to have your book?"

"He told me he found it on the train." Guy studied Gerard's sleepy, enigmatic smile. He had seen a trace of it the night Gerard called at the house, but not like this. This smile was a professional weapon, calculated to inspire dislike. Involuntarily he looked at Bruno.

"And you didn't see each other on the train?"

"No," said Guy.

"I spoke with the waiter who served you two dinner in Charles's compartment."

Guy kept his eyes on Gerard. This was annihilation he was feeling, even as he sat upright, looking straight at Gerard.

"So what?" Bruno said shrilly.

"So I'm interested in why you two"—Gerard wagged his head amusedly—"take such elaborate trouble to say you met months later. Well, the answer is obvious. Within a few days, your wife was killed, Mr. Haines. Within a few months, Charles's father. My guess is that you both knew those murders were going to happen—"

"Oh, crap!" Bruno said.

"And discussed them. Pure speculation, of course. That's assuming you met on the train. Where did you meet, Mr. Haines?"

"Yes," Guy said, "we met on the train."

"And why've you been so afraid of admitting it?" Gerard jabbed one of his freckled fingers at him.

"I don't know," Guy said.

"Wasn't it because Charles told you he would like to have his father killed? And you were uneasy then because you knew?"

Was that Gerard's trump? Guy said slowly, "Charles said nothing about killing his father."

Gerard's eyes slid over in time to catch Bruno's tight smirk of satisfaction.

"Pure speculation, of course," Gerard said.

Guy and Bruno left the building together. Gerard had dismissed them together, and they walked together down the long block toward the little park where the subway kiosks were, and the taxicabs.

"All right, he still hasn't anything," Bruno said. "Any way you look at it, he hasn't anything."

GERARD poked a finger between the bars and waggled it at the little bird that fluttered in terror against the opposite side of the cage. Gerard whistled a single soft note.

From the center of the room, Anne watched him uneasily. She didn't like his having just told her Guy had been lying, then strolling off to frighten the canary.

"Do you have any idea why your husband didn't want to say he met Charles, June before last?"

The month Miriam was murdered, Anne thought again. June before last meant nothing else to her. "It was a difficult month for him," she said. "It was the month his wife died. He might have forgotten almost anything that happened that month."

"Not in this case," Gerard said casually, reseating himself. "No, I think Charles talked with your husband on the train about his father, told him he wanted him dead, maybe even told him how he intended to go about—"

"I can't imagine Guy listening to that," Anne interrupted.

"I don't know," Gerard went on blandly, "I don't know, but I strongly suspect Charles was planning his father's murder and that he may have confided to your husband that night on the train. Charles is that kind of a young man. And I think the kind of man your husband is would have kept quiet about it, tried to avoid Charles from then on. Don't you?"

It would explain a great deal, Anne thought. But it would also make Guy a kind of accomplice. Gerard seemed to want to make Guy an accomplice.

"I'm sure my husband wouldn't have tolerated Charles even to this extent," she said firmly, "if Charles had told him anything like that."

"A very good point. However . . ." Gerard stopped vaguely, as if lost in his own slow thoughts.

Anne stared at the tile cigarette box on the coffee table, and finally took a cigarette.

"Do you think your husband has any suspicion who murdered his wife, Mrs. Haines?"

Anne blew her smoke out defiantly. "I certainly do not."

"How about March of this year?" Gerard asked. "Do you think your husband could have been seeing Charles now and then around the month of March without your knowing about it?"

Anne stood at the bar with her back to Gerard, remembering March, the month Charles's father was killed, remembering Guy's nervousness then. Had that fight been in February or March? And *hadn't* he fought with Charles Bruno?

Of course, she thought, that might explain it: that Guy had known Charles intended to kill his father, and had tried to stop him, had fought with him, in a bar. "He could have, I suppose," she said uncertainly. "I don't know."

"How did your husband seem around the month of March, if you can remember, Mrs. Haines?"

"He was nervous. But I think I know the things he was nervous about."

"What things?"

"His work . . ." Somehow she couldn't grant him a word more than that about Guy. Everything she said, she felt Gerard would incorporate in the misty picture he was composing.

She waited, and Gerard waited, as if he vied with her not to break the silence first.

Finally he tapped out his cigar and said, "If anything does occur to you about that time in regard to Charles, will you be sure and tell me? Call me anytime, during the day or night. There'll be somebody there to take messages." He handed his business card to Anne as he left.

When Guy came in about an hour later, Anne was in the kitchen, tending the casserole that was nearly done in the oven. She saw Guy put his head up, sniffing the air.

"Shrimp," Anne said. "I guess I should open a vent."

"Was Gerard here?"

"Yes. How did you know?"

"Cigars," he said laconically. "What did he want this time?"

"He wanted to know more about Charles Bruno. If you'd said anything to me about suspecting him of anything. And he wanted to know about March."

He stepped toward her, and Anne saw the pupils of his eyes contract suddenly.

"Wanted to know if you suspected Charles was going to have his father killed that month." But Guy only stared at her with his mouth in a familiar straight line.

She moved aside and went into the living room. "It's terrible, isn't it?" she said. "Murder."

Guy followed her. It tortured him to hear her say murder. He wished he could erase every memory of Bruno from her brain.

"You didn't know, did you, Guy—in March?"

"No, Anne."

"Do you believe Charles had his father killed?"

"I don't know. It's possible, but it doesn't concern us."

"That's right. It doesn't concern us. Gerard also said you met Charles, June before last, on the train."

"Yes, I did."

"Well—what does it matter?"

"I don't know."

"Was it because of something Charles said on the train? Is that why you dislike him?"

Guy shoved his hands into his jacket pockets. He wanted a brandy suddenly.

"Listen, Anne," he said quickly. "Bruno told me on the train he wished his father were dead. He didn't mention any plans, he didn't mention any names. I didn't like the way he said it, and after that I didn't like him. I refuse to tell Gerard all that, because I don't know if Bruno had his father killed or not. That's for the police to find out." He felt himself false, totally a lie, and put his hands over his face.

"Guy, I do believe you're doing what you should," Anne's voice said gently.

His face was a lie, his level eyes, the firm mouth, the sensitive hands. "I could use a brandy."

"Wasn't it Charles you fought with in March?" she asked as she stood at the bar.

There was no reason to lie about this also, but he could not stop. "No, Anne." He knew from the quick sidelong glance she gave him that she didn't believe him. She probably thought he had fought with Bruno to stop him. She was probably proud of him! But Anne would not be satisfied with this. He knew she would come back to it and back to it until he told her.

That evening Guy lighted the first fire of the year, the first fire in their new house. Anne lay on the long hearthstone with her head on a sofa pillow. The thin nostalgic chill of autumn was in the air, filling Guy with melancholy and a restless energy. The energy was not buoyant, but underlaid with frenzy and despair, as if his life were winding down and this might be his last spurt. Couldn't Gerard guess it now, knowing that he and Bruno had met on the train? What were they waiting for, Gerard and the police? He had the feeling that Gerard wanted to gather every gram of evidence against them both, then let it fall suddenly upon them and demolish them. But however they demolished him, Guy thought, they would not demolish his buildings.

Anne had fallen asleep. He stared at the smooth curve of her forehead, paled to silver by the fire's light. Then he lowered his lips to her forehead and kissed her, so gently she would not awaken. The ache inside him translated itself into words: I forgive you. He wanted Anne to say it. No one but Anne.

DISTRICT Attorney Phil Howland, immaculate and gaunt, smiled tolerantly through his cigarette smoke. "Why don't you let the kid alone? It was an angle at first, I grant you. We combed through his friends, too. There's nothing, Gerard. And you can't arrest a man on his personality."

Gerard recrossed his legs and allowed himself a complacent smile. This was his hour.

Howland pushed a typewritten sheet to the edge of the desk

with his fingertips. "Twelve new names here, if you're interested. Friends of the late Mr. Samuel Bruno, furnished us by the insurance companies," Howland said in his calm, bored voice.

"You can tear them up," Gerard said.

Howland hid his surprise with a smile, but he couldn't hide the sudden curiosity in his dark, wide eyes. "I suppose you've already got your man. Charles Bruno, of course."

"Of course." Gerard chuckled. "Only I've got him for another murder." He was smoothing out a number of papers, folded in thirds like letters, on his knees.

"Who?"

"Curious? Don't you know?" Gerard smiled with his cigar between his teeth and pulled his chair closer. Howland disliked him, personally as well as professionally, Gerard knew. Howland accused him of not being cooperative with the police. The police had never been cooperative with him, but despite their hindrance Gerard in the last decade had solved an impressive number of cases the police hadn't even been warm on.

Howland got up and leaned against the front of his desk. "But does all this shed any light on the *case?*"

"The trouble with the police force is that it has a single-track mind," Gerard announced. "This case, like many others, simply couldn't have been solved without a double-track mind."

"Who and when?" Howland sighed.

"Ever hear of Guy Haines?"

"Certainly. We questioned him last week."

"His wife. June eleventh of last year in Metcalf, Texas. Strangulation, remember? The police never solved it."

"Charles Bruno?" Howland frowned.

"Did you know that Charles Bruno and Guy Haines were on the same train heading for the Southwest on June first? Ten days before the murder of Haines's wife. Now, what do you deduce from that?"

"You mean they knew each other before last June?"

"No, I mean they met each other on that train. Can you put the rest together? I'm giving you the missing link."

The district attorney smiled faintly. "You're saying Charles Bruno killed Guy Haines's wife?"

"I certainly am." Gerard looked up from his papers. "There's my proof. All you want." He gestured toward his papers, handing them to Howland. "Read from the bottom up."

The last statement, from the Metcalf taxi driver who had driven Charles to the Kingdom of Fun amusement park at Lake Metcalf, had come in this morning. The next papers were signed statements from Hotel La Fonda bellhops, from the barman in the roadhouse where Charles had tried to get a drink of Scotch the night of Miriam Haines's murder, plus telephone bills listing long-distance calls to Metcalf.

"That taxi driver was certainly hard to find," Gerard remarked. "Had to trace him all the way up to Seattle, but once we found him, it didn't take any jostling for him to remember. People don't forget a young man like Charles Bruno."

"So you're saying Charles Bruno is so fond of murder," Howland remarked amusedly, "that he murders the wife of a man he meets on a train the week before? A woman he's never even seen?"

Gerard chuckled again. "My Charles had a plan. Can't you see it? Plain as the nose on your face? And this is only half."

"Slow down, Gerard, you'll work yourself into a heart attack."

"You can't see it. Because you didn't know Charles's personality. You weren't interested in the fact he spends most of his time planning perfect crimes of various sorts."

"All right, what's the rest of your theory?"

"That Guy Haines killed Samuel Bruno."

"Ow!" Howland groaned.

"I haven't finished checking on Guy Haines yet," Gerard said with deliberate ingenuousness. "I want to take it easy, and that's the only reason I'm here, to get you to take it easy with me. I didn't know but what you'd grab Charles, you see, with all your information against him."

Howland smoothed his black mustache. "A man like Guy Haines?" He laughed.

"Against a fellow like Charles? Mind you, I don't say Guy Haines did it of his own free will. He was made to do it for Charles's unsolicited favor of freeing him of his wife. Charles hates women," he remarked in a parenthesis. "That was Charles's plan. Exchange. No clues, you see. No motives. Oh, I can just hear him! But even Charles is human. He was too interested in Guy Haines to leave him alone afterward. And Guy Haines was too frightened to do anything about it. Haines was coerced."

Howland's smile went away momentarily at Gerard's earnestness. The story had the barest possibility, but still a possibility. "Hmm-m . . . and how do you propose to prove this?"

"Oh, he may yet confess. It's wearing him down. But otherwise, confront Charles with the facts."

"Well"—Howland let his breath out in a long sigh—"what do you want me to do, work over your little boy with this stuff? Think he'll break down and tell all about his brilliant plan with Guy Haines, architect?"

"No, I don't want him worked over. I like clean jobs. I want a few days more or maybe weeks to finish checking on Haines, then I'll confront them both. I'm going to Iowa for a vacation, and I'm going to let Charles know it." Gerard's face lighted with a big smile. "Incidentally"—he picked up his hat and shook it at Howland—"you couldn't crack Charles with all that, but I could crack Guy Haines with what I've got this minute."

"Mind telling me what you've got that'll crack Guy Haines?"

"The man is tortured with guilt," Gerard said, and went out.

11

"You know, in the whole world," Bruno said, "I wouldn't want to be anywhere else but here tonight, Anne." He leaned his elbow jauntily on the high mantel.

"Very nice of you to say so." Anne smiled and set the plate of melted cheese and anchovy canapés on the sawbuck table. "Have one of these while they're hot."

Bruno took one, though he knew he wouldn't be able to get it down. The table looked beautiful, set for two with gray linen and big gray plates. Gerard was off on a vacation. They had beaten him, Guy and he. He might have tried to kiss Anne, he thought, if she didn't belong to Guy. He took great pride in being a perfect gentleman with Anne. "So Guy thinks he's going to like it up there?" Bruno asked. Guy was in Canada now, working on the big Alberta bridge. "I'm glad all this dumb questioning is over, so he won't have to worry about it when he's working. You can imagine how I feel. Like celebrating!" He laughed, mainly at his understatement.

Anne stared at his tall restless figure by the mantel, and wondered if Guy, despite his hatred, felt the same fascination she did. She still didn't know, though, whether Charles Bruno would have been capable of arranging his father's murder, and she had spent the whole day with him in order to make up her mind. He slid away from certain questions with joking answers; he was serious and careful about answering others.

"Why didn't you want to tell anyone you'd met Guy on the train?" Anne asked.

"I guess because it looked bad. Miriam killed so soon after, you know. I think it was quite nice of Guy at the inquest on Miriam not to drag in anybody he'd just met by accident."

"But that didn't have anything to do with the questioning about your father's death."

"Of course not. But Gerard doesn't pay any attention to logic."

Anne frowned. She couldn't believe that Guy would have fallen in with Charles's story simply because telling the truth would have looked bad, or even because Charles had told him on the train that he hated his father. There was a great deal she had to ask Guy. About Charles's hostility to Miriam, for instance, though he had never seen her. Anne went into the kitchen.

Bruno strolled to the front window with his drink, and watched the red and green lights of a plane in the black sky. He wished Guy might be on that plane, coming home. Bruno had driven by this morning instead of telephoning, and Anne had invited him to spend the day and stay for dinner. She was terribly sweet to him, and he really loved her! He spun on his heel, and saw her coming back with their plates.

"Guy's very fond of you, you know," Anne said during dinner.

Bruno looked at her, having already forgotten what they had been talking about. "There's *nothing* I wouldn't do for him! I feel a tremendous tie with him, like a brother. I guess because everything started happening to him just after we met each other on the train."

His heart was pounding. The stuffed potato was beautiful, but he didn't dare eat another mouthful. Nor touch the red wine. He had an impulse to try to spend the night. "You're expecting Guy back this weekend?" he asked.

"So he said." Anne ate her green salad thoughtfully. "I imagine we'll go for a sail."

"I'd like a sail. If you wouldn't mind company."

"Come along." The moment she said it she found herself thinking, Charles could probably do anything, atrocious things, and fool everyone with the same ingratiating naïveté, the same shy smile. Yes, he could have arranged his father's murder. And he would have enjoyed killing Miriam, Anne thought. A fragile suspicion that he might have killed her crossed her mind, like a dry leaf blown by the wind. She might be sitting opposite a murderer. She felt a little pluck of terror as she got up, a bit too abruptly, as if she were fleeing, and removed the dinner plates.

"So you went on to Santa Fe after you met Guy?" she almost stammered, from the kitchen.

"Uh-huh." Bruno was deep in the big green armchair.

"Have you ever been to Metcalf?" she asked.

"No," Bruno replied. "No, I always wanted to. Have you?"

Anne came back into the living room and sat on the sofa without replying. She tipped her head back so the curve of her throat above the tiny ruffled collar of her dress was the lightest thing about her. Bruno sipped his coffee. *Anne is like light to me*, Bruno remembered Guy once saying. If he could strangle Anne, too, then Guy and he could really be together. Bruno frowned at himself, then laughed and stood up.

"What's funny?"

"Just thinking." He smiled. "I was thinking of what Guy says about the doubleness of everything. You know, the positive and negative, side by side. Every decision has a reason against it." He noticed suddenly he was breathing hard.

"You mean two sides to everything?"

"Oh, no, that's too simple! People, feelings, everything! Double! Two people in each person. There's also a person exactly the opposite of you, like the unseen part of you, somewhere in the world, and he waits in ambush." It thrilled him to recall Guy's thoughts, though he hadn't liked hearing them, he remembered, because Guy had said the two people were mortal enemies, too, and Guy had meant him and himself.

Anne looked up slowly. It sounded so like Guy, yet he had never said it to her. Anne thought of the unsigned letter last spring. Charles must have written it. Guy must have meant Charles when he talked of ambush. There was no one else besides Charles to whom Guy reacted so violently. Surely it was Charles who alternated hatred with devotion.

She loathed him. She knew all that Guy felt now about him. But she didn't yet know why Guy tolerated him.

"These things come out in actions," Bruno went on. "Take, for instance, murderers. Punishing them in the law courts won't make them any better, Guy says. Every man is his own law court and punishes himself enough." He was so tight, he could hardly see her face now, but he wanted to tell her everything that he and Guy had ever talked about, right up to the last little secret that he couldn't tell her.

"What's the matter?" he asked suddenly.

Anne laid her cold fingers against her forehead. "Nothing."

Bruno fixed her a drink at the bar Guy had built into the side of the fireplace. Bruno wanted a bar just like it for his own house.

"Where did Guy get those scratches on his face last March?"

"What scratches? I didn't see them."

"He fought with you, didn't he?"

"No!" Bruno laughed. He sat down. "Where did he say he got

the scratches? I didn't see him anyway in March. I was out of town then." He stood up. He suddenly didn't feel well. Suppose he was in for another attack now. He mustn't let Anne see *that*. "I'd better go soon," he murmured.

"What's the matter? You're not well? You're a little pale."

She wasn't sympathetic. He could tell by her voice. What woman ever was, except his mother? "Thank you very much, Anne, for—for the day."

She handed him his coat, and he stumbled out the door, gritting his teeth as he started the long walk toward his car at the curb.

The house was dark when Guy came home a few hours later. He prowled the living room, saw the empty coffee cups, the depression in a small pillow on the sofa. There was a peculiar disorder that could only have been created by Bruno.

What did Anne mean by doing this to him? Now of all times, when half of himself was in Canada and the other half here, caught in the tightening grip of Bruno. There was no enduring much longer.

He ran up to the bedroom and knelt beside Anne and kissed her awake, frightenedly, harshly, until he felt her arms close around him. He buried his face in the soft muss of the sheets over her breast.

"I've missed you," were the first words Anne said.

Guy got up and stood near the foot of the bed with his hands clenched in his pockets. "I'll be here three days. Have you really missed me?" he asked tensely.

Anne slid up a few inches in the bed. "Why do you look at me like that?"

Guy did not answer.

"I've seen him only once, Guy. He was here this evening."

"Why did you see him at all?"

"Because . . ." Her cheeks flushed. He had never spoken to her like this before. "Because he came by—"

"He always comes by. He always telephones."

"Why does it bother you so?"

"Because he's dangerous. He's half insane."

"I don't think that's the reason he bothers you," Anne said in the same slow, steady voice. "I don't know why you defend him, Guy. I don't know why you don't admit he's the one who wrote that letter to me and the one who almost drove you insane in March."

Guy stiffened with guilty defensiveness. Bruno hadn't admitted sending the letter to Anne, he knew. It was just that Anne, like Gerard, with different facts, was putting pieces together. Gerard had quit, but Anne would never quit. However, she didn't have the picture yet. It would take time, a little more time, and a little more time to torture him!

"Tell me, Guy," Anne said quietly. "Tell me, will you?"

"I shall tell you," he replied, hearing himself say it now, believing himself. He *would* tell Anne.

"Guy, come here." She held up her arms for him, and he sat beside her, slipped his arms around her, and held her tight against him. "There's going to be a baby," she said. "Let's be happy. Will you be happy, Guy?"

He looked at her, feeling suddenly like laughing for happiness, for surprise, for her shyness. "A baby!" he whispered. "When, Anne?"

"Oh—not for ages. I guess in May. What'll we do tomorrow?"

"We'll go out on the boat. If it's not too rough." And the foolish, conspiratorial note in his voice made him laugh out loud now.

"Oh, Guy! It's so good to hear you laugh!"

SATURDAY morning Bob Treacher and Guy were finishing their late breakfast in the living room. Bob had also flown down to New York, and Guy had invited him for the weekend. They were talking of Alberta and the men they worked with on the committee. It was a fresh, sunny November morning, and when Anne got back from her marketing, they were going to take the car to the Long Island marina and go for a sail. Guy felt a boyish, holiday delight in having Bob with him. Bob symbolized Canada and the work there, where Bruno could not follow. And the secret of the coming child gave him a sense of impartial benevolence, of magical advantage.

Just as Anne came in the door, the telephone rang. Guy stood up, but Anne answered it. Vaguely he thought, Bruno always knows exactly when to call. Then he listened incredulously to the talk drifting toward the sail that afternoon.

"Come along, then," Anne said. "Oh, I suppose some beer would be nice if you must bring something."

Guy saw Bob staring at him quizzically.

"What's up?" Bob asked.

"Nothing." Guy sat down again.

"That was Charles. You don't mind too much if he comes, do you, Guy?" Anne walked briskly across the room with her bag of groceries. "He said Thursday he'd like to come sailing if we went, and I practically invited him."

"I don't mind," Guy said, still looking at her. He knew she wanted to see them together again. He felt a rising resentment, and said quickly to himself, She doesn't realize, she can't realize, and it's all your own fault anyway for the hopeless muddle you've made. So he put the resentment down and determined to keep himself under control all day.

They stopped for Anne's friend Helen Heyburn in Manhattan, then crossed the Triboro Bridge to Long Island. The autumn sunlight had a frozen clarity at the shore: it lay thin on the pale beach, and sparkled nervously on the choppy water. The *India* was like an iceberg at anchor. As Guy rounded the corner of the parking lot, he saw Bruno standing under the shed of the dockhouse, saw the familiar anxiety of his waiting figure.

Bruno picked up the sack of beer and strolled toward the car. "Hello, Guy. Thought I'd try and see you while I could." He glanced at Anne for help.

"Nice to see you!" Anne said. "This is Mr. Treacher. Mr. Bruno. And you know Helen, Mr. Bruno."

Bruno greeted them with a shy smile and handed Anne the sack of beer.

They had to row out from the dock. Guy pulled in long deep

strokes, and Bruno, beside him on the center thwart, matched him carefully. Guy could feel Bruno's erratic excitement mounting as they drew near the *India*. Bruno's hat blew off twice, and at last he stood up and spun it spectacularly into the sea.

"I hate hats anyway!" he said, with a glance at Guy.

When they boarded the *India*, it was too gusty to raise sail. So they entered Long Island Sound under engine power, with Bob steering.

"Here's to Guy!" Bruno shouted. "Congratulations, salutations!" He brought out a flask and presented it to Anne. "Napoleon brandy. Five-star."

Anne declined, but Helen, who was already feeling the cold, drank some, and so did Bob. Under the tarpaulin, Guy held Anne's mittened hand. He could not bear to look at Helen, who was encouraging Bruno, nor at Bob's polite, vaguely embarrassed smile as he faced front at the wheel.

"Anybody know 'Foggy, Foggy Dew'?" Bruno asked, brushing spray fussily off a sleeve. His pull from the flask had pushed him over the line into drunkenness.

Bruno was nonplussed because no one wanted any more of his specially selected liquor, and because no one wanted to sing. He wanted to sing or shout or do *something*. He tried to look at the pennant at the top of the mast, but the mast's swaying made him dizzy.

"Someday Guy and I are going to circle the world like a plastic ball, and tie it up in a ribbon!" he announced, but no one paid any attention. Guy was explaining something about the motor to Bob. Bruno noticed that the creases in Guy's forehead looked deeper, his eyes as sad as ever.

"Don't you realize anything!" Bruno shook Guy's arm. "You have to be so serious *today?*"

Helen started to say something about Guy's always being serious, and Bruno roared her down and produced the flask again.

But still Anne did not want any, and neither did Guy.

"I brought it specially for you, Guy. I thought you'd like it," Bruno said, hurt.

"Have some, Guy," Anne said.

Guy took it and drank a little.

"To Guy! Genius, friend, and partner!" Bruno said, and drank after him. "Guy *is* a genius. Do you all realize that?"

"Certainly," said Bob agreeably.

"As you're an old friend of Guy's," Bruno raised his flask, "I salute you also!"

"Thank you. A very old friend. One of the oldest."

Bruno frowned. "I've known Guy all his life," he said softly, menacingly. "Ask him."

Guy felt Anne wriggle her hand from his tight hold. He saw Bob chuckling, not knowing what to make of it.

"Go on and tell him I'm your closest friend, Guy."

"Yes," Guy said.

He was conscious of Anne's small, tense smile and of her silence. Didn't she know everything now? Wasn't she merely waiting for him and Bruno to put it into words?

"Sure I'm mad!" Bruno shouted to Helen, who was inching away from him on the seat. "Mad enough to take on the whole world and whip it!" He laughed and struggled onto one knee.

"Charles, calm *down!*" Anne told him, but she still smiled.

"Awright, I'll sit down, but Guy, you disappoint me. You disappoint me horribly!" Bruno shook his empty flask, then lobbed it overboard.

"He's crying," Helen said.

Bruno stood up and stepped out of the cockpit onto the deck. He wanted to take a long walk away from all of them.

"Where's he going?" Anne asked.

"Let him go," Guy murmured, trying to light a cigarette.

Then there was a splash, and Guy knew Bruno had fallen overboard. Guy was out of the cockpit before any of them spoke.

He ran to the stern, trying to get his overcoat off. He felt his arms pinned behind him and, turning, hit Bob in the face with his fist and flung himself off the deck. He leaped high and far out into the water. Bruno's head was incredibly far away, like a mossy, half-submerged rock.

"You can't reach him!" Bob's voice blared, cut off by a burst of water against his ear.

"Guy!" Bruno called from the sea, a wail of dying.

Guy cursed. He could reach him. At the tenth stroke, he leaped up again. "Bruno!" But he couldn't see him now.

"There, Guy!" Anne pointed from the stern of the *India*.

Guy couldn't see him, but he threshed toward the memory of Bruno's head, and went down at the place, groping with his arms wide, the farthest tips of his fingers searching. A wave bashed the side of his head. He cursed the gigantic, ugly body of the sea. Where was his friend, his brother?

He went down again, deep as he could, but now there seemed nothing but a silent gray vacuum filling all space, in which he was only a tiny point of consciousness. He stretched his eyes desperately. The grayness became a brown, ridged floor.

"Did you find him?" he blurted later, when they got him back aboard.

"Lie still, Guy," Bob's voice said.

"He went down, Guy," Anne said. "We saw him."

Guy closed his eyes and wept.

He was aware that, one by one, they all went out of the bunk-room and left him, even Anne.

12

CAREFULLY, so as not to awaken Anne, Guy got out of bed and went downstairs to the living room. He drew the drapes together and turned on the lights, though there was no shutting out the dawn that slithered now under the venetian blinds. Bruno, he now realized, had borne half his guilt. If it had been almost unbearable before, how would he bear it alone? He knew that he couldn't.

He envied Bruno for having died so suddenly, so quietly, so violently, and so young. And so easily, as Bruno had always done everything. A tremor passed through him. He sat rigidly in the armchair, his body under the thin pajamas hard and tense. Then slowly he got up and went upstairs to the studio. He looked at the big sleek-surfaced sheets of drawing paper on his worktable. Then he sat down and began to write, slowly at first, then more and more rapidly. He wrote of Miriam and of the train, the telephone calls, of Bruno in Metcalf, of the letters, the gun, and his dissolution, and of the Friday night. His writing blackened three of the big sheets.

He folded the sheets, put them into an oversized envelope, and sealed it. For a long while he stared at the envelope, savoring its partial relief. This was for Anne. Anne would touch this envelope. Her hands would hold the sheets of paper, and her eyes would read every word.

Guy put his palms up to his own hot, aching eyes. The hours of writing had tired him almost to a point of sleepiness. His thoughts drifted, resting on the people he had been writing about—Bruno, Miriam, Owen Markman, Samuel Bruno, Arthur Gerard, Anne—the people and the names danced around the edge of his mind. *Miriam.* Oddly, she was more a person to him now than ever before. She was not worth a great deal as a person, he thought, by Anne's standards or by anyone's. But she had been a human being.

Neither had Samuel Bruno been worth a great deal—a grim, greedy maker of money, hated by his son, unloved by his wife. Who had really loved him? Who had really been hurt by either Miriam's death or Samuel Bruno's?

Guy remembered Miriam's brother on the witness stand at the inquest, the small eyes that had held only malicious, brutal hatred, not grief. And her mother, not caring where the blame fell as long as it fell on someone, unbroken, unsoftened by grief. Was there any purpose in going to see them and giving them a target for their hatred? Would it make them feel any better? Or him? He couldn't see that it would. If anyone had really loved Miriam, it was Owen Markman.

Guy took his hands down from his eyes. He hadn't thought of Owen at all until he wrote the letter. Owen had been a dim figure in the background. But Owen must have loved her. He had been going to marry her. She had been carrying his child. Suppose Owen had staked all his happiness on Miriam.

"Owen," Guy said.

Slowly he stood up. An idea was taking form in his mind even as he tried to weigh his memories of the long, dark face and tall, slouching figure that was Owen Markman. He would go and see Markman and tell him everything. If he owed it to anyone, he owed it to Markman. Let Markman kill him if he would, call the police in, anything. Suddenly it was an urgent necessity. Of course. It was the only step and the next step. After that, after his personal debt, he would shoulder whatever the law put upon him. He would be ready then. He could even catch a plane this afternoon, if he was lucky. Where was it? Houston. If Owen was still there. He mustn't let Anne take him to the airport. She must think he was going to Canada as planned. He didn't want Anne to know yet. The appointment with Owen was more urgent. It seemed to transform him. Or perhaps it was like the shedding of an old and worn-out coat. He felt naked now, but not afraid any longer.

On the plane for Houston, Guy felt miserable and nervous, and yet he was convinced that what he was doing was necessary.

Gerard had been at the police station to hear the questioning on Bruno's death. He had flown back from Iowa, he said. It was too bad, Charles's end, but Charles had never been cautious about anything. It was too bad it had had to happen on Guy's boat. Guy had been able to answer the questions without any emotion whatever. He didn't want Gerard to follow him down to Texas. To be doubly safe, he had not even canceled his ticket on the plane to Canada, which had left earlier in the afternoon.

The thick letter in his inside pocket crackled as he bent over the papers in his lap. They were sectional reports of the Alberta work, which Bob had given him.

He found a page from an English architectural magazine torn out and stuck between the mimeographed sheets. Bob had circled a paragraph in red pencil:

Guy Daniel Haines is the most significant architect yet to emerge from the American Southwest. With his first independent work at the age of twenty-seven, a simple, two-story building which has become famous as The Pittsburgh Store, Haines set forth principles of grace and function to which he has steadfastly held, and through which his art has grown to its present stature.

An asterisked paragraph at the bottom of the page said:

Since the writing of this article, Mr. Haines has been appointed a member of the Advisory Committee of the Alberta bridge project in Canada. Bridges have always interested him, he says. He estimates that this work will occupy him happily for the next three years.

"Happily." How had they happened to use such a word?

A clock was striking nine as Guy's taxi crossed the main street of Houston. Guy had found Owen Markman's name in a telephone book at the airport, had checked his bags and gotten into a taxi. It won't be so simple, he thought. You can't just arrive at nine in the evening and expect to find him at home, and alone, and willing to listen to a stranger.

"Pull up at this hotel," Guy said.

He got out and reserved a room.

Owen Markman was not living at the address in Cleburne Street, but a man on the steps of the small apartment building told him that he might find Markman at a certain café in the center of town.

Finally Guy found him in a drugstore, sitting at the counter with two women whom he did not introduce. Owen Markman simply slid off his stool and stood up straight, his brown eyes a little wide. His long face looked heavier and less handsome than Guy remembered it.

"You remember me," Guy said.

"Reckon I do."

"Would you mind if I had a talk with you? Just for a little

while." Guy looked around him. The best thing was to invite him to his hotel room, he supposed. "I've got a room here at the Rice Hotel."

Markman looked Guy slowly up and down once more, and after a long silence said, "All right."

Passing the cashier's desk, Guy saw the shelves of liquor bottles. It might be hospitable to offer Markman a drink. "Do you like Scotch?"

Markman loosened up a bit as Guy bought it. "Coke's fine, but it tastes better with a little something in it."

Guy bought a carton of Coca-Cola, too.

They rode to the hotel in silence, went up in the elevator, and entered the room in silence. How would he begin? Guy wondered. There were a dozen beginnings. Guy discarded them all.

Owen sat down in the armchair, and then divided his time between eyeing Guy suspiciously and savoring the tall glass of Scotch and Coca-Cola.

Guy began stammeringly, "What—"

"What?" asked Owen.

"What would you do if you knew who murdered Miriam?"

Markman's foot thudded down to the floor, and he sat up. His frowning brows made a black, intense line above his eyes. "Did you?"

"No, but I know the man who did."

"Who?"

What was Owen feeling as he sat there frowning? Guy wondered. Hatred? Resentment? Anger?

"I know, and so will the police very soon." Guy hesitated. "It was a man from New York whose name was Charles Bruno. He died yesterday. He was drowned."

Owen sat back a little. He took a sip of his drink. "How do you know? Confessed?"

"I know. I've known for some time. That's why I've felt it was my fault. For not betraying him." He moistened his lips. It was difficult every syllable of the way. "That's why I blame myself. I—" Owen's shrug stopped him. He watched Owen finish his drink; then automatically Guy went and mixed another for him. "That's why I blame myself," he repeated. "I have to tell you the circumstances. You see, I met Charles Bruno on a train, coming down to Metcalf. In June, just before Miriam was killed. I was coming down to get my divorce." He had a huskiness in his throat he could not get rid of. Guy studied Owen's long, dark, attentive face. "And . . ."

"Yeah," Owen prompted.

"I told him Miriam's name. I told him I hated her. Bruno had an idea for a murder. A double murder."

"Jesus!" Owen whispered.

Guy clenched his hands. "My mistake was in speaking to him. My mistake was in telling a stranger my private business."

"He told you he was going to kill her?"

"No, of course not. It was an idea he had. He was insane. I told him to shut up and to go to hell. I got rid of him!"

"You didn't tell him to do it."

"No. He didn't say he was going to do it."

"Why don't you have a straight shot? Why don't you sit down?" Owen's slow, rasping voice made the room steady again.

He didn't want to sit down, and he didn't want to drink. He had drunk Scotch like this in Bruno's compartment. This was the end and he didn't want it to be like the beginning. He touched the glass of Scotch and water that he had fixed for himself only for politeness' sake.

"Well," Owen drawled, "if the fellow was a nut like you say— That was the court's opinion finally, too, wasn't it, that it must have been a madman?"

"Yes."

"I mean, sure I can understand how you felt afterward, but if it was just a conversation like you say, I don't see where you should blame yourself so awful much."

"But you see, if not for me, Miriam would be alive now." Guy watched Owen lower his lips to the glass again. What was Owen going to do? Leap up suddenly and fling the glass down, throttle him as Bruno had throttled Miriam? He couldn't imagine that

Owen would continue to sit there, but the seconds went by and he did not move.

"You see, I had to tell you," Guy persisted. "I considered you the one person I might have hurt, the one person who suffered. Her child had been yours. You were going to marry her. You loved her. It was you—"

"Hell, I didn't love her." Owen looked at Guy with no change whatever in his face.

Guy stared back at him. Didn't love her, didn't love her, Guy thought. His mind staggered back, trying to realign all the past equations that no longer balanced. "Didn't love her?" he said.

"No. Well, not the way you seem to think. I certainly didn't want her to die, but I was glad enough not to have to marry her. Getting married was her idea. That's why she had the child. That's not a man's fault, I wouldn't say. Would you?" Owen was looking at him with a tipsy earnestness, waiting for Guy to say something, to pass judgment on his conduct with Miriam. Guy turned away with a vaguely impatient gesture.

"Do you think so?" Owen kept on, reaching for the bottle on the table beside him.

A hot, inarticulate anger was rising inside Guy. He slid his tie down and opened his shirt collar. "Listen," he began quietly, "I am a—"

But Owen had begun to speak at the same instant, and he went on, droningly, ". . . the second time. Got married two months after my divorce, and there was trouble right away. Whether Miriam would of been any different, I don't know, but I'd say she'd of been worse. Louisa up and left two months ago after damn near setting the house on fire." He droned on, pouring more Scotch into his glass.

"Listen!" Guy said, unable to stand it any longer. "I—I killed someone, too! I'm a murderer, too!"

Owen's feet came down to the floor. He sat up again and started to set his glass on the table, then didn't. "How's that?" he asked.

"Listen!" Guy shouted. "Listen, I'm a dead man. I'm as good

as dead right now, because I'm going to give myself up. Immediately! Because I killed a man, do you understand? Don't look so unconcerned. Doesn't it mean anything to you that I took a man's life, something no human being has a right to do?"

Owen drank again, slowly.

Guy stared at him. The words seemed to congest even his blood, to cause waves of heat to sweep up his arms from his clenched hands. The words were curses against Owen, sentences and paragraphs of the confession he had written that morning, that were growing jumbled now because the drunken idiot in the armchair didn't want to hear them.

"It doesn't mean anything," Guy began again, "it doesn't mean anything to you, does it?"

"You're not the first man I seen that killed another man. Or woman." Owen chuckled. "Seems to me there's more women that go free."

"I'm not going free. I'm not free. I did this in cold blood. I had no reason. This was just as if I pulled a gun on someone in a public park and shot him," Guy went on, though it was as if he talked to an inanimate thing in the chair. "I was driven to it," Guy said. "That's what I'll tell the police, but that won't make any difference, because the point is, I did it. You see, I have to tell you Bruno's idea."

At least Owen was looking at him now, but his face, far from being rapt, seemed actually to wear an expression of pleasant, polite, drunken attention. Guy refused to let it stop him. "Bruno's idea was that we should kill for each other, that he should kill Miriam and I should kill his father. Then he came to Texas and killed Miriam, behind my back. Without my knowledge or consent, do you see?" His choice of words was abominable, but at least Owen was listening. "I didn't know about it, and I didn't even suspect—not really. Until months later.

"And then he began to haunt me. He began to tell me he would pin the blame for Miriam's death on me, unless I went through with the rest of his damned plan, do you see? Which was to kill his father. The whole idea rested on the fact that there was no reason for the murders. No personal motives. So we couldn't be traced, individually. Provided we didn't see each other. But that's another point. The point is, I did kill him. I was broken down. Bruno broke me down with letters and blackmail and sleeplessness. That's what I'll tell the police, but it won't matter, because they'll say I shouldn't have broken down. It won't matter, because they'll say I was weak. But I don't care now, do you see? I'll accept whatever they want to do to me. I'll say the same thing to the police tomorrow."

The bottle slipped out of Owen's fingers and fell onto the floor, but there was so little in it now that almost nothing spilled. He righted the bottle clumsily, leaving it on the floor. "You sound a little touched—if you want my honest opinion," he said.

Guy groped for a concrete idea to present to Owen. He didn't want his audience to slip away, indifferent as it was. "Listen, how do you feel about the men you know who've killed somebody? How do you act with them? Do you pass the time of day with them the same as you'd do with anybody else?"

Under Guy's intense scrutiny, Owen did seem to try to think. Finally he blinked his eyes and said with a smile, "Live and let live."

Anger seized Guy again. For an instant it was like a hot vise, holding his body and brain. The word formed itself and spat itself from between his teeth: *"Idiot!"*

Owen stirred slightly in his chair. He seemed undecided whether to smile or to frown. "What business is it of mine?" he asked firmly.

"What business? Because you—you are a part of society!"

"Well, then it's society's business," Owen replied with a lazy wave of his hand.

Guy turned his back on Owen. He knew well enough who society was. But the society he had been thinking about in regard to himself, he realized, was the law, was inexorable rules. Society was people like Owen, people like himself, people like—Brillhart, for instance, in Palm Beach. Would Brillhart have reported him? No. He couldn't imagine Brillhart reporting him. If people from

Owen to Brillhart didn't care sufficiently to betray him, should he care any further? Why did he think this morning that he had wanted to give himself up to the police? He wouldn't give himself up. What, concretely, did he have on his conscience now? What human being would inform on him?

"Except a stool pigeon," Guy said. "I suppose a stool pigeon would inform."

"That's right," Owen agreed. "A dirty, stinking stool pigeon." He gave a loud, relieving laugh.

Guy looked at Owen's big scuffed brown shoes extended limply on the carpet. Suddenly their flaccid, massive stupidity seemed the essence of all human stupidity. It translated itself instantly into his old antagonism against the passive stupidity of those who stood in the way of the progress of his work. His work, Guy thought. Yes, there was his work to get back to. Think later, think it all out later, but he had work to do.

He looked at his watch. Ten past twelve. He didn't want to sleep here. He wondered if there was a plane out tonight.

Guy picked up his topcoat from the bed. He looked around, but he hadn't left anything because he hadn't brought anything. It might be better to telephone the airport now, he thought.

"Where's the john?" Owen stood up. "I don't feel so good."

Guy couldn't find the telephone. There was a wire by the bed table, though. He traced the wire under the bed. The telephone was off the hook, on the floor, and he knew immediately it hadn't fallen, because both parts were dragged up near the foot of the bed, the handpiece eerily focused on the armchair where Owen had been sitting. Guy pulled the telephone slowly toward him.

"Hey, ain't there a john anywhere?" Owen was opening a closet door.

"It must be down the hall." Guy's voice was like a shudder. He was holding the telephone in a position for speaking, and now he brought it closer to his ear. He heard the intelligent silence of a live wire. "Hello?" he said.

"Hello, Mr. Haines." The voice was rich, courteous, and just the least bit brusque. "I'm in the next room."

Guy's hand tried unavailingly to crush the telephone, and then he surrendered without a word.

"There wasn't time for a Dictaphone. But I got most of it down. May I come in?"

"Come in," Guy echoed. Gerard must have had his scouts at the airport in New York, Guy thought. He must have followed him in a chartered plane. It was possible. And he had been stupid enough to sign the register in his own name. He put the telephone on the hook and stood up, rigidly, watching the door. His heart was pounding as it never had before, so fast and hard, he thought surely it must be a prelude to his dropping dead. Run, he thought. Leap, attack as soon as he comes in. This is your very last chance. But he didn't move. He was vaguely aware of Owen being sick in the basin in the corner behind him. Then there was a rap at the door, and he went toward it, thinking, Wouldn't it have to be like this after all, by surprise, without my thoughts ordered, and worse, having already uttered half of them in a muddle. Guy opened the door.

"Hello," Gerard said, and he came in with his hat on and his arms hanging, just as he had always looked.

"Who is it?" Owen asked.

"Friend of Mr. Haines," Gerard said easily, glancing at Guy with his round face as serious as before. "I suppose you want to go to New York tonight, don't you?"

Guy was staring at Gerard. Gerard was the law, too. He had to face Gerard. It was inevitable and ordained, like the turning of the earth, and there was no sophistry by which he could free himself from it.

"Eh?" Gerard said.

Guy tried to speak, and said something entirely different from what he had intended. "Take me."

ACKNOWLEDGMENT

Page 67, lines 33-36: from "Button Up Your Overcoat," copyright 1928 by DeSylva, Brown and Hen-
derson Inc., copyright renewed, assigned to Chappell
& Co., Inc. International copyright secured. All rights
reserved. Used by permission.